Praise for Shatterworld

"I've enjoyed Shatterworld! It has fact flavored with the fantastic, all built upon a backbone of faith…An interesting place to visit. Take the journey yourself!"

Robert Don Hughes
Author of the *Pelmen the Poweshaper* and *Wizard and Dragon* series

"There's an intriguing astrobiological premise, an alien character we can truly cheer for, and plenty of room for a sequel."

Kathy Tyers
Author of the best selling *Truce at Bakura* and *Fusion Fire*

"This trilogy has Shatterworld, Circumnavigation of Shatterworld, and Pacifists' War. Don't let…the 12 year old heroine in the first book deter you. These are seriously good novels. The basic plot is an old one: a group of persecuted Christians escapes Earth and flees to a remote barren, seemingly uninhabited planet.

In the first book of the series, Rejoice is a 12 year old genius who saves the planet. In the second, she's a teenager sharing in a missionary journey around the planet. In the third, she's married and back to saving the planet again [well, sorta]. This is serious, powerful Christian fiction."

David Bergsland
Author of the *Tales of Mighty Men* trilogy

Redemptive Fiction Award of Excellence:
Shatterworld, Circumnavigation Of Shatterworld, and Pacifists' War

LELIA ROSE FOREMAN

A Shattered World

Dedicated to

Doris Irene Bane Rose

who led me to the dictionary and
encyclopedia and who always listened.

Thanks also too: Susan Thogerson Maas,
Ellen Dodson, Barbara Hummel, Dixie Mace,
Ralph Hutchinson, Kurt Spicer, Ruth Spicer,
Larry and Kara Brake, Jeanne Zelen, Aletha
Bakke, Trisha Search, Melissa Heinlein, Dr.
Debi Miller, Dr. Frank Foreman

Contents

I

BOOK ONE: SHATTERWORLD

SHATTERWORLD CHAPTER ONE

As elders and deacons in blue overalls, and deaconesses in brown dresses entered the spaceship's bridge, twelve-year-old Rejoice retreated. She crammed herself into a corner behind her tutor, Sister Guthry. Standing on tiptoe, she peered over her tutor's shoulder to watch the colony leaders study the displays.

Elder Smith tapped his thick, pale fingers on a screen that showed one of the planetary photos from the satellite sent before the Starflower. "The astronomers told us this planet had life. Where is it?"

The Elders and Deaconesses looked at Sister Eunice Guthry. The round woman stumbled over her words. "It must have had life at one time, or it wouldn't have that kind of atmosphere. There must be plants in the ocean to keep up the oxygen level."

The elders studied the images and charts with squinted eyes and furrowed brows. Deacon Carden pointed with slender, brown fingers to a column on a screen. "What does that mean?"

Elder Sims, a man tall, thin, and as dark as Lights Out, turned and noticed Rejoice. He shook his head and gestured with his thumb toward the door.

Sister Guthry turned awkwardly in the tight space and laid her hand on Rejoice's shoulder. "As my apprentice-pupil, she helped me amass the data. She knows she must not talk about this meeting."

Rejoice glanced at her. She knew now.

Elder Sims turned to the column and sighed.

Rejoice bit her lips as Sister Guthry frowned at the column. "It means

"

that because the atmospheric chloride levels are so high, the ozone level is low."

Elder Chin shook his head. The droops of skin over his eyelids quivered. "The ultraviolet is murderous. It will kill all our crops. It will kill us."

Elder Sims sighed again and rubbed the back of his neck.

After a silence: "Doesn't glass block ultraviolet?" Deaconess Hernandez drawled.

"Yes!" Rejoice said.

All the elders turned and scrutinized her. Cheeks warming, she looked at her feet. "Please forgive me for interrupting," she mumbled.

Elder Smith fingered his sparse gray beard. "We need our geologist. Please fetch your father, Young Lady Rejoice."

With her heart hammering, Rejoice squeezed out of the bridge and jogged down the long corridor lined with educational posters to the Holly family quarters. When she burst into the living room, her older brother Stronghold leaped off the worn sofa bolted to the floor. "Well?" he shouted. "Are we going down?"

"They want to talk to Father."

Brother Holly's eyebrows lifted. "I wonder why?" He stretched out his legs and examined his bare feet. "I wonder where I left my slippers this time?"

Rejoice jiggled from foot to foot while Father and Mother searched for his slippers and six-year-old Makepeace sniffed her dress. Why was he so interested in the smell of her sweat?

Stronghold dropped to his knees. "Please tell me we're getting off this ship. If I don't get off this ship, I'll explode. Seven years! Seven long years!"

"I know. I was with you. I know every molecule on the Starflower." And every face and every personality and every quirk.

"So what's the planet like?"

"I can't tell you yet."

"It's not fair you get to know all about it and I know nothing. Come on, a hint."

Mother interrupted. "Stop wheedling. She tells you something; you tell someone else. And then the ship fills with rumors, most of them wrong. People get all excited for nothing. We will wait for the official announcement when we can all know the same thing at the same time." Father slid on his slippers. "And you don't want fair. You want grace."

Stronghold ignored him. "Sis, just a hint. I'm dying here."

As they stepped over the threshold, Rejoice said, "It has clouds."

Stronghold leaped. "Clouds! That means water. Or dust. Or methane. Hey, are they water clouds?"

The door sealed shut.

When Rejoice returned with Father, the elders were discussing the feasibility of glassing over entire fields and checking the information on plants in the database to find out which plants were resistant to ultraviolet light.

"Eh, Theophilus," Elder Smith said, side-hugging Rejoice's father. "We have a mystery for you. What is this?" He pointed at an image of a six hundred kilometer circle of peaked islands near the only continent. The steep peaks thrust through the ocean like the teeth of a giant steel trap. In the exact center of the circle a lone island reared its steep cliffs.

Father's dark, almond eyes widened and his khaki-colored skin paled. "Did we see any asteroids on the way in?"

Sister Guthry nodded and the blond hair piled up on her head trembled. "A wide belt and a number of loose ones off the ecliptic."

Rejoice glanced at her tutor. That number of loose asteroids was in the millions.

Father rubbed his smooth chin. "Are there many of these craters?"

"Smaller ones," Sister Guthry said. "Here, here, and here."

Father relaxed and pointed to the round lake near the center of the continent and the two doughnut-shaped islands on the other side of the giant steel trap. "Have you seen Crater Lake in Oregon? Those islands are the remnants of volcanoes that blew up. Bigger than Krakatoa. The erosion on the slopes here shows the eruptions happened hundreds of years ago."

Father tapped the image of the giant bull's-eye "But this looks like a massive asteroid or comet smashed into this planet. Yes. You can see here the ridges on the continent, and here the shock waves from the impact. It would have caused an enormous tsunami, earthquakes, perhaps a lot of volcanic activity. I'll guess that's when those Krakatoas popped. See how the circles line up? Could be the asteroid hit right on a fault. The vaporized crust and ocean and ash would have condensed high in the atmosphere, causing it to rain for, oh . . ."

Elder Smith suggested, "Forty days and forty nights?"

"To be sure. It must have blackened the sky for years. Is there life here?"

Sister Guthry stroked her hair with a trembling hand. "Atmospheric conditions say there is life somewhere, likely hidden in the oceans. It all fits. The asteroid and the volcanoes could have splattered lots of gases and particulates that destroyed the ozone layer. The heat from the meteor strike could have burnt up all the plants. The volcanic gases could have suffocated what was left."

Rejoice fisted one hand inside the other. Had they traveled seven years only to find death?

"Gases? Poisonous to humans?" asked Elder Chin.

"Yes," Sister Guthry said. "But atmospheric analysis shows the concentrations are low enough now that we could get by with simple filter masks. Vegetation would absorb the gases. Already the ozone is rebuilding. It's not like the ultraviolet light or gases would kill instantly. It takes lots of exposure. Our crops would speed the process of cleansing the atmosphere."

Elder Chin frowned. "So we could live there unprotected someday." "I think so. I'll need to crunch some numbers, but I think it would take less than a generation. I think. You can tell only so much from up here and a month away. We need to go down and look closer."

Elder Chin shook his head again. "But, as we move the ship around, we use up the fuel we would need to get back to Earth if this planet will not sustain us."

"I bought all the fuel I could." Elder Smith crossed his arms across his wide torso. "There might be enough."

Sister Guthry laid her fist on one of the screens. "This planet has a twenty-five-hour day, land in a temperate zone, and gravity a little less than Earth's. Where else are we going to find a planet this good? Where?"

Rejoice held her breath. Was anyone allowed to talk back to Elder Smith like that?

Elder Smith clasped his hands together. "Do we stay and build a new life, or do we go back? Is this worse than Earth?"

Elder Chin folded his arms and studied more data.

Deacon Kim said, "Suddenly I feel inadequate for my role as agronomist. I studied, but—bare rock?"

Elder Sims cleared his throat. "I made my decision eight years ago. I don't know why I need to make it again." The lights from the computer bank reflected off his dark eyes.

Elder Smith's already florid face reddened some more. "Amen to that."

"How corrosive are these poisonous gases?" Elder Chin seemed to address one of the screens.

From the back of the crowd, Pastor Wiseman said, "Brothers and Sisters, instruments can tell us only so much. They cannot tell us the will of God." The silver cross on his black uniform glittered. The elders and deaconesses stood motionless and silent, their heads bowed reverentially. Pastor Wiseman smiled. "Whether we live or die, we are in God's hands. Let us pray for wisdom and guidance."

The men and women knelt in silence.

Rejoice knelt also, but she stared at the data screens. What would it be like to step onto another planet?

Half an hour later, Elder Smith stood. The others rose slowly and waited for him to speak. Though every family on the ship had sold everything they had to provision the ship, it was Elder Smith, once the fifty-ninth wealthiest man in the world, who had purchased the Starflower.

Elder Smith stood with his feet apart and arms crossed, studying the images of the watery world with one mountainous continent the size of

Australia and millions of islands. He gestured over to Elder Chin, who nodded to him. "It seems good to me to stay. I believe God cleared off this planet so we could move onto it. Amen?"

"Amen," the others echoed.

* * *

Rejoice held onto her little brother's hand as she waited in line for the airlock to open. Children went to New Earth last, and as Makepeace was the youngest child, she and he would be the very last to board the shuttle.

Not Worthy shouted, "The first thing I'm going to do is jump in the ocean and swim for kilometers."

Every scoffed. "You think the adults will let us do that? I don't think so. And what if there are monsters in the water?"

"Then I'll wrestle them to land and have a barbeque."

Rejoice snickered.

Eight-year-old Sing asked, "What's a barbeque?"

Makepeace tried to pull out of Rejoice's grip. "Okay, but don't go far."

He peeped as he sped away.

"Makepeace!" She chased and caught him before he turned into the first cross corridor.

He squealed as he wriggled in her grasp.

She swung him by his arms in a wide circle as she reeled toward the line of children. She hoisted him and blew on his tummy. His laughter echoed off the bulkheads.

A clunk within the airlock riveted the gaze of everyone.

Rejoice held Makepeace close and whispered in his ear, "Are you ready? We're about to start a new life."

* * *

Only twelve years old, and her life was over.

Rejoice Holly hugged her knees as she sat on top of Ocean Shore Boulder and gazed at the three moonlets. Big Potato and the two Small Potatoes proceeded across the evening sky. High tide shushed at the foot of the boulder and bore the dead scent of salt and iodine.

She adjusted her breathing mask to scratch under it and studied the lumpy Big Potato, pocked with craters and grooves. If she had a telescope and a way to measure the distance between the pits in the grooves, she could figure out the depth of the regolith, or dust, on the moonlet. Desperately, she concentrated on the dust and shoved on the door of her mind, trying to shut out the thought that nagged her.

A poke in her back startled her. She squealed and tottered on the edge of the boulder before turning to glare at her laughing older brother standing on the boulder's broad top. "Stronghold! You know I hate it when you do that."

He laid big-knuckled hands on his hips, squinted his brown eyes above his mask, and laughed again. "Then don't forget what time it is. I knew you'd be up here staring at the stars."

She brushed back her hair. "The stars aren't complaining all the time. She pushed past him and dropped onto the damp sand below the boulder.

Stronghold leaped over her head, rolled on the sand, and stood in front of her. Together, they strolled toward the Quonset-hut apartments, accompanied only by the sounds of the weak tide lapping and their feet crunching the black sand. The shore stretched barren before them, and on their left, broken basalt, the remnants of a volcano ripped and smashed by tectonic forces, jutted dark against a violet sky.

Rejoice could just barely remember a beach back on Old Earth, a beach filled with shouting people, sand littered with glass and bits of seaweed, rope, and tar mingled with burnt sticks, potato-chip sacks, and shattered clamshells. Seven years ago in ship time. What she remembered best were the screaming seagulls with gaping beaks that had balanced delicately on the salt breeze, seagulls that had swooped to steal her hotdog.

She stopped and gazed at the Angel constellation backed by the blazing Milky Way. If she had a telescope, she would be able to see Old Earth's sun on the Angel's shoulder, thirty light years away.

Stronghold hunched his shoulders. "Why do you waste your time looking at the stars? You'll end up a farmer's wife, so why are you trying to become an astronomer? Do you think the history books are going to call you the famous Dr. Rejoice In The Lord's Salvation Holly?"

Again. Why couldn't he shut up? "I like astronomy and I'm good at it. You aren't good at anything except hologames."

Stronghold stiffened and his eyes smoldered.

She had gone too far. "I'm sorry. I didn't mean it that way."

"Sure you didn't!" Stronghold sprinted toward the domed apartments, his shoulder-length, black hair streaming behind him.

Anger and sadness wrestled in Rejoice's heart as she stopped to study the three moonlets again. He was upset. She was upset. Had God really needed to clear off the planet so thoroughly?

The only life they had found were algae and protozoans under river rocks and some seaweeds and insect-like creatures a meter below the ocean's surface.

Rejoice wanted seagulls.

As she gazed at the moonlet Big Potato, a memory came of seagulls balancing on the air, yellow-webbed feet and bright, white bellies. Never again would she see a seagull. Never.

The only animals they would ever see were farm animals. The only scenery would be crops or bare rocks. The only work was hard work, nasty work, or boring work.

Rejoice covered her ears and pressed. Stop it! If she kept whining she would turn into Stronghold.

Rejoice jerked her gaze away from the moon and trotted after Stronghold running far ahead of her. When she reached the door of her family's apartment, the only one with a plastic holly wreath on it, she wiped her eyes. She entered the airlock, hung up her mask, and straightened her long brown dress.

When she entered the two-room apartment, Father, sitting at the table with the rest of the family, said, "Well?" Tiredness lined his face, as it did all the adults of the colony. Next to him, Makepeace observed a shriveled holly berry that had fallen off the female holly bonsai in the middle of the table. The male holly bonsai basked under a grow-light atop the refrigerator. The smell of gravy rose from the covered dishes surrounding the little tree.

"I'm sorry, Father. Pray forgive me as I endeavor to improve my ways." Rejoice slipped into her chair.

"To be sure. But this is the third time. Next time we shall eat without you, for we shall assume you wish to fast."

"Yes, Father."

Mother grinned at her. "After supper, why don't we all go out and look at the stars? They're so beautiful in these clear skies."

Stronghold growled.

Father said, "Maybe tomorrow. I need to rest."

"All right." Mother led the family in a hymn of praise. They prayed and ate in silence. The quiet was interrupted only by Mother humming now and then.

What would it take to upset Mother? How could anyone be so happy all the time? Once, when she had been called Rejoice In The Lord's Salvation one too many times, she had asked why Mother had the simple name Carol, when everyone else was named after a biblical phrase or concept. "I'm named after carols of Christ's Birth Day because that's what I like to sing best," she had answered with a lilt. So Rejoice had asked sarcastically why Mother hadn't named herself I Like To Sing Christ's Birth Day Carols, Especially Deck The Halls With Boughs Of Holly? Mother had laughed and answered calmly, "Perhaps I should have."

Makepeace put down his spoon and rubbed a spot of reflected light on the tabletop.

Mother announced, "Tomorrow is our family's turn at soil-making."

Stronghold jabbed at his food. "I don't want to."

"Grumbles and rumbles dusted surround," Makepeace said.

Father cleared his throat. "I don't recall you being asked whether or not you wanted to."

"Why can't I keep on constructing the glass pavilions? Brother Hammer told Elder Ruiz I'm the best extensioner he's got in construction. He says I've got," he turned to glare at Rejoice, "good hand-eye coordination."

"I'm proud of you," Mother said. "However, as none of us enjoys soil-making, we all must take turns at it." She warbled, "Toiling on, toiling on . . ."

Stronghold laid his fists on either side of his plate. "What did I ever do to you to make you hate me so much?"

Mother's spoon clattered on the table. "What?"

Stronghold reddened and his eyes became slits. "Why did you drag me across the galaxy to drop me here?"

Father and Mother glanced at each other. Mother stammered, "We did it because we love you and wanted you to grow in a godly community."

Stronghold scowled at Father. "Isn't that just like a loving father to dump his kids on a bare rock?" Father opened his mouth, but Stronghold continued, "I don't want to wear a mask for the rest of my life, my life which you condemned to death."

Mother ran her fingers through her hair.

Father frowned. "Son, all men die."

"Not on Old Earth! The scientists were working on immortality."

"They've been working on it for a hundred years. When we left, they were no closer to it than when they began. I'll live, God willing, to one hundred, perhaps one hundred and ten, and so likely will you."

"A hundred years of living on this." Stronghold's voice rose and cracked. "I want to go back."

"We don't have enough fuel."

"Yes, we do."

Father glanced down at his plate, looked back up at Stronghold. "All right. Yes, we do. If all the gauges are reading exactly right. If nothing goes wrong or needs adjusting on the way back. But, most likely, we'd come out of warp a light year from Old Earth. And then what?"

"We could live on the ship."

Mother said, "Be reasonable. You know why we can't live indefinitely on the ship."

They all turned and gazed at Makepeace, who slowly leaned over the table, studied the reflection of his chocolate-almond eyes and beautiful elfin face, and licked the top. Of all the babies conceived on the Starflower during its warp travel, only he had survived. Most were miscarried and the rest died shortly after birth of multiple defects. Makepeace had not died of his particular defect, or gift, which on Old Earth might have been called autism.

Rejoice shook her head as her stomach twisted. Why wouldn't Stronghold shut up? How long did he think he could push everybody around like this?

Stronghold gestured toward Makepeace. "And why do you keep sending him to morning school? He embarrasses me."

Rejoice's heart shuddered. Makepeace had never embarrassed him on the ship.

In the quiet voice that meant that you had better give the right answer, Father asked, "Would it be better if he stayed home to lick the tables?"

Stronghold's face contorted. He crashed his fist against the table. "You lied to me! For seven years you told me we were going to the Promised Land. You said there would be freedom here, and animals, and happiness. You never even asked me if I wanted to go."

"You will not speak to your mother and me that way."

"No, no. You want me to be a good little boy like she's a good little girl." He jabbed his splayed fingers toward Rejoice. "I hate this family!"

Mother covered her mouth with one hand.

Father said evenly, "May I remind you that you are one-fifth of this family?"

Stronghold pounded on the table. "I know it and I hate it." He kicked over his chair and shot out the door. The double slam rattled the walls.

"Your mask." Mother gasped, and then bowed her head. Tears dripped on to her plate. Father stood, sat again, and placed his arm across her shoulders and wound his fingers into her curly, brown hair.

"Tables fisting. Hurt earring. Hurt to bang to tongue and dance little lights," Makepeace said.

Now she knew what it took to upset Mother. Rejoice whispered, "May I please be excused?"

Father rubbed his face against Mother's hair.

Rejoice left the table, crawled into her bunk set into the wall, and pulled the curtain shut. But the curtain could not block Father murmuring and Mother weeping. Rejoice hated this planet as much as Stronghold did. But why did he need to hurt them like that?

SHATTERWORLD CHAPTER TWO

eyond the horizon and under the sea, six-legged and six-tentacled Ur-Veena poked among the seaweed holdfasts writhing through deep muck to anchor on stone. The tiny electric pulses of grubs, worms, and maggots tapped against his skin.

There was the pest.

Ur-Veena grabbed the furry maggot and pulled it out, squeezing the pest to death. An eager spiney, a worm with sharp jaws and barbs, rippled the water near his articulated legs and bumped against the toothed sliver of stone resting on Ur-Veena's spurs.

He waggled the limp maggot behind the spiney, which spurted and stirred up more muck as it flipped and snapped at the morsel. In the growing murkiness, Ur-Veena withdrew his three main eyes and switched to clicking and listening to faint echoes of his surroundings and even fainter static from the roiled mud. His main eyes crinkled into lumps protected by his smooth, round shell. Light and olfactory sensors peeped from behind opercula dotting his shell.

Ur-Veena grasped the next plant and pulled himself forward. He was working much closer to the edge of the world than he liked. If he stayed much longer, he would blister from the ball of heat far above the world that peppered his skin with stray magnetic blips against the constant flow of north and south, and with harsh uvi forces. But since this was where the children and best seaweed grew, this was where he worked. Fortunately he was nearly finished with this patch.

In the time of darkness, En-Teppi, the one who had been lot-chosen to wander, would replace him. Then Ur-Veena could retreat to the deeper waters.

He pulled himself to the next plant. No maggots on this one, and only slightly grazed, one broad ribbon was ready for harvest. Ur-Veena reached for his blade, and the stone sliver edged with shatterstone teeth rasped on the stem above two buds. Done, he set the sliver on the spurs of his articulated legs on the port side and impaled the leaf on the starboard spurs. This task finished. Time to check the children's nursery again.

SHATTERWORLD CHAPTER THREE

Rejoice woke to the sound of Mother's humming. How could she be so cheerful? Last night had been the biggest fight their family ever had, and now she acted like nothing had happened. Why didn't she care that nothing was the way they thought it would be?

Rejoice rolled over in the tight bed space and yawned. A stomach cramp reminded her that she had not eaten much at supper. She slid out of bed and pulled on another long brown dress. All the women wore the same high neck style and colored dress so that none would grow proud in her appearance. No one would look down on someone more shabbily dressed. Rejoice washed the dress she had worn the previous day in the sink and hung it up to dry next to her bed.

Stronghold should have been getting dressed. Where was he? She pulled the curtain aside from his bunk over hers. He wasn't there.

Mother's humming faltered, slid into a squeak, and ceased.

"Ah," Father said, as though punched in the stomach.

Her parents looked at each other with eyebrows drawn together in worry, but did not break the spiritual discipline of silence before the common breakfast.

Mother tugged a blue shirt over Makepeace's shaking head and stuffed his wriggling body into his overall. He whined until he was distracted by a teardrop on his knee.

Mother wiped her face and stepped to the door. Makepeace threw himself upon the door so that he could be the one to tug it open.

Stronghold slept curled on the floor of the airlock, his head cradled by a wadded raincoat.

Mother knelt to shake his shoulder.

"Mmph? Oh. Right." He got up slowly and stretched. Then he made a shooing motion with his hand. "I'll . . . I'll meet up with you later."

They snapped on their masks and strolled under glass cover to the Meetingplace for common breakfast. Makepeace limped and fluttered his hands. Rejoice kept glancing at Father out of the corner of her eye. His shoulders hunched and his frowning face had dark arcs under his eyes.

In the plain meeting hall, they took their places between the Byers with their pale girls and the Whites with their obnoxious, blue-black triplet boys. Pastor Wiseman read a passage of Scripture. Deaconess Hernandez made announcements. And then they all sat down to a breakfast of oat griddlecakes and lentil sprouts.

Every time Rejoice raised her eyes, people were staring at them. Makepeace pressed his hand in the syrup and licked his fingers. Mother grabbed his wrist and led him into the kitchen to wash. Stronghold entered, and every eye swiveled to watch him slide onto the bench beside Rejoice. One would have thought he was the only one who was ever late.

Conversation rose around them, but Stronghold said nothing and acknowledged no one. He ate slowly, hunched over, with his mask dangling behind his neck. Hands in her lap, Rejoice fiddled with her mask. Please, please let Stronghold smile and be her laughing big brother again. Her throat hurt when she remembered the games of tag in the corridors of the Starflower. His eyes held no expression.

When had he come back last night? Were his lungs all right? Dr. Cruz had told them that they could breathe outside without masks for several weeks before their lungs corroded. But who knew if the lungs could heal after that kind of damage? Young Man Redhorse and some of the older boys had made a show of not wearing their masks at recess, but several days of detention caused even them to be diligent about wearing the filters.

During opening classes, Teacher Be Still And Know That I Am God Hardesty, pulled Makepeace away from licking the windows. He made

Stronghold wash off the smudges because Rejoice was busy tutoring eighteen-year-old As Far Hernandez in calculations concerning the flow of irrigation water.

At recess, Rejoice and Harmony, paced around the solar-panel-shaded courtyard. Even in the shade, Harmony's wavy, red hair seemed to glow. Rejoice twisted a strand of her straight, dark-brown hair. Too bad she couldn't make her hair glow like that.

"Is your brother sick?" Harmony asked. "He's just sitting in the corner. He looks so sad."

Rejoice did not want to talk to the colony's chatterbox about this. "Remember that storm we had the week after we landed? Sister Guthry told me we can expect a lot of them because so much of New Earth is ocean. When the temperature of the ocean reaches—"

"You know who thinks your brother is cute?"

Rejoice sighed. "Every Knee Shall Bow."

"Oh, you do know. Do you know who thinks you're cute?"

"It doesn't matter. I don't intend to marry."

"Don't say that!" Harmony screeched. Her hands flew to her face. "It's a sin not to marry and have babies."

"Says who?"

"The Bible."

"It does not. In fact, St. Paul said it's better not to get married."

"He did not."

"Look it up. It's in First Corinthians."

"I will."

Harmony studied her intertwined fingers. "But why don't you want to get married?"

"I don't want to be a farmer's wife and milk cows every morning. I want to be an astronomer."

"Oh, that again. Why?"

"I like it."

Harmony shook her head. "How can anyone like that much math? I'll never understand you."

No. She wouldn't. No one on this planet ever would.

Another memory of Old Earth popped up. A lake, where the water lay as smooth as polished stone. The fire her family had made to roast marshmallows cast a yellow flickering light on the grass that grew up to the water's edge, but the light that lay on the smooth water was the moon's silver glow. The warm, wooden dock that stretched far out into the lake was transformed into a shadowy bridge to the light.

Rejoice had tiptoed to the end of the dock and stared at the great silver circle of the moon and the silver path on the dark water that ran from her feet to the great globe. "Yes," she laughed, "I'm coming," and stepped onto the shimmering path. But it was too slippery, and she fell into the cold water. The lake swallowed her down. She choked and thrashed until Father pulled her out. Mother cried while she dried Rejoice off with a thick towel. Everyone laughed when she tried to explain how she fell off the slippery path to the moon.

So she never told them again, but she vowed in her heart that someday she would go to the moon. She had never made it. They had come here instead. Here where they were supposed to breathe in rhythm with nature. Except there wasn't any nature.

The bell rang, and the children filed back into the classroom to study mathematics, Greek, Hebrew, and logic. Rejoice rhythmically opened and closed her hand in her peripheral vision as she became more deeply engrossed in the calculus of planetary motion. A note popped up on her screen reminding her to move on to Greek. She had gone thirty minutes over on math.

No Confidence In The Flesh Cruz gawked at her from the far side of the Meetingplace. *Oh, gah!* She flipped her screen onto Greek. She hated to be stared at, especially by him. A few years older than her, he was pudgy, and furry eyebrows met over his nose. She had never seen him speak, but his intense eyes seemed to see through whomever he was looking at. She shivered.

After lunch, while the sun baked the bare rock into blistering temperatures, Rejoice curled on the sofa in the air-conditioned apartment. Once they had trees, would they throw away the air conditioning?

Mother sang sprightly hymns as she scrubbed the walls. Father rocked slowly and hummed tunelessly as he did when in deep concentration.

He frowned over the maps he composed from satellite pictures. "Well, dearest mine, I've cataloged and examined every island and rock on this planet as closely as I can with the limited resolution of our cameras. There is no sign of green life anywhere. All are black, grey, or brown rocks."

"Don't you think that we should fly over them with the shuttle for a closer look?" asked Mother.

"That's a thought. But most of the islands are pretty small. There's one larger archipelago on the other side of the planet that might be worth a fly over. But I believe that the priority should be to thoroughly explore Sole first." He rubbed his dark eyebrows and brushed at the straight hair hanging over his ears. "Need a haircut."

Mother widened her round, hazel eyes at Father. "Why don't you let it grow long and pull it back into a samurai style?" She sang the first two lines of *Sakura*.

He grimaced and shook his head.

Stronghold slouched on the sofa with his legs stretched out before him, screen on his lap set to a textbook, his eyes unfocused. Rejoice glanced from her brother to her mother. Would Stronghold blow up again and make her cry? How could Mother keep on singing? What was there to sing about?

Humming, Mother stepped past her daughter, stopped, stepped back, and tapped on her screen. "Your assignment was to study bovine disease."

Rejoice blanked out the astronomy text and positioned the screen on the table. "Mother, we have no cows, and we won't grow any until the fields are successful. When we do grow them, they won't have any hoof-and-mouth disease."

"We have no idea what latent viruses we may have brought with us."

Rejoice gritted her teeth a moment, then sighed. "Mother, have you ever considered that maybe it was God who put this desire to study space in my heart? Have you ever considered that somebody in this colony should know astronomy?"

Father looked up from his maps. "Good point. I'll believe it the day the colony needs an astronomer. In the meantime, you'll obey your mother and study bovine disease. And don't roll your eyes."

Rejoice reset her screen. Her tongue worried at a cucumber seed stuck in one of her molars. They would never understand. Was she the only one that thought it stupid to use so much technology to start the colony and then throw most of it away?

Her mother watched her a moment while she tugged at a thread on her washrag, then leaned on the edge of the table. "Honey?" she whispered. "I know it's important to you, but sometimes one dream has to die so that God can give us another one. I had big plans to be a famous singer. God delivered me from that vanity."

Makepeace hooted under the table, crawled over, and stroked Rejoice's ankle.

Someone rapped on the door.

Mother jumped, hurled her washrag into the sink, and hurried to the airlock.

"Come in, come in!" she cried as Deaconess Redhorse oozed in, a warm pudding of a woman, bulgy, with wide, dark eyes sunk in a broad face. The deaconess waddled in with a wide grin showing gap teeth. She plumped down on the sofa. Stronghold drew in his legs and looked away.

"Brother Holly," Deaconess Redhorse announced, "the Elders have considered your request to have your oldest son transferred from Elder Petrovich to Elder Ruiz as apprentice pupil in construction and engineering."

Stronghold's head jerked up. Makepeace snuffled over to Deaconess Redhorse and stroked her fat cheek. She smiled and patted his hand.

"The Elders agreed. Elder Chin said he would accept the young man No Confidence In The Flesh Cruz as apprentice, so there is a space open for your son."

Rejoice covered her smile. Last week, Stronghold had pointed out a pile of smashed glass, the result of No's fumbling, and laughed. "Brother Grace To The Humble Hammer nearly lost his sanctification when he saw that. Elder Ruiz only managed to calm him down by promising to keep No Confidence away from the extensioners after that."

Deaconess Redhorse continued, "But we do have a question about your request to be exempted from soil-making."

Stronghold sat up straighter. Mother cleared her throat and twisted her fingers together.

Father pointed to the maps on his desk. "I am not seeking to evade duty. There are some promising formations a bit inland that Stronghold and I should investigate."

"Promising?"

"To be sure. I think the basaltic buckling here and the ignimbrite between us and New Krakatoa could have trapped a pool of oil."

Deaconess Redhorse frowned and shifted. "Oil?"

"Yes. For the making of plastics, medicine, and fabric. We could even use it to make furniture and houses."

"Ah."

"Wait a minute," Mother said, tapping her temple with a forefinger. "Doesn't ultraviolet light degrade plastic?"

Father pressed his fingers together. "Not all kinds of it. We could embed sand on the outside to shield plastic walls if we had to."

Deaconess Redhorse waved a broad hand to cut them off. "The point is that you hope to find resources the colony can use. The point also is that you are overworked. You have depleted yourselves emotionally, Brother Theophilus and Sister Carol."

Father and Mother exchanged glances.

"Our Lord and Savior took time to rest, and so should you." Deaconess Redhorse leaned her great bulk forward, and Makepeace scuttled out of the way. She laid her great hand on Mother's knee. "You can't even rest on the Lord's Day because you need to watch this sweet little one to be sure he does not harm himself."

Mother folded her arms. "We aren't complaining."

"Are you so proud that you cannot ask for help?"

Mother swallowed. Father gazed at Deaconess Redhorse for a moment, and then said, "Pray forgive us for our self-sufficiency."

The sofa groaned as Deaconess Redhorse leaned back. "This Lord's Day, I shall take Makepeace. And if this lad can stand this fat old lady, I shall take him every other Lord's Day. Agreed?"

Mother nodded.

"You still have to make soil this afternoon, but for the next two months, you are exempted. You may have one rover and one trailer for your equipment." Deaconess Redhorse heaved herself to a stand and smiled at Rejoice. "Are you still satisfied with Sister Eunice Guthry as her tutor?"

Mother nodded again. "Oh, yes. In fact, though I know she's still young, could we have her permanently apprenticed to Eunice? We'll still need a meteorologist when Eunice is gone."

Deaconess Redhorse pulled on her mask. "Ask us again in four years." She waddled out the door.

After she had been gone a few minutes, Father glanced at his watch. "It's nearly time to go."

"Father," Stronghold said.

"Yes?" Father prompted.

"I should thank you," Stronghold said in a strained voice.

"I meant to request the transfer a long time ago."

"But I can't thank you," Stronghold continued. "I don't want to be with you. I don't want to hear you. I don't want to see you. But where can I go? I can't walk away from the colony because there's no food out there. I can't go to someone else's house because I'm under your authority. I'm stuck. I'm trapped here where nothing will ever happen until the day I die."

The family focused on him. "How, how can you say such things?" Mother sputtered.

Father touched her arm. "Carol, we taught him to speak the truth. I once felt that way."

Stronghold made a truncated raspberry. "Your father imprisoned you on a ball of rock?"

"My father abandoned me and my crippled mother to poverty when I was ten."

"So you decided to do him one better."

Father and Mother slowly sat down, he at his desk, and she on a dining chair. They closed their eyes, bowed their heads, and took slow, deep breaths.

Rejoice placed her hands on her cheeks. She needed the inner discipline to do what they were doing: praying and waiting until they could speak words of peace. She too bowed her head, but she kept glancing up at Stronghold.

Clenching and unclenching his hands, Stronghold watched them, almost spoke, and then slapped his screen to another text. Every minute or so, he tightened his jaw. Slowly, the anger in his face transformed to grief.

Rejoice looked away. Makepeace chewed on his sleeve.

Father said in a low voice, "It's sixteen hundred and time to go. Will you go with us?"

"As if I had a choice," Stronghold said.

"Will you go with us?"

Stronghold shrugged and stood.

The family put on masks and wide-brimmed hats and left the apartment. They strode past the hydroponics sheds, disconnected the boat batteries from the solar collector, and clambered into the Sea Squirt.

Twenty minutes later, they rounded the point of shattered basalt, a wall of dragon's teeth that marched between the colony and the next field-to-be.

When Mother pulled out the hot, cumbersome body suits they needed to keep the nanobots from disassembling them into dust, Rejoice blurted, "Please, Mother, could I be the one to gather the seaweed?"

With a soft, grating sound, the Sea Squirt beached on black sand. Mother rummaged through a box on the side of the little motorboat and pulled out an orange flag emblazoned with the number twenty-one in black. "Use this to mark the patch. Remember, take no more than half."

Mother placed her forehead against Rejoice's. "Don't go too far. I see some dark clouds over there and a storm might be brewing."

"Don't worry." Rejoice pushed off in the Sea Squirt. She wanted to roar off with a mighty spray behind her, but the boat's top speed left only a gentle wake. She putted along and prayed, "Lord, we used to be such a happy family. Please make us happy again." But it was a foolish prayer. One should not seek happiness; one should seek the glory of God, and happiness might follow. Seeking happiness makes it run away. So said Pastor Wiseman. She sighed. This job should have gone to Stronghold, but she hated the boring job of sprinkling nanobots as much as he did.

Heading farther out, she searched through a clear section on the boat's hull for a patch of seaweed not yet harvested. A gentle wind rumpled the water, sighed through an oarlock, and dried the sweat gathering on her face. The scent of iodine and salt air muted by the filter mask brought the memory of seagulls balancing on the air. She dipped her hand in the cool water. When would the sea fill with the diatoms and plankton and fish? The colonists were growing those in experimental tanks close to the hydroponics shed, but had yet to release any of that tiny, teeming life.

A sinuous line of dark orange fishtail kelp wavered under the boat. Squinting her eyes against the sun's late-afternoon glare, Rejoice scanned the sea. No orange flag bobbing in the waves. She screwed together the long harvesting rod and entered the position of the patch and the date on the log. In thirty days, Brother Hancock would come and check to see how much of the seaweed had regenerated after harvest.

Rejoice lowered the pole, clipped a length of seaweed a half-meter above the sea floor, and hauled the strong iodine-scented strand into the boat. Drift, clip, and haul. Drift, clip, and haul. Her shoulders ached and her eyes watered from the stench of the slimy seaweed piling up. If only there were seagulls she could throw bits of sandwich to, or pale white jellyfish pulsating in the clear waters. Clip and haul.

A drop of sweat ran into her eye and stung. She wiped her eye, glanced up, and gasped. Where was the shore? How had she gotten so far? A black cloud billowed high and stretched out arms to envelop the sky. Although she had not gathered the quota of seaweed, she needed to go in now.

"Come on!" she urged as the boat putted along much slower than the black cloud growing higher and higher. A skirt of rain ran under the gloom. She beat on the motor casing. "Go faster, you stupid thing!"

A gust of wind smacked into the boat, shoving it off-course. The brim of Rejoice's hat flapped and tore. The oarlock squealed. Rejoice turned the boat toward the shore again, but the vessel bucked and tipped.

Sideways rain drove into her face; and the wind howled. Lightning crackled and lit the black sea. Thunder boomed over the staccato drumming of the rain. Rejoice struggled with the boat, trying to steer to where shore should lay hidden behind a thick curtain of clouds and rain. A fierce squall spun the boat, and the tiller ripped out of Rejoice's hand. She snatched the handle, and the tiller beat into her side. The motor coughed and quit. She fumbled for the start button and pushed it repeatedly.

Nothing.

Her stomach lurched as the boat rocked and slid up a crest, down a trough. Rejoice huddled, sobbing, "What time I am afraid, I will trust in God."

The shrieking wind pushed her where it would.

SHATTERWORLD CHAPTER FOUR

The current surged. Ur-Veena wrapped his tentacles around a rubbery stem to keep from being rolled. The world's edge roiled and shivered under bursts of light. Sediment swirled about him. He huffed to clear his gills.

Had the children all retracted? He braced himself and tenderly palpated through the nursery. One poor child had a pebble stuck between its stalk and base. Its tendrils writhed in the muck. Ur-Veena flipped out the stone and siphoned clear water on the child. It promptly plopped into place and retracted into a blue ball capped with cartilage. Ur-Veena splayed out his tentacles. All the rest of the children had withdrawn and were safely capped. Good. Now he could search out the watch niche and wedge himself in.

* * *

Pale light streamed down in columns. Ur-Veena brushed off the accumulated muck from each child and blew clear water on their caps. One by one, each unfolded and extended its tendrils to filter-feed.

He caressed each child. How big the swelling at the base of each had become. A few more times of light, and each base would split open, releasing the triangular proto-swimmers. He loved the sight of proto-swimmers rising in a shimmering cloud, slowly coalescing into more discrete pinwheels as the triangles joined into groups of three and fluttered toward the deeper sea.

Maybe this would be the batch that developed into talking females.

Ur-Veena burrowed into the mud near the nursery. A disturbed guck-sucker blundered away and sank into the ooze. Guck-suckers fed on the scum that grew on the edge of the world in the time of darkness. Protected from the glare of the world's edge by leaf and mud, Ur-Veena waited and watched the silent children.

Clunk.

His eyes swiveled up. He gripped his stone sliver and rose. Rarely, perhaps five or six times in a lifetime, did torpals or other deep-sea horrors plunder the plant beds and nursery. The sound of a hollow stone tapped on stone came again. If not a torpal, then what made that sound?

Something huge pressed in the edge of the world. His hearts spasmed and his gills flared. Edgeworld-pressers meant churtrees!

SHATTERWORLD CHAPTER FIVE

Rejoice shivered awake the next morning. Water sloshed in the boat halfway up her shin. She gasped. Her wrinkled hands slipped on the lid of the toolbox. Like an arthritic old woman she bailed, trying to ignore how her arms hurt, how her stomach cramped with hunger, and how her wet clothes chafed her skin. She brushed back her dripping hair and searched for the shore of Sole. She sat up, clutching the bailer, and gazed at the empty sea and tattered fragments of clouds.

Father God, where was she? She turned, and oh, a stony spire lifted from the sea, there another, and there another. And past those peaks, barely visible, rose the single island in the center of Bull's-Eye.

The waves lapped on the thin ridge of rock. Was she between Bull's-Eye and the continent of Sole, or had she been blown clear to the other side of Bull's-Eye?

She shivered again, wrapping her arms around herself. The locater, the radio, the motor, nothing worked. She tilted the motor up. Water dripped out of a seam and numerous strands of shredded seaweed wrapped tightly around the propeller.

"Ouch, ouch, ouch," she whispered as she pawed through the toolbox for a knife. She hacked at the slimy mess until the propeller was free. And now the motor did work; and so did the radio, as did the locater, for a minute at least, long enough to show on a satellite image that she was between the continent and Bull's-Eye. With a spit of static the locater and the radio shorted out and died before she could call home.

Tears trickled down her face. *Baby! Stop it! God gave you a brain to use, so use it.* She rummaged through the toolbox again. She unfolded a solar collector and hooked it up. There was still some power left to the motor, but she would need more to reach the mainland. She unpeeled a ration bar. What had she learned in her survival lessons? Number one: Assess the situation. Be realistic, not fearful nor hopeful.

The clear section of the hull showed seaweed here, lots of seaweed—three kinds, in fact—the orange fishtail, red threads, and wide, brown ribbons. Wouldn't Brother Hancock be interested in that? She screwed together the long harvesting pole and guided its clipping end toward one of the red threads.

A large blue creature with tentacles darted through the weeds. The thing grappled with her pole and sawed at it with a blade, nearly twisting the pole out of her hand. A blister on her palm popped. She grabbed the pole with both hands and tried to shake the creature off, but it clung stubbornly to the pole and continued to saw. She held on and watched. What was that thing? What should she do?

The creature wore a bushel-sized, round, bright-blue shell, dotted with rainbows. Six jointed, dusky blue crab legs around the rim of the shell were as long as her arm. Six pearly blue tentacles writhed in front of the jointed legs as the creature slithered up the pole.

Let go! she commanded her disobedient hands. The thing's heavy tentacles flopped over the gunwale. Under its weight, the boat tipped, tools rolled out of the box, and the knife on the bench clicked onto the side and bounced into the sea. Rejoice scrambled toward the bow, slipping on the pile of seaweed. With a whoosh, the creature hauled itself out of the water and flopped into the boat. It jabbed the blade at Rejoice, just missing her.

Rejoice backed up and grabbed an oar. The creature lunged at her with the blade. She whacked aside the blade with her oar. Its tentacles curled up. The tentacle holding the blade uncurled in a blur to thrust the blade toward her knee. She blocked with the shaft of the oar. They strained against each other. Another tentacle wrapped its tips around the shaft and jerked. The blade slid down the shaft toward her hand. She let go of the shaft and clutched the paddle part. She thunked the creature's shell with the butt of the oar.

The creature backed a step, lowered the blade, and then lost its strength. Those blue, jointed legs scrabbled on the floor before folding flat. The creature raised its blade, dropped it, and deflated. Water squirted from under its shell. The tentacles fumbled with the blade. Rejoice waited, shifting the oar.

The two combatants faced each other as seconds ticked by. The creature convulsed and lay limp. Its rainbow dots faded.

Rejoice stared at the stub-handled blade and gulped back hysterical sobbing. Was it dead? She prodded the creature with her oar. It lay on the clear section of the boat, so she could not see whether or not there were others below. She stepped closer. Trembling, she reached out and touched a smooth, thin tentacle. Her fingers traced up the tentacle to the polished lip of the shining shell. The articulated legs were gritty and covered with an intricate mottling. Such an odd shape, and such beautiful colors. She swept her hand along the shell. A tentacle quivered. She stopped.

Two of its three main eyes looked straight at her, nestled between the shell lip and the tentacles. Bright blue they were, with flecks of gold. They did not seem like the flat, dead eyes of fish, but rather like the eyes of people, with round, black pupils.

Words stuck in her throat. She watched as the eyes slowly closed. "You—you're dying. Did you think I was attacking you? I—we—we don't want to hurt you. We came here to get away from war."

Its legs and tentacles subsided a little further.

Rejoice took a deep breath, slid her arms under the creature, and groaning with effort, shoved it up against the side of the boat. With her and the creature both on the same side, the boat tilted dangerously. The pile of seaweed she had gathered shifted and slapped into the sea. "Oh!" She gasped, and rolled the creature over the edge.

Splash! The boat pitched, tossing Rejoice like a ping-pong ball. Ration bars plopped into the sea and sank.

The oar floated nearby. She used the other oar to snag it and the harvest rod. She peered at the blue creature which lay where it had sunk, its limbs as purposeless as the seaweed around it. She had returned the creature to the water too late.

Rejoice let herself cry, though whether the tears were relief or sorrow, she could not tell. Before more of the creatures came, she needed to leave. She wiped her eyes and pushed the start button on the motor. After three attempts, the motor stuttered into life. "Thank you, God."

* * *

Under the wrath of the late afternoon sun, Rejoice licked cracked lips. She had been forced to stop and charge the motor seven times. Now the coast of Sole lay before her, but where was the colony? Should she go to the right or to the left? She scrutinized the shore, muzzy minded, exhausted. *How do I choose?*

She cradled her head on her knees. The idea seeped into her brain that she should beach anywhere and decide where to go after a night's sleep. She dozed off.

The dream of a giant bee woke her. Blearily, she looked up. Overhead, the colony's vertical takeoff-and-landing aircraft droned. On the water, a half kilometer away, the colony's other boat, putted toward her. Mother stood, waving and screaming, in the boat.

Rejoice lifted her hand.

Mother jumped, tottered, and fell into the ocean. Father tried to pull her back in, but she shouted, "I'll hang onto the boat. Just get my baby!"

Rejoice laughed and wiped her eyes.

Her parents and the men in the boat yelled to each other as they wrapped her in a blanket and gave her water and hot soup and salve for her sunburn. They praised God and hugged each other and talked about the search.

But nobody said a word when she opened her hand to show them the creature's blade.

SHATTERWORLD CHAPTER SIX

The hot circle had begun its slide into dark when Ur-Veena shuddered. Blindly, he groped for a plant, and pulled himself upright. Some of the blistered skin on his tentacles peeled off. He panted over raw gills.

He lived!

Painfully, with his sun-blasted eyes still closed, he stretched each tentacle one at a time, and then each leg. He probed with a double tipped tentacle. Each of his eyes still occupied its column, so that edge-presser had not been a churtree. That shape, too. Never had he seen anything with that shape. His tentacles quivered. If only he had the lost libraries to tell him what that monster in the air-ocean was.

The nursery. Had he saved the nursery? He palpated delicately about him, tracing the tiny arms of the children, wincing every time a plant rubbed a burn. Each child accounted for, he searched for his blade. He must have left it on the edgeworld presser. His tentacles closed over something alien with odd electric currents and a strange smell. One side of the object sliced through the broiled skin of a tentacle.

He dropped the odd blade. Trade? Had the thing offered to trade blades?

A whiff of rotting plant puzzled him. He dared to open his opercula and saw in dark and light the mass of plant pressing the edge. Enough floated there to feed the cluster for many days. Enough to give him time to form a new blade. But in his burnt and suffocated state, he could not reach the mass.

With one erratic step after another, he dragged himself toward the cluster until he happened upon another alien thing, a rectangle with flaps. He drew the small thing toward him and tasted it with his palps. He bit off a corner with his beak hidden in the middle of his tentacles. Its mantle tore easily, as did the dead material inside. Food. Not good food, but possibly the not-churtree had a different idea from Ur-Veena's people about what was good. He chewed. What new thing had come upon them?

SHATTERWORLD CHAPTER SEVEN

"Please, Mother. Just for a few minutes? I need some peaceful time," Rejoice said.

"You're feverish from your sunburn. You can have your peaceful time in bed."

Rejoice slumped in her chair at the table. Her mind still spun from all the people hugging her and telling her they were so glad they had found her and the party to celebrate her return and the doctor examination and Mother fussing over her. She never wanted that much attention again. The embarrassment was punishment enough for not paying attention to the weather. Tomorrow, after the relief had worn off, every father would tell his children not to be foolish like Rejoice. Her finger rubbed a circle on the smooth table top.

Mother bent and kissed her on the forehead. "Oh, all right. I don't know when Father will get back from the Elders' meeting, so Stronghold had better go with you. Get back before dark."

Only twenty minutes then. "Yes, Mother." Stronghold followed her to Ocean Shore Boulder and sat beside her facing the sea. Big Potato rose, but she gazed steadily at the sea.

"Uh, Sis?" Stronghold said. "I'm glad you didn't drown."

"I'm glad you weren't disappointed."

"I'm serious. I don't know what I would have done if you had drowned."

"Felt sad for a while, and then gone on, I suppose."

"No. There's nothing to go on for. I hate this planet. I hate the way we live." He balled up his hands and rubbed them on his thighs.

"That's no secret." Rejoice reached to scratch her cheek and stopped with her fingertips pressed against the skin. She must not do that. Already she glowed like a baked turkey. Rejoice changed the motion to rub the salve around "Someday you'll have to forgive Father and Mother for bringing us here."

"No. I'll have to stay damned, because I won't do it." He studied his fists.

Rejoice picked at the bandage covering the blister on her palm. Her heart sank.

"Sis, do you remember Old Earth?"

"A little. The beach. A birthday party. I think I had a friend named Charity. Not the Charity here."

Stronghold resumed rubbing his thighs. "I had a friend named Ricky, a normal guy with a normal name. But he wasn't holy enough for Father." He kicked his heels against the boulder. "A couple of weeks before we left, his folks came to Father and Mother and offered to take me. Ricky wanted me for his brother, and they wanted me for a son. Father snatched me away so fast my teeth rattled. I never saw Ricky again."

"What did you expect them to do? How would you have felt if they had said, 'Sure, you can have him. We didn't want our son anyway?"

"I wanted to stay with Ricky. Do you think this is a good place we're trapped in?"

She hunched her shoulders. No seagulls and no moon speckled with the lights of research stations. "They did the best they could. They made a mistake. Didn't you ever make a mistake?"

"Yeah, I did. I didn't run away when I could have."

Rejoice swallowed hard and stared at Big Potato's reflection on the sea. She whispered, "Well, here we are. It's too late to run away, so we need to make the best of it. There's life here and that creature is intelligent."

"Come on. Bees build hives. So what?"

"I studied the blade for hours. It was carefully chipped. There was a groove on the edge, and tiny, sharp crystals were glued into the groove to make teeth. Like a saw. Father said they were diamonds."

His hands shooed away the thought. "Crows pick up shiny things."

"Diamonds aren't naturally shiny or sharp. They have to be cut!" She swayed. "Oh-oh. I feel dizzy."

He rolled off the boulder and reached up for her. "Come on, then. Let me get you home."

* * *

A few hours later, Rejoice opened her eyes. The slit where her bed curtains overlapped let in a thread of light that fell jagged on her crumpled sheets. The resinous smell of salve permeated her tiny bed space. Her face burned and itched. She shivered with chill. Her joints ached. If she moved her head just so, she could see the side of Father.

Outside, her parents spoke in low voices, and there was an occasional light thump and a rustle. She didn't need to see them to know that Father sat at the desk, patting his Bible to emphasize a point, and Mother curled on the sofa, embroidering dark green holly leaves on cream colored placemats.

"...and if we can't set up some sort of amiable relationship with them, how can we use the seas without armor-plated vessels?" Father said.

"Well, I don't know if I can shake hands with the thing that tried to kill my baby."

"That one's dead. I pray we haven't begun a war."

Rejoice started to speak, but her lip split in two places. She licked her lips.

Father continued, "I guess it's a good thing that Elder Chin was a professor of linguistics. I had no idea that calm, sedate man could be so excited. He hopes to begin trade with them."

"And what do you propose to trade?" Mother softly sang the first few bars of a sailors' chantey.

"Fish, maybe. Depends on what they eat. Depends on what they think is pretty. Depends on whether or not they have the concept of trade."

"But what do we want from them?"

"Peace. Information. Diamonds."

Mother laughed again. "Oh, Theophilus, what will we do with diamonds?"

"Industry, my dear. If I'm to drill for oil, diamonds will come in handy. Our factory can make diamonds, but I'd rather that time was spent on making new homes." Silence except for the constant hum of the air purifier followed that. Then Father murmured, "It scares me when I think of the colony relying on me for geological information. I studied it on the ship, but I never once held in my hands a piece of gabbro or gneiss. I keep thinking that what I don't know is what's going to trip us up. What we don't know. Here we are, not a single one of us a scientist before we began our journey. Not a single one of us has had any practical experience."

"God will provide. Rejoice In The Lord's Salvation wants be a scientist."

"Astronomy is not practical."

Rejoice opened her mouth, but then Mother said, "Did you see how Not By Works Lest Any Man Should Boast was hanging around tonight? He kept asking if there was anything he could get for Rejoice to make her feel better."

"Seems like a nice boy. Brother Worthy overheard him tell one of his friends that he likes Rejoice because she doesn't giggle. If Not proves out, he may be a good choice for her. Though I'm not too sure about his parents."

"Oh?"

"Anybody named Worthy who hands his kid that name knows the kid will end up being called Not Worthy."

Mother laughed loudly. "Ha! Remember the Barbone family back—I don't know, some hundreds of years ago during Oliver Cromwell's rule of England? They called their son If Christ Had Not Died For Thee, Thou Hads't Been Damned. And all his friends called him Damned Barbones, as if it would have taken a big effort to call him If Barbones."

"Exactly.

"I think I'll start calling him Lest and see if that catches on." Fabric rubbed against fabric as Mother shifted. "You know who else was worried about Rejoice? No Confidence In The Flesh Cruz."

"Dr. Cruz's boy."

"He's such a sweetheart. But he's so shy. He won't talk with any of the girls. Yet he's always trying to help people who are hurting. Do you know that he's been trying to talk to Stronghold and encourage him?"

"He is a sensitive boy. But I doubt that Stronghold will listen to him. I heard Stronghold call him 'No Coordination in the Flesh Cruz.' And yes, I did reprimand him. I grow tired of reprimanding my son."

Mother sighed. "With all the glass panes that No Confidence has broken, it is accurate. Not a nice thing to say, but accurate. It's a good thing he switched as apprentice to Elder Chin."

Father scratched his chin and nodded. "Well, he won't need coordination to talk with the creatures." After a pause, Father said, "He's a few years older than Rejoice. But he is the only child from an excellent family."

"Well, he's presently an only child. We'll see what happens over the next year." This time they both laughed.

Oh no, not him! Rejoice covered her eyes and her palms slid on the salve. His eyes were so creepy.

"Yes, anyway, Rejoice is too young to be thinking about marriage now." Mother shifted again.

"But not too young to be thinking about her career?"

"She would be very good at it."

"To be sure. But you're asking for heartache, letting her think she can get out of milking cows and cutting hay. As soon as we shift to a simple agrarian lifestyle and start weaving, milking, and shoveling by hand, she won't have time to study the stars. You're setting her up by letting her think anything else."

"Farmers need meteorologists."

"Part-time meteorologists. Carol, don't you see that she hears you saying she can please herself and be whatever fancy enters her head? Remember when Stronghold asked me if there would be animals on New

Earth? I said maybe. He asked if there were trees. I said there might be. He asked if he could go on explorations. I said it depended on circumstances. What did he hear me say? He heard me say that there would be circuses and zoos and holo arcades here. There aren't any, and now he hates me. Rejoice will too when she discovers that the real world doesn't bow to her whims. And how can she know what she wants to be? She's only twelve. When she starts noticing how good Not, uh, Lest looks, she'll forget all about this. What childhood dreams do you still have?"

There was a long silence. Then Mother whispered, "Every single one of them." A longer silence, then, "You were one of them."

"Mother!" Rejoice cried.

The curtains swished open and blinding light leaped in.

"I hurt everywhere," Rejoice said.

Mother placed her fingers on her daughter's face. "And such a fever you have, too, my poor sweet love. I'll get you some medicine."

* * *

During the common breakfast, Deaconess Hernandez announced, "Brother Hancock has discovered a small, armored fish with three eyes. Tune to Announcements, and you'll see a picture of it on your screen. Laboratory analysis showed its proteins to be composed of the same amino acids as life on Old Earth. This should mean that when we introduce salmon in the ocean, they will find food."

"Fishing!" one of the triplets shouted.

Deaconess Hernandez cleared her throat and frowned at the triplets until they had subsided. "This might also mean that we have a source of protein that will allow us to discontinue the vat-grown meat sooner than our original plan."

"Next: the perennial wheat has sprouted in the first field and seems to be growing well."

Rejoice dragged her fork through her syrup, making a brown and white design on the plain white plate. She could guess why Deaconess

Hernandez was not bringing up her discovery of the hexacrab. Two tables over Brother Hancock grinned as he pointed out some detail on his screen to Elder Hernandez. Brother Hancock deserved his time in the light. And his discovery hadn't been made by being foolish.

After breakfast, Mother interrupted Rejoice's syrup doodling by touching her cheek with cool fingers. "You need to go home and rest."

"Mother. Why should I go home and feel bad when I can be studying? This is my apprentice day."

Makepeace hovered close and stroked her red hands. "Skin hotted."

"Ow! Stop that!"

Mother hesitated. "All right. But if you need to lie down, you tell Sister Guthry, and I'll come and get you."

Rejoice trudged a half kilometer south of the apartments, climbed the stairs to the weather station set on a mound of tumbled basalt, and sat down by the instrument banks blinking their varied lights. Sister Guthry hurried in, her thin, yellowed hair loose and gauzy around her head. She fumbled with her mask. "Let me show you this satellite sequence from the day before yesterday." She paused. "If I ever see this pattern again, I'll know a storm is coming here." She clicked through the satellite images of cloud swirls. Then she stopped and went over and carefully hugged Rejoice. "I'm so sorry."

Rejoice sucked in her breath at the painful embrace. "I'm not blaming you. I understand we're still learning the weather patterns. I'm the one that forgot to look up from time to time." She turned to the instrument banks. "May I set the ship's telescopes on space scan?"

Sister Guthry shook her head, and the skin under her chin vibrated. "I'm so sorry. I just can't do it with a clear conscience. We need every telescope we have on the Starflower trained on New Earth until we understand the weather here. You said it yourself. I don't want to risk losing you again."

Rejoice shifted in her chair. Her joints still ached and her skin throbbed in pain with each heartbeat. She couldn't use the ship or satellite telescopes even for a little bit. Maybe it was all punishment for damaging one of the colony's boats.

"Rejoice, are you all right? Do you want to go home and rest?"

"No." It would take a day to explain what she did want, and likely Sister Guthry wouldn't care anymore than her parents. She had signed the charter along with them.

Sister Guthry settled into the rolling chair beside her and watched her for a while. "All right, then," she said and pulled Rejoice's screen to her. "Let's do some review. We'll survey the trigonometry the Starflower used to calculate your position yesterday."

"Could I please name the other planets? New Earth, First City, Big River; I think that's carrying plainness too far. Please? I don't want to beg to look at Gas Giant or Near Sun."

Sister Guthry covered her mouth and then lowered her hand to her chest, revealing a grin. "After trig, you can name the planets anything you want."

Rejoice smiled. It wasn't seagulls, but it was something.

SHATTERWORLD CHAPTER EIGHT

Ur-Nissi emptied the bag of clingers, spineys, and basalt flakes in front of Ur-Veena who opened one eye a slit and surveyed the growing pile before him. Ur-Veena had not had the strength nor his blade to pry off clingers from the basalt as he had dragged himself to the cluster, so Ur-Nissi had done the gathering for him. The spineys tried to wriggle from their thready seaweed nets. Ur-Veena squirted some fresh water over his gills and chose a splinter of basalt to make a stele to describe the not-churtree. He broke off spines of varying sizes from the spineys, dipped the spines into the clinger's glue glands, and then attached them to the splinter. A wriggling spiney scraped off another patch of dead skin on his tentacle.

Ur-Nissi, the largest male in the cluster, grabbed the denuded spiney and flung it away to regenerate elsewhere. "What is it?"

"Not-churtree," Ur-Veena answered. "What else, I do not know. Perhaps it is described in the lost libraries."

"We have searched for the lost libraries for two hex hex hex years. I doubt that we will ever find them."

"We will find them, or we will make new ones."

Ur-Nissi stroked a raw patch on Ur-Veena's tentacle. "If you live, you will bear many scars."

Ur-Veena clicked his beak, "I will live. I will scar. I will touch this new thing that has come into this world."

SHATTERWORLD CHAPTER NINE

One week later, sheets of rain cascaded from the roof of the Meetingplace, bubbled down the drainage ditches, and cast a wavering light over the colonists at breakfast.

Deaconess Hernandez gripped her screen. "Soil building is canceled today." Thunder growled over her voice. She waited and took a deep breath. Another rolling growl hid whatever she had to say. She shook her head and clumped to the table where Elder Hernandez rubbed her shoulder as she shouted in his ear.

The colonists stood and sang, "Praise God, from Whom all blessings flow. Praise Him all—"

BOOM

Makepeace jumped and squealed.

"—here below." The people's lips moved but could not be heard over the thunder and squealing and drumbeat of rain.

As they finished singing, the lightning moved past First City and the rain eased, but Makepeace continued to squeal.

Dishes clattered and benches scraped across the floor as the people parted to attend to their chores after breakfast. The sharp smell of ammonia cleanser replaced the sweet smell of syrup.

Rejoice caught up to the glass-factory foreman on the covered sidewalk and tugged on his sleeve. "Brother Hammer?"

He stopped, glanced at his watch, and planted his feet far apart. He ignored the ropes of rain and gusting wind flung at them through the arches of the loggia. "Yes, Young Lady Rejoice."

She tugged her coat tighter. "I was wondering if you could make a little batch of optical-grade glass for me. I want to grind lenses to make an optical telescope."

He frowned at his watch. "What for?" The wind howled through gaps in the grids of thousands of panes of glass sheltering the fields.

Rejoice shouted to be heard, "I want to look at the stars. I want to follow the weather on Wimbleweather." She paused. "The largest gas giant planet in this system." A cold raindrop trickling down her neck made her shiver.

"Why don't you use the ship's telescopes?"

"I'm not allowed to. They're being used to watch the weather on New Earth."

"Rightly so," he said. "Why should you care anything about space? We're never going back. And after what you've been through, I'd think you would be glad they're watching the weather. We were among the stars for seven years. Wasn't that long enough?" He glanced at the rain with a rictus of disgust. "I've work to do."

"Please. We couldn't see the stars in warp. All I saw were pictures. I'll grind the lenses. I'll even cast them if you want, if you're too busy."

He shook his head. "What would you grind them with?"

"The optical equipment. If you'll tell me where it is, I'll go get it. I promise to put everything back exactly the way it was."

He shook his head again. "We won't need that stuff for years. It's still on the Starflower."

"Oh! I thought—well, then, on the next supply run."

"Young Lady, the last supply run to the ship was two weeks ago. We won't be going back up for another six months at least."

"But I—" Two weeks ago! "Then how can I make a telescope?"

Brother Hammer tapped his watch. "Young Lady, you want to look at the stars, here's what you do. Tonight, when it gets dark, go outside and look up. Right now, we both have work to do. God be with you." He turned and stepped into the rain. The wind flipped off his hat. He caught the brim of the hat and jammed it back on his head. From the fields came a loud rattle, and then the crash of a pane of glass smashing.

Rejoice retreated into the Meetingplace and stood, dripping on the ceramocarbon tile. The rain streaked through the air and bounced on the ground.

* * *

Rejoice trudged through the steady rain to the weather station. On the rain-slick stairs, she stopped to watch the sea churn and dash over the dock and fret at the tethered boats. Breakers crashed against Ocean Shore boulder. No Confidence In The Flesh had broken quite a few glass panels. Could she grind some of that broken glass on the grinding wheel? The grinder made hoes sharp, but what would it do to the glass? No, she needed thicker glass and a much finer grinder.

She slid her feet across the stair tread texture to wipe off sand, and did it again when she reached the landing mat. The wind blasted open the outer door when she moved the lever. She pushed against that wind to close the door and leaned against it, panting. The floor was all sandy mud and water. She hung up her dripping coat and mask, and shivered.

After opening the inner door, welcome dry heat blew on her wet face. She dried off her face and hands with the towel hung on the inner door and laid her shoes on a rack.

Inside, Sister Guthry stood at the massive, reinforced window, arms folded, watching the spray and foam scudding across the beach. She glanced at Rejoice and then surveyed the roiling sea again. "I hope we find out this is the rainy season. We can't harvest the wheat if it stays like this."

Rejoice still shivered.

Sister Guthry bustled over. "Oh, you look so cold. Here, you sit down right in front of the heater. Would you like some hot tea before we begin?"

"No."

Sister Guthry sat in the other rolling chair and blinked. "Something's wrong. What is it?"

"Nothing." Rejoice sighed.

"Hmm." Sister Guthry rolled to the inset microwave oven, poured chamomile tea into a buttercup-yellow mug and rolled back to set it before Rejoice on the cloudy glass counter. "I think it's more than rainy-day blues. Ah. You're almost thirteen. Could be hormones."

"That's not it," Rejoice said, her face heating up. "I wanted to make a telescope since I can't use the ship's. But Brother Hammer doesn't want to help me. It would take him ten minutes to make the right kind of glass, but he won't do it. And the optical equipment is on the ship, and the last supply run for months was two weeks ago."

"I heard the announcement."

"I didn't." That's what she got for letting her mind wander during the boring announcements. She stared at the screens on the wall opposite the window. They showed weather over three places on the planet and temperature stats. On the far end of the wall a line jiggled, marking temblors somewhere on New Earth. Stronghold was lucky he went with Father to set up more seismometer stations. Maybe if she got interested in geology she could get a chance to obtain the equipment she wanted. And maybe she could have a chance to get away from the colony for at least a little bit.

"Perhaps your mind was on other things. You sound frustrated."

Rejoice sipped her tea. What? What were they talking about?

Sister Guthry caught her lower lip between her teeth and studied her apprentice pupil. "Are you warm enough now for a good problem?"

Rejoice nodded. Sister Guthry entered a problem on Rejoice's screen that involved sixty-three steps at minimum to solve. Rejoice shoved aside her mug and studied the problem. The last time she had been given a sixty-three-step problem, she had needed sixty-nine steps to solve it. She meant to come closer this time. Slowly, as the tea cooled, she considered how best to attack the problem. When she saw the pattern, she moved surely and deliberately, each step and calculation soothing her, each step easily leading to the next step in an orderly progression. The minutes melted away as hidden numbers revealed themselves in new patterns. Her left hand opened and closed close to her left eye, blocking out distractions in her peripheral vision.

Finally, Rejoice crowed, "I got it!" She handed her answer and proof to Sister Guthry. "It took me only sixty-five steps."

A gust of wind tore at the windowpanes of the weather station. A blanket of water slapped the little building. Rejoice had forgotten about the storm.

"That's elegant." Sister Guthry handed the screen back. She ran a plump hand over her tidy hair and leaned in her chair. "You know, that's one of the things I really like about you."

"That I'm good at math?"

"Well, that too. I like to teach math, and you like to learn it, which is a happy combination. But I was referring to something else. I like how. . ." Her hands circled as she searched for the words. "How even when you're upset, you can still think. You can do what needs to be done."

Rejoice cocked her head. "Isn't that what we're supposed to do?"

"Oh, my, yes. But it isn't something all of us can do. Most of us are better at screaming than we are at thinking. Are you ready to scan space?"

Rejoice gasped. "Do you mean it?"

"I think we can spare one of the telescopes for twenty minutes. But one sign of lightning, I'll need to pull in the receiver. Then we're leaving, all right?"

"Right." She hurried over to the instrument banks and sat poised with her fingers over the key board. What should she ask for first? She set the ship's cameras at near space scan. Five minutes later, she yelped, "Look at this! An asteroid we haven't catalogued yet."

Sister Guthry bent to examine the screen. "Well, well. You are good at discovering things, aren't you? Now what do you do?"

Rejoice frowned as she directed the satellites to turn their lenses toward the new object, the ship to beam lasers on the object and the satellites and compare the different times it took for the laser to reflect back, and the computer to perform an analogous object search. In ten minutes, she grinned and pointed at the spectral analysis. "Metallic meteor. Eleven kilometers long, eight wide, of two fused pieces. Eight hundred thousand kilometers away. Oh, that's close, isn't it?"

"Yes, it is. Command the ship's computers to track it every two days for the next few months."

"I don't know how to do that yet."

Sister Guthry rolled closer. "Okay. Pull up the scan page again and touch the further instructions button."

Rejoice followed the directions, her lips stretched back in a grin.

Sister Guthry took the screen, opened the catalog, and tapped through to the designations. "Congratulations, dear. Asteroid Rejoice is in the catalog."

"You named it after me?"

"You discovered it."

The station shook under a blast of wind and rain, and metal crashed outside the door.

"Oh, dear," Sister Guthry said. "We're coming apart. I'd better see what that is." After closing the inner door she pulled the lever of the outer door, and the wind whipped it open. With one hand on the door frame, she stepped out to the landing. "Just as I thought. The antenna ripped off the wall. The bracket tore loose." She stepped back into the airlock and stammered, "Rejoice, I'm going to hold the antenna shaft before it snaps. You run to the maintenance shed and get a repairman. But be careful."

The antenna creaked, and Sister Guthry plunged outside without her mask or coat. Rejoice snatched up her coat and followed. Both airlock doors banged against walls. The antenna snapped and Sister Guthry slipped over a step.

She fell, landed head first, rolled, flipped, and crashed at the bottom of the stairs. Rejoice pounded down the stairs and crouched by her head. "Sister Guthry! Are you hurt?"

Sister Guthry grunted and clenched her teeth. Cold rain spat in her face as her eyes pleaded with Rejoice and her breathing hitched. Rejoice threw her coat over Sister Guthry and paused. Her teacher's head lay on rock. Rejoice pulled off her dress, wadded it up, and slid it under Sister Guthry's cheek. Then she sprinted off in her petticoat toward the clinic.

* * *

Rejoice shivered in her blanket on the sofa and sipped sweet mint tea. Her body had warmed long ago, but cold dread still made her shiver. *Oh, God, please God*, she thought over and over in numbing refrain. Was there a God to hear her pray for her teacher?

The apartment door banged open. She jumped. So did Father at his desk and Stronghold on the sofa beside her. The tea in her cup sloshed, and she set it aside on the tiny end table.

Mother strode in and tossed her mask on the table. The mask skidded until caught by the female holly bonsai tree.

Mother slumped into a dining chair. "Praise God for His mercy."

"She'll be okay?" Rejoice asked.

"Yes, she'll recover. Though not right away. She broke her hip and one rib."

Father edged over to the chair, nearly tripping over Stronghold's legs and knelt by Mother. "Your first severe trauma surgery. I am so proud of you and your team."

Mother smiled and laid her head on his shoulder, made a noise of contentment, and said quietly: "Brother Carlson handled the anesthesia perfectly, and Dr. Cruz never hesitated."

"And you?"

"I was terrified." She swallowed and sat up. Father moved into a chair next to her and held her hands as she continued, "But I assisted her like it was a hologram and not Sister Guthry. I took too long stitching up the incisions, but Sister Cruz said I did fine."

"When can I see her?" asked Rejoice.

"Oh, probably tomorrow. But, it'll be two months at least before she can get out of a cast. Maybe longer. It depends on how well she responds to electrotherapy and implants. Let's pray it takes only two months. You won't have any free time until she's back on duty."

"What?"

"That's how it works with apprentice tutors and pupils. If Elder Ruiz was hurt, Stronghold would have to take on as many of his responsibilities as he could."

"I'll be the meteorologist?"

"Not quite. Every day you'll be responsible to get the weather data to Sister Guthry before school and before lunch. After lunch, you'll need to take her place in the fields. And then you'll have to get her the data after supper."

Rejoice blinked a few times while she thought, and then she flung off the blanket. "Does this mean I can skip school and study astronomy instead?"

"No," Father said. "That means no astronomy for two months."

Disappointment punched her in the stomach.

Stronghold snorted. Makepeace crawled out from under the table, grabbed Stronghold's knees, and looked up into his face.

Mother sighed. "I'm afraid that's what it means."

Rejoice's anger stomped over her attempt at staying calm. "Father! What do you have against astronomy? God made the universe. What's so wrong with studying it? We live in it, and it's important."

"Rejoice," said Father gently, and she stopped. "Do not whine," he said in an even quieter voice. "Yes, the universe is important. But those stars are not going to cry if you starve because you watched them instead of planting beets."

"Planting beets is better than crunching over lava fields searching for iron ore that isn't there," muttered Stronghold.

Rejoice's ears and neck burned. How could she make them understand? Mother knew about dreams. She turned to her and struggled to keep her voice even and quiet. "Mother, how would you like it if someone told you that you mustn't sing for two months?"

"I wouldn't like it. But if there were sufficient reason, I suppose I'd tape over my mouth and pray fervently for the two months to go by quickly." Rejoice fought to keep her lip from trembling. What could she say to that? That's exactly what Mother would do. What did it take to believe like her parents did?

"You know," Stronghold said, "if we were back on Old Earth, she could be an astronomer and you couldn't say anything about it."

Mother and Father looked at each other. Father tightened his lips and shook his head.

"Ah," Mother said. "Maybe, maybe not. Things were changing when we left."

"She could be an astronomer." Stronghold leaned forward "And you could buy your groceries at a store like normal people." He pointed to Makepeace, who had his ear pressed to the corner of his screen. "And he wouldn't have been autistic or whatever he is. He's brain-damaged because you had to take us here."

"That's enough." Even though Father said it quietly, his eyebrows drew together and lines pointed toward his thinned lips.

Rejoice's hands grabbed each other and bunched in front of her mouth.

"He didn't have to be brain-damaged, but Elder Smith said it was time to go, and you went."

"I said that's enough."

Stronghold slumped against the sofa back. Makepeace whimpered and crawled onto his lap. Stronghold glanced down, brushed his knuckles across his little brother's cheek, and whispered, "I'm sorry, Makepeace. I didn't mean to make you feel bad." Makepeace snuggled against him. Stronghold wrapped his arms around him and stroked his back.

Rejoice refused to look at her parents, but she felt their utter stillness, their unwillingness to speak lest the speaking turn into shouting. She folded her hands together and clamped them between her knees. If they were loose, she would slap Stronghold's mouth. She hadn't asked him to butt into her argument. Why didn't he care that he had made *her* feel bad?

And yet, he was right. If they were back on Old Earth, she could be an astronomer, and no one would suffer for it. She could use the telescopes set on Charon that could tell whether or not a far-off planet had an atmosphere that indicated life. She could use computers that jacked directly into her brain and worked on massive networking systems.

She stared at her knees. But what good did it do to think like that? She and Stronghold could scarcely steal the Starflower and fly back to Earth. They were here, and here to stay, and griping about it wouldn't let her watch the stars any sooner. She resolved to do her work and Sister Guthry's for the next two months without complaining. But after that, she would study space even if she had to skip school to do it.

* * *

The next day was The Lord's Day. The family took their rest after the morning prayer and sermon. Mother and Father met with the Hancocks and Copulos to play their weekly board games.

Rejoice enjoyed the Hancocks' energy and humor. But the Copulos, despite having five children, including Harmony, their youngest, did not seem to like children. So all the younger kids went outside while Rejoice, Stronghold, and Harmony watched Makepeace.

"I sure like your Aunt Hancock," Rejoice told Harmony while still sucking on the hard candy that Sister Hancock had snuck into her hand. Rejoice kicked a clot of sand on the beach.

Harmony smiled. "I like her too. But why do your parents seem so sad?"

Rejoice watched Stronghold pull Makepeace in his little red wagon to the beach for their weekly throw-stones-in-the-sea contest. What could she say that wasn't gossip or discouraging?

Harmony said, "He's still pretty angry about everything, isn't he?"

"I don't know if he'll ever be happy again."

"Oh, I think he will."

Harmony gazed at Stronghold with that mushy expression. Rejoice's stomach turned. "Race you to Ocean Shore Boulder." She darted away.

"No fair!" shrieked Harmony. They both ran, spraying sand, panting, arms pumping. Rejoice barely touched the boulder first.

* * *

In her bed space that night, while working on her screen, muffled cries invaded her tiny space. Makepeace? She blanked out the article about determinants of albedo and reached for the curtain.

Father said, "Carol, wake up. It's a dream. Wake up."

Rejoice let go the curtain. The cries stopped.

"Oh." Mother gasped. "Oh."

"Same one?"

"Oh, yes. Stronghold reminded me yesterday. Then having such a good time with the Hancocks and Copulos made me miss all the ones we left behind."

"Let me get you some water."

A curtain rustled, feet padded across the hard floor, water spurted from a faucet, and Mother gulped noisily between gasps for air.

"Thank you, dear. I keep thinking of Duke and Nell and Chancy and Shawn and precious baby Amandala." Mother gasped one more time, and then sighed.

"Not a baby anymore. Thirty-one at least."

"If."

"Yes, if. But if it did happen, it happened a long time ago. They didn't want to go. They tried to keep you from going. You can't blame yourself."

If what had happened? Rejoice jerked upright and thumped her head on the ceiling of her bed space. Bright lines streaked across her vision.

Her parent's voices dropped to whispers. Rejoice slid back under her blanket and rubbed the painful spot on her head.

* * *

A week later, Rejoice washed her brown dress in the sink, pulled on her blue Lord's Day dress, and tucked into one pocket a handkerchief embroidered with blue holly leaves and yellow berries.

With Mother humming a happy march, they walked straight to the chapel, for the colony fasted together every Lord's Day morning. Make-peace munched on a rice cake as they walked, because little children were exempt from times of fasting.

Golden sunlight streamed in through the wrinkled glass of the arched chapel windows, shone on drifting dust motes, and cut the air into shafts of dark and light. The pews still smelled like new plastic and gleamed golden brown against the only carpeted floor in the colony. The deep blue pile of the carpet muffled sound so the colonists could meditate in silence for the first half hour of the church service. It worried Rejoice that usually she meditated on how hungry she was or questioned why she seldom heard from God. Today, though, she fretted about Mother's nightmare.

What had happened on Old Earth? Or rather, what had possibly happened on Old Earth? All she could remember were seagulls and the moon and Charity and the slick top of the coffee table with some bright pennies on it she had swallowed. The coins had tasted cold and sharp. Whistles and the clackaty-clack of trains that shook the walls of her home. She shivered. Charity would be thirty-five now, not twelve. Relativity worked in strange ways.

When the pastor rose and read from the Psalms, Rejoice sighed in relief. What did everybody think about for half an hour?

Next the choir, led by Mother, sang five hymns. The congregation rose and sang five more hymns. Rejoice winced at Father's enthusiastic and off-key singing. After that the different Elders prayed, and then Pastor Wiseman preached a two-hour sermon about the verse in Isaiah, "Come now, let us reason together."

Rejoice watched Stronghold, who sat slouched with his arms folded across his chest. He leaned over and whispered, "He can really shovel it, can't he?"

Father frowned at him and shook his head. Stronghold resumed his slouch.

After the sermon, everyone rose, and the Elders prayed for the safety and growth of the Sisters and Brothers back on Old Earth. The congregation was dismissed for a cold feast that featured lots of pies and ice cream at the Meetingplace attached to the chapel. After lunch, the Holly family headed home and Deaconess Redhorse dragged Makepeace to her apartment for the afternoon.

At home, Father lay down on the sofa and hummed as he read a commentary until he fell asleep. Mother lay on the floor at right angles to him and raised her feet to lay them on his stomach. Stronghold climbed into his bed space and pulled the curtain.

Rejoice sat alone at the table. Why did kids always want to play and run whenever there was free time, and grown-ups always wanted to take naps? What was so attractive about sleep?

She toyed with her screen for a few moments. Nothing interested her. All she wanted to know was what Mother dreamed about enough times that Father could tell what the dream was. She couldn't ask about a private conversation because seven years of close ship-board living had bred a strict set of rules about privacy.

Her fingers tapped idly down the screen's menu. *Oh!* She knew how to ask.

Rejoice stretched out on the floor with her head next to Mother's. "Mother? Are you awake? Why did you leave Old Earth?"

Mother shifted, but kept her eyes closed. "To start a new life here. One where we could follow God."

"Couldn't you follow God on Old Earth?"

Mother laughed. "Yes, of course. That's what most of our Brothers and Sisters are doing."

"So why did you come here?"

"To be God's people in another part of the galaxy."

"But when you left, you didn't know for sure that you could live here. Why didn't you wait until a probe got here, checked it out, and came back with a report of the conditions?"

"That would have taken sixty years. I would have been eighty-seven and too old. Did you notice that, except for three people, nobody older than forty came on the ship?"

"But there might have been something here to kill us all."

Mother shrugged as much as one can while lying on the floor. "Living is risky. You could choke to death on your next mouthful of oatmeal."

Rejoice rolled onto her stomach, propped herself up on her arms and studied Mother's face. "That's inconsistent. The grown-ups in this colony are so careful. We get safety lectures all the time, and first-aid lessons, and procedure reviews. We have to wear safety glasses during construction work and filter masks every time we step outside. But you wildly flew to a planet you didn't know anything about."

Mother opened her eyes. "Young Lady, we knew it had a good atmosphere. And we knew what we were leaving."

"What?"

Mother closed her eyes and sighed. After frowning a moment, she said, "Do you know why we had to live on the poor side of town?"

"We did?"

"You were too little to notice, I guess. Anyway, we lived there because I had you." She craned her head around to smile at Rejoice. "The government was trying to discourage people from having more than one child. You could adopt all you wanted, but if you bore more than one child, employers had tax incentives to fire you. And there were no welfare benefits for those so imprudent as to bring an extra child into the world. Even so, some people still wanted more than one child. That's why the Apgils were so eager to adopt Stronghold."

"Who?"

"Ricky's parents. You probably don't remember them. We were afraid they were going to kidnap your brother and hide him until after the launch date."

"Would you have left without him?"

The blankets in Stronghold's bed space rustled.

"No. Of course not. We made sure it wouldn't happen. Many more people wanted to come than could fit on the ship. We had to draw lots."

Why wouldn't she answer her question? "Mother, why did you put our name in a drawing of lots? You could have joined a commune."

"Some of us did."

"So why did you come here when you could have done something else?"

Mother snorted, crossed her arms, and whispered, "Are you going to be like Stronghold and criticize us for every single move we make?"

Rejoice averted her gaze. "No, Mother. I'm sorry. Pray forgive me."

"You're forgiven. Now please, may I take my nap?"

Rejoice picked herself up and walked out of the apartment, grabbing her mask along the way. So, her mother wasn't going to tell her. "I hate secrets," muttered Rejoice as she walked to Ocean Shore Boulder. She clambered up to survey the land. A drizzle began, dampening her dress. Although she had forgotten her rain coat, she did not want to return to the apartment. It was low tide so she walked under the dock and leaned against the pilings underneath until the rain stopped.

Just after she settled, footsteps clunked above her as two men walked to end of the pier. She recognized the voices of Elder Smith and Brother Hancock. They were probably telling each other secrets. Rejoice stood still and squinted against the sunlight glinting off the sea between cloud shadows. A strip of their faces appeared through one of the gaps in the plastic boards of the pier.

They sat side by side, facing the sea and dangling their legs over the edge of the dock.

Elder Smith said, "I can't help it. The way I see it, it's all foolishness, chasing after savage octopuses."

Brother Hancock braced himself against the dock, closed his eyes, and leaned into the cool drizzle on his face and the fresh breezes skipping over the cold waters of the sea. "Those diamonds for our drill bits are not foolishness. The composite drills we brought along will last for years, but then what? Besides, our colony will grow, and we'll need more materials. You were happy enough when I announced that as soon as we get plankton levels up, I'm going to seed this beach with crab and clam larvae."

"That's close to shore and doesn't interfere with developing our fields and barns."

"Was I or was I not called to develop whatever ocean resources our planet might have? Is or is not this planet ninety percent ocean?"

Elder Smith cleared his throat and tugged at his gray beard. "The percentage depends on what's under the polar ice." He waved a hand. "No. I don't interfere with another man's calling. But I tell you, it would have been a lot more convenient if that Holly girl had discovered them five months later."

Rejoice's face, neck, and ears heated. Eavesdropping was rude, and banned. But if she moved, they would know that she had been eavesdropping.

"You don't mean that," Brother Hancock said. "Suppose our plankton had been poisonous to them?"

"Then we would have never discovered them, eh?"

Brother Hancock sat silent.

Elder Smith waved his hand again. "I know. It would have been terrible, for we need to respect all of God's creatures. I know. We're to take dominion, not crush and kill. I know. I also know we're behind schedule, and I won't get my farmhouse with the willows set around and ducks in the front yard and leghorns in the back as fast as I want it. Which is yesterday."

Brother Hancock chuckled. "You won't be happy until you're out there shoveling manure."

"You got it, Brother."

Brother Hancock sniffed. "The sea smells better."

Rejoice agreed and smiled. The men rose, stretched, and ambled back over her head and down to the beach and toward the apartments. When they disappeared around the corner of a warehouse, Rejoice breathed easier and meandered barefoot along the shore until the skin of her feet wrinkled.

SHATTERWORLD CHAPTER TEN

Ur-Veena reached through the bars of the corral and stroked one of the mute females. En-Teppi shoved seaweed through the bars.

Ur-Veena whistled and clicked, "Good day to you, my lovely. Do you like the fresh seaweed? I have a pretty slug shell for you to examine."

Passing Ur-Nissi grated, "Why do you bother talking to them?"

Ur-Veena snapped out a tentacle at Ur-Nissi. "I think this one understands some of my words. If we keep breeding with the more intelligent females, perhaps a future generation shall have talking females restored to them. Perhaps a future generation shall again feel females with lives of honor."

Ur-Nisse snapped a tentacle back at Ur-Veena and continued his crawl to the east.

"I hear the not-churtrees approaching with their stink-pusher." said En-Teppi.

Ur-Veena cocked one eye up to the edge of the world. Beside him, En-Teppi shifted and coiled one blue tentacle.

Ur-Veena clicked a broken spine against the stele of basalt and spines he was working on. This stele recorded the last visit of the not-churtree. "They come often. They want more trade than we can give them."

En-Teppi crawled to his niche and returned with a net woven of plant fiber. "Perhaps they will accept the shatterstone unworked." He rolled out a diamond the size of five spines bundled.

Ur-Veena palpated the stone. "Perhaps they will."

SHATTERWORLD CHAPTER ELEVEN

"**B**ut, Father, when can I go out to see the hexacrabs?" Rejoice said after morning school. She set her screen on the apartment table. "We could count it as an afternoon school field trip."

Next to her, Makepeace rubbed a holly berry into pieces. He tilted his head and sang, "Slosh waters under shadows and sharp legging, soft legging, basket round shine."

Stronghold scowled. "Why are you so interested in a bunch of primitive squids?"

"They sing such lovely songs," Mother said.

"They're another reason we shouldn't be here," Stronghold said. "We came here to be peaceful, right? And the first thing we do is steal all their seaweed. It's just like what the fifty-nine states did to the Native Americans. And just like the Native Americans, they're going to fight back when they find out what we're doing to them."

Father nodded gravely. "If we find a tribe of hexacrabs using the seaweed beds we're harvesting from, we'll have to stop harvesting. But you're misremembering some American history, son. William Penn treated the Native Americans fairly, and they had a good relationship."

"Penn's children didn't. We need to leave before we harm them."

Father raised his eyebrows. "You need to make sure you treat the hexacrabs fairly." He leaned back in the chair. "Every day I'm more encouraged about our life here. Our clover-wheat fields are growing well. Brother Higoshi discovered moss growing in a cave mouth southeast of here. We've got algae and zooplankton that's fairly ultraviolet resistant, so we can fill that upper layer of ocean where nothing grows yet. The hexacrabs tolerate our plants and eat our fish with relish. They're intensely grateful that we're going to expand their food chain. Praise God that things are looking good. When you consider the odds . . ." He smiled at Mother as though they shared a secret. She reached across the table to squeeze his hand.

Rejoice envisioned the holly berry she had planted in one corner of a field. If it sprouted and grew, she would dig it up and give it to Mother for a present when they moved out to their farm. First the fields, then the barns, then the farmhouses. But she still didn't have an answer to her question. "When am I going out to visit the hexacrabs? I discovered them."

"When we know for certain that it's safe."

Father hated whining. Rejoice opened and closed her fist near her left eye for a few seconds before saying in a low pitched voice, "But you've been talking to them for two months now."

Father shook his head gently. "To be sure. But did you learn Greek in two months? On Old Earth, it takes years to know a foreign people. How long will it take us to understand these native sea people?"

"Why can't we just go to another planet?" Stronghold asked. "One with people we can already talk to. Normal people."

Rejoice pressed the side of her face. Why, why, why did he keep butting in?

Father held up a hand and counted finger by finger. "Three, no, four reasons. One, we're making it here."

"You call living on a rock and wearing a mask everywhere you go making it?"

"Two, God called us here."

"What did He do? Use the comm-line?"

"Three. We don't know that any of the other planets are as good as this one. Nobody had returned from any of them before we left Old Earth. Four. The names of all other stars with planets that had life were erased from our database. So we wouldn't go anywhere else than to the planet whose charter we paid for."

"Who erased it?"

"The government. Believe me, we wanted the information."

Stronghold slammed down his fork. "You win. You're always right."

Mother sang the first line of an old song: "How are you going to keep them down on the farm after they've seen Paree?"

"Stop laughing at me," Stronghold said.

A knock at the door interrupted. Mother rose and ushered in Elder Ruiz.

"Theophilus," he said. "What do you make of these?" He turned over a box and poured out on the table a dozen long splinters of basalt covered with bristling white thorns and bumps. "We're dredging them up by the thousands."

Father jumped up and grabbed two of them. "I saw one of these in the hexacrab cluster. Don't—You're not destroying them?"

"Well, the dredger isn't exactly gentle."

"Dig elsewhere until I tell you otherwise. I mean, until the Elders tell you. You can move the dredger away from the area where these are, can't you?"

"It will be a lot of work and put us behind schedule."

Father turned away from Elder Ruiz, staring at the rocks in his hands, and narrowed his eyes. He worked his jaw silently for minute, grinned, and handed one of the slivers to Rejoice. "You're right. We do need a field trip. Let's go see those hexacrabs and ask them about this."

Rejoice clutched the stone and danced inside.

* * *

Three hours later, the Holly family leaned over the gunwales of the Sea Star to wave at Brother Hancock in the Sea Squirt. Protective clouds softened the sunlight to a pearly glow on the smooth sea. Father fastened the two boats side by side so they rose and fell together on almost imperceptible swells.

Brother Hancock, a reedy man with gentle blue eyes and a bulbous nose, turned up the reception on the monitor, and pointed to the screen set in the bow of the boat. On it, Elder Chin in scuba gear talked to a mottled hexacrab.

Elder Chin spoke, and bubbles rose, bursting and obscuring his voice. A small computer beside him translated his words into the clicks, grinding, and song of the sea people: ". . . and above our ocean of air lies another ocean of space. It is a place we cannot ascend to unless we wear protection, or else we would die. It is in that space-ocean that the sun which makes your light swims."

The pod of hexacrabs before Elder Chin rubbed tentacles together and ground their beaks in excitement. The mottled hexacrab spoke and the computer translated: "Exist ocean above space-ocean, question?"

Elder Chin swept one hand over his head, and that tangled his feet in the improvised foothold. The largest hexacrab reached out with three tentacles to place the human facing them. "Thank you, Ur-Nissi. There is another ocean, yes. But it is not above space as space is above air, and air is above water. Extend your leg and draw it back." The hexacrabs extended articulated legs, and then folded them under their shells. "That ocean we call warp. It folds all the other oceans into itself as you fold your legs into yourself. More than that I do not understand, and I cannot explain."

The hexacrabs squealed their astonishment.

Elder Chin reached into a net bag and pulled out a small, stoppered bottle. All eyes swiveled toward the bottle.

"Good," Father said. "I wonder what they'll make of that."

"They seem so bright," Mother said. "You can tell they're honest, or they would have accused us of being liars by now. How can they learn so much so fast?"

"Shh." Father leaned closer to the screen. Their boat bumped into the other boat.

Elder Chin spoke. "Under your feet is another ocean."

The mottled hexacrab with one stubbed tentacle stirred up the muck. "Exist under feet this, then rock."

"Yes, an ocean of rock. And under the ocean of cold rock, there is an ocean of hot rock. Sometimes the hot rock squeezes through the cold rock and squirts into your ocean."

Grind. Grind. "Therefore exist cause of boiling water and hot rock during Dark Death. Therefore . . . Therefore . . ." The hexacrab coiled his tentacles.

Elder Chin said, "We seek many things in the cold rock ocean. You give us shatterstones. We give you knives. We give you containers. Will you trade shatterstones again?"

"Containers you make possess much use. We will trade. You hold new container, question?"

"This is another thing we search for in the cold rock ocean. This is oil."

Father pulled Makepeace away from licking the screen. The little boy tilted his head. "Therefore exist cause of boiling water."

Stronghold snorted. "They talk like he does."

"Shh." Father gestured at the screen. Rejoice held Makepeace close and laid her chin on his head so she could see Elder Chin unstopping the bottle. A small tendril of black, like heavy smoke, slithered out of it.

The hexacrabs recoiled and spurted away.

Elder Chin slammed the stopper into the bottle.

The mottled hexacrab crept back, swishing the water with its legs like a child waves its arms to rid a room of smoke. "Nasty you want. No understanding. Another ocean you come from. I show you several days' journey place where oil squirts from cold rock ocean. No trade. You take. We thank you."

Father sat back, grinning. Then he frowned. "An oil drill will be harder to construct in the ocean than on land. I may try inland from that off-shore site. There must be oil. I simply haven't looked hard enough yet. Well." He rubbed his chin. "Rejoice and Stronghold, suit up. We're going down."

Surprise animated Stronghold's face above his mask. "Really? You're going to let us kids go down?"

Mother stuttered, "Maybe I should go instead. I don't want—I mean, what if they try to hurt Rejoice again?"

"I'll be right beside her. Let's go."

Rejoice fumbled slightly as she exchanged the filter mask for the scuba gear and elation made her hands tremble.

The descent through the four-meter-deep waters carried Rejoice into another world, another ocean, and she laughed at the thought. The shifting light seemed charged with magic, and her heart beat to the rhythm of the words "I'm glad I'm here. I'm glad I'm here." For this, they had crossed the galaxy.

The bubbles rushed up as they floated down. Mud swirled about their fins as they touched bottom. When she and Stronghold and her father reached Elder Chin, the man swept his hand slowly over the smooth shell of the largest one. "Ur-Nissi. He keeps me in my place."

Father snorted.

"Ur-Pita. En-Teppi. Something chose him to wander. I don't know what his title means yet. And here is Ur-Veena." Wavering light flowed over the shells and legs.

Rejoice reached out to softly stroke the mottled shell of the hexacrab in front of her, and it, in turn, rubbed the smooth rubber of her wetsuit. Her heart hammered with joy.

"Exist you smaller," said the hexacrab. "Exist you not-churtree child, question?"

Rejoice thought. She was smaller than Stronghold and the two men, but she was not as small as a child. What was it asking her?

"Yes," Elder Chin answered for her.

Rejoice ran her fingers over the curve of a tentacle. "What is a churtree?"

Elder Chin's eyes crinkled behind his face mask. "Something they don't like from the air ocean. At one time the hexacrabs tried to kill every churtree they could reach. When I told them everything on the surface had died, they had a big celebration. Since the churtrees aren't around anymore, I haven't asked them much about it. Why don't you ask?"

She turned to the hexacrab, delighting in the flow of water over her hands. "Did you think we were churtrees?"

"Yes. One time."

"Do hexacrabs always try to kill churtrees?"

"Yes. Churtrees eat children. Churtrees take dead people into air-ocean. Maybe eat. Take some live people into air-ocean and cut legs into pieces and throw back into ocean to die. Churtrees pull off eyes. Churtrees—"

"Ugh! So that's why that poor hexacrab attacked me."

The mottled hexacrab reached up with three tentacles and traced her fingers. "Exist you child. You dropped me into ocean to live. Therefore you not-churtree. You give food, blade for trade."

Rejoice placed a hand under one of its tentacles and felt muscles rippling under the skin. "You were the one that crawled into the boat." Her veins tingled.

"Yes."

"You didn't die! I'm so glad!" The wonder that it was not angry at her made her catch her breath. What was she asking about? Oh, yes, the churtrees. "Were you at war with the churtrees?" She waited as the translator tied to an anchor whistled and grated.

"Exist what war, question?"

"Did you hexacrabs kill very many churtree?"

"Only if they fall into sea. We cannot breathe in air-ocean. If we leave world, we die. Churtrees cut into pieces and throw back into world. Two, three times hexacrabs lived long enough to tell story what see before eyes pulled off, what feel before legs cut off."

She was going to be sick. Rejoice placed her hands on her stomach. She waited a deep breath before saying, "You thought you were going to die when you attacked me."

"Yes. I abandon life to protect children, cluster."

"You could have hidden. I didn't see you."

"Must protect cluster, children."

"That's beautiful!"

"Exist what beautiful, question?"

"She swallowed the lump forming in her throat. "Our Savior said—"

Elder Chin touched her shoulder and shook his head. "I haven't translated those kinds of words yet. I don't know if they have those concepts. Try 'Teacher.'"

Rejoice licked her lips and almost giggled nervously. She waited another deep breath. She needed to calm down. In her peripheral vision Stronghold waved. Not yet; she wasn't finished. "Our Teacher said no man has a greater love than the one who lays down his life for his friends." Her bubbles rose as the hexacrab coiled and uncoiled two tentacles.

"Also, we say. Therefore we think same in different oceans."

Father swam forward and opened his hand to show the basalt splinter. "We found these near our colony. Can you tell us what they are?"

The mottled hexacrab shivered. Its gills flared out from beneath its shell. The creature gently took the splinters from Father's hands and caressed them. The other hexacrabs crowded in. "Where?" was the only word the computer could translate in the surge of grating and clicks.

"Near our colony. We can take you there if you wish."

Rejoice wanted a screen. She swam up under her bubbles, marveling at their silver dance, and splashed up beside the Sea Squirt, grabbed her screen from her seat, and floated down again.

The mottled hexacrab traced great circles in the water with its tentacles. "Before the Dark Death, clusters stretched from cold water edged with hard water to suffocating hot water. We send lot-chosen to wander from ocean where small lights not see. Everywhere walk, these see, touch."

"What are they for?"

Elder Chin said, "Question? Exist purpose?"

"Exist see, touch. Tell story, information."

"They're books? What does this one say?" Father touched one nearly hidden in one of the hexacrab's coiled tentacles.

"Not say. See, touch. Tell shape plant in air-ocean. This one tell shape churtree."

"Stelai," breathed Elder Chin. "Each stele is a document." He entered something into the computer.

Rejoice settled softly in the mud, her fins stirring up little of the muck.

"Can you draw us a picture of a churtree?"

"Exist what draw picture, question?"

Rejoice sketched a picture on the screen of a hexacrab with its six tentacles and six jointed legs and round shell. The hexacrab took the screen and peered at it, then traced the lines with a tip of a tentacle. "Question? Exist what?"

"This is a picture of you. I can show this to someone else, and then they would know what you look like."

The hexacrab turned the screen every which way, closed some opercula and opened others, and rubbed a tentacle across the screen. "Exist you wonderful to see me in lines. What by means see, question? Exist you space-ocean, air-ocean, water-ocean. All membranes open to you."

"I think—" Stronghold said.

"Is there any way you can show us what a churtree looked like?" Rejoice said.

After the computer had translated her speech, the hexacrab folded its legs, curled up its tentacles, snapped shut each opercula, and sucked in each eye.

"Oh! Oh! Did I make it mad?"

"No." Elder Chin laughed. "They do that when they're thinking hard."

A few minutes later, the hexacrab opened up, scuttled off, and brought back a long strand of seaweed. He chewed on it, spitting out little fibers. Ur-Pita brought some shells with little wriggling animals inside that it squeezed until each animal extruded an amber drop of fluid that resisted dissolving into the surrounding ocean. The mottled hexacrab kneaded the fluid and fibers together and made clay that it modeled into a cylinder with four legs supporting half the cylinder and four arms spaced evenly at the other end around a circular mouth filled with spiky teeth. He bent it into an L shape with the short legs on the bottom and the arms on top, bent the circular maw forward, and put round knobs between each long arm.

"Ick," Rejoice said. "Why did they hate you?"

"Hate all. One time, more time, churtrees throw chopped baby churtrees in water-ocean. All time throw broken bones in water-ocean. They safe in edgeworld pressers like you. Catch us with nets, blades."

"And then the churtrees ate you."

"Not know. Take us to air-ocean. Cannot see. They eat children."

"Why didn't you use your blade to punch holes in their boats?"

"Young Lady!" Elder Chin said.

The hexacrab trembled. "Question? Happen what?"

"Then their boats would have sunk."

At this, Elder Chin and Father grabbed Rejoice by the arms and yanked her to the surface. They threw her into the Sea Star and clambered in after her. Stronghold bobbed in the sea beside them, gripping the gunwales with his strong hands.

Rejoice pulled off her mask. "What happened? What's wrong?"

Red-faced, Elder Chin said, "You just told them how to hurt us."

"I told them how to defend themselves against the churtrees."

"There are no churtrees left. We have boats, and now they know how to sink them."

Father rubbed his eyes and shook his head.

"See!" Brother Hancock pointed to the screen.

Like a man doing deep knee bends, the mottled hexacrab jerked up and down, up and down. So did several of the other hexacrabs. The ones that weren't doing this dance coiled and uncoiled their tentacles. The monitor picked up the voice of the mottled hexacrab. "The not-churtree expose soft spots. Expose child. Trust us. We must expose soft spots. Expose children."

"Ah!" As he strapped on his air filter, Elder Chin said. "They have never let me know where their children are."

Below, Ur-Nissi, waving a stub of a tentacle toward the mottled one, said, "Torpal ate this while I save children. Expose children to no one. Churtrees make food traps. Question? Not churtrees make children trap?"

The mottled hexacrab flared out its gills. "Not-churtrees good. Trust us. Not-churtrees give us stelai, food, truth. I will go to not-churtrees cluster."

Elder Chin shook his head and grinned. "Can you beat that?" The boats rocked as he leaned forward to shake Rejoice's hand. "Praise God, Young Lady. He worked it out for good. You did exactly the right thing. Even after I gave him nutrition bars he would ask me twenty times a day what I ate. Now that we know about the churtrees, I can see why he was wary. We needed to expose our soft spots; to not hide in our hard shells. We had to trust them enough to show them our children. We had to show them how our boats were vulnerable. Now they'll trust us enough to open up to us more."

Mother brushed back her daughter's dripping hair. "Was that the same one you fought? My poor baby." She hugged Rejoice, soaking her dress in the process.

"Mother!"

A few minutes later, Rejoice, Stronghold, and their father had dressed and given food and a plethora of glass bottles to Brother Hancock and Elder Chin.

Father headed the Sea Star back toward the settlement they had officially named First City.

"Elder Chin will certainly be talking about this at his next Bible study." Father chuckled. "Elder Smith and Elder Sims complained to him at the last study that he was talking too much about the hexacrabs. He just smiled."

Mother laughed and took Father's hand.

"He's always been a great Bible teacher. Now he's like a kid in a candy shop. I believe that he's delighting in finding out why God included him on this pilgrimage."

Stronghold sat in the back of the boat and glowered at her. She edged closer to him and whispered, "What did I do?"

She could barely hear him over the bubbling of the motor as he hissed, "I can't stand how no matter what you do, it turns out right and you're the hero. I never had a chance to say a word. Do you know what it's like to have a sister who's always right when you're always wrong?"

"I'm—" She stopped. She wasn't sorry her blunders had worked out.

Stronghold exaggerated his turn away from her and stared out to sea. Makepeace tried to climb into his lap, but Stronghold pushed him away. Rejoice bit her lip. Stronghold used to bounce Makepeace on his knee, playing pony. They used to chase each other up and down the narrow corridors of the Starflower, their laughter echoing off the walls. But ever since they had set foot on this planet, all that had evaporated, like a pleasant dream ruined by waking up on test day. And that she was sorry for.

SHATTERWORLD CHAPTER TWELVE

Ur-Veena danced in the dark from the stelai to the plastic net to the glass jars stacked in the center of the cluster. The not-churtrees would take him to the lost libraries! He stroked a jar. He ripple walked to the stelai. He had searched his entire life for the libraries and now the air ocean people had found them for him. His three hearts pumped faster. He pushed against the ground with all twelve appendages and, like a newly hatched, wriggled every part of his body as he descended.

SHATTERWORLD CHAPTER THIRTEEN

Rejoice's gaze drifted from the text about beneficial soil organisms while the rain pattered on the walkway. Mother sang a lullaby and embroidered holly leaves on what appeared to be a small blanket. "I hate composition," Stronghold muttered next to Rejoice on the sofa. He typed, "Duh duh duh duh duh!" on his screen. Makepeace licked his screen in between bouts of pointing to shapes that an animated bunny held.

Rejoice thought about the giant gas planet Wimbleweather spinning on its side in a shudderingly long orbit around New Sol. One burnt ball close to the sun, Hell's Gate; New Earth; one frozen ball of rock, Harfang; and then the two gas giants, Wimbleweather and Queen with at least twenty moons apiece made up the new solar system. She was still considering perfect names for those moons. There were asteroids, too, which no one had begun to count, and which no one but Rejoice was interested in counting.

"You're doing it again, dear," Mother said, fitting her comment into the lullaby she was singing.

Rejoice blinked and stopped opening and closing her left hand. "Pardon me? Are you talking to me?"

"I am," Mother said melodiously.

"What am I doing again?"

"You're thinking about astronomy instead of your lesson."

Rejoice redirected her eyes to her screen.

"No. Look at me. I need to talk to you." Mother put down her embroidery on the table and regarded Rejoice. "I had to go to the Meetingplace today, and I watched you at recess."

Stronghold set his screen down. "You tell her, Mother."

"Excuse me, Young Man, but this is none of your business. Pay no attention."

"How am I supposed to do that when you're yelling at her right in front of me?"

Mother's hand darted forward and ruffled his straight black hair. "Move your front so we won't be in it. Go in the bathroom and comb your hair."

He scoffed, slammed his screen down on the sofa, and clumped into the tiny bathroom. The faucet taps squealed and water roared, muffled behind the thin door.

"Yes, now," Mother said, turning to Rejoice. "I saw you and Harmony talking. Or rather, she was talking and your mind was a million kilometers away. I doubt you heard a word she said."

"Mother, she never says anything worth listening to. It's all, 'This boy likes this girl, this girl hates that boy.' She doesn't talk about anything exciting."

"Such as?"

"The planet we're on, and the hexacrabs."

"Since Brother Hancock is her uncle, hexacrabs may be all she hears about at home. Maybe she's sick and tired of them."

Rejoice set her screen down. "I'm sick and tired of boy, girl, boy, girl."

"Whether or not Harmony says anything worthwhile, Harmony is worthwhile. She's your sister in Christ. She worries about boys because she's worried about her place in the new society we're creating here."

"So am I," Rejoice said. "You won't let me be what I want to be." She bit her lip to keep it from trembling, and then added, "Is it so wrong to think about astronomy?"

Mother sat beside her and slipped her arm around her. "No. Of course not. Scripture says the heavens declare the glory of God. What's wrong is making it all you think about."

"It isn't all I think about. I think . . ." She hesitated. Stronghold could hear every word if he chose to, and she didn't want him to hear what she thought of him. She couldn't talk about Mother's dreams without violating the rules of privacy. What was safe to say? Rejoice leaned back against her mother's arm and sighed. "I wish I could make someone understand how beautiful astronomy and math are. Mathematics is so balanced. You do one step and the next, and the next, like a dance. It's like a crystal, too. And all the planets obey the laws of math. The most beautiful shape in the universe is the ellipse." Why couldn't she say what she meant without sounding like an idiot?

Mother squeezed her. "I believe you. I'm merely asking you to sometimes think about drab things." Mother stared off and said softly to herself, "Accept the discipline of obscurity."

"What?"

Mother smiled and stepped back to her chair. "I was remembering how badly I wanted to be a famous singer. It embarrasses me to think of it now, but once I sat down and designed several posters of me that I imagined boys would hang on their walls and drool over. When I gave that up, it was a relief not to be chasing after the big break and searching like a badger after rats for agents and producers."

Rejoice picked up her screen and ran her fingertips along the top edge. "That's not my problem."

"I beg your pardon?"

"I don't want to be famous. I just want to study astronomy."

Mother winked. "And name asteroids after yourself?"

"That wasn't my idea. I would have called it Sightseer. Honest, Mother. I don't want people to look at me. I don't like being the center of attention."

Mother blinked several times. "Then, I don't know what your problem is."

"Maybe I don't have a problem. Maybe the colony does."

Mother froze. "Are you upset over the spiritual disciplines we adopted when we drew up the covenant for the colony?"

Yes, no, yes. "I don't care about the fasting and the clothing." She fumbled for the exact words. "I don't understand why we all have to be farmers. Even the computer repair people are required to have home gardens. Why? We could automate the farms."

Mother shook her head. "We don't want to reproduce the hectic, jangled life of Old Earth. We intend to live peaceful, quiet, gentle lives of praise and love and harmony with nature. We intend to live in such a way that our bodies and souls are not sundered."

Mother sounded like the preamble to the Covenant. "That's fine. But why can't some be farmers or builders, and some be astronomers?"

"Ah. Now I know what your problem is. Selfishness. You want others to produce your food while you study the stars and produce nothing of benefit to anyone else."

Rejoice opened her mouth to protest, but then shut it. Okay, okay, she needed a good example. How about, okay, doctors. Um, nurses. Vets. They wouldn't need to be full time farmers as their population grew. But then Mother would say those vocations benefit people. Rejoice didn't know what the benefit of astronomy was except she would die if she couldn't do it.

"That's okay, sweet-love. You'll outgrow it." Heat
rushed to Rejoice's cheeks. "On Old Earth—"

"I'm sick and tired of hearing about Old Earth." Mother's usually musical voice sharpened. "What is it about Old Earth that makes you and your brother unable to think about anything else?"

Rejoice rubbed her thumbs on her screen. A tear crept into each eye. "Seagulls. I miss the seagulls."

Mother rose and then sat again. She picked at the threads in her embroidery work and bit her lower lip. Her eyes glistened, too. "They have such compelling calls, don't they? 'Come fly with me. Come fly and be free.' The surf and the cry of the gulls. Mockingbirds. The swish of tires on wet pavement. I would have gone mad on the ship if we hadn't had recordings of birdsongs and raindrops." She paused. "Do you remember the jazz musician who lived on the next street, behind and over from ours?"

"No."

"He was an old man, retired. He had calloused, gnarled fingers the color of molasses. He'd sit on his back porch surrounded by mangy dogs, and he'd be playing his saxophone. Sometimes the dogs would howl along. I had to hang over the corner of the fence to watch him play. Oh, he was sweet. When he played his spirituals, I forgot all about the peeling paint and dingy sky and the stench." She sighed, then shook herself. "You know, we haven't had any calypso music in the choir for the last couple of years. I'm going to search through my files and pull some out. We could sing it at the dedication of the fishing boat we should build next year."

The bathroom door opened a crack, and Stronghold hollered through it, "Are you still yelling, or can I come out now?"

Mother laughed. "Come on out."

Stronghold clumped back to the sofa with wet hair and crashed down beside Rejoice. He switched on his screen.

Rejoice kept her eyes riveted on her screen, but she didn't see a single word on it. Inside, she prayed, *God, if you don't want me to think about astronomy, please take the desire away from me. I don't want to hurt Mother. If she gave up singing, then I can give up—Wait a minute. She didn't give up singing. She leads the choir. She gave up—*

The front door swung open and Father strode in, pulling off his mask. His slick blue coat dripped on the floor. "Carol, what happened to the wreath on the door?" He leaned forward to kiss his wife as he held back his coat to keep from dripping on her.

"I took it down."

"Why?" He hunched his shoulders.

"Sister Olson told me I was being vain by making my door more special than anyone else's and elevating the name of Holly above that of Christ. Anyway, let me heat up your lunch."

"I'm not having lunch," Father said. "Did you tell Sister Busybody

Olson you put the wreath up originally so you could find your door on the Starflower?"

Mother reddened. "No. And you shouldn't call her names, especially in front of . . . She's a saint of God."

"She's a saint of God with a nose too long. Put the holly wreath back up. If anybody asks you why it's there, you tell them your husband's so stupid he can't find his way home without it. How's that? Has Stronghold eaten yet?"

Rejoice glanced from one to the other. How could her parents carry on two or three conversations at the same time?

Mother's eyes lit up and her lips tightened to hold back laughter. "Why aren't you having lunch?"

"Glitches on the aquarium track. Ur-Veena should be here in a few hours. Elder Ruiz says we need the best extensioner we've got to dip the aquarium in the ocean, load up the hexacrab, and set it on the trailer."

Stronghold shot up. "Me?"

"You're the man," Father said.

Stronghold whooped and darted for the door. As he threw on his rain gear, Father watched him with an expression Rejoice couldn't interpret, perhaps pleading. Mother kissed him on the cheek and squeezed his hand. Another message. Maybe they were telepathic. The rain drummed harder as Father and Stronghold went out the door.

Mother gazed pensively at the door for a minute and then said, "That's another thing about you and Stronghold."

Now what? Rejoice studied her.

"When it's so easy to be happy and everything is going so well, why do you and your brother choose to be unhappy?"

Rejoice could not think of even one respectful reply. How could she tell Mother, who had been born with some kind of happy gene that made it impossible for her to be sad for more than twenty minutes, that for normal people, it was hard to be happy. Of course she was happy. She was doing what she wanted. Stronghold and Rejoice would never be able to do what they wanted. Their parents took those choices away from them.

Ack! She mustn't think that, or she would end up as angry as Stronghold.

Mother sighed. "I always wanted a big, happy family, my own personal choir. Well, maybe the next one will be a happy child." She stretched out the small blanket she was embroidering.

Rejoice's eyes widened. "Mother! You're not pregnant?"

Mother laughed. "You needn't sound so horrified. And no, I'm not. But I intend to be as soon as the barns are built and the farmhouses started. I don't have that many more years to bear children. I told you: I want a big, happy family."

Rejoice sat back. "I think I'd better read up on these worms and springtails," she stammered. "There's a test on them tomorrow."

Mother jumped up from her chair, snatched the towel by the sink, and cried, "No, Makepeace! You use a towel to wipe the floor. You don't suck it up!"

SHATTERWORLD CHAPTER FOURTEEN

Ur-Nissi watched the edgeworld presser move away, roaring and bubbling. He clicked his beak a few times, then crawled to Ur-Tista, the one who had taught him how to speak and the ways of honor. He told Ur-Tista he wished to track the other not-churtrees, for they were meandering toward the edgeworld nursery.

Ur-Tista sucked in his eyes for a moment, then turned and dragged himself to his niche. The three legs on his port side had been eaten by a torpal twenty-eight child-come seasons before. He sorted through his treasures, and handed his sharpest blade to Ur-Nissi. Then Ur-Tista also gave him one of the long-distance talkers from the not-churtrees.

Ur-Nissi asked, "Question? Do you believe that this box will really speak through Ur-Veena from the air ocean?"

"We will see. Ur-Veena said to hold this button if you wish to speak to him."

They rubbed tentacles. Ur-Nissi positioned the blade on one spur and the radio on the other spur and scurried after the not-churtree. The edgeworld presser moved faster than he, but if it stopped he would catch up to it.

SHATTERWORLD CHAPTER FIFTEEN

The clouds had emptied and moved on by the time the colonists assembled by the boat dock south of Ocean Shore Boulder. Steam rose from the damp sands, and the harsh light of the late afternoon sun cast long shadows. Like a giraffe balanced on the edge of the dock, the extension crane rose before them. Stronghold sat back in the control seat of the extension and wore what Rejoice thought of as his "I'm so cool, I'm bored." face.

A gleaming black wagon crouched on tracks that sloped from the walkway down to the sea, running parallel and close to the dock. The hot smell of oils and newly forged metal mingled with the sharp smell of salt and iodine.

"There he is!" squealed Harmony, bumping against Rejoice and waving frantically. Far off, a speck in the sea resolved into Elder Chin and Young Man No Confidence In The Flesh in the Sea Star. Ur-Veena hung onto a sling behind and under their boat. They coasted to a stop a few meters from the end of the dock.

As gracefully as a ballet dancer, Stronghold maneuvered the extension hands to pick up the aquarium and dip it into the ocean. A group of men rolled the wagon on its tracks under the gentle waves. Elder Chin watched through the bottom of his boat and then motioned thumbs up when the wagon was in position and Ur-Veena was safely in the aquarium.

Stronghold guided the robotic arms to set the aquarium on the wagon. The men grunted as they pulled on the massive rope tied to the end of the wagon and tugged it onto land. The top of the aquarium rose above the waves like a breaching whale with water and foam sluicing off its sides. Elder Sims capped it with a dark cover to protect the hexacrab within.

"It's so big!" Harmony breathed. "I didn't know it was so big!"

Rejoice shook her head. "I told you how big he is."

"But that's not the same thing as seeing!"

Rejoice twiddled the wind string on her hat. "You're right. I'm sorry I snapped at you."

The wagon halted on dry land and glistened in the sunlight. Ur-Veena's three sight-eyes swiveled about, and he trembled. Elder Chin pounded down the dock and dropped beside the aquarium. He pulled on the bubbler's tubing and readjusted his microphone. "How do you feel?"

The hexacrab clutched the translator in one tentacle and whistled. "New. Different. You swim water-ocean, but similar us in air-ocean you crawl on bottom. You swim fast. You more attached to bottom. Question? How see too bright?" His tentacles rubbed over the glass sides.

Stronghold swung down from the extensioner and pushed through the crowd to the aquarium. He patted low on a corner. "It's leaking here, see?"

Elder Ruiz squatted to examine it. "Sharp eyes. It won't drain dry for several hours. We can fix it after his tour."

Under Elder Chin's direction, several other men came up and pasted on the aquarium another layer of the same kind of film they used for their sunglasses.

Ur-Veena whistled. "See good some."

"Hup!" Elder Sims shouted. The men picked up the rope again and waited, poised, their sleeves rolled up, their clothes darkly wet from the waist down. "Pull three meters!"

As the aquarium rolled further onto dry sand, the colonists pushed each other closer to see Ur-Veena.

* * *

Brother Zystra nosed the Sea Squirt into a cleft on Bull's-Eye Island. "Close enough," Brother Hancock said, and stepped off the boat. He clambered up the steep sides of the island and disappeared over a ridge.

Brother Zystra looked back. With binoculars he could barely make out the bright orange, three-meter flag attached to a buoy that marked the hexacrab cluster. He checked his screen. "Resolved," he called out, "Ur-Veena should be at First City now. We're going to be late."

"In a minute!" Brother Hancock's voice came faintly. Several minutes later, his head popped up over the ridge. "Nope, no new plants or animals." The boat ducked as he stepped into it. "Maybe the next island."

"We need to get back."

"I know. I know. Though I don't know how much the hexacrabs will get out of his visit. I don't think they've completely grasped the concept of talking to each other long-distance."

"When they hear Ur-Veena talk about our city and they can't see him, they'll get it."

Brother Hancock's eyes crinkled above his filter mask. "Let's head back, then."

The motor purred at half-speed, which was faster than top speed had been when Rejoice became lost. The men sat without speaking, their faces shaded by broad-brimmed hats, Brother Zystra resting his hand lightly on the vibrating tiller. Brother Hancock hunched over, watching through the clear space in the hull.

"Hold it," Brother Hancock said. "Would you look at this?"

Two meters under them undulated a field of blue stars, five-pointed, finely fringed, with a golden dot in each center, set on spindly stems that broadened to a bulb at the base.

"I can't believe how beautiful those are," Brother Zystra said.

Brother Hancock slipped off his hat and unbuttoned his overalls. "I'm getting a specimen."

"We'll be late."

"Something might eat them before we get back. Will you help buckle on the back?" He donned his scuba gear, picked up a knife and a collection jar, and flipped over the side. When his bare feet touched the oozy bottom, the blue stars retracted part way. Hancock reached for one, hesitated, and wriggled on one of the rubber gloves tucked in his belt. Then he reached with his gloved hand, grasped a blue star, and tugged. The star shrank into a lump. He sliced under the bulbous base with his knife and jerked out the blue star.

A shrill whistle disconcerted both men. Brother Hancock dropped his jar.

Ur-Nissi enfolded him and coiled a tentacle around the man's knife. The hexacrab plunged his blade into Brother Hancock's arm. Brother Hancock rolled back, and a red cloud swirled around him.

Brother Zystra punched the emergency button and shouted. "The hexacrabs! They're killing Brother Hancock!" He seized the harvesting pole and thunked Ur-Nissi's shell.

Ur-Nissi slashed Brother Hancock's air hose and bit into the man's side. Blood clouded the sea.

Brother Hancock jackknifed and pushed off from Ur-Nissi's shell. He groped and caught the harvest pole. The hexacrab and man grappled for the pole. Brother Hancock kicked Ur-Nissi's eyes. With the arm not slashed he pulled toward the surface.

Brother Zystra grabbed his hand and hauled. The boat tilted.

Brother Hancock gripped a bench and kicked against grasping tentacles. Another hexacrab reached for the pole.

Brother Zystra captured the pole and pinned Ur-Nissi to the sea floor.

The other hexacrab seized the pole and climbed.

Brother Zystra shoved the pole away. He grabbed Brother Hancock with both hands and dragged him into the boat.

Flinging away a clinging tentacle, Brother Hancock coughed and choked on swallowed water.

Brother Zystra, kicked on the motor, and they roared off.

* * *

The computer that Elder Chin carried wailed so loudly that he dropped it.

The emergency siren? Rejoice clapped her hands over her ears.

Elder Chin fumbled with the computer and slapped off the siren. Brother Zystra shouted into the radio, "The hexacrabs! They're killing Brother Hancock!"

Hexacrabs whistled and clicked over the radio.

SHATTERWORLD CHAPTER SIXTEEN

At the dock, a pilot, and Dr. Cruz scrambled toward the runway where the vertical-takeoff-and-landing aircraft sat next to the shuttle. Mother's hand flew to the beeping brown button on her dress. "Oh!" She gasped. "I'm the nurse on call." She pushed through the crowd and set Makepeace next to Rejoice. "Watch him!"

She pushed back through the crowd to run to the plane. Makepeace cried and struggled to follow. His fist whacked Rejoice in the face, so she inverted him, swung him to her back, and held onto his feet. Rejoice jostled closer to see Ur-Veena.

In the aquarium, Ur-Veena pulled his radio off his spur, and glared at it, flaring his gills and grinding his beak. After a tense moment of listening, he screamed, "Same churtree! Child trap!" He pounded on the side of the aquarium with his blade. "Kill child! Trap!" Cracks radiated from the place he struck.

"Hey, you'll break it!" Stronghold slapped his hand over the place. Ur-Veena struck again. The hexacrab's blade smashed through the glass and pierced Stronghold's hand.

Stronghold opened his mouth to scream, but he fell under an avalanche of broken glass and water. The hexacrab crashed on top of him and raised his blade. Father threw himself on Ur-Veena. They grappled for the blade.

Elder Chin wrapped his arms around the back of Ur-Veena's shell. "Quick! In the water before he dies."

Still struggling with the tentacle holding the blade, Father scrambled off Ur-Veena's shell and Stronghold's stomach. His foot crunched one of

Ur-Veena's articulated legs. Ur-Veena bit and ripped Stronghold's shirt. Father pushed and Elder Chin dragged Ur-Veena toward the sea. Other men pulled Stronghold out of the way, crunching glass under their feet. The airplane screamed over their heads.

Tripping over each other, Elder Chin, Elder Sims, and Father wrestled the flailing hexacrab into the sea. Ur-Veena grabbed their arms with his powerful tentacles and tried to pull them under. Twenty men splashed into the sea and shoved Ur-Veena away from the Elders and Father. Ur-Veena, still brandishing his blade in one of his tentacles, slashed Elder Sims' chest. The men raced back to dry land, half-carrying Elder Sims and Elder Chin, falling and pulling each other along.

Ur-Veena lunged at them, his legs and tentacles scrambling on the sand, but he got no farther than the edge of the sea. Father fell onto the sand and coughed up seawater. Elder Sims sank to his knees, frowning, as he held the edges of his gash together and diluted blood soaked his overalls.

Elder Chin shouted at the hexacrab through the translator. "Please get in the shade of the dock or you'll burn!"

Ur-Veena submerged and slid into the shadow.

Makepeace howled. Harmony sobbed. Brother Carlson examined Stronghold's hand. Rejoice couldn't bear to see the blood gushing out of her brother's wound. Brother Carlson ripped off Stronghold's shirt. The hexacrab had torn his chest with his beak.

Several young men grabbed stones, but Elder Chin shouted at them, "Have you forgotten we're men of peace? Move back! You are frightening Ur-Veena! Move back!"

Father rushed to Stronghold, tore off his shirt, and wrapped it around the wounded hand. Stronghold couldn't walk. Brother Carlson and Father linked hands, forming a sling, and carried Stronghold to the three-bed dispensary adjoining the Meetingplace. Other men massed about Elder Sims to help him walk to the clinic.

Rejoice wanted to follow Stronghold to the clinic, but she and Makepeace would be in the way. Why were the hexacrabs attacking them?

The crowd milled about, some shouting, some crying. Pastor Wiseman and Elder Smith stepped up on the edge of the wagon and bowed their heads. Rejoice and all the people around her bowed their heads and breathed deeply and slowly. Within a minute, everyone had stopped and quieted except Harmony and some of her friends, who sobbed on each other's shoulders. Makepeace flopped, twisted, and whined. Rejoice finally dragged him off the beach.

* * *

The next day Mother said, "Oh, Makepeace, what am I going to do with you?" She pulled him away from licking the footboard of Brother Hancock's dispensary bed.

"That's all right," Brother Hancock whispered. "I don't mind."

"I do mind," Mother said. "Rejoice, would you go find Deaconess Redhorse and find out what's taking her so long? Wait, cancel that. That would be an insult. She said she would take Makepeace, and she will, as soon as she is able."

"Mother, I could take him to the apartment and watch him there."

"I —no—yes. If she doesn't come in ten minutes, do that. In the meantime, don't you need to study for a test?"

"That was this morning. Teacher Hardesty canceled it because everyone was so shook up."

"Then you'll need to take it tomorrow. So study."

"Yes, Mother." How could Mother think about school right now? Rejoice looked at her brother in the bed next to Brother Hancock. Stronghold's stare was unfocused and his face held bitter lines around his mouth. Fleshmesh covered a glass cut above his left eyebrow. Elastic strips wound around his injured leg. Still, he appeared better than Brother Hancock, who had drainage tubes snaking out from his arm and his side and whose gentle eyes were sunken in. But Brother Hancock talked and Stronghold didn't.

"Could I have another painkiller?" whispered Brother Hancock.

A strong knock rattled the flimsy dispensary door. "In a minute," Mother sang. She gave Brother Hancock his medication before she opened the door. Elder Smith, Pastor Wiseman, and Elder Sims strode in and filled the room. Deaconess Redhorse squeezed in after them, collected Makepeace, and squeezed out again. The men and Mother laid their hands on uninjured places on Brother Hancock and Stronghold, and prayed for their health and thanked God for their lives. Rejoice held onto Stronghold's stiff foot.

After the last amen, they paused.

Elder Sims hitched up his overalls, keeping the material from rubbing on his chest where the hexacrab had slashed him. Pastor Wiseman said, "Elder Chin wants you to come and talk to the hexacrab."

"Which is nonsense as far as I'm concerned," Elder Smith rumbled. "I say we should shoot it and be done with it."

"No, no," whispered Brother Hancock. "You mustn't think that. The hexacrabs are a people who have survived terrible circumstances and still maintained a high culture. You have seen the thousands of stelai buried in the beach here. Each stele is a significant document."

"What they did to you lowered them to animals in my eyes," Elder Smith said.

Hancock laughed weakly. "As if humans haven't been doing this to each other for thousands of years. I promised my God I would be a man of peace. I will not war on these sea people." He coughed, and the lines around his eyes tightened. "What does Ur-Veena want to talk about?"

Elder Sims said reluctantly, "He says you killed some of their children."

"Nonsense," Smith said. "Brother Zystra said they were collecting plant samples. How could their children be plants?"

Brother Hancock struggled to sit up. Mother inserted herself between the men and raised the head of the bed. Brother Hancock's face became even paler. "Blessed Lord. Forgive me for doing such a thing." He reached up. Elder Smith reached down to take his hand. "Have you ever seen a jellyfish?"

"Dead, on a beach." Elder Smith said.

"When jellyfish have babies, the babies don't seem like jellyfish. They're free-swimming larvae. The larvae settle down and turn into polyps, like sea anemones. They look like plants. When the polyps mature, they have layers that float off that are jellyfish." He dropped his hand. "The blue star." He covered his face. "The poor child. It tried to get away. How could I have been so foolish? Why didn't I wait and ask a hexacrab about it? They know everything that grows in the ocean. And now they fear and hate us. Because I killed one of their children. Blessed Lord."

The men stood and watched Brother Hancock.

Rejoice's chest hurt. She squeezed Stronghold's foot. Larvae? Blue star? What had he done?

Elder Sims turned his broad-brimmed hat around and around in his hands. "One of Ur-Veena's legs was badly mangled during yesterday's melee." He looked at Pastor Wiseman.

Pastor Wiseman continued the news, "Dr. Cruz wants to try to piece together the exoskeleton and see if it can heal, but Ur-Veena won't let a human near him. He talks to Elder Chin on the translator, but he doesn't seem to know what to believe. Sometimes he calls us not-churtrees because we put him back in the water while he was trying to kill us. Sometimes he calls us same-churtrees because we killed one of the children. Do you think you can come and talk to him?"

"Absolutely not," Mother broke in. "That glucose drip and all those drainage tubes are not Christmas tree ornaments. After what we went through to save him yesterday, I won't have you kill him by dragging him around."

What were Christmas tree ornaments? Rejoice glanced from the men to Mother and back again. Was Brother Hancock going to die?

Elder Smith tugged at his gray beard. "Dr. Cruz said we could if we were very careful."

Mother flung up her hands. "All right. But I'm going with you." After she checked that all the monitors and other pieces of equipment were securely attached to the bed and she had placed a clear tent over all, she and the men slowly moved out, gently pushing the bed between them.

Rejoice edged closer to Stronghold's head. Would she ever hear him laugh again? "Stronghold? Does it hurt much?" He turned his face away. "Stronghold? I'm glad the hexacrab didn't kill you. I love you."

Stronghold spoke as though each word were a massive granite boulder he had to shove uphill. "You must be the only one."

"What do you mean? We all love you."

"Mother wouldn't nurse me. She ran off and let someone else do it."

"She left before you got hurt. She didn't even know you were hurt until she got back. And Father saved your life. Don't you remember him carrying you here?"

Stronghold answered in a monotone. "I remember him bringing us to this planet, which he wouldn't have done if he loved me. This planet hates me. Just when I think things might go okay, it kicks me down again. I'll never be able to handle an extensioner again."

"Dr. Cruz said your hand was going to heal up fine."

"What does she know? She's not a real Doctor."

"She was a physician's assistant, which is pretty close. And she studied hard on the ship to get her medical degree."

"They say my hand will heal to make me feel good. That's the only reason."

Her throat ached. What could she say to make him turn back into the brother she knew? "She—Brother—" She laid her head on his shoulder, whispered, "I love you," and cried. Stronghold stared straight ahead.

* * *

Rejoice struggled with the wheel chair where sand had drifted over the sidewalk. She stopped to catch her breath and observe the stars so bright.

Stronghold muttered, "What are you doing now?"

"There it is. It's a little hard to see because of the glare of the walklight, but that star there, the one that's a little blueish, that's Wimbleweather."

Stronghold sighed theatrically and kicked against his footrest. "Are you going to start whining about astronomy again?"

Rejoice shoved the wheelchair through the drift.

"Ow!"

"I move you, you complain; I stand still, you complain. At least what I whine about is physically possible."

"Do you really think that we can't go back to Earth?"

"That's what the Elders said."

"The Elders and adults are all sock puppets of Elder Smith. You are so stupid."

"I am not stupid. You think Father is lying to us?"

"Yes."

Rejoice stopped pushing the recalcitrant wheelchair and lifted the hair from her sweaty neck to expose it to the cool breeze blowing in from the ocean.

"Hey, let me help!" No Confidence called from behind them.

Rejoice jumped.

No Confidence In The Flesh jogged up to them and seized the handles of the wheelchair. "God is doing great things, isn't He?" No Confidence shoved at a pace that was a jog for Rejoice. He handed a small vial to her. "My mother forgot to give you the extra pain meds you might need tonight. Isn't God amazing?"

Stronghold's head slumped onto his chest.

God was amazing because his mother forgot? *What?* Rejoice jogged beside them through the pools of light and the shade until they reached the Holly airlock.

"I'll pick you up before breakfast, or sooner if you need to go back to the clinic before then. God be with you!" No Confidence trotted over to the third row of apartments.

"I hate him," Stronghold muttered. "He's just like Mother. Happy, happy face."

Rejoice pulled open the airlock door. "That's better than surly, surly face."

At the dinner table, Mother handed a plate of sliced hydroponic tomatoes to Stronghold, and said, "I feel as though I've been cursed by the Chinese."

Father smiled. "Oh, with the curse that says: 'May you live in interesting times?'"

"That's the one." Mother nodded. "I'm ready for some boredom."

Father glanced at Stronghold, who ate mechanically with his left hand. "I'm with you there. But aren't you glad you were there to see that today? I never knew Brother Hancock to be so . . ."

"Foolhardy? If this planet had flies, one would have flown into my mouth."

"He was courageous. Noble even. I hope the hexacrabs make a lot of stelai about Resolved Hancock. He really won Ur-Veena's heart when he said he'd go back to the sea people as soon as he could and let them execute justice."

Mother shook her head. "And what if they do decide to kill him? Why did we bother to sew him up?"

"I don't think they will kill him. He exposed his soft spot, and now they understand that we honestly don't intend to hurt them. Now they understand they must tell us more about themselves so we don't have any more accidents like that one."

"Do they?" Mother straightened Makepeace on his chair. "What happened after Brother Hancock fainted and I took him back to the dispensary?"

"First, it took about an hour to put Ur-Veena's leg back together. Then, he told us that not only do they have a blue-star-flower stage, they also have a swimming larval stage that lives in the deep sea. And their females don't speak. They haven't since the asteroid hit."

"You're kidding." Mother stabbed a pea pod with her fork and dabbed it in some dressing.

"Why?" Rejoice asked.

"I don't know," Father said, "unless only one mutated, brain-damaged female survived. Or perhaps the radiation after the asteroid had a greater effect on the female genes." He cut his potato. "Ur-Veena said he's lived through 200 child-come seasons. And he insists that comes only once a

New Earth year.

"That makes him, what, 250 years old?" Mother set back the bowl of gravy that she had picked up.

"Two hundred forty-nine Old Earth years," Rejoice said.

They sat and thought about that for a while. Makepeace cocked his head and studied his glass of water. "Crashes, smashes, splashes." he sang.

"Here's the best part," Father said. "After the next child-come, Ur-Veena wants to split the cluster and move part of it here. We've got the shallow water they need to grow their children in, and further out, the deeper water they live in. They moved to Bull's-Eye two hex, hex, hex child-comes ago to search for the lost libraries, and we've got one of them. I think they intend to turn this place into a university of sorts."

"So they use a base six number system!" Rejoice cried. "Oh, that will be fun!"

"Won't it?" Father said. "I believe that two, hex, hex, hex is two times six to the third power, which would be. . ."

'Four hundred and thirty-two years," Rejoice cried and clapped.

Stronghold rolled his eyes.

"Another interesting thing: every hex hex years . . ."

"That would be thirty-six!" Stronghold yelled and made a face at Rejoice.

"Yes, every thirty-six years one of the hexacrabs in each cluster is chosen by lot to wander. They go from cluster to cluster trading news and education. They probably also diversify their genetic pool. It took En-Teppi five years to find Ur-Veena's cluster. After he reads the stelai here, he'll go searching for another cluster."

"Who is En-Teppi?" asked Mother.

"One of the hexacrabs." Father speared a tomato slice. "I'm excited about this." He laughed. "Too bad Elder Smith isn't. He said, 'Fine and dandy. They trust us. I don't trust them. I don't want them living next door to us. And I don't want any more time wasted on them.'" Father sobered. "He does have a point. All the time we've spent on the hexacrabs is time we haven't worked on the fields, greenhouses, and barns."

"Are we going to starve?" Rejoice asked.

"No, honey," Mother said. "But we're behind schedule on producing the surplus we need to feed oxen and goats and donkeys. So we haven't grown the animals yet. And the barns are behind schedule. I wish we could hurry. But you have to finish the first thing before you can do the second." She smiled at her husband. He smiled back, and they briefly touched hands.

"Well!" Father said. "Elder Ruiz has come up with a scheme that would benefit both our peoples. If we build the structures for a kelp farm and the hexacrabs maintain it, we can share in the harvest. We'll need a good extensioner to build those structures."

They fixed their attention on Stronghold. He continued to eat mechanically, looking at no one, saying nothing.

SHATTERWORLD CHAPTER SEVENTEEN

Ur-Nissi turned from the radio. He had heard enough from Ur-Veena. He churned up the sediment until he was completely concealed by a mud cloud. Ur-Tista reached in a tentacle and tapped him on the shell. When Ur-Nissi folded his legs under his shell and churned up more sediment with his tentacles, Ur-Tista dragged him out of the cloud.

Ur-Nissi clacked his beak. "He is bereft of reason! He would embrace a naspy! For the morsel of a library, he would cut down every plant! What have the not-churtrees done to Ur-Veena? What are they to kill our children and twist Ur-Veena's beak?"

"Am I not the oldest and wisest?" Ur-Tista answered. "Do I not say 'Come and go,' and you come and go? Listen to me. Ur-Veena is as diligent to protect our children and advance our people as you are."

Ur-Nissi snapped out three tentacles with contempt. "Shall Chan-tot kill our child and not be killed in turn? Would we spare a torpal?"

"Ur-Veena is correct that we should not spear justice on these ignorant not-churtrees. The killer has lost the use of his tentacle. It promises to never hurt us again. Do not forget the killer volunteered himself to face our justice. It promises to never take anything from the water ocean without the permission of one of us. Would a torpal make such a promise?"

"Words. Words that will not swim if he brings weapons to our ocean again. You listen to me. The Ur should move far, far away from these odd new people."

"Who would tend the nursery and females?"

Ur-Nissi hesitated. "Many would volunteer to stay behind."

Ur-Tista reached three tentacles forward and stroked Ur-Nissi's tentacles. "We know the not-churtrees are cowards. We know how to kill the not-churtrees. I say we will do as Ur-Veena says; but we will always hold the blade, and we will watch the not-churtrees."

"And if they hurt us again, will we kill the not-churtrees?" Ur-Nissi raised his blade.

"Yes," Ur-Tista hissed. "If they bite us again, the world shall run black with their blood." He stepped away, his shell dragging a shallow furrow in the mud. He stopped a few paces away and boomed to the entire cluster, "Ur-Nissi shall take my place as master of the cluster when I go to live next to the not-churtree."

All eyes swiveled to Ur-Nissi, who lowered his blade in astonishment. Then he raised his blade again and said in ritual agreement, "May the kraken let us live. Against all torpals, against all naspies, against all churtrees, against all those who would tear our flesh."

"And against all unjustified fear," Ur-Tista added.

* * *

Only for this had Ur-Veena allowed himself to be towed away from the libraries he was organizing on stands the air-ocean people provided him. With Ur-Tista on his left, Ur-Nissi on his right, and before him the cliff of the continental shelf, the beginning of the abyss, Ur-Veena stood with the entire cluster. He clutched his blade with two tentacles and a not-churtree-made net, peering into the dark with visual, electrical, and olfactory senses.

He pulled up his broken leg again. The air-ocean people had glued together the fragmented exoskeleton but his muscles did not feel firmly attached and they ached. When he did not focus on the leg, it dragged.

Ur-Nissi clicked. The line of hexacrabs listened for an echo.

Ur-Veena blew water over his gills.

Ur-Sti clicked.

A small echo returned.

The hexacrabs jostled each other as they raised their nets higher.

Ur-Tista clicked. More small echoes returned.

Ur-Neepa slid a foot over the edge of the cliff, and the two hexacrabs on either side of him helped haul him back from the brink.

And then the children swam among them. Three sided, three eyed, with sealed mouths and three muscular fins, the children returned from the dark sea and swam among them.

Ur-Veena swung his net above toward the nearest child. But the hard little nub that was the beginning of a shell passed beyond the rim of the net before he could draw it in, and the child wriggled on to the second line of hexacrabs. Young Ur-Tinti flung his net made of seaweed fibers and caught the child in its mesh. Ur-Tinti whistled, sharp and clear.

Ur-Veena gathered his net.

Ur-Nissi caught a child and whistled.

Ur-Neepa rose high, caught his child, and toppled backward, tangling himself in the nets of those around him. They clicked gleefully. This time, the first time in hex hexes of years there were enough children for everyone to have at least one. Several children fluttered by as the first line disentangled. The second line caught them. Whistling grew into a mighty, joyful sound.

Ur-Veena flung his net and wrapped it around a beautiful child that watched him with quivering fear. He blew water over the child's gills and the little one relaxed. Ur-Veena whistled.

A larger echo returned from the whistles.

Ur-Veena scuttled back, turned, and using legs and arms and blower he hastened away from the edge.

All those who had not yet caught a child dropped their nets and raised their blades. Ur-veena grabbed a dropped net and gave his blade to Ur-Sisisi who scuttled past him toward the cliff. Ur-Tista clicked and clicked.

The hexacrabs rushing toward the cluster and the hexacrabs lining up on the edge of the cliff heard the echo growing larger. The free children scattered, piping in panic. The hexacrabs churned the muck into deep clouds.

All the small echoes of children passed the cliff edge. Behind them, the large echo grew ever larger.

Ur-Tista commanded, "Pile up! Torpal!"

Ur-Veena used his deep rage and fight-urge to propel him faster away to take the child to a safe place.

A darting child rammed into Ur-Veena's broken leg and burrowed under him. He wrapped that child in the extra net and now towed two of them.

The large echo grew larger and closer.

The hexacrabs piled onto one another, two, three, four, five hexacrabs high and eight across to form a larger echo shape in the pings from the torpal.

Ur-Veena grated, "May the kraken let us live!"

The torpal hesitated, looped back.

A tentacle, Ur-Nissi's, grabbed one of Ur-Veena's outflung arms and pulled him behind a boulder.

The torpal rushed toward the pile of hexacrabs and closed its terrible teeth upon Ur-Tasi while the others stabbed with their diamond-lined blades through its rough hide. Bloods mingled with the mud and sea. The torpal tore off Ur-Tasi's right side and flipped away. Its tail smashed into the pile.

Two of the hexacrabs were battered off the pile. One was caught by reaching tentacles. The other swirled too far away and drifted in the torpal's wake and then down until the torpal swung back and snatched him in its wide jaws.

The torpal dove then, leaving behind the bitter taste of blood and loss.

The hexacrabs scrambled over each other to reform the pile.

Ur-Tista clicked. They waited. He clicked again. They heard no echoes from the abyss.

The hexacrabs crawled apart and searched for their nets and the scattered children. Ur-Tista stayed at the edge and clicked until all the sediment had settled.

* * *

Ur-Veena laid the sleeping child within the niche he had chipped out of the basalt many hexes of years ago. He surrounded it with seaweed, taking care to leave circulation space by the gills and propped shards around the entrance. Other hexacrabs had claimed the names of the fallen to name their children. He would name this one Sa-Issi. May the Kraken let him live.

SHATTERWORLD CHAPTER EIGHTEEN

Rejoice was glad to hold Harmony's proffered hand as they stood in front of the Elder and Deacon Board seated at long tables. Behind the girls, Father sat, head bowed, eyes closed. Rejoice suspected he was taking a nap. *Please, please, God, make them say yes.* This time she was asking for something a lot of people wanted.

Elder Smith shifted his gaze from his screen to Rejoice and Harmony. "No."

Harmony shivered. Rejoice blinked back tears.

Elder Chin coughed. Elder Sims shook his head slightly and poked at his screen.

Rejoice set her shoulders back. "But did you see how many people signed our petition?"

Elder Smith cleared his throat. "Yes, we did see that. We considered your petition carefully. And the answer is still no. We should not spend needed colonial resources of material or labor on what is ultimately a frivolous project. It does not advance the goals of this colony."

It did too. The project would help them commune with this planet's nature. She opened her mouth to say so when Father rose behind her.

He lightly clasped her shoulders, and said, "Thank you, Board, for the time you took to consider and pray about this matter." Then he steered her toward the door.

On the sidewalk, Rejoice jerked on the strings of her hat and pulled her mask farther down on her nose. "But what's wrong with building a floating bridge to the kelp farm? What's wrong with more of us getting to know the hexacrabs?"

"Nothing," Father said mildly.

Harmony whispered, "They might hear you."

Rejoice strode off in the direction of Ocean Shore Boulder. When Father and Harmony caught up to her, she pointed with her whole arm to the three boats in the ocean, black against the setting sun. "Brother Hancock and Elder Chin and No Confidence get to spend all their time out there. But none of the rest of us can. How can we when we only have three boats?"

"How can we indeed?" Father said.

Rejoice folded her arm and glared at him. When he got like this, he was expecting her to think of something creative.

Harmony backed away.

"They won't let us build a bridge," Rejoice said.

"Funny," Father said, "I didn't hear them say that." He turned to Harmony. "Did you hear them say that?"

"Yes?"

"Hmm." He stretched and then placed his interlaced fingers behind his neck.

"Oh, I know," Rejoice said, "I'll take Makepeace's little red wagon and haul rocks out and build a causeway. How many rocks do you think it will take to build a half kilometer long causeway?"

Father chuckled. "What's wrong with a floating bridge?"

"They won't let us build one!"

"They did not say that. They said it could not be built using needed colonial resources or labor."

"What's left?" She studied him as she tried to ignore the gathering teenagers who had been waiting to hear what the Board decided. "Ooooooh."

Father let his arms fall to his side. "Well, Young Ladies, I have data to fuss with. Please don't worry your mothers by staying out too late." He sauntered to the apartments.

Harmony drew near, her forehead a mass of wrinkles. "What's he talking about?"

Rejoice gestured for the teenagers around them to come closer. "What do we do after supper?"

Harmony glanced around her friends. "We walk around the apartments and Meeting Place and along the beach?"

No Confidence said, "We go cruising. That's what my dad calls it. He won't tell me why."

Every said, "That's what my father calls it too. It's like our parents have a secret language."

Rejoice waved it away. "Whose parents work in the repurposing warehouse?"

Give Glory raised his hand.

"Okay. Ask them if we can't go in and find stuff that nobody can use for a long time, stuff that we could use as planks. And who here is apprenticed with glass making?"

As Walk and Charity raised their hands, No Confidence said, "But didn't I just hear you yell that the Board said no?"

"They said we could not use needed material or labor. After supper is free time. We can do whatever we want after supper."

Harmony tugged on Rejoice's sleeve. "You mean build it all by ourselves?"

"Why not?"

And so Charity and Walk blew glass balls for the floats, and Give Glory and his friends flattened the huge, empty seed cartons to make the planks. So My Soul, Be, and Great Is The Lord constructed a wind generator to produce more energy for melting glass; and Love, Industry, We Have Received, and Persuaded built sections of planking with see-through glass plates between the buoyant seed cartons.

Brother Holly drilled in several places along the bridge route. "I have to drill for oil somewhere," he had said. A number of other fathers decided the best time for their children to practice diving to keep up proficiency was after supper. And if, during the dives, a few rods were inserted in the basalt drill holes to hold anchoring cables to the half-kilometer-long bridge, what was wrong with that? The rods and cables weren't needed for the original purpose of building suspension bridges over mountain valleys; and who said wasting unneeded material was godly?

They even built a glass observation deck directly over the kelp bearing structure anchored to the sea floor so they could watch the hexacrabs with tiny hexacrabs tied to their backs swing among the struts like slow-motion acrobats.

The strong storms subsided into a much milder weather cycle. The builders hoped the bridge would hold up to the next season of storms. Or rather, most did.

Elder Smith glowered but said nothing about the bridge. He did not stop glowering until a certain evening he spent walking on the First City Bay beach with his wife. She was a small woman who was seldom noticed and preferred it that way. "I'm so glad the hexacrabs moved close by," she said, as the two of them approached the kelp farm. "They're taking such good care of the abalone and fish. I was afraid I would end my days on a barren moon of a planet. But now there's life."

"The fields," Elder Smith said.

"Oh, yes, the fields. But those are tame. I like wildlife. And speaking of wild, look at those kids whooping and hollering and chasing each other on that bridge. Doesn't it make you happy all over to see that?"

It did not, but although Elder Smith had intimidated thousands of men in his lifetime, when his wife expressed one of her rare opinions, life went far better for him if he agreed. "It's a right cheery sight," he said, nodding and forcing a smile.

* * *

Rejoice perched on Ocean Shore Boulder, watching the sun slide toward the horizon, humming the tune to *Bolero* by Ravel, and swaying.

Harmony sauntered toward her. Rejoice jumped down, and together they walked toward the bridge.

They strolled to Stronghold, sitting on a rock watching the other teenagers shrieking and splashing each other in the cold seawater. By the time his hand and leg had healed enough so that he could help with the construction, most of it had been done. He scratched absent-mindedly at the scar on his hand.

Harmony cast a quick grin at Rejoice and then nudged Stronghold's foot with hers. "We're going to the hexacrab cluster. Want to come?"

"No," he said, scowling. "Why is everybody so crazy about those slimy things anyway?"

Harmony drew back her foot. "Oh, I guess you're still mad at them."

"I'm not mad."

"I would be. And scared, too. I don't know how my uncle visits them every day."

"I'm not scared."

"Then how come you've never been to the floating deck? Not once."

Stronghold stood and walked toward the bridge. "I don't think they're interesting. And I don't know why we should trust them."

Harmony gave him a little push. "Because we exposed our soft parts to each other and now we have to take care of each other." She whistled the last phrase in Hex.

"I can't stand it when you talk like hexacrabs."

In the distance Sister Guthry pulled herself up the stairs to the weather station. Rejoice dashed over to the stairs and clattered up them to Sister Guthry. "What do you want? I'll get it." She panted.

"No, Young Lady." Sister Guthry tapped her cane on the tread. "You've gone up and down these stairs enough for me. You go on and play."

Rejoice bounded down the stairs and danced across the sand back to Stronghold and Harmony. Her teacher getting better, Stronghold beginning to talk, the salt air and golden slanting light, these filled her heart with joy. She skipped along the floating bridge sections as the sea sloshed and gurgled under them, each section dipping when she stepped on it and bouncing up when she stepped off. It became a game to run without lurching from side to side or tripping over the open spaces between each section. She and Harmony and Stronghold tried to skip the full length of the bridge without stopping.

"Move over," Abiding whistled in Hex as they squeezed past him.

All three were panting when they reached the deck. The sun kissed the horizon. Rejoice and Harmony threw themselves flat on their stomachs to peer over the edge. Stronghold knelt beside them.

"There's the corral with the females. I feel sorry for them," Harmony said.

"That's the one thing about the hexacrabs I do like," Stronghold said. "If all the women were behind bars and kept silent, everything would be a lot better."

Rejoice hid her fists under her armpits so she wouldn't smack him.

"You're mean," Harmony said, keeping her eyes on the cluster.

"What else can they do?" Rejoice asked. "If the brain-damaged females ran loose, the torpals, kraken, and naspy would eat them. Ur-Veena said that sooner or later we'll see one of them, and then we'll wish we hadn't." Her fingers stroked the pebbled glass of the deck. She enjoyed the deck's slow, rhythmic rocking.

"Uncle Resolved calls Ur-Veena Ur-Leonardo de Veena and says he is a true Renaissance crustacean. I wonder what that means?" Harmony wrinkled her forehead.

Stronghold laughed. "You'll study Leonardo de Vinci in Old Earth history."

"Oh, look!" Harmony cried. "There's one of the little ones. He's tied to—oh, who is that? Ur-Pito. He's showing the little one a spiney."

Rejoice peered into the green and brown dappled sea. The current dragged a kelp strand back and forth across her vision like a windshield wiper. Ur-Pito broke off a spine and presented it to the little one. The little one chomped on the stiff spine and dropped it. Ur-Pito retrieved the spine and tucked it into a mesh bag hanging on one of his spurs.

"They're so cute!" Harmony said.

Stronghold peered over the edge. "Hunh. You've got a weird definition of cute. Cute is you."

Harmony pushed herself up and stared at him with her eyes wide and shining above her mask.

Stronghold backed up. "Wouldn't you know it? I just remembered a chore I have to do at home. God be with you." His feet went *thunk thunk thunk* on the bridge.

Harmony watched him until he was halfway across the bridge, then whirled to face Rejoice and squealed, "Did you hear what he said?"

"Yes, and so will the whole colony before breakfast, I daresay."

Harmony splashed her. "Not unless you tell. It would be vain of me to repeat it. God help you if you're vain around here. And if God doesn't help you, Sister Olson will."

Rejoice rolled onto her back and laughed. Harmony leaned over the edge to plash the water with her forefinger. Rejoice finally sat up and saw the sun, a red-gold dot, wink out on the horizon and the turquoise sea shade to gray. "Uh-oh. It'll be dark before we get back."

* * *

When Rejoice entered her apartment, Mother straddled Makepeace on the floor, pinning his arms with her knees, prying his mouth open with one hand, and brushing his teeth with the other. Mother smiled at Rejoice. "There you are, dearest. Could you grab a flashlight and get your brother? Your father is at an engineers' meeting, and Stronghold went to string up mesh for the beans. Why he decided at this moment to get diligent about the beans, I don't know. If you could gently remind him that I want all my children home when it gets dark, I would appreciate it." Mother put down the toothbrush, ruffled Makepeace's hair, and smothered his face with kisses while Makepeace wriggled helplessly.

On the way to the bean fields, the farthest fields out, Rejoice stopped and gazed at Big Potato and the trailing Small Potatoes. The sea's gentle hiss could not be heard here, and the velvet air caressed her skin. The Milky Way blazed near the horizon. The bluish point of light winking near the Well Constellation was the gas giant Wimbleweather. In its atmosphere, storms raged and lightning crackled ceaselessly. But here, the air lay still, and seedlings stretched up out of the cooling soil. "Thank you, Lord," breathed Rejoice, and the calm and peace that her parents said filled the heart of every person who followed God enveloped her. She breathed deeply.

The beam of her flashlight outlined Stronghold sitting on a mound of mesh. She held the flashlight beam on his feet. "What are you doing?"

"I'm thinking. Is there something wrong with that?"

"I haven't heard any sermons against it. But Mother wants you to think at home when it gets dark."

He sighed and rose to follow her. "What does she think is going to happen to me in the dark?"

Partway back, she veered to a side path and motioned for him to come before she realized he couldn't see the path. She took his hand. "Let me show you something I'm working on for Mother and Father."

"Sure."

She knelt by a corner of a perennial wheat field and shone her light on a tiny, prickly holly plant.

"Were you authorized to do that?"

"No. I'll dig it up before the harvest. No one is going to miss a cup of dirt. I'll give it to Mother when we move into our farmhouse to grow beside our front door."

"Where's the other one?"

"What other one?"

"Don't I need one for my front door? I'll have my own farm in three years."

Rejoice grinned and elation danced in her heartbeat. "I'll plant it tomorrow." In the dark, she gazed in the direction of his voice. "You plan to marry that soon? You'll only be eighteen."

"Married or not, I intend to leave Father's house as soon as I can."

Her joy burst and fell in tatters under her feet.

The two of them walked from the field in mutual silence, Rejoice wiping her eyes with her sleeve. When they were close to the apartments, a cry broke the stillness of the night. They stopped.

"Over there," Stronghold said.

The cry came again.

"It's Sister Guthry!" Rejoice said. "She must have fallen again!"

They ran toward the cries and saw a flashlight's bobbing beam. Sister Guthry hobbled, wailing, toward the apartments. Her cane rattled against the stony path.

"What's wrong?" Rejoice cried.

Sister Guthry dug her fingers into Rejoice's shoulder and sobbed. "I just checked the orbit of your asteroid. In three years it's going to hit New Earth. We'll be splattered to kingdom come!"

SHATTERWORLD CHAPTER NINETEEN

U r-Veena rubbed tentacles with Ur-Pito. They examined each other's little ones for cuts and fungal growth, and then pressed together, side by side, to let the little ones wrestle and throw kelp at each other. The adults discussed the progress of the salmon fingerlings. That done, Ur-Veena trudged toward his niche.

His little one, Sa-Issi, peeped, "Let's swing on the kelp structure."

"No. I choose not to."

"I want to play with Sa-Lati."

"No, I choose not to. As long as you are tied to me, you must go where I go."

"I'm hungry. Give me some plant."

"No. I choose not to."

Sa-Issi's little legs clicked as he strained against the rope crossed under his beak. "Then untie me and I shall get plant."

"No."

Sa-Issi strained harder. "Question? When will I get off you so I can choose where to go?"

Ur-Veena coiled his tentacles in pride. His little one was the first to ask that question. "You will get off when you can break the rope by yourself. Then I will know that you are strong enough to fight the torpal and the naspy and the gut-wrigglers."

Sa-Issi pushed harder.

SHATTERWORLD CHAPTER TWENTY

Rejoice glanced at the colonists sitting in solemn array in the Meetingplace, heads bowed. Her eyelids felt heavy as she covered a yawn. Makepeace stirred restlessly, clutching Mother's arm with one hand and sucking on the other. With her yellowed hair tangled about her shoulders, Sister Guthry stared at the floor and from time to time sniffed and dabbed her eyes. Elder Smith slumped in his chair, his large hands jerking on his lap like stepped-on crabs. Rejoice's stomach gurgled. She crossed her arms over her stomach, hoping to muffle the noise. She had a slight chest ache and headache to plague her as well. How did fasting help them pray for hours?

Elder Smith's boots scraped the floor as he rose heavily, wearily, and turned to face the congregation. "If any of you lack wisdom, let him ask of God, who will give it generously," he muttered, quoting from Scripture. Elder Smith cleared his throat and gazed out the windows at the glassed-over fields of wheat, barley, corn, and amaranth flowing under the caress of the sea breeze. His throat worked. "It doesn't take much wisdom to know that we must leave this place. We must leave our fields. We must leave our labor and the dreams for what we had hoped to have here. The sooner we settle that in our hearts, the better."

The congregation stirred at that.

"Since none of the other planets in this system are habitable, the next question is where we will warp to. I'll tell you this: I won't go back to Old Earth like a beaten cur with my tail between my legs."

Rejoice shivered and waited for the rebuke of that vain and prideful statement. A long minute passed. The pastor tensed.

Father rose and waited, his head bowed until Elder Smith had sat down. Rejoice gazed up at Father as he ran his fingers along the top of the pew in front of them. He said, "There are some who would call that a decision based on pride."

The eyes of all the men flashed to him, most seeming to communicate, "I wouldn't, Brother, but say on."

Elder Smith reddened.

"But," Father continued, "that sin is as deep in me, for I agree. One reason: and this is the one that stems from pride, is that if we did reach Old Earth, we would be total paupers. We would arrive with no food and no jobs. Second: I don't think we can reach Old Earth. Maybe we could have gone back a few minutes after coming out of warp here. Maybe. But with all the positioning we've done of the ship around this planet in the last seven months, I think it's no longer possible. Third: we must remember why we left Old Earth six months sooner than we had originally planned. We spent years planning carefully. And then we had to race like refugees. If we do reach Old Earth and find the Leechies have blown it up, where will we be then?"

The whole congregation tensed and looked at each other over their children.

Rejoice pulled at her mother's sleeve. "Someone blew up Old Earth?"

"Shh," Mother said, and whispered fiercely, "We don't know if India and Brazil carried out their threats against the Fifty-nine States and Quebec. We assumed the probabilities were good. So did eight other colony ships that fled at the same time we did." She reached across Rejoice to grab Stronghold's wrist. "But we won't ever know. That's why we never told you. We didn't want you children to share our nightmares."

Sickened, Rejoice let go of Mother's sleeve. Stronghold stared at Mother and then Father.

Father glanced at the family. "We would do better to head for a nearer star. But that is a counsel of desperation, since our chances of finding a habitable system are hopeless unless God guides us."

Elder Smith shifted in his seat. "I remember the names of some of the stars the other colonists went to. We have three years to learn how to reprogram our warp drive toward one of them."

"Three years isn't long enough to stock our ship," said Deacon Kim.

Father responded. "We can't stay here unless we wish to die. If we can't provision the ship with enough food for everyone, then I'll stay behind and send my children on."

"Why can't we just blow up the thing!" Deaconess Hernandez asked. Her dark eyes flashed.

Her accountant-turned-engineer husband shook his head. "We didn't bring any bombs with us, and we can't build enough bombs to blow up an asteroid that size."

Sister Olson, with her blond braids in disarray, rose and spoke, her voice brassy and shrill. "But why must we leave at all? Why can't we move out of its way and go into space until after it hits?"

Many people nodded. But Sister Guthry, dabbed at her eyes, saying in a halting voice, "Because when it hits, it will do at least as much damage as the asteroid that created Bull's-Eye. What isn't killed by the heat waves, shock waves—" She gasped. "—tsunamis or volcanoes will die afterward, when the sunlight is blocked for months by ash from the explosion. Whatever lives through the cold and dark will die from the acid rain. And whatever lives through that will die from the ultraviolet as the ozone layer is destroyed again. We can't hang on for that many years."

A few of the people shuffled their feet. Rejoice bit on her finger to keep from crying out loud. What about the hexacrabs? The Meetingplace seemed to creak and groan with tension. Pastor Wiseman reached for the pulpit and pulled himself up to it like a drowning man straining toward a pier.

"We need to pray more." With a trembling hand, he blessed the congregation. "Go to your homes in peace. We will meet here again tomorrow for common fast."

They started to disperse, silently, but then Sister Olson sobbed loudly.

Deaconesses Hernandez and Redhorse went over to her and patted her shoulders. She screamed, "We need to repent! God is punishing us for secret sin!" Mother, Pastor Wiseman, and Brother Olson raced over to escort her into the sound-proof room where the babies were to be nursed. Dr. Cruz followed a minute later. Rejoice shivered.

Elder Smith rose up again and raised his hands. "Sister Olson will be fine. Please, let us follow the Pastor's advice and seek for God's wisdom."

Rejoice's family stopped at their door with the wreath casting a black shadow on it, but Rejoice kept going. She didn't check behind her to see if anyone approved, and they didn't ask where she was going.

In several minutes, she reached Ocean Shore Boulder. The sea whispered of sorrow against the dark sand and lapped at the base of the stone. Rejoice leaned forward against the back half of the boulder, which rested on hot, dry sand, and poised to climb it.

Elder Chin stood near the floating bridge, helping Brother Hancock put on a wetsuit. Brother Hancock's left arm hung at his side.

Rejoice trotted toward them. The men embraced, spoke briefly to each other, and then parted. Brother Hancock headed to the floating bridge, Elder Chin back toward the colony. Elder Chin trudged past Rejoice with eyes downcast.

Brother Hancock was adjusting his face mask when she reached him.

"Are you going to tell the hexacrabs?" she asked.

He pulled the mask off with his good hand. "We thought we should."

"Oh. Is Elder Chin coming back?"

"Well. Not immediately. He decided he couldn't do it because he's too upset."

Rejoice plucked at her brown sleeve. "Stronghold runs away when he's upset, too."

"Eh. Children always see more than they should. Are you here because you want to tell the hexacrabs too?" He wiped away the sweat on his forehead.

Rejoice licked away the bead of sweat that had trickled down to the corner of her mouth. "Yes, please."

"I'll wait for you." Brother Hancock walked to the side of the bridge and sat with his feet dangling over the edge.

Rejoice darted into the oven-like cabana and changed into a wetsuit. Sweat had plastered her hair against her forehead by the time she stepped out.

She sat beside Brother Hancock, slipped on a pair of fins, and took a deep breath. "Brother Hancock? Why didn't you grown-ups tell us children about the Leechies blowing up Old Earth?"

He sighed as he gazed at the horizon with sad eyes and blinked slowly. "Eh. They might not have. We didn't stay around long enough to find out. Adults are supposed to protect children, not give them nightmares. If we'd had to turn right around, that would have been seven years of dread for you to live through before we found out for sure."

"You should have told us."

"Maybe so. But we left in a hurry, and we made a lot of decisions in a hurry. Not telling you was one of them. I'm sorry if it was the wrong decision."

"That's not the only one," Rejoice muttered.

"Pardon?"

"Why does everything have to be the way it is? What made you decide we had to be farmers? Why couldn't some of us be farmers and some of us be something else? Why do we all need to fast at the same time, all wear the same clothes, and—" She stopped to take a breath.

One side of Brother Hancock's mouth curled up. "We don't want industry because we don't want to drown in a sea of possessions. We were going to start a new world. We were trying to hear God on how best to do that. We surveyed history and chose the traditions we thought would help us the most. We didn't want to repeat the errors of Old Earth. You've studied the Covenant. That's what we chose."

"I didn't choose. And Stronghold didn't choose."

Brother Hancock dabbled one of his fins in the water. "No, you didn't. Nor did we choose the world we were born into. We didn't choose to be persecuted for our faith. We didn't choose to lose our jobs or be blocked from the universities because we wanted to serve our Lord. Your father is brilliant. He qualified for one of the top universities in the world. When they found out he was a Christian, they took away his full scholarship."

"He never told us that." Now her throat hurt along with the chest and headache.

"Again, he didn't want to burden you with Old Earth garbage. We were wiping the dust off our feet when we left."

"But you had the choice of not being a Christian," she whispered.

"Yes," Brother Hancock sighed. "Separation from God is always an option. None of us chose to be born under our father Adam's curse. But we can choose to be redeemed by the blood of God's Son. We assumed our children would follow in our footsteps. Eh . . . If you want to strengthen your heart, it doesn't matter much if you do it by jogging or swimming. We knew we would need unity and a single vision to survive seven years on a tiny ship. We needed unity to work together and sacrifice to create this new world. So, we chose to follow the same spiritual disciplines. No one can say they are more spiritual than someone else. But maybe, if we survive, we'll need to examine other spiritual disciplines for those who want to do something else."

"What would the Elders do to someone who doesn't want to do any of the disciplines? I don't think my brother—I mean—"

"I don't know." He pulled his withered hand onto his lap and studied his knuckles. "Young Lady Rejoice, I'm not criticizing you. I'm asking you a question. Why are you asking me these things instead of your parents?"

Rejoice looked away, but the sun's glare hurt her eyes, and squinting, she looked back toward him. "I—I don't want to hurt them."

"From what I know of your father and mother, honest questions won't hurt them. Isn't the real problem that you're afraid you don't believe?"

"No! I believe. At least I think I do. Nobody understands. You think you know what my problem is. And Mother thinks she knows what my problem is. But you don't. Nobody does, because I'm different. I stay up late at night reading about planets and orbits under my covers. In logic class, I think about the stars. When I'm sowing turnips, I think about asteroids. It's all I can think about. Why did God make me like this and then put me on a planet where I can't do anything about it? Why can't I be boy-crazy like Harmony? Then my mother would be happy." Rejoice wiped her eyes with the backs of her hands, acutely embarrassed. The hot air, heavy with the smell of iodine, turned her stomach. Her feet kept shifting as though they wanted to hide away as badly as she did.

Brother Hancock smiled and shook his head. "You're very thirteen."

"I won't be thirteen for another month and a half," she said in a tight, tiny voice. Why had she told him anything?

"Close enough. When I was thirteen, eh. You don't want to hear an old man's stories. But listen to this. It doesn't matter. The cages on Old Earth were just as tight as the ones here. It's just that the bars looked different. You had to wear what was fashionable. You could only work at jobs that were available. You could only go to schools you were admitted to. And God help you if you expressed an opinion differing from the media's current ravings. Here or there, the human heart is whatever it wants to be."

"But—"

"Can I finish my old man's speech?"

"Yes, sir."

"Thank you. This colony can make you sing a hundred hymns, but if you want to blaspheme in your heart, no one can stop you. Your body can pull turnips, but your mind can be on the sun if you want it to be. You're as free to love the stars here as you would have been on Old Earth. Here or there, believe me, if God put that in you, He'll give you a chance to use it. Someday."

"Mother says I'm being selfish. She says I want to make other people work and produce my food while I just please myself and produce nothing."

"I hate to say this, and you better not repeat this. But your mother's wrong on a couple of things. You're not selfish, or you wouldn't be so worried about your family and the hexacrabs. And you did produce something. Panic. Don't we all have ulcers now?"

"I don't—what?" Her forehead wrinkled, making her headache worse.

"I'm sorry. Bad joke. Astronomy produced our crisis. Or rather, it showed us that we have a crisis." He adjusted his mask over his bulbous nose. "Young Lady, as important as your problem is, it takes a back seat to telling the hexacrabs they're all going to die. We need to tell them so they can do whatever it is they need to do before they die."

Rejoice studied her knees as shame replaced embarrassment. Her problem was nothing compared to the ones the colony and the hexacrabs were facing. Why had she wasted Brother Hancock's time? She snapped on her mask and shoved herself off the bridge. The shock of the cold water made her gasp. Brother Hancock splashed in beside her and tapped on her tank of air.

Right, breathe regularly. She moderated her breathing to an even rhythm and they swam to the hexacrab cluster nestled in the shade of the kelp farm.

Little Sa-Issi scrabbled and danced on Ur-Veena's shell as the mottled hexacrab chipped a diamond next to the translator post. Like a piccolo, the little one piped, "You did not come. Question? Did you not come to see what we would do? We waited. I am hungry. Question? Are you hungry when you wait?"

Rejoice snickered. How could Ur-Veena chip diamonds with a small hexacrab jerking so hard on his rope? Oh, what was she doing? How could she laugh at a time like this?

Brother Hancock settled in front of Ur-Veena. Flattened silver bubbles raced to the surface. Ur-Veena stowed his rocks in a net and swiveled all eyes to face them. Brother Hancock waited a long minute before saying "I need to speak to Ur-Tista."

Ur-Veena turned with undulating tentacles and crept toward Ur-Tista's niche. His crushed leg dragged behind him.

Sa-Issi whistled, "You and Chan-tot are the same." He tap-danced on Ur-Veena's shell.

"Question? How are we the same?" asked his guardian.

"Both of you have broken legs."

"No, he has a broken tentacle. Brave Ur-Nissi broke it before we understood each other." Ur-Veena reached the pile of stelai he had been working on and caressed the stone slivers. "I shall ask Ur-Tista to cut off this leg. It is plain that it shall not heal."

"Question? Will air ocean Chan-tot cut off his tentacle?" piped Sa-Issi. Rejoice watched Brother Hancock. They could not hear Ur-Veena's reply as the hexacrabs moved out of range of the translator. She moved closer to Brother Hancock. Her heart beat frantically and her hands clenched and unclenched rhythmically. How would the hexacrabs react when they found out they were all going to die?

Languidly, Ur-Veena and Ur-Tista strolled toward them. Rejoice wished they would hurry, and then she wished they would take forever. Now she knew why Elder Chin had left. This was too hard.

Finally, Ur-Veena and Ur-Tista stood in front of them.

"I have bad news for you." Brother Hancock reached out and gently took one of Ur-Tista's tentacles. "The Dark Death came because a giant rock from the space-ocean hit this water-ocean. In the space ocean there swims another asteroid that will hit this water ocean in three years. We have seen this asteroid, this giant rock. We cannot stop it. In three years—" He took a deep, shuddering breath. "In three years will come another Dark Death."

Ur-Tista and Ur-Veena clicked a few times and backed away. Ur-Tista whistled a high, urgent note. The hexacrabs of the cluster gathered, clumping and rolling into a writhing mass of tentacles and legs. A babble of whistles and clicks caused the translator post to squeal.

Brother Hancock switched it off. "There are too many voices for it to follow."

"What are they doing?" Rejoice asked.

"I don't know. I've never seen this before."

Rejoice and Brother Hancock watched sand and sediment swirl around the grappling hexacrabs. Their shells clinked against each other.

Then they fell apart and most of the hexacrabs crawled back to the kelp beds. Brother Hancock turned the translator on.

Ur-Veena advanced toward them and held out his blade. "We do not ask for trade. We will give you all the blades you need to attack this asteroid."

"Oh, no," Rejoice cried. "You don't understand. It's too big to be poked out of the way." Her hands gripped her mask.

Ur-Veena gurgled to Ur-Tista as they intertwined tentacles. Then Ur-Veena offered the blade again. "We will make bigger blades and longer shafts. Come with us to the deep ocean. There we will fight torpal and teach you courage. We do not ask for trade."

"You don't under—"

Brother Hancock touched Rojoice's elbow, and then reached out his good hand, palm upward. As Ur-Veena laid the blade on his palm, Brother Hancock said, "Thank you. Could you please make twelve of these, twice as large? I will go with you to fight the torpal. Thank you." His fingers closed around the blade. He turned, and Rejoice followed him back to the dock.

They slogged up out of the shallows and onto the beach and sat on the side of the bridge, where wavelets washed against their ankles. Brother Hancock reverently laid the blade beside him. Rejoice unbuckled his equipment. He wiped off the seawater glazing his face and whispered, "Bless them. They think they're superior to us. I think they're right. Did you catch that, what Ur-Veena said in Hex? The translator said, 'teach you courage,' but what he said literally was 'shell the movement of your soft parts with strength.' Did you hear him? God bless them."

"Why did you take the blade? It won't do any good." Rejoice pulled back her dripping hair.

Brother Hancock picked up the blade again and held his hand out flat. The diamond teeth shone in the harsh light. He took several breaths and swallowed before saying, "Young Lady, do you know that Micah, Perseverance, and Joy are not my only children?"

Rejoice cleared her throat and licked away the saltwater from her lips. "Joy told me she had a sister that died."

"Devotion was such a pretty girl," Brother Hancock said softly. "She had her mother's nose, not mine." He smiled a little. "And hair the color of corn silk, and soft gray eyes. She was just a few years younger than you when she got leukemia. Ninety-nine percent of all children with leukemia can be cured now, but my daughter was in the one percent. We prayed. We drove across the country to another doctor and hospital. We tried all the drugs that were allowed and few that weren't. It didn't matter. She died in my arms screaming for a bedpan. I'm sorry. You don't need all the gory details. What you need to know, is that during every moment of her illness, we were doing something. We didn't sit by and let her die without trying everything we knew how to do." He stroked the blade. "These brave hexacrabs are trying to save themselves the only way they know how. Shall I take that away from them?"

"No," Rejoice whispered. She blinked back tears. The sun simmered her skin under the black wetsuit.

Brother Hancock studied the blade as the ocean hissed and sunlight rode the waves; then he turned to face her. "Oh, Young Lady, I didn't mean to make you cry. It's all right. Devotion is in God's hands. We'll see her again someday." He sighed and scanned the beach. "If we die, I can't complain. We gave it our best, and we knew our chances weren't good. But the hexacrabs . . . I don't understand. We killed ourselves, but what did the hexacrabs do? Why should they be killed, Father God, why?" He bent forward and gripped the diamond-studded blade so hard that blood seeped between his fingers.

Rejoice could think of no answer. She got up, fled to the cabana, and, trembling, changed back into her long brown dress and filter mask. When she came out, Brother Hancock was still praying. She left him there and ran home.

In the cool apartment, Father knelt beside the sofa with his face buried in its cushions. Mother knelt beside him, holding his hand and humming a hymn about trusting God. Makepeace and Stronghold sat silently on the edges of their bed spaces.

Rejoice watched her parents, her stomach cramping in fear and hunger. How could they pray so calmly? An onslaught of dizziness forced her down into her bedspace. She hadn't slept since Sister Guthry told her about the asteroid. Now sleep caught her.

SHATTERWORLD CHAPTER TWENTY-ONE

Sa-Issi dozed, tangled in his ropes. He woke when Ur-Veena swung from one strut to another on the kelp-farm structure. The little one's legs scraped across Ur-Veena's shell. The larger hexacrab said, "Taste the current. That is the taste of good weather to continue." Sa-Issi extended his palps. "Question? Which flavor is good weather?"

Ur-Veena let go, and sank down beside Ur-Tista, who was chewing on a blade of pungent kelp. The elderly hexacrab flicked away an Old Earth snail. Salmon streaked by. The two hexacrabs trudged toward the cluster.

Ur-Tista turned his eyes to Ur-Veena. "What will you do if you cannot teach these other-ocean cowards the courage they need to defeat the asteroid?" Leaving off the particle that indicated that the following sentence would be a question showed his agitation.

"Then I shall go and fight the asteroid."

Ur-Tista expelled some water and slid a tentacle tip along one of Ur-Veena's scars. "You cannot live in that ocean."

"Neither can the air-ocean people. They wear protection in the space-ocean, as they do in our water-ocean. I shall wear protection." He flared his gills. "I shall go into the air-ocean and the space-ocean and the warp-ocean. But first, we must make sure the asteroid is defeated."

They passed by the corral, and Ur-Veena reached in through the bars to stroke a female. Before he touched her he jerked upright and then rolled into a writhing ball. He sucked in his tentacles and closed all his opercula.

A few minutes later, Ur-Veena shot out his tentacles, popped open his opercula, and whistled to Ur-Tista, "The air-ocean people say our water and rock-ocean are two shells placed together. Perhaps on the other side of our ocean are females that talk!"

"We have never heard of it. En-Teppi has not heard of it."

"The other side of the water ocean must be much farther than any of the lot-chosen have wandered. When next we have lots, I will be chosen."

"The lot chooses."

"I shall tell the lot to choose me. I will trade with the air-ocean people for an edgeworld presser that I can direct from beneath. Then I could travel over the great chasms."

"Me. I will go too," piped Sa-Issi.

"Yes." Ur-Veena, reached back to stroke the little hexacrab. "You shall go, and many, many stelai will be made of our voyage from one side of the ocean to the other."

SHATTERWORLD CHAPTER TWENTY-TWO

Rejoice woke late that afternoon, dry-mouthed, crusty-eyed, and with panic clogging her throat. What had woken her?

The door whooshed shut. Feet tapped past her bed and sheets rustled on the other side of the apartment. The fold-up bed creaked.

She rubbed her eyes and swallowed several times.

Father asked, "How is Sister Olson doing?"

Rejoice laid still in her bed with her eyes closed and listened.

"She kept having panic attacks and hyperventilating. I called Dr. Cruz and she came and gave her another sedative."

"Did Pastor Wiseman and elders reprimand her for her inappropriate behavior?"

"Theophilus, I don't believe you understand Sister Olson." Mother sounded impatient.

"No, I don't!" Something thumped on the table. "She frightened a lot of children and quite a few adults."

"Do you remember her before we started the voyage?"

There was a pause. In the bed niche above Rejoice, Makepeace sang, "Pum pump um pum."

"I see your point. Yes, she was an impressive woman of faith. But why would seven years on a ship change her so much?"

"You haven't shared Deaconess Redhorse's Bible studies with her like I have. Sister Blessed Are The Pure In Heart Olson could not in good conscience start using birth control as most of us women did. Theophilus, she lost seven children on the voyage. She has little memorials for every one of them arranged in her apartment. When we arrived here and found an almost dead planet, she saw it as a sign that God was not pleased with us."

"She certainly has a right to her opinion. And yes, I am sorry. I never stopped to consider the effect of her losses on her. But still, we've all suffered loss. Has Deaconess Redhorse talked to her about how sharing her opinions so loudly are not beneficial?"

"Of course she has. But Theophilus, she's pregnant again and is very emotional. Now she's been told this baby will not live to age three."

There was a long pause. Water dripped in the sink. Rejoice slid off her blanket and rubbed her forehead. Her headache was gone, but starvation pinched her stomach.

Father said, "Carol, please forgive me for my attitude to a suffering Sister in Christ. I'm feeling like her in some ways. I was overjoyed when we were chosen for this pilgrimage on the Starflower. I wanted to protect our children. I was not going to do to them what my father did to me."

Rejoice rolled over and blinked. Her parents sat on the sofa with Father clinging to Mother, and could be seen through her partially-open curtains.

His voice broke. "I will never forget that moment. My father turned and winked at me and said, 'I'm off to greener pastures,' and out the door he went. When it closed behind him, I knew I would never see him again. And I knew another thing. I knew I hated what he had done. When the lock clicked shut, in that instant, I vowed that I'd never abandon my wife and children. I would die before I let them be hurt. So when the Leechies threatened to incinerate us, I couldn't . . ."

"I know, honey, I know," Mother whispered as she stroked his fore-head.

"I thought God had called us here."

"He did," said Mother with firmness in her voice that surprised Rejoice. "Sometimes He calls us to die. At supper every night, let's read a part of

John Wesley's diary. He stood by the bedside of hundreds of dying saints and recorded their last words. Those people knew how to die. Maybe it's time we studied how."

"Good idea. Though if we leave, we might not die."

"No!" Rejoice screamed, bolting out of her bed space. She sucked in her breath in shock. You don't scream at your parents. You don't speak unless you can speak words of peace. She held her hands against the hammering of her heart. Her throat tightened further with knife-stab pain. "Father, we can't just leave this planet. We have to save the hexacrabs!"

He stared at her with hollow eyes and shook his head. "They lived through it once before."

"Barely. And now their females can't talk. The ocean used to be filled with them, and now it's almost empty. Another asteroid, and they'll be gone like the churtrees."

Father placed his head in his hands. "We have no place to put tanks of hexacrabs on the Starflower. They need the ocean on this planet for their life cycle. If we take them away, they will still die."

"The Bible tells us that we need to lay down our lives for our friends."

"You expect us to lay down our lives for a bunch of squids?" Stronghold shouted from his bed space.

Tears gathered in Father's eyes. Rejoice nearly stopped breathing. She had never seen her father cry before.

"I would save them if I could," he whispered. "But I don't know if I can save even you."

Making a strangling sound, Stronghold bolted out of his bed and slammed through the door. Rejoice hurried after him.

She found him leaning on the side of Ocean Shore boulder, his face buried in his arms. She climbed past him, sat on the edge of the boulder, and scanned the empty sky purpling with dusk. The sea hissed on the bare sand. Slowly and steadily, Big Potato rose. Its white reflection wavered on the sea.

After the Small Potatoes had cleared the horizon, Stronghold climbed up beside Rejoice. He sat, breathing heavily for several minutes. "Sis, call me a jerk."

She bit her lip and shook her head.

"Call me a stupendous, colossal, gigantic jerk! Father really did mean to do right by me. It's not his fault. All I could think about was getting away from this place. I didn't understand that getting away from here meant we would die."

"I'm not leaving." Rejoice braced her feet against the boulder. "God called us here to this time to save the hexacrabs."

Stronghold sucked in his breath. "Don't give me this 'God called us' business. If He loved us, would He be sending that big rock to smash us? I can just see Him. He's laughing, "Ha! Ha! I'll wipe the smirk off that kid's face. 'Splat!'" He smacked his fist into his palm.

"Oh yeah, I'm sure God put that asteroid there just to ruin your life. No wonder you don't want to believe in God. I wouldn't want to believe in a God who could be pushed around by how I felt."

Stronghold glared at her. "Do you believe in God?"

Rejoice hugged herself. *Give me time to think!* "Mother and Father do . . ."

"I know that. That's how we got into this mess. Do you believe?"

She bit her lip again and twined her fingers together. She studied the sea, and then Stronghold. "What I feel is abandoned and helpless. But what I say is this: There is a God who gives wisdom to those who lack wisdom if they ask for it. I didn't choose to be here. And you didn't choose to be here. And none of us chose that big asteroid to come hit this world. But here we are, and the hexacrabs need us. What are we going to do about it?"

"That's easy. We're going to die."

"No, we're not. God gave us brains to use, and I'm going to use mine. And I'm going to sit here and fast and pray until God tells me how to save the hexacrabs."

Stronghold's shoulders slumped. "Okay, Sis." He swallowed a few times, and then slid off the boulder. He walked along the shore, away from the apartments.

Something in the way his shoulders hunched chilled her bones. "Stronghold!" she screamed.

He stopped and waited with his back to her.

"Promise me!"

"What?" came his answer, faint over the hiss of the sea.

"Promise me you won't kill yourself!"

He stood silently as his head dipped lower.

Rejoice pulled her legs up under her. She was right. She poised herself to jump off the boulder and chase him.

"Okay."

"Promise!"

He turned, his mask a bright white in the gathering dusk. "I said okay. What more do you want?"

She wanted him to be happy and play with Makepeace again and grow up to play with his own babies on his knee. The words stuck in her throat.

He trudged back to her, his feet dragging long black lines in the sand.

She laid flat on the boulder and rubbed the gritty surface.

He came close and searched her face. "I guess I shouldn't deprive Father and Mother of the joy of personally watching their son die."

She reached out and grabbed his hair. "Promise!"

"Ow! Promise what?"

Rejoice wanted more, but they were not allowed to swear. She let go. Stronghold's eyes examined hers as though he were seeking a particle of sanity. He turned and strode away.

She sat up and faced the sea and hugged her knees to her body. A shelter wouldn't protect the hexacrabs if an earthquake shook it apart. And it didn't solve the problem of the food supply dwindling under an ashy sky. The Starflower wasn't big enough to push the asteroid away. They couldn't build a rocket big enough. They had brought enough supplies to start a city. After that, they expected to use native materials. They had little transportation: two shuttles, one plane capable of vertical takeoff and landing, three boats.

Rejoice dangled her feet over the edge of the rock and kneaded her growling stomach. There must be a way to save the colonists without abandoning the hexacrabs. But the only reality she could see was the asteroid and the planet like trains running on converging tracks until they crashed at the switch. The asteroid would splatter the planet's crust into the atmosphere. She had three years to throw the switch.

Where was God? Where was the answer? And who was she to think that she would get the answer? She pressed her fists against the boulder. God had used a donkey to speak to an evil prophet. He had used a little servant girl to tell a general how to be healed of leprosy. He had used a boy with two fish and five loaves of bread to feed five thousand people. He could use Rejoice if she waited long enough. "Please, please," she whispered. "How can we save the hexacrabs?"

Plunk! A small blur arced in the purple air. A rock chunk flew by and splashed into the sea. *Plunk!* Makepeace had pulled his little wagon of rocks all the way from home.

"Makepeace." Rejoice exclaimed. "Where's Mother?"

She jumped down and ran to catch him. "Thank heavens you've got your mask on. Oh, here, it's snagged on your ear. Come on, let's go home."

Rejoice started to lead him home and then she remembered she had vowed not to leave the boulder until she had an answer. She slapped her thigh, changed direction, and tugged her brother toward the giant rock. "This will be the first place they search for you anyway." She hoisted him up.

They sat together, side by side, and watched Big Potato. The warm breeze off the land ruffled their hair and brought the scent of grass and mint. Makepeace tossed another rock. *Plunk!* Licking another stone from a stuffed pocket, he studied with bright eyes the small moon and its smaller companions. Then he climbed down and studied the rocks at the base of the boulder. Rejoice stayed on the boulder and watched him dump out his wagon.

He sorted through the rocks, old and new, found one, and held it up to the moons, studying it before he placed it in his wagon.

Rejoice climbed down next to him and leaned against the boulder. His added rock was shaped almost like the smallest Potato.

He pushed around more rocks until he found one almost the same shape as the second Potato and then a large one the shape of the Big Potato. He needed both hands to lift the Big Potato stone into his wagon. Puffing with effort, he pulled the wagon onto a large flat stone at the base of the boulder close to the water. He lined the Potatoes up in the pattern of the moons. Whining, he kept shoving at largest rock. He squinted his eyes in concentration and pounded a rock on Big Potato. *Tik! Tik! Tik!*

"You'll hurt your fingers." Rejoice reached for the rocks.

Makepeace pushed her hands away and rearranged the rocks. He had chipped a notch in the rock that matched the divot in Big Potato. He pointed. "Big Potato, Small Potato, Smaller Potato. One potato, two potato, three potato, four. Not four."

Rejoice peered at the rocks laid out in precise distances in the wagon. Makepeace sang, "Five potato, six potato, seven potato, more!"

Like the seagulls that had hovered over the beach on Old Earth, an idea hovered in her mind, teasing at her understanding. Sister Guthry and Father said the Potatoes might be the remnants of the moon broken into pieces by Dark Death.

Makepeace climbed into the wagon and stood. He picked up a small rock and shouted "One Potato!" and threw it into the water. *Plunk!* The wagon rocked back with his momentum.

Rejoice shouted, "Be careful!" and leaped next to the wagon.

Makepeace picked up the second rock held it up to the moons to study its shape. He shouted, "Two Potato!" and threw it hard. *Plunk!* The wagon rolled back a few more centimeters, close to the edge of the flat rock that was the first step up the boulder.

"Makepeace, be careful, or the wagon will roll off the rock." She halted in the action of reaching for him. That seagull of a thought cried close to her ear.

Makepeace picked up the biggest rock with both hands and lifted it over his head. He shouted, "Three Potato!" and heaved it over the front of the wagon. It clattered on the beach. The wagon jerked back and the rear wheels fell over the edge of the flat rock into the sand. Makepeace fell backwards.

Rejoice got one arm under him, fell, and rolled on top of him, catching herself with her hands just before they bumped heads. Makepeace smiled at her, laughed, and hugged her.

Rejoice looked into his brown eyes and laughed, too.

"Newton's Third Law!" Makepeace hugged her neck. She seized her little brother, rolled over a few more times in the sand, and hugged him so tightly that he squealed.

"That's it, that's it, that's it," she sang. She jumped up and brushed the sand off both of them. "Into the wagon, little brother. You get a free ride home. I'll drop you off, and then I need to see Sister Guthry and the Starflower computers. Thank you, Makepeace, God bless you, Makepeace. That's it, that's it, that's it! One Potato, two potato, three potato, four." They both sang all the way back.

Rejoice's arms hurt and her knees were buckling by the time she'd dragged Makepeace and the wagon back to the apartments. Yet she nearly flew to the meteorological building.

The sea gulls cried in her mind.

SHATTERWORLD CHAPTER TWENTY-THREE

In the soft darkness, Ur-Veena shifted the rope Sa-Issi had pulled over one of Ur-Veena's legs. He grated, "You disturb my rest."

Sa-Issi piped, "I hunger."

"I fed you plenty of plant before sleep."

Sa-Issi tugged on the ropes. "I still hunger! Feed me!"

"No."

"Enh! Enh! Enh!" Sa-Issi's feet clacked on Ur-Veena's shell as he jerked on the fibers. "Enh!"

Ur-Veena would not laugh. No, he would not, although the temptation pulled as hard as Sa-Issi. He scraped his beak.

"Enh! Enh!" The last threads snapped. Sa-Issi tumbled off Ur-Veena's back. The little hexacrab danced in the muck and wriggled all his tentacles. "Now I am adult. I will eat whenever I want!"

He scuttled to the blade of seaweed Ur-Veena had impaled on a stone splinter to keep it close.

Ur-Veena clamped a tentacle around his beak. He would not laugh, nor would he exalt his child over the others. But in his eyes he would treasure this memory of the first child broken free in the new colony.

* * *

Ur-Veena stirred the water. "Feel this."

Sa-Issi probed through the mud, trying hard to use his growing sense of electrical perception. "Yes, but I cannot find it. Here it is! Do I eat it?"

Ur-Veena rolled back on his legs. "If you want to, you may. Usually we feed the maggots to the spineys. Because we feed them, they stay with us, and that makes it easy to procure spines for the stelai." He flared his gills. "Now I know what I shall trade to the air-ocean people for an edgeworld presser. They need weapons to fight the swimming stone."

SHATTERWORLD CHAPTER TWENTY-FOUR

he hot morning sun stoked the crowded Meetingplace. The futile humming of the air conditioner could not cover the creaking of the pews, and the whimpering of children. People squinted at the platform where Rejoice and Sister Guthry sat behind Pastor Wiseman. Rejoice shifted in her seat and twisted her sweat-damp hair around her fingers.

Sister Guthry, with every hair pulled neatly back, glowed, smiling at all, even Sister Olson.

Sister Olson's eyes were vacant. Her husband and Dr. Cruz sat on either of her. Deaconess Hernandez sat right behind her leaning forward and patting her shoulder.

The people bowed their heads as Pastor Wiseman read from Scripture the story of Moses leading the Israelites through the Red Sea. He finished and closed the Bible with a thump. Rejoice jumped. Sister Guthry reached over and squeezed her fingers.

In the following silence, several people coughed. Others wiped their faces and necks.

Sister Guthry gripped her cane and pulled herself up. She shuffled to the pulpit. In a strong voice, as though she were preaching to thousands, she said, "The night before last, I discovered something that scared me out of my wits. I forgot to trust in God. Instead I acted in animal fear. I apologize to all of you. And now I ask you to listen to someone who kept her wits. Listen to the one God prepared for this occasion. Listen to the Young Lady Rejoice In The Lord's Salvation Holly." Still grinning, Sister Guthry shuffled back to her seat.

Face burning, Rejoice unrolled the screen behind the pulpit and activated the graphics. She could not believe her tutor said that. Pointing to some dots orbiting a picture of their sun, she said in a voice that wobbled, "First of all, this asteroid isn't named Rejoice anymore. I renamed it Opportunity. If the asteroid continues on its present course, in three years it will hit New Earth. We don't have the ability to blow up anything this big." She took a deep breath and glanced at Makepeace, who appeared to be studying a floating dust speck in the sunlight. Father, Mother and Stronghold watched her with hope flickering in their eyes.

"What we can do is fly to the asteroid, land on it, and break off a piece at a time." She switched to a close-up drawing of the asteroid. "We can get oil. People used to use oil for fuel and explosives, and we could use it to mine pieces from the asteroid."

"Excuse me, Young Lady." Brother White in grease-stained overalls rose and held out his hands as if begging. His triplets swiveled to stare at him. "Why go through such trouble? It would be much easier for us to run an electric current through water. We have no shortage of water or solar electricity. The current will separate the water into hydrogen and oxygen. That is easy to liquefy and is a much better fuel than oil." He shook his head. "But it wouldn't be enough to blow up the asteroid."

Rejoice suppressed a giggle. The answer was in the water. Elder Smith and Stronghold always complained that there was too much water on the planet. Would they notice? "I don't plan to blow up the asteroid. I plan to use Newton's law that for every action there is an equal and opposite reaction. My little brother, Makepeace, demonstrated this to me yesterday. He stood up in his wagon and threw a big rock off the front of it. What do you think happened?" Oh, God, she was teaching just like Father did. This was no time to teach by questions.

Makepeace laughed and sang "One Potato, Two Potato, Three Potato, Four."

She continued, "The rock goes one way and the wagon goes the other way. Right?"

The people nodded. They may not have been scientists, but after seven years of study on the Starflower, they all knew simple physics.

"So we use the hydrogen and oxygen to blast off pieces of the asteroid, like in mining, and then we use rockets or catapults or electromagnetic mass drivers to throw the pieces off the asteroid. The small pieces would be pushed a lot, and the asteroid would be pushed a little. And, if we throw and throw and throw for three years, all the little pushes could change the asteroid's course by one degree or slow it for a couple of hours—and it would miss New Earth!"

Everyone held their breath.

Would it work?

Rejoice dropped her screen onto the pulpit. As if the clatter were a signal, people turned to each other and whispered until Elder Sims rose. "How would you build a living space on the asteroid for the workers who would need ready access to it?"

"We don't need to. We can have the Starflower sit on it."

Sister Guthry pushed herself up. "And we can set up tons of solar panels to power our operations and the ship, can't we, Brother Hammer?"

Brother Hammer, the glass-factory foreman, stood holding his hat in his hands, and said in a voice that broke, "There's no problem churning out as many panels as we need." He turned his hat with shaky hands. "But I'm going to move the factory to the other side of the river so it won't eat up our beach. I want a place for my grandchildren to play."

"Wait a minute," Elder Sims held up a long finger. "If we're talking rockets and mass drivers and oxygen tanks and increased solar-panel production, then we're talking major industrialization. We would have to automate the farms to release people to set up factories. We can't plow by oxen and milk by hand. We can't do what we came here to do."

Everyone turned their eyes to Pastor Wiseman and Elder Smith. The two men looked at each other until Sister Smith reached over and squeezed her husband's hand. He studied her face for a minute, and then he cleared his throat and said slowly, "Here's the way I see it: if God shuts the door in your face, you look for a window. I thought God called us here to be farmers. Maybe he called us to save the hexacrabs."

The people whispered and laughed until Father stood with slumped shoulders. "It won't work. I'm sorry, but I can't see how we can build these electromagnetic mass drivers. Our factory-bots make manufacturing easy, but where are we going to get the raw materials? I need to find iron, titanium, copper and aluminum ores. And if I can find them, then we have to mine them. Then we have to get chemicals to purify them. And then we need to build train tracks to transport them, and on and on and on it goes. We can't do that in three years."

The whispering and laughing stopped.

"But it's a metallic asteroid." Rejoice swept her hand up. "We can take one of the factory-bots up there and mine the asteroid. And if you want, we could shoot iron bars to orbit New Earth for the shuttle to pick up. We could even make shuttle parts so you could build a fleet." Rejoice glanced at Stronghold. "Of course, to assemble the factory-bot, mass driver, and solar array on the asteroid, we're going to need some good extensioners."

"Yes!" Stronghold shouted. "Yes! Yes! Yes!" He leaped up and started dancing around the room. "Yes! Yes!"

Harmony danced around with him, clinging to his neck.

Everyone but Rejoice and Sister Guthry surged to their feet and danced among the benches and hugged each other and cried and praised God and sang songs. The parents kissed their children.

Makepeace squealed and swung on Mother's arm as she and Father pushed through the dancing mob. They crushed Rejoice between them, and Mother sobbed over and over, "Rejoice In The Lord's Salvation! Rejoice In The Lord's Salvation!"

* * *

Thirteen-year-old Rejoice stifled a yawn and tried to appear solemn as she stood stiffly in line with Stronghold, Elder Ruiz, Brother and

Sister Carlson, Brother Mfume, and Brother and Sister White and their seventeen-year-old triplet sons. She gripped one of the diamond-toothed blades the hexacrabs had given to the "warriors" setting off to battle the asteroid. She clenched her teeth against another yawn as Pastor Wiseman walked slowly down the line, pausing to pray for and kiss each person. The people of the congregation waved the straw blades they made after receiving the blades from the hexacrabs. She suppressed a nervous giggle. A pacifist people waving blades in the chapel!

She searched for Harmony, Not Worthy, Abiding, Constancy, and Behold. They were staring at her. Already she missed them desperately. She had spent every night of the last three months searching for asteroids, and many of the days talking with Sister Guthry and the engineers about the building of the electromagnetic mass-driver catapult. Bless the technician who had thought to include the construction details in the ship's data bank.

She looked at Mother smiling through tears, and Father with his arm around Mother's shoulders. His eyes shone.

Pastor Wiseman stepped in front of Rejoice and laid his hands on her head. His breath smelled of mint. "Lord of Heaven and Earth, we ask that You would protect this young one and bless her with all spiritual blessings. May she be guided by Your hand. 'The Lord bless you, and keep you; the Lord make His face to shine upon you, and be gracious unto you; the Lord lift up His countenance upon you, and give you peace.' Amen." Pastor Wiseman kissed Rejoice on the cheek and whispered, "Thank you for answering God's call." His beard scratched her face.

Her eyes popped open. Astronomy wasn't just something that she wanted to do, that fulfilled her personal dreams? It was something God had called her to do? As Pastor Wiseman stepped away, Mother rose and led the choir in singing *O God, Our Help in Ages Past.*

At last the ceremony ended, the wall was folded away, and the congregation moved in a chattering, tumultuous mass to the Meetingplace to feast and honor those chosen to work on the asteroid. They would be flying to Opportunity in an hour.

Rejoice watched Father and Mother speaking with many hand motions to the Carlsons and glancing over at Rejoice and Stronghold as they talked. Rejoice retrieved the package she had hidden under a pew.

When they had finished talking, Mother walked over to the sidewalk and swung her arms around her Stronghold and Rejoice, and kissed them both. "Go ahead," she said. "We'll save your places while you say good-by to the hexacrabs."

With her hands behind her back, Rejoice smiled at Mother.

Mother smiled back and said, "What do you have behind your back?"

"A surprise for you."

"But you hate surprises."

Rejoice laughed. "Only if someone is surprising me. You love surprises, don't you?"

"You know I do."

Rejoice swung the potted holly plant out from behind her back.

Mother gasped. "Where did you get that?"

"That's our secret," she said and nodded at Stronghold who grinned. "I want you to plant it by our farm house so we can see how big it is when we get back."

Mother cried and motioned at them to leave as she went over to show the little tree to Father.

"We'll be right back," Stronghold called.

Holding hands, Stronghold and Rejoice trotted past the Meetingplace, the apartments, and Ocean Shore Boulder. Brother Hancock waved to them from the floating bridge. On the beach, they ducked into separate cabanas, changed into scuba gear, and clumped out again. Brother Hancock, already dressed in scuba gear, waved at them again. They followed him across the bridge to the observation deck, where Brother Hancock splashed in first. Rejoice started to follow, but Stronghold tugged on her elbow.

"What?"

"Uh, Sis? I'm glad you're coming with me."

"Space is the best place to search for asteroids. I need to go out there.

I'm glad you're coming with me."

Smile lines gathered around Stronghold's eyes. Wind whipped his black hair around his scuba mask. "I was thinking, as we stood up there getting blessed, about how, you know, three years is a long time, even if I am getting to work with machinery. A long time. I wish the whole family was going."

"Me, too. If Father and Mother could come, it would be like when we were warping here, only less crowded. But somebody needs to watch Makepeace. And Mother pregnant! I can't believe we won't see little Opportunity until she's two and a half years old." Good thing the colony had never thought to jettison the technology that helped pregnant women.

"We'll see her. On the screen." He pulled his hair behind his ears. "You know, Father isn't such a bad guy once you get to know him."

"Hello-o!" A shout drifted toward them. Harmony stumbled over the bridge with her dress hiked up.

"Harmony!" Rejoice stood and waved. When Harmony reached them, panting, they embraced, laughing.

Harmony sucked in several breaths. "Rejoice, could you explain to me again about this action-reaction business? I can't seem to get it."

"Oh, Harmony," Rejoice groaned. "The next time you come to the deck, bring some roller skates and a handful of rocks. Put on the skates, back up to the edge of the deck, start throwing rocks, and see where you end up."

"I got it!" She spun and fixed on Stronghold. "You're so brave, Stronghold, to be going out like this. Please don't tear your space suit! You could die! Promise me you'll call every day!"

Rejoice rolled her eyes. An explanation wasn't what her friend had come out to get. The wind stung Rejoice's eyes as she gazed over the bridge and wished Not Worthy or Constancy had come to talk to her.

With a burst of bubbles, Brother Hancock's head surged out of the water. "Are you coming or not?"

Harmony handed something hidden to Stronghold and said, "I'll be waiting at the Meetingplace." Then she scurried back across the bridge.

"What did she give you?" asked Rejoice.

"Let's say 'God be with you' and get it over with." Stronghold jumped into the sea.

Rejoice splashed in after him. She sank to the seabed under the observation deck and faced Ur-Veena. She stroked his mottled tentacles and his smooth blue shell. He stroked her arms through her wetsuit and the radio-computer leads attached to her oxygen line. Sa-Issi dangled from Stronghold's arm and pretended to give him seaweed to eat. Brother Hancock bobbed beside them, silent except for his bubbles, his useless arm floating at odd angles.

"I'm leaving today," Rejoice said, blinking hard. "I will be gone for three years."

"Yes," whistled Ur-Veena. "Your work is to catalog every stone that swims in the space ocean."

"I'm going to miss you," Rejoice said, and sniffed.

Stronghold disentangled himself from Sa-Issi, shot four meters up to the surface, and flung himself onto the deck. The pounding of his feet echoed on the bridge.

Rejoice swallowed. "Today is hard for all of us. We're happy that we are going to save the world from a Dark Death. But it's hard to say God be with you to so many people. People are crying everywhere. I'm not, but I'm still sad. I'm not going to see my little sister, Opportunity, until she is two-and-half years old. I will see her pictures, but it's not the same."

"No," agreed Ur-Veena. He never had learned how to see a flat image.

"But before we left, I, we wanted to say God be with you, and thank you." She stepped back so she could swim to the surface without kicking Ur-Veena, but he wrapped his tentacles around her knees.

Brother Hancock chuckled. "He has something to show you."

"Come and see-touch the biggest stele our people have ever made," said Ur-Veena. He towed her three hundred meters away from the cluster, his gait only slightly affected by his missing leg. He pulled her to a jagged spire of basalt thrust up from the sand almost to the ocean's surface. An

Old Earth crab scuttled deeper into one of its crevices. One of the stone's faces had been chiseled smooth to a plane.

Rejoice gasped and reached forward to rub the massive diamond glued in the center of the plane. Surrounding it were ellipses marked by diamond chips, and somewhere on each ellipse shone a glass marble tinted the color of the planet it represented. Her lips moved as she touched and named each one: Hell's Gate, New Earth, Harfang, Wimbleweather, and Queen. Jagged shards dotted the space between New Earth and Harfang: asteroids. Opportunity, Anger, Boredom, Cynic, Deceit, Effete, Foment, Greed, Hatred.

"As you discover more stones, we will add to this," said Ur-Veena. "Someday, all oceans shall know of each other."

"It's beautiful," Rejoice whispered.

"This is my special gift to your people. We hope that your people will help us explore our world and search for more of our people. Perhaps we will find females who can still speak."

"That would be wonderful." Rejoice pressed her hand against her heart. "Maybe I could go with you."

Brother Hancock swam closer. "I have presents for the both of you." From his pouch he pulled out a carved figure that he handed to Ur-Veena, and a screen that he showed to Rejoice. "Your mother told me how badly you missed the seagulls from Old Earth. We didn't bring any along. We brought only animals we could eat, if it came down to that. But we did bring a few of these. I'll grow them after we have fish enough to spare. They look fine hopping around on rocks and diving for fish. They're lively little things."

Rejoice studied the picture of a fat bird with orange webbed feet, a white breast, black back and wings, a candy-striped beak, and eyes set in white circles with black vees radiating from them. "It looks like a clown. What is it?"

"A puffin. They should be all over by the time you get back. Do you like it?"

She studied the bird more closely. The tears she had promised herself she would not shed blurred her vision. "It's not what I had in mind, but, yes, I like it." Her finger stroked the image. "I like it very much."

II

BOOK TWO: CIRCUMNAVIGATION OF SHATTERWORLD

CIRCUMNAVIGATION CHAPTER ONE

Rejoice Holly wiped damp palms against her plain, brown dress and swallowed. Acceleration pressed her against the shuttle seat. The cracked upholstery shoved a jagged piece of itself into her shoulder blade. She tried to wriggle so the piece would end up in the middle of her back instead, but the netting and acceleration held her too firmly. Her dry tongue licked dry lips.

She swallowed with a sandpapered throat. Wasn't there some way they could have humidified the air? Would Not Worthy be there? He had seemed distant lately. And Mother promised Rejoice a wonderful surprise when she got back. Why did Mother do that when she knew Rejoice hated surprises? And why couldn't Rejoice hold a thought for more than two seconds? Maybe Mother's surprise was another baby?

The acceleration lessened, and Rejoice took a deep breath of stale air.

Her eighteen-year-old brother stretched in the seat next to hers. Stronghold's large hands rubbed a sparse beard. His skin had paled to a washed-out khaki after three years of living on a spaceship. His heels drummed on the floor of the shuttle. "I'm so tired of waiting to get home."

"Me, too," Rejoice said.

"Real food."

Rejoice grinned. "And Harmony. What more could a man want?"

Stronghold grinned back and brought the ring he had cast of stainless steel out of his shirt pocket. "I wish they would give us a day or two before the welcoming party. I won't be able to see Harmony alone for hours and hours. It's hard to carry on a courtship with everybody listening."

"You're telling me," said one of the triplets in front of them. He switched to a falsetto voice, "Oh, darling, I'll count the heartbeats until you arrive safely."

"Consuming Fire, hush up," Brother White said to his son. "You're just jealous because you don't have someone gazing into your round, brown eyes with adoration."

The triplets erupted into snickers and elbowed each other. Stronghold kicked the back of the seat and the triplets laughed louder.

Rejoice hid a smile. Melodramatic Harmony. She reached into a seat pocket and pulled out a tiny replica of asteroid Opportunity as it had been before the mass driver and mines had diminished its size and pocked it with giant pits. She rubbed the metal model and found the motion soothing. She should have made a second one for herself. Too late now. Would Ur-Veena like the model? Had he learned to see pictures yet?

Sister Carlson, her skin faded to a delicate peach, reached over and squeezed her hand. "I just had a thought. Wouldn't it be wonderful if we could translate your textbook into the hexacrab steles?"

Rejoice bumped the back of her head against the seat. "Right now the last thing I want to think about is astronomy. I can't even remember why it was so important to me."

Sister Carlson squeezed her hand again. "We're grateful it was. How many other people have saved a world and written three textbooks before they were sixteen?"

Oh, please. Rejoice turned her face to study the model so that Sister Carlson wouldn't see her face. Writing the grade school version had not been tough, and Sister Carlson had written half the high school text.

The shutters at the window whirred as they pulled back to reveal the brown continent of Sole. Rejoice craned to look past her brother as they dropped lower and lower. The rectangular fields rolled by lined with the dark windbreaks of eucalyptus, holly, and chinquapin.

Brother Mfume announced, "Pray that I'll remember how to land on a place with gravity." Indicator lights reflected off his black, shaved scalp.

"Pray? I'll pilot if you can't," said Wheel Within Wheel, another triplet, even darker than Brother Mfume.

The shuttle shuddered, rattling Rejoice's teeth. The asteroid model plopped on her lap. A sickening swoop, and the shuttle wheels scraped the runway. The shuttle bounced, then settled, then slowed. Rejoice swallowed hard to relieve the pressure against her eardrums.

The triplets and Stronghold cheered. "Praise God," Sister Carlson murmured. "I'm looking forward to working in the cannery and clinic. I'm never setting foot off this planet again."

Rejoice nodded. Where was she going? Whenever she asked Mother what her new duties would be, Mother only smiled in her round-eyed, aggravating way and said, "Wait and see."

Well, they were here, and now was time to see. The opening hatch clunked and let in faint music and singing, as well as the welcome smell of sea and grass. Rejoice's eyes watered. She fidgeted in the aisle. The boys clogged the aisle ahead of her.

Hot, moist air rolled over her. Reluctantly, she pulled on her filter mask. She had hoped she wouldn't need the mask when she returned. She stepped out into the bright sunlight and blinked. Hundreds of people stood on the runway and waved. Some lifted black banners with silver asteroids emblazoned on them. They sang the hymn *O God Our Help in Ages Past* to the music of guitars, violins, drums, and keyboards.

She clasped her hands. Had the whole colony come? Didn't anybody have anything better to do? God, couldn't they just skip to tomorrow?

"May I help you down?" asked Brother White.

"Oh, no, I'm fine," Rejoice squeaked. She clattered down the steps. The eight hours a day she's spent suffering in the centrifugal force machine they'd built on the asteroid to maintain their strength finally proved worth the effort. There was Mother hugging Stronghold. "Oh, my goodness," Rejoice breathed. Mother's head reached his chest. He was much taller than Father now.

Mother released Stronghold and engulfed Rejoice in a backbreaking embrace. She rocked back and forth and whispered in her ear, "I missed you so much." Then she held her at arm's length and gazed in Rejoice's eyes, her own eyes filling with tears. "My baby is a young woman. I can look you straight in the eyes."

Father encircled them all while Makepeace bobbed around them like a toy going down the bathtub drain. Little Opportunity squealed with excitement. Why Mother had named her baby girl after the asteroid Rejoice had spent three years nudging away from New Earth baffled her. But then, almost everything Mother did baffled her.

Rejoice disentangled and caught Makepeace, cupped his face, and gazed into his chocolate-almond eyes. It was hard to believe that such beautiful eyes had such a fractured brain behind them. "I'm home, little brother. I can't believe how tall you are now."

"Party, party,' he crooned.

Rejoice turned to Mother. "He just made sense!"

Mother laughed, her hazel eyes crinkling above her filter. "If you listen carefully, he usually does."

Rejoice picked up her little sister with lustrous, long hair, Opportunity, who gave her a big hug. "Edoy! Edoy! Edoy!" the little girl yelled as Rejoice spun her around in circles shouting. "Oppy! Oppy! Oppy!"

The little girl reached for Stronghold. He took her out of Rejoice's arms and swooped her up into the air. Opportunity screamed and giggled.

Father and Mother went over and embraced the Carlsons. Father said, "Thank you for your care of our children."

Makepeace tugged on Rejoice's hand. She followed him through the clusters of people hugging and laughing and stared at all the new buildings. On a tiny screen they had looked like doll houses. All the new, massive structures dwarfed her. The crowd streamed toward a hexagonal glass pyramid that began with clear panes at ground level. The glass gradually grew darker blue until the panes adjoining the central spire were midnight blue with tiny, clear stars speckled on them.

"Oh," breathed Rejoice. The cobalt mined from the asteroid Opportunity had made the blue glass possible. Oh-oh, she was going to embarrass herself and cry.

Stronghold stopped beside her and whistled. "Would you look at that? I can't believe the elders let the engineers build anything so beautiful. If that was back on Old Earth, you know how many BB holes there would be in it?"

Rejoice snorted in disgust. That rescued her from tears.

A squeal pierced her ears.

Harmony threw herself on Stronghold.

Rejoice plugged her pained ears. Wow, Harmony had changed.

Harmony's golden red hair mingled with Stronghold's black.

Rejoice tried to repress her envy that came automatically whenever she compared Harmony's lovely hair with her own plain brown. What were her chances of looking that beautiful when she turned seventeen? She stood on tiptoe to scan the crowd. So, where was Not?

There, he stood talking with Every Knee Shall Bow and Brother Jefferson, Every's father.

Rejoice pulled Makepeace through the crowd until she arrived, panting, in front of them. Her mouth fell open. "Oh, my goodness," she breathed again. Not Worthy was gorgeous. Three years had also changed him a lot. She had seen the dark moustache that lined his upper lip and heard his deep voice over the comm-link. But to see him as tall as Brother Jefferson and a head taller than Every took her breath away.

Brother Jefferson extended a calloused hand. "Congratulations, Young Lady Holly. We owe you an incredible debt of gratitude."

Rejoice stammered as she shook his hand. "I hardly worked alone. Without Elder Ruiz and the Whites and Stronghold and Brother Mfume, we couldn't—I mean, I can't pilot."

"Of course." Brother Jefferson turned, bent, and touched his molasses-brown forehead on his daughter's café au lait forehead. "Why don't you kids plan for a good time?" He winked and walked away.

Every kept her left hand in her pocket and ran her right hand over her tightly coiled hair. "Uh, maybe a picnic?"

Rejoice beamed at Not. "What are you doing tomorrow?"

Not shifted. "I was planning to extend the fence at the Jefferson's dairy.

We were just discussing that. He has to expand . . . you know."

"I wouldn't mind going along to help."

"Well, sure, why not? Every and I and you could picnic halfway through. Sure, let's do that." He looked at Every.

Every watched him, dark eyes glittering before she shrugged. "Okay."

Makepeace jerked at Rejoice's arm. She let him tow her away and said over her shoulder, "I'll call you later."

He nodded and turned to Every. Rejoice smiled at the people welcoming her as she walked toward the blue glass pavilion, but inside uneasiness roiled. Not Worthy didn't need to get wild about her return like Harmony, but he could have been a little more demonstrative than that. Wasn't he happy to see her back? And Every sure had grown up to be beautiful.

The crowd pressed through arched doorways into a solemn blue-tinted space. Long tables covered with white cloths, blue crystal, white plates rimmed with blue, stainless-steelware, and symbolic stone blades stood in proud rows on the midnight-blue- floor speckled with silver. The people pulled off their filter masks and slung them behind their necks as they positioned themselves around the tables.

Six huge glass tanks of sea water lined the wall on the right. Stronghold already stood in front of one with his scarred hand extended up to the rim. Ur-Veena stretched his five crab-like legs and reached one of his six blue tentacles over the tank edge to grasp Stronghold's hand. His three large eyes for vision glistened and his tiny light detectors sparkled through opercula on his indigo, rainbow shell.

Rejoice grinned. Even with one leg missing and sunburn scars on his tentacles, Ur-Veena was one of the loveliest things on New Earth.

She pulled Makepeace to the tank and laid her hand beside Stronghold's. Ur-Veena slipped over another tentacle and grasped her wrist. She enunciated into the translator attached to the tank. "Here is a model of the asteroid Opportunity as it used to be. It's much smaller now and swimming far away. I want to thank your people for encouraging us to fight the Dark Death bringer."

The translator whistled and clicked as Ur-Veena wrapped his double-tipped tentacles around the model and pulled it into the tank. He whistled and the translator said, "It is good to see you again after your long swim in the space ocean. You are larger and changed. So is Sa-Issi. Now we look forward to swimming the longest journey in the water-ocean."

Rejoice dried her hand on her dress and puzzled over the words. He had said literally *our gills huff*, which meant *we look forward to*. But what did *longest journey* mean? No, that was the same in both languages. She glanced away and cleared her throat. She should have studied Hex more diligently. Maybe he meant that now she could visit him a lot in the village. Well, why not? She liked scuba-diving and playing with the baby hexacrabs. "Yes," she whistled back.

Elder Chin, the linguist, with all his facial wrinkles arranged into a massive grin strode up and slapped the tank. His eyelids drooped so much, it was a mystery how he could see. He cheerfully whistled and clicked in perfect Hex. He glowed with good cheer.

Mother retrieved Makepeace. Stronghold and Rejoice hurried to say hello to the other hexacrabs.

Mother returned to push Stronghold and Rejoice to the head table. "We can't start without you."

Rejoice wished she could sit with her family instead, but the colony wished to honor them, and honored they would be, whatever Rejoice wished.

Pastor Wiseman stood to pray before the feast. She closed her eyes in relief. For a few minutes anyway, people wouldn't be staring at her.

The prayer ended. Great bowls of food were passed down the table: green beans, corn, hot wheat buns with real melted butter and strawberry jam, chapattis, boiled eggs, salmon filets, hard and soft cheeses, cucumber sushi, burritos, creamed new potatoes, five kinds of salads, noodles, fried white radish patties, fruit and carrot pies, watermelon ice cream, cobblers, crumbles, cheesecakes, guava tarts, molasses drops, and peanut crunch. The food kept coming.

Rejoice couldn't eat all that food. She could hardly choke down a little of it past the lump lodged in her throat as she counted down the minutes.

What Rejoice couldn't eat, Stronghold could. He ignored the streak of butter on his chin as he shoveled salmon into his mouth and grinned at Harmony seated ten tables away. Rejoice looked for Not Worthy and found him seven tables away next to his father and mother. Rejoice spread jam on a bun. Maybe Not wasn't happy to see her. She needed to talk to him.

Not's parents were talking to Brother and Dr. Cruz. Their son, No Confidence In The Flesh, stared at her. She turned her eyes back to her fork. She never had been able to withstand his intense gaze. He must be an adult by now. Hopefully, he was engaged to some poor girl who could teach him not to stare at other girls.

Pastor Wiseman rose, and the people subsided to a respectful silence. "We have come here today, the first annual Opportunity Day, to remember what brought us to this place and position."

Rejoice concentrated on her fork. To save her life, she couldn't think why he had to go into the history of the revival on Earth that birthed their movement, and then the entire history of the colony. They had been there. So why tell everyone what they already knew?

Rejoice swallowed another breath. On the other hand, as long as he was talking, she wasn't, which was good, except that it gave her that much longer to dread when she would need to talk. She glanced at her family attentively watching Pastor Wiseman. She would give a speech if Father had to come up and move her mouth for her like a ventriloquist's dummy. Why did she need the experience when speaking was the last thing she planned to do for a career? And why didn't Stronghold need the experience?

She looked over at Stronghold covering a yawn. When it came to Stronghold, some things even Father couldn't do. She tapped her fingertips on the table. They should have named him Strong Willed instead of Stronghold. Maybe if she was as stubborn as him, she wouldn't be forced to give a stupid speech.

She concentrated on the fork again and the blue light reflecting from it. No, she had promised herself that she would never hurt her parents the way he had. Besides, he didn't have to speak because he had become an adult, and adults couldn't be forced to do anything. Certainly none of the adults had volunteered to give a stupid speech.

She felt every gaze directed toward her. Oh, no. Pastor Wiseman must have stopped and now it was her turn.

Why was it so hot? Had it been this hot before? Sweat pooling in her armpits, Rejoice rose. What had she planned to say? She started by stuttering, stopped, and tried to take a deep breath. It was hard to breathe in this hot, humid air filled with the smells of food and farm and sea. Why couldn't everyone look somewhere else while she struggled to catch her breath? Ah, Makepeace wasn't staring; he was alternating licking his spoon and studying his reflection in it.

Gone. Her speech had abandoned her, but she must say something. She said, "I don't deserve any special honor. Who does deserve it is my brother, Makepeace. He gave me the idea for the mass driver. But even if he hadn't, the engineers would have thought of it."

Deaconess Redhorse reached her fat hand across the table and stroked Makepeace on the head.

Please, everyone, stay kind to him forever. She scanned the room. She needed to say more than that. And then she noticed the babies. She followed the news and knew how many babies had been born, but it had been ten years since she heard squalling in a service and seen babies scooting down the aisles. Everywhere she looked, a nursing baby gazed intently at its mother or was being patted over a shoulder while blowing innocent bubbles.

"I'm so glad we can have babies again," she said, and then heat rushed along her neck and face. Surely she hadn't said that.

The people laughed, with a few pounding a table. The clamor woke several babies. Their cries joined the echoing noise.

"That's all," she mumbled as she sank into her chair and covered her face.

Everyone clapped as though it had been the best speech in the universe. Then they all rose and cleared the tables.

Rejoice sat and took a deep, shuddering breath. It was over.

Stronghold said in her ear, "Great speech, Sis. It was short."

CIRCUMNAVIGATION CHAPTER TWO

Pastor Wiseman took Rejoice's hand and led her to the greeting line.

Rejoice spotted Sister Olson, her blonde hair tightly braided and pinned to her scalp and her brow furrowed, working her way through the crowd toward Rejoice. People wanting to shake her hand penned her in. She forced herself to smile. This should get all the nasty stuff out of the way at once.

Sister Olson took her hand and held it firmly. "Pride goes before a fall, you know. God gives grace only to the humble."

"Yes, M'am," Rejoice said as humbly as she could.

It wasn't good enough. "You should have let your elders speak."

Rejoice studied her hands caught in Sister Olson's. Let them speak? She would have loved for anyone else to speak. No—peaceful thoughts. A soft answer turns away wrath. "Yes, M'am. I'm sorry. I'll try not to do it again."

"I don't like to be mocked."

Unless it was Sister Olson's wrath.

Mother came and rescued Rejoice. "Sister Olson, I'm so glad to see you. I know you haven't felt well, so I appreciate the extra effort you made to come. Your brand new baby girl looks so healthy!" The two women hugged and Sister Olson left.

Stronghold and Father walked up to join her and Mother.

"Good speech," Mother shouted over the clicking of plates and the jolly chattering of the crowd.

Rejoice covered her face and shook her head. Right. It was short.

Father said, "I am so proud of the two of you. You sacrificed more than any of us can understand." He put one arm around her and the other around Stronghold. "Now you have to come over and see our first annual Opportunity Day Fair."

"Is that the surprise you promised us?" asked Rejoice.

Mother laughed. "Not at all."

"You're going to have a baby."

Mother jerked her head back and widened her eyes. "No, not yet. Whatever gave you that idea?"

Stronghold shouted, "Rejoice hates surprises. She's been crabby ever since you told her you had a surprise. Just tell us what it is before she explodes."

Mother and Father glanced at each other. Father handed Makepeace to Deaconess Redhorse and Mother gave Opportunity to Sister Toshimoto who whisked her out of the building. They walked to a far corner of the room and sat at a small table smelling of ammonia cleanser.

Mother's round hazel eyes sparkled as she leaned forward. "Tomorrow we begin to circumnavigate the globe on a mission." She grinned.

Rejoice processed the words. "What?"

Father cleared his throat. His slanted eyes concentrated their gaze on Stronghold. "Tomorrow morning our family, except for Makepeace, is boarding the water-ocean ship Magellan."

Mother clapped and bounced on her seat. "And so is Ur-Veena and Sa-Issi. Only of course they're riding under the ship. We're going to take a year to visit half the major archipelagoes. We'll seed them with life while Ur-Veena looks for more hexacrabs. He's hoping to find females who can talk. And—"

"You're crazy!" Stronghold jumped up. "We just got back. You want me to say, 'Hi Harmony, bye Harmony,' just like that and leave again? I can't believe you'd ask that of me."

Mother stammered, "I was thinking it would be a really nice way for our family to get to know each other again."

"No. Absolutely not! I'm ready to start my own family."

Father held up his hand. "You don't have to go." He ran his fingers through black hair and sighed. "We have reasons for thinking it would be a good idea, but you can reject them if you wish."

Stronghold sat again and watched his father warily.

The skin between Mother's eyebrows wrinkled as she brushed back brown curls. "Father and I are going whether you do or not. I thought you would be thrilled to be part of the very first voyage around New Earth."

"Maybe we'll run into some of those monsters the hexacrabs told us about," Father said mildly. "Maybe we'll even find some churtrees."

Mother shuddered. "I hope not. But here's a chance to see new lands and spread life."

Rejoice held her hand against her cheek. But what about Not Worthy? The picnic was tomorrow. She licked her lips. If it got any hotter, she would suffocate. "Isn't saving New Earth enough?"

Mother picked up a napkin and twisted the white fabric. Her mouth wobbled.

Rejoice's heart ripped. She didn't want to hurt Mother. She wanted to see Not. She wanted to stay and watch the colony grow. "Can't you just fly the shuttle over to the islands and check them out?"

"Yes, we could," Father answered. "But some of the islands are quite small and steep. We're not sure that we could land. Also, our mission includes seeding the ocean and searching for hexacrabs. A ship is the way we decided to go."

"What about drones?"

"That would be nice. Too bad a storm destroyed all the ones we had. Too bad the corporation that sold us the factory managed to leave out the instructions for building new drones."

Rejoice gritted her teeth. "Mother . . . does it have to be tomorrow? Can't the trip wait?"

"No, it can't," Father said. "We postponed it more than we should have to wait for your return. The storm season is approaching, and we must be off."

"Why do the Hollys have to go?" Rejoice asked, and winced. She hadn't meant to sound so whiny. "Can't some other family go?"

"Elder Chin, for his linguistic ability, and Brother and Sister Hancock, for their expertise in marine biology, are also going. I'm going to do geological surveys of the islands. Your mother is our medical help. Opportunity is going because she's attached to your mother. There's room for only two more people. We had hoped Stronghold would be the mechanic and you would help us analyze the satellite and undersea imaging."

"There are other mechanics," Stronghold said.

Father looked around the blue pyramid. Everyone had left except them and some young men across the auditorium rolling the hexacrabs in their tanks out of the building. One of young men was No Confidence In The Flesh Cruz. No stopped to stare at Rejoice. She quickly looked away.

Father studied his knees. "This would be a good time for the Holly family to leave town."

Stronghold leaned forward. "Why?"

Mother dropped the napkin. "It's not that bad. It's just . . ." She glanced at Father. He nodded. Mother picked up the napkin again and picked at lint. "It's just that Elder Smith is having a struggle right now and, ah, we seem to represent all that has gone wrong for him."

Rejoice sat up straight. "Elder Smith wasn't here."

"No, he wasn't." Mother glanced around as if checking to make sure no one else was near. "He's, ah, not very happy about you right now."

Her skin prickled all over. Rejoice whispered, "What did *I* do?"

"You discovered the asteroid that was going to hit New Earth."

"If I hadn't, we'd all be dead this very moment."

"Yes," Father said. "He says that would have been a quick, clean death. We would have been happy farming until the very last moment, and then we would never have known what hit us. We'd have been with the Lord in blink of an eye."

"That's fine for us," Rejoice said, her voice rising, "but what about the hexacrabs?"

"Shh," Mother said. "He's not happy about them, either. He feels the colony is wasting all its energies on the hexacrabs. And again, you were the one who discovered them."

"I didn't put them in the ocean. God did. What does he want?" Rejoice slapped the table.

Mother laid her hands on top of Rejoice's. "He wants life to be the way he meant it to be. He gave up all his wealth to pay for us to come here to live simply. We were to make everything by hand and live quiet lives on farms. Instead, we have factories and all kinds of industry. The youngsters spend most of their time with the hexacrabs."

"But . . ."

Mother raised a hand, "Yes, we did what we had to do, but it didn't fit his dream."

"Rejoice," Father said, "Elder Smith dreamed big. We all dreamed big. He thought those big dreams were God's plans. We all agreed. The bigger the dream, the harder it dies. First there was the agony during the warp journey of watching our babies die. Then there was the disappointment of finding his perfect farming world decimated and polluted by the Dark Death meteorite. Why would God allow that? Then Elder Smith was forced to agree that it was necessary to divert resources from farming to industry, just to make this shattered world livable. The dream had to be deferred. But now that the young people have been introduced to technology in the new world, they don't want to return to manual farming."

"I never wanted to do manual farming."

Stronghold snorted. "Me either."

"How do you keep them down on the farm, after they've seen Paree?" Mother sang and then sighed.

Father tapped the table with his knuckle. "Then there was the discovery of hexacrabs and the confusion about how they fit into our theological framework. The elders are disappointed, divided, and confused. We all are. It happens when God chooses to fulfill His will in ways that don't comport with your hopes and dreams. Now, you may not know this, but

Elder Chin and Elder Smith have been close friends ever since Elder Chin led Elder Smith to the Lord. However, right now, they hardly talk. It's why Elder Chin wants to leave with us, too. Elder Smith had jumped to the conclusion that God had cleared this shattered planet of life so we could occupy it. Elder Chin argued that God appointed us to land on this planet at this time to save His creatures, the hexacrabs, and to lead them to a knowledge of the true God."

Nobody spoke for a minute. Everyone else had left the room. The babble from outside receded.

"Finally," Mother said, "two years ago, Sister Smith had a stroke. She is everything to her husband. Now, instead of farming, he spends most of his time nursing her. He's not happy."

Rejoice leaned back as if to escape cognitive dissonance. "Can't you cure a stroke?"

"If you treat it right away and have the right equipment. But we don't."

"I thought we stocked the Starflower with everything."

"We had budgetary constraints. Elder Smith chose to buy more cow embryos instead. He said we should trust God for our health."

Stronghold's fists hit the table. "Then it's his fault Sister Smith is still sick."

Mother covered one of his fists with her hand. "Don't you think he tells himself that every morning when he picks her up out of bed to put her in a wheelchair? Every time I do physical therapy with her, he's reminded of the decision he made ten years ago. All the time he spends nursing his wife, he's reminded that herds of dairy cows were more important to him than his wife's health. He trusted God and God let him down." Mother sighed. "He won't allow himself to be angry at God, so he's angry at us instead."

"Carol," Father said, "It wasn't just Elder Smith's decision. We were all in on the planning for the journey and all the elders together had the final say."

Mother gave Father a hard look.

"To be sure," Father said. "Elder Smith's opinion carried a lot of weight.

He was paying for everything."

"And he does blame himself," Mother said. "I can see it in his eyes."

A tear trickled down Rejoice's face. "I thought we came to build a perfect community, and now you're telling me our leader is a vindictive, old man."

"Rejoice!" Father snapped. "Are you perfect?"

Rejoice wiped the tear with her sleeve. "No. I—no."

"And neither is Elder Smith. Can you understand that he's not God?"

"Yes."

"Can you understand that the mind may understand something when the heart can't understand at all? When that happens, the heart usually wins. Elder Smith is broken-hearted."

Rejoice nodded.

Father continued, "I want to get out of his way for a while. He's making sure all my requests are turned down. He'll likely do the same to you."

"So what?" Stronghold held his hands out, palms up. "I already arranged for Harmony and me to work the kelp farm. The crops need the kelp for fertilizer. Elder Smith never goes there, so I can't be in his way. I'm sorry you're leaving the second I get home, but I'm staying."

"So be it," Father said. "We'll get a substitute. What about you, Rejoice?"

She put her hands in her lap and twisted her fingers together until they hurt. "I had planned to come home and stay home. I didn't know home was going to go away. I wanted to see all my friends and . . ." She bit her lip.

After a long quiet moment, Mother said, "We'll be in contact with the colony every day. You can still visit your friends."

"Comm-link isn't the same as face to face. After talking on the comm-link for three years, I need to be able to touch people. I'm sorry. I want to stay."

More silence. "So be it." Father shoulders sagged. "We haven't had a house built for us yet, so you'll need to stay in our apartment for a while. I'm sure that Sister Carlson would be happy to be your substitute mother for another year."

Rejoice nodded as a hollow space opened in her stomach. "How is the holly tree? I was hoping to see it growing in front of our new house when I got back."

"It's in a big pot now growing happily on our sidewalk. You'll need to keep it watered and fed until we get back," Father said.

Mother set aside the napkin. "I shouldn't have made it a surprise. Let's make our first and last evening together in a long time a pleasant one." She stood, smoothed the wrinkles in her brown dress, and snapped on her filter mask.

They walked under pergolas draped with kiwifruit vines, flaming bougainvillea, and heavy-scented honeysuckle. White orchids lined the paths. Where once had been bare rock, lawns of clover, dwarf daisies, and fescues stretched between buildings. Carob trees—grown man-high so far—formed little groves in the center of each lawn. Rejoice wanted to hug each wrinkle-barked tree. Each tree was delightfully different from its neighbor. Stingless bees probed the purple clover heads. One bee landed on Rejoice's arm and contemplated the mysteries of brown fabric. Rejoice studied its pollen-dusted hairs and the vein patterns on its clear iridescent wings: so beautiful, so intricate.

The filter mask itched under her chin. She'd had let the mask slip once three and a half years ago, and Sister Olson had berated her for five minutes. Aha, that was why Sister Olson tore into her about pride. Sister Olson had sided with Elder Smith.

Who else hadn't come? The Hinojosa family hadn't come, but Sister Hinojosa was in labor with her third child in as many years, so that was understandable. Had she seen the Nguyens? No. Had they not come because they, too, were mad at her? Oh, Elder Sims hadn't been there. He was close to Elder Smith. She hadn't seen the Coopers either.

Oh, and Sister Guthry hadn't come, but she was sick. Rejoice needed to make a special point to see her tonight and thank her for all the math puzzles. Immersing herself in the puzzles was the only thing that kept her sane sometimes when the triplets really got on her nerves.

They passed under a blue banner proclaiming Opportunity Day Fair and entered a huge barn built of thick, white glass and stainless steel trusses. The glass walls and white-and-gray swirled floor tiles echoed with the din of cackling chickens, baaing lambs, quacking ducks, and people shouting jovially at each other. Rejoice wiped the sweat from her neck as she moved from stall to stall and looked at Rhode Island Reds,

Silver Laced Wyandottes, Araucanas, and Banty chickens. Harlequin and Peking ducks, quail, and fat turkeys stared back at her with shining eyes. In one stall, a camel scratched the back of its front leg with a spilt hoof.

Right. When Elder Smith did away with motorized vehicles, they would need camels for transportation.

The Holly family walked down an aisle of flower arrangements, and then, as bright as the flowers, quilted blankets and embroidered computer covers and bags. They viewed a display of the fifty kinds of cheeses the colony could now make.

After joining them, Harmony hung on Stronghold's arm and squealed over the Jack Russell Terrier puppies and Holstein and Jersey calves.

After three years of sterile space-ship living, the noise and heat and overwhelming colors and smells assaulted her. A headache joined Rejoice's discomfort. She needed a cool, quiet place to sit for a few minutes.

Mother showed her a whistle hand-carved from a stick. Not Worthy walked around a display of wooden pinwheels. "I'll be right back," Rejoice shouted at Mother, and followed him. The Mahmoud family blocked her way, and by the time she got around them, Not had disappeared.

She walked down the aisle of bleating miniature goats. Three women stopped Rejoice to hug her. "Thank you for making the planet safe for babies." Rejoice nodded and got away.

She rounded a corner and found a quiet aisle filled with sacks of grain. The girl Every sat stiff shouldered on a bale of hay with her back to Rejoice. Not sat beside her and griped, "I don't know what your problem is."

Rejoice backed up.

"So when are you going to tell Rejoice?" hissed Every.

Against every rule of privacy the colony had, Rejoice pressed herself against a stall to hide and listen.

Not scoffed. "What's the hurry? She's probably leaving on that voyage tomorrow. We can tell her when she gets back."

"No. You tell her today. I don't know why you didn't tell her while she was still in space."

"Come on. We can't announce it to the colony because you aren't seventeen yet, and you want to broadcast it on the comm-link?"

Rejoice peeked around the corner. A shiny band on Every's finger flashed as she flung her hands up.

"The girl has to know! She thinks you're her boyfriend!"

Not shrugged. "We're just friends. Something wrong with that?"

Just friends! Rejoice snapped her head back and blundered back the way she came.

Mother held her by the shoulders, asking, "Rejoice, are you ill? Rejoice, can you hear me?"

Rejoice took a deep, juddering breath. "Mother, I want to go with you tomorrow. When do we leave?"

CIRCUMNAVIGATION CHAPTER THREE

Since the people of the colony did not believe in elaborate pageants, the wedding of Stronghold and Harmony needed only a few hours' notice. The people, each one bearing a bouquet of flowers from home, assembled at the chapel. They watched the couple recite vows that were centuries old; vows to love and cherish, have and hold, and to stay together in sickness and health until death separated them.

Harmony, as did all the women, wore her blue Lord's Day dress and a wreath of flowers in her hair. Stronghold looked suddenly grown-up in his gray suit with a flower stole. As they knelt before Pastor Wiseman and the flickering wedding candle, and as they prayed, Rejoice swallowed hard. They had had such a good time together on the Starflower and the asteroid. And now he was married and staying at First City, and she was sailing away. She missed him already.

The hexacrabs in tanks at the back of the chapel whistled and clicked softly to one another.

Rejoice wiped away a tear. Stronghold and Harmony exchanged rings and a kiss. She had thought her homecoming would be so happy, but all she felt was anguish.

The people stood and flung flowers at Stronghold and Harmony as they ran down the central aisle.

Father and Mother embraced. Makepeace jiggled and Opportunity danced on her chair. Rejoice's cheeks burned. Who would ever have and hold her? No one, no one, no one.

Mother squeezed Rejoice and said in a trembling voice, "Oh, honey, we'll see them again in a year."

For once, Rejoice was glad Mother didn't understand her. She hugged Mother back.

The banquet was nearly a repeat of the one the day before with the clatter of steelware and plates and the scraping of chairs across the tile floor, mounds and heaps and piles of food, people laughing and shouting cheerfully at each other. Rejoice watched the families one by one go up to the new couple and give them a present and a blessing. When Not and the rest of the Worthy family went up, Rejoice decided to watch the hexacrabs instead. Food stuck in her throat.

She turned to Mother. "Did you get a substitute for Stronghold?"

"Sure did." Mother dropped some peas into Opportunity's mouth. "Young Man No Confidence In The Flesh Cruz. We're going to have so much fun together."

Rejoice hoped her face wasn't showing what her mind was thinking. She grabbed her glass of raspberry juice and sipped to help hide her face. No Confidence Cruz! Of all the people to be stuck with on a ship for a year! The Hancocks would be fun, but No Confidence was the young man who gave Brother Hammer such fits by accidentally smashing so many glass panels. No gave her shivers because whenever she was working on a hard math problem in class and happened to look up, she would usually find him staring stupidly at her. Maybe it wasn't too late to back out of the voyage.

It was too late. Father stood and said it was time to go.

Rejoice followed him out the door. Surely this was just a dream. She would wake up soon and she would still be on the Starflower getting ready to come home.

The salt air blew her hair across her eyes, billowed her dress, and flopped the brim of her hat. The hot, moist air, despite the breeze, stifled her breath. It took all her willpower to keep from pulling the mask away from her nose and mouth and trying to gulp in air.

A ten minute's-walk brought the chattering crowd to the docks. Then, "Oh," Mother said. The people stopped talking and stared at the two people on the dock in front of the dove-white Magellan. Elder Smith stood huge and grim over his withered wife in a wheelchair.

Pastor Wiseman and Elder Chin strode forward first and Elder Smith hugged them both ponderously. Then they knelt before Sister Smith to talk to her, and she nodded. Brother and Sister Hancock joined them, and Elder Smith slowly and seriously shook their hands. Now it was the Hollys' turn.

Mother carried Opportunity and Rejoice grabbed Makepeace's hand. Father tentatively held out his hand. Elder Smith seized it and pulled Father into an embrace.

"Eh, Theophilus," murmured Elder Smith. 'May God bring you back safe and sound. May your work pull back the ocean."

"I'll do the best I can," Father said.

Elder Smith turned to Mother. "Sister Holly, Naomi here wants to tell you something."

Mother knelt by Sister Smith, activated the communication board, and supported her arm as Sister Smith, letter by letter, typed out, [Love U and miss U. Report to me everyday.]

Rejoice marveled at the patience of Elder Smith and all the adults as they waited for Sister Smith to press each letter. No one shuffled their feet or glanced at a screen. When Makepeace tried to push his head between Sister Smith and the communication board, Mother gently and firmly hugged him to her side with one arm and continued to help Sister Smith with the other. How did one become patient like that?

And then Rejoice had a thought: maybe God was forcing her to live on a boat with No Confidence on it so she could learn patience. Why else?

No stared at Mother as Sister Smith typed, [Real news better than vids.] Mother nodded tearfully.

No Confidence joined them, and Elder Smith shook his hand too. Pastor Wiseman laid his hand on everyone's head in turn and prayed a blessing on each one.

After the blessings came the final good-byes. Harmony hugged Rejoice tightly. "Thank you for saving the world, sister-in-law," Harmony said.

They hugged each other even tighter.

"Thank you for making my brother so happy," whispered Rejoice in her ear.

Then Harmony looked over Rejoice's shoulder, stiffened, and said "Oh, no!"

"What?" Rejoice said.

"Sister Olson's coming. Let's walk over to your parents and stand behind them."

Both girls turned and pattered to where Stronghold squeezed Father. The girls stood behind Harmony's parents, Deacon and Deaconess Copulos as they hugged Mother. Mother then hugged Deaconess Redhorse with Makepeace sandwiched between them.

Sister Olson did not zero in on Rejoice to complain as she had anticipated. Instead Brother and Sister Olson walked up to Young Man No Cruz. Sister Olson's head was buried in her husband shoulders as she wept. Brother Olson talked with No and shook his hand. No leaned over to talk with Sister Olson, but she kept her head buried and wouldn't look up. No Confidence Cruz talked some more to Brother Olson and then hugged them both and the couple drifted away.

What was that all about?

The Hancocks came up, aunt and uncle to Harmony. Deaconess Copulos, Harmony's mother, cried on her sister's shoulder and Harmony cried on her Uncle Hancock's shoulder.

Deaconess Redhorse took Makepeace's hand. Her son and daughter came up to help as Makepeace screeched and struggled to get away. In the confusion of his wailing, Harmony and her mother breaking into tears, Elder Smith trying to roll his wife off the dock so the people could board, and everyone pulling on life-preservers, Mother's face crumpled and she fled into the Magellan.

"I'll take Makepeace for a walk every day," Stronghold shouted as Rejoice followed Mother. She looked back and was surprised to see

Harmony holding both of No's hands and talking to him with more tears dripping off her face. No patted her on the shoulder and turned and ran up the gangplank. Black silicon and metal sail slats slid up the masts and rotated to catch the wind. The gangplank slid back.

Rejoice ran back to the deck to grasp the railings and wave frantically at Harmony, Persuaded, Abiding, Behold, and Constancy. Harmony threw her bouquet of flowers to Rejoice, but it fell short. Then everyone threw flowers that landed on the deck and in the ocean, creating a confusion of colors on the gray-blue water. The wind hissed through the solar composite sails.

It seemed the farewell would never end, and then it ended with the dock and people blurred by distance. Puffins rode like corks on the ocean swells, just as Brother Hancock had promised her. Bits of seaweed, brown and muted orange, floated past. Waves spanked against the ship's side and bubbled under.

Father hoisted Opportunity onto his hip and clapped his hand on Rejoice's shoulder. "We're off! After these last two days, I'm ready for a quiet sea voyage." Rejoice put her arm around his waist and Opportunity's leg as he continued, "You know, when I was a youngster, I dreamed about sailing around the world. I didn't know it would be around a different world than Earth."

Rejoice sighed. "I dreamed about going to the moon."

"Hmm. Yes. I remember when you fell off the pier at the lake the day before we left Old Earth. You said you were trying to walk the silver path to the moon."

"Father, I was only three." Alarm prickled her skin. "You haven't told anyone else that story, have you?"

"To be sure, but not lately. Is it something you want to keep private?"

Rejoice nodded. "Yes. Please." As if anyone who had heard the story would forget.

Father smiled. "I'll advise Mother." Then he scrutinized her. "Perhaps, when we get back, we should pay a visit to the Potatoes. We could use some instrumentation up there and see what metals might be hiding in their craters."

"Oh, Father, when do I get to stay home?"

Father chuckled and gave her a shoulder hug while still gazing out at sea. "Magellan is home, for a year. Oh, I nearly forgot." He turned to Brother and Sister Hancock who also leaned on the railing. "Do you have the fish bits?"

Brother Hancock grinned, shoved aside his paralyzed arm, and with his good hand dug into his pocket. First he pulled out a wooden whistle which he presented with a flourish to Rejoice. "Blow one long note and two short ones."

Rejoice pulled down her mask, blew softly, and made a peep.

"Louder than that!" commanded Brother Hancock.

Rejoice took a deep breath and blew it shrilly.

The puffins, which had become far-off dots, erupted from the waters and flapped toward the ship.

Brother Hancock pulled out a greasy bag filled with pieces of fish and offered them to Rejoice. "They're coming for their reward."

Rejoice and the Hancocks laughed as she threw the pieces into the ocean and the puffins dove after them. Father held squealing Opportunity over the railing so she could see the puffins rubbing striped beaks and grunting at each other.

"They are so darling," Rejoice said. She threw her arms around Brother Hancock. "Thank you so much."

He patted her back. "Eh. I probably shouldn't have released them so soon. We've had a huge drop in our fish numbers."

"Those little puffins ate them all?"

"Eh, maybe not. Could be some of the predators the hexacrabs told us about; could be disease; could be the fish moved. I'm hoping this voyage shows us the reason."

Sister Hancock reached for his hand and the two looked at each other, he with his faded blue eyes and she with sea green, the way Father and Mother often did, in a silent communication that baffled Rejoice.

Did marriage make one telepathic? When she got back, would

Stronghold and Harmony be looking at each other like that? Would anyone ever look at her like that? She crumpled the empty bag. Maybe back on Old Earth amid the teeming billions there was someone, but here on New Earth, there were precious few young men to choose from. And all of them were interested in someone else. Except maybe No Confidence Cruz. Only God knew who or what interested him.

She crunched the paper tighter. What was that quotation? "Nothing's so bad that it can't get worse."? She tried to tell herself that the hexacrabs had it worse. At least she could talk to the human males. She just couldn't think of any she wanted to.

A puffin cocked its clown-colored head and watched Rejoice with a shiny eye. She smiled in spite of her gloom. The Hancocks moved away hand in hand, and she watched them, wondering idly if Harmony's red hair would gray with age the way her Auntie Hancock's had. Mother had a few white hairs Rejoice couldn't remember seeing before she left to deflect the asteroid. Father seemed much older, but she couldn't see exactly what had changed. His hair remained as glossy black as ever.

Rejoice jumped when Father slid his arm across her shoulder. "It's hard to believe how much you've grown. You're not my little girl anymore." He paused. "You and Sister Carlson seemed to get along."

Rejoice nodded and bit her lip. "I owe her a lot. She was very good to me." Then she looked up and tried not to cry. "But I really missed you and Mother every day."

He looked out to sea and squeezed her tighter. "We missed you two so much. Mother was overjoyed when you changed your mind and decided to come with us. We were just wondering why you did."

Rejoice looked up at Father and this time tears did leak out of her eyes. She stammered and shook her head.

"It's okay," Father said. "We don't need to know. We're glad to have you with us. But at the moment your mother is upset that we couldn't safely bring Makepeace. We all understand why. We know he'll do fine with Deaconess Redhorse and Stronghold. But knowing all that is not making it any easier." He studied Rejoice.

"So what do you want me to do? Lick the tables?"

"No. You don't have to be Makepeace. All I want you to do is remember that Mother just lost her oldest child to another woman, and her middle child to disability. We wanted to bring him, but can't. Try to be as cheerful as you can around her." He took a deep breath. "I know you're not happy about Young Man No Cruz."

"How could you tell?"

"Something in the way you rolled your eyes when Mother told you he was coming with us."

"Oh."

"We're going to be in tight quarters for a long time. It will be worse than on the Starflower because there are fewer people and less room. We won't have climate control. We may get sea-sick."

"Not me."

"This is a placid day. Storms are something else. What I'm saying is that we're all going to need to work hard at being pleasant to each other."

Rejoice wiped the sweat on her forehead with her sleeve. Didn't he realize that spending three years with the White triplets and not going insane had trained her to put up with anything? Well, thinking of No, maybe not. "I've received the message."

How to change the subject? "Father, what did Elder Smith mean when he told you to pull back the ocean?"

Father sat Opportunity down and hooked her retractable line to the railing with a snick that echoed in the white railing pipes. Then he unlatched and pulled down two folding seats on the outer wall of the sail housing, and motioned for Rejoice to sit beside him. He studied some far off cumulus clouds. "It's a theory. It may be generations before we find out whether or not it's correct, but it's partly why we put First City where we did."

Rejoice held up her fingers. "Because of the river for irrigation and navigation, the fairly-close inland lake, the semi-protected, navigable bay, and sandy beach for glass. Oh, and the largest, ah, the only continent with room to for us to expand. Did I get them all?"

"No. Don't forget the average temperature."

"How can I? Why didn't we settle where it's cooler?" She sagged.

Father laughed. "You got used to it the first time you were here." Opportunity wobbled over to him and buried her face in his knees.

"It took me over a month to get used to the heat after the rainy season stopped."

Father ran his fingers through Opportunity's fine hair, black as Stronghold's and his. "So it did. Back to the theory, which is: if we re-vegetate the planet with algae and grasses and trees and so forth, then all the new growing plants will suck out a lot of the carbon dioxide from the atmosphere, and thereby cool things down. Even if First City cooled a great deal, it would still be good for agriculture. We tinkered with the crop's genes to make them tolerate the new day lengths and heat. We could modify them back to tolerate cold, if it ever gets cold."

Rejoice straightened up. "I remember now. I had forgotten."

Father laughed again with an easy, relaxed smile. "Apparently, so did Elder Smith. Someone must have reminded him."

Rejoice hadn't seen him this happy in years. Maybe the voyage would be good. She leaned back against the wall. "But what does that have to do with pulling back the sea?"

"The atmosphere cools down, the ice caps at the poles grow larger and sea levels drop."

Rejoice finished it, "And the shallow parts of the ocean become land and the ocean pulls back. Oh, but what happens to the hexacrab cluster?"

"They've moved many times. They can move again. We can move our kelp farm with them."

"What do the hexacrabs think about our changing the climate?"

"We haven't told them. Why fret them with something that may never happen?"

Rejoice frowned. "That seems dishonest."

"I don't think so. We can't say what will truly happen nor how fast. They do know we are planning to sow life on every island we touch. They know I'm looking for minerals. Brother Hancock is looking for more species. Elder Chin is looking for more hex cultures. And the hexacrabs are looking for adventure and females that talk. We're all happy."

"So why am I on board?"

"To help interpret satellite pictures, and be a lab hand, deck hand, galley hand; and to have fun with us."

"What satellite pictures?"

"After supper. Right now the ship is navigating itself through well-known waters and we all intend to rest after a strenuous leave-taking." Father gently pushed Opportunity back and folded his seat into the wall. He unlatched two hinged bars above the seat and swung them out. Then he opened a small hatch and pulled out a wad of string that he shook out and hung on the bars.

"I don't believe it," Rejoice said. "That's a hammock."

Father winked. "Astute observation." He swooped up Opportunity and carefully placed himself and her into the hammock. As the little girl snuggled against him, he shifted her bonnet to shield her eyes and murmured "N-A-P time. The engineers had fun designing this when I told them I intended to nap on the deck. There's even a little shelf I can pull out to hold lemonade. Care to join us? There's a hammock next to your seat."

Rejoice shook her head. How could Father be so fond of naps? And how could she sleep when she had to find out where everything was?

CIRCUMNAVIGATION CHAPTER FOUR

Rejoice folded up her seat with the methodical neatness that tight quarters on the spaceship had taught her. Since they had kept this ship a secret from her, she didn't know the first thing about it, from where they were supposed to eat and sleep to where they were supposed to do research.

The wall behind their seats had to hold the sail mechanisms. She walked toward the rear of the ship, the stern, passing stairs that led below, some little boats, and three metal objects that looked like rockets with propellers and handholds that were hanging from scaffolding. Circular life preservers and coils of rope lined the walls. She counted twenty preservers. For a crew of eight. Perhaps that hyper-cautiousness was why no one had died yet on New Earth.

Behind the ship, a gentle wake furrowed the sea. Walking toward the front, the bow, she passed sharp-tipped, long poles fastened to the walls, a first-aid kit, fire extinguishers, a hatchet, more preservers, radar equipment, another boat, stairs to the top of the sail housing and another set of stairs below. A large box screwed to the deck held coils of cable.

In the bridge, she found a wheel turning itself and a bank of computer, radar, sonar, and radio equipment. She unslung the screen she wore over her shoulder, and plugged it into the main computer. A quick scan showed the schematics of the ship. The sun's heat burned through the glass windows as she checked the sonar map of the sea floor they were gliding over. The heat drove her out before she could check on anything else.

Behind the ship, the dark line of Sole Continent hovered on the horizon with flashes of sunlight from the multitudes of glass panes at First City. Before them, the sea stretched blankly. To the southeast rose the sharp peaks of the Bull's Eye Islands obscured by sea haze and distance. The deck thrummed faintly with the vibrations of the engine and propeller. The wind sung through the slats of the metal sail.

The puffins fell back. The air smelled of salt, and sunlight sizzled on the deck. Rejoice stood in the shade of the sail, alternating watching the empty ocean and watching her little sister doze on Father. Rejoice turned away and muttered, "Well, for an exciting round the world trip, this is really boring."

The schematics had shown another radio room under the bridge. It might be cooler down there. Maybe she could call someone and talk. Not Harmony. She was sure to be busy. Even though no one was around, Rejoice's face heated even more.

Sister Guthry. She had forgotten her apprentice tutor, Sister Guthry. She hadn't come to either banquet or the wedding because she was sick. Despite all the scrubbing and medication they had taken before boarding the colony ship Starflower, cold viruses had still come with them. With the change of plans, Rejoice never did get to visit her and thank her for the math puzzles. Yes, she would call Sister Guthry.

At the stairs, she hesitated. If she went downstairs, she might run into No Cruz. Would talking to him be better than mind-numbing boredom, or would it equate? She pulled her shoulders back. He couldn't be avoided for an entire year. She descended into an empty, white hallway lined with labeled, white doors. First door on the right: Storage 1. That could wait. On the left: Hancock. Next door on the left: Rejoice and Opportunity. She held the door lever. No, she should finish exploring first.

Next door: Holly, with a message in the tiny slot under the name that read: Do Not Interrupt. Rejoice would need to be dying before she knocked on a door with that message on it, and maybe not even then. Still, since she was feeling lonely, she didn't like the exclusion. Next door: Chin and No. So they shared a room. What would that be like?

Lest she be caught staring at No's door, she moved on to the hall's end, a door marked Radio and Hexacrab Access. The door had a wheel on it instead of a lever.

The wheel turned easily, and the thick door opened inwardly with a soft whoosh. Elder Chin, sitting on the floor, looked up and arranged the wrinkles of his face into a smile. "Young Lady, you may come in if you wish."

Rejoice looked down at the floor and gasped. Lights surrounded a thick, transparent glass floor. Under the floor, Ur-Veena and the much smaller Sa-Issi hung from handholds. Their gear floated in net bags suspended from hooks in the transparent, sloping walls of the keel. A microphone in their triangular room jutted from their ceiling/the human's floor, and a wire snaked from it to the translator/recorder on the shelf next to Elder Chin.

He pushed a button and announced, "Entering this session is Young Lady Rejoice In The Lord's Salvation Holly. Please be seated."

She lowered herself to the floor and shivered. Cold. Slightly damp. Ur-Veena pressed one tentacle against the glass. She placed her palm on the other side. "Am I interrupting?"

Elder Chin grinned as he turned off the recorder. "You are welcome to interrupt. You may provide some insight into our learning sessions."

"Learning? What are you learning? We haven't gone anywhere yet."

Elder Chin laughed. "We have known the hexacrabs for only three New Earth years. You cannot think that we have learned their entire history and culture and language in three years. I doubt three hundred years will achieve it."

Rejoice gathered up some folds in her dress. "I guess I haven't thought about it."

"You had other thoughts to occupy your mind, and we thank God you did," he said kindly. "Now, what brings you here if it isn't to study the hexacrabs?"

"I was just exploring the ship. I thought I would look at the radio room, maybe call somebody."

"Not this one, not at this time of day."

"Oh, because you'll be in here."

"Young Man No has reserved thirty minutes of every day except the Lord's Day at this time to talk to Harmony. You may call at another time. Here you may visit any time."

Harmony's first day of marriage was not reserved for Stronghold alone? Rejoice intertwined her fingers and bit back her questions. If she wanted to know why No Cruz talked every day with Harmony, she would have to ask No to his face. You weren't allowed to ask questions about another person behind his back unless you were asking your father or mother.

Rejoice could wonder, but she could not see herself asking No why he had to talk every day to the woman her brother had just married. Did Stronghold know about it? And why had Harmony never mentioned this to her? Harmony was the closest thing she had to a best friend, but there were obviously a lot of things she had never shared. Rejoice shivered from something besides cold.

Elder Chin pulled an orange cushion from a cabinet and offered it to Rejoice. "It takes a while to get used to the cold floor. Sitting on this should help."

Rejoice slid it under herself.

"Is there anything that you wish to say to Ur-Veena or Sa-Issi?"

Rejoice spoke into the translator, "I am so glad that I get to spend more time with you during our voyage. Sa-Issi, you are much larger than when I left three years ago."

"I have broken a hex of shells since we talked last." piped Sa-Issi and puffed his gills.

"Yes, but you must break a hex more shells before you will be large as I am." said Ur-Veena.

Rejoice frowned. What did that mean? Elder Chin said, "Like Old Earth crabs they must break out of their small shells to grow into new ones. It's news to me that it requires two hex of shells to achieve adult size. I must note that."

"What do you hope to find on our journey?" asked Rejoice into the translator.

"We hope to find the lost clusters of the people. We hope that some survived and have grown again like us. We hope much that their females talk and may live lives of honor." answered Ur-Veena.

"I hope so too," Rejoice said.

The lever clicked on the radio room door. No was inside. He might come out at any moment. She couldn't face him yet. "Please excuse me," she whispered, and backed out of the room. Elder Chin paid no attention as he tapped at his computer.

She fled down the short corridor to her room and slammed the door behind herself. She slung herself on one of the two narrow bunks lining the walls and rolled over to stare at the ceiling. Her life was becoming narrower and narrower. First she left the wide Earth with seven billion people on it, to live for seven years on a spaceship with seven hundred people on it. Seven months on New Earth, and then three years on the space ship with nine people. And now a tiny ship with only seven people besides her.

Rejoice bunched the pillow under her head. Adding the hexacrabs made it nine. Whoopee. And one of them was No Cruz. The only way her life could become any narrower was for them to shipwreck and leave her on a desert island with just No. Ha, Not and No, the two big negatives in her life. One was Not for her and the other was No way.

Three hours later, she was still staring at the ceiling when somebody knocked on the door. Rejoice rubbed her forehead. "Yes?"

The knocking resumed. Soundproofing must have blocked her reply, so she opened the door.

Mother grinned. "Ready for supper?"

Rejoice glanced at her screen. It was that late. "I guess so. Where's the kitchen?"

"The galley. On a water-ocean ship, it's called a galley."

"Okay." Should she classify that under really important information?

They walked to the end of the hall, turned right down a short corridor, and right again into the hall on the other side of the ship. Here was the galley, dining room, entry to the engine room below and the Hancock's lab.

"You cut the radish roses while I peel the carrots," Mother said.

They cut and peeled in silence for a few minutes. Rejoice's eyes watered when she cut the green onions for the salad.

"Rejoice, I don't think you're very happy about this trip."

"No. I'm not."

"I thought it would be such a pleasant surprise."

"I hate surprises. I must have told you that a hundred times."

"I love to be surprised. I don't understand why you don't."

"Then don't understand." Rejoice stopped and took a deep breath. That had been said much too sharply. "I mean, please accept that I am different from you. I like to see what's coming."

"You would have liked to mentally prepare for this voyage."

"Yes."

"Then, Rejoice, my dearest, I am sorry. I should have let you know what we were going to do."

"Yes, you should have."

Mother cut hard-boiled eggs in half and plopped the yolk into a bowl to mash with mustard, salt, and pickles. "Well, here we are. Even Elder Smith gave us his blessing. I'm glad for that."

"After what you said, I was surprised to see him."

"I wasn't. Not really. Elder Smith has always done what Sister Smith has asked him to do. And she is very fond of me. And of you for that matter."

"That's good," Rejoice said without enthusiasm.

"Rejoice, why must you deliberately make yourself unhappy? Here we are, as I said, and we have a chance to see new things, see what kind of animals live on the Large Archipelago, get to know each other."

"What animals?"

"The moving blurs we think are animals in the satellite photos."

"Oh oh oh!" Rejoice popped open her screen, but couldn't see any place to plug it in.

"Every seat has a hook-up in the dining room." Mother sang, "I had to see what I could see . . ."

Rejoice darted out the door, then darted back. "Do you need me to help you finish?"

Mother laughed. "Go ahead."

Rejoice zipped through hundreds of weather satellite photos until she found the file named Anomalous Movement. She was studying them when Father came into the dining room stretching and blinking.

"Father, why are these pictures so bad? I can't tell anything."

Father dropped into a chair and yawned. "Resolution. The resolution of our satellite cameras are fine for tracking weather. Who needs to see anything smaller than a meter for weather?"

"So why didn't the colony put up some better cameras?"

"Perhaps because you had taken a shuttle and the Starflower to Opportunity?" Brother and Sister Hancock entered the room. Brother Hancock slapped Father on the back with his good hand as his paralyzed arm brushed the table. Sister Hancock arranged the curtains over the portholes so sunlight wouldn't glare on the tables.

"The colony had the other shuttle. They could have put up a better satellite," Rejoice said.

Elder Chin came in bearing plates and a mug of silverware, and smiling.

Father grimaced. "All right. I had asked for better satellites and more satellites so I could do a better geological survey, but we needed to build an irrigation canal from the river to the fields."

Rejoice frowned. She remembered when they did that. They had to dismantle the desalination plant because the extra salt being pumped back into the ocean had bothered the hexacrabs. The closed plant had been dumped to form an artificial reef.

Brother Hancock laughed. "You should see the fish cavorting around the old desalination plant. Last time I checked, there were four kinds of those armored fish—"

"Hard heads," Elder Chin said to Rejoice.

"—ten kinds of seaweed, three of those from Earth, five kinds of sailor-cap snails, and four kinds of New Earth sponges."

Mother, with Opportunity clinging to her dress, came in with baked potatoes. Sister Hancock scurried out to get the salad.

Everyone seemed jolly except Rejoice. "But after the canal was built, why didn't they put up better satellites? Is it because Elder Smith didn't want you to have any?"

Father studied her a moment. "Because there were tractors to build. And homes. And a birthing center. And a veterinary clinic. And air purifiers for the barns, and dozens of other things. Like this ship."

"Which is only solar and wind powered. I thought you were going to drill for oil so we could have oil powered engines that are stronger and more reliable."

"Ah, yes," Father said. "Actually, I was hoping this voyage would show us where some drill sites are."

"But the hexacrabs know where the oil is seeping into the ocean."

Elder Chin leaned forward. "If only we could understand hexacrab directions."

Rejoice looked at him, puzzled. "They can't say: turn right at the big rock and crawl for five kilometers?"

The adults burst into great laughter. Brother Hancock slapped the table. Rejoice looked from one to the other. What had she said? What were they laughing at her for?

Elder Chin wiped his eyes. "You're the one who kept trying to show them pictures, aren't you?"

"That was before I found out hexacrabs can't see pictures for some reason. They're not blind. They have eyes. But they don't see pictures. I don't understand how they can see and not see."

"Thank you," Elder Chin said to Brother Hancock who handed a slice of bread to him. The aroma of fresh-baked bread filled the room. "Let us pray."

After the grace, Elder Chin buttered his bread. "There are two issues here concerning hexacrab directions. No, they can't say five kilometers. They can say it takes five days to get somewhere, but that can be a short or long distance depending on how difficult the terrain is, what the temperature is, what the currents are, and on and on."

He took a large bite of bread and relished it while Rejoice waited. "You wondered how they can see and not see. They wonder how we can feel and not feel, smell and not smell, taste and not taste. They wonder how we can get around when we're blind to the electric and magnetic fields they see so easily."

"Feel and not feel? What are you talking about?"

"I've done some tests with them," Sister Hancock said, leaning over a plate of steaming corn. "They perceive the tiniest gradations of water pressure, and have a word for each one. Just like we look at visible light, and call one wavelength blue and another red and call the lengths in between purple and maroon and mauve and wine and so forth."

"Oh." What color was wine?

"Their sense of smell and taste are exquisitely more refined than ours. The children smell their way back home. They don't say: turn right; they say: follow this smell, this taste. And they use words we can't translate because we can't sense what they can sense."

Brother Hancock pointed a carrot stick at Rejoice. "You may have noticed that we run the sonar only one minute out of ten. That's because if we do it more, the hexacrabs will have headaches."

"Oh." What more could she say? She bit into a radish rose, and remembered she hated radishes. She hadn't had one for three years and had forgotten. She put it down and looked around. "Where's No?"

"He knows when and where supper is. If he chooses to fast, that is his business," Mother said cheerfully. "Would you like some green beans?" A speaker in the ceiling beeped. Brother Hancock plugged in his computer and studied the screen. He glanced at Rejoice's screen beside her plate. "Tap in under Magellan. Hancock. Underwater Camera. Active, and you can follow along."

Rejoice did so. A murky silver flash crossed the screen. Opportunity smeared butter across the screen with a chubby hand. Rejoice snatched her little sister's hand away, and Opportunity shouted, "No! No!"

Brother Hancock pressed a key. "Ur-Veena, Sa-Issi, would you catch one of those salmon for me?" He grinned and rubbed his bulbous nose. "We may have found our missing salmon."

Something fell past the porthole. Rejoice shrieked and jumped up. "What was that?"

Father reached across the table to pat Rejoice's hand. "We have a control panel on the side of the ship the hexacrabs can access."

Another metallic shape fell past the porthole.

"The hexacrabs just released their sea scooters."

"How they love their sea scooters!" Elder Chin said. "It's like the invention of the automobile for humans. It gives them freedom of mobility."

"They catch the fish; I dissect it; and they get it back for lunch," Brother Hancock said. "Switch to Scooter Camera."

"The screen split into two murky views, one obscured by a hexacrab foot.

After several minutes of this, Rejoice decided that nothing very exciting was going to happen, and she cut a baked potato grown lukewarm. She should be glad that at least the hexacrabs were happy with their freedom. Somehow 'should' seldom became 'is' for Rejoice

.

CIRCUMNAVIGATION CHAPTERFIVE

R ejoice halted to peer past the white railing at the spot far starboard. She stared at the empty sea sparkling under an empty sky. What had she seen? Nothing apparently. Or some random flash of reflection from a wavelet.

Opportunity pulled Rejoice's broad brimmed hat and chanted, "Go, cama, go."

Rejoice shifted her little sister higher on her back and resumed her swaying walk. "Camel is tired."

"Cama not tired. No want nap."

This ship was too small. Why had she agreed to go? What were Father and Mother thinking? She swayed around the bow of the little ship and entered the blessed shadow of the rigid slats mounted on masts and encrusted with solar cells that powered the Magellan.

Stepping out of the shadow felt like pushing through a wall of heat. She was glad that the light brown fabric of her pants and dress let the sea breezes breathe through readily. Unfortunately there were no breezes today.

She stopped again to search for the flicker glimpsed out of the corner of her eye. She was seeing things, but there was nothing there. Why would there be anything there?

Her nose itched under the filter mask. Since both hands were holding Opportunity, who was growing heavier by the minute, she could not scratch it.

No Cruz broke into her reverie. "What are you looking at?"

Rejoice jumped and teetered until she pushed Opportunity back into her center of gravity. "Uh. Nothing."

As he did every day, No had been hurling a blunted spear toward a target he had contrived by tying circular life preservers together at a ninety degree angle so that one floated flat and the other rose above it. Rejoice always found the clouds to be interesting to look at as she walked past him. The spear splashed. No grunted as he hauled the spear back in by the rope tied to the hollow, metal spear's end. As soon as he had it in hand, he hurled it again.

This was the first time he had stopped to talk to her. "Excuse me." She stepped around him and headed toward the doors. She patted her sister on the rear. "Hi-ho, little girl, let's go see what the hexacrabs are doing."

"No wanna nap."

"I didn't say nap; I said hexacrabs. Down we go."

The lighted, white stairway and hall seemed dim after the sun's glare. The cool, filtered air chilled the sweat on Rejoice's neck. She let down her sister and pulled off their filter masks. She breathed deeply and choked.

She had expected dry air free from the scent of iodine and salt, but what she inhaled reeked of a nasty chemical.

Sister Hancock in the hallway turned her eyes to Rejoice. "Oh hello. Would you be a dear and reroute the venting while we clean up the preserver solution that Brother Hancock dropped?"

"Didn't either drop it," came Brother Hancock's voice from the lab, followed by some coughing. "It jumped out of my hand."

Sister Hancock snapped on the filter mask that had been hanging around her neck, reentered the lab, and closed the door.

Rejoice swung Opportunity to her back and galloped down the hall. Happily, the heavy door that opened into the hexacrab access and primary control board stood ajar so she could hurry in. She lowered her sister; pressed her palm twice rapidly against the thick transparent floor in the gesture that meant, I see you but cannot linger; murmured aloud, "Excuse me, Elder Chin," and darted around him. In the primary control room, she routed the ventilation to air out the hallway and lab. "I need to vent the lab. A bottle jumped out of Brother Hancock's hand."

"Aha. The source of that wonderful scent."

Ur-Veena released his handhold and squirted off to one of the tiny intake holes. Sa-Issi tumbled after.

Elder Chin and Rejoice almost bumped heads as they leaned over the floor to watch. Ur-Veena grated and whistled. Rejoice caught most of the words, but needed to wait for the translator to understand the entire sentence: "A torpal desires the dance of death!" One of Ur-Veena's tentacles grabbed Sa-Issi, one pulled the lever that released the sea scooters, one opened the hatch, two pulled diamond-toothed spears from the wall, and one pressed the alarm with a fluid grace that made Rejoice catch her breath. A few seconds of swirling water, and they were gone.

"What's a torpal again?" Why hadn't she studied Hex harder?

Elder Chin upended the delighted Opportunity. "I think it is akin to a shark. Shall we go see?" He rose and carried the little girl like a package slung under his arm out into the hall.

Sister Hancock stood in the hallway glaring at her husband and hanging onto his sleeve. "You're not ready. You can't, not with that arm."

His blond hair stuck up at all angles and his eyes narrowed. "Excuse me, but that arm will never be ready." He gestured toward his paralyzed arm. "It's been three years since the hexacrabs offered to shell my soft parts with courage by going on a torpal hunt. Do you honestly think I'm going to turn down my first chance to go?"

Rejoice shrank back. She had never seen adults disagree loudly before.

Sister Hancock clenched his sleeve tighter. "We don't even know what you're getting into."

"The purpose of this voyage is to find out." Brother Hancock suddenly leaned forward, kissed his wife, turned, and raced up the stairs.

Sister Hancock stood a moment with clenched fists. She followed with slow steps. Rejoice and Elder Chin followed her to the deck.

Brother Hancock pulled on his wetsuit with Young Man No helping him. Father lowered a boat into the water and tossed in several coils of rope, a sea scooter, and the long spears that had been hanging on the mast and solar cell housing.

Rejoice tried to look anywhere but at Sister Hancock glowering with her arms folded across her chest. When Rejoice saw the spears, she laughed nervously. "I thought we were supposed to be pacifists."

"We are pacifists," Elder Chin said. "We are not Jainists."

"What's a Jainist?"

"Look under World Religions," Mother said as she twisted her brown, curly hair into a bun. Then she shouted over the railing, "Be careful, Theophilus!"

"Resolved," Sister Hancock said, "why don't you let Young Man Cruz go instead?"

Brother Hancock snapped the last tab and checked the air mask connection. "Instead? He's coming with. What do you think we brought this bundle of muscles for?"

No Cruz grinned as he tied a sling around Brother Hancock's paralyzed arm. Then he stripped off his blue work shirt, dropped it onto the deck, and helped Brother Hancock into the boat. Father, No, and Brother Hancock roared off.

"Oh my," murmured Rejoice. The colony had upped the power in their boats' motors since the time she was lost in one. Please let her get a chance to take one out. However the power of the motor was not the biggest change she saw. No Cruz used to be pudgy and somehow pasty despite his brown skin. Now, obviously well-used muscles stood out on tanned arms. Black hair hung down to brown eyes and black eyebrows that nearly met each other. His jaw had lengthened, and his nose, which had been too large, now fit an adult face. Right. He was twenty now. Now that she could watch him without him staring back, she did.

She hadn't noticed his new build. Whenever he came up on the deck, she went below or looked the other way. And when he was below, she worked in the galley or stayed in her room or gave Opportunity rides. He had missed most of the meals doing only God knew what. Once she had seen him in the hall tracing some pipes and wiring, but she had scurried away before he could turn his intense eyes upon her. He still made her skin crawl. Whenever she looked his way, he was always staring at her. She sighed. Rejoice could hardly avoid him for an entire year. She should talk to him. But about what?

The boat grew smaller as it followed the locaters in the sea scooters piloted by the hexacrabs. They headed toward where she had thought she had seen something. Mother attached Opportunity's tether to the railing and plumped her daughter down on the box of cables. Sister Hancock held the railing so tightly that her knuckles turned white.

Mother plugged in her computer and popped up the screen. "Here we go."

They crowded around to see a split screen with two views of murk, one half-occluded by a hexacrab tentacle.

After gazing at featureless water on the screen for several minutes, Rejoice looked up to directly see the boat made tiny by distance. Tinier figures stood and moved in it. One of the figures went over the side.

The screen showed Brother Hancock in a confusion of bubbles mounting the sea scooter and purring toward the camera.

Rejoice reached to scratch her nose, and her fingers skittered across her filter mask. Bother! "How is he going to pilot the scooter and dance or fight or whatever with one good arm?"

"Ask him!" Sister Hancock said with an anger that startled Rejoice.

The camera mounted on the front of the Ur-Veena's scooter swung around and showed the humans their first sight of a torpal. Rejoice could not tell if it was a fatter skate or a flatter shark than Old Earth had. Teeth rimmed its underslung mouth. Barbs projected from its side flaps. Instead of a shark's tail, the animal had a whip lined with more barbs. Three eyes gleamed milk-white in its rust-colored, armored head.

The muscles in Sister Hancock's neck grew more defined. "There's no fool like an old fool!"

Rejoice gaped. Who would reprimand her? Mother put her arms around Sister Hancock.

"Look," Elder Chin said.

Rejoice gasped. A salmon darted under the torpal's belly and provided scale. The torpal was at least five meters long and the whip-tail added another three meters. Five meters! The hexacrabs swung around, approaching the gliding torpal from behind, one on either side. The torpal rolled its eyes and twitched.

Rejoice held her breath as the hexacrabs drew nearer. One side of the split screen showed a terrifying view of teeth coming toward it, and the other side showed a hexacrab lance piercing the gills.

Black blood swirled as the torpal arched back. Sister Hancock moaned as the second lance slit the gills on the other side.

The torpal thrashed. Its tail snagged a scooter. The torpal doubled back and gnashed the scooter. The teeth descended and the camera went black. The computer switched to Brother Hancock's view of Sa-Issi squirting off the scooter and falling.

Brother Hancock swerved down to catch him as Ur-Veena circled the thrashing torpal and whistled, "You who demand death shall swim to it!" The diamond-toothed lances worked out of the gills and drifted. Sa-Issi snatched one with a quick tentacle as Brother Hancock's scooter rose. Brother Hancock gripped the scooter with his knees, released the steering lever, and fumbled with his spear.

Above him, Ur-Veena darted his second lance at a milk white eye, but the weapon glanced off the bony plates.

Brother Hancock thrust his spear up into the torpal's belly. The scooter spun sideways as the torpal slashed down. Sa-Issi plunged his lance into the torpal's gaping mouth. They were knocked over as the torpal flipped and lunged toward Sa-Issi. Tail barbs scraped across Sa-Issi's shell.

The torpal gnawed on the stone lance. Teeth chipped off both. Brother Hancock struggled to right himself. His torn sling wrapped itself around the scooter's propeller. Frantically, he tried to free it, then ducked as the torpal charged him. His paralyzed arm floated out. The torpal twisted and snapped.

The arm disappeared.

Rejoice screamed. Sister Hancock fainted. Her head thunked on the deck. Opportunity wailed.

Mother, bending over Sister Hancock, cried out, "Rejoice, get my surgical kit from the dispensary, the door between the dining room and lab. And lock Opportunity in your room."

Rejoice, who had started for the stairs, doubled back, unhooked Opportunity's tether, and grabbed her off the cable box. The little girl howled and flailed her arms and legs. Rejoice almost dropped her sister on the stairs, and caught her own fingers on the door when she shut it. She raced back with the kit and banged into the doorway. The ship rolled in that moment, and instead of falling down the stairs; she fell out onto the deck.

Elder Chin swung a boom with a huge canvas seat over the railing.

On one side of the screen, No swam toward Brother Hancock with a line trailing behind him.

"Hurry, oh hurry," breathed Mother to the image of No struggling so slowly against the water. The view twisted as the torpal bumped the scooter. The torpal's wash turned No. The line and lance and his legs tangled together.

No kicked the torpal in his effort to free himself. The torpal turned and snapped his jaws upon the lance a few centimeters from No's fingers.

The other screen showed Ur-Veena's lance plunging again into the exposed gills, stirring clouds of dark blood. The torpal released No's lance and turned again. The barb on its tail scored No's arm. Teeth filled the camera's view, then receded as the torpal rolled and showed No's lance imbedded in the middle of its spine. One of the monster's flaps collided with the camera and shattered it.

The last view showed only the underside of a hexacrab tentacle. A long minute passed.

With Opportunity's screams still echoing in her ears, Rejoice regained her footing. Elder Chin lowered the canvas seat.

"Rejoice, stay here with Sister Hancock." Mother ordered.

Rejoice knelt by the woman, lifted her limp head and cradled it in her lap. Mother tore open the surgical kit.

Rejoice swallowed acid. She clenched her teeth together to keep from crying.

They waited forever for the boat to come. Finally No brought the boat alongside. Father crouched over Brother Hancock, using his hands as a tourniquet on the stump of Brother Hancock's arm. No slid the seat under Brother Hancock, and Elder Chin reeled him up. No climbed up the ladder beside him to hold the seat away from banging into the side of the ship. The crane swung the seat over the railing.

Blood, there was blood everywhere, all over Father and No, sloshing in the boat, dripping on the white deck.

Mother sprayed coagulant on the stump and hissed in some painkiller as Brother Hancock muttered, "Didn't have any use for that arm anymore anyway. Anyway. Glad to be rid of the nuisance." Then he shouted, "What's wrong with Arlene, I mean, Beth . . . I mean, what's wrong?"

"Bethany is fine," Mother announced. "Come this way."

No and Elder Chin linked hands to make a sling to carry Brother Hancock down the stairs.

Father came slowly up the ladder. His gaze flicked over Rejoice, Sister Hancock, and the blood on the deck. "Uh-oh."

"She fainted," squeaked Rejoice. Her head buzzed.

"Better clean this up before she comes to," said Father. "Hose. Where did the engineers put the hose?" He checked the box of cables, and then found the hose coiled behind a panel. He washed off the deck. Then he sat on the box and panted. "Out of shape. Don't have the breath I used to." Then to Rejoice, "Is she going to be okay?"

"She bumped her head."

"Concussion?"

"I don't know. How do you check?"

Father came over, and at that moment, Sister Hancock drew in a deep, shuddering breath and opened her eyes. Tears instantly filled them. She reached up for Father's hand and whispered, "Is he dead?"

Father held her hands and knelt beside her. "Not at all. Young Man Cruz dove in and got him right away. Carol is seeing to him right now."

"Oh, thank God." He helped her up and they embraced. He supported her as they went down the stairs.

That left Rejoice on the deck. If she went downstairs, she would be in everybody's way. Then she thought of the boat, the hose, and the sling. Everything needed to be put away. She might as well do it. Rejoice stood up, and needed to grab the railing because her legs were so shaky. Why hadn't this voyage stayed boring?

She glanced over the railing.

The hexacrabs were towing the torpal to the ship.

CIRCUMNAVIGATION CHAPTER SIX

Sa-Issi lay with his beak pressed against the top of Ur-Veena's shell, his tentacles splayed over the shell like the ribs of an umbrella, and his legs trailing behind as Ur-Veena piloted the sea scooter through dark waters. When they had gone beyond even the scent and vibration of the Magellan, Ur-Veena shut down the motor to let them drift. Far below, three salmon rippled the sea.

Sa-Issi unfurled his tentacles and sank a bit before wrapping one tentacle around Ur-Veena's front leg. He piped, "Question? The reason they take the torpal if they do not eat it?"

Ur-Veena gently swayed his tentacles as he tasted the currents with patches near the base of each tentacle. The magnetic north hissed as a background against which sparked the little lives that swam and floated near them. Something moaned kilometers away. Ur-Veena recognized the song, but he had never seen the singer. His gills flared as he thought of seeing things no adult hexacrab had ever seen.

"Question?" piped Sa-Issi again. "The air ocean people will form big spears with the teeth?"

"The air ocean people will cut the torpal so that they may see what is inside."

"Question? Reason?"

"They try to taste our currents."

"The torpal smelled good."

"They will return enough for us to eat. We catch; they cut; we eat. It is good."

Sa-Issi paddled the water. He stretched one tentacle up through the thermocline to feel where the water above was warmer than the water below. "My soft parts wanted to squeeze into my shell."

"You did exactly as I trained you. You carry honor as did Sa-Tsetse."

Sa-Issi clambered under the scooter to cling to Ur-Veena's other side. "This is where I swam for unknown days?"

"Perhaps. We do not know where in the deep ocean the children go when they leave us. No one remembers when he was a child."

The tips of one of Sa-Issi's tentacles softly probed the broken camera lens on the front of the scooter. "Many leave. Few swim back."

"Only those with courage return."

Sa-Issi's large, vision eyes extended even though it was too dark to see much by light. The little hexacrab chirped, "Question? Therefore I have courage?"

"Yes." Ur-Veena started the motor and turned the scooter toward the Magellan. "You have courage."

"Question? Air-ocean Chan-Tot has courage?"

"Yes. Only once did he need help to shell his soft parts with courage."

"When?"

"Wait. Taste."

Sa-Issi spread out his tentacles. "Another torpal. We shall dance?"

"No. There is no nursery here, and we have enough to eat. We do not wander to search for torpals." Ur-Veena accelerated the scooter.

Sa-Issi tightened his grip. "The torpal may smell us."

"Therefore we return to the ship."

The scooter purred. Far, far below, a creature stirred.

CIRCUMNAVIGATION CHAPTER SEVEN

Rejoice tapped on the Hancock's door, and then assumed she had heard a "Come in." Perhaps they shouldn't have soundproofed the rooms quite so well. Balancing the tray with one hand, she opened the door with the other.

Mother bent over Brother Hancock sleeping on the double wide bed. Sister Hancock sat on the desk chair watching them grimly.

"Breakfast?" Rejoice asked.

Mother looked at her with eyes rimmed with dark circles. "What a blessing you are, my young lady."

Rejoice felt glad now that she had awakened early to go into the dining room and toss out the dried and cracked cheese, the stale bread, and the wrinkled vegetables, and then scrub the encrusted plates and bake two batches of cinnamon-peanut rolls. She set the tray on the desk. "What are you doing?" she asked Mother.

"Drawing blood to culture it."

Sister Hancock barked something that might have been laughter. "Does he have enough left to give?"

Rejoice frowned. Culture? Music and art? "What does draw blood to culture it mean?"

Mother held up a thin glass tube filled with blood. "I'll take this to the laboratory and spread it on some plates of bacteria food to see if he got an infection from the torpal."

Hyper-cautious again. Rejoice smiled. "That's silly. We know alien germs can't infect us."

"Do we? That's what we read during the journey through warp. But here we are. The hexacrabs and humans share the same amino acids. They can eat our salmon. We can eat their hard heads. Who's to say there isn't a germ there that can destroy us? Who can say this voyage won't bring back a blight to eat our crops?"

"A blight?"

"We can't say yet that there is nowhere on this entire planet a fungus that likes our grain. That's why the colony has seven years of food stored up so far. Just in case."

Just in case. So that's what those huge warehouses near the runway were. Instead of building and placing satellites, the colony had built warehouses to store food they would never need. That was probably Elder Smith's doing. Why couldn't Father run the colony instead?

Mother placed her equipment in a box and straightened up.

"I'm off to the lab. Call me when he wakes up."

Sister Hancock nodded abruptly.

Rejoice studied the monitor attached to the bed: blood pressure, electrolytes, clotting factors, enzymes. Swallowing became a chore. She could never be a nurse. How could Mother stand all that blood? She turned to Sister Hancock. "Would you like anything else for breakfast?" Sister Hancock's eyes never left her husband's face. "Thank you, dear, but I don't think I can eat yet."

Rejoice fiddled with the tray. Should she take it back? But then Sister Hancock might get hungry later. "Oh, Elder Chin told me to tell you, if it wasn't an inconvenient time, the hexacrabs want us to process the torpal before it spoils so they can have their share. They also caught a salmon for us."

Sister Hancock shook her head. "God bless their little, multiple hearts." Then she sighed heavily. "Well, Resolved isn't going to do it, so I suppose I'd better. Will you watch him please?"

"Sure."

Sister Hancock lingered at the door, gave an anguished look at her husband, and then shut the door behind her.

Rejoice settled in the chair. Brother Hancock slept on, the purple-red line on his neck where flesh mesh held a gash together showing starkly on his pallid skin. The few blond hairs he had left covered his scalp in disarray. A few minutes reflection brought her to the realization that she could be here for hours and that watching a sleeping man is intensely boring.

She didn't want to fall asleep. If she did, she wouldn't know when he woke up. And besides, every time she closed her eyes, she saw again the torpal tearing off his arm.

She plugged in her screen and pulled up the Starflower view of the last forty hours to see if its telescopes had spotted any more New Earth grazing asteroids. One, a meter and half across. Who cared? That size would burn up high in the atmosphere if it did hit New Earth. Still, she commanded the Starflower's telescopes to track it and log it as a possible hazard for future space travel. The space rock was so small that all it got for a name was NEG-2, 547-1.5m. That took five minutes. She pulled up her last math book and looked at some Penrose tiling problems, but could not concentrate.

She took one of the cinnamon-peanut rolls and licked off some frosting. Maybe she should check on the news from home. She scrolled through that day's First City Chronicles. No news about them. No one had called back to let the colonists know what happened to Brother Hancock? Apparently not. There was the day's sermon, the weather, the total of strawberries harvested, a poem, a note of thanks to the people who had helped with the Holly wedding. That had been only a week ago! After the notice of an upcoming choir practice, the Chronicles ended. Now what?

Maybe someone was calling back with the news. She pulled up the radio broadcast and found herself blinking at Harmony's face as she said to someone, "If you say so."

"I do," replied No. "In this situation your parents are not correct." A beeping sound interrupted. "I have to go help out in the lab. Now don't forget—"

Rejoice shut it off. Her ears burned. She shouldn't have listened to that much of a private conversation. At the same time she wished she had listened in earlier. What were they talking about? Sister Hancock would probably like to know what No thought that Harmony's mother was wrong about. They were sisters. Why hadn't No told Harmony what happened to her uncle?

Her questions were cut short by a change in Brother Hancock's breathing. She put the computer away and leaned forward.

Slowly his eyes opened and searched the room before resting on Rejoice. A smile crept across his face. "Young Lady," he whispered.

Rejoice called over the intercom. "Mother? Brother Hancock is awake."

"I'll be there," answered Sister Hancock.

Five seconds later Sister Hancock strode through the doorway, pulling off rubber gloves with quick snaps. "There you are! You couldn't even wait two weeks! Not one lousy week and you're out there getting body parts torn off! We're supposed to be gone a whole year. How much of you is going to come back?"

"Hello," he croaked.

"How are you supposed to top this? Tomorrow you go out to do one-armed battle with the kraken?"

He reached out feebly with his bruised hand. "It was glorious. It was the second most fun I've had in my life."

That stopped her a second before she said scornfully, "What was the first most? Getting stabbed by Ur-Nissi?"

"Getting married to you."

Her face crumpled. Her knees hit the floor and she laid her head on his chest.

He grunted. "Not there. It hurts."

She shifted down a few centimeters and sobbed.

After a grimace, he said, "I won't do it again."

"Liar!"

"Well, at least I'll try to not do it while you're looking."

"I hate you!"

He stroked her hair.

"Not there," she said in a muffled voice. "It hurts."

"I love you," he said tenderly.

Rejoice headed out the door and nearly collided with Mother.

Mother peeked in and then quietly shut the door. "I can check on him later."

Rejoice followed Mother back to the dining room where Opportunity tugged at her leash attached to the table. Elder Chin sleepily chewed on a roll. Father slumped over the table, apparently dozing. Mother sat heavily on her seat and handed a strawberry to Opportunity. "We need to call a ship's conference, and we need to call it now."

"Yes." Elder Chin solemnly pushed away his roll. He set the intercom to ship-wide. "Ship's Conference. Ready?"

Father sat up.

"Here," No Cruz said from the lab.

"Here," the Hancocks said from their room.

Ur-Veena whistled in the keel, "What paths are we climbing?"

"The question is: what should we do now that Brother Hancock has been badly hurt? First, let us pray."

Everyone bowed their heads except the hexacrabs who did not have necks. Ur-Veena whistled, "Is that to breathe air? The tentacle was useless. The torpal gave a gift to Chan-Tot male." Then to Sa-Issi's apparent question, he clicked, "They net their thoughts like fish with silence."

Rejoice looked down at her hands and tried to be quiet enough to let the peace of God guide her thoughts, but she was afraid to close her eyes and see again the blood and gore.

After several minutes of silence, Mother spoke, "We need to abort this mission, and we need to do it now. Humans cannot lose tentacles as easily as hexacrabs. I do not know how long it will take for Brother Hancock to recover. We left later than we should have and could be battling storms much of the way. We might as well go back and try again next year."

"Ah, no," breathed Brother Hancock. Rejoice had to strain to hear him. "Ur-Veena is basically correct."

"Excuse me," Mother said, "but Brother Hancock may still be in shock and not responsible for what he says."

"Sister Holly," came the wheezed reply, "I am shocked that you would say that about me."

"I agree with Sister Holly," Sister Hancock said.

"Young Man Cruz?" Elder Chin asked.

After a long pause, No answered, "Whatever you decide, I can live with. Though I would like to go on."

Elder Chin sighed. "I do not think the hexacrabs could be easily persuaded to defer their dreams yet another year. Brother Holly?"

Elder Chin looked toward Father, who scratched his unshaven chin. "Brother Hancock is the one who was hurt. If he said he wanted to go back home, I would go along with him. However, he wants to continue. The amputation was clean. He should be as able to recover on the ship as on land."

Everyone waited another minute of silence. No one asked for Rejoice's opinion, or for Opportunity's. Yet they had asked No Confidence In The Flesh. Of course, No was twenty, and two years an adult. While she had been on the Starflower, he would have gone through the affirmation ceremony. The colonists didn't believe in vows or oaths except for marriages. But each young man and young lady had the opportunity to add his or her signature to the over seven hundred other signatures at the bottom of the Covenant of the Colony. They were thereafter called Brother or Sister and could vote on church decisions.

After her eighteenth birthday Rejoice would have the choice of whether to add her signature or not. It wasn't much of a choice. What was the alternative? Living with the hexacrabs?

"All right." Mother sighed. "I'm going to bed. Elder Chin, will you please call the colony and tell them the good news?"

Before Elder Chin could reply, No broke in. "Could I call Harmony first? She's going to be upset that I talked to her and didn't tell her about this."

"I'll call her and my kids first, before you tell the colony," Brother Hancock said.

"So be it," Elder Chin said. He rose and left after Mother.

"I'll help you clean up," Father said. "Then we can take Opportunity for a walk." After washing the dishes, table and counters and vacuuming the floor, they went up on the hot deck with no shade. The sail slats had folded and retracted into their housing when the ship stopped for the torpal hunt, and no one had yet told the ship to resume. Even the two-meter-high box that housed the sail slats and mast, and the bridge cast no shadows under an equatorial sun that pressed on the ship and people.

Father strode into the bridge and restarted the ship.

Opportunity refused to walk. She clung to Father's legs and made sure he was between her and Rejoice. Every time Rejoice looked at her, she hid her face and whimpered. Opportunity pulled her hair across her filter mask and ducked behind Father's knee.

"My own sister doesn't like me," Rejoice fretted. The glare off the ocean made her squint.

Father scooped up Opportunity. "Right now you're the bad guy who locked her up when she was terrified. Tomorrow will likely be my day to be the bad guy."

They rounded the sail housing, and there was No, in his bib overalls with his shirt stripped off again. He hurled a blunted spear toward his target of tied circular life preservers. The spear missed and splashed close to the target. No grunted, and hauled it back in swiftly by the rope tied to its end. As soon as he had it in hand, he hurled it again. Sweat ran in rivulets down his neck and back. He paid no attention to Father and Rejoice as they walked past.

When they came to the box of cables on the other side of the ship, Father stopped and sat on the box and jiggled Opportunity on his knee.

Rejoice sat beside him, leaned for only a moment on the hot housing, and tried to say casually, "No seems awfully interested in Harmony. It seems like every time I try to call someone in First City, he's already on the radio talking to her."

"To be sure. He always has some project or other going."

Harmony was a project? What did that mean? But then a more urgent question presented itself. "Father, I don't understand a lot of things."

"If I can explain, I'll try."

She licked her lips and tasted the salt air, which meant her filter needed cleaning. She hoped this wasn't gossip. "We're supposed to speak carefully and use encouraging words, right?"

"Yes."

"Sister Hancock called Brother Hancock a fool and a liar. She said she hated him. And the whole time she was saying that, he never stopped smiling."

Father laughed until he coughed. "Oh," he said. "That hurt."

"You would reprimand me if I talked like that."

Father patted Rejoice's knee. "You give allowance to people who are badly frightened. Brother Hancock understood that what she was really saying was that she loved him so much that she couldn't bear the thought of anything happening to him."

"So why did something happen? Why did Brother Hancock get hurt? Why was Makepeace born brain-damaged? Why did the hexacrabs have an asteroid hit this planet? Aren't we doing God's will?"

Father shook his head. "I thought we taught you better that that. It was Jesus who promised us, 'In this world, you shall have tribulation.'"

"We left that world."

Father chuckled. "So we did. A better translation is 'cosmos or universe.' We're still in a fallen universe. Bad things are going to happen."

"But why?"

"I just told you. I can't make up another answer. Jesus said the rain falls on the just and the unjust alike."

Rejoice sat back and squinted at the bright, blank ocean. Behind them, the masts rose and the sail slats opened with a snapping sound like that of Sister Hancock and her gloves.

Father shifted Opportunity. "I don't think our ship has it, but you should be able to download it from the Starflower data banks. Look under Theology. Problem of Evil, Problem of Pain, Studies on Job. Something like that could show you how the best minds have wrestled with the same question."

But Rejoice was thinking about the Hancocks again. "Father, why did Brother Hancock call Sister Hancock Arlene?"

"That used to be her name. When we boarded the Starflower to warp here, we all changed our names."

"What was your name before you changed it to Theophilus?"

Father stood and deposited Opportunity on the deck. "That, I would rather not tell you. I wasn't at all fond of the name."

They marched around the deck again. No still hurled spears toward the target. He panted and his sweat spattered on the deck as he hauled in the spear as fast as he could, and threw again, hitting the target. He still ignored them.

Father coughed again. "Did you get Sister Guthry's first set of math puzzles yesterday?"

Rejoice smiled. "She sent it to you, too?"

"She always does."

"All the ones when I was up on the Starflower for three years?"

"Oh yes. Every one. And your answers."

"I didn't know that." She laughed. "They were fun. But I wished they'd take a little longer to complete."

"Braggart!" Father chuckled. "How many steps did you take on the third one?"

"Forty-seven. You?"

Father groaned. "Fifty-three. Well, that's better than usual. Most of the harder ones take me about ten more steps than you. Squirt your answer to my computer. I want to see how you did it."

"Okay."

When they passed the box again, Rejoice asked, "What's that box of cables for?"

"It's a bit of a long story. We were first going to coat the ship with a copper compound to keep the New Earth barnacles off. Barnacles growing on the ship's skin create turbulence. That slows the ship down. Anyway, the copper compound made the hexacrabs sick, so that was out.

"Then we thought we'd keep the skin slightly charged to repel the barnacle larvae. The hexacrabs nixed that too. So we ran up these cables and thought that every so often we would send the hexacrabs off on their scooters, attach these cables on the sides, and electrocute any barnacles that had settled.

"Then we realized that that didn't really solve anything because dead barnacles create as much friction as live ones do. So we decided that why we had really put in these cables was to have an easy way to quickly recharge the boats if we have to. And then we wondered why we hadn't thought of that in the first place."

"Weren't you following directions on how to build a ship?"

"To be sure. But we had to make a number of modifications. We had ship plans, but not research ship plans. The original plans also did not include a room for hexacrabs."

They turned the corner and watched as No did ten push-ups then rolled and grabbed the spear at the same time, leaped to his feet, and threw the spear without taking time to aim. The spear missed but came close to the target. He hauled it back and began push-ups again.

After reaching the other side of the deck, Father said, "That young man is making me tired. The next thing he'll be doing is jogging ten kilometers. Do you know how many times that is around the deck?"

Rejoice didn't care. "So what are you doing about the barnacles?"

"The hexacrabs scrape them off. They like to keep busy and they like to eat barnacles. They seem to think barnacles taste like candy."

"Ugh."

"Speaking of ugh, Young Man Cruz and I dumped the torpal back in the ocean after Sister Hancock got her samples, but she probably still has a lot of work to do in the lab. If No is out here exercising, she's probably alone and could use some help. Why don't you check it out?"

"Okay." Rejoice trotted past No who was now clumsily tossing the spear with his left hand. Why had Brother Hancock chosen to dance with death using traditional spears instead spear guns? The colony had decided that some technological use was allowed. Elder Chin talked about cultural accommodation. Maybe that was it. Or maybe the colony thought doing everything the hard way was spiritual.

In the lab, Sister Hancock was setting up the camera/microscope. Little trays of bloody bits of torpal covered the counters and tops of machines. "Hello, dear. What can I do for you?" she said crisply and calmly as she peered into the microscope.

"Well, No isn't helping you anymore, so I wondered if you needed me to help."

Sister Hancock looked up, and a strand of gray-streaked red hair escaped the bun at her neck to fall across her cheek. "Young Man Cruz already did the heavy work of butchering the monster for me. I told him to go and follow his own schedule. But if you wish to help me, you may."

Had Rejoice been rebuked? "What would you like me to do?"

Sister Hancock looked around the lab and frowned. Then her face cleared. "Here. Take this sample of torpal blood to the gas chromatograph and the magnetic resonance force microscope and analyze it, comparing it to both human and hexacrab blood."

Rejoice took the thin glass rod filled with brick red blood. "This is orange-red. On the screen it looked black."

Sister Hancock said distantly as she adjusted the microscope, "The lower you go in the ocean, the blacker red looks."

Rejoice looked at Sister Hancock moving with deep concentration. This was the same woman who had shown her love an hour earlier by screaming at her husband when he woke up from the anesthetic? And now she spoke as though she had never said a harsh word in her life. How did she do that?

She found the gas chromatograph, a shiny box in one corner with instructions on the screen. After she inserted the rod, the screen showed the next step and the next. A colorful printout of spectral lines emerged. It looked nothing like the spectral lines of stars, so Rejoice could not interpret the findings. She keyed in instructions to compare the torpal blood to human blood. "The computer is asking which of the four types of human hemoglobin it should compare it to."

"It doesn't matter. Whatever the computer highlights as a reasonable choice, pick."

"Okay." She did that, and then the record of hexacrab blood. She did the same routine on the massive magnetic resonance force microscope. It occupied nearly a quarter of the lab, and she winced at how much power the machine drained from the ship's batteries.

Sister Hancock came over to look at the results. "This is amazing. Torpal hemoglobin is eighty-five percent identical to hexacrab hemoglobin, and sixty percent identical to human. Oh, would you like to look at these slides of torpal blood? The red cells are nucleated, and what I think are white cells are ciliated."

Rejoice had seen enough blood, but she looked through the microscope anyway. If she said she wanted to exercise, could that get her out of the lab?

Sister Hancock handed her a bowl. Rejoice shuddered. The bowl was full of bloody torpal teeth. "Could you run this down to the hexacrabs? They want to use them to make some kind of weapon."

"I thought they used diamonds for their blades. Don't you need these for your samples?" asked Rejoice.

"I've already sectioned and photographed dozens of them, and analyzed the constituent parts. I've got dozens more in the deep freeze. If the hexacrabs don't want them, you can throw them away or save them for souvenirs."

Rejoice shuddered again as she examined the curved teeth, serrated on one side and coming to a wicked point. The torpal had hundreds of these teeth, and yet the hexacrabs had attacked the giant fish like it was a game. "The hexacrabs don't seem to care about death."

"It does seem that way." Sister Hancock sat on a stool. "I couldn't believe it when they gave us the body of one of their females who had died to dissect. They watched us do the dissection, and then Ur-Veena asked if we would give them a body to dissect if one of us died. I said, 'No!' before Brother Hancock could say something stupid."

"You mean he would have offered his body?"

Sister Hancock sat with her lips tight together for a few moments. "He won't now. Anyway, they made sure we didn't eat her and we put all the pieces on their, hmm, it's not a burial ground, because they don't bury. But it's where they drag the bodies to."

"They thought we'd eat one of them?"

"They don't have us figured out all the way, any more than we have them all figured out."

"But they don't seem to mind being eaten after they're dead."

Sister Hancock stood and picked up one of the trays. "They don't mind the little scavengers. Big predators irritate them very much. Don't forget they used to think we were big predators."

She picked up a knife and poked into the tray. "Truly, they aren't that much different from us. We don't like to think about it, but little scavengers eat our bodies after we're buried as well. We see the ancient Egyptians as weird for attempting to indefinitely preserve their dead bodies through mummification. We also don't like to see our dead bodies eaten by big scavengers. In the Bible it was a great curse to die in a war and have the crows and vultures and hyenas pick at your corpse."

They needed to talk about something else. The chemical smells prodded Rejoice's growing nausea. "How come they're not afraid of death, when we are?"

Sister Hancock snorted, "Are we? I certainly wish that Resolved was a little more afraid of death, the idiot." She used some tweezers to pull something disgusting looking out of the stuff on the tray. "I don't think that I'm particularly afraid of death, though I'd rather not die at this point. There's so much to do."

"But you . . ." Rejoice bit her lip.

Sister Hancock set down the knife. "Yes, I am afraid of Brother Hancock dying. If I could have one wish, it would be that we could go together, but I never pray that wish. It comes too close to telling God how to run things.

God knows better than I do what kinds of life experiences I should have."

Rejoice swallowed. "I'll go take these down." She held the bowl away from her as she scurried down the hallway.

In the hexacrab access room, Elder Chin smiled. He took the bowl reverently from her hands and laid several teeth on the transparent floor. "I will put these with the basalt flakes in the storage compartment. When we reach an island, the hexacrabs can pick up some clingers and make some teeth-studded lances."

"Why don't they just make more diamond-studded lances?"

"Did you hear that, Ur-Veena?" Elder Chin spoke into the translator.

Ur-Veena whistled as the tips of one tentacle traced the outline of one of the teeth on the floor. "Shatter-stone cuts, yes. On another leg, a lance of torpal teeth tastes like trist to the eyes."

Rejoice looked at Elder Chin.

"On another leg means 'but' or 'however', like our 'on the other hand'. I transliterated it because I liked the phrase. Trist is a fungal growth on some of their seaweed they cherish as a special treat. So he said that he thinks lances made of torpal teeth are more beautiful than those made with diamonds." He picked up one of the teeth and examined it. "Ur-Veena, do you have a story about torpal that you can share with us?"

Ur-Veena sucked in his eyes and was silent for a minute, then extended them again. "Yes." Sa-Issi clambered onto Ur-Veena's shell and reached up two tentacles to touch the glass where the teeth lay. Elder Chin leaned forward.

"The story is told by Sa-Fassi about Sa-Tsesta in the Sa cluster before the Dark Death. The nursery had endured sickness and maggots beyond the count of sand. The people bit maggots until their gills clogged with their bodies."

"Excuse me," said Elder Chin. "Do you know where that Sa cluster is?"

"No. No lot-chosen to wander from the Sa have come since the Dark Death."

"Then why was your returning child named Sa-Issi?"

"The coloring and shape of his shell is Sa."

Elder Chin entered a note on his computer, as he muttered, "I hadn't noticed any difference, but we'll figure that out later." He said out loud. "If you please, continue."

"A great weariness weakened the people after the cleansing of the maggots. Sa-Tsesta alone stayed to watch. In the time of dark when eye vision fails, the teeth of a single torpal came to trouble the waters. Single it was, but longer by two tentacles than most, and lean with an empty belly. It swallowed even the bits of maggots. It smelled the nursery, small prey, but larger than maggots, and our enemy chose to open its mouth upon the children.

"Sa-Tsesta lunged and thrust his lance, but the cloud of dead maggots blinded him, and his lance only scraped the hard head. The torpal turned his mouth and sheared off three legs.

"Sa-Tsesta tumbled away and thrust again, severing the cord of tail. The torpal turned his mouth again and cut off three tentacles. Sa-Tsesta rolled, limbless on the portal side. The torpal turned again. Sa-Tsesta thrust and pierced the torpal's middle eye. The torpal crushed Sa-Tsesta's shell with half a bite before it vibrated and turned its belly toward the edge of the world. Sa-Tsesta pinned its jaw to its brain.

"The next day, the people found them. They feasted on torpal for a hex of days. Sa-Tsesta, they carried to the cluster in honor and fed him the first of all they gathered. This continued until child departure season. The people carried Sa-Tsesta to the edge of the deep waters, and with his remaining eye, he saw the children he had protected swim away. Sa-Tsesta asked to stay and sing his song of victory. The people waited and he sang. They sang for victory also.

"As they sang, a kraken rose from the deep. They submitted to the beak, Sa-Tsesta first, and then half the cluster before the kraken turned back. One half remained, and Sa-Fassi tells the story. May the kraken let us live."

The hexacrabs released their grips on the handholds and drifted away from the ceiling. Elder Chin stared at them and did not move or speak.

Rejoice stared at them also. Submitted to the beak? The kraken ate their hero? She swallowed. May God grant they never met what could beat a hexacrab.

CIRCUMNAVIGATION CHAPTER EIGHT

Far below the Magellan, lower than any living adult hexacrab had ever gone, Ur-Veena and Sa-Issi drifted on a shut-off scooter. Pressure squeezed Sa-Issi. He whistled, "Question? Why did we come here where the water presses so hard?"

"To feel the currents"

"Who lives in the deep where we go as children but do not remember?"

"The Ancient Ones, may they let us live. Do not speak of it now."

Sa-Issi toyed with the mesh bag filled with torpal teeth. "Question? When was air-ocean Chan-Tot afraid?"

"When you were still tied to my shell. Another dark death swam through the space-ocean, searching for rocks to make them bleed. The air-ocean people saw it with their metal eyes. They could not breathe until we gave them blades to fight the dark death."

"My soft parts are shelled with courage. I will fight whoever harms the nursery."

Ur-Veena stroked the little one's tentacles. "Yes, you will. My eyes extend to see the day when females fight beside you."

Sa-Issi curled his tentacles. "Females cannot even speak."

"Before the Dark Death, they did. We wander the world over to search for females who can speak and live lives of honor as we do."

"You say the eating of barnacles on the library is the female's honor."

"Lay eggs; eat barnacles, what else can our females do? That must be their honor." Ur-Veena switched on the scooter. "It is time to rise."

Sa-Issi clutched his bag. Next time he would fight a torpal with a blade rimmed with teeth.

CIRCUMNAVIGATION CHAPTER NINE

ejoice awoke to an incessant beeping from her computer on the desk. She fumbled her way through the dark, turned it on, shifted the tiny desk light so the glow wouldn't wake Opportunity in the next bed, and checked the screen. Harmony wanted to talk to her. After rubbing her eyes, she accepted the call.

"Rejoice? Is that you? I can't see you."

Rejoice whispered. "Of course you can't see me. I'm in my room. Do you know what time it is?"

"I can't sleep. I need to talk to you and I want to see you. Please go to the camera."

"I got to bed real late and just got to sleep. I'm going to need to get up in a couple hours and I don't want to wake up my sis—" Opportunity blinked at her with solemn eyes. Too late. She sighed. "Look, give me ten minutes to wash my face. I'll call you back."

"Don't tell anyone I called, okay?"

Rejoice switched off the call with a suppressed growl in her throat. She wasn't about to agree to keeping a secret. Secrets were for little girls like Opportunity who thought you wouldn't notice the smear around the mouth from the stolen chocolate. "Come on, little girl." She picked up silent Opportunity and carried her to the women's bathroom/laun- dry/shower room. Splashing water on her face helped her wake up, but didn't improve her mood, especially when she found out Opportunity had wet and needed to be changed.

Fifteen minutes later, she tip-toed over the hexacrab floor, trying not to wake them. The vibrations of the circulating pump tickled her bare feet. She turned the light on low in the radio room and flipped on the screen and camera.

"Oh, hello sweetie," Harmony crooned to Opportunity, but worry lines creased her face.

"Why this hush-hush call?" If she got this call over with quickly, maybe she could still get some sleep before getting up to make breakfast.

"I want to find out what really happened to Uncle Resolved."

Rejoice rolled her eyes. Her best friend had driven her crazy during the warp voyage of seven years, had driven her crazy in the colony, had driven her crazy with nonsense calls during her mission in space, and apparently intended to drive her crazy now. "Didn't you read the reports everybody sent in? Didn't Brother Hancock talk to you face to face?"

"Of course I read the reports. Everybody read the reports. That's all anybody in the whole colony can talk about. The whole cluster too. Sa-Pisa says the child he catches he'll name Sa-Chan-Tot."

"Sa-Pisa is old enough to catch children?"

Harmony waved the question aside. "I'm afraid they didn't tell us the whole story so we wouldn't worry. You didn't send in a report."

Rejoice rolled her eyes again. "We all saw the same thing. All I can add is that I felt like throwing up the whole time."

"Rejoice, you're my best friend. Please tell me the truth. Is Uncle Resolved going to die?"

"I don't think so."

"He was so white when he talked to me."

"I know. None of us are the right blood type to give him any. And what Mother pumped into him isn't red."

A noise made Rejoice turn. No entered the access room, rumpled, but dressed and his black hair combed. What was he doing up at this hour?

He knelt and briefly pressed his palm against the floor twice for 'Hi-Bye', the human approximation of the hexacrab gesture that meant 'I see and acknowledge you, but have no time to visit.'

The hexacrabs were awake. Right. They slept very little. She had rudely walked by them.

"Is everything okay?" No whispered as he walked into the radio room. His eyes lit up when he saw Harmony. "Good morning."

"Uh, hi, No," Harmony said.

No grinned. "Okay. Out with it."

Harmony looked beseechingly at Rejoice for a moment. "I was calling to see how Uncle Resolve is."

No said gently, "What did Brother Hancock tell you yesterday?"

"Not to worry."

"What are you doing?"

She cast down her gaze. "Worrying."

"That should remind you of something we discussed just last week. What was it?"

"Um . . ."

As Harmony worked on remembering, Opportunity grew heavier and heavier. Rejoice tried to set Opportunity down, but her sister whimpered. So she picked her up again and left.

She walked rudely past the hexacrabs again and lay Opportunity down in their room, but the girl cried. Finally, she flipped the light off and snuggled with Opportunity in her bed. She fumed at the black ceiling while she patted her sister's back.

Before she had left to move the asteroid, Harmony had often come around, supposedly to talk to Rejoice, but really to be near Stronghold. Was that what she was doing now? Using Rejoice to have an excuse to talk to No? If so, what sense did that make? She had been married for only a week. Was she already so disappointed in Stronghold? But what—? Rejoice rolled over and moved her pillow. None of it made sense. What was she not seeing?

The next thing she knew, the morning bell was ringing, so she must have fallen asleep after all. She rolled out biscuit dough while Mother washed and combed Opportunity. She took breakfast to Brother Hancock and made it back to the dining room after everyone else but No had sat around the table. Elder Chin recited the Morning Prayer.

Rejoice rubbed her eyes again. It seemed unfair that No could sleep in while she had to work in the galley. "Where is No?"

"Studying," Elder Chin spread blackberry jam on a biscuit.

"Here's my find for the morning papers." Sister Hancock triumphantly set three small jars on the table. In one floated a whitish ribbon, in one a black, slug-like mass, and in the last one, a mottled ball with sharp barbs.

"What have we here?" Father picked up the jar with the mottled ball and held it up to the light.

"Torpal parasites," Sister Hancock said.

Rejoice put down her fork.

Mother picked up the ribbon. "Looks like a tapeworm. My goodness, look at the size of it."

Rejoice didn't want breakfast anymore. How could these people be so delighted with bits of bodies and parasites? Even Elder Chin peered at the jars.

She was saved from gagging by a call from Constancy. After Rejoice had described in great detail the previous day's events, she got another call from Abiding. After her sixth call, she told her friends to read about it in the news, and that cut conversations short. The thirteenth call was the last.

Then she escaped to her room for some peaceful time. However, peace eluded her. Two of the calls had been from Sister Guthry and Sister Carlson. Rejoice yawned as she thought about them. Why did she like older ladies better than people her age?

She scanned the Bible, but she couldn't concentrate on the words. She yawned again and put on a math program. Usually, solving equations calmed her, but not this morning.

Was No avoiding her? He had not yet sat down to a meal with the rest of the crew. When did he eat? Elder Chin had said he was studying. What did a person like No study? Hmm. She tuned her screen to his. He had pulled up a manual on ship engine diagnostics. Made sense. He was supposed to be the ship's engineer, though how anyone as fumble-fingered as him could be engineer of even a child's wagon escaped her.

Father wasn't on-line. Mother was talking to Deaconess Redhorse back at the colony. Rejoice quickly switched away before she heard any of the discussion. Sister Hancock was working on a manuscript for a textbook about torpal anatomy. Elder Chin was flipping through notes about Hex. Rejoice turned back to No's computer. He was still on the same page.

Was he trying to memorize it? Probably he had fallen asleep on his computer because he had gotten up so early.

Rejoice jumped when someone knocked on her door. "Come in," she shouted.

"Hello there. I wanted to see what you were doing," Mother said.

Rejoice's scalp prickled. Mother didn't spy the way Rejoice had just been doing. She resolved to stop.

Mother came in and tugged on the brown sleeve of Rejoice's dress and studied her screen as her hazel eyes crinkled. "Now why did I think you would be doing math?"

"I should be doing something else?"

"Actually, yes," said Mother as she sat on Rejoice's bed. "I've been looking through your academics, and this voyage could be long enough for you to earn your first bachelor's."

Unmarried men? "Bachelors?"

"College degree."

Weariness dropped onto Rejoice. "Mother, when do I get to graduate and stop studying?"

"Ha!" Mother said. "When did I graduate? We all need to study all the time because the colony is still too small for anyone to learn only one job and then quit."

"Okay." Rejoice shrugged. "I'll learn how to milk cows too."

Mother giggled. "That should be hard to do on this trip. No. I would like you to go ahead and earn a degree."

"We're a thousand light-years from the nearest university. Who's going to give me this degree?"

"I am. Now, as your college advisor I've drawn up a list of the classes you need to take to get a bachelor's of science in astronomy." She popped up the screen on her computer.

"I need to take more astronomy?"

"No. You're already PhD level on that. But you can't get a bachelor's without broadening your horizons. Here's the list. You tell me what you would like to start with."

Rejoice studied the list with bewilderment. Western Literature, Eastern Literature, World History, The Puritans and Quakers in England, Art History, Physical Education, Old Testament Poetry, Economics, Psychol- ogy . . . What did these have to do with anything? "I thought all the psychologists back on Old Earth taught lies."

"Not all the psychologists. Not all the time. And even the false teachings can show you how far from God man can wander when he tries to. Did you want to start with psychology?"

She didn't want to start with any of them, but what was the point of arguing? "No. Economics, please." At least that would have numbers in it.

Mother hummed a brisk sea chantey as she set up the program to download the economics course from the Starflower the next time the spaceship orbited overhead.

"Mother, how did you meet Father?"

Mother closed the computer and sat back with a smile that spread across her face until her eyes danced. "The choir from our church went to another church to put on a special program. The whole time we sang, one handsome young man kept staring so hard at me that I wondered if I had something stuck in my teeth. Afterwards, he introduced himself, and then he introduced me to his mother, a saint whose trials had burnished her to pure gold. We went for a walk, we started talking. And we never stopped talking. I'm a very blessed woman."

Rejoice traced the infinity sign on her desk with a fingertip. She should have dusted the desk that morning.

Mother tugged at the ribbon that pulled back her curly brown hair. "You seem sad, Rejoice."

"I don't know. You had another church to go to find someone. I don't have another church to go to."

"Hmmmmm. I remember before you left to fight the asteroid, you said you never wanted to marry."

"A person can change her mind, you know." Rejoice breathed in deeply the smells of the room, salt air, cotton blankets, the sharp tang of ammonia that still lingered even though the bedding on Opportunity's bed had been changed. "But it doesn't matter. There's no one on this whole planet for me to marry."

Mother placed her hand on Rejoice's. "Don't fret. If God calls you to singleness, you can find great joy in that. Anyway, you're still young."

"What's going to change in two years? Are new colonists going to warp over any time soon? I did do some reading on the Starflower. I found out that on Old Earth teenagers are allowed to date people they're not married to, and they can get engaged before they're eighteen years old."

Mother's expression did not change. "So?"

Rejoice sighed. So why had she bothered to bring it up? "Why did you let Harmony marry Stronghold even though she's too young?"

"Stronghold is old enough. Also, since we couldn't be home to help supervise the courtship, it seemed best to let them marry. Oh, Rejoice. Why do you deliberately make yourself unhappy? There are plenty of good young men in the colony."

That was too much. "Name one."

Mother sat back. "Well, here's Young Man Cruz, right on this ship. He's a fine young man, diligent and hard-working."

And stupid. "What about Not? I suppose you think he's a fine young man too."

"Of course. He's been a good friend to you."

Mother had no understanding of reality, none whatsoever. "Mother, I don't understand this trip. Why am I here? All I do is babysit and wash dishes."

Mother arched her eyebrows. "You mean you haven't been analyzing the satellite photographs?"

"I've analyzed them enough to know that analysis is useless. Our satellites can't resolve anything smaller than a meter. Yes, there are unknown moving objects in Half Moon Bay, and they're going to stay unknown until this ship physically reaches Half Moon Bay and we look at those UMOs with our own eyes. Why do we have a few satellites with crummy cameras? The colony has had three years to build and place better satellites."

Mother smiled as though Rejoice had told a joke. "The satellites with crummy cameras were all we could afford. And they were good enough for weather forecasts."

Rejoice tried to keep the impatience out of her voice. "I understand why we brought only three satellites. I don't understand why we haven't built more. I sent over one hundred thousand tons of metals to New Earth. Or why couldn't we just fly over the islands with our shuttle and take pictures with better resolution?"

"You'll have to ask your father that. I believe that he said that it was suggested. But there wasn't a camera with the right specs. Making the camera was tabled due to other priorities."

"What other priorities?"

Mother took a deep breath and started ticking off points on her fingers.

"We needed to build a birthing center. We needed to build barns. We needed to build houses for all the new couples. We built the ship. We—"

"One ship. Even Columbus had three. Why are we mounting an exploration with so few people and supplies? Why?"

Mother held up her hand. "Rejoice, I can't give you an answer that will make you happy. Why don't we maintain peace by moving on to another subject?"

"Like economics?"

"That will do." Mother laughed and waltzed out singing a song about the hills clapping their hands for joy.

Rejoice watched her walk out of the room. How had Rejoice lost out on her inheritance? Why couldn't she have gotten the happy gene that made Mother bubble everywhere? Father liked to say, "Be grateful to God that life's not fair, and learn to live with it." She tuned her screen to look at the gathering clouds.

* * *

A week of rain drenched the Magellan and Rejoice's spirits. The ship was too small to endure staying below deck all the time, but going above deck meant risking being blown off. Father had warned her about sea sickness, but all were blessed that none seem to suffer from it much. Only Elder Chin on the worst days had to take the medication that made him drowsy.

No still missed half the meals, and when he did show up, he stared at whoever spoke while he wolfed down more food than Rejoice thought any one person could eat. And when no one was speaking, he stared at Rejoice with a mournful gaze that reminded her of begging dogs.

Rejoice spent that wretched, wet week trying to think of ways to converse with No. Once, she saw him typing in the dining room after everyone else had eaten and left. She sat across the table from him. "What are you doing?"

He closed the screen. "Writing a letter to Sister Olson."

Sister Olson, the woman who never missed a chance to criticize Rejoice. She tried to say neutrally, "Oh. What about?"

"It is a private matter," he said with a gloom that matched the low, gray clouds outside and the rain that washed the porthole behind his head.

"Oh, ah, excuse me then." She returned to the galley to wash dishes and scrape carrots for a carrot cake. She hoped No Cruz wasn't reporting prideful behavior on her part to Sister Olson. She couldn't think of anything prideful she had done, but when it came to Sister Olson, nothing you did was safe. Her mind raced back to the last humiliating confrontation with Sister Olson after the speech and then Sister Olson crying on No as they were leaving.

Rejoice rinsed a bowl. Her cheeks heated at the memory of Sister Olson. And No was writing to her. On purpose. About something private. She went to the freezer and counted out the frozen eggs for the cake. Who cared whom No wrote to? She had satellite photos to look at and asteroids to track and name.

She thought of Not By Works. He was happy with Every and working hard extending fences for Brother Jefferson. All her friends worked twelve hours a day in the fields or the mutable factory making beams this week and tractors the next.

Stronghold worked the kelp farms. Smart of him to refuse to come. No, maybe not. She was getting to know Opportunity and he wasn't. But then he was getting to know Makepeace again and she was not. God grant that he would be as kind to their little brother as he was on the Starflower and not as fractious as he had been when they first arrived. Finally he was happy and getting to know Harmony. Rejoice had thought she knew Harmony, but she couldn't figure out what that girl was talking about with No.

Rejoice carried flour from the huge pantry that held enough staples for a year. Math was so neat and precise. Two plus two was always four in the decimal system. But who could figure out people?

* * *

Hurricane Nasty tossed the ship around so much that Rejoice had been bounced off her cot. Poor little Opportunity had thumped into the wall. Her nose bled over herself and the bedding. The day after that the sky shone with a brittle clearness that called everyone to the deck. Father replaced a broken solar cell. Mother laid mattresses and sheets on the railings. Sister Hancock tossed some bright orange radio transmitters overboard to be tracked for the next ten years so the currents could be charted. Rejoice held Opportunity's leash and walked her around the deck.

When they rounded the curve of the bridge, No and Elder Chin leaned on the railing of the bow and stared out to sea. They both wore the blue work overalls, but Elder Chin wore his white shirt neatly buttoned and Noble's shirt hung in a wad from his back pocket. The wind carried Elder Chin's words to her, "No, I absolutely forbid it. You are who you are, and that is either accepted or it is not. It is better by far to find out before it's too late."

A private conversation. Rejoice quickly turned her little sister to retrace their steps. What was he forbidding? Then, to distract her mind from the sinful desire to pry into other people's business, she pulled out her screen and called Stronghold. She pulled down the folding chairs from the wall, and sat Opportunity on her lap so she could talk.

"I'm glad you survived the storm, Sis," he said.

"Made me wish I was home with you," Rejoice said. Opportunity wiggled out of her lap and sat on the deck to play with her cloth doll. Rejoice wrapped a loop of the leash around her hand. "Today is nice, though, with a breeze so it doesn't feel so hot. We're trying to air everything out. Let me see, we're about a week from the Necklace Chain Islands."

"Wish I were on a ship," said Stronghold. "It's so hot here, the hens are laying hard-boiled eggs."

Rejoice rolled her eyes. "How's Makepeace?"

"He's changed a lot in the three years that we were gone. His talk makes a lot more sense now. But he's still sad and misses Father and Mother. I do wish I could see my littlest sis grow up. How are you two getting along?"

"Well, you saw what close quarters we have. She's such a sweetie, but Mother says that she's as strong-willed as her big brother."

"Uh-oh. You better keep a tight hold on that leash."

"I always do."

They said their good-byes and Rejoice felt better. They got up; walked around the sail housing and came upon Sister Hancock who bent down to pat Opportunity on the head. A dip net dripped on her shoes.

"Trying to catch a naspy?" teased Rejoice.

"I'd like to," Sister Hancock said. "We haven't seen much native life yet, and I'm dying to find out what the sting of the naspy is."

Opportunity tugged on her leash and pulled Rejoice away. What a useless trip. All they had discovered so far was one torpal, their own salmon, and two new kinds of hardhead fish, one with ridges, and one with spikes. No naspy, no kraken, no churtrees, none of the other creatures the hexacrabs told them had populated the sea before Dark Death.

Perhaps it was just as well. Everything the hexacrabs described sounded icky, especially the air-ocean churtrees. They ate hexacrab eyes.

Rejoice and Opportunity walked up the other side of the bridge.

No and Elder Chin still talked.

No's hands wrapped around the top railing. "But it's so hard."

Elder Chin snapped back, "Who told you that it should be easy?"

Rejoice steered Opportunity around again. She walked her in a U-shaped course from the bridge, past the doors to below, around the solar-cell-encrusted sail slat housing to the stern and up the other side.

This time she found No alone doing push-ups on the deck. It seemed to her a shame to waste the first good day in weeks on push-ups. Furthermore, he blocked the walk.

"Oppy, about face!"

No turned his face up to stare at her. "Why don't you join me?"

Rejoice stared back. "Excuse me?"

"I noticed you never exercise. You should, you know."

"I can't say that I do." Why did he think it was any of his business? He smiled as he lay with his chest and palms pressed against the deck and his elbows up. Rejoice tried to think what that reminded her of; a memory of Old Earth, where she had lived until she was five; and then she had it. He reminded her of a grasshopper. But grasshoppers didn't stare with such intensity. She looked away. Let him win the staring contest.

"Brain cells work better in a body that is not sluggish."

Rejoice took a deep breath and counted to three slowly. Staring wasn't enough, he had to insult her too. "My brain cells seem to be working fine, thank you."

With a grunt, he pushed himself up and stood. "Isn't there something about yourself you would like to improve?"

Her situation. She wished she was sitting on Ocean Shore Boulder having a picnic with Not By Works. "Not really."

"What?" he mocked. "Have you achieved perfection already?" Before she could reply, he grabbed the railing, jumped, and stood again, wobbly, on the top railing. "Wouldn't you like to improve your balance?"

Rejoice clutched her throat. "What are you doing? Get down before you get hurt!" Opportunity squealed and clapped.

He wobbled a step, then jumped off. His shoes thumped on the deck. "Why don't you try?"

"I'm not interested in falling into the ocean. There's torpal in there."

"If you feel like you are going to fall, you simply jump back to the deck. Come on. I'll hold your hand to keep you steady."

Opportunity squealed again and swung her leg over the lower railing. The rest of her could not squeeze between the lower and middle railings, but she tried anyway.

"Come on. You don't know what you're missing."

Rejoice eyed the railing and the blue sea sparkling beyond. The sheets on her right rippled slowly in the cool breeze. Actually, it did look fun, something in short supply on the voyage. She attached her sister's leash to the railings with a click that echoed in the pipes. "Okay." She hiked up her dress past her knees. Somehow, she had ripped her pants near the left ankle. She climbed cautiously.

"Here, put your hand on my shoulder."

She did, and the feel of his warm flesh under her hand made her wish he was wearing his shirt. She stepped up to the top railing. He took her hand and slowly raised it as she teetered. The deck seemed unreasonably far below, and when it came to the sea— She closed her eyes. She hadn't had this much vertigo floating in space. She had ceased to notice the rolling of the ship weeks before, but she became anxiously aware of it now.

"I think—" she said; and then her feet slipped. She plummeted over the side.

No squeezed her hand and pulled. She arced through the air and whacked into the side of the ship. Her hand tore out of his. She splashed into the water.

Her hip radiated pain. Salt water sluiced over her face. She clawed frantically at her dress as bubbles and hair and water obscured her vision. Suddenly, she was three years old again and panic filled her heart. It was like when she had tried to walk onto her imagined silver path to the shining moon off the end of pier. The lukewarm water pulled her down and filled her mouth when she tried to scream for Father.

When she bobbed up in the air, a white life preserver floated near her. She choked on water and slipped off her filter mask. She went under again. She was going to drown. Despite the pain in her diaphragm drawing up her knees, she forced her legs down, scissored them and propelled herself up again. She had her face in the air again, but how could she get the water out of her lungs?

The alarm clanged on the ship sliding away from her. The propeller could chop her into bits if she were sucked into the whirling blades. She forced herself to kick again. The life preserver drifted nearer. Rejoice grabbed the ring. The stern of the ship passed, and the wake smacked her in the face. She swirled in an eddy. She pulled herself onto the preserver and coughed until she thought her throat would tear out.

Rejoice pushed back hair and hat. On the deck No tied a rope around another life preserver. She sucked in breath as the solar slats rotated about the mast and the ship began a ponderous turn. When she was rescued, she was going to give him a piece of her mind.

The sea sloshed in her shoes and drug on her skirt, making it nigh impossible to swim. She ought to kick off her shoes, but if she did, she would have only one pair left, and when they got wet, she would need to go barefoot.

Something gripped her leg.

She screamed and thrashed with everything she had. She twisted and kicked. "Torpal!" Her heel rammed into something hard. She screamed again and tried to put the life preserver between her and the teeth.

Then she saw the blue tentacle.

She clutched the life preserver to her chest as her heart skidded. This was Ur-Veena. She hadn't been kicking the armored head of a torpal; she had been kicking Ur-Veena's scooter. Her shoes had departed sometime during that fit. Rejoice looked back to the ship, praying that Sister Hancock wasn't recording this for the edification of the colony. No dove into the sea with the tied life preserver in his hands. His shirt fluttered behind.

After he reemerged, he swam toward her with long strokes. The rope trailing behind him lifted out of the water as the end tied to the railing pulled away from him.

Rejoice pointed. "No! Look!"

The rope pulled taut and jerked No back. A tangled loop lifted his ankle out of the sea. His hands groped for the knot as his body twisted in the ship's turbulence.

Father grabbed an ax snapped to the housing wall, and with one slash severed the rope.

Their lifeline fell into the sea, and No righted himself. The ship continued in a large radius.

After he had freed his foot, No swam to Rejoice and floated before her with his arms crossed on the life preserver. "Are you all right?"

"No," she said curtly.

He wiped his sea-glazed face. "You jumped the wrong way."

"You idiot!" she shouted. "I didn't jump! I fell!" Whoops, she had just earned a reprimand.

He watched the Magellan's slow arc for a minute. "I should have had you practice on a pipe lying on the deck first."

"You should have left me alone."

He wiped his face again. "I'm sorry."

Rejoice looked away. She couldn't say, "I forgive you," yet. "Why isn't Ur-Veena scooting us to the ship?"

Silence made her look back at him.

He was staring at the water thoughtfully. "That's a good question." He ducked under the water, swam alongside the scooter, and then spurted back. "Out of charge. The hexacrabs can't read our dials. Ur-Veena's using another scooter to drag it back to the ship. Someone should invent one they can read. I don't know why we haven't done that yet. It should be easy." He shook his head, flinging water like a dog. "You could do it."

Rejoice shivered in the breeze, and submerged more of herself to get out of the wind. Her screen! She pulled it out of the water. Smashed, crushed when she hit the hull. No wonder her hip hurt so badly. Rejoice stared at the broken screen, trying not to cry. She must say peaceful things, think peaceful thoughts, but all she wanted to do was hit No on the head with it.

"Looks bad," No said.

Rejoice gritted her teeth. Seek peace. Seek peace.

"I guess you get the spare computer."

"*The* spare? There's only one?"

"Now there's none."

The Magellan occluded the sun. Rejoice grabbed the bottom rung of the ladder on the port side of the ship. Her hip felt like it was broken. Tears dripped from her eyes as she pulled herself up each rung. Father helped her onto the deck as Sister Hancock and Opportunity laughed. Mother alternated between wiping tears and laughing.

When Father took the two life preservers from No, he said quietly, "May I assume you had good reason to pitch my daughter overboard?"

"Uh, no, Sir."

Rejoice limped away from the chortling group. God, how could she live through a year on this ship with him?

CIRCUMNAVIGATION CHAPTER TEN

Ur-Veena pushed the scooter into its charging chamber, grabbed the handholds, and pulled himself to where exhausted Sa-Issi lay huddled on the hull. "I speak loudly of Sa-Issi," he whistled.

Sa-Issi chirped, "Question? Reason for the air ocean people to swim in a herd of slow-bobs?"

"I think they did not know the slow-bobs were floating here. You acted with honor to keep the slow bobs away from them." He did not mention that he had needed to rescue Sa-Issi when his scooter ran out of charge. Ur-Veena poked the clear sack which held a gray green ball with tiny flaps on one section. "You rest while I present this to the Female Chan-Tot."

Sa-Issi snaked a tentacle in front of Ur-Veena's three main eyes. "It still hurts here."

Ur-Veena pulled the tentacle below his eyes to the palps about his beak and gently pressed it. "All the bristles are gone. The poison will hurt for another time of light."

"Question? Slow-bobs can kill the air-ocean people?"

"I do not possess that knowledge. It is possible, for their skins tear more easily than ours." Ur-Veena remembered the foul taste of human blood.

Sa-Issi wrapped five tentacles around Ur-Veena's legs. "Tell a story about slow-bobs."

Ur-Veena clipped the bag holding the slow-bob onto a handhold. "The story is told by Ni-Issa."

"Ni?"

"Before the Dark Death, the Ni lived closer to the libraries than the Ur did. The Nis tended the libraries, and most of the lot-chosen to wander of the Ni joined the Ur. Therefore the Ur came to know much of the stories of our peoples throughout the great ocean."

"There are no Ni in the Sa cluster."

"There are no Ni anywhere. Their nursery has risen above the edge of the world, the water-ocean I mean. Until the air-ocean people found the libraries where air, water, and rock meet, we had no trace of the Nis."

"The Dark Death?"

"Yes," Ur-Veena whistled. He thought of all the shallow seas the Magellan had swum by that should have been crawling with his people populated only by hardheads and worms. "The Ur cluster disappeared, buried by rock that flowed like mud and burnt like the great light. Eight Ur survived and chose to look for the libraries. They hoped to find wisdom to instruct them in that time of death."

Sa-Issi pulled himself closer to Ur-Veena. "You were shelled with courage."

The tips of Ur-Veena's scarred tentacle rubbed Sa-Issi between his eyes as they withdrew. "I was not one of the eight. Ur-Teevi caught me many Child Return seasons later."

"Question? By what means did you know where to follow the Ur adults?"

"I may have started life as a Ni or Ees. My coloring is not recognized. That may be why I have always searched for the libraries, searched for our lost knowledge, searched for all we have lost." He looked at the clear bag with the slow-bob lazily rotating within it. The slow-bob had pricked another tiny hole in the bag. Dozens of tiny holes perforated the bag. In like manner did the hexacrabs prick away uselessly at their loss. Ur-Veena recognized by scent and sight the green gonads strung like beads around the one orifice of the slow-bob. It needed to mate. Being mindless, it would not mind the mindlessness of the female it sought.

Ur-Veena, with a rippling motion, simultaneously shoved the slow-bob toward the entry way, opened the hatch, and tore the bag. The slow-bob drifted out, then caught by the sea the ship was sliding over, spurted out of sight.

"Question? Reason for releasing the slow-bob?"

"I will catch another later." Ur-Veena thought of the air ocean people who had talking females, who bore one child at a time and knew who the father and mother were, who grew their children within themselves. They were a strange people, nearly deaf and blind, unable to taste with accuracy, unable to sense magnetism or electricity without their metal eyes. Still, they possessed females that spoke and swam in warp-oceans. His skin changed a shade darker.

Sa-Issi piped, "The air ocean people wear metal gills and another skin to swim in our ocean. Question? We should wear another skin to visit the air-ocean?"

Ur-Veena seized a handhold, and pulled them further into their niche. "We lack the inside bones in our tentacles that the air-ocean people possess. Therefore, without water, our tentacles fall to the ground. Therefore, we ride in glass niches to visit the air-ocean."

Sa-Issi pressed against the clear hull with two tentacles. "The air-ocean people then push us around. We steer our scooters. The air ocean people steer this world edge presser. Question? We could steer our glass niches?"

Ur-Veena swiveled all three eyes toward Sa-Issi in astonishment. His people saw clearly and accurately much that the air-ocean people could only guess at. But the air ocean people compensated for their blindness with an enormous ability to see what was not but could be. Sa-Issi had just done the same thing. Could that ability be learned to a greater degree? Ur-Veena trembled.

CIRCUMNAVIGATION CHAPTER ELEVEN

Brother Hancock began to shuffle in for meals. He had always been thin and now he was gaunt. The joy in his face as he examined the torpal specimens was good to see, even if the specimens themselves were not. Against her will, Rejoice became interested in torpal physiology and anatomy.

Several days after Rejoice's plunge into the ocean and she had healed well enough she no longer limped, she walked on the deck to breathe fresh air while she contemplated a mapping problem.

No threw something besides spears.

Rejoice watched as he lobbed a greenish-brown ball through a life preserver. "What are you throwing?" She immediately regretted the question. She'd promised herself to steer clear of No Cruz.

No handed her a ball that stank like concentrated ocean. "Algae-kelp balls. They're made up of thirty kinds of algae and kelp, and dozens of kinds of zooplankton and phytoplankton in time release capsules. Brother Hancock told me to put these in the ocean because his samples showed this was like a barren desert here. He doesn't know if that's because of currents or toxins or what. So this year we seed it, and when the voyage is repeated, he'll check this area to see if the seeding did any good."

"So why don't you just dump them over the side?

"And pass up the chance to practice hitting targets? Come on, let's see how you do."

"I'd rather not," Rejoice said, trying to hand back the ball. Small bits of it flaked off.

"Don't give me that limp-wristed, frail female act. See if you can hit the target."

Rejoice stared. Had she heard what she thought she had heard? He had said it in a friendly manner, but the words were rude. She frowned at him, but he still smiled. At least he wasn't asking her to risk her life. She stepped up to the railing and heaved the ball which arced up, then down, and splashed considerably short of the target. "There."

"You can do better than that." He tossed a ball, and it splashed several meters closer to the target. "See if you can beat that."

"You threw it left-handed."

"That's right. I want to become good with both hands. Here you go." He handed her another ball. "I'll do it left-handed, and you do it right-handed, and we'll have a little competition. Now throw!"

Rejoice grimaced and threw. The ball sank only a few meters from the ship.

"That was pathetic." No threw left-handed again, and the splash wetted the preservers.

Pathetic. Rejoice scooped up a ball from the container and stepped up to the railing. She studied the target, practice swung, and then hurled with all her might. The ball splashed within a meter of the target.

The tossing grew into a race, and by the time the container had emptied, Rejoice had hit the target twice and No had done it once, and they were laughing, and the sun was shining, and life was much better than it had been in a long time.

"Same time tomorrow?" No asked.

Rejoice wiped flakes of algae off the skirt of her brown dress. "Yes." There was precious little else to do. And this was fun without getting hurt.

* * *

The next day, Rejoice emerged on the deck rubbing her throbbing shoulder. "I can't do it today. My arm hurts too much."

No dropped the container to the deck with a thump. "Of course it hurts. So what? Here you go."

Rejoice refused to take the proffered ball. "Did you know my arm was going to hurt like this today?"

"Certainly. Anytime you do something new, it hurts. You keep practicing, you get stronger and better, and it stops hurting. But you have to keep practicing." He grabbed Rejoice's hand and placed the ball in it. Then he hefted a ball, and threw it left-handed, and missed the target by several meters. "Your turn."

Rejoice tossed the ball back into the container and winced. Making breakfast and doing the dishes had been an agony. Everything she did with No ended up hurting her. She had never been this sore before. "I don't see the point. What does it matter whether I can hit a target or not? You can practice by yourself."

No shrugged and said pleasantly, "I suppose you can wimp out if you choose to." He turned his back to her and plunked the balls left hand, right hand, left hand near the target.

Rejoice stared at him with her mouth agape. Her chin pulled the mask down her nose. What had she done to earn that kind of rudeness? She walked away before she said something that would earn her a reprimand.

In the privacy of her bedroom, she kicked the bed several times. A year she had to spend with that arrogant young man on a ship that had already grown too small. Why had she agreed to come? Restlessly, she paced her room; four steps this way, four steps that.

Then she thought how much better it would be to pace the deck and simply stay on the side of the ship that No wasn't on.

So she went above deck again and prowled back and forth several times. No splashing occurred on the other side. She peeked around the corner. No was gone. The container lay on its side, half-empty, with some of the balls rolled onto the deck. One ball, in a wet spot, was oozing itself into a greenish slime puddle.

Where was No? She looked over the side, half hoping he had fallen overboard, but only waves curled away from the ship as it plowed through the sea.

Rejoice fumed. He hadn't finished his job. He left this mess here for someone else to clean up. She picked up the slimy ball with forefinger and thumb, and gingerly dropped it over the side. She shoved the container toward the railing so she could tilt the balls out, but she stopped at a thought. If she practiced when he wasn't around, one of these days she could walk casually by, pick up a ball, and pop it on the target when he didn't expect it.

She aimed, threw, and hissed as the ball flew wide. Agony threatened to rip her arm off. She gritted her teeth. If that idiot No had persevered through pain, then she could too. She ignored the fire in her muscles and the occasional tear that seeped out of her eyes, and she emptied the container, ball by ball. She didn't hit the target, but she came close enough to think she might the next day.

That night, she refused to look at No during supper, even when Father leaned forward and asked him jovially, "Young Man Cruz, are you able to sleep through Elder Chin's snoring?"

"Elder Chin snores?"

Brother Hancock and Father chuckled.

Elder Chin arched an eyebrow, which pulled up some of his wrinkles. "So that Young Man Cruz may get the sleep he requires, I wait until he is asleep before I retire."

No sounded dismayed. "Sir, you shouldn't wait up for me."

Elder Chin speared one of the last strawberries. "The longest I've had to wait so far is twenty seconds. It takes me that long to arrange my pillows."

Brother Hancock and Father laughed again, and Brother Hancock said, "Ah, the blessing of a healthy, young body and a clean conscience."

Rejoice crumbled her bread. Why did the adults think No was such great stuff?

* * *

The next day left-over balls littered the deck again. This time she hit the target once, but her arm still hurt. The day after that, she got the container of balls from the Hancocks before No did, and she threw every single ball. Her arm hurt less and she hit the target three times.

The next day, the Hancocks didn't want any algae-kelp balls dropped into the ocean, so Rejoice got permission to raid Mother's embroidery box for material to make bean bags. She found some fabric she could only think of as snot-green. Why Mother had any fabric that nauseating color, Rejoice couldn't imagine, unless it was to make into vomit bags if any of them got seasick. That would be the fabric least missed, so she cut out squares and sewed them into heavy bean bags. From then on, she always kept one in her pocket, and when no one was around, she practiced throwing at various targets.

Several days later, they sailed near their first island chain, a string of forty-seven islands ranging in size from three hectares to boulders a few meters across.

The hexacrabs whistled joyfully as they scooted off in search of clusters. Father and Brother Hancock huddled over the satellite map and sonar maps of the sea floor and plotted the ship's course.

Sister Hancock collected water and sediment samples. Mother gave Opportunity piggy-back rides along the deck and sang cowboy songs to her. No readied two boats for going ashore.

Rejoice brought up the pictures from Half-Moon Bay in Large Archipelago and showed them to Father and Brother Hancock. "The moving blurs always seem to be at the water's edge or going into the water. The longer, larger blurs don't move much once they're on the beach. These smaller blurs seem to come and go from the larger blurs. The smaller blurs disappear when they get about this far from the water's edge. Caves maybe? Are we looking at mothers and babies maybe?"

Brother Hancock smiled crookedly, "Seals."

"Well, like seals maybe. But we'll have to call them something else."

"Sealoids then. But doesn't that sound silloi to you?"

"Excuse me, Rejoice," Father said, "but we're not at Large Archipelago."

"I've checked through the last year and a half's worth of photos of the Necklace Chain. There are no anomalous movements on these islands. They're dead."

Father arched his eyebrows. "Very good. Thank you."

Brother Hancock squinted at the bare rocks. "Actually, this is prime territory for hexacrabs. Most of the sea between the islands varies from one to four meters. Perfect for the nurseries. And further out along here," his finger traced an area on the map, "are kilometers of water five to seven meters deep for their clusters. But as the chain is surrounded by deep ocean, I don't know how they would migrate here. Of course, there might be survivors from before the change in geology."

Rejoice looked up. No stared at them. Father glanced up also. "Ready?"

"Yes, Sir."

No and Elder Chin clambered into the boat laden with jars and nets. Father and Rejoice settled into the boat nearly filled by a four-wheeler with enormous wheels.

Brother Hancock clung to the deck railing for support and watched them go with envy etched on his face. Opportunity wailed that she wanted to go.

"Why aren't Mother and Opportunity coming?" Rejoice shouted over the motor as she tried to look around the four-wheeler. Perhaps he did not hear her; he did not answer for ten minutes. He smiled as he rocked rhythmically. She smiled. The noise of the propellers overwhelmed any sound from him, but surely he was doing his usual tuneless hum. He rocked and hummed whenever he was in focused thought. That familiar motion wrapped her like a warm blanket.

As they neared the shore, Father cut back the engine to a purr and they slowed. "The water is only a meter deep here. See anything?"

Bubbles and reflected sunlight blocked the view of underwater until she looked in her shadow. A mottled, armored fish flicked its thick tail. A small cloud of sand drifted about its head as the dark-blue fish vacuumed the sea floor. A sudden flurry of many legs showed that it had caught a worm. "Hard head," Rejoice said, and then she squealed, "Look! It's a purple and white striped, uh, cucumber! It's beautiful!" She plunged her hand into the water to point.

"Hold it, hold it! What are you doing?" The boat rocked violently.

Rejoice grabbed the gunwales to keep from pitching into the water. "I was just pointing. Shouldn't we collect it for Brother Hancock?"

"Not us," Father said, leaning carefully over the four-wheeler. "You leave that to No and Elder Chin. Even they are not collecting anything radically new until the hexacrabs have looked at it. We are not going to repeat the mistake of harvesting a hexacrab child. How do you know that cucumber isn't another stage in their life? How do you know it isn't poisonous or waiting to bite off your fingers?"

Rejoice sat back and mentally sighed. "I don't know. Pray forgive my carelessness."

"No harm done." Father returned to his seat. "I'll bring Mother and Opportunity when I know the island is safe and not crawling with bloodsuckers or about ready to erupt."

The boat scraped softly on the bottom. Rejoice and Father pulled on long boots, and Rejoice tucked her dress into her pants. Together, they pulled the boat half onto the shore. They wrestled the four-wheeler out of the boat.

Then Rejoice had to rest. The glare from the ocean and the heat radiating from the bare rock threatened to melt her. She panted until Father offered her a drink from a canteen sloshing with ice. The cold water slid down her throat and puddled in her stomach. "Father, why is this the only four-wheeler on the ship?"

"I'm sure one is all we'll need."

Rejoice fanned herself. "I checked. There's redundancy for everything on the ship except some of the lab equipment and the four-wheeler. Why?"

Father climbed onto the seat of the four-wheeler and patted behind him where Rejoice should sit. She climbed on. The vehicle's motor purred, and they crawled up a slope. "This is the only four-wheeler left. It must be enough.

"What happened to the others?"

"The last time you were on the other side of New Sol, we had a hurricane we named Destruction. The building housing the four-wheelers collapsed and crushed all but this one. By the time you got back in communication range, it was old news. Guess you didn't read the back issues of the Chronicles."

"I read some of them." Rejoice leaned against Father's back to help her stay on as the four-wheeler tilted over a ridge. Bare brown rock stretched before them. "Was the warehouse one that No built?"

"As a matter of fact, yes, he was on the work crew that built that one. But it wasn't just his team's buildings that collapsed. We're not building anything with gable ends anymore. It's hipped roofs on everything that doesn't have a dome or barrel vault roof."

And what about the gorgeous blue glass Meetingplace built while she was in space? "Or a pyramid."

"A pyramid is all hipped roof." He slowed as they came to an area pocked with holes.

"So what happens if this breaks down?"

Father stopped the four-wheeler and dismounted. "We either walk or Young Man No fixes it."

"I guess we'll walk a lot."

Father looked at her as if he wanted to say something, but instead he knelt beside a perfect little bowl in the rock with a round stone inside it. "The wind blew this pebble around and around until the pebble and hole smoothed each other." With a flick of his wrist, he pulled out a rock hammer from his tool belt and tapped on the pebble. As Rejoice wandered over the other tiny bowls in the rock, the wind soughed over the island and her father muttered, "Looks like chromium diopside. Let's see. Can I check that in the lab?" He raised his voice. "Keep a lookout for diamonds."

"Why?"

"I think I've got a diamond-indicator mineral here."

"Okay." The hexacrabs used diamonds in their blades and the humans used them for drills and grinders. Carbon was such a wondrous element. One form was soot; rearrange the atoms into a lattice, and you had a bright gem; arrange them another way and you had buckyballs, giant soccer ball-shaped molecules. She rummaged through a cup with several rounded cobbles in it. Then she eyed a small lump of rock about seven meters from her, and pitched the cobbles at it.

"Hey, don't throw away my samples!"

She called back. "They're all the same. I'll save you one." She hit the projection twice. Then she brought the last cobble to her father.

His broad hat brim shaded his eyes. "What were you doing?"

"I'm practicing hitting a target. On the ship I use a bean bag."

"Oh, ho. That's what the thumps on the wall were. And here I thought you were tantruming."

Rejoice rolled her eyes.

"Well, I'm glad you're doing it. It's a good skill to have."

Rejoice leaned on the four-wheeler. The machine reeked of oil and dust and old vinyl. "Why? What difference does it make?"

"You don't know and I don't know. Maybe you'll need to throw something at a torpal someday."

Rejoice sighed. "I'm only doing it until I can hit a life preserver at fifteen meters. Then I'm going to walk up to No when he's sweating like a baked apple, hit that target ten times in a row, and walk away. And then I intend to never throw anything again as long as I live."

Father shook his head. "Rejoice, why can't you give No Cruz a chance?"

"A chance to do what?"

His eyes widened, then crinkled at the corners. He studied her a few moments. "A chance to prove that he is a human being, and a pretty decent one at that."

Rejoice rolled her eyes again.

Father chuckled, "Yes, to be sure. I wasn't very happy with him for inviting you to tightrope walk on the rail. His judgment needs a little more maturing. But I'm glad that he got you exercising."

Rejoice licked dry lips. She didn't want to answer. If she said she didn't like him because he was stupid, she would get a lecture about how God values all people, bright and dull; and if everybody despised the stupid, what would happen to Makepeace? If she said she didn't like him because he was clumsy, she would get the same lecture with the words clumsy or graceful inserted. She shrugged. "I don't like how he's always staring at me."

"Maybe he likes what he sees."

Rejoice grimaced. "I don't think so. He stares at everybody like that."

Father resumed tapping. "To be sure. It's a fact he does like people. And he's observant." He stopped and laid down fragments of rock. "And he's courageous."

"No is? How can you tell?"

Father sat down and clasped his hands in front of his knees. "Didn't you see what happened after the torpal bit off Brother Hancock's arm?"

"I was running to get Mother's surgical kit."

"And you didn't read my report?"

"No. I saw all I wanted to see. I still have nightmares every time I go to sleep."

Father scratched his neck under his filter mask. "So you didn't know that No helped finish killing the torpal which was slashing about everywhere. And then he shared his air hose with Brother Hancock whose air hose had been cut. And he got him back to the boat in time to save his life."

"Uh, no. I guess I thought you did it. Oh, that's right. You told Sister Hancock it was No. I forgot." Was she losing her mind? "The torpal was still alive?"

"It nearly got Ur-Veena before No speared it."

"Oh. Right. I think I even maybe saw part of that. Everything about that hunt is a blur to me."

"If I had tried to rescue Brother Hancock, I'm sure he would be dead today. That's why I wanted a strong, healthy body to accompany us old men."

Rejoice watched the wind blow a fragment of dried seaweed across the rock. Now she was supposed to say something like, "Yes, I will give No a chance," but she wasn't sure she could say it and mean it at the same time. She pressed her lips together.

The radio on Father's belt beeped. He pulled it off and thumbed the on switch. "Holly here."

"The hexacrabs are back," Brother Hancock said.

Whistling followed his words, and then the translation: "No people. Naspy only. Naspy everywhere."

CIRCUMNAVIGATION CHAPTER TWELVE

"The story is told by En-Teppi, the lot-chosen to wander. After the Dark Death, when clusters rose above the world's edge, and that which was in the air ocean fell on the sands, and the water grew so hot that many perished screaming, and the water itself fled and carried many brave people to regions beyond our knowledge; after this Dark Death, says En-Teppi, a hex of the En were left. The cluster now lay too close to the world's edge. Black and foul dirt rained from the world's edge to clog gills and peck like small beaks on the skin. They searched through the longest night when hex after hex of days did not come, and nowhere could they find the nursery."

Rejoice pressed closer to Mother. Perhaps she shouldn't have come. Did the hexacrabs have any stories that weren't horrible?

All the humans knelt on the transparent floor in the access room. Their knees jammed together, forming a sort of porthole into the the hexacrabs' niche. Ur-Veena with Sa-Issi on his back writhed three tentacles about the closest handhold.

"The only female, En-Totsa, died when a current of mud and stones engulfed the searchers like a torpal turning its mouth. En-Sissa lost two legs. Still they searched. They crept along the edge of the deep water and fled where the water burned. Everywhere floated dead bodies, prey and predator in the peace of death together, until they finally dissolved.

"Slowly days returned, and still the people searched. En-Chasti discovered a nursery, not theirs, but one whose cluster had disappeared. This nursery lay half buried, pale and weak from the foul rain. Most tenderly did the En clean the children and stand guard. But the rocks bled and one by one the children died and the En grew weaker."

Rejoice tugged on Father's sleeve and whispered, "What does 'the rocks bled' mean?"

"Oil seep." Father pinched the bridge of his nose. "Sometimes they mean lava."

"The people of En retreated to a far place where they could breathe and live. They thought long about the dead nursery. The currents and land had metamorphosed and the rocks bled to foul the taste, yet might not children return to the nursery? The world was new. No one could say."

Opportunity sneezed. Mother wiped the little girl's nose. Then she took another handkerchief and dabbed her eyes.

"They stayed where they could harvest seaweed until the next child return season. They crawled to the dead nursery and caught three male children. One died, but two lived and grew and learned the songs.

"The next year, they caught two, but as they came rejoicing back, a naspy stung En-Sissa. Year by year, more naspy came and increased like maggots. Some years adults would go and bring back children. Some years adults came back grasping nothing. Some years the adults did not come back and they fed the naspy. Every year the naspy lay in wait."

"So what are naspy?" whispered Rejoice.

"We don't know yet," Father said.

"En-Teppi was caught the three hex hex of years after the Dark Death. Two hex hex years later, he was lot-chosen to wander, and a hex and one-half of years of searching brought En-Teppi to the Ur. To the seekers of the lost libraries that were found, En-Teppi tells the story."

The humans still knelt and kept silence as Sa-Issi slipped off Ur-Veena's shell. The faint thrumming of the circulation pump filled the room.

Elder Chin licked his lips. "When En-Teppi wandered, how many En were there?"

The answer in base six was translated as: "Forty-seven."

Brother Hancock hissed in astonishment. "An increase of only forty-two in one hundred and seventy-four years! How many are females?"

Ur-Veena clicked, "All the females died shortly after capture. None laid eggs."

Brother Hancock groaned, "Then why? Why do the En stay in such a deadly place?"

Ur-Veena whistled and grated harshly. "Shall they allow the naspy to eat the children without fighting for them?"

Brother Hancock ran his hand down his face. "No. Of course not."

Sister Hancock asked, "And children were still returning over one hundred seventy years since the last egg was laid?"

"Yes."

"How can that be?" She chewed on her thumbnail.

Ur-Veena did not answer. He drifted away from the microphone.

Elder Chin switched off the translator. "I believe they are tired and discouraged. We should let them rest."

The humans moved into the dining room. They poured themselves cups of hot mint tea and sat around the table.

Brother Hancock fidgeted with his spoon. "You know, when they talk about naspy, it sounds different from how they talk about torpal."

"You caught that, did you?" Elder Chin said.

Rejoice hadn't. She sipped her tea and wrinkled her nose. It needed sugar. The other colonists had spent the last three years talking to hexacrabs, and she hadn't, so they were sure to see and hear nuances of communication that she wouldn't.

Elder Chin tapped his spoon on the table to emphasize his sentences. "When the hexacrabs speak of the torpal, it is almost with admiration. No, wrong word. Respect perhaps. They see the torpal as a worthy opponent. The naspy they see as more irritating and disgusting, the way we would see rats carrying bubonic plague. And the kraken . . . ."

"They worship?" Brother Hancock injected. Sister Hancock patted one of his few blond strands back into place.

Elder Chin frowned. "I don't think so. I think it's more like a deep reverence. But it's hard to say since they won't talk about it."

"The hexacrabs have had to endure so much." Mother's gaze focused at a far-distant point.

"So why don't we know what a naspy is?" Rejoice regretted the question as No swung his stare to bear upon her. She deliberately kept her eyes on Elder Chin.

"My department," Brother Hancock said. "I hope to find out here. Elder Chin is no help with at least seven different descriptions."

"Exactly what they gave me. I gave up asking after the seventh time. That's when I decided to call the creature naspy, a cross between nasty and an asp."

"So what we have here is either at least seven kinds of small, nasty, and deadly critters; or we have one critter with at least seven stages to its life."

Father slipped his arm around Mother. "Well, Carol, shall we go look at some rocks?" She smiled at him. Then he said to Brother Hancock, "Do you want us to pick up some samples for you?"

He shook his head. "Elder Chin and Young Man Cruz obtained enough to last awhile. Until the hexacrabs are willing to help us catch some naspy I'd like to wait a bit."

"I'll pack a picnic." Mother headed for the galley.

Rejoice watched the sugar crystals swirl in the bottom of her cup as she stirred the green spearmint tea. If Father, Mother, and her little sister boated to an island and the Hancocks consoled the hexacrabs, that left her and No at loose ends. He was still staring at her. Maybe Father was right and he was courageous, but he still gave her the shivers. She couldn't finish the tea. "Excuse me," she said to the room, "I need to do laundry."

Washing, drying, sorting, and folding of the women's laundry consumed ninety minutes. That left two or three hours before time to make supper.

In her room, Rejoice threw and caught the bean bag with one hand. Now what? Maybe she should start on the college curriculum that Mother had set out for her. Reluctantly, she pulled up the first lesson on economics: What is money? She read about barter and how money was a medium of exchange that was portable, divisible, stable, etc. "Who cares?" She shut off the screen. "We don't use money in the colony. Why should I study this?"

She thumped the bean bag against the porthole. A year minus four weeks still to go. It would be too early in the morning there to call someone back at the colony. And tonight the voyagers would be calling Stronghold and Makepeace as they always did, so she should wait until Father and Mother were back. She checked the radio to see if anyone had called the ship and left any messages.

The colony channel was blank, but another channel was being used. She switched to it, and the room filled with the whistles, grunts, clicks, and gratings of hexacrabs. They had their own channel for reporting back and forth? How nice. They spoke so quickly she could catch only an occasional word. Hexacrabs all sounded the same to Rejoice, so she couldn't tell who was speaking. Uh-oh. She was violating their privacy, so she turned it off.

Did the hexacrabs value privacy the way humans did? The next time she saw Elder Chin, she would ask him.

In the middle of a yawn, she scrolled through the ship's log searching for Brother Hancock's rescue. She fast-forwarded through the amputation.

The view swung wildly as Sa-Issi and Ur-Veena tried to impale the torpal. Clouds of blood obscured No's descent in a flurry of bubbles. He speared the torpal below the middle of its spine just as it opened its mouth to gnash Ur-Veena. The monster doubled back to bite him instead. No pulled back the spear in time for the torpal to bite the spear instead of his arm. Behind it, Ur-Veena stabbed the torpal in the gills. No stabbed it in the back again. That finished the monster. The torpal thrashed about in its death throes, but the giant fish no longer bit.

No kicked over to Brother Hancock who was wrestling weakly with his scooter as his air poured out like a fountain from his cut hose. No cut off

Brother Hancock's belt which had gotten caught on one of the scooter projections. Then No shared his air hose with the man as he pulled him to the surface.

Rejoice turned off the recording and started breathing again. Good thing she knew how it turned out before she watched it. No had not looked clumsy there, or at least no more clumsy than any human in scuba gear next to a hexacrab did. She shivered.

Maybe No had changed a lot in three years. Maybe she should try talking to him, though about what she still couldn't guess. Maybe the ship's engine? She laid aside the screen and picked up her comb. And it was nice that he hadn't reported her for calling him an idiot when they were in the ocean. She combed her plain, straight, brown hair.

Probably No was exercising now. Most of the time she went above deck, he was there, throwing spears or doing push-ups or stretching or running. She asked the ship's locater where he was, and found he was in his room.

Rejoice bit her lip as she struggled with the temptation to spy on him, and then she gave in. She tuned her screen to his and saw the last thing she expected: a page of calculus.

The page had examples and problems she had done five years earlier. In the solution blank, No entered hesitant, slow answers. He began to solve one equation incorrectly, and as Rejoice winced at his poor approach, he erased it and started over again, this time correctly. Rejoice could not stand his slow, deliberate pace at something she could whiz through in her sleep. She turned the screen off and thought. Maybe she could tutor him.

A minute later, she knocked on his door and heard faintly his shouted, "Yes?"

She walked in. "Can you talk, or are you busy?"

He stood so quickly he knocked over his chair. He set it upright and snatched his life vest off the back of it in one motion and turned off the computer. "Certainly." No threw on the vest and walked out the door.

Rejoice caught up to him on the deck. Why was he in such a hurry?

"Were you doing something secret?"

He looked at her with merry eyes as he continued walking. "Not at all. I was working on calculus, and frankly, I welcome the chance to take a break. What did you want to talk about?"

Rejoice pulled her hat around so the brim would shade her eyes. The hot sun bounced heat off the deck and a faint shushing sound came from the waves breaking on the Necklace Chain. "Nothing in particular. I was wondering where you wanted to go after you were done with calculus."

"After calculus? Please, I've been beating my head against calculus for the past four years. I must have memorized and then forgotten the formulas and principles thirty times. I'm finally beginning to see the top of the peak. How am I going to reach it if you remind me there are twenty more mountains beyond that?"

"Why do you keep studying it if it's so hard for you?"

"The colony might need me to use calculus someday."

They completed a circuit of the deck and began another. "When did you learn to repair engines?"

"I don't know that I have. I studied once a week under Brother Nguyen. He helped me memorize engine parts and I helped him memorize Scripture. We were about to tear down a tractor engine when I was called to join the Magellan."

Rejoice fiddled with the bean bag in her pocket and the beans sliding under the fabric. "You were called? Everyone before you said, 'No,' huh?"

No Cruz laughed. "That's a terrible pun. Dozens of us applied. I feel honored to be the one chosen."

Rejoice looked off at the sea. Dozens? She had assumed that everyone had been talked into going the way she had been. Yet dozens had applied and been turned down. So why had No, who didn't know what he was doing, been picked? "If dozens of people wanted to go, why did the voyage wait on Stronghold and me to get back from space?"

No shook his head. "Because your father wanted you two to have the first chance to go."

"Didn't that make the dozens who wanted to go angry?"

"Only a petty person would begrudge a father wanting to spend time with his own children. Especially after they had been away for three years."

"So Stronghold turned down what everyone else saw as highly desirable?"

"I'm glad he did, though your father is sorry."

"I think he expected Stronghold to say no."

"He did."

Rejoice was startled by No's certainty. How could he know what Father was thinking? Despite the arrogance implied by thinking he could read people's minds, Rejoice was surprised to feel her heart warming toward him. You had to admire a person who was willing to work so hard at something he was no good at because he thought it might be useful. At least he was trying. Maybe he could be talked to. "I've been wondering why it is that you call Harmony every day."

"I suppose you have."

What kind of answer was that? She pulled away the hair that had blown across her face. Oh, technically she hadn't asked a question yet. "So what is it that you and Harmony talk about?"

"I'm sorry, but I can't talk about it. It is a private matter."

She stared at him. He looked back with begging-dog eyes. "Pardon me?"

"I said that I will not tell you what we talk about."

Right. Now Rejoice saw how the rest of the conversation was supposed to go. She would say, "Why?" and he would say, "Because," and she would ask "Why?" again, and he would laugh, and she would beg, and he would drop a hint, and so forth and so on. Already she couldn't stand it. She saw no reason to go on with that kind of conversation. "Okay." She turned, and walked back to her room.

* * *

The next week filled with activity as the Hancocks set up aquariums in the lab and one of the storage rooms, and stocked them with hardheads, worms, and clingers.

The hexacrabs used the torpal teeth to make several lances, and gave the largest weapon to Brother Hancock. He hung it above the door to the lab.

The hexacrabs saw no use to hunting the naspy, and refused to do it, saying they preferred to spend their deaths on protecting children.

So finally, with thick gloves, long-handled nets, and double-walled jars with thick screw-on lids, No ventured out and collected the purple and white striped cucumbers, lavender anemones, puce bristle-balls, maroon saber-toothed fish, powder-blue sponges, pale-purple jelly blobs, violet knotted strings, sea bladders, squirters, hard heads, mollusks, and snake-like gulpers.

They seeded the seas about the Necklace Chain with ultraviolet-resistant seaweeds and corals. Mother and Rejoice sprayed sandwort and dune grass seeds in a fertilizer gel on the bare rocks, and dusted over that with powdered lichens and mosses. The soil-makers had been used up long before in making of farmlands on Sole. Since the colony lacked the resources to make any more of the nano-machines, they needed to rely on natural processes to create soil on the islands.

* * *

The rains started again, and didn't let up for nearly two months as they visited three more island chains of bare rock. Two were black, volcanic islands. One was low, humped mounds of granite streaked by lines of white quartz. All were desolate.

The clouds closed in, pressing the narrow halls and tiny rooms into prisons. Opportunity cried every day, and every day she cried for a longer time.

Mother started harmonica lessons from Sister Hancock. Father started also, but quit after the third lesson, saying he didn't have the patience for it. Every afternoon, he took a long nap. Sometimes he took one in the morning as well.

One morning, as the rain ran in rivulets down the thick porthole glass and Rejoice mixed pancake batter while Mother heated frozen berries for syrup, Rejoice asked, "Mother, doesn't it seem like Father is sleeping an awful lot lately?"

Mother licked the stirring spoon to see if the syrup was sweet enough. "He has always liked to take naps. When we were courting, I learned to keep him away from horizontal surfaces, or else the date would consist of me watching him snore."

Rejoice sprinkled some water on the griddle. The drops sizzled and danced. Hot enough. "I know he likes to nap. But it seems like he's doing it more than normal."

The plates chinked against one another as Mother pulled them from the cupboard. "He's been working hard for the last several years. If he chooses to relax now, I suppose we can let him. He gets busy enough when we reach land."

"But . . ."

"But what?"

But he didn't look the same as when she had left to dismantle the asteroid. He was three years older, but it was more than that. It was . . . it was what? "I think he sleeps too much."

"I think you should concentrate on your behavior instead of your father's."

"Yes, M'am." Rejoice slid the spatula under the first pancake. Maybe she was letting the rain and Opportunity and close quarters get to her. She was finding it harder and harder to get out of bed herself.

CIRCUMNAVIGATION CHAPTER THIRTEEN

Ur-Veena nipped a wedge from the seaweed frond he had brought with them, and his palps scraped the piece across the edge of his beak. He maintained a kilometer's length from the Magellan behind him. The ship's irritating sonar could still be heard, but did not hurt as it did when he was closer. He pondered on ways to break the sonar. He had not understood how far sonar could reach when he gave permission to the air-ocean people to use it from time to time.

He nipped another wedge, and then handed the frond to Sa-Issi to finish. One tentacle twitched near the lance mounted on the side of the scooter.

Sa-Issi scalloped the edge of the seaweed all around as he watched his elder with all three vision eyes. The light and dark sensors within each opercula of his shell sparkled like flakes of mica. He too thought about the sonar. "It is difficult to believe the air-ocean people can see so far, even to the bottom of the deep."

"They should not," clicked Ur-Veena. "They will disturb the Ancient Ones, may they let us live." His tentacles twitched. "They grow naspy within their world edge presser. They taste the currents with their metal eyes. They cut open every creature, every plant, every rock. They persist in asking us about the hidden things. Egg laying season comes closer with every time of darkness, but still they drift like slow-bobs and cut like little beaks. And nowhere do we find water-ocean people. Nowhere do we find females who can speak. Perhaps our currents diverge."

Sa-Issi stopped nibbling. "Diverge? How can we swim another way? The scooters must be recharged. There is little food for us in the deep." Ur-Veena grated, "I taught you how to crawl. Do not you teach me. We are caught like our females in a corral, a corral the air-ocean people have built."

Sa-Issi chattered with fright. "The air-ocean people gave us these scooters. They gave us a niche in their world edge presser. They take us where we may search for females."

"In such a manner do we care for the kelp beds and destroy all the maggots that would bore into the kelp. That we do so when the kelp is of the proper size, we may eat it."

Sa-Issi released the frond and clambered onto Ur-Veena's shell. "The air-ocean people shall never eat us! We have exposed our soft parts to each other!"

Ur-Veena sucked in his eyes and clicked slowly, "I cannot taste the air currents."

CIRCUMNAVIGATION CHAPTER FOURTEEN

On another morning, dark before dawn, Opportunity wet the bed again and woke up crying. Rejoice took her to the women's laundry to bathe and change her.

No Cruz come out of the men's laundry, yawning.

Rejoice checked her screen. Four-thirty! Did he wake up every morning at four-thirty?

Opportunity kicked and squealed and splashed water all over Rejoice and the floor, which added mopping and more laundry to the nasty business. Rejoice finally got her sister into dry pajamas and a dry bed where she promptly fell asleep. Rejoice lay in her bed and fretted. It was none of her business why No was up at four-thirty. It was none of her business what No and Harmony talked about. Stronghold seemed happy. He seemed ecstatic, in fact. So why was she worried?

And why couldn't she figure out how to get along with No? Thinking he was stupid and arrogant made her feel guilty. She was the evil one being so judgmental and harsh. It was Rejoice's responsibility to think good things about him, but it was so hard.

She had tried to ignore him and avoid him for the past two months. When Rejoice walked around his exercises on the deck in the rain, she pulled her rain coat hood over her eyes. The rare times he showed up for meals, he inhaled food and stared at Rejoice like he wanted to eat her too. At their small Lord's Day services in the galley she made sure that she sat on the other side of Father from No, so that Father's body would shield her from his eyes. The only times he didn't stare at her were when Elder Chin spoke. Then he glued his gaze on Elder Chin, and whatever Elder Chin wanted, No was quick to jump up and get.

The colony had strong privacy rules, and it had them for good reason. The Elders had figured out long ago that the most prevalent sin of a colony with less than a thousand people would be gossip. Still, what was No doing up at four-thirty, no, now five o-clock?

She opened her screen and checked the radio. He was not talking to Harmony. The hexacrabs were talking again, with long pauses between bursts of speech. Rejoice felt sorry for them. They seemed so discouraged after such a long trip and finding no other hexacrabs at all, let alone any talking females.

"Are you studying calculus?" she muttered as she tuned her computer to No's. The screen showed a text from the Bible. Was he reading it in the dark, or was he waking up Elder Chin? Rejoice split her screen and tuned one side to Elder Chin's computer. It showed the same text. Then both screens shifted to another text. So they were studying together. Rejoice turned off the computer. Now she wasn't sure whether she was relieved or aggravated that she hadn't caught No doing something wicked.

She was sure she had to get off the ship before she went insane.

Small quarters she was used to, but constant rain, naked rocks, empty ocean, and a tiny deck were wearing her down.

Perhaps they were wearing everyone down. After breakfast, Rejoice went to help in the lab by cleaning the aquariums. Cleaning the aquariums was tricky, as half the creatures in them were lethal. Rejoice had to wait until the probable naspies had congregated at one end of the tank to insert a partition. Then she could scrub the side they weren't in. Even that was tricky because the aquarium bases were gimbaled so they could tilt with the motion of the ship which meant she must not press hard while scrubbing or she might spill the whole thing into her lap.

One of the partitions jammed halfway down. While Rejoice wrestled with it, Brother Hancock came over to help. When he pushed on it, the partition suddenly broke free and slammed into place. His hand on the top of the partition dipped into the water, and in that fraction of a second before he could pull it out, the sabertooth fish had flashed over and gouged his thumb.

"Ach!!" he shouted as he jerked his hand away. Then he stared ruefully at the gash and the blood running down his hand. Rejoice frantically searched for a towel as he said, "Eh, you don't need to mention this to Sister Hancock."

"Mention what?" Sister Hancock said as she stepped into the lab. The look of intense irritation that crossed Brother Hancock's face told Rejoice she should be elsewhere and be there soon. But even in the galley with the door closed, she could hear them arguing, so she climbed the stairs to above deck and walked in the rain.

Mist and rain had shrunk the world into a wet, grey circle less than a kilometer in diameter. Rain dripped from the sail slats. As the ship pitched, water sloshed about the deck before cascading over the edge. The bright orange raincoat Rejoice wore trapped moisture; the rain pattered against it with dull plops. The air smelled sodden, with less salt, but still permeated by the stench of iodine.

Rejoice turned the corner. No juggled three dark grey balls. Hatless and shirtless, he tossed the balls with evident great effort as the rain flattened his hair against his skull and streamed down his arms and ran off his elbows.

Rejoice stood watching him. Maybe she should try again. There were about nine months and twenty-two island chains yet to go. Maybe now that he had learned she didn't like to banter or flirt, he would behave better. She tugged a little at her filter. "What are you doing?"

Between gasps for air, he said, "Juggling."

Well, yes. Rejoice cleared her throat and tried again. "Let me rephrase the question. Why are you juggling?"

No caught the balls, one, two, three, and set them carefully on the deck where they still managed to thunk loudly.

Rejoice asked, "What are they?"

No leaned on the railing and gulped in air. "The lead weights we use to get the deep ocean samples. They weigh a quarter kilogram each."

That explained why she hadn't seen the balls before. The Hancocks always did their ocean sampling while she was in the galley making breakfast. "You couldn't find anything lighter to juggle?"

No wiped rain out of his eyes. "I find that juggling lead weights gives me a great incentive to not drop them on my feet."

"Why juggle at all?"

He took a deep breath. "I want to be useful to the colony."

Rejoice looked at him and thought about the answer. She had asked, "Why juggle at all?" and he had answered that he wanted to be useful. What was the connection? The colony didn't need jugglers.

His next sentence did not clarify things. "Do you remember when I broke all those glass panes during the building of the pavilions?"

How badly should she hurt his feelings? She did not want to. "Yes."

"After I was transferred to a less dangerous job, I thought for a long time about what had happened. I hadn't just embarrassed myself. I had also damaged a lot of property and set back several hundred people in their ongoing projects." He took a deep breath and wiped his face again. "Saint Paul says that bodily exercise profits only a little, but I saw that I wasn't profiting the colony by even that little bit. I knew that I could never be as coordinated as your brother or the triplets, but I certainly could become more coordinated and stronger." He nudged the balls with his foot. "So I worked out a program to increase my coordination and strength. I learned to juggle and walk on my hands and walk on a balance beam. I lifted weights and ran. And I studied first aid and engines and whatever I could think of that I thought might be useful"

"Astronomy?"

No laughed. "You've got that sewed up."

Rejoice smiled and tugged at the shoulders of her raincoat. The garment felt like her personal sauna. Maybe she should take it off and just get rain-wet instead of sweat-wet. "Do you get up every morning at four-thirty?"

"Yes. Elder Chin is leading Old Testament Studies right now. In two weeks, we'll start Patristics, and after that, the Pauline letters. By the time the voyage is finished, I should have a degree in Biblical Studies."

Now was not the time to bring up the fact that she hadn't started on her degree yet. "You worship Elder Chin."

He looked horrified. "Not at all. I worship only God. But I do respect Elder Chin. It is such a privilege to be spending this time with a great man of God."

Rejoice had never thought of him as great. He just was. "How is he great?"

No motioned to her as he began to walk. She caught up to him and they walked with the wind at their backs. "Think about it. Elder Chin gave up a prestigious job that paid well and gained him a lot of respect to follow Christ. His wisdom and ministry led Elder Smith to the faith and touched many through the Christian university that they founded together. Their goal was to establish a society founded on the precepts of the Gospel, a society without war. When Old Earth refused to allow such a society to exist, they left for a New Earth, not knowing whether he would live or die."

Rejoice laughed. "By that reckoning, then all our parents are great."

"Exactly so."

Rejoice thought about that as they walked around a corner and the wind blew into their faces. They walked in silence until they had turned two more corners and had the wind to their backs again. "Even Sister Olson is great?"

No hunched his shoulders and said, "About her I have thought a, hmm, great deal."

That was a poor play on words. She didn't answer.

"When you're faced with a difficult person like that, I think you have to ask yourself, what would she have been like if she weren't trying to follow Christ? In addition, I think you have to realize that however hard she is on everybody else, she is at least twice that hard on herself." He studied Rejoice's face until they walked into the wind again. They both wiped their eyes when they reached the other side of the ship and No looked earnestly at Rejoice again. "You know, it's funny you should mention Sister Olson. You and she are somewhat alike. Both of you—"

Rejoice's mouth dropped open, though, of course, No couldn't see that through the filter mask. She clicked it shut and then said, "You don't know what you're talking about."

She turned away and ran down the stairs. What was the point of trying to talk to No? He was obnoxious. Nine more months and then back to the colony and far, far away from No. As she pulled off the filter mask, she prayed, "Father God, give me patience. And give it to me right now."

Rejoice reached her door and the faint sounds of Opportunity screaming inside the room. A sign on the door read 'Do Not Interrupt'. So where was she supposed to go to calm down until she could speak words of peace?

Rejoice threw her raincoat at the door and left it slumped and dripping on the hall floor. She headed for the galley to make herself some mint tea and found that someone had already brewed a pot. After pouring herself a cup, she walked into the dining room.

On the closest chair, Mother rubbed some bruises on her leg. Sister Hancock looked woebegone and stared into her cup of tea. Was this a good time to join them?

Mother smiled at Rejoice. "Come sit beside me." She hugged her daughter when Rejoice had done so. "I'm so glad I've got one daughter who won't kick me in the shins to get her own way."

Sister Hancock still stared morosely at her tea. She dabbed at her eyes with her handkerchief. Had she been reprimanded for her argument with Brother Hancock?

Mother patted Sister Hancock's hand. "She will recover."

Sister Hancock blew her nose. Mother turned to Rejoice. "We got word two minutes ago. Sister Olson had a psychotic break."

Rejoice's ears burned. She had just criticized Sister Olson behind her back.

Sister Hancock sighed and said, "The colony is not equipped for something like this."

"Yes, we are," Mother said. "The Ivanovs took the baby, and the

Minkowskis took the two year old. The neighbors on either side are doing the meals and laundry. We take care of each other. What more is needed?"

"I don't know," Sister Hancock said sadly. "If we had it, she wouldn't have had a psychotic break."

Father came in. "Rejoice, I don't expect to see your coat in the hallway."

Rejoice jumped. "Yes Sir. I'm sorry." As she darted out the door Mother said, "Theophilus, sit down."

Rejoice hung up her raincoat in a shower and mopped the hallway. How dreary would it get before the voyage was over?

She sat on the vibrating dryer. Its warmth comforted as she meditated on the dismal days behind and before. She had always thought of Sister Hancock as a calm, placid person. Either she had changed or Rejoice was finally seeing the real person under the mask. Father had said he wanted to spend time with her, but whenever she had free time to talk with him he was sleeping.

And then there was No Confidence In The Flesh Cruz. She had expected him to be obnoxious, and he was, but now and then, like a flashing pinwheel in the wind, he would show traits that Rejoice admired: perseverance, love of God, an ability to analyze, and consideration. Though not toward her.

Then she had another thought. No was glad Stronghold hadn't come so that he could. Maybe he had also hoped Rejoice would reject the offer and someone he liked far better would have gone in her place. Maybe he wasn't trying to be obnoxious, but it just slipped out because he really wished she were someone else.

So who would No rather have been with? Despite the warmth of the dryer, Rejoice shivered. If Harmony had gone, then there wouldn't have been that hurry-up wedding of Stronghold and Harmony. Rejoice slumped and drummed her heels on the dryer door. That didn't make sense. If Harmony had gone, then Stronghold would have gone, and that would have left No on the shore.

If only people made as much sense as numbers. Numbers always did what they were supposed to do and had no hidden motivations. Who could tell what people would do?

Mother danced into the laundry, singing, "This is the way we wash our clothes, wash our clothes, wash our clothes," to Opportunity riding on her hip.

Rejoice smiled and pushed herself off the dryer. One person she could count on. Mother would always find a way to sing about what she was doing. Mother and math: the two constants in a spinning galaxy.

"Edoy, Edoy!" Opportunity said, reaching out her arms.

"Oppy, Oppy." Rejoice picked up her sister and hugged her. Sometimes Opportunity could be a lot of fun.

"Hide 'n see?" she said.

"Not now," Mother said. "I'm giving you a bath. Then you can play hide and seek." She placed Opportunity on the dryer, unsnapped her leash, and said to Rejoice, "Dear love, would you make some potato soup for lunch? Garlic breadsticks with that. And a salad?"

Rejoice ruffled her sister's smooth hair. "Aye, aye."

When Rejoice had everything ready for lunch, she walked down the hall to her room to change her flour-dusted dress for a clean one. Brother Hancock was knocking on her door. A white bandage swathed his thumb.

"Eh, there you are. I want to show you something in the lab." He skipped down the hall. "I found out what the sting of the naspy is. It's great!" He stopped and Rejoice nearly ran into him. "Actually, it's appalling. But it's interesting. Come on!"

In the lab, Sister Hancock focused a camera into one of the aquariums crowding the room. "I'm set."

Rejoice peered into the water. Two purple and white cucumbers lay on sand. One crawled on its belly. The other—Rejoice's stomach lurched—the other looked like a marble wrapped in the loose skin of a cucumber. "What's wrong with that one?"

"I think it's pupating," Brother Hancock said. "I'm keeping a monitor on it to see if it changes into something else. Right now, though, watch the other one." He netted a small armored fish from its tank and dropped it into the tank with the cucumbers. The fish changed color from mottled green to mottled grey and zipped about as if in a panic.

The cucumber reared up the end that was puckered into a six-pointed star and tracked the fish. With small jerks, the cucumber hunkered down.

Rejoice blinked.

A point shot out of the cucumber and imbedded in the flank of the fish. The fish writhed and pulled against the white cord connecting the point and the cucumber. Then the fish stopped. Its eyes glazed over. The cucumber sucked the cord in. The star disappeared into the side of the fish, and the fish skin deflated.

"The sting of the naspy is a poison harpoon," Rejoice said. She had put her hand in the water pointing to the first cucumber she had seen. She might never scuba dive again.

"Isn't it remarkable?" Brother Hancock said. "I can see why the hexacrabs have a hard time defending against that."

"Is it poisonous to humans?"

"I don't know," Brother Hancock said.

"I'd be shocked if it wasn't," Sister Hancock said. "Tomorrow I'll try to run a chemical analysis of the venom and see if it resembles any known Old Earth toxins."

"If it doesn't look like anything from Old Earth, how will you test it?"

Sister Hancock glared at Brother Hancock as his blue eyes widened innocently. "Since we are not asking for volunteers, we shall need to wait until someone is accidentally stung and we can record the reaction. May God grant that doesn't happen for centuries." She shifted the camera over to the pupating cucumber.

Rejoice looked at the rows of aquariums. "Do you want me to finish cleaning the tanks?"

"Ah," Brother Hancock said. "We decided that it's too dangerous a job for you to do."

Rejoice stared at the cucumber sucking the fish. Was the job worth fighting for? She didn't especially like cleaning the smelly tanks, but the chore let her watch little creatures and got her away from No's constant stare. "I'll be very, very careful. I am almost an adult."

Sister Hancock smiled. "Almost."

"Nobody seemed to mind my doing dangerous things on the asteroid."

"Didn't Sister Carlson check every part of your space suit before you went out, and monitor you and your safety?"

Rejoice left without answering. Once they made a decision, they wouldn't unmake it, so why had she tried?

She went above deck. The rain had softened to a drizzle. No hurled spears. He scowled as he grunted and hurled and hauled. Rejoice retreated.

Opportunity was still out of her room, so Rejoice flipped the sign over to Do Not Interrupt, and locked the door behind her. She wasn't hungry anyway. She sat on her bed, brooded, and tossed the bean bag into the far left corner of the ceiling. The room smelled stale and damp.

Finally, in desperate boredom, she called up her last program in quantum mechanics and settled down to a world of sense.

Two hours later, someone knocked on her door. Irritated, she flipped the screen shut and opened the door. There stood Mother, smiling. Rejoice pointed. "The sign says, Do Not Interrupt."

"Good afternoon to you, too. I thought perhaps you had forgotten the sign was up."

Rejoice took a deep breath and released it slowly. "Did you want me to help you with something?"

Mother entered the room, sat on the bed, and motioned for Rejoice to sit in her chair. When Rejoice had done so, she said, "I want to discuss your academic career. As near as I can determine, you haven't started a single class."

"No, I haven't," Rejoice studied her hands. "None of them interest me."

"Nonetheless, you should study them."

"Why?"

Mother sat silent a moment as she tugged on her brown sleeve. "The other colonists are not the only ones who need to broaden their perspective. You need to understand more about the world and the people in it."

"There's only seven hundred eighty-one people in the world. And I'm never going back to Old Earth, so what does it matter?"

Mother sighed. "I see a very narrow minded girl who is getting deeper and deeper into a rut. You need to grow, girl."

Rejoice flipped open her screen and showed a complicated equation to Mother. "Can you do that?"

Pain filled Mother's eyes. "You know I can't."

"Then who are you to say I'm narrow? Maybe I'm deeper than you can stand to see!" Even as she spoke, Rejoice knew she mustn't say that. You don't mock others for their gifts or lack of gifts because God distributed as He willed. Where would Makepeace be in a world that scorned the deficient? Even so, Rejoice burned. "Mother, you tried to keep me from studying astronomy when we first arrived. But after we discovered the asteroid, then you said that God had led me to study astronomy. All I knew was that I thought I would die if I didn't study the stars. Well now I feel like I'm going to die if I don't get off this ship. Is that God leading me?"

Mother stood and glowered at Rejoice.

Rejoice stood and glowered back. "I never wanted to come, but you insisted."

Mother's face changed from anger to sorrow. "You sounded very like Stronghold when you said that."

"Well maybe now I know how trapped he felt!"

"But you weren't forced to come. Why did you change your mind and decide to come, if you didn't want to?"

Sudden tears dropped onto her hot cheeks. She wailed, "I don't know!" She ran at the door, shoved it open, and wailed. "Just leave me alone!"

As she blundered down the hall, she nearly ran into No coming out of the men's laundry, toweling his hair. The stairs echoed hollowly as she pounded up them. Rain spattered on her head and back and she turned, looking. Where was there to go?

Dark sea and dark sky lay before her with no hint of welcome as she walked to the bow and sat on the lower railing and held on to the top railing. She drummed her heels on the side of the ship and stared at the sea splashing into foam against the keel. She had promised herself years before that she wouldn't hurt her parents the way Stronghold had, and here she had just done it. She had belittled Mother's abilities. To top it off, she had embarrassed herself in front of No.

Her thoughts were interrupted by the sound of splashing and the whisk of wet rope. No was target-shooting again. He had finished his exercise routine earlier, so the real reason he was out there was to watch her. Did he fear she would jump?

On the Starflower with its minimal crew, there had been many places to hide and be alone. There was no place on this ship to be alone.

She wiped tears that were quickly replaced. Away from the room and Mother's face, she remembered exactly why she had come. Not By Works had humiliated her, and what was worse, he was totally unaware that he had humiliated her. She had wanted to be loved by Not, and she wasn't, and nobody would ever love her, and why should anybody? She had run away from the pain, only to be jammed into a tighter box with more pain.

She stared at the foam. Maybe jumping wasn't such a bad idea. Yes, it was. No would try to rescue her and the hexacrabs would have to rescue both of them and everyone would make a fuss and then she would never be left alone.

Behind her, the splashing continued. Why wasn't there someplace she could be alone? Rejoice twisted the hold strings of her hat. She didn't want to be alone. She wanted to be with someone who would hold her and say I love you and care about this ache in her heart. The sea and her life stretched out empty before her.

CIRCUMNAVIGATION CHAPTER FIFTEEN

Ur-Veena stared at the two blurs beyond the translucent ceiling. The largest blur moved slightly, spoke, and then the translator crackled, "What else might we meet in this deeper ocean?"

Ur-Veena understood nearly all of the air ocean people's speech without the computer translation, but he had not told them. He found it instructive what they told each other when they were not speaking to him. After pulling the microphone closer, he whistled and grated, "We are not a people of the deep water ocean. We do not remember our swimming lives. We cannot name all that swims." He released the microphone and drifted down to tap his jointed feet on the clear walls of the niche. He had not anticipated his longing to crawl in his cluster again. How had En-Teppi endured his loneliness until he found the Ur cluster? And what had the lot-chosen to wander from the Ur found as they searched an ocean emptied of its people?

Dimly he perceived the hand of the air-ocean male Chin pressed against the transparent ceiling. "We do not ask for what you do not know. Many new sights will cross the vision of our air-ocean and water-ocean peoples. Perhaps a deep swimmer has come for a short time to swirl the shallow waters of your people."

Ur-Veena reached out with two tentacles to stroke the reassuring roughness of his torpal-toothed blade. "My eyes have seen swirling of water seven times. Five times the teeth of torpal, two times in dim distance the Ancient One."

Little Sa-Issi danced in excitement. "Your eyes have beheld the Ancient One?"

The other human spoke. It sounded like the air-ocean male that swam like a slow bob. "Wait a minute. What you call kraken, they call the Ancient Ones, if I'm understanding hex correctly."

"Yes. I translated that phrase as kraken, because when I asked for a description, it sounded like a larger version of themselves, like the Scandinavian myth of the kraken."

The other blur pressed a hand against the ceiling. "How do you fight the kraken?"

Ur-Veena should never have spoken the name of the Ancient Ones in the hearing of the air-ocean people, but once the naspy has laid its eggs, how do you find all of them? He clicked, "We do not."

The other blur pressed both hands against the ceiling. "The kraken don't eat you? No, wait, the story about Sa-Tsesta says they do."

Anger clotted Ur-Veena's words. "May eat. May not. Ancient Ones decide. May the Ancient Ones let us live."

Male Chin said, "They do not like to talk about the kraken."

Male Cruz lifted his hands. "But when they are such fierce fighters, why would they let the kraken eat them?"

Sa-Issi peeped, "I will fight them."

Ur-Veena swiveled his eyes toward Sa-Issi. "I should tie you to my shell."

Sa-Issi curled up and sank away from the translator.

Male Cruz tumbled over his words, "Suppose, suppose the kraken are the next stage of a hexacrab's life. I mean, look how many stages that we know they have."

Male Chin said, "I think not, but it will be interesting to see how they respond." He spoke into the translator. "Are the kraken what you become when you grow old?"

Ur-Veena unrolled a tentacle as the translator whistled and clicked. "No. We cease to breath and become food for the gut wrigglers and tight threads. Our empty shells are chewed into sand by the little beaks. Our legs become tunnels for—"

"I understand," Male Chin said.

Male Cruz said, "Do they think the kraken are gods?"

Ur-Veena seized the translator. "Not Creator of All, rock-ocean and warp-ocean. Ancient Ones are Spear of Creator." Then he dropped to the keel and curled up beside Sa-Issi.

Male Chin muttered, "That's a new phrase. Rock-ocean and warp-ocean. Could that be like our Alpha and Omega? And Creator of All. God who made all things through Jesus Christ?"

"Spear of Creator sounds more like the Greek furies than anything in the Bible."

"Incomplete analysis. God often sent armies to accomplish His will."

"But God never asked any of the people run over by an army to reverence that army."

"That's an important distinction. Good for you."

Ur-Veena's tentacles rippled with disdain. These air-ocean people probed with sound and poked with metal and pried with words. They brought much good, but every good thing they brought yielded needles when bitten into. He pulled Sa-Issi out into the ocean and mounted a scooter he hoped had been recharged.

CIRCUMNAVIGATION CHAPTER SIXTEEN

Two months and five island chains later, Rejoice threw the bean bag over her shoulder and caught it behind her back as she studied the last lesson on economics. She still hated the subject, but it, Art History, and The Puritans in England were nearly done. Could she get away with juggling for physical education? She was glad she had suggested New Earth Marine biology as a possible course. Being tutored by the Hancocks who were the textbook writers turned out to be fun, and they let her clean the aquariums again.

Now they knew the cucumbers turned into bristle-balls. The balls ate algae, but each bristle was tipped with venom, venom much like tetradotoxin which poisoned those who ate the gonads of fugu puffer fish back on Old Earth. The bristle-balls laid eggs that grew into knotted strings. What the strings did was an on-going research project.

Rejoice reread the last paragraph on economics again. Why would anybody spend more than two minutes of their life thinking about this stuff? Why would anybody care about anything so boring? But she had promised Mother after a tearful and embarrassing apology that she would finish the class before they reached the Broken Lands. She closed her eyes and tried to remember the last paragraph, but couldn't. She sighed and reread it again.

Over the intercom came Father's voice. "Ready to go?"

Grateful for the break, she shut the computer. "I'll be right up."

The Circle Chain arced away from the ship. Jagged basalt formed each dark island. Sunlight sparkled on blue water.

The hexacrabs helped Sister Hancock and Mother in their boats adjust underwater cameras. In another boat, No and Brother Hancock headed east for specimen collection. Elder Chin stood stolidly on the deck holding Opportunity's leash and watching her show how far she could jump.

Rejoice joined Father and the four-wheeler crammed into a tiny boat for a long trip west to the largest island in the chain. She was glad for the cool breeze as they roared along and jolted against the waves. Since they couldn't talk over the noise, she thought about the last two months. Her studies had proven to be a good excuse to avoid No Cruz. If only she didn't want to avoid him, but she never knew when he would say something ridiculous. He ate only every other day, so that meant she had to avoid looking at him only half the meals. Once she had caught his eye and been startled to see him looking sad. Wasn't he happy, being surrounded by great people?

Maybe he was missing the calls to Harmony. They were out of direct contact with the colony. When the Starflower was overhead, they sent messages up, and downloaded the messages sent by the colony several hours before. They would not be able to contact the colony directly again until the Magellan reached the Large Archipelago, and even then it would be for only an hour or two at the time when it was night at the colony. If the Elders had bothered to add communication relays to the satellites they would not have had these difficulties.

As aggravating as the short-sightedness of the colony Elders was, at least Father had fun calculating when and where the radio waves would bounce off the atmosphere. Then he would assign what seemed like random times for radio use.

Father slowed and putted around the rim of the island, looking for a spot to land, "What does this chain look like to you?"

"Another Bull's-Eye."

"That's what I think. I think that the asteroid that hit New Earth split into two pieces when it started to burn in the atmosphere. Sound good to you?"

"No. The impact sites would have been closer together."

"Okay. How about the asteroid splits somewhere in its last trip around the sun. An explosive venting of volatiles, something like that. So the leading, smaller piece hits here twelve hours sooner than the one that made Bull's-Eye."

"Why one asteroid that breaks? Why not two separate asteroids that impact hundreds of years apart?"

The skin around Father's eyes crinkled. "You're ruining my last chapter on New Earth geology. Okay, what are the chances of two huge asteroid strikes within that time frame?"

"Uh…" Rejoice grinned. "Astronomical. About as good as Opportunity hitting about five hundred years after Dark Death."

"Got me there. But I still think this happened about the same time. That would explain why the devastation was so total. What this asteroid didn't burn up, Dark Death did. I think this was first, and smaller, because we don't see any shock waves crunching on the other side of the planet the way we see the Broken Lands exactly opposite the Bull's-Eye. Ah, here we are." He nosed the boat onto a plane of rock that rose gently from the sea like a boat ramp.

By now, they had gotten the loading and unloading of the four-wheeler to a routine. Only this time, when they positioned the machine on the land, Father bent over the seat and turned pale.

"Father, what's wrong?"

He struggled for breath. "Asthma . . . maybe."

"You never had that before."

"Don't worry. Sometimes . . . it develops . . . late in life. I'll be okay . . . in a minute." He lowered himself to the ground and sat with his arms around his knees.

Rejoice sat beside him. How could she obey Mother by not worrying about Father? Yet he didn't look worried, and Mother didn't think anything was wrong. And she was the nurse. She should peacefully move on to another subject. "I've been thinking a lot lately."

"You do that . . . when you're sailing."

"I've been studying the Puritans. We're a lot like them, but they weren't pacifists."

Father nodded.

"I noticed there was a course on the history of pacifism. I want to take it even   if it delays my degree. I want to understand it, because sometimes I think you need to fight."

Father nodded again.

"You agree?"

"No. But it is . . . good to ask the questions. We have all . . . struggled with the issue. Now it's your turn."

"I keep thinking about the churtrees. What if an asteroid hadn't wiped them out? How would we be able to live with a people that like to pluck out hexacrab eyes?"

"You're sure they were . . . intelligent enough . . . to be morally responsible?"

"They built world-edge-pressers and nets and spears."

"So the hexacrabs say. That's why . . . your boat got the hexacrabs so riled up when we first met. Suppose . . . you had tried to kill Ur-Veena when he attacked? Would we . . . be friends today?"

Rejoice squinted at the white Magellan floating on the blue sea. The boats about it were specks. "But suppose I was in danger? Like somebody was going to kill me. Would you fight them?"

Father put his arm around Rejoice and squeezed. "I would negotiate. I would try to . . . interpose my body between you and the attacker. I might try to disarm the attacker, but I would not . . . try to harm him."

"But what if the only way you could stop him was to kill him? Would you just let me die?"

Father took off his filter mask and wiped his mouth with his sleeve. One could go weeks, maybe even months breathing unfiltered air before the lungs would be damaged, and everything they planted helped remove more of the poisonous gases. But it still shocked her to see a careful adult take off his mask in the open air. He pulled the mask back on. "Everybody dies eventually. We have to realize that many things are more important than whether one lives or dies. For the Christian, it almost doesn't matter, for whether . . . one lives or dies, one is still with Christ." He stood and mounted the four-wheeler. "I've caught my breath. Let's go."

Rejoice got on behind him and readied the bag of lichen balls she would drop to mark the trail. The jagged ground gave them a teeth-jarring ride. After fifteen minutes of careful negotiation around spires of basalt, she tapped Father on the shoulder. "There's nothing here."

Father looked back. "You might be right."

A wheel caught in a crevice and slewed the four-wheeler. The back smashed into a spire, jolting them half off the seat. Time seemed to slow, and yet Rejoice could not react. The recoil bounced them over the decimeter ledge. Father and Rejoice fell off when the four-wheeler crashed and tilted.

Before Rejoice could think what had happened, Father sat her up. "Are you all right?"

Rejoice examined herself. Her sleeve was torn, and her elbow stung and bled a little. "I don't think I'm going to enjoy sitting down tomorrow, but I think I'm all right. What about you?"

"I'll live." He turned and looked at the four-wheeler with its left back wheel splayed awkwardly. "That is thoroughly broken." He squatted down to look at the wheels and axles. "Thoroughly broken." He rubbed his eyes and muttered, "How am I going to get this back to the ship?"

His radio beeped. He pulled it off his belt and thumbed it on. "Holly here."

The hexacrabs whistled, "Another torpal desires to die."

"Resolved," Sister Hancock's said. That was all she said, but that word spoke a volume.

After a moment's pause came Brother Hancock's voice. "Let it swim."

The hexacrabs gurgled disappointment.

Father spoke up. "Brother Hancock, Young Man Cruz, I need your help. We've had an accident and the four-wheeler is broken."

Mother said, "Are you hurt?" at the same time Brother Hancock replied, "What are you going to need?"

Father wiped sweat from his forehead. "We're fine. Do you think the dollies in the lab are strong enough to haul the machine?"

"Guess we'll find out," Brother Hancock said.

Father slipped the radio back onto his belt. "Let's go. We've got a long hike ahead of us."

Rejoice had been sitting on the hot rock, simmering from more than heat. "If we had another four-wheeler, we could use it to pull this one."

"To be sure," Father said mildly. He extended his hand to help Rejoice stand up. "If kelp could fly, the hexacrabs would go hungry."

"So why didn't the colony build more? There are other uses for them besides exploring pagan rocks."

Father walked so slowly Rejoice had no trouble keeping up with him. "Other priorities," he said.

"So what's more important than four-wheelers and satellites?"

"A printing press."

"A printing press? You mean a machine that makes books out of paper?"

"To be sure."

Why would anyone make books when we have—" She reached for her screen. Right. She had left it in her room. "When we have computers?"

Father shaded his eyes. "Who says we're going to have the computers forever? We have a growing collection of broken ones. In another year or so, we're going to run out of replacements."

Father was intelligent. If there was anybody in the colony smarter than she, he was it. Why was he being so obtuse? "So why doesn't the colony build more computers?"

"We can't. We don't have enough minerals."

"I sent you five hundred million tons. That's not enough?"

Father laughed, and then wheezed. "We're very appreciative of the iron, nickel, lead, copper, zinc, ah, cobalt, etcetera mined from the asteroid. But you didn't send us any germanium, gallium or yttrium."

"Can't we make those from other heavy metals on the Starflower's nuclear reactor?"

"If we had enough of the right heavy metals, which we don't, we could. But even then it would not be in large enough quantities to be worth it."

Rejoice frowned. "That's all the more reason you should have been given enough material to do a proper search. Giving you one four-wheeler is a joke."

"Breathe deeply," Father said. Rejoice did so, inhaling the scent of sea, hot basalt, and her own sweat. Father continued. "Just because you look, doesn't mean you're going to find. We wanted to prepare for the eventuality that we don't ever find the minerals we need. The first thing we printed was three thousand copies of the Bible. That used up nearly all our kenaf, flax, and cotton. So now we're downloading more slowly and printing eleven copies of every manual, document, and book we have stored in Starflower's files. We'll put five copies of each in the First City library, three copies in a repository we have yet to build inland, and three in one we'll build on Large Archipelago when I find a proper site."

Which question first? None of this made sense yet. "Why are you putting libraries where nobody lives?"

Father held up his hand. "The main reason is preservation of the books. Suppose there's an earthquake at sea and a massive tsunami wipes out First City? If all our books are there, then we will have lost our history and knowledge. We'd be like the hexacrabs when they lost their library and all their history."

"But all the people would be dead, so why would it matter?"

"You're taking a very short range view. We won't always all live in First City. Within five hundred years, there could be a million or more of us, and we'll be scattered over the face of this world, inland Sole, the Large Archipelago, floating cities. You need to learn to think beyond this week."

Rejoice stepped carefully over the uneven ground and hung her head. None of those million people will be descended from her. She scrunched the beanbag in her pocket, pulled it out, and tossed it from hand to hand. "I am thinking beyond next week. I think we need those minerals and the colony should be going all out to find them."

"Again, you're assuming that if we look hard enough, we're going to find them."

"If we look hard enough, of course we'll—" She stopped as she finally understood what he was saying. The crust of the lunar moon had a slightly different composition from the crust of Old Earth. The asteroid she had mined had a different composition from the basalt she was walking on. New Earth had twice as much water as Old Earth. Maybe it had half as much yttrium. Or maybe it had none at all.

Rejoice sprinted for a spire, and then stood panting in its shade. When Father drew near, she said, "How will we live without computers?"

"The same way people have for thousands of years." He stopped in the shade, took off his hat, and fanned himself with it. "We can still have radio and industry. We might be able to have slower, less powerful computers. They are made mostly of sand and carbon. But listen to me, Young Lady. Even if we lost all our technology and had to plant crops with sharpened sticks, we could still have godly lives, good lives, enjoyable lives. But without the Word of God, where are we? *I* voted to build the printing press instead of more four-wheelers. So you can be angry at me instead of the colony. All right?"

Rejoice tried to swallow, but her mouth and throat were dry. "I'm sorry." She put the bean bag away. "It's just that I can't stand it when I see you get the short end of the stick."

"What stick?"

"Well, Elder Smith and all his friends have big farmhouses now. You and Mother still have a dinky apartment. And—"

"Stop there. Your mother and I do not live on a farm. The people with big farm houses have big families. Elder Smith's house is smaller than our apartment. His barns are bigger, but you have to put the cows somewhere where they can breathe filtered air. And once you and Stronghold moved out, we had plenty of room."

Rejoice resumed walking. The island seemed a lot bigger on foot. No matter what, Father would never say anything bad about the colony and its leadership. It was time to stop complaining. "But..." she said, "but if we lose our technology, then asteroid Deceit will impact New Earth in five hundred and seventy-one years!"

"That's why as soon as this voyage is over, the Starflower is going out to bust an asteroid again."

Rejoice stopped. "I have to go into space again?"

"No. Not you. You've done your tour. No one is going to make you go where you don't want to go again. And we'll make sure you have lots of time to make your decisions from now on. I let your mother talk me into keeping this voyage a secret from you. We will never do that to you again."

Rejoice walked. Her cheeks burned.

Father said, "There are more than enough volunteers for the next trip out." They walked in hot silence for several minutes. "One of them is Young Man Cruz. When he first filled out the application, he said he would go if not enough people signed up. Yesterday he told me he wanted to upgrade that to he wants to go very badly."

"First this voyage, and then space. He wants to escape Elder Smith too?"

"That's not how I read it. He likes to be useful." Father stopped and scanned the jagged landscape. He grunted and pointed to one of the white lichen balls Rejoice had scattered while he steered. "This way. Here's something I've noticed. You and Young Man Cruz still aren't getting along."

Rejoice said nothing. If she spoke, she would say something she would regret.

"You know, some personality types simply don't mesh. People like that can love each other in the Lord and pray for each other, but still need to stay away from each other to maintain peace. Perhaps that's the case with you and Young Man Cruz."

Rejoice's muscles relaxed at the implied permission to stay away from No.

"Over here!" Father shouted.

Rejoice startled at the shout. Brother Hancock and No stood by the boats and shouldered poles with wheels. Those two quickly bounded past Father who turned around to trudge back. Rejoice stayed with him, even though his pace was snail-like. It took the rest of the day to drag the four-wheeler to the boats.

* * *

During the next two weeks, No spent every spare moment on the machine until it was fixed.

Another week after that, they came to the Broken Lands, an eerie place of broken cliffs and jumbled rock and tortuous ocean valleys. The shock waves from the impact of Dark Death had rippled through the crust to meet each other on the opposite side of the globe and there crunch up the crust like an old paper bag. The hexacrabs complained continuously of the foul taste of rock blood and the constant sonar needed to map the irregular ocean floor lest the Magellan hit an underwater ridge. Black tar smeared the rocks. It took weeks to navigate through the dead land.

Once they were past the crumpled formations, the humans turned off the sonar and radar except for one minute an hour, to give the hexacrabs rest before they reached Large Archipelago.

Two days later, as he was leaving the galley, Elder Chin mentioned that Ur-Veena was discouraged. They had seen so many places that would make excellent locations for clusters. Yet they found no signs of other hexacrabs at any of their many stops. Elder Chin said, "Ur-Veena is getting very crabby."

Rejoice glanced at him as he turned to leave. Then she whispered to Mother, "I lived with triplet's puns for three years. I didn't think that Elder Chin was capable ofpunning."

Mother grinned. "I'm sure it was an accident."

* * *

Near the end of a sunny day, a week and a half after they had seen the last of the Broken Lands and were over a place in the ocean four kilometers deep, Rejoice played hide and seek with Opportunity. Since she had to hold Opportunity's leash, the little girl couldn't hide all that well, but she shrieked with laughter when Rejoice looked in all the wrong places first. No came up the steps and watched them for several minutes. He obviously wanted something, but seemed afraid to ask. Rejoice tired of the game and decided to have mercy on him. "Do you need help with a calculus problem?"

"Uh, no, thank you. But can we just talk for a little bit?"

He scooped Opportunity up and swung her around onto his shoulders as she squealed. They walked, and Rejoice waited. He studied the deck as they paced it. Finally, he took a deep breath. "I can talk to every single person in the colony, except you and you're—"

Rejoice waited several steps. "And I'm what?"

He took another deep breath. "Look. Can we start over again? I guess I got started on the wrong foot, or else I never got my foot out of my mouth. What will it take to start talking again?"

Rejoice pondered. One was never to reject any offer of peace. Their lives were built on achieving peace. If he wanted to try, she must try also. She twisted the leash into loops around her fingers. "Well, I guess you could apologize."

"Certainly. What do you want me to apologize for?"

He didn't know? How stupid was he? She fought down her irritation so she could say neutrally, "One thing is comparing me to Sister Olson."

"Yes. I'm sorry I told you that."

"So you agree that it's not true?"

"No. It's still true, but you weren't ready to hear it yet."

Rejoice jerked the leash off her fingers. "That makes me feel a lot better."

"I don't mean to make you angry. It's simply that I noticed that you both—"

"You look! When I want a personality analysis from you, I'll ask for one."

He nodded. "Fair enough."

Fair enough! This wasn't going to work. "I need to study. Give me Opportunity."

The alarm clanged, making Rejoice jump. Over the intercom, Elder Chin shouted, "The hexacrabs have stopped breathing!"

CIRCUMNAVIGATION CHAPTER SEVENTEEN

No swung Opportunity down and sprinted over to the panel where they kept the ready scuba gear.

Rejoice gathered up her little sister. What could she do to help? As she watched him tear out the equipment, a rounded hump rose beyond him. She stood paralyzed for a moment, watching the white hill plowing through the seas toward them. Then she ran to an alarm, flipped its lever, and shouted, "Something big and white is coming in from the north. It's headed straight for the ship!"

No turned and stared with an oxygen tank hanging off one shoulder. The Hancocks ran up from below and looked where Rejoice pointed. "Whoa!" Brother Hancock shouted. Mother clattered up the stairs with brown flour on her hands. She snatched Opportunity from Rejoice's arms. "I'm taking her below!" She bumped into Father coming up the stairs.

The white monster struck the ship with a thud that unbalanced Rejoice.

Elder Chin shouted over the intercom. "A giant octopus is trying to rip off the hexacrab's hatch!"

No dropped the tank with a clang. He seized a long spear from the wall. "I'll try to distract it."

Brother Hancock picked up the tank. "I'll try to get the hexacrabs out from the other side. Theophilus, throw down some scooters."

"No-o-o!" Sister Hancock shrieked.

"Help me with the buckles."

"No-o-o." She pulled the straps tight.

No leaned over the railing and prodded the monster with the butt end of the spear. The mass rolled to reveal an umber eye that glared at him. No braced and shoved harder.

The ocean erupted as three tentacles burst from the water and the white mass rolled with a spray to show three huge, lidless eyes. The tentacles shot through the railings and wrapped around No.

Rejoice screamed. Brother Hancock jumped over the other side of the ship. Father ran for the axe. Another tentacle gripped his ankle and knocked Father into a sprawl.

No flipped the spear around and jabbed the monster. A harsh screech filled the air.

Rejoice stared at the water streaming off its pebbled scales. Spears wouldn't pierce that. The electrical cables!

Rejoice leaped over Father clawing to stay on the deck, snatched the hatchet, and slid it to his outreached hand. She threw open the cable box and frantically pulled out coils.

Father whacked the tentacle around his ankle as another tentacle snaked through the railings to grab No's elbow and pull.

Something popped. No yelled and grabbed the spear with his left hand and darted it into one of the umber eyes.

The monster jerked back and screeched. It tried to pull No through the railings, but he didn't fit.

Crack! Crack!

She ran to the railing and hurled the terminal ends at the monster. No's face turned dark. Father slashed at the tentacles holding No. Rejoice turned the discharge lever and pulled.

Electricity tore through the monster's wet hide. The tentacles released No. He collapsed on the deck in a pool of dark orange blood. The monster spasmed one second, two, three, four, five, six, seven. The ship's engines stopped as the main battery discharged all its electricity into the monster. The monster steamed and blistered.

Rejoice shut off the electricity. The monster drifted, its limp tentacles sometimes twitching like the emotional residue of a nightmare.

Rejoice and Father knelt beside No.

Elder Chin pounded onto the deck. He grabbed up the tank and mouthpiece, snapped on a mask, and still holding the tank and without bothering to strap it on, hurled himself over the railing.

No lay gasping and shuddering.

Sister Hancock joined them. "Can you understand me? Can you nod your head?"

No nodded weakly.

Her face and bearing were rigid. "Neck's not broken. Let's see about his spine." She gripped his ankle. "Can you feel this?"

He continued to gasp with small, animal whines with every breath out, but he nodded. He rolled over to his back and looked up at Rejoice. "Thanks," he whispered. Then he looked at Sister Hancock and pulled off his mask. "I can't breathe," he mouthed.

Sister Hancock unbuttoned his shirt, took one glace at his chest, and ran to the intercom. "Carol we've got a collapsed lung up here!"

Father coughed. He hunched his shoulders and kept on coughing. Unable to stop, he turned away from No and coughed into his handkerchief.

Rejoice prayed a s Mother ran up with her equipment and bent over No. She had to look away when Mother stabbed him in the chest with something that looked like a stake, but she could still hear the soft sound of gristle being torn and the hiss of air. Then Mother inserted some flexible tubing that filled with red foam and dripped on the deck.

Father coughed as though his lungs were coming out. Then he stopped and stared dully at his handkerchief with a smear of red on it. He wheezed, "This isn't good. Rejoice . . . when Mother is done . . . please tell her . . ." Another coughing fit took him, and then, instead of breathing in, he slumped unconscious on the deck.

"Mother!" Rejoice jumped to Father and hauled on his shoulder, trying to turn him over.

Sister Hancock pushed Mother. "Go!"

No pushed away the oxygen mask and gasped. "Him."

Mother finished turning Father over. "Theo! Theo!"

Sister Hancock jammed the mask back onto No's face. "Take one breath!"

No's chest rose.

Sister Hancock swiveled and slapped the mask onto Father's face.

Rejoice raced to the locker with the stretchers and dragged one back.

Sister Hancock switched the mask to No.

Rejoice shoved the stretcher beside Father. Mother slid her arms under his shoulders and Sister Hancock grabbed his feet. "One, two, three!" They lifted him and placed him on the stretcher. They grunted as they lifted the stretcher and staggered to the stairs. Rejoice opened the door for them. Then she ran back to No.

Brother Hancock clambered onto the deck, knelt beside No, and dripped on him.

No grabbed his wrist. "The hex—" He wheezed.

"Let's just worry about you right now," Brother Hancock said.

Rejoice ran for the other stretcher and skidded on the water and blood.

Brother Hancock glanced at his one hand. "We'll have to wait."

The oxygen mask bobbled as No nodded.

Sister Hancock burst through the door. She touched Brother Hancock's shoulder. "You. Attend Carol. Rejoice, grab No's feet. One, two, three!" Rejoice and Sister Hancock hoisted No onto the stretcher. Brother Hancock carried the oxygen bottle and opened the door. Rejoice strained to lift her end of the stretcher. Oh, God, she was a wimp! She promised to exercise if God would give her the strength she needed right then. Brother Hancock propped open the door and ran to grab one of the poles of the stretcher. He and Rejoice squeezed through the door together and bent as Sister Hancock hoisted to keep No from sliding off the stretcher while navigating the stairs. They placed No on the lower bunk of his room.

Brother Hancock knelt by No's head, laid his hand on No's hair, and rubbed his thumb against his forehead.

Rejoice pulled the stretcher out of the room as Sister Hancock brought in a beaker to catch the fluids dripping from the tubing.

When Mother came out of her room, Rejoice dropped the stretcher in the hallway. "Is Father going to be okay? May I see him?"

Mother halted, rubbed her face with both hands. "Uh."

Sister Hancock kicked aside the stretcher as she ran down the hall.

Mother looked at the corner Sister Hancock swung around. "Uh. No. Not yet." Her gaze drifted to the floor. "Uh, the best thing you could do is clear the hallway and take care of Opportunity. And—and stay out of the way. I don't have time." Mother jogged to No's room.

Rejoice gathered the stretchers and dragged them up the stairs. *Oh God oh God oh God.* A heavy weight filled her chest as she propped the stretchers in their locker. Her throat constricted as she descended the stairs.

Holding a large box, Sister Hancock entered her parent's room.

Rejoice opened the door to her room. Opportunity charged into her and pummeled her, wailing. Rejoice pulled her sister up and got slugged in the face. She pulled shut the door, sank onto the lower bunk, restrained Opportunity, and then she cried.

* * *

Sometime that night an anguished cry from No startled Rejoice awake.

Darkness filled her room. She held her breath until she grew dizzy waiting for the announcement that her world had ended. Would she cry out like No, or scream, or take the news calmly? But no one came to her room. Opportunity had woken too, and she wailed as Rejoice rocked her. Leaving the door ajar so she could hear some of what was happening had been a mistake. She closed the door so her sister's crying would not disturb anyone.

The next thing that awakened Rejoice was ported sunlight shining on her face. She took her sister to the laundry and dressed her with fingers grown clumsy with dread, and listened, listened to silence.

She shuffled past her parents' door with heavy Opportunity on her hip. If only she had the courage to look in. She rounded the hall corner.

Brother Hancock slouched in the dining room chair, looking aged and glum, and clutching a cup of applemint tea. He looked at someone Rejoice could not yet see and murmured, "Our first death."

Elder Chin replied in a leaden voice, "And such a death."

Rejoice reached the doorway and carefully set Opportunity down. *Oh, God, no!* She screamed inside, but her tongue and lips would not move. Slowly she straightened. The next word would smash her into a thousand pieces. She stared at the two men facing each other over their cups of tea and waited, waited for what she did not want to hear.

Elder Chin saw her and sighed, "Young Lady, you look as though you've had a hard night."

Her hands crept up to her face and she stared at him.

He inclined his head as Brother Hancock turned and looked at her. "You might as well know, though this seems scarcely the time, but sometime yesterday Sister Olson killed herself."

Rejoice's knees buckled. They weren't talking about Father! As she fell, Brother Hancock and Elder Chin leaped up.

They dragged her to a chair and propped her up in it while she struggled against wild laughter.

"Young Lady." Elder Chin tied Opportunity's tether to her chair as Brother Hancock rushed to the galley.

Rejoice bit her lips. It wasn't Father! Her hands shook so hard that when she took the tea Brother Hancock brought her, it sloshed out of the cup. Her knuckles turned white. It wasn't Father!

"Will you pray with us?" Elder Chin asked.

She nodded because she was afraid to speak, afraid of what would bubble out.

Brother Hancock held one of her hands, and Elder Chin held the other as he led in an earnest prayer for the comfort of Brother Olson, the nurturing of their children, wisdom for the colony, and healing and peace for all.

As he prayed, Rejoice sucked in air. Her heartbeat slowed. By the time he had finished, she could control herself better, but she still just nodded when Elder Chin asked if he could get her breakfast. She stared at the pale, green tea as he rose and strode to the galley.

Brother Hancock scrutinized her while he sipped his tea. Opportunity cried. He scooped her up one-handed, and clumsily deposited her in her high chair.

Elder Chin returned with a tray of waffles and boysenberry syrup. "I'm sorry I'm not much of a cook. Heating frozen waffles reaches the limit of my culinary abilities." He set a plate of three in front of Rejoice and one in front of Opportunity. He cut the single waffle into pieces for the little girl and poured syrup.

"More, more," she said.

Elder Chin responded by making faces at Opportunity until she laughed.

Rejoice nibbled a waffle. When would she trust her voice enough to ask how Father was?

A clang in the hall made her jump. No cried out, and then whimpered, "That hurt! A lot!"

Elder Chin hurried out the door and dragged in No. "Young Man, I left you in bed and I expected you to stay there."

Rejoice widened her eyes at the sight of No's chest wrapped in multitudes of bandages. His right arm nestled in a sling and was pinioned to his side. What wasn't covered in bandages was covered with mottled bruises.

No stumbled as he was led to a chair. He mumbled, "I don't want Brother Holly to run out of oxygen."

"He won't. He has enough to last a week. I'll take the bottle to him. You need rest."

"I'm hungry," No said plaintively.

"I imagine so," Elder Chin said. "No more fasting until I say otherwise, do you understand? No, stay there. Oh, why did your parents give you such a ghastly name? I'll get your breakfast. Sit!"

Brother Hancock chuckled. Rejoice switched her gaze from No's bruises to him. He motioned toward No. "Between the two of us, we almost have two good hands. We spent the night filling oxygen bottles. We also finished shifting the decompression chamber into a hyperbaric chamber."

She squeaked, "Why?" and bit her lips again.

"That's right. You weren't there." He reached across the table and held her hand. "Your Father has a New Earth fungal infection in his lungs. He has probably had it for a long time. We think he may have picked it up when his mask broke during the exploration of the Nefarious Caverns in the northern part of Sole. The fungus blocks his air sacs so that he has trouble breathing. That's why we're giving him straight oxygen. Right now, that's enough. If his lungs get worse, we'll put him in the hyperbaric chamber to force oxygen into his tissues."

Rejoice nodded. This sounded bad. If it was a New Earth fungus, would they have any medicine against it?

As though he could read her thoughts, Brother Hancock said, "My wife is testing hundreds of chemicals, even as we speak, to see what will kill the fungus. And when your mother wakes up, they'll test hundreds more. If anyone can find a cure, they will."

Father had told Rejoice, "Just because you look, doesn't mean you'll find." Rejoice closed her eyes for a minute and tried to find the place of peace.

Elder Chin came in with a plate of cut-up waffles and set it in front of No who was staring with glazed eyes at the table.

No brought his head up and tried to focus his eyes on Elder Chin. "The, the hexacrabs . . ."

Elder Chin's face shifted. "We'll talk about them later, after you've eaten and gone back to bed."

Rejoice's fingers tightened on her cup. *Oh, no.* What had happened to the hexacrabs?

Brother Hancock rose and set down his cup with a click. "I'll be in the lab."

Rejoice looked at No shoveling the last bit of waffle into his mouth. Red syrup dripped down his chin.

Elder Chin brushed No's hair away from his eyes. "Remind me to cut your hair tonight. After you've rested. Would you like more waffles?"

No nodded.

"Young Lady, this Young Man is sleep-walking, and dopey from the painkiller as well as exhaustion. Please make sure he stays here until I get back."

Rejoice licked the syrup off her fork and watched No slumped in his seat. Bit by bit, he straightened and gazed around the dining room until his eyes came to her.

"Oh, hello," he said, apparently noticing her for the first time. "Did, did I thank you for saving my life?"

"Yesterday." She felt sorry for him. "How much of you is broken?"

No laughed, and then grimaced. "Four ribs. My shoulder was dislocated." He grimaced again. "Elder Chin and your mother popped it back in place last night. Some torn ligaments in my arm and chest." He sat back and took several shallow breaths. The smell of the medicines slathered all over him mingled with the sweet smell of syrup and the warm smell of waffles.

Rejoice's chest and throat hurt. She hated to think how badly No's chest hurt. The thought made her shiver.

"Rejoice?"

"Yes?"

"I—" He pushed himself up a bit. "I'm glad you're a fast thinker. It only took you a minute to figure out what had to be done." He stared morosely at the table. "And I with all my huffing and puffing and practicing was absolutely useless. I thought I could help and I couldn't. I . . . just . . . couldn't . . . figure . . . out . . . ."

"Please, No," Rejoice said. She reached across the table to take his hand, his hand with scraped knuckles. "You held off the monster until I could get the wires to it. You were brave."

He stared at her hands enfolding his. "Useless again. And now Brother Holly is sick. What can I do?"

"No, you're not listening to me."

"I must listen," he slurred.

"Yes, listen to me. You were wonderful."

"I thought I could drive it off or kill it, but I couldn't. Nothing has turned out the way I thought it would. I thought." He turned his eyes and looked hopelessly at Rejoice. "I should have stayed home. I didn't. It didn't work."

"I know." Rejoice sighed. "Life doesn't work out the way you think it will, or hope it will." Please God, don't let Father die. She let go of No's hand and rubbed her face. "We're sad here, and the colony is sad. I don't know how much more sadness I can take."

"The colony?"

"Yes, Sister Olson committed suicide. How can you believe—"

His face shifted into horror. "Sister Olson?" His voice broke.

She nodded.

He lay his head on the table and groaned, "Oh, no. Oh, no. Oh, no!" He took a spasmed breath. His shoulders shook as he cried with deep racking sobs that must have tortured him.

Opportunity's thin wail joined his.

Elder Chin burst into the dining room. "Son of my soul," he moaned. "Come, come" He tried to help No stand, but No couldn't or wouldn't cooperate.

Brother Hancock came in. He saw what Elder Chin was trying to do and got on the other side of No to help support him.

Once No was up, he laid his head on Elder Chin's shoulder and continued to weep as they walked him out.

"Is there some way to tie him down so he stays in bed?" Elder Chin said.

"Sheets tied together?" Brother Hancock suggested.

The sound of No's cries went down the hall, turned the corner, and stopped when the sound-muffling door of his room shut. Opportunity screamed and kicked her chair. Rejoice shuffled over to her and un-snapped one of the chair buckles.

"Don't do that, Young Lady," said Elder Chin as he came through the door. "I will baby-sit, and you will go back to bed."

Rejoice stopped and thought fuzzily.

Elder Chin held her lightly by the shoulders and peered into her face. "Before you go, I want you to tell me what happened."

"We were just talking, and then I told him about Sister Olson and he started to cry. I'm sorry."

Elder Chin's jowls shook. "This was not the best time to tell him. I told you only because it looked as though you had overheard us." He sat heavily in a chair next to Opportunity and patted his knees as an invitation to climb on. "You're probably not thinking any more clearly than he is."

"I'm sorry." No had written at least one letter to Sister Olson. Why her? "They weren't friends, were they?" Who could possibly be friends with Sister Olson?

Elder Chin dipped a piece of waffle into the syrup and then inserted it into Opportunity's mouth. She stopped screaming and sucked on the sweetness. "He saw that Sister Olson was not coping well with her little ones. Three or four times a week, when he was finished with his work, he would drive out to the Olson farm for two hours or so to baby-sit and clean house for her while she napped or went on walks. Did you see her state when she came to see us off?"

She nodded. "No never told me about that." When had she given him a chance to tell her anything?

"He wouldn't." Elder Chin shook his head. "He never tells anyone about his good deeds."

Rejoice sat down again and thought about No quietly helping Sister Olson, waiting on Elder Chin, and trying to help Father when he himself was badly injured. No matter what he did, she had always thought the worst of him. And now she knew why No had compared her to Sister Olson. Wasn't she exactly as judgmental and harsh as Sister Olson? Her ears and cheeks flamed.

"Do you need help to get to your room?"

Rejoice covered her eyes. The shame, Father maybe dying, Sister Olson dead, the crying of Opportunity, the monster, it was all too much. She tried to hold it in, but couldn't. She cried as deeply as No had. Tears ran over her hands as she tried to make herself stop. "Oh, oh, oh," she sobbed.

Brother Hancock came into the dining room "Who let these children stay up past their bedtime?"

Embarrassment burned down her throat, but she still couldn't stop crying.

Sister Hancock ran into the mess, hugged her, and wiped her face with a handkerchief. "There, there," she crooned. "It's been a bad night, but your father will be all right. Oh, sweetie, it's okay to cry. We love you. Everything is going to be all right."

Nothing would be all right again. Rejoice wrapped her arms around Sister Hancock and held on desperately. She would drown in this flood of fear and sorrow.

Elder Chin took screaming Opportunity away.

Slowly, the flood ebbed, and Rejoice was left with hiccups and exhaustion. Sister Hancock helped her up and led her to her room. Then she fetched a drink of water and gave Rejoice a clean handkerchief. Why couldn't one die of embarrassment and be done with it? Sister Hancock tugged the quilt up to Rejoice's neck and pulled the door shut. Rejoice fell asleep.

CIRCUMNAVIGATION CHAPTER EIGHTEEN

A kiss on her forehead woke Rejoice.

Mother smiled. "Good afternoon, darling."

If Mother smiled, perhaps things weren't too bad. On the other hand, Mother always smiled. "Good afternoon." Rejoice sat up. The blanket slithered off the bed with a whisper. She pulled it up and bunched the quilted fabric at her feet. "Did you need me in the galley?"

"Not unless you feel like it. We can survive just fine on waffles for a while. I thought you might like to talk to your father. He's awake now."

Rejoice jumped up and headed for the door. Mother grabbed her by the hem. "Not so fast. Wash your face and brush your hair first. It's bad enough for one of you to look ghastly."

Rejoice nodded and scurried into the women's laundry. The tiny mirror reflected eyes still puffy from weeping. Ugh, her dress smelled bad. Or maybe that was herself. A quick shower and change made her feel better. As she combed her wet hair, she prayed that Father would recover quickly.

When she came into the hallway, Mother whispered in her ear, "Now try to be cheerful."

Rejoice nodded. If Father was alive, why shouldn't she be?

And then she saw him.

The part of his face that wasn't covered by a mask hissing oxygen was white. His fingertips were tinged with blue. His eyes had narrowed to slits. Every breath seemed a struggle. How strange to be standing over him.

Rejoice forced the corners of her mouth up.

Father's gaze flicked from her to the chair pulled up beside his bed and back.

The chair scraped as she dropped into it and took his cold hand. With long pauses for breath between each whispered word, he said, "Rejoice. You. Did. Good. Yesterday. I'm. Proud. Of. You."

Rejoice swallowed. "Thank—thank you."

He held onto her hands as he strained for each breath.

Rejoice tried to think of something cheerful to say, but she couldn't. She wiped away a tear, hoping he wouldn't see it. "I'm going to see if I can work in the lab to find medicine for you."

Slowly he nodded and squeezed her hand. "I. Love. You. Too."

Mother touched her on the shoulder. "We'll let him rest now." As Father released Rejoice's hand, Mother said to him, "Bye, my heart. I'll be back in a few hours."

Rejoice nearly tripped over an empty oxygen bottle near the door. "Oops. I'll take this down to be recharged." She picked up the cool bottle and cradled it in her arms. "I'm surprised No didn't take care of this."

Mother softly closed the door. "Young Man Cruz was so agitated that I had to sedate him. You won't see him until tomorrow."

Rejoice looked at the floor. Why did she automatically think the worst of No? "It's my fault."

"A little bit." Mother gave her a quick kiss. "We're very grateful to you. You seem to be awfully good at rescuing people. That you made a little mistake later is something none of us hold against you. Please don't fret. We all remember being sixteen, and frankly, you've done a lot better than any of us would have. After you recharge the tank, why don't you take it easy? No chores until tomorrow. Try to be cheerful, okay?"

"Okay."

As she recharged the tank and tagged it, Rejoice thought about how selfish she had been during the whole voyage. She resolved to do better for the rest of the trip.

She checked her screen. Two o'clock. And suddenly she felt ravenous.

In the galley, the counter was covered by the collapsed and dried dough Mother had been working on when the monster attacked. Had that been only a day ago? She threw out the mess. Mother had told her not to do any chores, but she didn't want waffles again, and probably no one else would either. So she rolled out cinnamon-raisin rolls, made a potato-onion casserole, and put on a vegetable-rice soup. Good smells permeated the galley and wafted down the hall.

Then, while everything was simmering or baking until done, she went to the women's laundry, and put on the first load of wash. Blood spattered a distressing amount of the clothes and bandages.

Back in the galley, she mixed a large pitcher of raspberry-grape juice and brewed a pot of mint tea.

She poked her head into the lab. Mother and the Hancocks rolled swabs over red gel in small dishes and stacking them in incubators. With incubators, aquariums, and people, there was no room left in the lab.

Mother looked up. "I'm sorry, sweetheart. I know you want to help, but I don't have time to teach you how to do this."

No time to waste. And no room either. Rejoice swallowed her disappointment. "I made lunch."

"Did you? Thank you. But you were supposed to take it easy."

"It was easy."

Mother smiled. "We'll be in, in a bit."

Rejoice closed the door. Her legs could not rest. Back in the galley, she made a batch of shortbread and oatmeal cookie dough, which she then refrigerated to bake the next day when No woke up. She set the table and cleaned the galley. What else could she do?

She went up on deck and paced around the ship several times, seeing only empty ocean. What had that monster been? The hexacrabs would know. Something had happened to the hexacrabs, but Elder Chin hadn't said what. The last thing she could remember was Elder Chin shouting that the hexacrabs had stopped breathing. Or maybe that the monster was trying to attack them. Oh, Ur-Veena couldn't have died.

Rejoice ran down the stairs and through the hall to the access room. Elder Chin sat glumly on the transparent floor, watching the hexacrabs huddle in a corner. Beside him, Opportunity built towers of fabric blocks and then with a shout punched them down. Whenever a block fell between Elder Chin and the hexacrabs, he moved it absentmindedly.

Rejoice's hand went to her throat. The hexacrabs lived!

"So," Elder Chin said, "do you, therefore, say that we, the air-ocean people should submit to the beak?"

Ur-Veena ripped open a bag and chirped, "Barnacles." He and Sa-Issi grabbed scraper blades out of the bag and swarmed out their door and out of view.

Elder Chin slapped the floor, then sat back, closed his eyes, and took several deliberate, deep breaths.

Rejoice backed part way out of the room, but Elder Chin said, "Please do not go yet. You may be able to help me."

He continued to breathe deeply as she got an orange cushion to sit on. "Edoy! Edoy!" shouted Opportunity who ran and clambered over her. "Oppy! Oppy!" Rejoice said, and hugged her little sister.

Rejoice watched Elder Chin. Since he didn't seem to mind the noise Opportunity made, she tickled her sister until Opportunity was gasping.

Finally, Elder Chin opened his eyes. "Perhaps another perspective will help me see what is going on." His face sagged as he looked into the hexacrab's room.

"Why did they say "Barnacles," and leave?"

"It was an honorable way to get out of talking to me." He picked up a block and traced the seams with his thumb. "The only other time I have seen Ur-Veena this upset was when Brother Hancock killed one of the children."

"How can you tell when a hexacrab is upset, anyway? They don't have facial expressions. Ow!" Opportunity had stepped on her knee.

"They change color somewhat. When they speak, they use fewer and fewer parts of speech. Instead of saying, "We are going out to scrape barnacles and think things over," they say, "Barnacles."" He sucked on his teeth. "I think they are going through a dark night of the soul."

Rejoice moved Opportunity out of her face. "A what?"

"In humans it is a time when one faces such agony that one cannot hear God, which increases the agony so much, that one leaves the experience either strengthened in a faith that has changed in some way, or else one is shattered by a total loss of faith."

"What faith? I thought the hexacrabs weren't Christians yet."

Elder Chin set down the block. "Young Lady, you have not been reading my columns."

"Uh, no, Sir. I'm sorry." Heat washed over her face. Humans change color when they're upset, just like the hexacrabs.

He frowned, then smiled. "Good. No preconceptions. What you question will help me clarify." He leaned forward. "I think that submitting to the kraken and being killed is a religious experience for the hexacrabs. We saw the story of Sa-Tsesta, the one who fought the torpal and then was eaten by a kraken as a tragedy."

Rejoice shivered.

"Perhaps the hexacrabs did not think it a tragedy. Perhaps they think that is the happiest of all endings."

Rejoice stared. Mental gears shifted and stripped their teeth in a sudden surge backward. "But that's—that's—horrible." Opportunity jabbed in her armpits in a vain attempt to tickle her sister. Irritated, she pushed Opportunity away. "So that was a kraken?"

"Oh, yes. Last night, Brother Hancock and I found out why the hexacrabs submit."

"Because of the religious experience?"

"No, physically, why they stop moving, why they stop breathing. Last night, I pulled the hexacrabs from their room and scooted them far away. I was hoping that if I could keep water flowing over their gills, I could keep them alive until they recovered from their paralysis, if they could recover. And half a kilometer from the ship, they did." Elder Chin gently took Opportunity who was hopping between Rejoice and him, and snuggled her into his lap. He stroked her on the back.

"And?" Rejoice said.

"When I got close to the ship, they stopped breathing again. So I took them away, and they recovered again, though they seemed confused. I waited until I was afraid hypothermia would do me in and I was low on oxygen. I went back to the ship again. By this time, the ship was several kilometers past where we encountered the kraken. Oh, by the way, congratulations."

He extended his hand. Rejoice took it and felt his dry, papery skin. Why was he congratulating her?

"I didn't find out until this morning that it was you that killed the kraken and saved several people's lives thereby. With all the emergencies, we haven't had time to notify each other of events. I don't think you know what happened next, but if you do, you can stop me."

Rejoice nodded. When would he get to the point?

"So we got back to the ship, and this time the hexacrabs could breathe. I put them in their room, got on board, and talked with Brother Hancock. He had the brilliant idea of swishing some kraken tentacle parts in sea water, putting that water in a stoppered bottle, and giving it to the hexacrabs. When Ur-Veena unstopped the bottle, bingo, within a minute, neither hexacrab was moving."

Rejoice frowned. How curious.

"This time, Brother Hancock took them out, and I, hmm, I was going to say I aired out the room. I circulated fresh water into it and when the hexacrabs returned, they could breathe again. So. So. So. Brother Hancock theorizes that kraken exude a neurotoxin that paralyzes hexacrabs. He tested it on some naspy, but they seemed unaffected. Two kinds of hardhead slowed down. The rest of the experiments will wait until we find a cure for your father."

Rejoice sat up a little straighter. "So the hexacrabs don't fight the kraken because they can't?"

Elder Chin nodded and his jowls shook. "That leads to several questions." He counted them on his fingers as he listed them. "During the paralysis, are the hexacrabs unconscious, or are they conscious but unable to move? Or are they hallucinating? Or in a state of euphoria? They were upset when they found out we had not only diverted the kraken, but had killed it. Are they upset because we killed their god or agent of God? Are they upset because we denied them a chance to enter paradise? Are they upset that we unbalanced nature? Or because something bad will happen to them or their cluster because of divine retribution? Will they consider humans evil or good now? Are they afraid of us? Or do they fear for us? Or are they in shock because their universe turned upside down?"

"Wait," Rejoice said. "That's too many questions. What do you mean by entering paradise?"

"Some Muslims believe that anybody who dies doing Jihad, or holy striving, goes straight to paradise. Some Hindus believe that if they are crushed to death by a juggernaut, they will get to bypass reincarnation or at least develop a better karma. Many Christians welcome martyrdom, knowing that once the agony is over, they'll be with Christ. Is that how the hexacrabs view death by kraken?"

He sighed and ran his fingers through Opportunity's fine black hair. "I have tried a hundred different approaches to talk about the kraken, but the hexacrabs won't talk. That story about Sa-Tsesta is it. I can guess on a human level what is happening, but how can I find out whether or not hexacrab psychology is the same there?"

"Same where?"

Elder Chin pursed his lips as he patted Opportunity on the rump. After a minute's reflection, he said, "Suppose that someone were to prove to you that Jesus had never risen from the dead. What would that do to your faith?"

"How could anybody prove a thing like that?"

"A skeleton, a time-machine. It doesn't matter. Just imagine that proof exists and you accept it. What happens next?"

Rejoice felt queasy. "Uh, well. It would mean that I had believed a lie."

"Would you say that didn't matter?"

"No, because Jesus said He was the truth. I want to follow the truth."

"So what would you do on Lord's Day morning?"

"I don't know."

"And what if no one else believed the evidence, and you alone saw the truth?"

"I guess I would try to talk to them."

"And if they refused to believe you?"

"I'd be, uh, lonely. I guess. Maybe an outcast." Rejoice's heartbeat sped up. She could end up an outcast. If Father died, that would leave Mother and the Hancocks the only people between her and Elder Smith. On Old Earth, she could have moved to another city. There was no other city on New Earth. Rejoice held her hand against her thudding heart. She missed Elder Chin's next question. "I'm sorry. Will you repeat that?"

"And what would you do for Christ's Birth Day and Resurrection Day?"

"I don't know."

"So without your habits and thought patterns built in you by faith and culture, you cannot decide how you would act or what you would do. Would you be confused? Would you be depressed?"

"I think so. It would be terrible to find out I had wasted my life on a lie."

Elder Chin shifted. Opportunity wriggled away and plopped into Rejoice's lap. Then she bounced over to the blocks and tossed them. Her shoes went tap, tap, tap on the glass floor.

"I think that is happening with the hexacrabs. But how can I read their molluscan minds?"

"So why won't they talk about it?"

Elder Chin shrugged. "It's not necessary for taboos to be logical."

"What does taboo mean?"

"It means something in a society that is not to be touched, or not to be done, or not to be talked about."

"But why would any society have something that can't be talked about?"

Elder Chin sat, rubbing the corner of his mouth with his forefinger and studied Rejoice. What was he planning? Finally, he said, "Suppose Ur-Veena were to crawl up to the microphone and say to you, 'Tell me about your sex life.'"

Rejoice's cheeks and throat grew hot. The heat spread down her arms as she stuttered, "First of all, I'd tell him I don't have one." A roaring filled her ears. She closed her eyes to avoid his gaze. He laughed. She opened her eyes and glanced at him. "Then I'd tell him it was none of his business!"

Elder Chin grinned. "There's a taboo subject we don't discuss in public. It isn't until the night before the wedding that the mother takes her daughter and the father takes his son out to discuss the detailed mechanics of sex and give the code that will open the documents on sexual techniques."

So that's what Father and Stronghold did the night before the wedding. Rejoice's heart beat harder. Why was Elder Chin embarrassing her like this?

"The way you feel now may be the way the hexacrabs—"

"Excuse me," If Rejoice got any hotter, her clothes would catch fire. She ran out of the room. She wanted to shout, "Barnacles!" and slam the door behind her, but she restrained herself.

Father's door stood ajar, but she didn't want to see him in this state. She ran into the women's laundry and splashed cold water on her face repeatedly until her breathing and heartbeat had slowed. Then she went to see Father.

He looked up from his computer resting against his drawn-up knees, and the skin around his eyes crinkled.

Rejoice sat beside him. His fingers had grown puffy and his breathing faster and shallower. He cleared his screen and tapped it. She flipped open her screen to follow what he typed.

"What were you working on?" She tried to ignore the odor of sickness and the tubes running into his arms and nose and the hiss of oxygen.

[Report on yesterday/last night. Everyone else too busy.]

"Oh, I could have done that. I'm not busy."

[Sure. Please add what I miss.]

What had she just done? She hated to write.

[Problem?]

"No. But an awful lot happened. It will be hard to write about."

[U are so red. Sunburn?]

Her cheeks heated up again. Why did she have to be so easily embarrassed? She changed color when she was upset much more than the hexacrabs did. Other people could talk in front of crowds. Other people could talk about difficult subjects. She twiddled with the edges of her computer and stammered, "Elder Chin embarrassed me."

[?]

"He, he asked me about my sex life. No, I mean, He—"

Father seemed awfully still. Had he stopped breathing? Fire ran down her neck. She glanced at him. He typed, [Go on.]

She took a deep breath. "Elder Chin said the hexacrabs won't talk about the kraken because they're taboo and I asked what is taboo and Elder Chin asked me how I would feel if Ur-Veena asked me about my sex life and I got embarrassed and left."

Father's face turned red as he laughed without sound. After gasping for a while, he typed, [U had me worried for a moment. Elder is fantastic teacher.]

Right. Father attended a Bible study at Elder Chin's apartment every Fourth Day evening. Mother attended one at Deaconess Nkruma's home. "He didn't need to embarrass me like that."

[U won't ever forget taboo.]

Rejoice studied her screen and listened to the oxygen hiss.

[I will talk to him.]

"No, don't do that. Then I'll really be embarrassed."

He reached out a swollen hand and held one of hers. He typed one-handed, [Love U.]

"I love you, too," she whispered. They held hands in silence. Why was it Father who had the lung fungus? Oh, what if they all had it, and he was simply the first to get sick? "Father?"

[?]

"Why was it you who got sick?"

[Probably because I breathed spores in cave.]

"No, I meant," she stuttered. She meant why him and not Elder Smith? Why him when he was the best person in the colony? She must not say those thoughts.

[Why not?] He typed slowly. [Better me than you I think.]

She gently squeezed his hand. He was so wrong.

Mother came to the door and beckoned to Rejoice. When Rejoice walked into the hall, Opportunity was sucking her thumb and clinging to Mother's leg. Mother looked harried. "Rejoice, would you please watch Opportunity again? Elder Chin has been up for thirty-seven hours. It's his turn to rest."

"Sure, I'll make sure she doesn't pull out any of Father's tubes."

"Actually, I need you to take her away. I'm going to set up dialysis for Father and a bicarbonate drip and a respirator and well, a lot of things to help him fight off the infection. Once I get everything set up, Opportunity mustn't come in at all."

Rejoice took Opportunity's leash. "I wish I could help find a cure."

"You are helping. Thank you for the meals. Thank you for watching Opportunity."

"I wish I could help more."

Mother shut her eyes and frowned in concentration. "Yes. You can help more. You could squirt over my treatment plan for Doctor Cruz to look at and give me advice on. And you could check through our lab data base to see if there's anything we can obtain that we haven't tried against the fungus."

"How are we going to get medicines from the colony?"

"We won't. We took half the colony's medical capacity with us. What we don't have, they don't have. I've already put Father on a course of five antibiotics on the off-chance that one of them will affect a New Earth fungus."

"Mother?"

"Yes."

"How bad is it?"

"People with illnesses worse than this have lived. Don't worry. It won't help." Mother went into the room and firmly shut the door.

Rejoice stared at the door. Would being cheerful help? She checked her screen. The Starflower would be able to receive data transmission in an hour. Send up treatment plan, check data base, oh, and finish report for Father. She picked up sleepy Opportunity and took her to their room.

While Opportunity dressed and undressed her doll, Rejoice set up the treatment plan for transmission to Doctor Cruz. As she read the treatment plan and looked up the purposes of each treatment, Rejoice found it harder and harder to swallow. Dialysis and the swelling meant Father's kidneys were failing. Enzyme levels indicated the liver was failing. A bicarbonate drip meant lactic acid was building up in his body. She didn't know what those things meant, but they all sounded bad. However, Mother wouldn't lie. Sicker people had lived, she said, so surely Father would get well too.

Uneasily, Rejoice switched over to the report. What she read made her cheeks heat again. Father's report about her raved as though she had single-handedly dispatched the kraken and saved the hexacrabs and humans from a bloody death. They would make her give another speech if she let this stand.

She deleted some of the more effusive statements and replaced them with a more accurate portrayal. Father would have thought of the cables too, but he had been grabbed by the kraken. Elder Chin's and Brother Hancock's jumping into the water had taken more courage than what she had done. All she had done since then was sleep, baby-sit, and cook.

Rejoice wrote about No and how when his right shoulder had been pulled from its socket, he had thrown the spear with his left hand. She could not have done the same thing. First of all, she would have been screaming her head off. Secondly, she couldn't do anything with her left hand alone. What if the kraken had grabbed her right hand? Would they all be dead today?

That was why No had practiced so hard with his left hand. He had been smart enough to prepare for unforeseen circumstances. Maybe she needed to do the same.

She read through the report one more time and added that the hexacrabs had been paralyzed by something the kraken put in the water. She squirted it to the transmitter. Just before she closed the screen, she noticed that Father had also been working on a document titled Letters that day. Since he couldn't speak, he had probably written a letter to Stronghold telling him not to worry. Should she send that too? She opened the file and found in it not just a letter to Stronghold, but letters to every member of the Holly family, even to Opportunity.

Opportunity could sing the alphabet, sort of, and recognize some letters, but she couldn't read yet. Why was there a letter for her?

Rejoice opened the letter with her name on it. He surely meant for her to read it or he wouldn't have put her name on it. [My dear Rejoice In The Lord's Salvation, I didn't mean to leave U so soon, but our lives and times are in God's hands. I thank God for the time He allowed me to share with U. U are so precious to me.]

The words blurred. The screen crashed to the floor and Opportunity jumped as Rejoice bent over in agony. Whatever Mother had said about living, Father was preparing to die.

CIRCUMNAVIGATION CHAPTER NINETEEN

Ur-Veena scrapped the hull with a blade grown dull from overuse. He had scraped this spot three days before, but he went over it again with careless, slow moves as he meditated on the air-ocean people and the Ancient Ones. Sa-Issi adjusted the flow shield that kept them from being swept away from the skin of the ship. Sa-Issi kept one tentacle wrapped around one of Ur-Veena's legs at all times. The mottling on his blue skin pulsed with an inner rhythm.

Ur-Veena had not spoken for hours as he thought over the stories of his people, the devastation of Dark Death, the coming of the new people who discovered his people's libraries. He had rejoiced in new knowledge and the recovery of old, in a new mobility, in a regaining of hope that his people would again fill the shallow seas and share honor with complete females.

The sea eddied and bubbled past him with flavors he could not recognize. He scraped the bare hull. What niche could his people find that the air-people could not?

Sa-Issi climbed onto Ur-Veena's back. "Sing to me," he whistled mournfully.

Ur-Veena paused in his aimless scraping, sucked in his eyes, and snapped shut each opercula. He inhaled water to stretch tight his membranes for the lowest singing. After three slow clicks, he sang a sacred song:

"Dark is the deep.

Dark is sleep.

Dark is the joining of shell and flesh.

Dark is the ending we call death.

The current flows whether dark or light.

The deepest knows in the day or night.

Dark is the deep.

Deep is the dark."

He grated the last words:

"Yet even in the deep, an eye shines."

CIRCUMNAVIGATION CHAPTER TWENTY

A few days later, Rejoice knocked on the door of No and Elder Chin's room. She almost tipped over the lunch tray when she pulled the door open, but No didn't look up from the screen balanced on his lap. He sat in bed with his knees drawn up and typed slowly with one hand.

Rejoice set the tray on the desk. "What are you doing?"

No frowned at the words on the screen and deleted some. "Writing a letter to Brother Olson."

Rejoice stood and shifted around the things on the tray.

No looked up. "Did you want something?"

She licked her lips and stammered, "Are you too busy to talk?"

No looked surprised. He cleared the screen, set it aside, and swung his legs over the side of the bed. Rejoice sat down on the desk chair to be level with him, but he rose slowly, wincing, and walked to the door.

He had the door half open before Rejoice could say, "I wanted to talk privately."

"No one will bother us on the deck. Oh, I forgot." He took his mask from its peg. "Will you help get this on? I don't seem to do as well as Brother Hancock does with one arm."

Rejoice slid the strap over his hair and followed him up to the deck. There they trudged the tiny circuit, passing by a container of kelp balls that she and Brother Hancock had wrestled up the deck that morning.

Now that the point had come, Rejoice's courage failed. She grabbed two balls and offered one of them to No. He shook his head. Right. He wasn't supposed to make any violent moves for at least another two weeks. She tossed three balls overboard with her left hand. No ignored it. Why didn't he comment on how pathetic and weak her throws were? She had planned to show him how she could hit the target using her right hand, but it seemed inappropriate now. They walked in silence accentuated by the susurration of a breeze flowing through the sail slats and their footsteps on the metal deck.

Rejoice clasped and unclasped her hands. Why was a simple apology so difficult? She glanced at him. For once, he was not staring at her. Nor did he look at the sea; the deck seemed to hold his interest. Stronghold had been like this during his recovery after Ur-Veena had stabbed him. Did all men do this after they got hurt?

"You seem awfully sad."

"Yes," he said. "I should never have come on this voyage. But, obviously, I must finish it."

Rejoice held her tongue a moment. He almost hadn't finished the voyage. Mother had told her that he was only a minute or two from death when she had released the air from his chest that had been squeezing his heart into immobility. Then she had told Rejoice she expected her to try to be cheerful and encourage No. Rejoice had never succeeded with Stronghold, and she didn't see how she would with No, either.

Finally, Rejoice said, "My mother said that when several bones are broken, the body spends all its energy on healing them, even emotional energy. And it's natural to be depressed when bones are knitting."

"I'm sure that's true. I still should not have come."

"You, ah, you have done a lot to make this voyage, ah . . ." She had been going to say successful, but she couldn't say their journey had been. They had found that two of the major monsters the hexacrabs had mentioned were still alive in the ocean, but now the hexacrabs weren't talking about anything with the humans. They hadn't met any talking females or any other hexacrabs at all. They hadn't found any rare minerals they needed for computers and industry. Brother Hancock had lost an arm. No had torn ligaments and broken ribs. Father was—

No broke into her thoughts. "Someone else could have done just as well."

She looked up at him. "You saved Brother Hancock's life."

His pace slowed to a crawl. "True," he muttered. "But any young man would have done the same. But I believe it's also true that Sister Olson would be alive if I had not come."

Rejoice looked back toward him and stopped.

He sighed. "Nothing worked out the way I thought it would. Blinded by pride or, I don't know what, I . . ."

He stared up at the sky. "I badly wanted to impress you, but now Sister Olson is dead and—"

What? "Why on New Earth would you try to impress me?"

He scuffed the deck as they walked. His shoes were worn. How would the colony replace them? Rejoice had never considered the question.

He said, "It doesn't matter. I was mistaken . . . about a great many things. I thought Sister Olson would be all right because I had assigned five people to go over to her house on a schedule and help the Olsons out. But now she's dead. Brother Olson, Morning Star and Rose Of Sharon have more grief than anyone needs. I should have seen and done the duty I saw before me instead of chasing after some fantasy. If I had stayed home, Sister Olson would still be alive."

"In other words, what God and the colony couldn't do, you could."

He stopped. He took a deep breath.

Rejoice grimaced. Why had she said that? She was supposed to be cheering him up, not berating him. "I'm sorry."

No resumed his slow pace. "Don't be sorry," he said in a voice so sad it broke her heart. "Thank you. I needed to be reminded." He adjusted the sling on his arm.

She had to do it or she would never get it over with. "No, I am sorry, about a lot of things. Will you please forgive me for being angry? You were right. I am just as critical as Sister Olson."

No finally looked at her. "Is that what you thought? No wonder you were angry."

They walked several steps before Rejoice remembered that she had told him not to analyze her personality unless she asked. She was sure she didn't want to know, but she should. "So . . . how are we, were, we the same?"

He shook his head slightly. "You have to remember that I liked Sister Olson. I like to see people have high ideals. Even if they don't reach those ideals, where they end up is still higher than someone without ideals. Unfortunately, the person with high ideals can have a weakness, which you and Sister Olson shared; when you don't reach those ideals, you can be too hard on yourselves."

Rejoice was stunned. She had never thought of Sister Olson as idealistic. She blinked and thought as they walked about the deck. He liked Sister Olson. Nobody else she knew did. Unless it was Brother Olson. She had never heard him speak a single word so she had no idea what he thought. No Cruz liked her. And he didn't think Rejoice was critical. Maybe he was stupider than she thought. He was certainly proving to be nicer.

No interrupted her thoughts. "How is your father?"

Rejoice could not make herself say: He is dying. Mother says he is sleeping but I think he's in a coma. I don't know if I will ever get to talk to him again. What she could say was, "My father is very, very sick." The lump in her throat precluded any more.

"My mother says your mother is doing everything correctly. He couldn't be getting better care."

Yes, he could be getting better care. But better care was a thousand light-years away. Tears gathered in her eyes.

No stumbled, and then took several breaths sucked in through gritted teeth. "I think I had better go back and lie down before you have to carry me down." He turned and trudged toward the stairs.

Rejoice had meant to say more. "No, one more thing. Just before we were so rudely interrupted by the kraken, you said you wanted us to start over again. I wanted to tell you that, yes, I would like to start over again."

He stopped and took a long time to respond. Was he going to say he had changed his mind? When he finally answered, his voice sounded as though he were suppressing some great emotion. Joy? Relief? "Thank you." He seemed to want to say more, but he chose to walk down the steps, and did so with a straighter back.

Rejoice wanted to follow, but she had kelp balls to throw in the ocean. Sighing, she tossed the tied lifebuoys overboard and tried to hit them left-handed. As she aimed and threw, she meditated on the stark beauty of quantum mechanics versus the messy complexities of human motivation. No Cruz seemed to care what she thought about him. Why he should care escaped her. But at least she had finally accomplished something Mother had told her to do. She still couldn't cheer up herself on command, but she had cheered up No. Strange.

Once the balls were gone, she dragged the container back down to the storage room and went to No's room to pick up the dishes. A Do Not Interrupt sign stayed her hand from knocking.

The sound of whistling lured her to the hexacrab access room. Opportunity wound dark green embroidery thread around Elder Chin's fingers, and Mother knelt on the glass floor and sang/whistled to Ur-Veena.

Mother frowned hard as she tried to reproduce a grating sound that ended with a double click. When she saw Rejoice she whistled into the microphone, "I ask you not to turn your shell as I turn my eyestalks in another direction for three breaths." At least, that was what Rejoice thought she whistled, but it was still hard for Rejoice to understand hex spoken quickly.

Mother hugged Rejoice and grinned. "Isn't it wonderful? Ur-Veena consented to teach me a child departure song. And he's going to let me make a recording of two hex of his people's songs."

Rejoice scrambled to come up with an appropriate response. Father was dying, and Mother was excited about singing in Hex? Oh, that meant the hexacrabs were speaking again. "Are any of the songs about the kraken?"

Mother put her forefinger on Rejoice's lips. "They're songs about the children. And Ur-Veena made one about Opportunity. I'll talk to you about them later. Right now, I'd like you to visit Father."

"Father?" Rejoice's heart quickened.

"He's drifting in and out of sleep. Don't wake him if he's asleep. If he wakes up, don't be disappointed if he falls asleep again in five minutes. Do you understand?"

"Yes."

Mother kissed her and turned back to Ur-Veena. Rejoice raced down the hall to Father's room.

He slept, panting rapidly as pure oxygen hissed over his face. Rejoice sat beside him and stroked his hand, still swollen, and now yellow. If only she could will away the yellow, the color that showed the failure of his liver and the build-up of toxins. She looked away from his hand and stared at the heart monitor until she thought her own heart would fail from seeing how irregular his heartbeat had become.

After an hour of watching Father sleep, she gave up and went to the galley to wash stacks of dishes and cook three dozen carrot hand-pies. After setting them on the table with biscuits and fruit gels, she went to the laundry and folded clothes. Everyone kept such irregular hours now there were no set meal times or chore times. Rejoice mopped salt off the stairs. Why did travel adventure books never mention the tedium and drudgery that formed most of every day? She thought to make tea for the Hancocks and walked back to the galley.

In the dining room, she found them already sitting with cups of rosehip tea. She prepared and brought them a tray of seaweed crackers.

"Thank you, dear," Sister Hancock said. Dark half-circles drooped beneath her eyes and limp strands of grayed hair loosened from the bun trailed down her neck. She took some crackers, and then a carrot hand pie. The seaweed crackers crunched between her teeth as she meditated on the bottom of her cup.

Rejoice sat beside them and licked a flake of salty, bitter seaweed. "I've been thinking."

"Now there's a dangerous activity," Brother Hancock said.

Elder Chin came in with Opportunity on his back. He set her in her high chair and teased her, pretending to give her a cracker, and then flicking it out of her reach.

"I've been considering the cranial capacity of kraken."

Brother Hancock laughed. "Who's been teaching you such big words?"

"You," Rejoice said. "The kraken has a big brain. They are built a lot like the hexacrabs. The hexacrabs venerate them. What if the kraken is intelligent?"

Elder Chin set down the cracker with a crunch. The good humor in Brother Hancock's face drained away. His fingers twitched around the base of his cup.

Sister Hancock said, "It acted like a beast. It carried no artifacts, used no tools, did not study us, and only attacked us. It can't be intelligent."

Brother Hancock raised his trembling hand. "Artifacts and tool use are definite signs of intelligence. But a lack of them does not necessarily mean a lack of intelligence. How intelligent are the anemone and swimming stages of the hexacrab?"

Elder Chin sucked his teeth. "Perhaps we should step down the voltage on the cables, so that if we encounter another kraken, we could discourage it rather than kill it."

Glumly, Brother Hancock tapped the table. "I don't know how you would determine the dividing line between discouraging and lethal." He closed his eyes and slumped. "Merciful God."

Elder Chin laid his hand on Brother Hancock's shoulder. "We have no proof, only a question. I know that we saved the hexacrabs."

"For which they are not thankful," Brother Hancock muttered. He sighed. "Not again. I had hoped that we would move in less ignorance with hexacrabs along. But they haven't helped nearly as much as I thought they would. Our purposes do not always coincide."

"Why would they?" Elder Chin asked.

Sister Hancock had been sipping tea and watching her husband with sorrow-filled eyes. Suddenly she set down the cup with a clack! on the table. "That's it!"

All turned to look at her. She made a cage with her hands. "Fungal cell walls are different from human cell walls. The cellular transport mechanisms would be different also. So we couple the drug with, oh, say a peptide of some sort. One the fungal cell wall admits and the human cell wall doesn't."

Brother Hancock sighed again. "How do we do the analysis, synthesizing, and coupling with the equipment we have on board?"

She looked at him wide-eyed. "Well, we can sit here and wring our hands, or we can tear the lab apart until we figure it out, can't we?"

Brother Hancock sat up and checked his screen. "Right. We have forty-five minutes before Starflower gets overhead. Then we'll have ninety minutes to ask it the right questions."

"I did an analysis of cell wall components day before yesterday."

"When did you have the time?"

"When you were sleeping."

Brother Hancock grinned. "Time's a' wasting." They rushed out of the dining room together.

Rejoice watched them go. Would they be successful? She had been an at-home secretary and he had been a shoe store manager before boarding the Starflower. On the star ship, they had all studied hard for new roles on a new planet, but who could say how much any of them really knew?

"Gampa, gib me dink peez," Opportunity said.

Elder Chin gave her a drink of cooled rosehip tea.

"What do you think?" asked Rejoice.

"I know nothing about cell walls."

"No, about the kraken."

"I think we don't know enough yet. I'm glad you brought the question up." He gave Opportunity another cracker. "Your father told us you would make us question our assumptions. Keep up the good work. Also, would you please care for this little one? I have a new line of questions for Ur-Veena."

"Yes, Sir." She sat beside her sister and blew on a piece of carrot pie until it had cooled. Babysitting, cleaning, cooking, and more cleaning. She would have had more fun working in the cannery. She had wanted to help with the research on the fungus in Father's lungs, but she didn't have the background to understand what she read. If she ever had time to study again, she intended to add courses in organic chemistry, molecular biology, zoology, botany, and human physiology.

* * *

Two days later, Rejoice walked Opportunity on a deck shrouded with fog. Condensed fog dripped from the sail slats and plopped on the deck and the brim of her hat. "I don't understand," she said to No, "why Elder Chin doesn't turn this ship around and go straight home."

No looked at her with his brows drawn together.

He would probably tell her they had passed the halfway point and with the currents and prevailing winds, it would be faster on the present course. Or he was going to tell her whether or not they were at the colony, Father would still die. Or maybe he would tell her they were on a glorious mission and mustn't cancel it for any reason.

But No said none of those things. Instead, he cocked his head. "Are you telling me that you don't know that the person in charge of this voyage is your father?"

She gaped. "I thought Elder Chin was."

No shook his head and laughed. "Why do you think your father could choose who came and who didn't? How do you think he was able to delay the start until after you came back?"

"But it was Elder Chin who led the ship's conference back when Brother Hancock got hurt."

"Of course. He's the elder. But who did Elder Chin ask last for the final word?"

Rejoice's filter mask felt stuffy. Perhaps it was time to change the filter. "I guess I thought my father was asked last because he was the least important."

No laughed again and quoted scripture, "The last shall be first and the first shall be last. Your father is in charge of this voyage and where it goes and whose interest is pursued. He's also in charge of the next space mission to destroy asteroid Deceit."

"He was going to go into space after this voyage?"

"No, but he decides who does go."

So that explained why No told Father he wanted to go to space. She had assumed that No talked to Father only because Father was a friendly ear. "But Father can't talk now. Why doesn't Elder Chin take over and order us home as soon as possible?"

"Next in command is Sister Hancock. But your father has already left his orders. We are to skip the next chain and head straight for Large Archipelago. There you are to collect rocks for his apprentice pupil using the same methods of collection you have been taught."

"He didn't tell me that!" Rejoice said. Oh, those instructions might have been in the letter she had never finished reading. Everything clicked into place, and Rejoice felt like a fool. She also felt as though she would drown in sorrow. Before she broke down, she tried to change the subject. "I understand you are going to be on the team to destroy asteroid Deceit. As long as the triplets don't go, you should have fun."

No said nothing. He stared ahead as they walked around the deck and fat water drops splatted on their hats. Rejoice resisted the urge to fill the silence. Was he upset that she had been critical of the triplets? He didn't know that because of them, she had learned to inspect her bed every night.

Opportunity babbled to herself as she imitated the preaching style of Pastor Wiseman. They walked four times around the ship. Rejoice tried not to think of it, but, as always, her thoughts returned to Father with his bloated, yellow fingers, and labored breathing. Every day he looked a little bit worse. Mother never left his side now except to sing with hexacrabs.

The hexacrabs still talked to no one but Mother, and then only about the songs. Gloomy Elder Chin now worked in the lab entering data as the Hancocks measured fungal growth.

Once, bleary-eyed Sister Hancock dropped an entire stack of Petri dishes, and the subsequent screaming and raging seemed to echo through the ship for hours, though it only lasted a few minutes. Brother Hancock would not allow Rejoice to clean up the mess because he didn't want her to be exposed to the fungus. Sister Hancock's public apology at dinner for disturbing the peace of the ship had been thoroughly embarrassing. The last few days had been terrible.

And now, as they walked about the deck, No seemed to have fallen into a depression again. Rejoice could not think of a single way to cheer him up. Certainly, she had nothing to be cheery about. She checked her screen. Time to start lunch.

She reeled in Opportunity and left No, who didn't seem to notice. On the way to the galley, through the open door, she heard Mother singing *Rock of Ages* to Father. She peeked in. Mother washed his face as he slept.

In the galley, Rejoice brooded as she stirred tomato paste into the barley-lentil soup. Opportunity had to help with everything, and she managed to spill the entire bag of barley. After that was cleaned up, Opportunity shoved a bowl full of biscuit dough on the floor and smashed it to shards.

It took two hours to make lunch. Rejoice was exhausted by the time she set the bowls on the table. How did Mother do anything with Opportunity under foot? "Lunch is served," she called softly over the intercom, not wanting to disturb anyone, and not knowing if anyone would come. After delivering a bowl of soup to Mother, she came back to find the Hancocks and Elder Chin sagging over their bowls. Exhaustion lined their faces.

They ate in silence interrupted only by Opportunity's demands. The Hancocks dragged back to their lab as Elder Chin slowly tore apart a biscuit and ate it. Suddenly he looked up. "Where's Young Man Cruz? Did he eat already?"

"Last time I saw him, he was walking on the deck."

Scattering crumbs everywhere, Elder Chin surged up and out of the dining room. A few minutes later, he dragged in completely wet No and said, "I don't care if it's spiritual or not, right or wrong, convenient or inconvenient, when I tell you to do something, I expect you to do it. Now, eat."

Rejoice tiptoed over to give No a bowl of soup. Had he been walking the whole time?

No did not look at her as he pulled the bowl closer. Water dripped from his hair into his soup. He scooped up a spoonful with his left hand and fumbled it. Some splashed on his shirt. He closed his eyes and clenched his jaw.

"It's hard to do things left-handed," said Elder Chin more gently. "Do you want me to feed you?"

"No." He swallowed twice. "Sir."

Rejoice escaped into the galley. She resolved to not make any more soup until his right arm had healed. In the galley, she remembered Opportunity. If only Elder Chin would watch her sister for a while, but she couldn't think of a good excuse to foist the little girl on him. Rejoice couldn't concentrate hard enough to study. She couldn't call anybody in the colony because they were still out of range. Sure, she could record a message, and watch a recorded message back, but that did not appeal.

"Rejoice," Mother said over the intercom. "Please come here."

Oh-oh. Her heart stuttered. She peered into the dining room, but before she could ask, Elder Chin flicked his hand. "Go."

She raced to Father and Mother's room, and then stopped at the door and opened it slowly.

"Come on in," said Mother, laughing. "Why do you look so worried?"

Rejoice struggled to maintain her composure. Did all mothers ask stupid questions?

Father's eyes were open. Mother rose and Rejoice took her seat. "Hello, Father."

He typed slowly, [U OK?]

Rejoice nodded, afraid to ask how he was. And she couldn't think of a bit of news that could interest him.

[Tired of Op yet?]

"Well, yes," Rejoice said. While it wasn't a good answer, at least it was a true one. Then she told Father about the smashed bowl and how hard it was to clean up while trying to keep Opportunity from cutting herself.

When she had finished, Father nodded slightly, closed his eyes and fell asleep again. Rejoice waited several minutes, and then tiptoed out. She regretted that the last thing he had heard from her was a complaint. She would not do that again. Yet it had felt good to talk to someone about how hard life was.

* * *

Over the next several days, as the ship plowed its way toward Large Archipelago, Father woke for longer and longer times. Together, he and Rejoice studied the pictures of blurs in Half-Moon Bay on the south-east end of the largest island. They could not come to a conclusion. Rejoice pointed out the very small, odd cloud formations that appeared each morning just inland from the shore. They hadn't seen such linear, tinted clouds anywhere else on New Earth. Father looked thoughtful, but didn't say anything.

Once, she asked him, "Father, how come you never told me you were in charge of the ship?"

[U want to call me Captain and salute?]

"No, it just would have been nice to know."

[I'm in charge. Glad to make your life nicer.]

While Rejoice pondered how to respond to that, he fell asleep.

CIRCUMNAVIGATION CHAPTER TWENTY-ONE

Ur-Veena scraped his jointed legs and shell with his diamond studded blade, and then turned to inspect all of Sa-Issi's hard surfaces for barnacles and other growths. He tapped the tips of his beak together. Sa-Issi kept still as he watched him with all three eyes.

"The Dark Death is not done with us," grated Ur-Veena.

"Question? Question?" stammered Sa-Issi, unable to form any more words than the particle that indicated a question.

"Dark Death came from the space-ocean. These air-ocean people claim to come from another rock sphere in the space-ocean. Perhaps. Perhaps." He reached for the handhold near the hatch and pulled himself forward. With a delicate touch he stroked one of the scooters. It tingled slightly. "They give us scooters with information we cannot read. They surround us with machines we cannot understand or use or make for ourselves. They do not let us search by ourselves for females. Do they seek for the last of us that they may finally cleanse the water-ocean of our presence?"

Sa-Issi squeaked, "They give us kelp. They give us salmon. They answer our questions. They exposed their soft spots. They play with me."

Ur-Veena positioned one tentacle by an intake hole. "Yes. Taste the currents. Watch with all your eyes."

Sa-Issi popped open all his opercula. "You teach the songs to Female Cholly."

"Yes. I remind them why we wander."

"You do not speak with Male Chin."

Ur-Veena stared out the hatch. "He probes too far with his questions. I weary of questions."

"I ask too many questions?"

"Yes." He did not look at his small companion.

Sa-Issi retreated to a far corner and curled into a lump.

CIRCUMNAVIGATION CHAPTER TWENTY-TWO

A week later, Father shuffled into the dining room to sit down opposite Elder Chin. Behind him, Mother wheeled a cart holding his oxygen tank and nutrient/medication drips. He shook hands with Elder Chin, and then typed, [Congratulations.]

Elder Chin beamed. "Thank you. It is most gratifying to become the grandfather of the most beautiful baby in the world. Heart's Desire is perfect."

Father typed, [I expect to be dangling a cute red head on my knee next year.]

"Perhaps so," Elder Chin said, "but there is no comparison. Sorry, Brother."

Brother Hancock chuckled. He seemed as giddy as Rejoice at seeing Father up. "I'm partial to curly hair, myself." All his children had straight blond or red hair, but two of them had married people with blue-black skin and hair so tightly coiled it could scarcely be combed. What his grandchildren would look like was anybody's guess.

Father typed, [So what happens when Hide God's Word In Your Heart gives birth?]

"Ah, then her baby is the most beautiful baby, and Heart's Desire becomes the most beautiful toddler."

Everyone laughed. It didn't matter that the jokes were vapid. They were happy to be alive. Healthy babies were being born at the colony, the sun shone that day on the ship, and Father could walk, slowly, yes, and with an oxygen mask and tubes snaking from his arms, but he could walk.

Rejoice brought in mugs of peppermint tea for everyone but Father. He still had to work too hard at breathing to be able to eat or drink yet. Opportunity pounded her candied yam chip on the table until the chip disintegrated into dust. No sipped out of his mug holding it with his right hand newly released from its sling. He winced and transferred the cup to his left hand.

"So," Sister Hancock said, "How excited were the hexacrabs when you told them about the thousands of islands north of Largest Isle?"

Elder Chin's smile subsided. "I cannot tell. I am still being given the silent treatment."

Mother rubbed her eyes and yawned. "After I recorded the songs, Ur-Veena stopped talking to me too, except to say all he wants to do is taste the currents."

Rejoice sat pressed against Father. "If the Large Archipelago is the spot on New Earth least damaged by Dark Death, why did we settle on Sole?"

Elder Chin gave Opportunity a new yam chip. "We thought that if we started on bare rock, we would have fewer worries about damaging the ecosystem, or having the ecosystem damage us before we learned about it. Ultimately, though, it was God's guidance. If we had not settled where we did, we would not have met Ur-Veena and discovered the lost libraries."

Still, the elders had decided, and not Father. "We might have met other hexacrabs."

"I hope there are some here, and that we meet them," Elder Chin said.

Father looked at her and typed: [Also first photos showed no green life. Only brown and gray rocks.]

Rejoice laid her head on Father's shoulder and ignored the smells of disinfectant and sickness.

Later that day, while Rejoice was walking Opportunity, she came upon No carefully hefting a spear. He returned it to its bracket and joined her for the dawdle.

"It is good to see your father feeling better."

Rejoice tugged at the strap of her mask. "Yes, it is. But when I asked, Mother told me it could be months or years before he's totally healed." Or maybe never. She tried to close the door on that thought. He would get better and better and better. He must. She crossed her arms and felt a small hole in the elbow of her dress. She would have to patch that right away. Now all her dresses would be patched. There were holes in the elbows of No's shirt as well. "Would you like me to sew patches on your shirt?"

"Huh?" No held out his arms and inspected them. "I can do it, sort of. I've been repairing Elder Chin's clothes." He thought a moment. "However, if you want to, I would be relieved to have someone who is good at it do it for me. Or maybe you could show me how to do it better."

Rejoice thought of the cotton and flax that were going into the making of books instead of into fabric and the subsequent slow down in the issuing of new clothes. "I don't understand the colony at all. This voyage we're on needs so much to succeed; and the colony needs us to succeed. Why didn't the colony give us more four-wheelers and clothing and satellites and ships?"

"Scarcity of resources and labor. In fact, in a few years we should have a real crisis with a scarcity of labor that should last a good ten years."

A ten year crisis of scarcity of labor? Rejoice had heard these words before. What did economics have to do with the colony which didn't use money? "What scarcity of labor? We're all working as hard as we can."

"That we are," No said, clasping his hands behind his back. "But when you watch Opportunity, what else can you do?"

"Precious little. I can cook, but it takes twice as long."

"Exactly. And as we who were children during the voyage on the Starflower grow and marry and have children, half of us are withdrawn from the labor of building into the labor of raising children. Of course, the raising of children is the most important task, but it does mean fewer hands for the making of things. That's why the colony is in such a hurry to get the infrastructure in place before we're all consumed by baby care."

No husband, no babies for her. Rejoice picked at a thread at her elbow.

She would get to be the labor. Whoopee. Why would the labor crisis last only ten years? Oh, of course.

She watched Opportunity hop over the seams in the deck plates. In ten years the present crop of babies and toddlers would be old enough to do serious work. She had needed to go into space when she was thirteen. What would Opportunity need to do?

"Well, I still think the colony made a mistake in how it decided to allocate its resources." There was a good economics statement.

"So do almost all of us. Only every one of us has a different idea of what the mistake is. That's one reason why we're switching to money and a modified capitalist economy in two years."

"What? When was this decided?"

"Before we left Old Earth. The adults have always known it. I guess that's why it's not a big topic of conversation. Before we left Old Earth, the colonists studied the histories of communes and utopias and colonies. Looking at the difficulties of those before us have had taught us what kind of economy we wanted."

"Capitalism!" she said scornfully. "I prefer socialism. From each according to his ability, to each according to his need. That was the only phrase in my economics course that sounded Christian."

"True. It does sound Christian on the surface. But denying the consequences of the Fall is not Christian."

Rejoice studied him.

"Socialism is what we have now. The elders are getting really tired of dealing with the feuding that inevitably results from what we have. Sister so-and-so is not working as hard as me. Brother so-and-so refuses to do the work the way I tell him to. Why are we building this instead of that?"

Rejoice wanted to giggle as he imitated a whiny five-year-old. At the same time, what he was saying alarmed her. Worse, he was indicating she sounded like a whiny five-year-old. "I never heard about this feuding."

"I suppose sharing a room with an elder means hearing things not everyone hears."

And having a deaconess for a mother didn't hurt either. "It must be nice to be one of the elite."

No stopped and closed his eyes. Opportunity tugged on her leash and Rejoice followed, looking over her shoulder at No. She must have offended him. When would she learn to control her tongue?

After a few moments, he opened his eyes and rejoined Rejoice. "Thank you. Tonight I will pray about and meditate on this serious charge you have brought against us."

"I didn't bring any charge against anybody."

"Excuse me, but you did indeed do so. You charged me and I assume Elder Chin and the rest of the elders with elitism. That can occur with any spiritual and economic structure, and no man is immune to it. If I and the elders truly do hold an attitude of pride and superiority, then God will judge us. We need to repent before that happens."

Rejoice feared that whatever happened next, she was bound to end up in a lot of trouble. "Please ignore what I said."

"When God may have guided your words? I think it will be good to examine our hearts. At any rate, you just pointed out the major weakness of socialism."

When had she done that? Were they having the same conversation? "Could you tell me what I pointed out?"

"The problem of elitism. One group of people, the government, tells everyone else what to do and tries to allocate resources evenly. What a joke."

"I don't think being fair is a joke."

"I notice you don't eat the radishes. Suppose everyone on this ship had to eat two per day, whether they wanted to or not."

"But I wouldn't like that."

"But it would be fair. If you think about it, we really don't want a fair allocation of resources. Everybody wants more of this and less of that. When we switch to a capitalist economy, then everybody can buy what they want the most and not buy what they want less. And whoever wants to get a project funded will need to persuade other people to put up the cash to fund it. Voyages to find more resources such as the one we're on should get plenty of support, especially after all the excitement this one has raised."

Rejoice frowned as she tried to remember the lessons. She had fallen asleep every time she studied economics. "But capitalism leads to deep poverty here and excessive wealth there."

No nodded. "There is that danger. Every human endeavor has danger. Mankind's inherent sinful nature ensures that. Nothing prevents you, however, from seeing a need and giving to it. Under any system, you can give your wealth away. Capitalism tends to create more wealth to give away."

"You mean like Elder Smith did?"

"True. He had a gift for business and God blessed him in it with great wealth. Through that gift, he blessed many others. Including you and me."

"But not the hexacrabs."

"If he had not given away all his wealth, and flown us here, all the hexacrabs would be dead."

Rejoice blinked. That was true, but that was an accidental byproduct.

No looked out at the blank sea and flat horizon. "It pleases me no end to see the most important people in the colony leading the simplest lives."

"Such as?"

No widened his eyes. "Such as Elder Chin and your parents."

"My parents? My parents are important?"

No laughed. "Yes. Your parents. Your mother directs the choir and all the special programs at the church. Your father organized all the expeditions. They both have a lot of authority."

Rejoice tilted her eyebrows. "They're not the least bit bossy." Except for telling her what to study.

No laughed again. "Authority does not equal bossiness. You have great authority."

"I have authority? If that's so, why is it everybody tells me what to do?"

"Because you're still only sixteen. But you are the one that caused the colony to change all its plans and send a lot of people into space for a long time."

"I didn't do that. The asteroid did."

No said nothing to that, but the skin around his eyes crinkled.

Rejoice frowned. "But if my father is so important, why isn't he a deacon or an elder? Why aren't Brother and Sister Hancock a deacon and deaconess?"

"That you will have to ask them," No said. "But my understanding is that they were asked, and chose not take the offices."

Rejoice frowned harder. Why would they do that? She would ask Father.

After a few steps, he said, "Back to socialism. When I studied Old Earth history, I was struck by something I decided to call the rule of perversity. Every human endeavor attempted without the rule of God always achieves the opposite of what is intended. Socialism attempting to produce equality produces a ruling elite and oppression. People attempting to obtain freedom from the bondage of church rules, end up slaves to bad habits and their passions. People attempting to create the Kingdom of God without the power of God create hypocrisy and evil." He studied the deck with his shoulders hunched.

Intriguing. He saw everything so differently from her. "What are you thinking about now?"

"Hmm? Oh, two things. One is how perversity is working in my life. A private thought. I'm sorry. The second is something I just realized from my studies in the history of architecture."

"Why did you study the history of architecture?"

"Because to get my degree in Biblical Studies, I have to study something besides theology as well. Elder Chin insisted I take bonehead physics and bonehead chemistry, but—"

"What is bonehead physics?"

"Physics without the math. Anyway, I still had to pick up some other courses as well, and when I went through the listing, I saw the history of architecture. I thought it might teach me how to build buildings that don't fall down."

"My father said your building wasn't the only one blown down."

"That's true. But the collapse is the main reason why we have only one four-wheeler and a thousand spare parts. So, think about the gothic cathedrals in Europe. No artist signed any of the works in the cathedral because the buildings were supposed to glorify God and not man. The names of the priests and builders are not recorded. And yet, when you walk in, what are you surrounded by? Pictures of people, kings, beggars, saints, the damned. The walls are crawling with stained glass images of lords and ladies. There are statues of gargoyles, imps, plowmen and bakers. Everywhere you look you see people."

Rejoice could vaguely remember seeing a picture of a gothic cathedral in France. It had something called a rose window which she hadn't understood because there was no rose in it.

"Then we come to what was called modern architecture. The founders of the style intended to construct buildings focused on man. The style was to be scaled to man, fit for man's needs, radiant and helping man achieve perfection. So what was built?"

"I don't know."

"Boxes. Big, ugly, faceless boxes that were inappropriate for almost any climate. Boxes with no trace of humanity in them. Boxes that people hated to work in and hated to live in. Boxes that had nothing to do with the stated goals of modernism."

Rejoice grinned inside her filter mask. "And we, a people devoted to simple lives, build an absolutely beautiful Meetingplace."

"The Meetingplace is simple."

"It's beautiful with all that blue glass and stars."

"Beautiful and simple are antithetical?"

Rejoice opened her mouth and then closed it again. She had assumed they were. Okay. She would study the history of architecture. She wanted to look at bonehead physics too. If you took out the math, what was left? "If the rule of perversity means that humans automatically get the opposite of what they work toward, does that mean we pacifists are going to end up in a huge war?"

"May God have mercy on us," No murmured. "I pray not."

"What would we do if the hexacrabs declared war on us?"

No hung his head and thought. "Stay out of the water, I guess. Or throw Brother Hancock to them again."

Rejoice giggled. Opportunity tripped and sprawled on the metal deck. Rejoice picked her up. Opportunity saw her bloody knee and then screamed.

Rejoice carried her below deck for Mother to fix, and then she made supper. She watched Father sleep while Mother ate with the other people and then showered. Then Rejoice bathed Opportunity, patched her dress, washed the dishes, made a rice pudding, and went to bed with her little sister.

She stared into the darkness as she meditated on what No had said. Maybe other subjects could be as exciting as mathematics. Perhaps the rest of the voyage might not turn out so dismal after all.

CIRCUMNAVIGATION CHAPTER TWENTY-THREE

nother week passed as the yellow in Father's skin faded and the swelling shrank. One evening after Rejoice had kissed Father on the forehead and said good-night, she remembered a question.

"Father, why aren't you an elder or a deacon? Why isn't Brother Hancock? You're two of the smartest men in the colony. Is it because Elder Smith hates you because you love the hexacrabs?"

He looked over at Mother and typed, [U explain please.]

Mother looked up at the ceiling and shrugged. "Not all people have the same gifts and callings. I consider both your father and Brother Hancock deeply spiritual and godly men. However, the office of a deacon and an elder require gifts and callings that, that are stronger in other men in the church."

"Were you asked to join the deacon board?"

Mother looked at Father. He typed, [Yes. Several times. Both of us. We chose not to.]

"But why? Father, you need to be making the decisions for the colony. You're the wisest, most intelligent man here."

Father smiled. [Thank U,] he typed. Then he looked at Mother again.

She smiled wryly. "There are a lot of responsibilities to being an elder and deacon. It requires a lot of time, focus, and energy. Your father and Brother Hancock feel that they need to put all of the time and energy into figuring out how this New Earth works to help us survive. They are both gifted scientists and researchers, as is Sister Hancock. We have few of those in the colony."

Rejoice frowned and looked at Father.

[OK,] he typed. [I also hate church politics.]

"I thought so!" Rejoice said.

"But you should know," Mother said, "that it was Elder Smith who personally asked your Father and the Hancocks on multiple occasions to accept nomination to the deacon board."

Then Mother rose and kissed Rejoice and told her. "Your father is doing much better, but is still very tired. We can answer more of your questions later. Good night."

* * *

The ship was now positioned so that direct communication with First City was available at least an hour per day, during First City's midnight. So many people wanted to speak to those on the Magellan, that all the conversations were limited to five minutes each.

Rejoice started a radio chess game with Abiding who had the night shift at the mutable fabrication plant which was now producing and stockpiling wall units for farmhouses. On a day when the moist air pressed in like a smothering blanket and the ship's air conditioner had broken, Rejoice was trying to decide whether to move her queen or knight when she stepped into the radio room and bumped into No.

He whirled and pushed the door open again. "Excuse me, but I have not finished this private conversation."

Rejoice caught a glimpse of Harmony's worried face on the screen before No took her arm and turned her out. The door clicked shut behind her. Rejoice fumed. Who did he think he was, tossing her out like that? What was going on with all those secret conversations? Harmony had always tried to keep secrets from Rejoice, maybe because she knew how much Rejoice hated secrecy and social gamesmanship.

She stormed past the hexacrabs and ran into her room. With a flushed face and trembling hands, she plugged in her screen and entered the radio channel.

Harmony stood beside Mother's holly bonsai. "Are you sure Rejoice doesn't know?"

No replied in a soft voice, "I have not told her. Instead of worrying about Rejoice, why don't you concentrate on what you need to do next?"

Rejoice's ears burned as Harmony said, "But it's been so long since I've been able to talk to you."

"I see. Then let's start over at—"

Harmony screeched, "Someone's listening in!"

Rejoice ripped the computer cord out of its jack before Harmony could have the tell-tale trace her down. She slammed the screen shut and jammed it into its case. Father and Mother had to know about this. She marched to the door, but when she touched the handle, she stopped and considered. What exactly was she going to tell Father and Mother? She hadn't heard them making plans to run off with each other when No got back. Even if she had, where would they go?

All she had truly heard was that Harmony didn't want Rejoice to know something. What? Anything that secret had to be illicit, but again, what? And if she went to Father about this, she would be the one censored for violating privacy.

She dropped her hand and rested her forehead on the door. Stop. All the adults knew he talked to her. They might even know what about. But she was still a child even if she had saved the world. So everybody could keep secrets from her. She hated, hated, hated secrecy. Just who did he think he was? Why was he talking to Harmony instead of fixing the air conditioner? Why had Father brought him if he couldn't fix anything?

A few minutes later, Mother called her on the intercom. "Rejoice, please come to the bridge radio."

On the way up, she passed the Hancocks standing arm in arm watching the empty sea and exclaiming to each other how wonderful it was that Joy And Crown was expecting a baby.

In the bridge, she joined Mother and watched Harmony and Stronghold, also arm in arm, talking about Makepeace and how the hexacrabs in the new Sa cluster were acting strangely. They were harvesting the kelp as before, but they no longer sang or talked around the humans. When asked why, they only replied that they were tasting the currents. Rejoice could hardly made herself look at Harmony. Harmony talked about her behind her back, yet she was also her sister-in-law forever and ever.

In the middle of Stronghold's question about whether or not Elder Chin had any suggestions about how to talk to the hexacrabs, the transmission wavered and blanked as the satellite carrying it drifted out of range. So much for Rejoice's five minutes with Abiding.

On the way back to her room, she came across No doing slow, trembly push-ups on the deck. She started to brush past him, but changed her mind and stopped. She folded her arms and stared at him to see how he would like it. It seemed he didn't care because he continued the pushups. After several minutes of getting hotter in the sun, Rejoice burst out, "What secret things do you and Harmony talk about every day?"

No lowered himself and lay face down for several breaths. Then he sat up and laid the back of his head on the solar slat housing. Misery creased his face. "Can you understand that privacy and secrecy are not always the same thing?"

"No, I can't! I hate secrecy!"

"I have many conversations with people that I never repeat to anyone else. You are going to have to accept that about me."

"I don't have to accept anything about you!" Rejoice turned and fled to her room before she could say something she would truly regret. A difference between privacy and secrecy indeed! Another half a year on the same ship with No. The thought gave her a headache. For a while there, he had seemed like someone who was interesting to talk to, but now she wanted to never see his face again.

That night at supper, No did not come in to eat. Would Elder Chin drag him in again? Elder Chin rose without a word after eating and took a tray of food with him.

The same thing happened at breakfast the next day. Rejoice surmised that No was sick. But the only virus they had brought with them was the cold virus, so how he could be sick was more than she could figure. Maybe the steam they were all sweltering in had wilted him. Why didn't he fix the air conditioner?

Mother suggested that Rejoice spend the morning studying while she took over the care of Opportunity and the galley.

Rejoice opened her studies and groaned when she self-tested and saw how much she had forgotten since the kraken attack. As she looked at her scores in previous economics tests, she realized that she had settled for any score that passed just so she could get the course over with. She would start over from the beginning and this time think about how the principles applied to the colony and how they applied to her.

Then she scowled. It was No who had opened her eyes to what economics was about. Why did he have to be so nice one day, and so horrid the next? The triplets hadn't managed to do it, but No would. He would drive her crazy before this voyage was over.

Lunchtime came, and still No didn't show, and again Elder Chin took his meal to him. Rejoice had to clench her teeth to keep from asking what was wrong with No. Mother excused her from all chores and told her to study.

In her room, she found a message on the computer from Father listing who had what times on the radio that afternoon. Rejoice was to go first because she had missed her time from before. That still left three hours for study.

Since she had worked so hard that morning on economics, she would spend the afternoon on something she liked, so she pulled up quantum mechanics and immersed herself in the sweet, orderly world of mathematics.

In the midst of a knotty problem, someone knocked on her door. Sighing, she placed the problem on hold and opened the door.

Mother entered, smiling, with her hands behind her back. "I have a surprise for you." But when she saw the look on Rejoice's face, she added, "Wrong word, I mean present. I have a present for you." She brought her

Hands forward and showed a neat stack of six handkerchiefs embroidered with tiny dark green holly leaves on snot-green fabric. "I worked on it while I was sitting up with your father and you were working so hard to keep the ship together."

Before she could stop herself, Rejoice blurted out, "Mother, those are horrid. I hate that color."

Mother stammered, "I thought you liked it. Why else would you have picked the material for your bean bags?"

"Because it was the ugliest cloth you had and it wouldn't matter if I accidentally threw it overboard."

Mother sighed. "Sometimes, child, you are hard to please."

"No, I'm not! All you had to do was ask me what I wanted instead of trying to surprise me. I would have been happy to pick out the fabric."

"But then I would have felt like your maid for hire instead of your mother making you a present."

"Fine!" Rejoice said as she rushed past Mother and shoved open the door. "The solution for keeping both of us happy is obvious: don't give me any presents!" She ran into the hall and saw No staring at her.

What was he doing there? Had he been trying to listen in? "Leave me alone!" Elder Chin stood in the hallway also, holding Opportunity's leash. Great, why didn't she just broadcast the entire argument? With her cheeks growing hotter, she turned and ran up the stairs.

She jogged to the back of the ship, sat with her legs over the edge, and watched the water churning behind the ship. She should apologize, and the sooner she did, the sooner it would be over, but she didn't want to face anybody just now.

Why hadn't she simply taken the ugly handkerchiefs, said "Thank you," and then hidden them in the bottom of her drawer? The water churned ceaselessly, as did her thoughts. What was wrong with her? She should be happy. She had saved the planet for humans and hexacrabs; Father looked like he would live after all; everyone was getting married and having babies.

Rejoice leaned her head on the railing. She was not jealous of stupid

Harmony who got married just because she never would. Not her. She was not jealous because everybody else would have babies and she wouldn't. Not her. She was not jealous because all her friends could pick who they spent time with and she had to look at No every day. Not her. And unless she could stop lying, she was going straight to hell. Yes, her.

She wiped her eyes and blew her nose and stared at an empty sea until it was nearly time for the satellite contact. Wearily, she rose and walked toward the bridge.

She stopped when she saw No taking three lead weights out of a box. Had he been watching her the whole time? He stopped too, momentarily, on sighting her, but then he turned to face the sea and started juggling.

Rejoice watched him for a bit. "I thought you were sick when you didn't come for meals."

He watched the dull gray balls as they rose and fell. "Not physically."

Was he saying he was mentally ill? Somehow she doubted that. She checked her screen: several minutes yet before she could place the call.

No added, "I'm having a struggle accepting something I don't want to accept."

You didn't pry past such vague words unless you were counseling the person who said them. She wasn't about to counsel No. She watched the skin tighten around his eyes and listened to his panting as he juggled the heavy balls. "Doesn't that hurt?"

"Yes."

"So why don't you stop?"

He kept his eyes on the balls. "You don't want to know."

"So why did I ask?"

He paused before he answered, "I don't know."

She didn't need this aggravation. "Why can't you answer a straight question with a straight answer?"

Thok! Thok! Thok! He caught the balls. "Okay. Two reasons. One: after Elder Chin held me down and force-fed me, he booted me up here and said if I don't exercise for two hours, I can sleep in the hallway."

"How could Elder Chin do that? That's terrible."

"I must have needed it or he wouldn't have done it. Two: only a coward holds back from doing what he must because it might hurt. Straight answer."

Rejoice thought how she had stopped practicing throwing with her left hand because she couldn't stand the pain and never got any better. "I don't see the point in beating yourself up."

"Quitters never see the point." He began to juggle again, but missed the ball. It crashed with a tremendous boom next to his toes. It should have landed on his head. "See if I ever show any concern for you again."

He scooped up the lead ball and tossed it. "I accept that."

Rejoice shook her head. He didn't make any sense at all. She checked her screen. Nearly time for her to call Abiding.

She ran to the bridge. The sun's rays concentrated on her through the windows the way they do through a magnifying glass. She fanned herself with her hat. Perhaps she should have used the radio room below deck. No, then she would have faced the adults and needed to apologize. She still didn't feel ready. She felt hot. She felt trapped. Another half a year with No Cruz and hexacrabs that wouldn't talk and bare rock islands and a nasty welcome from Elder Smith when they did get back. She wiped her eyes again and hoped they weren't too red.

Sweat stained her dress by the time Abiding's face came into focus. Rejoice opened her mouth to announce the queen's move, when she thought of a way to find out what she wanted to know without going through No. "Abiding, can you tell me what girl No is interested in?"

Abiding looked up from the corner-screen view of the chessboard and laughed. "No? Ha! That young man is interested only in God. Every time he sits down with a girl to start a project, he begins with a speech about how he isn't courting her and she mustn't ever think he is. And then he makes sure there's somebody else in the field or room listening in on them."

Except in the case of Harmony. Father had mentioned something about No's projects. She hadn't asked what that meant then, and she had forgotten about it since. She pulled off her hat and fanned her face with it. "What do you mean by project?"

"He hasn't started one with you? You must be the only one."

"So what's a project?"

It's different for each person. He sits down with you and he asks something like, 'What would you do if God had given you all the resources and talents to do it?' or 'What is a weakness in your life you would like to overcome?' Then he works out a project with you and monitors how you practice and improve."

"Improve what?"

"It's different for each person. For example, when he asked me what I wanted to do that I couldn't, I said I wanted to write but I couldn't figure out how to arrange words to mean what I think. So he gave me the assignment of going verse by verse through Psalms, and each day take only one verse and rewrite it so it would make sense to a hexacrab. Once a week, he checked what I did. After a couple months of that, he had me write one short paragraph about something I found interesting. Now I'm writing the crop reports and birth announcements for the Chronicle. I love it."

Rejoice gazed at her, speechless and wilting under the intense heat.

"Are you sure No hasn't started you on some self-improvement project? That doesn't sound like him."

There flashed into Rejoice's mind the image of the kelp ball container on its side and the balls rolled out on the deck. The ball throwing contest. He had tricked her.

"Abiding, excuse me, I'll call you back tomorrow." She fled the hot room.

Drenched with sweat, No groaned with each sit-up. When he saw Rejoice glaring at him, he rose and gazed at her warily.

"You manipulated me," Rejoice said with tight jaws.

"Pardon me?"

"You manipulated me into learning how to throw kelp balls."

No picked up a lead ball and tossed it from hand to hand. "You can say I manipulated you or you can say I encouraged you to develop a facet of yourself that you hadn't developed yet."

"I can say that I hate sneakiness and I hate manipulation and I hate secrecy. I can do fine without your encouragement. I managed to kill the kraken without it, didn't I?"

No nodded and added a second ball to his juggling.

"And what's with you and Harmony? What is the big secret between you two?"

No kept his eyes on the balls. "Please, Rejoice, I hate making you angry. Please don't ask me for what I can't tell you."

Rejoice stomped back to the radio. She had a minute and a half of private conversation left. She punched in the code for Harmony and Stonghold's apartment.

A bleary-eyed Harmony answered. She yawned. "I had the alarm set for ten minutes from now. I thought you all weren't calling for another fifteen minutes."

"I want to know what all the secret calls between you and No are about."

Harmony folded her arms. "If I tell you, it won't be a secret anymore, now will it?"

"Does Stronghold know about it?"

Harmony's mouth dropped open. Then she shouted, "I don't like how your mind works, girl! If all you can do is think nasty things about me, then I'm not ever talking to you again!" Her fist darted to the control board and the screen blacked.

Rejoice's brain sizzled out of control. A tiny voice in the back of her mind chanted, *Stop! Breathe deeply. Invite peace.* But the heat and frustration roared louder.

Like a shuttle cock, she clumped to No still juggling lead weights. She stopped and glared at him. "She won't tell me either." She swallowed hard. The swallowing hurt.

No set the weights on the deck with a hollow, metallic sound. He wiped the sweat off his forehead with his arm and leaned against a railing. After some deep breaths, he said, "You're still angry."

"You better believe it. Why won't either of you tell me what's going on?"

No lowered himself to the deck. "It's not hard to figure out why Harmony won't tell you."

Rejoice wanted to hit someone or something. *Stop this! Invite peace.* She closed her eyes and took three deep breaths. Okay. She sat down, too. "Why?"

"You intimidate Harmony. She feels like a very dim candle next to your floodlight."

Rejoice stared at No as the sail slats turned and creaked. Stripes of light and shadow crossed them. "What?"

"You're brilliant, like your father, only more so, in the kind of intelligence that can be easily measured. Harmony is afraid that if she attempts anything intellectual around you, you will laugh at her because she can't come close to what you can do. She wants to show you after she has reached her goal, so you won't mock her for how long it took her to reach it."

Confusion paralyzed Rejoice's tongue, until she blurted out, "Harmony is doing something intellectual?"

No's mouth turned down. "You just proved my point."

Rejoice had failed a test, but she didn't know what the test was. "Look, I overheard you and Harmony." Shame burned her cheeks at this admission. "It was just a minute. I, well, you sounded awfully tender."

His dark eyes narrowed and he looked away for several moments before returning his gaze to Rejoice. "I need to be tender with Harmony. She's very sensitive."

"Harmony? She's as sensitive as a rhinoceros."

"Excuse me, you are wrong."

Rejoice sat back. "You sure don't talk tenderly to me."

"I don't need to. You're tough. I like that."

Rejoice stared at him, aghast. He liked that. He liked her? That arrogant young man liked her? She lowered her eyes and stared at the deck where a piece of white paint had chipped off a bolt. The sails shifted a degree.

"Too bad you don't understand people at all."

She snapped her gaze back to him. "Mother said I should study psychology."

"I like your mother. She and Elder Smith are much alike."

Rejoice's skin flared. No was a lunatic. "They're not at all alike. Elder Smith is a mean, vindictive, old man; and my mother is always kind and happy and always singing. Why are you saying such outrageous lies?"

The skin creased between his eyebrows. "Why do you say Elder Smith is vindictive?"

"Because he is. He won't let any of my father's projects go through, or if they do go through, he makes sure father doesn't have the equipment he needs."

"It's the decision of the entire board of elders, not one man."

"But whatever Elder Smith wants, the board gives him."

He lifted a hand. "That's not true. Elder Chin has mentioned many ideas that Elder Smith brought up and was talked out of. He is no dictator and the elders are by no means rubber stamps. And none of the projects that you're thinking about have been killed. Many have been deferred. Instead of an oil derrick, we built a nuclear power plant. You can't do everything at once, can you?"

"No."

"Also, isn't this voyage your father's project? And didn't Elder Smith come to wish us well?"

"Father says he came because somebody reminded him that we might shrink the ocean. Mother says he came because Sister Smith told him to."

No templed his fingers and thought a moment before answering. "Your parents are wise people. They are both at least partially correct. You must understand that Elder Smith wants to be a great leader. He wants to be a godly man. Sister Smith has never asked him to do anything he didn't already want to do, but couldn't see how to do until she asked him. Yes, your mother and he are much alike."

Again the lie. "They are not the least alike. He is self-important and always serious. Mother is always happy."

"Your mother is not always happy."

"What, you know my own mother better than I do? She's always happy. Sometimes it drives me crazy."

"Your mother is not always happy. Listen to me. Elder Smith carries the entire colony on his back. He is afraid that if he is not always strong, if he is not always decisive, the colony will dissolve into chaos and fear. Your mother is carrying everyone on this ship. She is afraid that if she is not always cheery and encouraging, that everyone will be sucked into the same kind of grief that threatens to overwhelm her."

"Grief? My mother? My mother? Carol Dove Holly?"

Now he spoke as gently as he had with Harmony. "Your mother was very close to her family left behind on Old Earth. Family is the most important thing to her. And what does she have on New Earth? Her husband is sick. He nearly died. Her first son rebelled. Her second son is brain-damaged, and will be brain-damaged for the rest of his life, unless God performs a miracle. Every gift she gives her first daughter is rejected."

Rejoice licked her lips and fought against tears. The salt air tasted bitter. She wanted truth, but not this truth. "How do you know this?" she whispered. "How do you see what I can't see?"

"I like to watch people."

Shadow and light lines striped the deck. "No?"

"What?"

"Do you remember when we went to school together, and," she gulped, "and when I was doing math, you were always staring at me?"

"Yes."

"Why? Why did you watch me?"

"Because I like to watch beauty."

What? She pulled at a strand of her plain brown hair. The colony did not encourage the use of mirrors, but she had looked into enough of them to know that she was not beautiful. "Beauty?"

"Yes. You've seen the vids of the ice skaters, the gymnasts. These are people who have trained their bodies and perfected their art. They're beautiful. The farmer plowing a straight furrow is beautiful. The cook preparing a delicious meal is beautiful. You doing math is beautiful."

Rejoice gazed at No. A lump in her throat kept her from speaking. For a moment there, she had thought he was going to say she was beautiful and he loved her or some such ridiculous thing. *Fix it in your mind, Young Lady, no one is ever going to say that to you. You need to settle for being as beautiful as a farmer plowing.*

He continued, "I used to tune my screen to yours so I could follow your steps. At home I would try to recreate what you had done in class. I never could. But I got better at math for trying."

Rejoice cleared her throat and examined her knuckles. She had been wrong about everything, had always been wrong about everything. A new thought tightened her throat. She was like Elder Smith too. He was mad at God and taking it out on the Holly family. She was mad at God because life didn't turn out the way she wanted, and she was taking it out on Mother and No. Poor fellow, he must truly be tired of her rudeness. She looked up at him. And she had thought he was stupid.

"Why didn't you ever speak in school?"

"I already knew what I thought. I wanted to hear what everyone else had to say."

Wonder at the kind of person she was sitting beside caused her to look away. And what she saw made her gasp and spring to her feet.

"Look!" She pointed over the ocean at the last thing any of them had expected to see: a canoe floating less than a half kilometer away.

CIRCUMNAVIGATION CHAPTER TWENTY-FOUR

No vaulted past her and pulled the alarm lever. Shrill ringing tore the air as he shouted, "Canoe on the starboard side!"

The cacophony of people charging up the stairs joined the alarm. Sister Hancock dragged up a camera so the people of the colony could also see what happened. Elder Chin peered through binoculars and then thrust them toward Brother Hancock. "Looks like that model of a churtree that the hexacrabs made for us."

Mother, with Opportunity on her hip, gasped and said, "What am I doing up here with this little girl?" She bore her away and Opportunity's "No! No! No!" followed like a fading echo until the door to her room was closed and locked.

"Got it in focus," Sister Hancock said. "What? Oh." She looked at the screen next to her viewfinder. "Young Man Cruz, Brother Holly says to check all sides to make sure that's the only one."

No jogged about the ship looking out at sea. "Only one," he said when he got back.

Though Father seemed a prisoner in his little room, he kept his eye on everything through the computer and camera system, and one never knew when his messages would pop up in the midst of one's work. Still, how much better it would have been if Father had breath enough to climb the stairs.

The masts groaned as they turned and the ship changed course to head for the canoe.

"It's paddling toward us," Brother Hancock said.

Mother came up the stairs, breathless, and Brother Hancock handed the binoculars to her. "Ooooh. It looks…it looks…"

"Hideous," Sister Hancock said.

"The vulture thinks its babies are cute," Brother Hancock said.

Rejoice leaned over the railing to peer at the canoe. From so far away it looked like a black spider floating on a twig. She moved to look over Sister Hancock's shoulder at the viewfinder.

She licked her salty lips. The churtree had a black cylindrical body with four stubby legs. Four long, thin arms radiating about a circular, red mouth lined with teeth. The ugly thing paddled on both sides of the canoe at the same time with spoon-shaped paddles marked with red and black spirals.

With no hesitation it paddled straight for the ladder on the side of the Magellan and quick as the sting of the naspy picked up two spears and bolted up the rungs.

No Cruz unlatched the gate at the top of the ladder and reached down a hand to help it up.

It yowled like a cat and thrust one of its spears at him.

No flinched aside, so instead of being stabbed through the throat, the spear furrowed his cheek and slashed through the mask strap. The mask flew off and fell into the ocean. No flung himself back and sprawled on the deck.

The churtree leaped onto the deck. With its four black chameleon eyes set between the arms, it watched the wall of people back away. The skin on its meter long body twitched. The arms splayed out like a black pinwheel a meter high. It made Rejoice think of a giant, mangy weasel with a starfish perched on a long neck.

Rejoice backed into the camera stand. Both she and it crashed to the deck.

The churtree darted toward her with its spears aimed at her.

No threw himself on it and they rolled against the railing. Elder

Chin stomped on one spear. Brother Hancock grabbed the other and wrestled it out of the creature's hand. The churtree twisted and lowered its mouth to sink several rows of teeth into No's shoulder.

No shouted and thrust it past the railing. One of its arms grabbed the lower metal pipe. Screeching and spitting like cats fighting, the churtree pulled itself up. No pried its fingers from the metal pipe.

The churtree pin-wheeled into the ocean, splashed, and bobbed up again.

Sister Hancock leaned over the railing with the camera she had pulled off the tripod. Brother Hancock looked at the gash on his hand and Mother ran to get her medical kit. No clapped his hand over his shoulder, stood, and looked over the railing. Blood welled over his fingers.

Elder Chin picked up the spear from the deck and joined No. "How can we let it know we won't hurt it?" They watched the creature swim toward the canoe that had drifted away as the ship's momentum continued the ship forward.

The churtree rotated its black eyes toward Elder Chin holding its spear. The thing screeched, jerked backward, and then collapsed into a limp, floating mass.

The puzzled people leaned farther over the railing.

The churtree rolled over to reveal a hexacrab lance imbedded in its belly and blood streaming out to sully the water.

Elder Chin screamed, "What have you done?" He rushed to the jack under the alarm and with trembling hands plugged in his screen and tuned to the hexacrab scooter radio.

The hexacrabs whistled, "Celebrate with us, for we have killed the churtree!"

"No," Elder Chin rasped. "We didn't want you to kill the churtree. We wanted to keep it alive."

Ur-Veena grated, "Attack you? Yes?"

"Yes. But we understand that it is the way of this ocean, water and air, to attack first and ask questions later. We ignore attacks because we want to become friends with the churtrees, as we did with you."

The hexacrabs did not answer. All that could be heard were the creaking of the sail slats as they folded and Elder Chin's breathing. No's blood seeped through his fingers and trailed down his arm. Tears ran down Sister Hancock's face and the camera canted forgotten on her shoulder. Mother stared at them all with her face white and her mouth open.

Sa-Issi peeped, "Question? Churtree friend?"

Ur-Veena broke in. "Question? Churtrees teach air ocean-people the eating of hexacrab eyes?"

"Never, my friend. Never." Elder Chin's voice broke. "But we, all of us, must not kill the churtrees."

A shrill whistle with no translation issued from the computer, and then silence.

Brother Hancock squeezed his eyes shut. "We need to retrieve the body."

No looked over the side of the ship and took a deep breath.

"I'll do it," Rejoice said before he could volunteer. She tucked her dress into her pants so it wouldn't hinder her feet, and scrambled down the ladder while Sister Hancock found a huge net and lowered a boat.

As Rejoice putted over to the body, she glanced up at the camera aimed at her, and nearly froze with the thought of everybody in the colony watching her. She turned her face away. Of course Sister Hancock should be recording what she did. The alternate view was of Mother patching up No. Would the hexacrabs react violently to her retrieving the body? Where were they?

She pulled up beside the churtree. Bare patches of dark skin with red incised lines spotted its pelt of coarse fur. Gold circles banded its arms. Down the center of its back, tiny gold hoops pierced the skin in a meter line. Its eyes were still open. Rejoice shuddered as she dipped the net under it. Because it was heavier than it looked, she couldn't pull it in the first time she tried. She braced herself for the second try and pulled the body in. Blood and water puddled around the jutting black limbs.

By the time the hoist had pulled the churtree onto the deck and the boat had been secured, mother had pasted the last of the meshflesh on

No's shoulder. Rejoice picked up his blood-sodden shirt from the deck. "Maybe I won't patch this after all."

Sister Hancock, huddled over the body, called out, "Young Man Cruz and Young Lady Holly, I'd be taking a shower right now and scrubbing well. This churtree is crawling with parasites."

"Ewww!" Rejoice cried.

No muttered, "Determined to get us one way or another."

Elder Chin burst out angrily, "Theophilus, wait a minute!"

Shocked, Rejoice turned from the body to Elder Chin. He sat on the deck and frantically punched something into the computer. The radar dish revolved. His jowls shook as he studied the screen and then punched in something else. He studied the screen again. In disgust, he slammed the computer into his lap, sagged against the bridge wall and covered his face. Mother and the Hancocks went about their clean up with nervous glances toward him.

Elder Chin moaned, "They're gone."

Brother Hancock left the body to kneel on one knee beside Elder Chin. "The hexacrabs?"

Elder Chin dropped his hands to rest on the computer screen. "I'm sorry, Brother Holly. I tried. They've either smashed or ripped off the locaters. I can't find a trace of them. The scooters and hexacrabs are gone."

* * *

Ship's conference in two more hours. Rejoice sat folded on her bed and traced the outline of her screen with her fingers. More than sixteen hours had elapsed since the hexacrabs had disappeared, and they had not come back. Perhaps by now they couldn't.

After showering for a good hour upon the discovery of two black mites trying to burrow into her wrist, she had emerged wrinkled to find that everyone else had already eaten supper and cleaned up. That suited her, for she had a lot of apologies to make, but she needed time to think about what to say.

The next morning, when she had requested over the intercom some quiet time with no interruptions, Mother agreed. Then an hour later, she had been interrupted by Elder Chin's announcement over the intercom that everybody was to watch the recording they had just gotten from the colony.

Rejoice tuned her screen. Harmony and Stronghold stood side by side in the office overlooking the kelp farm. Tears glittered on Harmony's cheeks as she cried. "Last night the hexacrabs packed up and moved away. They took the females and all the scooters. And nobody is answering us at the Ur cluster. Where did they go? Did we do something to make them mad?"

Stronghold added, "We got up at the usual time and went out to harvest section 12-B, but the hexacrabs weren't there. So we went to the Sa cluster and it was empty. Nobody here knows what is going on. Do you?"

Red-faced, Harmony sniffled. The last thing she said was, "I'm including a message just for Rejoice." The recording ended and Elder Chin announced a ship's conference in two hours.

Now Rejoice sat and fiddled with her computer. After what she had said yesterday to Harmony, she was sure she didn't want to hear this message. Yet whatever horrible thing Harmony might say, Rejoice deserved it. She swallowed hard and thought about life with a sister-in-law that hated her for the rest of her life. Why had she worked so hard to make everyone mad at her? She sighed and pressed the play button. The sooner she heard it, the sooner she would get through it.

The screen showed Harmony in the apartment with a holly bonsai that looked as though she had forgotten to water it. Tears dotted her cheeks. That girl. If she wasn't crying, she was laughing her head off. Why couldn't she ever just be calm? Then Rejoice thought about how calm she had been lately.

"Rejoice, I need to apologize. Stronghold reminded me that you have this thing about secrecy and—"

"She's neurotic!" Stronghold said off screen.

Rejoice tightened her lips as Harmony glanced off screen. "Anyway, I know you don't like secrecy and Stronghold told me to let you know before you made everybody miserable. And No called to ask me to release him from his promise. And well, I guess I'd better tell you. I didn't want to because I wanted to finish it first. You don't know what it's like to grow up stupid when you're surrounded by brilliant people. Mother always rolled her eyes and said I did stupid things, and I guess I did that a lot. So when No asked me what I wanted to change, I said I wanted to stop being stupid."

Harmony sighed and glanced off screen again. "And No asked me what I could do that would prove to me I wasn't and I didn't know. So he asked me if memorizing a whole book of the Bible would do it, and I thought it would, so we've been working on it. I picked Luke because it's the longest book in the New Testament. I haven't finished yet, but you wanted to know, so you'd better listen. Here goes:

"Many people have undertaken to write an account of the things that have been fulfilled among us . . ."

Rejoice rubbed her throat where it hurt as she listened to Harmony recite verse after verse. "Then an angel of the Lord appeared to him and stood at the right side of the altar of incense. When Zechariah saw him, he was startled and filled with fear . . ."

Rejoice huddled into a tighter and tighter ball as she listened. Shame flamed her ears. How had she been so quick to assume No and Harmony had been up to something evil? Why couldn't she shrink into nothingness?

"Mary was greatly troubled at his words and wondered what kind of greeting this might be . . ."

Maybe what No was struggling to accept was the fact that he had to spend another six months with Rejoice. She didn't want to either, but how do you leave your own skin?

"He has brought down rulers from their thrones but has lifted up the humble . . ."

Yes. An apology to Harmony, if she could get one past the lump in

Her throat. An apology to Mother. An apology to No. An apology to the entire ship's crew for disturbing the peace. Again. Why hadn't she stayed in space?

"In those days Caesar Augustus issued a decree that a census should be taken of the entire Roman world . . ."

Rejoice shut off the message. Her dry eyes burned, but she could not cry. She had cried before and it hadn't done any good. When had she ceased to be rational?

She set the screen aside. She knew exactly when: when she discovered Not Worthy loved Every Knee Shall Bow instead of her.

With a new and hideous insight, she realized she was jealous of Every. She was jealous of Harmony. She was jealous of the Hancocks. She was jealous even of her parents, jealous of everyone who could find someone to love who would love them back. Instead of thanking God for the unwelcome gift of singleness, she had spit bitterness on everyone around her. Would she be this suspicious and spiteful the rest of her life?

So . . . there was the disease. Where was the cure? Rejoice pulled the grimy bean bag out of her pocket and rubbed the beans between her fingers. Sister Olson had a cure, but it wasn't the right one. The pain she left behind pierced more deeply and savagely than the pain of putting up with her.

She rolled out of bed and knelt on the floor. "God, you've got to help me. I can't go on being like this. How do I change? How can I be grateful that I'll be single all my life?" She listened, but all she could hear was a faint ringing in her ears and her breathing. After a while, her knees hurt. All she could think of were the apologies she needed to get through.

Sooner started, sooner done. She rose and rubbed the wrinkles in her knees. Who first? Mother?

She peeked in her parent's open door. Mother sat with a screen in her lap and embroidered some violet-blue cloth with red thread while Father checked the maps of the ocean floor.

Mother looked up and smiled. "Come on in." She patted the bed by Father's feet. "You can sit here." She shook out the cloth she was working on. "Since you hated the yellow-green material so much, I thought maybe this dark purple would please you more. Is this acceptable, or should I try something else?"

Rejoice took a deep breath. "Mother, it's not the material. It's me."

Mother watched her, eyebrows raised.

"I'm sorry that I've been so difficult. It's just, well, I'm not making an excuse, but maybe you want to know. Why I went on this trip was because I couldn't stand the thought of having to look at Not Worthy while you were gone. When I yelled at you, I was really upset at Elder Smith and Young Man Not By Works Worthy. I'm sorry I broke peace with you."

Mother thought a second. "What did Young Man Not By Works Worthy do?"

"He didn't do anything. I guess I fell in love with him." She squirmed. This was why the colony made peace-breakers confess. This was so embarrassing that no one wanted to sin and need to confess again.

Mother tapped her chin with her forefinger. "Why would you let yourself fall in love with somebody who's engaged to someone else?"

"You knew? Not Worthy thinks it's a secret."

"It amuses me how much you children think we adults don't know."

Rejoice's grip on her composure had been tenuous, and now she lost it altogether. "I didn't know! He never told me!"

Mother threw everything on Father, sat beside Rejoice, and hugged her tightly. "Not only that, you were in space and couldn't see how they look at each other. Now I understand. I'm so sorry I didn't even know you were struggling with a broken heart." She stroked Rejoice's hair. "That maggot! I hope he nails himself to a fence post again."

Rejoice pulled back. "That's—that's not a peaceful thing to say."

"What he did to you wasn't peaceful. I assumed you knew all along. I can't believe he didn't think that he needed to tell you! That coward! He sure lived up to his name. He's certainly Not Worthy of my daughter. Men are so stupid!"

The screen beside her flashed. Rejoice read, [Thanks.]

"No, dear love, you're not stupid."

[Then why do I remember U call me stupid back in]

"Oh hush," Mother said. "You're aggravating. Don't you understand Rejoice is in pain? It hurts to have your first love turn you down."

Rejoice huddled closer to Mother and a faint scent of vanilla and soap. How couldn't she have seen before that Mother was not against her? Mother wanted her to study so she could understand the world. Only now was she beginning to understand how little she did understand. Mother wanted her to be happy. Mother was on her side.

She wrapped her arms around Mother and squeezed. If only she could start this voyage over again. "I'm so afraid nobody will love me the way Father loves you."

A loud silence followed. Rejoice looked up. Mother and Father gazed at each other in that kind of silent communication she would never share with anyone.

The words formed on the screen: [Don't be too quick. Your assumptions can be incorrect.]

Rejoice dried her eyes. Her assumptions about Harmony and No had certainly been incorrect. No was the next one who deserved an apology. She started to stand, but Mother pulled her back.

"Honey, I want you to know something. We didn't know this voyage would be this bad. If we had, we wouldn't have gone. When I think of how you've coped through all this, and a broken heart besides, I'm impressed. We're very proud of you."

Rejoice nodded dumbly. What was Mother proud of? She was unwilling to ask.

"God has given you a challenging lot. You spent three important years of your life in space away from all your friends and peers. Your father and I didn't realize how that might affect you socially."

"Is that why I can't understand anybody?"

[I was pretty clueless when I was sixteen.] typed Father.

Mother laughed. "You were still clueless at eighteen. You're clueless now."

[Thanks] he typed. His eyes laughed.

Rejoice wanted to get through the apologies. Mother squeezed her one more time, and let her go.

CIRCUMNAVIGATION CHAPTER TWENTY-FIVE

Rejoice stood at No's door for at least a minute dithering. Then she knocked, assumed she heard a 'Come in,' opened the door, and walked in.

No lay sleeping on his back, with no shirt on and the bib of his denim overall folded down. What did that man have against shirts? The bruises on his skin had faded to yellow and the scab where Mother had stabbed him was shrinking. The lacerations on his shoulder were a maze of dark red lines. The furrowed line on his cheek flared a brighter, spreading red. A thin, white scar on his arm showed where the torpal had scraped him. This voyage had been a bad one for him, too.

Rejoice startled. She had no business being there, and she turned to leave, but No opened his eyes. Rejoice stammered, "I didn't mean to wake you up. You know how you can't hear through these doors."

He rubbed his face. "Is it time for the conference already?"

"Not yet. I wondered if we could talk first."

No rubbed his face again, "I'm sorry. I don't feel up to another fight."

"No, I promise, I won't ever fight with you again as long as you live."

No covered his face and his shoulders shook.

Alarm chilled her spine until she realized he was laughing. "What did I say?"

He swung his legs over the edge of the bed and sat up. "Even someone as persistent as you can't make a promise like that. As far as I'm concerned, you never said it." When he stood up and reached for his shirt, he winced, and left the shirt on the back of the chair. Yawning, he brushed past Rejoice and opened the door. "Let's go."

"I wanted to apologize in private."

"Let's talk over tea. It might wake me up."

Rejoice followed him into the galley and found trays of shortbread, peanut-butter cookies, corn meal muffins, and candied yam chips. No said, "I'll take these into the dining room while you make tea."

Rejoice lifted the hinged lid of the metal tea box and was greeted by the mingled dusty odors of mints, lemon grass, hibiscus tea, and dried herbs. "What kind do you want?"

"Peppermint. Oh, wait, how much of that is left?"

Rejoice estimated. "About seventy packets."

"What is there the most of?"

"Chamomile."

No made a face. "Of course. Who can stand the stuff? Oh, right, I can. Make me a cup of that, please. I'd like to save the peppermint for Elder Chin." He pushed through the door with the stacked trays.

Rejoice set up two tea pots, one with chamomile for her and No, and one with peppermint for the rest of the crew. While she waited for the water to boil, she looked out the porthole at the empty sea. Where were the hexacrabs?

When she brought in the two cups of steaming, tan tea, No bit into one of the few remaining peanut-butter cookies. "Wonderful. Did you make these?"

"Not this time." She slid into the seat opposite him. "Harmony sent me a recording of her reciting the book of Luke."

He swallowed and widened his eyes. "She did?"

"Yes, and there is a difference between privacy and secrecy. I'm sorry I pretended I didn't know the difference." She closed her eyes. "I'm sorry I've been so wicked during this whole trip."

"Wicked? Not at all." Rejoice opened her eyes. He gestured with the cookie. "Hasty in judgment perhaps, but then, you're quick at everything." He pointed to the scar on his chest. "I have reason to be grateful you're quick."

Relief flooded her veins. He was not angry as he had every right to be. "I'm still sorry I've been giving you a difficult time."

"I've found that people who give me a difficult time are usually people that are having a difficult time."

His compassion and insight awed her. What had changed him so much in the last three years? Or was it that she was finally seeing who he was? Should she tell him about Not By Works? She took a sip of chamomile and added honey.

"You don't have to tell me about your difficulty. You don't have to tell me anything you don't want to. I just ask you to return the courtesy."

"Yes, Sir."

No winced.

"I really am sorry, No, and I will try to be courteous from now on." She took another sip. "Would you help me with a project?"

No shifted in his seat. "What did you have in mind?"

"Well, Abiding told me how you do projects with people. If it's a young lady, you get permission from the parents and you tell the girl that you're not courting her, and then you meet once a week to see how the project in going."

No took several deep swallows of tea. "Uh, what kind of project do you have in mind?"

"I want to stop being so wicked."

No pushed aside the tea and laid his head on his forearm. His shoulders shook again.

"You don't think that's a good project?"

No sat up and tried to rub the smile off his face. "I should have known that the young lady who can save an entire planet would want more than a piddly little project."

"It's that hopeless, huh?"

No swallowed some more tea and picked up another cookie. He thought while he ate it and picked up another one. "The problem is that it's the wrong focus. One, you are not going to achieve goodness on your own. If you could reach total goodness in every thought, word, and deed, then why did Jesus hang on a cross for you? If you could be good on your own, He could have just come, led a good, long life, and on His deathbed whispered, 'Now you people do it the way I did it'. It didn't happen that way because every one of us needs forgiveness. Right?"

Rejoice nodded.

"Two. If you're trying hard to not be wicked, who are you focusing on? You. You either feel as though you did pretty good today, so therefore you're proud of yourself. Or you feel as though you did badly, therefore you feel bad about yourself. You end up leading a yo-yo life, focused on how you feel you did."

Rejoice nodded again. Yo-yo. Yep.

"Instead of focusing on you, you should focus on God and the people God has put into your life. Think about God's goodness instead, and the duty to the people around you. What would help them? What would serve them?"

Rejoice thought about that as he popped the cookie into his mouth and grabbed another one. There were only two left. How did he manage to eat two dozen cookies in less than five minutes? "No, how old are you? How do you know all this stuff?"

He smiled. He had a nice smile. "That's a sermon sixty-year-old Elder Chin gave me three months ago. I had to write it from memory the next day, and when I missed a point, he gave it to me again. Then I had to recite it five mornings in a row. He wanted to make sure I got it."

Rejoice sipped her tea. "Does that mean you won't work on a project with me?"

"I'd be happy to work on a project with you. But it needs to be something we can measure, and it should be something short-term, like from now to the end of the voyage."

"And then after the voyage we go our separate ways and never speak to each other again?"

No slumped back in his seat and studied his cup. "If that's what you wish. I will respect your desires."

"That's not what I wish. What I wish is we could be friends forever and ever, and be able to talk to each other without being afraid that we're going to hurt each other's feelings."

He sat up and a broad grin spread across his face. Oh, he had more than a nice smile. He had a very nice smile. If only his gaze weren't so intense.

"So, do you want to be my coach for learning how to throw left-handed?"

"I'd be happy to."

Elder Chin stepped into the dining room, and stopped. His eyes met No's, and No nodded slightly. Elder Chin grinned, made a fist that dipped and came up, turned, and danced out of the room.

What was that all about? Rejoice looked at No with another cookie in his hand. Ah, Elder Chin was happy to see him eating on his own.

"You know," Rejoice said, "people fast for different reasons. Some do it to discipline their bodies. Some do it as a way to focus their prayers when there's something they want a lot. Me, when I fast, all I can focus on is how hungry I am." No smiled at that. "You fast more than anybody I've ever seen. Why do you fast?"

No switched his gaze from Rejoice to the cup he held. His face grew darker and redder.

He was blushing!

He licked his lips but missed the collection of crumbs in one corner.

"You don't have to tell me," Rejoice said.

He stood abruptly. "I need more tea."

Rejoice watched him go. Water splashed in the galley. Moody fellow. Of course, her saying that was like the maggot calling the tinsel-worm slimy.

The Hancocks came in. Sister Hancock scanned the dining room, and headed for the galley. No came back and sat down. Brother Hancock touched him on the shoulder with his bandaged hand. "Young Man, you and I are in a competition."

No smiled. "That's all right, Sir. You can win." Then he frowned. "Just a minute." No left again.

Sister Hancock brought in a tray of tea things and the pot of peppermint tea. Elder Chin came back, and after him, No dragging some metal rectangles and circles. Mother came in and took No by the chin to turn his face and look at the furrow on his cheek.

"I'll bet that spear was dipped in poison. How do you feel?"

"Fine."

"Poison?" Brother Hancock said. "That young man is getting ahead of me."

Elder Chin waited until everyone had settled and plugged in their screens. [Brother Holly present] glowed in the lower quarter of each screen. Elder Chin entered the date and started the camera. Future historians would be able to watch the conference and with the luxury of hindsight analyze what they did right or wrong. "Let us begin with prayer," said Elder Chin.

They bowed their heads and breathed slowly. Rejoice rubbed sweaty hands on her dress and invited in peace and wisdom. Would they come?

After several minutes of silence, Elder Chin said, "Young Lady Holly. Do you have any observations of the churtrees or hexacrabs you would care to mention?"

Rejoice pulled up the satellite pictures of anomalous move-ments. "I don't think these pictures of Half-Moon Bay show babies and mothers anymore. I think these long blurs are canoes and the small blurs are churtrees."

Elder Chin hissed. "Of course. Why didn't we see that sooner?"

[Didn't expect to.] Father's words appeared on their screens. [But should have suspected. The blurs indicated land animals. The churtrees were the only land animal we knew of.]

Rejoice continued, "I reviewed photos of other parts of the Large Archipelago. I found a few indicating the bigger blurs in other areas besides Half-Moon Bay. There are some a few kilometers out to sea. Sometimes they're in groups, sometimes just one. I'm still trying to figure out the odd shaped clouds that form near the shore of Half-Moon

Bay every morning. When I reviewed again I saw some other places where the clouds formed in the morning scattered in other places."

[If all agree, I'll change course to Half-Moon Bay now.]

Elder Chin looked around the room. All nodded. "It's agreed. Now, Young Man Cruz?"

No rose and walked to the metal shapes. "I spent last night researching historical methods of defense that don't involve hurting the other person. I didn't find many. I think I can fabricate some kind of armor, but with the time and materials I have, it's going to be heavy and clumsy. I made some shields here. The first one I made out of a repair pane for the hexacrab room. I thought it would be advantageous to see through the shield, but it turned out to be too heavy. So I made these metal ones. They're still not what I want, so I'll keep working on it."

From behind one of the shields, he pulled out a wad of filaments. "I modified this net with weights on the edge and this cord so that if you throw it correctly, it will spin out into a circle, drop on the churtree, and then close when you pull this cord."

Brother Hancock grunted.

"If we knew their physiology, we could try sleeping gases and such like. We could try to spray some of our instant hardening insulation on them, but we don't have much, and there is the danger of getting them in the face or wherever it is they breathe. That's all I have so far." He sat down.

Rejoice shuddered. Unless you could consider a pit of teeth, eyestalks and arms as a face, they didn't have faces.

Elder Chin said, "Brother Hancock?"

"I'm entering into the record all we have on the dissection. Five kinds of parasites, many tattoos, four eyes, four arms, a bazillion teeth arranged like that of sharks. The food is shredded in its throat with a grater-like arrangement. Lungs are full of scars, perhaps from residual atmospheric sulfuric and nitric acids. Two sets of vocal cords. Two spinal cords, one dorsal, one ventral. Oh, four finger tips on each arm. Zero finger nails. Each foot has four, small, clawed toes. No positive sex determination yet, but we suspect that it's a male with obvious genitalia. He was liberally studded with gold ornamentation. That's all for now."

"Sister Hancock?"

She placed a transparent bag of gold hoops and circlets on the table. "Here is the ornamentation. I've been . . ." She sighed. "I've been thinking about the family of this poor churtree. He's got to have a parent or egg-mate or children. Somebody has got to be worrying about him and wondering where he is. How do we notify the family without endangering the hexacrabs, or making the churtrees think we killed it? If we returned its jewelry, perhaps that would convey the message of its death without implying how it happened."

"How could we endanger the hexacrabs who aren't even with us anymore?" Mother pushed brown curls behind an ear. She gave Opportunity in the high chair another cookie.

Sister Hancock pressed her chin. "If the churtrees learn there are murderous hexacrabs about, they might mount a search, and they might be better at finding the hexacrabs than we are. Anyway, we've hidden the body in the deep freeze and set loose the canoe after photographing it. I don't like hiding what we've done here, but I don't see what else we can do."

"How do we know where to return the gold?" No said.

Sister Hancock fiddled with the bag of rings. "Everything at this point is guesswork. If Rejoice is right, there's a churtree village in Half-Moon Bay. If you have a better idea where to return these, I'll listen."

"Maybe we should just stay away from the churtrees," Rejoice said. No one replied to that. She had spoken out of turn.

After a minute of silence, Elder Chin said, "Sister Holly, please continue."

"I wish I knew where the hexacrabs have gone. Can we restore fellowship with them without declaring war on the churtrees?"

Elder Chin looked as sad as Rejoice had ever seen him. "They seem to think that the friend of their enemy is their enemy also."

Rejoice had a thought. "Maybe they went to deliver themselves to a kraken."

Sister Hancock cleared her throat. "Maybe they went churtree hunting."

Rejoice had another thought. "What happens when the scooters run out of charge? Do they sink to the bottom of the ocean?"

Brother Hancock said, "Not if they filled the air tanks first. I've often seen them paddling spent scooters. They have trouble reading the charge meters. I guess we haven't made meters they can read because we're still trying to do everything at once."

"Why aren't we looking for them?" Rejoice said. "They could be in danger."

"Young Lady," Elder Chin said in a voice filled with grief. "Doesn't the departure of the two clusters and our two crew members tell you that they no longer want to associate with us?"

Brother Hancock made a fist. "I don't understand how they could throw away four years of friendship. Ur-Veena and I—I spent more time with him than I did my own kids. I guess we have different ideas about what friendship means."

"They feel betrayed," Elder Chin said.

"I feel betrayed," Brother Hancock said.

[They will be back.] glowed on the screen.

"How do you know?" Mother said.

[If naspy and pollution didn't stop the En, do U think humans will keep the Ur and Sa from coming back during Child Return?]

"You're right," Sister Hancock said. "Elder Chin, did they say anything to you that could give you a clue to their intentions?"

"You mean besides calling me a maggot-riddled, small-beak-brained, churtree friend? No."

Rejoice typed a note to Father: [Any use for gold?]

[Yes, but copper and silver usually found with gold more useful. Also may indicate rare earths. Non-issue if churtrees own and don't want trade.]

Rejoice tapped her screen. At one time she had been horrified that all surface life had been exterminated by Dark Death. If only it really had been. *Oh dear, that was not a peaceful thought.*

"Elder," No said. "What should we do if we meet the churtrees again? I didn't mean to kill the churtree, but what I did led to its death. I have trouble thinking what I could have done differently."

Droops of skin concealed his slanted eyes as Elder Chin frowned. "I have been thinking of nothing else for the past eighteen hours. What we need to keep foremost in our minds is Whose people we are. Who will protect us? Who will call us home when it is time? Our warfare is not with man or hexacrab or churtree. I am not sure that the defenses that Young Man Cruz has kindly come up with at my request are a good idea. They give us the mindset of trying to save our lives." He opened his eyes and took a long swallow of peppermint tea. "We should not care whether they kill us or not. Our behavior is to be based on God's love, who loves all men, all hexacrabs, all churtrees equally."

"Then why did we leave Old Earth?" Rejoice asked. Why did she keep coming up with stupid and irrelevant questions?

Fortunately, Elder Chin did not look offended. "Some of us think that it was because God wanted to use us to save the hexacrabs." He took another swallow of tea.

"Elder," No said. "I think I might be able to allow a churtree to kill me. I don't think I can stand by and let one kill someone else on this ship." He glanced at Rejoice.

Elder Chin nodded. "Thank you for your honesty. The rest of you, can you agree that under no circumstances will you hurt a churtree?"

"Yes," said the Hancocks together. Mother twisted her fingers together before she whispered, "Yes."

[Yes.]

Rejoice was startled when Elder Chin looked at her. She hadn't realized she would have to agree or disagree. "I don't know."

Elder Chin said gravely, "I understand."

"I don't understand," Rejoice said. Why did they need to record this? "The humans could stay on Sole and the churtrees could stay on Large Archipelago. Wouldn't that be peaceful enough?"

"Pass up the chance to meet another people?" Elder Chin asked as though Rejoice had just told him to put out the sun with a bucket of water. "Pass up the chance to establish a relationship with a people who appear to need the Good News?"

"In four years, the hexacrabs haven't accepted the Good News." *Shut up.*

"Four years is a short time."

Maybe if you're sixty it is. Rejoice gritted her teeth.

Elder Chin continued, "It may take many human generations."

Ur-Veena was over two hundred and fifty years old. Rejoice stared at the table, unwilling to contradict the elder any more than she already had. She closed her eyes and took a breath. If the way of peace were easy, then everyone would walk in it.

"Brother Holly."

[If the hexacrabs were with us, I would take them home first. But they are gone. I have set the sonar on continuous so they can find us if they want to. Until they show up, now is the time to visit the churtrees and notify them of the death.]

After several minutes of silence, the conversation began again, but this time Rejoice and No were not asked for their opinions as the others decided that not only would they give the churtrees the rings, but also a present of food, a gift that on Old Earth was a fairly unambiguous gesture of good will.

Brother Hancock pointed out that the churtrees were obvious carnivores, so kelp meal for them was out. They wouldn't give the hexacrab's salmon they had in the freezer, since the alien fish might be poisonous for them. They could give several slabs of torpal meat. They also decided to give the kraken tentacle they had coiled in the freezer. Best to get rid of it while the hexacrabs were gone.

Then they decided they would wear light, padded chest, and head armor after all, for they would wear as much if they were going among bears. No shields. No weighted nets. They dismissed with prayer.

Soon everyone had left the dining room but No and Rejoice. No looked morose as he shredded a corn meal muffin. "I thought I had enough faith for anything," he said.

"Well, if it's any consolation, I'm glad you fail at faith when it comes to watching me get killed and not caring one way or the other about it."

"It's not that you don't care."

"That's what Elder Chin said."

"You misunderstood. You don't care for yourself. Excuse me. You do care for yourself, but you don't seek revenge for yourself. You always care for others. However, all of us need to reach the point where we trust God for the others. I'm not saying this well."

"The Bible says you're supposed to protect the helpless."

"So it does," he said. "I've got a lot of thinking and praying to do."

"I don't," Rejoice said. "I've already got it figured out. We're crazy!" She reached for a shortbread cookie. Oops. Now she had gone and made him angry. She needed to stop working so hard at antagonizing people. But when she dared to look at him, he was grinning.

"Rejoice, don't ever change."

She blinked. "I'm supposed to change; into the image of Christ, remember?"

"You can do that. I guess I mean don't change who you are." He stood up and stretched. "I've got armor to make. Landfall tomorrow. Then we'll see what adventure God gives us." He left, leaving a pile of crumbs for Rejoice to clean up.

As she wiped the table, she pondered the fact that No liked her the way she was. But that was what she wanted desperately to change. How could he like the way she was when he was the victim of her moods? She thought of the other people on the ship and realized with surprise that she didn't want any of them to change either. And part of who they were was the principle of peace-making. To be true to the principle, they must go to Half-Moon Bay and try to establish peace with the churtrees. Maybe she also had some thinking and praying to do. If nothing else, she should pray for wisdom for tomorrow.

Oh, and she still needed to finish listening to Harmony's message and record an apology. Harmony memorizing the book of Luke. That was a very long book. She started wiping faster. Tomorrow meant dozens of churtrees. One had been bad enough. How would they cope with dozens?

CIRCUMNAVIGATION CHAPTER TWENTY-SIX

The next day, as Rejoice brought back the empty tray from the shop where No pounded on metal, she passed Elder Chin seated in the hexacrab access room motioning to giggling Opportunity. She stopped and watched as he touched his forehead, chin, and chest with his hands held in different positions. "What are you doing?"

"I am practicing my sign language. I had a deaf roommate once, but it has been many years since I used it. I've gotten rusty, I'm afraid."

"Do you think the churtrees use sign language?"

Elder Chin looked up at her and chuckled. "I don't know yet. But we humans can and will. I've already installed a sign language course in your computer."

Rejoice set down the tray and flopped onto the floor in front of him. "Why?"

"We just discovered that Heart's Desire is deaf."

"Oh no! I'm sorry."

His eyebrows arched up. "What are you sorry about?"

"That Heart's Desire is disabled."

"Excuse me. Heart's Desire is perfect. She simply cannot hear."

"Isn't there a surgery for that?"

"We don't possess the proper equipment. Now I have a question for you."

Please don't let it be about my sex life. "What?"

"Which is more disabled: the person who cannot hear, or the society that cannot find a way to deal with that?"

Rejoice thought about that and the courses she had filling up her computer. She sighed. "This voyage is not going to be long enough."

"None of our voyages ever are."

"Land ho!" Brother Hancock called over the intercom.

Rejoice snagged the tray on her way out the door.

Everyone on deck crowded in the bow. Sister Hancock looked through binoculars at the fuzzy horizon. "I don't believe it!" she squealed.

Brother Hancock had the next look. His eyes widened and he silently handed the binoculars to Rejoice.

The autofocus zoomed in and out as she tried to hold the binoculars steady despite the ship's rolling in the sea. Finally she held a spot long enough for the focus to clear. She, too, squealed. "Trees! Those are trees!"

As she passed the binoculars to Elder Chin, she repressed the automatic anger at the colony for providing such a low class satellite that saw only visible light. The trees were brown and grey, and because of the poor resolution of the camera, they had been identified as rock. If the colony had known there were trees here, it would have sent an expedition years sooner. Of course, then they would have met the churtrees that much sooner. Perhaps it was just as well.

"The trees aren't green, but I know who will be as soon as we transmit these pictures," Brother Hancock said.

"Poor Brother Carver," Sister Hancock said of the colony's botanist.

"Oh, I hope the churtrees will let us explore this land," Mother said. "Who would have guessed the trees would be brown?"

Rejoice glanced at her screen. They would reach Half-Moon Bay in three and a half hours, mid-afternoon. Two trains raced toward each other for a head-on collision and no matter how many flags she waved, they weren't going to stop. How was it that no one else was worried?

Mother watched her.

"I know," Rejoice said. "Don't worry, it doesn't help. Does not worrying help?"

"Yes, it does." Mother laughed and slipped her arm around Rejoice's waist. "Look, we're not going to walk up to them and say, 'Please stab us so we can show our devotion to God.' If they start throwing spears at us before we even reach the beach, we'll put the jewelry and food in a life preserver and shove it toward them. Then we'll sail in and out of the bay for four or five days until they get used to us and see we aren't planning to hurt them."

"How many months do we plan to stay here until they get used to us?"

"We haven't discussed that yet."

Rejoice leaned on the railing and studied the horizon. Maybe the voyage would last long enough for her to finish her degree and extra courses and sign language after all. God grant she wouldn't have to learn Churt. Two vocal cords! If they did establish a relationship, Elder Chin would want to stay here for years learning the language and culture.

Maybe that was just as well, too. As long as she was in Large Archipelago, she wasn't having her stomach curdled every time she saw Not Worthy. If they stayed here long enough, maybe No could teach her how to juggle with her feet.

That led to another thought. Why wasn't No Cruz courting anybody? That was absolutely none of her business. He could have any number of legitimate reasons. Still, why not?.

The ship plowed on through the sea, dividing the waves and splashing up foam. Bits of orange seaweed flecked the surface.

"Something new!" Brother Hancock chortled. Then he muttered, "Not yet. churtree first."

* * *

Three hours later, they rounded the southern tip of Largest Island and saw the first headland that protected Half-Moon Bay. Two headlands curved around a perfect bowl of blue sea. High land crowned with towers of a soft, gray stone that Father identified as tef marched toward the sea until it fell in steep cliffs a quarter kilometer from the water. The waves had ground the tef into grey sand that rimmed the bowl. Weathering had pulled down parts of the cliff and scattered boulders on the beach. On the right side of the crescent beach, twenty-seven churtree canoes lay in a crooked row. A small waterfall cascaded down the center of the cliff. Its stream disappeared into fifty meters of forest and reappeared on the other side, dividing the beach in two.

To the right of the stream, the churtrees had carved the soft stone cliff into apartments stacked atop each other with hundreds of barred windows facing the sea. At ground level, doors shaped like fat T's yawned darkly. Small columns of smoke snaked up from behind the apartments. That explained the small, long clouds on the satellite photos.

On the beach, some churtrees mended nets, and others sharpened bone fragments into spear heads.

As the white ship with black slat-sails entered the bay, the churtrees stood and watched for several minutes. When the slats lowered and the ship stopped in the middle of the bay, they turned and galloped toward the cliff.

No's eyes shone as he leaned on the railing. "A man would be happy to give his life to bring the Good News to a people such as these."

Rejoice gazed at him from the corner of her eyes. She would be happy to stay far, far away from the churtrees.

He gripped the railing and stared at the village as Sister Hancock set up the camera and Elder Chin lowered the loaded boat. Brother Hancock put away the hats, and Mother passed out the helmets No had made from four-wheeler fenders and insulation.

"Please, Elder," No said, "let me go with you."

Elder Chin smiled and laid his hand on No's uninjured shoulder. "Not this time. If we don't come back, you need to help Brother Holly sail this back to the colony and organize another voyage."

No paused. "Yes, Sir."

Rejoice hooked Opportunity's leash to the railing. *I'm not going to worry. I'm not going to worry.*

Mother interrupted her thoughts. "I would be more comfortable if you and Opportunity stayed in your room for the next few hours."

"I'll take her down at the first sign of anything."

Mother turned and buckled on her chest shield: a shaped fender with tiny holes pricked around the edges and sewn onto a life vest.

Elder Chin, the Hancocks, and Mother held hands in a circle and prayed one last time. Mother led them in the hymn, *Savior, Like a Shepherd Lead Us*. And then they climbed down the ladder, arranged themselves in the boat, and putted off. No tracked them with one of the cameras.

Rejoice knelt by Opportunity to wave bye-bye. She looked past the boat to the village and gasped. Black bodies poured out of the openings in the cliff and ran to and fro on the beach like a disturbed anthill.

She moved closer to No.

He looked up from the camera. "Yes?"

If she said how worried she was, she would start crying. "That armor you made is really clever. But I never did see the shield you made from the glass plate."

"Did you want me to show it to you?"

"Yes, please."

"Here, take the camera. I'll be right back."

Since Sister Hancock held the camera that was recording the reaction of the village from the boat, Rejoice kept her camera focused on their boat. But she often glanced up at the split screen view of the beach and counted. It was hard to tell with all the frantic jostling and fitful running, but Rejoice estimated at least fifty churtrees now crowded the beach. *You can turn around now.*

No pounded up the stairs, and she turned to greet him. But as she did, something splashed behind her. She whirled and looked over the side of the ship right into the maw of a water-slicked churtree leaping up the ladder.

Opportunity! The little girl sat on the deck with her shoes and socks scattered, counting her toes.

Rejoice grabbed the beanbag in her pocket and threw in straight into the tooth-rimmed mouth.

The creature choked. It backed a step, folded its long neck, then spit beans and shredded cloth into the sea.

Rejoice charged toward Opportunity, scooped her up, and ran down the deck until she hit the end of the leash. Rejoice's feet jerked out from under her. She crashed onto her back.

The churtree vaulted over the railing and raced toward her on its stubby legs with an upheld spear.

Rejoice curled around Opportunity.

The churtree hoisted back the spear to throw it. Then it crumpled sideways as a lead ball slammed into its side. Its long arms flailed as it yowled.

No unlatched the leash and flung it toward Rejoice. He stepped carefully toward the churtree and stopped when it hissed and raised its spear. Its legs scrabbled on the deck, but it did not rise.

Rejoice tried to breathe and couldn't. It felt as though her chest had broken.

"I've hurt it!" No cried. "I didn't want to."

Rejoice tried to suck in air and hold onto screaming, flailing Opportunity. A second churtree vaulted over the railing behind No as he stood watching the first with his hands stretched out toward the monster.

She pointed frantically and whimpered.

No turned and threw himself toward the glass shield he had dropped on the deck. He brought it up just as the churtree's spear flew toward his head. The spear glanced off the shield and cracked into the sail housing and then clattered onto the deck.

The churtree darted forward and seized the spear. Then it stood and watched No back away slowly. Its chameleon eyes glittered as it studied the glass pane covered by netting.

No set the bottom of the shield on the deck and dragged the heavy glass as he hunched behind it. "Get up, Rejoice."

Starbursts danced across her vision. She sat up and drew in a breath that felt like fire searing her lungs. She staggered up. No backed two more steps.

The first churtree, now behind him, drew back its spear.

Rejoice wrenched off one of the life preservers and swung it toward the churtree at the same time it threw the spear. The spear pierced the ring, and its momentum tore the ring from Rejoice's grasp. The spear tumbled and its shaft whacked No in the back. Rejoice stumbled over Opportunity. The weaponless churtree screeched and lashed out its black arms. She twisted away.

Still hanging onto Opportunity with her right arm around the little girl's waist, Rejoice reached out with her left hand to grab the netting that encased the shield. No and she hauled the shield back past the churtree wriggling on the deck. Now both churtrees were on the other side of the shield.

The second churtree leaped to its fallen companion and stabbed it where the trunk bent up into a neck. Then it turned, and *chink, chink, chink* hit the glass shield with the spear it had taken from its fallen comrade. The monster stood with its short legs crouched and its toes splayed on the deck, and rotated its eyes to study them again.

"Get to your room and lock the door." No said.

Rejoice sucked in another searing breath. "What about you?"

"I'm trying to cover your retreat. I can't hold this up much longer. Go!"

Rejoice turned and fled. She rounded the corners of the housing and raced for the stairs to their rooms. At the top of the stairs she slipped on a wet patch and crashed into the door jamb.

"Owee!" Opportunity cried. Her leg had been smashed between Rejoice and the jamb.

Rejoice stopped. Water puddled on all the steps. Why? Dreading the answer, she held Opportunity close and descended one step at a time. A churtree skittered out of Father's room. It left red footprints on the white floor.

Rejoice screamed.

The churtree jerked its spear up and yowled in a dual voice.

Rejoice raced back up the stairs. Behind her, the churtree's claws

Clicked on the decking. She slammed the weather door behind her.

"Owee! Owee! Owee!" screamed Opportunity.

Gulping air and with eyes blinded by tears, she lunged toward the box of cables. There she dropped Opportunity who screamed again. She threw open the lid, snatched the cables, and hooked one to the railings and one to a sail housing projection.

Opportunity was shoeless! Rejoice grabbed her again and put her hand on the rubber-coated lever as the churtree banged open the door.

It sprang toward them.

Her one hand flipped on the inverters to generate AC power while the other pressed the lever.

The churtree yowled and danced on the deck. Answering yowls echoed from the other side of the solar slat housing.

Rejoice started to press the lever harder. No wore shoes and should be safe. This churtree had killed Father. She intended to see it smoke.

But even as she began to press harder, something stayed her hand. Should she kill this churtree and make her father's death meaningless?

Sobs tore her chest as she released some of the pressure on the lever. The churtree took another step toward her. She nudged up the power. It pranced back a step. She lowered the power.

The solar slats began a weird dance, flapping up and down out of sequence and the alarm shrilled.

The churtree jerked its eyes, trying to watch the slats and Rejoice at the same time. It raised its spear, and Rejoice stepped up the current until the churtree shuddered and lowered its spear. It howled and the other churtrees howled back.

The churtree flipped its spear around, inserted the point into its mouth, and then ran head on into the sail housing wall. The spear ripped through its body. Its legs and arms spasmed.

Rejoice let go the lever and leaned dizzily against the sail housing. A mental fog obscured reality.

What about the other churtrees? She almost dropped Opportunity again. She spun and ran around the corner of the housing. Three churtrees lay reamed by their own spears. No Cruz writhed on the deck in a pool of red blood and streams of orange blood.

"No!" she screamed. She shifted Opportunity, stepped over No, and knelt in front of his face. Horror choked her throat. She softly touched his cheek.

His eyes opened and he gasped, "Thank God. I thought—" He clenched his jaw. His hands pressed against his right side and blood streamed past his fingers. "Another one came."

The shrill alarm stopped, but her ears still reverberated. "No," she sobbed, "you're bleeding and I don't know how to make it stop."

After two shuddering breaths, he said through clenched teeth, "Call your mother."

Fool! Fool! And worse than a fool! She ran for the computer jack, jouncing Opportunity all the way. Just as she reached the jack, Opportunity threw up on her. Rejoice set her down. Opportunity cried, "Mommy! Mommy!"

Rejoice plugged in the computer, turned to shout into it, and saw the boat racing toward the ship with a high white spray. "We've been attacked!"

"We're coming," Sister Hancock replied.

Rejoice set down the computer. Mother's kit; Mother had taken the little kit; she might need the big one. Rejoice stood near the steps to the lab side of the ship. She picked up Opportunity who screamed again. Who could think with all this screaming?

Halfway down the steps, she stopped. What if there were more churtrees? What if No had already died? She forced herself the rest of the way down.

She opened the cabinet door and paused. Rejoice couldn't carry the large kit and Opportunity. She had promised Mother to keep her sister safe in her room. What if more churtrees were even now climbing the ladder? With tears running down her face, she raced down the lab hall and up the bedrooms hall. She faltered when she saw the bloody footprints. Not yet. She almost threw up herself. Not yet.

She fumbled for the door handle, went in, and laid Opportunity in her bed. Against her sister's screams, she slammed the door.

At her parent's open door, she stopped. No? Father? Who should she go to first? She couldn't help either one. *Oh God oh God oh God.* All she could see through the half-open door was Father's arm and blood smeared hand over the side of the bed. His knuckles brushed the glass littered floor. The hand did not move.

She slammed the door. Her knees buckled. On her hands and knees, she struggled to draw a breath. She must not faint. No needed her; he needed the kit. *Not Father, oh God, not Father.* She held onto the wall to pull herself up and staggered to the cabinet. Its doors banged open and equipment fell in a clatter.

A minute later she knelt by No. His ragged breathing through clenched teeth terrified her. What could she do? Painkiller; she could at least ease his pain. She opened the kit and stared at all the bottles. She picked up one and stared at a scientific name that meant nothing to her. Then she saw written on the bottom of the label in Mother's neat handwriting the word: painkiller. She slid the bottle into the dispenser and held it against his jugular vein. The dispenser hissed. God grant that was enough and not too much.

She kept her gaze away from the spreading blood. "No," she said, "you can't die. I want to help you, but I don't know what to do." He reached up his hand and she took it.

The boat's motor roared, a clunked on the side of the ship, and feet pounded on the metal ladder. *Please let it be people and not more churtrees.*

"Rejoice?" Mother called.

"Here! Hurry!" She tried to stand but No would not let go of her hand.

Mother appeared around the corner, gasped, knelt beside Rejoice.

Brother Hancock crowded past them and knelt on the other side of No. "Young Man, you promised me I could win." He slid a stretcher pole toward Mother and coordinated getting No on the stretcher.

Rejoice looked at Mother frantically attaching needles and lines to No's arm. "Mother!" She choked.

Mother ripped open a package of gauze and pressed it against No's side.

Father's dead! Rejoice wailed, but her lips did not move.

"Hup!" Brother Hancock said. They lifted the stretcher. Rejoice almost dropped her corner.

As they headed for the stairs Elder Chin roared, "Where's the power? How can I sail the ship with no power?"

Rejoice dared a glance at the sea, expecting to see hordes of churtrees paddling toward them, but the sea sparkled calmly. Then they were down the stairs and laying No on the dining room table. Mother snapped out orders. She told Rejoice to prepare gallons of sterile saline solution.

The autodoc program told Rejoice how to do so and she did. Fortunately, the battery powering the kitchen had not run down.

She delivered the jars of saline. The sight of Mother probing with bloody, gloved hands into No's intestines drove her into the hallway where she gagged and shuddered.

Sister Hancock called her husband from monitoring the anesthetic to her place of assisting Mother, and marched Rejoice back into the kitchen, shoved her head under the faucet, and blasted her with cold water. "We don't have time for this," she hissed at sputtering Rejoice. "We have a ghastly mess to clean up."

"Father!" Rejoice sobbed.

Sister Hancock shoved Rejoice's head under the faucet again and jerked her back up, flinging cold water everywhere. "He can't come and do this, so you must. Make more saline! Now!" She grabbed the remaining jars on the way out.

Rejoice kept making more and Sister Hancock kept coming to get the saline. The next time Rejoice looked out at the porthole, she was shocked. A night sky glittered with stars and Large Potato glowed near a mountainous horizon. She went into the hallway and saw the stairs door closed and bolted. Was Elder Chin out on the deck alone? What were the churtrees up to? She leaned against the wall and listened to the sound of saline being poured out and gurgling down the floor drain.

She covered her ears to shut out the sound. She should not have stopped, for now that she had, grief threatened to swallow her.

A touch on her shoulder startled her into turning around. There stood Father. She screamed and jumped, banging into the bulkhead, and then stood staring and panting.

"Glad to see you, too," he whispered.

A blood-soaked bandage made from a torn sheet wrapped around his thigh. She grabbed him, laid her face on his chest, and bawled, "I thought you were dead!"

Brother Hancock skidded into the hall and looked around wildly. "Where's the churtree?"

Father flicked his hand and Brother Hancock ducked back into the mess hall.

Rejoice sobbed as Father gently stroked her back. "Are you needed here?" he whispered.

She shook her head. Five gallons of saline still stood on the counter.

"Help me back to my room." He leaned heavily on her as they shuffled down the hall. His face was gray.

In the doorway, Rejoice stopped at the sight of slashed tubing, broken glass, smashed panels and instruments, and blood splatters everywhere. Father fell onto the bed and groaned. "Oxygen, please."

Rejoice ran to the recharge room and got a tank which she rushed back. It took a few minutes to find the mask and enough intact tubing to make sure Father got the oxygen.

His face lost some of its grayness. He pulled out his screen. Rejoice's screen was still on the deck, so she leaned over to read what he typed.

[Why think me dead? Who played with the sails to distract the churtree and who called the others back?]

"Oh!" Rejoice said. "Oh! But I saw the churtree come out all covered with blood, and you didn't move, so I thought—" She faltered.

[So did churtree. Only stabbed me once, then destroyed room.]

Rejoice looked at his leg. He had to have devised his own bandage. "You need that looked at."

[Mother busy. After called others back and put on bandage, I passed out. When came to, saw Mother working on No.]

Rejoice nodded. Relief and dread and hysteria battled over her last bit of rationality. How could Father have stayed still while being stabbed and having his oxygen and food supply slashed? What if he had been stabbed in the gut like No? He would have bled to death while Rejoice ignored him. Why hadn't she checked further? "Can I get you something else?"

[Water. But first U change.]

Rejoice glanced down at her dress covered with dried splatters of blood and Opportunity's vomit. Right. A shower and grabbing of towels and sheets took only a few minutes. Father was asleep when she returned, but he awoke as she swept up the broken glass. She helped him as he struggled to drink the water and breathe. She then changed his bed and mopped the floor. What would Father do now that the respirator was broken?

And poor little Opportunity, who was taking care of her? Rejoice ran to her room. Her sister slept. A massive blue-black bruise covered her leg where Rejoice had crushed it against the door jamb. The room reeked of urine.

Rejoice sat on her bed to rest a bit before changing Opportunity.

The next thing she knew, Mother gently shook her shoulder. The gray light of dawn seeped past the open door. "Rejoice," Mother croaked, "how did Opportunity break her leg?"

CIRCUMNAVIGATION CHAPTER TWENTY-SEVEN

That afternoon, Rejoice jumped and squeaked when Sister Hancock entered the galley.

Sister Hancock patted her and said, "Don't worry. I won't push your head into the sink again. It is nerve-wracking, wondering if and when the churtrees are going to attack again." They both turned to glance at the screen which showed nothing moving on the beach. She poured herself some tea and held the cup with both hands as she sipped from it. "Young Man Cruz's vital signs are still stable."

Rejoice stopped stirring cookie dough long enough to draw a deep breath.

Sister Hancock put her arm across Rejoice's shoulders and squeezed. "I am so sorry about how I treated you last night. I am not a nice person when I am scared out of my wits."

Rejoice was still scared.

Sister Hancock fanned herself with a napkin. "This voyage has been a lot hotter than we expected. I wished we'd brought three extra air conditioner compressors. No fixed the air conditioning the first two times it broke easy enough, but now it looks as if we'll just cook until we get back. He needs a part we don't have."

Rejoice fanned herself as well and felt herself get even hotter. Why had she always jumped to the conclusion that No was incompetent?

The computer beeped. Sister Hancock wiped out the view of the shore and read the incoming message, saying "Huh," from time to time. After several minutes of this, she brought back the still view of the beach. "Your father agrees with the colony. We're heading home tomorrow."

Far louder than she meant to, Rejoice said, "Why not now?"

"Things to do," Sister Hancock said, rubbing her eyes. She picked up a scone. "Doctor Cruz reviewed the video of the operation and said it looks as though we did everything right. Since none of us trained as surgeons, I'm relieved. There's always the worry of intestinal adhesions and peritonitis, but we cleaned him well enough that he should be back to normal in a few weeks." She ate the scone thoughtfully and licked her fingers. "Did you get a meal up to Elder Chin?"

Rejoice nodded. She had found him slumped over the monitor, sleeping in the bridge. She looked at the screen again. The view changed as Elder Chin zoomed in on what looked like a churtree lying on the beach. Beyond it, several more black mounds lay among the boulders.

Sister Hancock sipped more tea. "It hasn't moved since I first saw it this morning." She covered a yawn. "Time to spell Brother Hancock. Thank you, dear, for putting up with crotchety people." She yawned again and went out to sit by No and monitor his condition. A few minutes later, Brother Hancock slouched by the doorway on his way to bed.

Rejoice added some dried currants to the cookie dough. While the first batch baked, she put on another load of laundry and put the first load in the dryer. Then she put another load of surgical instruments in the lab sterilizer. Back in the galley, she prepared peanut-butter cookie dough. Currant spice cookies were Opportunity's favorite and peanut-butter was No's.

She was taking the last of the peanut-butter cookies out of the oven when the computer beeped again. [Need to talk to U,] glowed in the screen. A few minutes later she sat by Father and watched him type, [Will U go with Elder Chin to churtree village?]

Rejoice felt her eyes widen with horror. "Why are we going back? Why aren't we getting out of here as fast as possible?"

Father tapped his screen as he studied Rejoice. [He wants to invest-

Igate what is wrong in village. U are the only one free to aid him.]

Rejoice gripped the edge of her chair. Mother was sleeping with Opportunity and needed to after spending all night operating on No, setting Opportunity's leg, and repairing Father's wound. Brother and Sister Hancock were alternating two hour shifts to watch No. Only God knew when Father would ever get out of bed again. That left her to help Elder Chin do something he had no business doing. "Do I have to?" she whispered.

[I made U a promise. Elder Chin can go alone.]

Rejoice closed her eyes. Sometimes worse than not getting your way was getting your way when your way was that of a creep. "I guess I'll go."

[I love U. Elder Chin is ready now.]

That took away the chance to fret before doing it. Good. She kissed Father on the forehead and went up on deck, being careful to lock the weather door behind her. Elder Chin lowered a boat laden with cameras and sample jars.

She climbed the ladder down to the boat first, and tried to hold the boat steady as he stepped into it. Scummy water sloshed about her feet. The sunlight reflected off the riffled water reminded her that she had not put on her hat before running out. She snorted. Why worry about harmful ultraviolet rays when the more immediate danger was churtree spears? "Aren't we going to put on armor?"

"I don't think we'll need it." He handed a camera to Rejoice. As they trolled toward the silent beach, Elder Chin said, "Young Lady Holly, you were correct."

Rejoice fumbled with the camera and squinted in the hot sun as she tried to think what she could have been correct about.

"We should not have undertaken a voyage of this magnitude with one ship and a tiny crew. We ought to have done it wholeheartedly or not done it at all."

"Well," Rejoice said, who had done a lot of thinking on that very issue, especially about why Father had planned it the way he did, "I suppose it seemed like a good idea at the time. The hexacrabs were pushing us to go, and we have technology and sort of satellite support, and everything was extinct anyway. Erik the Red, Columbus, and Magellan went out with less than we did."

Elder Chin turned the boat to meet the shore waves head on. "It is difficult to make decisions when so many must be made about urgent demands. You will see when it is your turn."

"My turn? Since when do I get to make the decisions?"

The skin around Elder Chin's eyes wrinkled a little more. "Did you think you would remain sixteen forever?"

"No, next year I get to be seventeen. Whoopee."

Elder Chin laughed.

Rejoice struggled with keeping the camera focused on the beach as the boat rose and fell with the swells. What was Elder Chin trying to tell her? There, on the beach in front of them, white paper glared in the sun, the paper that had wrapped the offerings of food.

A sudden stench, strong enough to penetrate the filter masks, the smell of bodies rotting under a hot sun, made her eyes water. "Ugh, what is it?"

"It is as I feared," Elder Chin nosed the boat toward the gray sand and slid onto it.

Rejoice gulped and wiped away tears before getting out to pull the boat farther in. The muscles in her back tightened in anticipation of being speared.

Elder Chin waded ashore and walked straight toward the paper. With shaking hands and a sudden urge to look for a bathroom, Rejoice followed and pointed the camera at whatever Elder Chin pointed at.

Mottled insects crawled over and buzzed about the spoiling torpal and kraken meat. A few steps farther in brought them to the torn transparent bag of gold rings and hoops. The scattered gold glinted.

Rejoice wiped away more tears. Her hands trembled as they walked toward the corpse of a churtree. It writhed with insects crawling over its body. A huge wound gaped in its neck. She gagged as Elder Chin used a metal rod to turn the body over so she could record both sides. He pointed to each tattoo.

Fifteen meters away lay another body. Rejoice recorded every marking and bit of gold on it as well. As they walked toward a third body buzzing with insects, Rejoice choked out, "What happened?"

As coolly as if he were discussing the weather, Elder Chin said, "Yesterday, as we approached the beach, we could see the churtrees were becoming agitated. Some of them appeared to want to get in their canoes, and some others prevented them. They all appeared to be threatening us. Sister Hancock threw the bag of gold and food strapped to the life preserver toward the beach. This caused quite a bit of commotion and some ran into the sea toward us. At that moment, we got the message from your father that the Magellan was under attack. We raced back. Behind us we could hear terrific screaming. I'm afraid we do not have a recording of what happened next. When I was able to get a camera pointed in this direction, only these few bodies were visible. Nothing moves in the village."

"Maybe they're waiting in ambush for us."

Elder Chin kept walking toward the village. When they reached the talus, they found bodies behind nearly every boulder. Again, Elder Chin stopped at every one and examined every mark, every ornament. Rejoice pretended that this was a nightmare and she would wake up soon.

Some of the corpses had stabbed throats. Others had run themselves through like the ones on the ship. For Rejoice, the bodies melded into a seething, buzzing mass of scars, red tattoos, black fur, tangled limbs, blood encrusted gold, and clouds of insects. Numbly, she followed Elder Chin to the cliff.

There, at the base of the cliff, they found the children. Small churtrees lay in mangled heaps. Elder Chin laid them out one by one. "You can see, some of the larger ones were slashed, but these smaller ones were killed by impact. They were either swung by their feet and dashed against the rocks, or they were tossed from high up the cliff."

They stopped when they came to a circular area cleared of stones and all plant life. Rejoice had thought she could not see anything worse.

She had been wrong.

She could not hold the camera steady as Elder Chin walked over to the churtree and crouched down beside the body. Its four arms had been stretched to the four points of the compass and then staked to the ground. The left hind leg had been pulled as far as it would go and then staked so that the creature lay impaled to the ground and unable to free itself.

Rejoice's voice quavered. "How could they do this to themselves?"

"Did you think crucifixion or necklace-tire burning is prettier? This one was killed differently, and I think over a longer period of time. You can see how emaciated it is. It may have come from an enemy village, or be a sacrifice, or a criminal. The red scars are the same as all the churtrees in this village that we've examined so far and as the first churtree that we saw two days ago in the canoe. Wait."

With the rod he pried up the stakes and turned the body over. After staring a minute, he muttered to himself. "Only the first churtree we met and this one have the row of rings down the back. One a sacrifice to the land gods and one to the ocean? Two queen bees battling for possession of the hive? Marks of rival village? The jewelry seems to denote rank. Only those with a double band on the upper left arm have pierced through themselves."

Rejoice hadn't noticed that. She wiped her eyes again and tried to steady the camera. Her nose dripped, but she wasn't about to lift the mask to wipe it.

"So why did the four churtrees that attacked us yesterday have orange scars, instead of red? Were they a warrior class or from a different family? But none of the churtrees from this village entered their canoes when we arrived, even though it appeared that they wanted to."

"The churtree that attacked us yesterday had orange scars and not red?" Rejoice said. "I hadn't noticed that." Of course she hadn't been looking too close at anything but teeth.

"Yes," Elder Chin said. "You were all busy below. So your father had me record all of the details above, before I cleaned up the deck and preserved the bodies."

Elder Chin sighed and turned in a circle, viewing the devastation. He shook his head. "Perhaps an entire people gone! Their language, their art, their customs, all gone! And who will explain them to us? Why did they do this? Are there any more hiding on this island?"

He rose to his feet. "I had feared our viruses had killed them. There is a doleful satisfaction in knowing that we were not the agents of their deaths. Or did our ignorance and pride somehow kill them all?"

He faced the cliff and its multitudes of openings. "Inside now. We may have to duck."

Inside? Rejoice's feet stayed rooted to the ground. Churtrees could be waiting ambush in those dark rooms.

Elder Chin bowed and entered into a puffy T doorway at ground level. He turned on his flashlight and directed its beam up and down, though at what she could not tell. Then he backed out, sat on a stone, held his head in his hands, and rocked back and forth.

"Elder?"

His eyes closed and he whispered.

A shiver vibrated up and down her spine. "Elder Chin, please, let's get out of here, please."

He looked up after several deep breaths. "Young Lady, I shall take the camera now. Will you wait here?"

"Not by myself, I won't!" The hairs on her neck prickled. What had he seen in there?

He stood and took her hand. "I am sorry I must put you through this; but we must document this people."

"Why? Wouldn't it be better to forget them?"

He turned and reentered the room. Rejoice followed. The light of his flashlight showed a roughly spherical room with a sandy floor and stacked against the walls were hundreds of hexacrab shells.

Rejoice's knees hit the sand and Elder Chin held her up by her shoulders. How had she gotten there? And she had wet herself. Dazed, she picked up the camera, brushed off the sand, and stood up. Mechanically, she pointed the camera at each stack Elder Chin pointed to.

They crawled through a doorway into a room filled with inverted hexacrab shells, each brim full of small white bones. She could never remember clearly the rest of that horror-filled exploration. They found rooms with dead churtrees, rooms with murals of churtree warfare and of giant waves and of battles with hexacrabs. They found bone shards and skin drums and boxes of knives. Some of the things, Elder Chin placed in his pouch. They found a forge and anvil and ingots of gold and copper, cradles made of hexacrab shells and filled with dead churtree babies, pouches of fresh water, carved tables of wood and stone, bone needles, dried fish, stone oil lamps, and rattles. They found nothing that involved cooking except for knives and drying racks. Perhaps they ate everything raw.

One room reeked with a different odor. Wooden cages lined the walls. Four-legged bats huddled in many of the cages. They perked up pointed ears and hissed, showing needle-sharp, stained teeth.

"The poor things," Rejoice neared the cages. The bats backed up to press themselves against the far side of the cages. "They're frightened, and who can blame them?" Crude pegs and bars held the fronts. She tugged at one peg, and the front flipped down.

The bat inside keened, then flung itself upon Rejoice. She screamed and ducked. The bat raked its claws across her neck. Elder Chin whacked it with his rod. The bat smacked into the wall and fell into a crumpled heap.

Elder Chin dabbed at her scratches with a handkerchief until they stopped bleeding. He gingerly picked up one of the cages with the metal rod and carried it to a window as the creature inside gnawed at the rod. There he flung it through the window to the ground. They watched as the cage smashed open and the bat hopped out. It fluttered to the nearest churtree and tore at its wound.

Elder Chin muttered, "Not the actions of a devoted pet. Are they used for falconing, egg-laying, lunch, or sacrifices?" He turned and looked at the cages. "I am loath to leave these to starve to death, but neither will I be their butcher nor release them to torment us. Let us go to the next room."

They crawled up a long, twisty tunnel until they emerged at the top of the cliff. Here, a breeze carried away the stench of death. In the sparkly bay, dove-white Magellan floated on bright blue water. The solar collectors and sail slats had turned row upon row to catch the sun's rays and recharge the batteries.

Rejoice took in deep breaths of spiced air. She turned to record the appearance of the brown and gray jungle on the mountain behind them. "Isn't there some way down that doesn't involve going through all those apartments again?"

Elder Chin looked over the edge of the cliff. "I cannot fly." He sat on a rock and looked at the jungle. "If this is not the last of the churtrees, then Ur-Veena and Sa-Issi are in serious danger. How I wish I could warn them." He stared at the brown spotted skin on the back of his hands. "Young Lady, how are you holding up?"

"The truth?"

"Always."

"I'm going to have nightmares for the rest of my life."

Elder Chin sighed. "As will I."

"I want to burn this dress and take a five hour shower. And I want to throw up and I don't know why we're here and I want to go home if I could just figure out where home is."

Elder Chin looked over the cliff at the scattered bodies. "How, how can we establish a relationship with a people who kill themselves when we try to say hello?"

"Maybe instead of torpal, which they obviously don't like, we should give them a box of hexacrab eyes."

"Young Lady, you go too far."

Rejoice lowered the camera. "I'm sorry, Elder, but I don't see why we want a relationship with anything this hideous. It is completely clear to me why the hexacrabs hate the churtrees. I hate the churtrees! Every atom in me hates the churtrees. I'm glad they killed themselves because that saves me the trouble of doing it." She trembled with anger. She had earned a reprimand, but she had only spoken the truth.

Elder Chin studied her and rubbed the side of his filter mask with his forefinger.

Uh-oh. The scratches on her neck stung as sweat dribbled into them.

Finally he spoke, "Forgive me. You were, after all, only whistling in the graveyard."

"I was what?"

"An expression. Also gallows' humor. What humans do sometimes to defuse their fear, a kind of humor that allows one to face the unfaceable." He turned to look down at the churtree again. "If ever there was a culture worth hating, this is it." He gestured toward another boulder. "Please sit."

"Shouldn't I be collecting some plant specimens?" She looked at the bush with leaves like wire spirals.

"Not now. We will let the second voyage handle that. Please sit."

Rejoice sat and braced herself for a sermon.

"Do you truly feel that you are all that different from the churtrees?"

"Have I started to sprout black fur?"

"Consider the statement: each of us has a churtree in our heart."

Rejoice rubbed her shoes on a rock. "I'm sorry. I don't know what you mean."

"Each of us is quite capable of acting like the churtrees. Each of us."

"Excuse me," Rejoice said. "But you're telling me that No, that my mother, that my *father* could act like the churtrees. I can't see that."

"It's much worse than that. I am asking you to understand that you could act like the churtrees."

"At this point, I'm supposed to say, 'Yes, Sir' and apologize; but I can't."

Elder Chin interlaced his fingers and said nothing for thirty seconds. When he spoke, Rejoice needed to lean closer to hear him. "I can name the ancestor of mine that tortured enemies of The People by the thousands. You cannot name, but doubtless there are in your ancestry, those who disemboweled pregnant women and snatched their blood-stained jewelry while laughing. The Reichmann's ancestors herded God's Chosen People into gas ovens by the millions to slaughter them. The taint runs deep in every one of us. A great English writer once said that original sin was the only Christian doctrine for which we have empirical evidence. If you do not understand the evil within yourself, then you do not understand Christianity. You do not understand what our Savior came to save us from."

Too hot and sick to puzzle the meaning of his words, Rejoice wiped her brow. "To keep me from becoming a churtree."

Elder Chin stood and pointed to the bodies. "Why did they do this?"

"You said you don't know."

"I don't know what reasons they gave themselves, but I do know what their underlying motives were: fear and hatred. Fear and hatred did this."

And she hated and feared the churtrees. Yes, and had good reason for it. "I'm sorry," Rejoice said, "but I have a headache and I will throw up if we don't get back to the ship soon. Please, are we done yet?"

Elder Chin held out his hand to help pull her up. "I think we've recorded all we should on this voyage. Let's go home."

CIRCUMNAVIGATION CHAPTER TWENTY-EIGHT

Mother peeked into Rejoice's bedroom. Opportunity played pat-a-cake with Rejoice on the bed. The little girl's leg in its inflated cast stuck out straight while the other leg swung back and forth. "Rejoice? If you wanted, you could visit with No a few minutes."

"Really? Yes!" She stood and Opportunity cried.

Mother sat down and pulled Opportunity onto her lap. "Before you go in, let me talk to you a minute. I don't know what possessed a smart man like Elder Chin to do the foolish thing he did. But I have discussed it with him and with your father. I'm not very happy with either of them right now." She drew her lips into a thin line. "I can understand why your father might allow Elder Chin to risk his own life going into that village. But that Elder Chin would even think of requesting that you go with him is outrageous And why your father would agree to even bring it up to you is beyond me."

"I volunteered."

"To take an ambush?"

"I think he knew they were dead." Why was she defending him? She was angry at him, too. "Father told me that I didn't have to go."

"We're still discussing it, and as soon as your father admits he is dead wrong, the discussion will end. I may ask Elder Chin to resign from all positions of authority."

Rejoice fidgeted. She didn't want to remember that day or know about her parent's arguments. Then she realized why she was defending Elder Chin.

"Mother, would you have gone?"

"Certainly."

"There's a discrepancy here."

"There is not. I am an adult. You are the child, and my job is to protect you. It is also Elder Chin's job."

"Well, maybe I like Elder Chin treating me like an adult."

"Maybe this discussion is closed until you're eighteen."

Rejoice studied the ceiling. Yes, the discussion was closed. She should never have started it. If only she were still in space looking forward to returning to New Earth. But how do you go back in time?

Mother squeezed Rejoice's hand. "I know it's hard. Please forgive me as I ask one more thing of you. Please don't tell Young Man Cruz what you saw yet. I don't want you to upset him."

Mother had to be thinking, 'like you did the last time when you told him about Sister Olson.' She nodded.

"You can visit for only a few minutes. And then I have supper for you in the galley. Do you think you can eat yet?"

Rejoice shook her head. She had no idea why she had waited until she and Elder Chin had gotten back to the boat to start vomiting, or why the rest of the day had seemed so completely unreal and everybody's words had echoed in an empty skull. Maybe when they left Half-Moon Bay, she could return to normal. Right now, she couldn't even remember what normal felt like.

Mother said gently, "Why don't I tell Young Man Cruz you need to rest? Both of you will feel better tomorrow."

Rejoice sat down by Mother. "How badly hurt was he?"

"Oh, bad enough, I suppose. He'll have to learn how to get along without an appendix."

Rejoice couldn't think what an appendix was. "Does that mean he'll be crippled?"

Mother laughed, "No, dear. Millions of people have lived long and healthy lives without one. It's a redundant part of the immune system."

"Oh." How could Mother stand doing what she did? How could she eat after doing an operation? "Is Father ever going to recover all the way?"

"I think so. Fungi grow slowly, and they die slowly. I can't promise you he won't be on a respirator for the rest of his life, but I don't think so."

Brother and Sister Hancock had cobbled the respirator together and got it working, but it looked as patched up and taped together as No did after his encounter with the kraken.

Rejoice nibbled on a fingernail. She hoped Mother was telling the truth. No, Mother always told the truth. She hoped Mother wasn't mistaken. "Can I see him now?"

"If you must. But just for a few minutes."

Rejoice trotted down the hall to the galley to pick up a bowl of cookies. In No's room, Elder Chin and No studied a screen together. The last working monitor hung on his bed. Bags of nutrient fluid and medication flowed into a tangle of tubes that ended up in his arms. Elder Chin had cut No's black hair crookedly.

Elder Chin saw Rejoice, turned to No, and kissed him solemnly on the forehead. After propping the door farther open, he left.

Rejoice took his chair and felt shy at how No beamed at her.

"Good evening," he said.

"How do you feel?"

"I've felt better."

"I brought you some cookies."

"Oh," he said, "I guess your mother didn't tell you that I'm not allowed to eat for four or five days."

Rejoice hurriedly set the bowl down.

"Don't throw them away," he begged. "They give me something to look forward to. If it isn't too much trouble, could you bake me some of the caramel rolls, too?"

"Sure, I'd be glad to." Rejoice found her eyes drawn unwillingly to the massive bandage on his side and some sort of drainage tube. She could never be a nurse. "Mother did tell me you don't have any shirts left."

"Good. Shirts always strangle me."

Rejoice laughed in a brittle, high pitch. Gallows' humor? "You don't need to destroy your shirts. All you need to do is make the collar larger."

"I don't know how."

"Surely one of your parents could do it for you."

"They don't know how to sew, either."

"Not even your mother?"

"Well, Mother sews up people fine, but she doesn't do clothing."

Didn't everyone in the colony know how to sew? When Father wasn't twiddling with the ship's controls or mapping, he was working on a quilt for Opportunity. He said he couldn't stand the thought of lying in bed doing nothing. "Let's see. The only one larger than you is Father. I'll modify one of his shirts for you so you can be dressed decently for our homecoming."

"As long as I don't have to wear it until then."

Thinking of his parents brought up a question. "Is your father jealous of the relationship between you and Elder Chin? Elder Chin seems to have adopted you."

"I choose to believe my father when he says he's proud of my being discipled by Elder Chin. I think he's relieved, too. Because I've failed at so many things, he worried for years that I would never find my niche."

"I found mine: astronomer and meteorologist. What are you going to become when you get back?"

He laid a bruised hand on his chest. "I won't become anything that I'm not already."

"I'm sorry, but I've been gone for three years. What are you?"

"A pastor. Perhaps I should say, a pastor-in-training."

Rejoice blinked several times. Someone with many private conversations, someone who encouraged people to better themselves, someone who did all he could to minister to other people's needs. Why hadn't she seen it before? "I never heard anyone call you Pastor Cruz."

He shrugged. "You might never. So what? Pastor Wiseman has the pulpit and he can keep it. I prefer one-on-one counseling and prayer."

Rejoice sat back. How many more surprises would No hand her before the voyage was over? If only she could see people as clearly as No did. She reached out her hand and No took it.

"Did I thank you for saving my life?" she said.

"Did I?" He squeezed her hand. "I didn't think so for a while. When you ran to your room and I heard you scream, I remembered the ladder on the other side of the ship. I was sure I had sent you out to be hacked to bits. Hearing you scream like that was the worst moment of my life."

"Mine too. When I saw the churtree tracking Father's blood—"

"Your father!" No stiffened, then groaned.

"He's okay," Rejoice said. "I mean, he's wounded and all, but he's okay. But at that moment I thought he was dead."

No closed his eyes a few seconds and exhaled. "What happened last night?"

She must not get him upset. "What did Elder Chin tell you?"

"Nothing. We just did a Bible study."

"I'd rather hear what happened to you."

"There's not much to tell. When I heard you scream I turned around to look, which was stupid because you can't see through the housing. The churtree got around my shield and skewered me. I shoved it off and accidentally dropped the shield on its foot. We both fell down. Then another churtree came around the back of the ship and started yowling. I tried to get up, but for some reason, I couldn't. Maybe I was hallucinating, but the deck felt charged and churtrees were dancing. My heart stuttered too. Do you think churtrees can discharge electricity like eels?"

Rejoice covered her mouth.

"Then they yowled at each other and killed themselves. I don't think I'll ever understand that. Then I saw you. Rejoice, what's wrong?"

Rejoice couldn't breathe. Her face flushed hot, then cold. "No, I nearly killed you."

"I think the churtrees came closer."

"No! Listen to me."

He reached over with his other hand and held her fist. "I'm listening."

She stammered, "I hooked up the cables to electrify the deck. That's why your churtrees were dancing and you couldn't move. But I wanted—I thought—I hated it and wanted to kill it. I thought it killed Father and I wanted to make it pay. I was going to kill it, but if I had, I would have electrocuted you. Elder Chin is right."

No's forehead crinkled.

"You don't know what I'm talking about."

"Not yet. But I'm working on it. What happened to the churtree that attacked your father?"

"It killed itself."

No's frown deepened. "I can't understand that." He shook his head. "What happened to the village?"

There was absolutely no way for her to tell him without upsetting both of them. "I don't feel very good. Can we finish talking tomorrow?"

"We can start again tomorrow. I hope we never finish."

Rejoice nodded and hurried out of the room. Maybe they never would finish. He liked one-on-one counseling, and it looked as though she would need counseling for the rest of her life.

She had meant to go straight to her room and spend the night meditating on hatred and peace. How could she leave the one and cling to the other? Her parent's door gaped open. She swerved into the room and sat by Father. He glanced at her and continued typing his report.

"How long am I going to feel this bad?"

Father wiped the screen and patted her on the knee. [Not for rest of life. Longer than U want. Shall we pray?]

"Will I feel better?"

[Is that why we pray?]

She bowed her head and breathed deeply. She found herself thinking of Harmony. The night before all this horror started she had watched Harmony recite the first twenty-two chapters of Luke. Harmony had to stop just as Jesus was praying in the garden of Gethsemane. But she hadn't just dully said the verses as Pastor Wiseman would have read them.

When she recited the chapters, she acted them out. She waved her hands, pointed her finger, and raised her voice in all the right places. Sometimes her voice rose in anger and other times it whispered compassion.

At the end as she recited Christ's prayer in the garden, tears fell from her cheeks almost like His sweat fell as drops of blood to the ground. It was right at this point that Harmony stopped, sobbed, apologized, and said that she would finish memorizing the last chapters and would recite them to Rejoice before she got home. Harmony looked totally exhausted by the effort. Stronghold had come into view to hug her and turn off the camera. Rejoice had cried, too, and had felt as exhausted as Harmony when she had finished. Did God arrange that to prepare her for the next two days?

Then Rejoice thought of the churtree staked to the ground and of Christ being beaten and nailed. Love let hatred do that to Him. Why the churtree had died, she didn't know, but maybe she understood why Christ did. Perhaps now she understood the agony of Mary, and why the disciples fled. The Bible stories that had seemed dull because of repetition began to fill with urgency and emotion.

Then she had another thought. "Father, I've been thinking about the satellite photos of the Large Archipelago that we've been studying for so long. Remember those odd little clouds we'd see sometimes?"

[Yes]

"I think that they were smoke from the fires in the village."

[That sounds right.]

"Father, I remember most of the clouds were over Half-Moon Bay, but some were from the other side of the island too."

[So you think that there are more churtrees on the island.]

Rejoice nodded.

She was still shivering at that thought when Mother hustled into the room. "There you are. I want you to take these." She deposited two white pills into Rejoice's hand. "And let me look at your neck again."

Rejoice pulled back her hair. "What are these for?"

"To help you get to sleep. I've already given some to Opportunity and

Young Man Cruz."

Rejoice flinched as Mother removed the bandage. "What does No need to do to be called Brother? He looks like he's been used for target practice; he's saved my life; he's saved the hexacrabs; he's a pastor; he's twenty. What more does he need to do?"

Mother laughed. "You got us there."

Father typed. [Habit only. Seem to wait til marriage. Only Cruz, triplets, and Revitch not married day or two after eighteenth birthday. We will change.]

The triplets weren't married because who wanted to marry anyone so obnoxious and have two brothers-in-law equally obnoxious? Eternity In Their Hearts Revitch was waiting for Blessed Assurance to get older.

"You've played a woman's part," Mother said. "Do you want us to call you Sister?"

"Not really. No has obviously grown up, and I haven't as much as I thought I had. Ouch! I wonder if I ever will."

"When you hit forty, you'll still be wondering."

[Need to remember to call Stronghold Brother, too. I'm not old enough to be father of a Brother.]

Rejoice squinted one eye and breathed out as Mother replaced the bandage. "Of course you are."

Mother and Father laughed together. Why were the adults always laughing at what she said?

Mother kissed her. "Good night, sweet-love."

* * *

Rejoice woke to the scent of poppy seed muffins cooling on her desk. Why hadn't Mother gotten her up to make breakfast? She checked her screen. Mid-morning!

She ate the warm muffin while watching Half-Moon Bay slowly revolve on her screen. Good, they were turning and leaving this cursed place. It took only a few minutes to shower, dress, and head for the galley.

In the dining room, Elder Chin and Opportunity played with dolls and little clay animals. "Wuff, wuff, wuff." Elder Chin's dog chased squealing Opportunity's cloth doll.

Rejoice sat down with lemon grass tea. Apparently Mother trusted Elder Chin with Opportunity, but then, the little girl couldn't hold a camera.

Elder Chin looked up. "Why don't you go see Young, er, Brother Cruz?"

"Sure." When she reached No's room, Mother was disconnecting him from everything. Rejoice sat on Elder Chin's cot and watched. "How are you doing?"

"Better than yesterday. I guess you were right."

"Right about what?"

"When you said I couldn't die. At the time I was pretty sure I could."

"Were you scared?"

No moved his arm so Mother could reach the tube connectors. "Believe it or not, I wasn't. At first I felt relieved in a sad sort of way. I figured it would be easier to die than to figure out how to go on living after I sent you off to be killed. And then you were back. It's funny what you think when you're dying."

"Did you have any visions or anything like that?"

"Afraid not. Guess it wasn't my time, though at that moment I thought it was. I wanted to apologize for dying right in front of you, and bleeding. I know how you hate the sight of blood."

"I should be getting used to it. I can't tell you how glad I am that we're finally heading home."

"Why? We just got here. What about the—"

"Don't move," said Mother.

"—churtrees? How are we going to talk to them?"

"Excuse me, Brother Can't Wait For the Churtrees To Have Another Shot At Me Cruz, but you've been hurt."

"So what? We're not leaving because of me, are we?"

"Not just you," said Mother. "We're leaving because of you and Brother Holly and Opportunity and—"

"What's wrong with Opportunity?" No asked.

"I broke her leg," Rejoice said in a tiny voice.

"You did it saving her life," Mother said. "It's a fair exchange. But I'm still nearly out of medical supplies."

"But what about the churtrees?" No asked.

Rejoice cleared her throat. "That's what the second voyage is for."

"When will that be? When can I sign up?"

"Don't move," Mother said. She wrapped sterile gauze around the needles in his arm. "Okay. When you're done, let me know, and I'll plug you back in again." She kissed Rejoice on the way out the door. "Have fun."

"Doing what?" asked Rejoice.

"Calling for help if I fall down," No slowly pushed himself up and shuffled out the door. The trip up the steps took ten minutes, and he was white-faced by the time he stood on deck, but his eyes brightened at the sight of mountains and jungle. He craned his neck to see Half-Moon Bay, but already the headland occluded it.

They stood and smelled the spicy air. "Look!" he shouted, and pointed to a cloud of tiny black shapes that wheeled above a ridge and then dove into the canopy. "Birds! There are birds!"

Maybe. Rejoice fingered the scratches on her neck.

"I wish . . ." His hands tightened on the railing. He stared with longing at the waves cascading over tumbled boulders. "I'm sure your father knows best."

This time he did. But if she counted his mistakes, could he count hers? She pulled her hat brim to shade her eyes better. Had she seen movement in the ship's wake? She stared at the spot. Yes, something swam in the ocean. Her heart sped up. More churtrees? *Please, no.*

Another splash and an uplifted lance three dozen meters behind the ship.

"Stop! Stop!" Rejoice screamed. She ran to the alarm and flipped the lever and shouted in the intercom, "The hexacrabs are back! Stop!"

CIRCUMNAVIGATION CHAPTER TWENTY-NINE

The sail slats creaked as they folded. The sound of feet pounding on the steps echoed through the ship as the Hancocks and then Elder Chin tumbled onto the deck. The Hancocks leaned over the railing. Elder Chin threw on scuba gear as a scooter fell into the ocean. Elder Chin soon followed.

Mother brought up Opportunity on her back and joined the others. She told Elder Chin through the radio that Father had turned off the sonar so the hexacrabs wouldn't be bothered. Elder Chin scooted out to the hexacrabs and towed them back. Rejoice prayed that there weren't any churtrees also swimming under the water.

When they disappeared under the keel of the ship, everyone headed back for the stairs. "Come on, old man," Brother Hancock said, wrapping his arm around No, and helping him down the stairs. By the time No shuffled to the hexacrab access room door, Elder Chin strode in grinning and brushing back his wet hair.

Elder Chin placed his hands on the floor. Ur-Veena and Sa-Issi reached up to touch the other side of the glass. A female's hexacrab's eyes swiveled everywhere as her gills flared.

"May the song give you joy," whistled Elder Chin. "We cannot eat, we cannot hunt, until you tell us your story."

With one tentacle holding the microphone and one stretched out to caress the eye stalks of the female, Ur-Veena began. "The tale is told

"

by Ti-Ista, the last of the Ti. The Tsa and Ist are all devoured. What the Day of Disturbance did not destroy, the predation of churtrees did. Gone are the nurseries; gone are the warriors; and only Ti-Ista lives to tell the tale."

Rejoice fought back revulsion as she remembered the stacks of hexacrab shells in the village.

"Only a hex of days ago, in number like breeding maggots, the churtrees came in their world-edge pressers to the Ti nursery. Ti-Issa, Ti-Ichta, and Ti-Satse fought and caused the blood of churtrees to darken the water-ocean."

The new hexacrab grated, and Ur-Veena shifted to listen.

"I cannot understand her language," Elder Chin said.

Sa-Issi peeped, "It is hard to listen to."

Ur-Veena turned back to the microphone. "I must re-speak the words I spoke."

"That proves it's a female," Brother Hancock breathed. His wife shot him a venomous look, but his gaze was glued on Ti-Ista.

"Ti-Issa, Ti-Ichsa, and Ti-Satse fought and caused the blood of churtree to darken the water-ocean. But as the heated light dwindled, so too did the light in the eyes of these three warriors dwindle and die. They were taken from the world and each child was ripped from its bed. Ti-Ista tended the kelp. When she returned she found only the eye-stalks of the people and the bodies of the churtrees. With no nursery left to care for, no cluster to defend, no male to fertilize her eggs, Ti-Ista sought to follow the churtrees that she might kill as many as she could before she was taken to fill churtree bellies."

Ti-Ista grated again.

Ur-Veena's tentacles writhed about his handhold. Sa-Issi dropped to the keel and jerked his legs. Ur-Veena swiveled his eyes from Ti-Ista to the humans above him. When he finally spoke, he spoke so slowly that Rejoice could understand every word even before the translation. "The Ti nursery was hid where the current flows toward the evening. But one must crawl along the edge of the world to where the current flows to the morning to find where the churtrees dwell.

"There we found Ti-Ista. The churtree live above this valley where your world-edge presser departed before the great light ceased and then returned."

The wrinkles of Elder Chin's face twisted into a pattern Rejoice could not recognize but heard as grief when he spoke. "We cannot see all in the air-ocean, but in this valley, today, there are no churtrees."

Ur-Veena grasped the microphone with another tentacle as No looked astonished at Elder Chin. "Where did they go?"

"They are dead"

"What?" No shouted. "How?"

"All?" grated Ur-Veena.

Elder Chin turned to No and hissed, "You will control yourself," and into the microphone he said slowly and carefully, "We found eighty-seven dead churtree yesterday. We saw none alive, though we searched."

No inhaled and exhaled noisily. Brother Hancock gripped him by the shoulder. Rejoice tried to join No's rhythm, but more quietly. How could she contain within herself the emotions of hatred for the churtrees, sorrow for the slaughtered hexacrabs, excitement over Ur-Veena's return, and pity for No?

Ur-Veena said even slower, "Therefore you are not churtree friend."

"Not at this moment. Always, as long as there is water to breathe, we will call the water-ocean people our friends. Always we will help defend your people from any churtree. If any surviving churtrees seek to harm the people, we will use all within our power to ensure that they will not succeed. If they attack you, we will put our bodies between you and them."

They would? Rejoice wrinkled her nose.

"Yes," Ur-Veena said. "You are a friend to the people."

Sister Hancock let out a long breath. She gave the thumbs up signal to the camera and Father watching. She and Mother grinned at each other. They froze at Ur-Veena's next words.

"Sa-Issi shall journey with the air-ocean people. He shall guide half the Ur and half the Sa here so the children may be caught. I shall stay with Ti-Ista to renew the Ti nursery."

Brother Hancock placed his hand on the floor. "Our hearts stop beating. There may be more churtrees we did not see. Surely Ti-Ista can crawl in the Sa cluster."

Ur-Veena clicked, "How long before the journey ends at Sa?"

Elder Chin plugged in his computer and read Father's answer, [With no storms or detours or mechanical breakdown, three weeks at the earliest.]

Ur-Veena replied, "The eggs must be fertilized, brooded, and planted within two hex days."

"Just a minute," Brother Hancock said. He closed his eyes, tapped his fingertips with his thumb as he counted out the dates, and opened his eyes. "He's right." Then he muttered, "Of course he's right. He ought to know better than me."

Sa-Issi peeped, "Two males. One female. Therefore I am to return to Sa."

Rejoice's cheeks heated. One female.

"Not yet," Brother Hancock said. "We're not leaving until we've built you a charging station for your scooters. We're not leaving until we've built you some kind of fort or retreat. We're—"

"Resolved," Sister Hancock said quietly.

Brother Hancock looked up at the camera and pulled back his lips into a grin. "Right, Brother Holly?"

[Agreed.]

Rejoice studied the ceiling. Maybe they would never go home. Yet she too agreed that they must not leave the hexacrabs defenseless. She stole a glance at No. Yes, he looked perkier.

* **

That evening, the Magellan anchored to a small rock of an island a kilometer from a tall cliff that descended almost directly into the sea. They called it Ti Bay, for under its waters the empty Ti cluster and nursery were hid. The bay dimpled the coast on the east side of Larger Island of the Large Archipelago. Toward the south, steep-sided islands flung out from Heron Peninsula and formed the Large Archipelago Keys. Past the Keys about thirty kilometers around the tip of Big Island on its west side lay the empty churtree village by Half-Moon Bay.

Rejoice and Father had gone back and reviewed the satellite photos from the week before and noted the concentration of big blurs that had left Half Moon and came to this spot. If they had arrived only a week earlier, the last slaughter of the hexacrabs might not have occurred.

Once they arrived at the spot, Ti-Ista pointed out where the nursery had been. She and Ur-Veena selected an empty niche and helped Brother Hancock and Elder Chin select locations to build defenses from any remaining churtrees, and a solar powered charging station for their scooters. Brother Hancock modified the scooter's charge gauge to emit a sound to allow the hexacrabs to know when the charge was weakening.

Sa-Issi was still in mourning about growing up too soon and being forced to leave his spot on Ur-Veena's back. But he was pleased when Father promised his return with many of the Sa cluster within a year.

The sunset glowed red, purple, and apricot behind jungle-covered mountains. The smell of spice permeated the soft air. Rejoice scanned the deck. She had gone to visit No after supper's clean-up, but he hadn't been in his room. There he was, silhouetted against the sunset, watching Brother Hancock and Elder Chin on the nearest island drilling mounting holes in the boulder.

Rejoice walked up to No. "How are you doing?"

He continued to watch the men. After a few seconds, he said, "You could have told me."

He was angry, and Rejoice could not blame him. "I could have told you," she said, "and disobeyed the adults who told me not to do so. It wasn't your fault; you can't do anything about it; and they didn't want you upset the way you were when I told you about Sister Olson."

The shadows from his hat and mask obscured his face as he watched the men load the equipment on the boat with the sound of metal striking metal. His hands kneaded the railing. Presently he said, "You were right to obey your parents. And they were right. I am upset and it's not doing anyone any good."

Rejoice stood beside him and watched the men get into the boat.

"What's with these churtrees?" No said. "Do they get into some kind of killing frenzy and if they can't kill the target, they'll kill themselves just to have something to kill?"

Rejoice held on to the warm railing and ran her thumbs along it. "I heard Father and Elder Chin discussing it in the galley. Father said the pattern seemed to be, if they decided that they couldn't win the battle, they would kill themselves rather than risk being captured alive. Elder Chin said that would be like the Japanese soldiers in the twentieth century. Then he made the oddest face and began to cry. I've never seen Elder Chin cry like that before."

"I have often seen him cry. But what did he say?"

"Do you remember when you told me about your 'law of perversity'?"

No moaned. "Yes and I think I know where you might be going, but I don't want to go there."

"Well, Elder Chin said it. He asked what if our pacifist gift of food was interpreted by the churtrees as a display of our overwhelming power. We demonstrated to them that we had defeated torpals and krakens and other churtrees, so what hope had they of defeating us?"

Noble turned and lowered his head. "So rather than allow their women and children to be captured and tortured they committed mass suicide."

"Elder Chin called it hari kari, I think. That's what the Japanese called it. But really I don't think we'll ever know. I recorded every wall, every basket, every body, every pile of bones; and nowhere did we find one scrap of writing, unless the tattoos are writing."

"You went into the churtree village?"

"Somebody had to hold the camera while Elder Chin flopped the bodies around."

"I wish I could have gone."

"I wish you could have gone, too. I'd much rather be recovering from surgery than carrying the memories of what I saw."

No finally looked at her. "Bad?"

"Much worse." She wrapped her arms around herself. "There were stacks of hexacrab shells from floor to ceiling. The worst were the dead baby churtrees." Her voice broke. "What kind of people would kill their own babies?"

"Uh, Rejoice, humans do."

"We do not."

"Okay, we the humans of the colony do not, but we the humans throughout history do. In ancient times many human babies were burned on sacrificial alters to appease demonic gods or crushed under the posts of sacred temples or . . ."

"Okay, I get the point!"

"And now for centuries we've aborted about half our babies to escape trouble."

Rejoice shuddered. "I just learned that lesson yesterday, and already I have forgotten it."

"Who wants to think about it?" He looked at Rejoice as though he wanted to say more, then turned to watch the boat approach the ship. "I keep wondering what I could have done differently that would have resulted in a different outcome. If I had not deserted my post . . ."

"If you had done anything differently, Opportunity and I would be dead."

His hands kneaded the railing again. "There are worse things to be than dead."

"I'm sure it is better to be dead than treacherous, but I can't help it; I would much rather die quietly in my sleep of old age than right now screaming and skewered to the deck."

"Please, don't. It was that close."

She had gone too far. Rejoice cleared her throat. "Okay. Change of subject. How happy do you think Elder Smith is going to be when he finds out we just committed the colony to ferrying hexacrabs around the world without even asking the elders?"

"Elder Smith won't be pleased at all."

Rejoice waited for several seconds. "What, no lecture on the godliness of Elder Smith?"

No sighed. "We all have our faults. I don't have it in my heart to condemn Elder Smith for being unreasonable when he watches his dream get shattered into smaller and smaller pieces. Certainly I didn't behave well when I lost my dream." He stared straight ahead. His knuckles whitened.

What dream was that? Rejoice watched him out of the corner of her eye as she pretended to watch the boat come in. Had he wanted to be a great builder instead of the klutz of the colony? She sucked in her breath. Maybe he hadn't married and refused to court because the one he loved had married someone else. Harmony? She directed her gaze to the boat. *Stop, stop, stop!* She had run down that road before and hurt everybody doing it. And what if he was in love with Harmony? He was acting honorably which was more than she could say about herself.

She thought about Not By Works breaking her heart and how she had behaved. Yet what had she lost compared to Elder Smith? Back on Old Earth, thousands of people had scurried to please his every whim. He had sold it all to build a farming community in harmony with God and nature in a new land, only to see all the young people taking to the sea and working in factories and chasing after hexacrabs. "Thank you," she whispered. "Sometimes I need to be reminded. And thank you for encouraging Harmony with your project. I was amazed at what she memorized and how the Word came to life when she acted it out."

No smiled. It was good to see. "She is a precious, talented woman. I would love to see her recite scripture in church. But she's still too shy."

The drone of the boat's motor ended. Elder Chin clipped the boat to the ladder.

When Brother Hancock reached the deck, he laid his hand on No's shoulders. "Eh, Brother, when are you going to quit bellyaching about that pinprick in your side and come out to help us?"

"As soon as possible."

Brother Hancock leaned on the railing and watched the sky darken.

"How are your folks handling everything?"

No smiled at him. "My mother says she's seen more of me inside and out than any mother has a right to see. Father says if he had known apprenticing to Elder Chin was so dangerous, he would have suggested another line of work."

As Brother Hancock chuckled, Elder Chin climbed the ladder and joined them. "Brother Cruz, shouldn't you be in bed?"

"I'll be down in a few minutes."

The men glanced at Rejoice and then went downstairs. The lights on the deck flickered on.

"Walk?" he asked.

Rejoice nodded, and they began a slow shuffle around the deck. The lumpy white shape of Large Potato rose and its reflected light streaked the sea.

"What a voyage," Rejoice said. "Yesterday I thought the whole voyage was a disaster. Almost everybody got hurt. We killed a kraken and we still don't know if they're intelligent or not or what they mean to the hexacrabs. We didn't find any of the metals we need. The churtrees are dead. The hexacrabs were gone." She pulled the strap on her mask. She intended to burn it the day the colony declared it safe to go outside without it. "But now they're back and I guess we're friends again because they can use us again. It turned out well, sort of, for the hexacrabs. But seeing all those hexacrab shells makes me wish we had come sooner."

"We didn't know. I hope we come back right away."

Rejoice watched him shuffle a few steps. "Don't you think you've done your share?"

He continued to slide his feet forward. "How do you measure 'share'?"

Rejoice didn't know. The question gave her something to think about as they crept from the bow to the stern. No and Father were sounding more and more like Elder Chin, answering questions with more questions and making one think about more than the surface. She studied Large Potato and thought about how No did not find her intelligence intimidating the way most of the boys, correction, most of the men of the colony did. "I guess you define share as the point where you decide you have suffered enough."

"Enough? Any is too much. I don't know anybody who wants to suffer. I know I don't."

"That's hard to tell. You're going to end up as scarred as Ti-Ista."

"You do what you should do and maybe suffering comes from it. That's when you have to decide whether doing your duty or avoiding suffering is more important."

"Hmm. Like apologizing instead of hiding in embarrassment."

"That's not an example I would have thought of, but that's actually a good one."

Rejoice looked at one of the lights. On Old Earth, dozens of insects would be flitting about the light, but no insects on New Earth were attracted to light. What made some insects search out light anyway? Would she find the answer in her zoology course? She barely remembered cockroaches. They hated light and hid in cracks. That thought reminded her of how she hid in her room until she had enough courage to apologize to No and the rest. "No, except when you were tied down, every time I came to your room privately, you shot out of that room faster than the sting of a naspy. Why is that?"

No answered slowly, "Are you sure you want to know?"

Rejoice suppressed a sigh. "I thought that was why I asked. But if you shouldn't tell me, I suppose I can live with the mystery."

No studied the deck for a long time. "Perhaps you ought to know, though what you'll do about it, I can't guess."

He sounded nervous. The torpal, kraken, and churtrees hadn't unnerved him, but whatever he was going to tell her did. "It's okay. I never asked."

"Your father told me that if he caught me alone with you anywhere on the ship where we couldn't be monitored, he would make sure I lost vital body parts."

Rejoice sputtered, "My father? Said that?" She clenched her fists and tried to calm down. "That's not, uh, a very peaceful thing to say."

"It's exactly what I would say to any young man interested in my daughter."

Rejoice's breath caught. *Our hearts stop beating.* "You're interested in me?"

"Of course. You're an interesting person."

Oh, well, then. She was interesting the same way a farmer plowing is beautiful. She pulled at a strand of hair and twisted it around her forefinger. She could handle that. But how do you respond to a statement like that? I think you're interesting too?

"When you turn seventeen and a half, I will ask your father for permission to court you."

Rejoice's breath caught again and she stopped. The ship rolled gently as she reinterpreted everything she had seen No do on the voyage. She didn't like having her mental gears stripped this way. Good thing she was wearing a mask and a hat to shade her face. "Don't you think you ought to discuss it with me first?"

"Isn't that what we're doing?"

Well, yes, they were. She walked again and had to remind herself to slow down so No could keep up. Something began to swell inside, but the voice of logic told her to stomp it down. She looked up at the sky. The first Small Potato cleared the horizon.

This was going to be hard to say, but she must. "When I started the psychology course, I found a sidebar article Mother had highlighted about shipboard romance. You might change your mind when we get back and you're surrounded by the other girls of the colony."

"I wish it were that simple. I fell in love with you when you were twelve."

Oh, God. Why hadn't she gone downstairs with Elder Chin? Rejoice had never been able to stand it when something didn't make sense, and this did not make sense. "I'm sorry, No, but I can't believe that. Not once in school, not once while I was in space, did you say even one word to me."

"I know," he said, hunching his shoulders. "Twelve is so young. I couldn't believe I fell in love with a kid. I couldn't sleep; I couldn't eat. I still can't."

"Elder Chin says you sleep fine."

"That's because he gets me up at four and makes me run until eleven at night. He says exhaustion is the best cure for lovesickness."

"Elder Chin knows you're in love with me?"

"I tell him everything. How else could he disciple me?"

"Wait a minute. Does everybody on this ship but me know about this?"

"Um, I don't think Ur-Veena knows or cares."

Rejoice looked up at the Potatoes. The only emotions she could identify out of the multitudes swirling through her were confusion and dismay. How long would she be the last person to know?

After a few steps, No said, "I tried to talk myself out of it. I thought, 'If this is love, who needs it?' I quickly saw that the way I felt about you meant I had to stay away from you or else I would get us in trouble. I had to wait until you got older. Then you went to space for three years, and I prayed every night that you would not be attracted to one of those triplets."

"That prayer got answered," Rejoice said.

No continued urgently, "I was hoping that on this voyage you'd get to know me and maybe you'd feel the same way back." He stammered, "It hasn't worked that way, and if it never does, I promise I'll stay away from you, even if it means staying in Large Archipelago for the rest of my life."

"Isn't that what you're planning to do anyway?"

"I don't know. What I plan to do next depends on you." He looked away and hunched his shoulders higher. "I should have kept my mouth shut. But it's been . . .so . . . hard."

Rejoice's emotions careened. "Why me? It's not like I'm beautiful or—"

"Oh, yes, you are," he said. "And you're lively. You say what you think. And you think about things. And you're kind to your little brother. And you have a toughness and tenacity that is amazing. And you care about people. I'd be crazy not to love that. Then I find out that you're a great cook and you can sew. And. And. There's nobody else like you on this planet. I'd bet there's nobody like you on old Earth. I'd be crazy not to want to live with a woman like you for all my life."

"You want to marry me because I can sew shirts?"

"No. I'm saying this badly. I meant to say you possess a lot of competencies. You're good at a lot of things."

Rejoice clasped her hands together. If she did marry No, she would share him with everyone else in the colony. She would be challenged every day to grow in godliness. She would live in the smallest, plainest house. She would follow him back to Large Archipelago in a search for churtrees to evangelize. Like Sister Hancock, she would get to worry every day over whether or not her husband had found a new way to kill himself.

He interrupted her thoughts. "So . . . is it all right to ask your father?"

She scrutinized him. Whatever he did, he did with his whole heart. Whatever he vowed, he would do. Could she live with that? She didn't know, but that was what courtship was about, finding out. And one could back out before the vows were made.

She reached out her hand. He wiped his hand on his overall and then grasped her hand. It trembled and felt damp.

All her emotions crystallized into one. She wanted to laugh. She didn't know whether she wanted to laugh from relief that someone really, truly loved her; or from joy that the one who loved her was as noble as No Confidence In The Flesh Cruz; or from the ridiculous situation that the man who wrestled kraken and churtrees and wanted to do it again could be so afraid that she would refuse him. She swallowed hard several times. *You will control yourself.* If she did laugh, he would think she was mocking him, and it had become very important that she never hurt him ever again. She took a deep breath. "Yes, I think I would like that."

III

BOOKTHREE: PACIFISTS' WAR

PACIFISTS' WAR CHAPTER ONE

Rejoice leaned forward to study the asteroid data on the large screen and frowned. A wave of dizziness swamped her and she accidentally hit the keyboard with her palm as she steadied herself. Static filled the large screen. She closed her eyes and concentrated on breathing.

The front door of their white, domed house opened and her husband Noble Cruz set his rifle in its brackets above the door with a click. With badly concealed irritation, he said, "Why are you up?"

She opened her eyes. He knelt beside her so his face was level with hers. She gripped the edge of the counter. "I'm checking on a New Earth grazer that's off the ecliptic. Today I verify its orbit."

"That's what your small screen is for. Let me help you back to bed."

She held up her hand in the 'don't touch me' position. "Excuse me, but I need the larger memory of the main board."

"You can remote in from the small screen."

She gritted her teeth. "I really need the larger screen to see what I need to see." She looked past him to the kitchen section with dirty dishes yet on the counter. The kitchen/dining/living/computer room had been swept except for the crumbs under the table which were already attracting all manner of insects. Triangular paintings pegged to the smooth white walls of their bubble home wore webbing of pseudospiders like lace. On the other leg, maybe she shouldn't expose herself to this aggravation.

Noble frowned, his dark brows moving together. He smoothed his face as he stood and pulled at the straps on his blue denim overalls. "What do you want for lunch?"

"Anything. It doesn't matter." Whatever he fixed, she would likely lose anyway. She felt sorry for him, doing her work as well as his, but she would never be able to persuade him to slow down.

He hesitated before walking over to the refrigerator.

It grated that he hovered so over her, and yet she could not blame him. It had nearly killed him when she lost every baby but Mark, each time for a different reason.

Rejoice inhaled deeply to keep the tears back. Six months into this pregnancy, it looked like this time this little boy would make it, but Rejoice wasn't so sure she would. She looked out the window next to her screen to see if Lad Mark was coming back from school yet. Yertles tried to flip each other in a melee for an apple that should not have been lying on the yellow brick road.

She inhaled and tried to focus as she called up the data on the asteroid again. Why she had thought to search in that section of space last week she did not know, but already she had found something.

Noble cleared his throat.

She glanced at him where he stood with the plates in his hands. He had that look on his face. She frowned at him. "I'm fine," she whispered, and returned to the screen. She opened and closed her left hand in her peripheral vision to help block out distracting sights.

And then the memory of her father humming tunelessly and rocking gently whenever he concentrated on his work distracted her. Why was she so determined to cry? She hated being so emotional.

When the computer beeped and a red light in the corner flashed, she jumped. Renewed dizziness made her clutch the edge of the counter, carefully this time so she wouldn't hit the keyboard. Faintly, she said, "We're all going to die."

Behind her, Noble snorted. "I heard that. You think I don't listen to you anymore, but I distinctly heard you say we are all going to die."

She looked over her shoulder as her lungs refused to draw in air. Black hair fell over his eyes as he sliced a loaf of bread. He looked up, grinning, then dropped the knife. "You're serious."

She stared at him, unable to say what she had just discovered.

He knelt by her side. "What do you mean?"

She pointed to the screen.

He glanced at the numbers. "I see the data. Now tell me what it means."

If only the baby inside her would let her take the deep breath she needed. "An asteroid, a fast one, is headed straight toward us. It will hit New Earth in three months."

"Three months." He swallowed. "Can the Starflower transfer the mass driver over to deflect it?"

"The Starflower is on the other side of the sun right now." Her fingers danced over the keys as equations flashed on the screen. "If we got the message to them right now, which we can't, and if they flew as fast as possible, they would still get here a week and a half after the asteroid hit."

"Shuttles," he stammered. "Could we send up all our shuttles with mass drivers?"

"The shuttles are not made for prolonged or deep space work."

"If it's a matter of being dangerous work, I'll volunteer to go."

Of course he would. She shook her head. "It's not dangerous; it's impossible." *Oh, God, two weeks after Opportunity's eighteenth birthday, one week after the baby's due date. Please, God, this can't be happening again.*

"Okay," he said, interweaving his fingers. "We humans can't escape, not all of us anyway. Three months. Ah, do you know where this asteroid is going to hit?"

Rejoice studied the screen. "I still need to calculate in the gravitational effects of the known asteroids it flies near and follow it a little longer. I can maybe tell you more precisely next week. It should be somewhere in the northern hemisphere, somewhat above our latitude."

His knuckles cracked as he kneaded his hands. "This island was not damaged too badly in the Dark Death. When you find out where on New Earth this new asteroid will hit, you could calculate the safest place to be. We could evacuate the colonists and our food to there. But the churtree;

how can we move the churtree? How can we save them?"

"We can't save a people who try to kill us every time we say 'hi.'" See how much she cared if God dropped a rock on their vicious heads.

"The logistics." He closed his eyes. "Is three months long enough to move the hexacrabs? They've scattered everywhere. And only God knows where the missing hexacrabs went."

Rejoice called up the calendar while trying to swallow the acid burning her throat. "We won't be able to move a single one of them. Three months is smack dab in the middle of Child Come season." *Father God, You must show me a way.*

"Well, well, how about this? We persuade Ur-Veena to tell half his people to go to safety. He's already split two clusters. He can do it again. And, ah, could we send up shuttles filled with explosives and, no. You told me once why that wouldn't work. How big is this asteroid?"

Rejoice shook her head. "Just stop."

He fell silent and clasped his hands.

The door opened and eight-year-old Mark shouted, "I'm home."

Rejoice winced. If only they could send Mark outside to play until they were ready to face him. But you didn't send children outside unsupervised, not here.

In two strides, Noble reached the door and called the slight man in blue overalls chaperoning a flock of children. "Hold, Brother Wu. Could you please take Lad Mark to the store and, ah, have him put ice cream on our tab? And, uh, one for everyone else, our treat."

Mark grinned with a gap-toothed mouth. "Yes!"

Brother Wu stepped closer to the door. "Is Sister Cruz all right?"

While Wu and Noble talked, Rejoice's mind spun around the facts. There was always an answer. What if they did send up unmanned shuttles? Stronghold had gotten awfully clever at robotics and programming.

"She's fine. We simply need to talk alone for a bit." Noble blocked Brother Wu's view of the screen Rejoice was working at.

Shuttles meet the asteroid when it's, what, a month, three weeks away.

"Can I have any kind I want?" asked Mark.

Place explosives . . . No, dig the tunnels first to channel the blasts.

Noble knelt to hug his son. "Not strawberry, no. Hours of itching eyes and a runny nose aren't worth ten minutes of pleasure."

Is it metallic like Asteroid Opportunity or stony like Deceit?

Brother Wu brushed aside a tomato leaf that was tickling his forehead. The tomato vine that grew over the curved doorway often snared unwary guests. He resettled the rifle on his back. "If you like, when we're done, I could take Lad Mark home with me for the afternoon."

Noble nodded. "Yes, thank you."

No time for tunnels. How many kilotons of explosives would they need to change the asteroid's trajectory?

Brother Wu scuffed the bricks. "As long as I have you here, I would like permission to rebuke Young Lady Opportunity. I saw Brother Makepeace alone on the Inner Ring Road."

The colony surely doesn't have enough shuttles to carry the amount needed.

Noble held the edge of the curved-top door. "I'll also talk to Opportunity."

Brother Wu said, "I looked everywhere for her. I had to get the children home and Makepeace wouldn't come with me. I told him to stay in the store, but I don't know if he understood me or not."

Mass, mass, mass; precisely how big is this asteroid?

"If Opportunity and Makepeace aren't home in ten minutes, I'll look for them." Noble said.

"Once I get Lad Mark and the other children under cover, I could do the search," Brother Wu offered.

Where is the spectral analysis? Why can't I think?

"No, thank you. I will call you if I need help." The door clicked shut, and Noble settled onto a stool next to Rejoice. His knuckles cracked as he pushed his hands together and pulled them apart.

"Oh," Rejoice said, then louder and sharper, "Oh!"

Noble leaned forward as she placed both hands on her cheeks.

"I am such a fool. It's not an asteroid."

"Is it a comet?"

Rejoice rolled her eyes, then wished she hadn't as Noble turned his face away. "It's a ship," she faltered, "a ship." She swallowed back acid. "Spectral analysis shows fuel expenditure."

"A ship? Like our Starflower?"

Rejoice nodded.

"How can that be? We have a contract with Old Earth. We paid a lot of money to ensure that no one followed us."

"You're assuming the ship is of human origin."

Noble stopped. They had settled on a planet with at least two intelligent races. Who could say how many more inhabited the universe? As Rejoice pressed more keys, Noble rubbed his mouth. "Whoever they are, I hope they're friendlier than the churtrees."

Rejoice sat back and wiped her sweaty hands on her dress. "Could you help me to bed now? I've had enough adrenaline to last me for years."

"What are you going to do about the ship?"

"I've set up the scanner to look for any transmissions they might be sending our way. If they're calling us, we'll hear them. I'll call them when I've had time to think. All we can do now is wait. I want to wait in bed."

Noble lifted her to her feet and helped her walk the meter to the bedroom door.

The radio announced, "Transmission received." Then a human female voice followed. "Colonists of Starflower, please respond. This is the colony ship Independence. We need assistance. During the Warp, two of our food synthesizers were destroyed. Our third one failed a week ago. If you possess any surplus food, we will purchase it. By the time our ship reaches you, we will have been fasting for a month. Colonists of Starflower, please respond."

"Radio off," Rejoice commanded. The silence echoed with the plea.

Noble's grip around Rejoice tightened. "Now can I go up in a shuttle? If we could meet them on the way, they wouldn't need to fast so long."

Rejoice leaned her head against the oval, plastic door frame to the bedroom bubble. She had managed to make him change his name from

No to Noble. She had never managed to make him less reckless. "No. We can send a greater quantity of food in an unmanned shuttle. I'll call Stronghold and the First City Airfield. You call the Elders and ask them to craft a friendly response that gives away no more than their message did. We still don't know their intentions."

Behind them, the front door opened. Young Lady Opportunity, with swinging, glossy black hair trailing down her plain brown dress, pulled in her twenty-four-year-old brother Makepeace. "We're home. Anything exciting happen while we were gone?"

PACIFISTS' WAR CHAPTER TWO

Three months later, Noble checked his screen. "Rejoice, they're almost here. Please hurry."

"No." Rejoice sat on the edge of the bed and thrust out her feet so Noble could slip on her shoes. In the corner of the bedroom, Opportunity patted the screaming baby writhing on her shoulder. He had been screaming for hours. Rejoice would join him soon. She opened her mouth, stopped, then shut it, clicking her teeth together. A pastor's wife should think peaceful thoughts and say peaceful things. Right.

Noble bent to kiss her ankle as he slid on the second shoe and smiled at her with one side of his mouth higher than the other. "Come on, what were you going to say?"

"Ick!" Opportunity said as the baby spit up and missed the spit rag altogether.

Rejoice sighed. "I was going to say, "And how eager would you be for a walk one week after getting your belly slit open?" Then I remembered you did do that once."

Noble's smile broadened and he winked, "We were much younger then." He helped her out of the bed.

Rejoice suppressed a snort. Fifteen years older hardly made them ancient; but if she kept up this rate of worry, she would be ancient in a few weeks. Why, did the first flight of the new people need to come to the churtree mission instead of First City where most of the colonists lived?

Opportunity wiped at the white, curdled mess on her dress. "Why don't I go and you stay here? I want to meet these new people."

Would that Rejoice could send her sister. "Because I'm in charge of the space program, such as it is. Because they requested me. Did you think I volunteered?"

Opportunity grimaced and turned away. Her black hair swished over her dress. Watching her sister, Rejoice again suppressed the desire she had inherited Father's black hair and Mother's curls instead of Mother's brown and Father's straight.

"If we leave now, we can take our time." Noble said gently.

"You told me to hurry."

"We can hurry slowly." He offered his arm and she held it, feeling under his black sleeve muscles that were still as hard as when they married, thanks to the hundred push-ups and fifty chin-ups he did every morning while praying. They crept toward the door, stopping long enough to sling rifles over their shoulders.

In the doorway, Makepeace ran his fingers up and down the door jamb as he examined the reflections on the white plastic. "Drying, crying in the night," he moaned. The image of their half-Japanese, half Scot father with beautiful almond eyes, Makepeace reached to touch where side and top of the door joined.

Rejoice's baby opened his eyes which were as beautiful as his uncle's when he wasn't screaming. She smiled at him as he quietly breathed for the moment.

He scrunched up his face and stuck out his tongue.

Mark, dark-haired and dark-eyed, a copy of his father, glared at them from the table. "Why can't I go with you?"

"I'm not giving you another answer than the one I gave you. Pouters pout in bed, lad," Noble murmured.

Mark's face crumpled as he rose to walk quickly to his bedroom with his back straight, his chin down, and his arms straight at his sides.

Outside, Rejoice breathed in the humid air and glanced up the lane toward the center of the mission. The white dome of the Meetingplace gleamed. In her mind's eye, she viewed the blue-tiled plaza surrounding the Meetingplace, and the first ring of seven bubble houses, school, store, and labs. Her house lay in the second ring of eighteen houses, on the road that ran to the cliffs along the Ti Bay. There the road curved to descend to the only other flat place on the island, which was where the missionaries had built a runway they never used. What would the newcomers think of their little mission station?

When they reached the perimeter of the mission compound, Noble stopped at the motion sensor to tap in the pass code so alarms wouldn't call out all the brothers. Rejoice glanced nervously up at Gap Pass. The Orange Scar churtree lived thirty kilometers away, on the other side of Gap Pass, a deep vee in the ridge that gnawed the sky. The Hancocks and Greens had spent the last week planting noisemakers throughout the jungle hoping to drive the churtree to their side of the ridge. Brother Zystra at the observation post above Half-Moon Bay reported an increase in churtree at their village, so the tactic might have worked. Or they could have been marshalling their forces for an all-out assault.

She tried to block the images, but the stacks of hexacrab shells filled her inner vision. The stench of the corpses and the buzz of the insects returned with a shuddering impact. *Focus, focus.* She needed to make sure she said nothing that could be misinterpreted by these new humans.

She visualized God holding her hand. Noble had been talking on the radio and missed her shivering. Rejoice sternly told herself to turn her mind to happier thoughts.

She scuffed her feet on the yellow brick she and Opportunity had requested the lane be made of. Had the elders had ever figured out why? Likely Elder Chin had since little passed by him. How had Oz ever made it into the Starflower library?

Noble took her arm again and kissed her as they passed the motion sensors. "You look beautiful, mother of my children. Thank you for carrying my son."

Rejoice smiled and shook her head. Noble could find the funniest things to be grateful for. Whose children did he think she would be carrying?

They passed a brown, cork-screw leafed bush with a rich odor of sage.

Like many of the plants on this island, one touch would raise huge blisters on the skin that oozed and itched for weeks. The road brushed the cliff and curved around a spire of rock. The rock had ages ago been carved into a multi-fanged monster, possibly by the churtree. They carved no statues now, possibly related to their severe depopulation after the Dark Death and again after the arrival of the humans.

At this point, a muscle in her abdomen burned. Why had Rejoice been too proud to insist on riding in a runabout?

A perfect blue sky arched over the brown and gray jungle, and the glittering waters of Ti Bay stretched below them. Beyond the frothy lace of surf floated platforms of solar cells generating electricity for the hexacrabs. Elevators from the bay rose up the limestone cliffs. To the north, limestone gave way to granite and basalt, a tortured terrain shattered by the impact of Dark Death.

Rejoice switched her gaze from the bay to Noble. He still grinned at her. The grin reminded her of the exaltation on his face six days ago as he had held close his still-bloody son and looked at her with shining eyes to announce, "His name is Jubilee."

Rejoice, looking everywhere but at what Doctor Carlson was doing with the caesarian, had said, "But that has three syllables."

"You named all the other children. I name this one Jubilee, The Year Of Jubilee Cruz."

"Are you all right?" Noble asked, breaking into the memory that was better than her churtree flashbacks.

She had named the other children: Luke, miscarried at five months, Mark, a 'keeper' as the nurse put it, John, miscarried at four months, and Ruth, lost at three and a half months gestation. She would have named this one Paul. At least Jubilee was shorter than Noble Is He Who Studies The Word or Rejoice In The Lord's Salvation. Before she married him, Rejoice had insisted that No Confidence In The Flesh Cruz change his name. She had hoped he would pick something shorter. He hadn't. "Jubilee it is," she had said, and then held her breath to keep from groaning.

Doctor Cruz, who was also her mother-in-law, and her own mother, who was also the nurse, descended on their grandson like yertles on a plum. They cleaned him and chuckled over him and did all the medical things for him that doctors and nurses do. They said that they would not operate on Rejoice because they did not trust themselves to work on family. How she was family and their grandson wasn't escaped her. But she used the problem in logic to distract her from pain and from listening to the patient instructions that Doctor Carlson was giving to nurse-in-training Sister Deng on how to stitch up her belly.

A scant day later, both grandmothers had flown back to Sole; Doctor Cruz to her practice and research lab in First City, and Mother to tend Harmony, who was dying of lung rot.

Why had Harmony gotten lung rot when Rejoice, who had spent much more time with Father, had not? Father was the first to catch it. What was the count now? Forty-one dead?

"Are you all right?" Noble asked again.

Rejoice tried to swallow a sudden lump. It had been five years already. When would she stop missing Father so desperately? "I'm fine." Her mind scattered from random memory to random memory when today was the day she most needed to focus on diplomacy. *Focus!*

Noble squeezed her shoulders. "You must be worried about these people from the Independence."

"How can you not be worried about a people who don't tell us anything about themselves? Who insist on coming to this island after we've told them as many ways as we could," she gasped for breath, "without giving away the hexacrabs and churtrees, that we don't want them to come here?"

"They're probably as worried about us as we are about them."

"What's to worry about us? In the entire universe, we should be the last thing they worry about."

"You're forgetting history. Many people are afraid of Christians, especially in small groups."

"We brought as many as the Starflower would hold."

"Yes, but seven hundred is a small group. Many small groups involute and turn psychotic."

"Like Elder Smith and Elder Sims."

Noble frowned and tightened his lips. "Not like them. You need to get over this irrational hatred of those godly elders."

"It's not irrational—I mean, I don't hate them." She winced, thinking of Elder Sims, tall, thin, and as dark as the deep, and next to him Elder Smith, shorter and massive with a florid face surrounded by gray hair. They both thought the only proper way to worship God was to do so after sitting with their foreheads pressed into a cow's flank and squeezing out milk by hand into a bucket.

Noble's gaze bored into hers. "For an example, somewhere around three hundred years ago a charismatic man named James Jones fled old America with a thousand of his cult followers and set up his personal Mount Zion in the South American jungle. When government agents threatened to check on the welfare of the children, he convinced all his followers to drink poisoned juice and then shot himself."

"That sounds like the churtree. What does that have to do with us?"

Noble sighed. "It has nothing to do with us. But these new people can't know that. Such bizarre cases are taught as the norm of Christianity in Old Earth schools." After a few steps, he added. "God allowed these people to come here for a purpose, and by faith, I look forward to finding out what that purpose is."

They walked by a gray tree with sweet scented leaves like bubbles. A tree urchin quivered on a branch. Its black spines clicked a warning.

She tripped over an upturned yellow brick. Her knees wobbled. "I think I need to rest." She licked something sweet from the corner of her mouth. Breakfast? She should have washed her face before they left.

"We're almost there," Noble said.

So they were. The paved lane ended and an opening in the jungle widened out into an airstrip the missionaries had used only once. The first time a colonial jet had landed there, a quartet of churtree on a hunting expedition nearby had impaled themselves on their stone spears.

Rejoice settled onto a camp stool next to seventy-five-year-old Elder Chin. His wrinkles rearranged into a broad smile as he embraced her, enveloping her with the smell of mint. "And how is my favorite daughter?"

That was how he greeted all his daughters and Rejoice. He considered Noble the son that he never had, ergo Rejoice was his daughter.

Stupid tears stung her eyes again. She squeezed Elder Chin's mottled hand. "I've felt better."

"Still screaming, eh?"

Please let him mean the baby. Her smile wobbled.

"He'll grow up to be a fine preacher."

Rejoice put on a smile and gazed about the group waiting for the jet. Gray and red-haired Sister Hancock adjusted a third camera and made sure the main board received its images. One-armed and now bald, Brother Hancock made faces for the camera check. Brother Higashi scanned the sky. Brothers Madison and Rutherford stood back to back scanning the jungle. Eight people there on the runway, and fifty back in the Mission watching on their screens. Twelve hundred in First City and in space. Maybe the three hundred in Promise were watching also.

Noble stooped eye level with the seated elder. "Elder, are you sure you want me to be the first to greet them? It is your place."

What could be seen of the Elder's eyes beneath droops of skin twinkled. "I prefer to watch. Thank you."

Noble straightened and fidgeted with the steel cross on his lapel. The smell of spice from the grayish brown jungle thickened in the hot sunlight.

Elder Chin wore black also. The rest of the men wore blue denim, and she and Sister Hancock wore their everyday brown dresses. For what was Elder Chin watching?

A far-off howler bag whooped. A shuttle roared. Lights at the edge of the runway flashed.

Rejoice took a deep breath and released it slowly. Watching the shuttle thunder in and taxi to within a few meters of them felt both unreal and inevitable. *Please, Father God, let these people bring peace and not a sword.*

She wiped her sweaty palms on her dress.

The door of the shuttle opened and stairs unfolded to the runway. A woman stepped out.

Rejoice gawked at the thin Caucasian dressed in tight purple pants, acid yellow shirt, and purple jacket. Bright red lipstick and fingernail polish resembled Old Earth pictures of neon signs. Black lined her eyes and eyebrows. Her short silver hair was shaved into repeating vees that ran in one line from her forehead to the nape of the neck. Bright silver earrings and a brooch on her chest echoed the pattern. A knife in a filigreed sheath clung to her thigh.

The woman stopped and studied the colonists in turn, especially at the women with hair the way God gave it them and unaugmented faces.

Not plain people. What then? Peacock people?

The woman stepped down the stairs, stopped two meters away from Noble, and said in a strong voice, "We were informed that you were pacifists."

"We are," Noble said. "Welcome to New Earth. Do you need more assistance than we were able to send you?"

The woman studied Noble with his rifle slung over his shoulder, "You are who?"

"I'm Pastor Cruz." He extended his hand. "We—"

"Where is Rejoice Holly?" She ignored his hand.

"Here." Rejoice stood. "Don't be afraid. We do mean you well."

"No fear, but why are you confronting us armed?"

"We're not confronting you. We're protecting you."

The woman's hazel eyes darted about. "A friendly warning; my people are armed in the shuttle. Should anything happen to me . . . you process?"

Rejoice and Noble exchanged glances. This was not going well. The woman was not going to speak to Noble who was the one with the people skills. When they had first married, he had assumed that anyone as intelligent as Rejoice could quickly master counseling skills. But her first attempt had been so disastrous that Noble joked afterward that it had taken him six months to repair the damage.

Rejoice licked her lips. Why couldn't Sister Hancock focus that camera on someone else? "Let's turn and taste the current."

Creases formed between the woman's drawn eyebrows.

"Please help me process this: your earrings."

The woman touched one with her forefinger and the sun's reflection dazzled Rejoice's eyes.

"They're vees with tails or short ys," Rejoice said. "Do they stand for your initials, or for vectors, or for thesis, antithesis, and synthesis?"

The woman's blackened eyebrows arched up, and she smiled. "Vectors, for truth. Reality may cause us to deviate, but also we change reality."

Oh, no you don't. But perhaps she meant it differently than Rejoice was hearing it. Language did change and involute. Noble's hand squeezed her shoulder. "If you wish, we've prepared a banquet for you in the Meetingplace. We thought that after you and the other passengers had eaten and rested, we could discuss your settlement plans."

The woman still toyed with her earring. "Explain, please, the guns." Her gaze traveled to the rifle slung over Rejoice's shoulder.

"The archipelago is not a safe place."

The woman's eyes swept the jungle and runway. "You live here."

Noble kept his smile plastered on his face. "Our reasons may not be yours. If you come to the Meetingplace, we can discuss the hazards here and your plans for settlement."

Brother Higashi interrupted with a shout, "Ware! Up! North!" He dropped to one knee, as did Brother Rutherford and Sister Hancock, and they readied their rifles, pointing them toward the northern sky.

Noble clapped his hand to his rifle, and then froze. A weapon glinted in the doorway of the shuttle.

The woman backed up a step. "What?"

Rejoice pointed north and whispered, "Shh. Don't move."

PACIFISTS' WAR CHAPTER THREE

A black speck spiraled above the jungle. Rejoice listened so hard she could hear the blood rushing through her ears. The black speck moved toward them. Then a wail pitched at such a high frequency that only the women and young men were able to hear it floated over them.

Sister Hancock fired. The black speck exploded and dropped.

Noble said softly, "We can join you in your shuttle for a discussion, or you can move quickly to our larger Meetingplace. Or you can postpone the talks. Your choice. We have enough food for everyone in your shuttle."

"What was that?"

"A pack bat. It's an animal that tears flesh from bone. The rest of the pack should be here in ten minutes or less. We're leaving now." Noble backed away, taking Rejoice's arm to support her. Brother Hancock rushed over to help Elder Chin stand.

Sister Hancock shouted at one of the cameras, "Pack due. Get your chickens in." She and Brother Higashi and Brother Rutherford formed a three man retreat formation, walking backward and scanning the sky. Brother Madison took the point position forward.

The woman held up her palm toward the shuttle. Its door slammed. She sprinted until she was even with Rejoice. "For truth?"

"Taste it." Rejoice pressed her lips together to keep from crying. Everything in her abdomen threatened to fall out. Why couldn't the woman have agreed to talk screen to screen? Her obvious distrust rankled. They scurried along the path through the jungle, along the bay, and rose through more jungle on one side of the path, and citrus, mango, apple, and plum orchards on the other. The woman loped easily beside them while Rejoice concentrated on putting her feet one before the other and not tripping. They passed the second ring of bubble houses, the first ring, and entered the large central plaza that surrounded a white, iridescent geodesic dome.

The woman stopped, and her eyes widened. Before them stood a rounded glass case with six sensor-whiskered legs and a black lid. Four extensions protruded from the front, and two from the rear. Two of the front extensions with finger-like claspers held rifles indistinguishable from the colonists'. Inside the case, water circulated around Ur-Veena. He touched a variety of controls. Two of his silver eyes swiveled toward the humans and one fixated on a control.

Noble grabbed the woman's arm and pulled her past the mobile aquarium while Rejoice gritted her teeth against the pain and aggravation. They had asked the hexacrabs to hide until the intentions of the newcomers were clear. The hexacrabs had studied enough Old Earth history to know the concern was justified. But the humans might as well have been begging mercy from a torpal.

Brother Higashi shouted, "They're in sight!"

The crackle of gunfire followed. Brother Madison reached the four-meter high, five-centimeter thick, double glass doors of the dome, hit the button, and the doors swung open. Brother Hancock and Elder Chin entered first, then Rejoice and Noble and the woman. Rejoice licked sweat off her upper lip. Brothers Higashi and Rutherford and Sister Hancock shot off three more rounds before hurrying in. A few seconds after the door swung shut, four-legged, black bats the size of roosters beat against the glass doors and swirled about the plaza. The hexacrab calmly aimed and fired, one rifle after another. Two bats splattered on the pavement.

The woman splayed her fingers across the smooth glass. A bat dove for her head and thunked against the door. She winced and her breathing grew audible.

Rejoice wanted to sit; no, she wanted to go home and lie down. She shuffled to the peacock woman and inhaled a rapidly-fading scent she could not recognize. "We would have preferred a more pleasant welcome." Which they would have had if they had gone to First City as the colonists had asked them to. "While waiting for the pack bats to disperse, may I introduce you to everyone?"

The woman did not turn her head. "What is that?"

Another LV, land vehicle, lumbered into view with a slightly smaller hexacrab inside that had six crab legs. The pack bats battered themselves against the glass cases for several seconds, and then rose like smoke and streamed away back north. "Those are our good friends, Ur-Veena and Sa-Issi. I believe they will be joining us for the banquet."

The woman turned to stare at Rejoice. "Friends?" she squeaked.

"Good friends." And aggravating.

The woman flushed and straightened.

Sister Hancock pulled out her computer and popped open its screen. "Good. Radar says the bats are flying straight away. We can try to get the rest of the people off the shuttle in twenty minutes."

The screen on Rejoice's hip beeped. She flipped it open. "Cruz here."

Whistles, gratings, and clicks answered. Then a translator intoned, "Our eyes celebrate the seeing of air-ocean person Rejoice. A new one is tied to your shell. When may we see him?"

Rejoice whistled and clicked back, "My niche is forever open to you. Enter soon."

"Also, when are we allowed to swim with the air-breathers from the warp-ocean?"

Before Rejoice could answer, Noble flipped open his screen. "The currents confuse them. They need time to taste the waters."

"We turn our eyes from you, but not our thoughts." The LVs turned and stepped away from the plaza.

When the hexacrabs had gone from sight, the woman exhaled. "So. Now what?"

"What would you like?" Noble said.

"A good, stiff drink."

Rejoice looked at Noble and he looked at her. Apparently he didn't know what that meant either. Ice?

Sister Hancock said, "I'm sorry. We have nothing like that. This is a 'bring your own bottle' planet."

The words had been English, but Rejoice did not know what they meant. Like Mother, Sister Hancock constantly used Old Earth phrases that she then needed to translate for Rejoice, such as 'get your chickens in' which meant more than getting the poultry into the coop. She couldn't figure it out at first because they had trained every chick on an electric grid to scurry into the coop every time it heard a recorded bat pack call or else be shocked. So the chickens took care of themselves. Rejoice returned her gaze to the woman. The weather, the creatures, the society; all shape the language. Had Rejoice used any phrases the newcomer would not understand?

"Reality reels," the woman murmured. She stepped away from the door, out of the alcove, and into the Meetingplace. She studied the translucent white walls, the gray tile floor, the three tables set for thirty-five, the small dais with a simple lectern at one side, the serving carts with covered trays redolent of rice, rosemary, and curry, the six adults waiting for them arrayed in brown dresses or denim overalls.

The colonists placed their rifles in the racks by the doors and followed the woman. Rejoice headed for a chair and dropped into it. Too bad it wasn't a bed. Sister Deng would need to check her over when this was through. Noble pulled out a chair next to Rejoice for the peacock woman to sit in. She frowned momentarily, but sat.

"Well," Rejoice said, "we can wait for your people, or we can eat now."

"Are those creatures joining us?"

Noble said, "No, I asked them to give us more time."

A look of relief crossed the woman's face before she relaxed it to an unemotional mask. "Initial negotiations first. We need to know how we can work with you."

Noble sat across the table from her. He motioned to Sister Hancock who set up a camera two meters away from them. "Would you like us to activate a screen so your people can be in on this?"

"They already are. What do you want in exchange for the food you sent us?"

"Nothing, Ms—?"

"We do not wish to impose on you. What sort of economic system do you have here?"

"Capitalism."

"Good. Necessity for working out a method of payment."

Rejoice rubbed her stomach. *Dear Father God, why do they use such grammar?* Was that involution?

Noble touched her hand. "It gives us pleasure to donate the food to you."

The woman closed her bright red lips for a moment and glanced at his hand. "Acceptance. Item one done. Item two: do you possess a food synthesizer we can purchase?"

"We scavenged all of ours for parts long ago. Frankly, we're surprised you were unable to repair yours."

"Sabotage." The woman looked up at the arched white ceiling. "Sabotage why we exited warp three months from our destination. Someone on Earth decided to ensure we never reached it."

Noble hunched his shoulders. "If you don't mind my asking, why is this planet your destination? Our charter specifically states that only we and those of our faith could come here."

"So go back to Earth and sue the vacuum-brains."

Sure. Seven years ship time, thirty years real time, and only enough fuel left to almost reach all the way back. Why hadn't they thought of that? Rejoice rubbed between her eyebrows.

Noble sat back and the feet of his chair squeaked on the gray tile. "I apologize. You're here and we need to deal with that. We can give you three to six months' worth of food until you get established."

"Necessity for eating our seed grains."

"We can donate as much as you need for your first crop. But I should warn you, this island is not a place to grow grains. We import every kernel."

"And what payment?"

"None. When I say donate, I mean donate. It gives us pleasure."

The woman blinked. "You are prospering."

Rejoice said, "We have seven years' worth of food warehoused. We can spare a few months' worth."

"Seven years." She seemed awed.

Rejoice ran her finger along the edge of the table. "Nine years ago, a blight struck all our cereal crops, and it took us two years to beat it. We like to be prepared." Rejoice had publicly and loudly opposed the warehousing of so much food as an unnecessary drain on their resources. God grant she wouldn't need any more lessons like that to teach her humility.

The woman nodded. "Four months' worth of food for six hundred ninety-seven people. Not a day more. We are not intending to parasitize." Brother Nguyen set cups of mint tea before everyone and placed, in the center of the table, jars of honey and molasses and lumps of pink sugar. The woman held her cup with both hands, but did not drink from it. She slowed her words as though speaking to children.

"Items two and three dealt with. Now to four. How long do you expect it will take to convert us to your faith? If we do not convert, how long before you decide to burn the infidels?"

Heat flickered on Rejoice's face. Noble needed to handle this.

Noble took a sip of tea and considered before answering. "You cannot deny us the right to try to share our faith. You might as well try to deny the sun the right to shine. However, we have no timetable for your conversion. And since we are pacifists, we don't burn infidels. We don't even toast them."

The woman hid her mouth behind her cup and chanced a sip before her next question. "These animals in the walking aquariums?"

"The hexacrabs," Noble supplied.

"These hexacrabs all converted?"

Rejoice admired how Noble answered evenly, "Not a one." He spent hours every week praying for the salvation of the hexacrabs. Their lack of response to the gospel was one cause of the split. The people in Promise refused to have anything to do with the pagan hexacrabs and little to do with the people who were fascinated by them.

"They must be very bright," the woman said slowly.

Brother Hancock broke into a fit of coughing, or something like, and excused himself. Rejoice glanced over at Elder Chin who sat immobile save for his eyes. When the colonists were trying so hard to have a good first contact, why was this woman being so rude?

"It gives you pleasure to donate those walking aquariums?"

"They earn their land vehicles," Noble said. "The hexacrabs work at an undersea mine on the other side of this island. They do ocean transport. They also help in the kelp farms."

"So the mine is why you live here despite the hazards?"

Close. Rejoice had the unholy wish that was the only reason.

When no one answered the last remark, the woman took a deep drink of the mint tea. "Permission to ask a personal question?"

Noble continued his intense gaze into the woman's eyes. "What would you like to know?"

"Two pregnant women here, no children. What did you do with the children?"

Rejoice clunked down her cup. Some of the hot tea slopped over her fingers. "I know I still look pregnant, but I gave birth last week, so you see only one. You don't see any children because we don't trust you any more than you trust us."

Noble's smile grew pained. It was this kind of bluntness that sparked grass fires in the congregation for him to put out. Several of the people shifted in their seats.

The woman looked at Rejoice and grinned. "I like you. I think we can talk. The name is Jax Lindsey. J-A-X. Mr. Henley Roberson has authorized me to negotiate on behalf of Independence Families." She reached over and shook Rejoice's hand. "Here is how I want to cut the cards."

Rejoice frowned. Greeting cards? Scissors? What?

"This island is a great place for culling the weak and unwary. I want to set up a training area with about fifty people rotating in and out, and ten permanent staff. We would be moving the six hundred thirty-seven others to a place near your First City. We want to be far enough away that we do not interfere with you, but are close enough for trading. Acceptance?"

Wasn't culling what people did with cattle?

Noble said, "It sounds acceptable except for the part about setting up a training area on this island. Please forgive us, but there are enough people on this island."

Jax smiled behind a fist. "What would you do to stop us?"

Noble sighed. "There is no need for conflict. We have an entire planet to split between the two of us. Just a hundred kilometers to the west is an island you could have all to yourself."

Jax continued smiling. "What would you do?"

Noble rubbed his open hand over his jaw and mouth before saying slowly, "Not cooperate. Sabotage non-violently if need be. We have no wish to quarrel with you."

"What are you hiding? Besides the children?"

Noble looked toward Elder Chin who nodded slightly. He looked back at Jax. "We do handle mining and botanical research here. However, the primary purpose of the mission is to evangelize the hexacrabs and churtree. You're not committed to pacifism or our God. We don't want you to be in a position where you could hurt one of these peoples."

Jax nodded. "Churtree giant hermit crabs also?"

"They're air-ocean people, as we are; half as tall as we, with twice as many arms and eyes; hundreds of times more teeth."

"If we promise not to hurt them?"

Noble grimaced. "It's not as simple as that. The churtree are easily frightened or challenged or . . . or something. Whenever they see us close by, one of our machines or anything large and new, they have to kill something. If they don't kill us, they kill themselves."

"You consider these churtree intelligent?"

"Not highly so. But they do have a complex language and a complex social structure."

Now Jax sat back. "Have they killed any of you?"

"Three," Noble said. He did not elaborate.

Rejoice glanced at Sister Deng. She and the two boys had stayed after Brother Deng was ambushed on the Cliffside Trail. Rejoice studied her slanted eyes and smooth, black hair knotted at the nape and the way her thin lips exuded calm as she slowly sipped the pale green tea. *God, why can't You fill me with love for the churtrees the way You did for Sister Deng?* Brother Yoder and his little girl had been killed while they were picking peaches.

Jax said, "You consider yourselves intelligent?"

"We get by," Rejoice said. Perhaps it would have been better if the Independence had been an asteroid. Space rocks had orbits you could calculate, mass you could measure, and trajectories you could predict. They weren't messy like people. Who did Jax think she was?

Jax smiled. "Now I apologize. Let item four sit on the table a little longer. Necessity for conferring with Henley Roberson over discussion so far." Rejoice glanced at Noble's impassive face. He wouldn't think much of a man who sent a woman into a dangerous point position while staying safely behind.

He cleared his throat. "If Mr. Roberson is in the shuttle, we can probably go get him now." He looked toward Sister Hancock who checked the radar readings and nodded.

"He's still on the Independence, but yes, let's get the others."

Everyone rose, scraping their seats across the tile floor.

Noble came around the table and whispered in Rejoice's ear, "You don't look well. Now that she's seen you exist, why don't I take you home and let you attend the rest of the discussions by screen?"

Before she could answer, Jax joined them. "I forgot to ask. Any of you mathematicians?"

"I am," Rejoice said. What did that have to do with anything? "I hold

PhDs in math and astronomy."

"Good," Jax said. "Henley is extremely fond of mathematicians." She moved on to stand by the door where the others were getting their rifles.

"You stay here while I get the runabout." Noble pressed down on her shoulder until Rejoice sat.

Rejoice watched them exit the Meetingplace and cross the plaza. When they had gone down to Airstrip Lane, she slumped. What if Jax was the most diplomatic in the bunch?

She jumped when Elder Chin dropped his hand on her shoulder. "Oh! Excuse me. I didn't notice that you had stayed behind, too. What do you think?"

Elder Chin eased into the seat beside her. "Some of us are going to be killed before this is over. Perhaps all of us are." Rejoice stared as he said, "Daughter, gird yourself to love them."

PACIFISTS' WAR CHAPTER FOUR

"Rejoice, you haven't even combed your hair yet," Opportunity thumped down a chair borrowed from the Meetingplace. Rejoice stopped stirring the tomato sauce to pull a strand of tangled brown hair into her field of vision. "You're right. I can't remember; did I comb it yesterday?"

"No. I combed it for you. Do you want me to comb it now?"

"No, I'll do it. Ah, why don't you help Makepeace set the table?" She scooted around the lengthened table, and opened the door to her darkened bedroom. When had the baby stopped crying? She looked into the crib and, by the light of the randomly orbiting night-light mobile, she studied the pimply face of her newborn son. Black hair wisped across his soft scalp. Tiny lips twitched at one corner, then relaxed into a flower bud under the nubbin nose. Rose petal eyelids squeezed shut, then popped open as the sweet baby face transformed into an angry gargoyle. He thrashed his tiny, clenched fists and his face reddened as he drew up his legs and screamed.

Rejoice sighed and checked his diaper. Dry. She had nursed him a half an hour earlier, another hopeless affair as he suckled desperately, but stopped every thirty seconds or so to scream or spit up. She rolled him over on his tummy to see if that would help, but it didn't. Nothing ever did. So she grabbed her comb and retreated to the dining room.

There she eased into a chair. Makepeace studied his reflection in a spoon. "Makepeace, we need forks and chopsticks too."

"Party, party," he crooned, and moved to the steelware bin.

She had scant energy to pull the comb through her hair. She should not have cooked the supper, and she should not have made it so elaborate. But, as much as she appreciated Opportunity doing the chores and fixing the meals, she couldn't help it, the best thing she could say about Opportunity's cooking was that it was edible.

Opportunity set down the plates hard. One cracked, and a chip flew off to ping against the stove. Opportunity looked at the plate's rim. "I didn't mean to do that." She pulled out a bin from under the counter and threw the plate away. "It just isn't fair."

Rejoice let her hands fall into her lap. "What isn't fair?"

"You got to marry when you turned eighteen."

Rejoice closed her eyes for several seconds. "Yes. I did. Circumstances allowed it. I'm sorry I got sick and needed you to come all the way out here to take care of me."

Opportunity put down another plate. The lines between her brows and around her mouth reminded Rejoice of the angry lines on Stronghold's face when he was fifteen. Her sister and brother were much alike.

"I know it's hard to be an ocean away from He Gives."

"Don't try to pacify me. If you cared, you wouldn't complain about the calling bills."

"I mentioned them once."

"Noble can call the mainland for eighteen and more hours a week, but if I call for one hour . . ."

Rejoice pressed her tongue against her palate to remind herself not to respond in anger. Those hours were pastoral duties and the church paid for it. The church would not pay for the hours those two spent breathing in each other's ears. "We've discussed this before. That isn't the issue. What is the issue?"

Opportunity slammed a mug onto the table and it disintegrated. She looked at the shards. The baby behind the bedroom door wailed. "I suppose you'll be too tired to do the dishes after supper again."

Fatigue lowered her voice and gave it a growl. "Oppie, I'm listening. What's the issue? If living with us for four months has pushed you over the brink, I'll send you and Makepeace home next week. I'll figure out how to function."

Opportunity swept the shards into her palm and said with a resignation that sounded close to despair. "It doesn't matter whether I go home or stay here. Wherever I go, I still have to watch Makepeace."

Their brother sat hunched over in his chair watching shifting kaleido-scope patterns on his screen. His tongue darted about his lips. Nervous. If Rejoice didn't get Opportunity calmed down soon, he was going to go off like a flare. "Maybe it's time for us to take a furlough. Then I could watch him."

"No you can't. You've got an eight-year-old and a baby to take care of. I'm the only one that's free. Free! Hah!"

Rejoice lowered her voice further. "We all do what we must, whether we want to or not."

Opportunity spun to face Rejoice and screamed, "After Harmony dies, Mother can watch Makepeace. Do you know what it's like to be tempted every night to pray that Harmony will go ahead and die so I can be free?"

Makepeace stood and rocked from foot to foot. His screen clattered to the floor.

All Rejoice wanted to do was lie down, but she needed to stand and deal with this. "Married isn't really all that free." Oops. She was trying to calm her, not correct her.

"You know what I mean. Free to do what I want! Free to paint and sculpt and marry He Gives and live in my own house and, and . . ."

"And you feel trapped."

Opportunity covered her face. "Oh!"

Should she hug Opportunity or Makepeace? They were both crying. She moved to hold and croon over Makepeace. If he became any more agitated, he would break furniture. But then, Opportunity had already broken two things. Her poor sister. No one bought her paintings save Rejoice and Mother, and there wasn't room enough in her house to buy one more. "It's okay, Makepeace. We're not fighting anymore." Rejoice pulled out a handkerchief embroidered with holly leaves and wiped Makepeace's nose. "Come on, I still need you to help me. Wouldn't you like to wash the windows for me?"

The screen on her hip beeped. With one hand, she continued to pat Makepeace on the back, and with the other, she turned on the computer. "Cruz here."

"Joy of my life, I'm not going to make it back in time. Do you think you could pick up our guests?" Noble drove with the Deng boys, Submit To God and Resist The Devil, as well as Mark in the runabout returning from the supply run to Brother Zystra at the Observation Post. Every bone within Rejoice wanted to collapse. She almost opened her mouth to suggest, "Why don't we simply delay the supper?" but he was a man who lived by tight schedules. She sighed. "Okay. I'll see you in a bit."

Opportunity handed a bucket of sudsy water and a cleaning cloth to Makepeace. He took the bucket and held it up to the light in such a way that he could see the iridescent swirls on the bubbles. Rejoice sighed again. "Opportunity, I don't suppose you'd like to run out and get them?"

Opportunity wiped one eye. "I don't want anyone to see me like this."

Well, for a few moments it would get her away from the demanding cries of the baby. If only she could understand what it was he was demanding. She moved to the screen and entered the code for the Hancocks.

"Yes, dear," Sister Hancock said when her face appeared on the screen. Her sea green eyes sparkled.

"May I borrow your runabout to pick up our guests?"

Sister Hancock looked off-screen a moment. "Certainly. Resolved will run it right over. While you're waiting for him, why don't you comb your hair?"

"Right. Will do. Thank you." She shut off the screen and sat. Her sister set the table and her brother washed the windows for the fifth time that day. Rejoice struggled with the snarls in her hair.

A few minutes later, Brother Hancock knocked at the front door. Opportunity fled down the short hall to the bubble bedroom Noble had added to the house for her and Makepeace. When Rejoice opened the door, Brother Hancock's face creased into a huge smile. "It's good to see you up. I thought that after last week you would need to stay in bed for a month."

Probably what she should have done. "They are overwhelming, aren't they?"

"Eh, Young Lady, you did wonderfully. I think they were deliberately trying to push every button they could think of to see what would make us blow up."

"Isn't that what I did?"

"Not really. Maybe by our standards." His faded blue eyes unfocused. "There is so much of Old Earth that is only electrons forming letters on a screen for you." His eyes refocused on Makepeace. "How are you, Brother Holly?"

Makepeace rubbed the window with a wet rag in small circles. "Crying, crying in the light."

"Which reminds me, I wanted to ask if Young Lady Holly would come over for supper tomorrow."

Her answer floated in from the hallway. "I have to baby-sit my brother."

"Of course Makepeace is invited too. You will come, won't you, Brother Holly?"

Makepeace touched the glass delicately with his fingertips.

"Okay," floated in Opportunity's answer.

Brother Hancock still stood in the doorway. The fingers of his remaining hand fiddled with his gun holster. "Your father would have been proud."

Rejoice slung her rifle over her shoulder. "I wish it had been Father who was here to do the negotiations."

Brother Hancock ran his hand over his bald head. "The only bad part about knowing a great man like that is missing him when he's gone."

Rejoice brushed past him so she could get in the runabout before the tears gathering behind her eyelids cascaded out. She could not cope with being this emotional. The thought of Father, the thought of the baby, the thought of Opportunity feeling trapped and part of that her fault:

everything made her want to cry.

Brother Hancock waved at her as she pulled shut the clear, wire-mesh reinforced door. The denser wire-mesh wheels squeaked faintly, like baby hexacrabs newly out of their niches. Rejoice smiled and waved back before driving off.

Through the orchards and jungle and past the cliff overlooking Ti Bay and then downhill by way of Airstrip Lane the runabout hummed. At the airstrip a new path had been plowed through the jungle. The inflated roof of the gymnasium showed above the shorter tree tops. Along the new path lay bagged plants from the cleared area waiting for the *Magellan* to pick up. They would be transplanted to nearby islands.

Popping sounds startled Rejoice. She slowed the runabout. Was something wrong with the engine? No, the sounds came from ahead. The pops sounded like gunfire, but they must have been noise from construction. She crossed the airstrip and entered the new path.

Men in camouflage and helmets ducked behind trees and shot at one another. One jerked back and spun, clutched his shoulder, and collapsed into a sticky thicket bush.

She slammed on the brakes.

"Halt!" shouted someone. "Civilian coming through!"

The boots of the man hidden in the brown bush did not move.

Someone tapped on her window and she jumped. A young man about Opportunity's age with blond hair curling to his broad shoulders, intense blue eyes, and finely chiseled features, leaned on a rifle and laughed. She swallowed two breaths, opened the door, and slowly stood to face him. Another person walked up to the car and pulled off his helmet to reveal a man about the age of Makepeace with chestnut colored hair in several braids, and blue-gray eyes shaped like the blond man's. He too laughed.

Rejoice looked from one to the other. Was Elder Chin's prediction already coming to pass? No, they were laughing, but they had just shot one of their own people. Her eyes were drawn to the still boots.

The blond one spoke. "That Carl. Always slow, always first one down."

"Next time he's on your team," the brown-haired one said.

Rejoice licked her lips with a tongue gone dry. "What?"

The blond one patted his rifle. "Quick anesthetic bullets. War games."

How could war be a game? She cleared her throat. "Well, will anesthetic bullets work against pack bats?"

"Don't know. Yet. Each rifle has five anesthetic bullets, the rest regular, so we can fire off the anesthetic bullets quickly and use regular bullets if pack bats show up."

"You need to count carefully during these games then, I take it."

"Exactly," said the brown one. "Intelligence test." Both men laughed.

"Do you play these games often?" Surely the men could hear the thudding of her heart.

"Not often enough," the blond said.

The brown one added, "We finished all the construction we could do and are waiting for next delivery, so Jax told us to redeem the time."

"Jax said that? Does she know Scripture?"

"Jax knows everything." The blond grinned.

"And what she doesn't know, she thinks she knows," the brown-haired man said.

"Myself, I wonder what going in a pawnshop and buying a watch has to do with using time wisely," the blond mused.

The brown one shook his head and looked speculatively at Rejoice. "Myself, I wonder if for truth these pacifists know only one position."

Rejoice opened her mouth to say, "What?" but the blond shouted, "You watch your mouth or Jax will slap it to the back side of your head. She told us to watch our steps."

The brown one held up his hands. "Easy. No harm."

Rejoice hoped it would take less time to decipher these fast-forward speaking newcomers than it did to come to a rough understanding of the hexacrabs. "I'm sorry I interrupted your, ah, game, but I came to pick up Jax and two others for supper."

The blond slapped his forehead with the heel of his hand. "I deleted!" He snatched up his rifle and sprinted down the path.

"Find Jax in our gymnasium." Gravel crunched as brown-haired turned.

Rejoice watched a few seconds as he strode into the jungle. When she saw that he was not going over to Carl, she called, "Wait! Stop. Ah, you with the brown hair, come back!"

He returned to the path. "Zack. Zack Roberson. You want?"

"You can't just leave Carl here alone." She waved toward the man in the bush.

"He'll be waking in a while."

"Not if the pack bats get to him."

Zack arched his eyebrows and reddened. "Good for learning lesson," he muttered.

"Murder is a lesson?"

He flicked his fingers. "No fear. I'll stay. I'll tell him how you saved his life. Don't expect gratitude from him."

Rejoice re-entered the runabout. Zack watched her as she drove the runabout down the path. A sudden wave of panic seized her throat. She gripped the steering wheel tightly. How could she go through with this? This rush of new people and new thoughts and new perils seemed as looming and inevitable as labor. She couldn't say with any of them, "I changed my mind. I'm not ready." She wasn't ready, never would be ready, and here was the gymnasium.

She stopped the runabout and took several deep breaths. *God, You're bigger than Jax and bigger than me. Hold us both.*

The huge double doors to the gymnasium stood open. Tiny eight-legged insects flitted about them in the hazy sunset light. The smell of freshly dug dirt and newly unwrapped plastic filled the clearing. She paused at the entrance and cautiously peeked in. "Hello?" Lockers lined one wall, mats lay scattered on the floor, and huge silver pots of soup simmered on a short counter next to a sink beside stacks of red plastic bowls with black rims.

She turned toward the sound of spattering water, and jumped back to the entrance. The shower corner was completely open and the blond man was showering. So this had to be the men's gymnasium. Where did the women shower?

The door to a small, enclosed room adjacent to the double doors opened and Jax stepped out to smile at Rejoice. Today she wore a black Japanese coat with trousers and black, divided-toe socks with orange sandals. Her lips, nails, and hair were marigold orange. Jax stopped and glanced behind herself. "Something wrong?"

"No, no, excuse me. Your colors remind me of the Orange Scar churtree."

"Tonight, we'll see the vids of churtree?"

"If you wish."

"For truth."

Rejoice kept her eyes away from the shower area. "We can go whenever you're ready."

Jax shouted toward the showers, "So hurry, Ernest!"

The sound of spattering water stopped. Rejoice and Jax walked toward the runabout.

A young woman, Caucasian, with black hair save for a white stripe down the middle that ran from front to back, joined them. She tapped on a flex screen inbedded in her forearm. "Delivery of fence is four hours away."

"Good. Time enough for visiting."

Rejoice held out her hand. "Hello. My name is Rejoice Cruz."

The young woman flinched back, eyebrows raised and mouth parted, before she stepped back and gently shook Rejoice's hand. "Myself, Myra."

"Youngest co-wife in B Family," Jax said.

Did Rejoice want to know what that meant? "We can go whenever you're ready," she repeated, then winced at sounding inane.

"Then now. Ernest Roberson can walk for taking so long."

As they got in the runabout, Jax knocked on the clear roof and clear doors. "For repelling pack bats?"

"Yes. And churtree spears. The runabout allows us a 360-degree view of what's around us before we get out."

Jax nodded. Ernest, dressed in shorts and a dark red sleeveless shirt, threw himself into the remaining back seat. He brushed back his wet, blond hair. Rejoice directed her gaze to the road before her. No man should be so beautiful. If he hadn't grabbed it all, maybe she would have gotten some. She shrugged it off. Some were handsome, and some weren't, and what difference did it make? When they drove past Zack, who looked bored as he stood over Carl, Ernest saluted and laughed.

PACIFISTS' WAR CHAPTER FIVE

A few minutes later, they pulled up to Rejoice's bubble. In front stood Elder Chin, leaning on a bamboo cane. The skin of his neck wobbled as he nodded. Rejoice introduced him to the newcomers who nodded curtly in return and shifted their gazes to the street or the other bubble homes.

Noble and Mark hummed in. Mark jumped out of the runabout. The boy ran to Elder Chin and hugged him so hard the old man tottered. Elder Chin slipped a hard candy from his pocket into Mark's hand. Then Mark looked up and saw Jax. His eyes widened as he ducked behind the elder.

The group funneled into the Cruz home. Rejoice almost sighed with relief when she heard nothing from her bedroom. Makepeace stood calmly behind his chair and studied the bubbles in his blue water glass. A streaming glass of mint tea with a peppermint candy stick in it sat at the head of the table. Noble helped Elder Chin into that seat.

Opportunity had reset the table with part of her dowry, the pottery she had formed and fired herself. Tomato sauce, fragrant with rosemary and sage, nestled in blue cups shaped like hexacrabs. Pale green pitchers adorned with kelp reliefs held apple juice and mint tea. Hardhead fish sported about the rims of the blue plates. Open weave baskets supported by crab legs held browned breadsticks sprinkled with cheese. Pale green serving bowls with jungle leaf patterns pressed into them held curried rice, salmon cakes, cucumber salad with fennel and poppy seed dressing, braised shitake mushrooms, steamed carrots with leeks, pickled eggs, and peach slices. Strawberry tarts piled on a green platter embossed with pattern of strawberry leaves.

Noble grinned at his sister-in-law. "You have outdone yourself today." He introduced the newcomers to Young Lady Opportunity Holly.

How could Noble possibly confuse her cooking for Opportunity's? However, fussing about it would be petty.

Ernest stared at Makepeace with an expression of horror when Noble introduced his brother-in-law. Myra appeared unsettled too, but Jax nodded with a fixed smile and elbowed Ernest until he nodded.

Mark plopped in the seat beside Elder Chin. Noble took the seat on the other side of the elder and asked Jax to sit beside him. Opportunity guided Myra to sit across from Makepeace and sat herself across from Ernest. Rejoice sat across from Jax and hoped she wouldn't need to get up again for a long time.

"Let us pray," Elder Chin bowed his head.

They bowed their heads, closed their eyes, breathed slowly, and silently invited the God of peace to guide their thoughts and actions. Mark's stomach gurgled.

The screen beeped. Rejoice squinted as her fragile peace shattered. Opportunity rose to turn on the screen. Round-faced Heart's Desire on the screen signed, {Grandfather he with you?}

"Shame on me," Elder Chin said. He rose, shuffled to the screen, and signed. {Sorry. I forget tell you. Tonight preacher I eat with him.}

Earnest stared even harder. "What are they doing?"

Rejoice said, "Young Lady Heart's Desire Han is deaf. She is one of Elder Chin's granddaughters and this year is her turn to help with his work. They are talking to each other with their hands."

Jax tilted her head. "An accident? Why have you not repaired it?" "She was born deaf. It's not the kind of deafness that can be repaired. The nerve is missing."

Ernest looked from Rejoice to the screen. "And you let her live to contaminate—"

"Shh!" Jax poked him. "We are here to learn."

Rejoice handed Jax the bowl of salad to cover her confusion. What did he think Heart's Desire could be contaminating? "We were hoping to learn a few things too. Did or did not the Leechies blow up North America?"

Jax smiled, revealing an orange lipstick smear on one eyetooth. "The reason why you left in the First Wave?"

Which question to ask first? "It's why we left sooner than we had planned. So what happened after we left?"

The skin tightened around Jax's eyes. "The USNA and Quebec blew up Calcutta and Rio de Janeiro. End of war." She still smiled.

Rejoice gulped. All those millions of people. Vaporized. Elder Chin seated himself and closed his eyes. She stuttered, "Ah, first wave implies a second wave. Are there more ships headed our way?"

Jax shrugged. "I can't know. No guarantees in universe."

There was a truth statement.

Ernest looked around the main room. "Religious reasons for soapy windows?"

Opportunity busily helped herself to breadsticks.

Noble chuckled. "Not at all. Simply an oversight."

Jax's eyes flicked from Makepeace to Elder Chin. "Religious reason for not repairing the arm of Mr. Hancock?"

"Again, no," Noble said. "We offered to make him a prosthetic, but he said he didn't want the factory to waste time on making one. And he didn't want to be bothered with learning how to wear one."

"Will it violate a religious taboo to ask how he lost that arm?"

"Not at all. First it was paralyzed after the hexacrab Ur-Nissi stabbed him and severed the nerves. Then on the first *Magellan* voyage, a torpal, something like a shark, tore it off."

"And Pastor Cruz here," Rejoice added, "is the one who rescued Brother Hancock from the torpal by killing it."

The newcomer's heads swiveled to stare at Noble with respect.

Ernest licked his lips. "But I thought pacifists—" Jax shot him a glance and he stopped.

Noble smiled at Rejoice and shook his head.

Ernest gazed with awe at Noble. "Then what happened?"

Noble glanced ruefully at Rejoice before turning to Ernest. "Have you tried the salmon patties? They're very good."

As they ate, Jax asked, "You directed us to save plants for the *Magellan*. What precisely for?"

Rejoice dipped her breadstick in the savory tomato sauce. Was this fatigue gnawing at her bones worth the good food? "Every year the *Magellan* goes on a year-long seeding and research cruise. We plant Old Earth type plants on most of the barren islands, but on the islands closest to Largest Archipelago we put the New Earth plants, the ones that don't blister you when you touch them."

"We noticed that except for where you are farming on Sole, the land is bare rock. Why?"

"Asteroids. Dark Death killed nearly everything some hundreds of years ago. Then eighteen years ago, Asteroid Opportunity threatened to finish the job."

Jax whistled. "Hazardous place this."

Tell her about it. "Well, we didn't have the fuel to go back to Old Earth. The government had locked the directions to New Earth in the navigation system. It also hadn't given us the designations of any other stars with habitable planets. So we were stuck."

Ernest started, glanced at Jax, and busied himself getting tarts.

Jax frowned at Makepeace who said, "Rocks smashing, oceans crashing." He jerked his hand around.

Jax tapped the tabletop with her painted fingernails. "Many asteroids in this system." No one said anything while Jax pushed around slices of mushroom on her plate with her chopsticks. "Where is your detection system? You did not notice us for weeks."

Jax had pushed her hot button there. Jax needed to ask the Senate that question. Rejoice pressed her tongue against her palate for a second. "Yes. After the scare you gave us, I daresay more scanning satellites will be built soon." If the people in Promise ever stopped vetoing her every request. "Unfortunately, when we arrived and deployed our satellites, we discovered we had purchased third or fourth hand junk." Just like their medical equipment. Thank God their flex factory had been well-made. "If you would hook up the Independence telescopes and any satellites you brought to our system of asteroid surveillance, we would greatly appreciate it."

"Not sure how. Your computers are so primitive."

Stay calm. "Believe it or not, we're proud of our computers. My brother Stronghold and a few of the engineers were able to revert our system to an earlier technology. If we hadn't, we would have precious few computers today."

Jax arched her blackened eyebrows.

"No germanium. No gallium either. We can't find any on this planet, and we haven't found any on the asteroids we've been mining."

"Not any?"

"The few molecules we've found aren't enough. I don't suppose you brought a couple kilos with you?"

Jax sat back and Myra with the striped hair spoke for the first time. "Lack of germanium means?"

"A lack of germanium-silicon compounds you use in your computers."

Mark reached for a strawberry tart, but his father sitting across the table from him intercepted his hand.

"No."

Mark frowned. "I was getting it for the elder."

Noble let go of his son's wrist. "Excuse me."

Mark set the tart on Elder Chin's plate. "Why did God have to make me allergic to the best-tasting thing in this whole world?"

Noble smiled. "You'll have to take that up with God."

Mark sighed. "Maybe it would help if God signed to me."

"Pardon me?"

"Maybe if God signed to me, I would get it. I can't hear God."

Elder Chin chuckled.

Jax slightly shook her head.

Noble said. "God usually speaks through the Bible. One thing He says there is to obey your parents, and I, the parent, am telling you to stay away from strawberries. Rejoice, would you please set the tarts farther down so Lad Mark won't be so tempted?"

The newcomers studied their food intently.

Rejoice exchanged the peaches and strawberries. *Huh.* They didn't like Elder Chin and they didn't like Makepeace for any reason she could discern. And they didn't like the colonists talking about God. What could draw them together in friendship?

After a minute, Jax looked up and about. "I'm confused. Your Meetingplace is bare, but your home is filled with beautiful paintings."

"Do you like them?" Opportunity leaned closer to Jax.

Ernest's blue eyes met Opportunity's. "You painted them?"

Jax rose and walked to the nearest painting, a large triangle attached at its top vertex to the wall and propped by short rods on the bottom vertices against the curved wall. She touched the nine-centimeter thick sides. "I have never seen canvas like this."

"They're panels left over from the Meetingplace. If any of the panels in the Meetingplace break, I suppose I'll have to scrape the paint off so that it can be put in its place." Opportunity scrunched the napkin in her hand.

Noble wiped his mouth before saying gently, "We have plenty of panels in storage. Your paintings are safe."

Jax pointed to the center of the painting at a white squid surrounded by blue hexacrabs holding stone spears at attention. Light from a silvered surface at the top of the painting fingered across a pale green background to disappear into a purple black abyss behind the white octopus which seemed to be embracing half a hexacrab. Tiny blue triangles flecked the painting. "This is what?"

Opportunity glowed. "That's from the story of Sa-Tsesta who saved the nursery despite being half-eaten by a torpal. While the Sa were celebrating Child Departure Day—that's what the little triangles are—a kraken came up from the deep sea and ate Sa-Tsesta and half the Sa. In the painting over here, you see how the line of hexacrabs with bundles on their backs dissolve into seaweed that are shaped like question marks. In front is Ur-Nissi. That's about the mystery of the missing hexacrabs."

"Asteroid Dark Death, for truth?"

"No. Half the Ur cluster never came back after the Reconciliation, and no one will tell us where they went. And the hexacrabs keep losing stuff, like an entire warehouse of hollow rods they bought so they could build another kelp farm like ours. They said the rods floated elsewhere during a storm."

Noble said to Jax. "We have enormous numbers of hurricanes on this planet because ninety percent of the surface is ocean. Make sure your buildings are windproof."

Jax blinked. "Much to learn." She moved to the painting above the stove and behind Elder Chin and examined the green leaves and red fruits. "The tomato vine growing over the doorway to this house?"

"Yes," Opportunity said. "Sister Cruz is a fanatic about tomatoes."

"I wonder why your paintings are not hanging in the Meetingplace. Oh, these are not religious paintings."

The glow switched off as Opportunity picked up her napkin and twisted it. "Painting is a sin."

"It is not," Noble and Rejoice said in unison.

Opportunity went on bitterly, "The only arts the colony will accept are quilts and embroidery and music. They don't allow paintings in the Meetingplace because they're sinful."

"Not sinful," Noble said. "Distracting."

"The Eastern Orthodox consider icons to be an aid to concentration," Opportunity flipped her long hair over her shoulder.

"We're not Eastern Orthodox. But if you want to put an icon in your bedroom, I won't stop you."

"No? The colony would shun me. You know it would. The people in Promise think painting is a sin."

Rejoice sucked on her chopstick as she watched her sister. Whatever was the girl doing? As soon as these people left, she was getting a lecture on public behavior.

Noble clasped his hands and rested his chin on them. "Some of them may. However, I'm a pastor. If I thought your paintings were sinful, I

would not allow Rejoice to buy them and clutter up our house with them."
Perhaps all that counseling training paid off after all. Rejoice knew as
well as she knew the times of the Potatoes rising above the horizon
that clutter was the exact wrong word for Noble to have used. Unless he
was telling Opportunity that he was angry at her for bringing up colony
divisions in front of strangers?

Opportunity opened her mouth, but Noble interrupted, "I hear
Jubilee crying."

She rolled her eyes. "I know. I listen to him all day long."

He murmured, "Would you please take care of him?"

"Oh." She dropped the napkin. "Right." The bedroom door clicked
shut behind her.

Rejoice lifted her warm cup to inhale the scent of mint tea. The next jet
would take Opportunity out of here. It was bad enough listening to her
own whining. Did Rejoice need to listen to Opportunity's, too?

Jax resumed her seat. "What type of government are you living under?"

How odd. Jax had asked about their monetary system a full week before
she asked about the government.

Noble answered. "A republic. We have a constitution much like that of
the old USA. But the only offices we've filled so far are two Senate seats,
one from First City and one from Promise. One constitutional law is that
the income tax is a flat rate and is never higher than nine percent of a
person's income. We intend to never give the government more than we
give God."

Jax tapped the side of her cup with her fingernails. "Your judicial
system?"

"Ah, based mostly on a combination of the Bill of Rights and a bit of
Mosaic law. Actually, we haven't set up our secular judicial system yet.
We all belong to the church and as such submit to church discipline."

Jax tapped harder, then seemed to realize what she was doing and
stopped. "We don't wish to be under your jurisdiction."

Noble considered that, his dark eyes watching Jax.

Since Jax liked rudeness, Rejoice supplied it. "You might have considered that before you settled right next to us. How do you propose to live among us and not live by our laws?"

"Comprehension," Jax said. "When we walk on your lands, we would adhere to your laws. I propose a division of land. This side of runway for you, other side for us. One side of river for First City, other side for Freedom."

Noble shifted in his seat. "I can't make that kind of decision. We would need to take it up with the Senate at the very least."

Elder Chin clicked a word in hex which meant caution. The Cruz family stopped all movement and waited. Jax looked from Noble to Rejoice.

How would that proposal divide the continent and Largest Archipelago?

Elder Chin addressed Jax. "If you do set up autonomous areas, does that mean that you will feel free to abrogate our agreements? Such as the one that we allow you to settle here in exchange for you retreating to your buildings whenever a churtree nears our compounds?"

Jax studied him as though this were the first time she had seen him before answering slowly, "I keep my word."

"Will your students keep your word?"

Jax smiled. "If not, they won't stay. For truth." After a pause, she said, "I wonder what you are getting from the churtree."

"Grief," Rejoice said.

Noble clicked, "Stop!" before turning to Jax. "I explained that our purpose here is to evangelize the churtree and hexacrabs. We came to this planet to expand God's Kingdom. That means we are to present the gospel to every creature that needs it."

Opportunity brought in the bawling baby. "He's hungry."

As Rejoice took her personal tyrant into the bedroom, Jax said, "May we view the vids of the churtree?"

No one should see churtree so soon after eating. Rejoice shut the door and dimmed the light. She lay on her side and tried to cuddle her squirming son. He alternated sucking and crying. Tears stung her eyes. Mark had been so much fun. She had spent hours delighting in his tiny toes and bowed legs and soft skin. This baby refused to let her enjoy him.

She closed her eyes.

The next thing she knew, Noble leaned over her and kissed her neck. She blinked him into better focus as he whispered, "They're gone. You don't have to hide anymore."

"What? Oh, I fell asleep. I'm sorry."

He kissed her again and deftly slid the baby from her side. "You have to admit that Jax has courage. I admire that."

"Why? I have courage too, you know. I did walk, without a single weapon, into the Red Scar village."

One corner of his mouth crooked up. "Uh, Rejoice, all the Red Scar were dead by then."

"I didn't know that at the time, now did I?"

Noble chuckled. "I didn't know that to acknowledge a characteristic in another person was to deny it in you. But now I understand my new rule: never admire another woman in front of my wife lest she grow jealous."

Rejoice opened her mouth to protest that she was not jealous. She closed it. Oh, yes, she was indeed jealous. Once she had been jealous of Harmony's red-gold hair. Now she was jealous of Jax's obvious strength. She was jealous of all women who could have babies as easily as cows do. She was jealous of everyone who had a body that didn't betray them. *Forgive me, God, yet again.*

Noble held his son to his chest and walked to the window, his right hand cradling the baby's head and his index finger stroking the soft hair. He looked out the oval window into the shady orchard. "I want what every father wants, I suppose. I want our sons to grow up safe and happy and serving God." He rubbed his cheek against the top of the baby's crown. "It's not faith, I know, but I do worry about these people. They call themselves rationals. I call them rationalizers." He kissed the baby's temple. "What kind of world is Jubilee going to grow up in now that these people have come?"

"Honestly, Noble, are these people any worse than the churtree?"

His face hardened as he swung away from the window and strode out the door.

Rejoice pressed the back of her hand against her forehead. Fool. After thirteen years of marriage, she knew his every trigger. Why would she keep squeezing them?

The sound of distant gunfire, which meant the hexacrabs, since the air-ocean people did not practice so late at night, reminded Rejoice that tomorrow she would dive for the first time in months. That was something to look forward to.

PACIFISTS' WAR CHAPTER SIX

When Rejoice parked the runabout by the Cliffside road barrier above Ti Bay, Jax and Myra were examining the carved, three-meter-high monster on the other side of the road. Much of it had eroded, but one could yet discern saber teeth and a serrated back ridge. Orange and dirty white lichens mottled the dark stone. On the craggy head and shoulders, brown ribbongrass bristled. Jax waved and Rejoice joined them.

At first, Rejoice thought Jax wore only paint and a matte black rifle on her back until the shifting gray and brown blotches on her body indicated fabric. Myra wore a similar outfit of black and gray. Both had knives strapped to their thighs.

Rejoice shivered. The rifles the colonists carried every moment they were outside were much slimmer than the rifles the dojo people carried. Their bullets were somewhat smaller, but the biggest difference happened to be the protruding objects from the bottom of the Rational's rifles, objects designed to carry many bullets—the word "magazine" floated up from some obscure place in Rejoice's memory. The Rationals had weapons ready to fire a high number of bullets at any time, unlike the single-shot weapons of the colonists. Another term floated into her memory—"machine gun."

Jax tapped the statue with chartreuse fingernails. "A churtree god?"

"I wish I knew. Elder Chin believes that it is possible that the churtree carved it. If so, their civilization must have really degenerated after Dark Death. They don't carve statues now. It could be a monument to one of their kings or one of their gods. There's nothing like it in the Yellow or Orange Scar villages. The other possibility is that it was carved by a land species unknown to the hexacrabs. We call it the Sentinel."

Jax pulled out of a gray pouch hanging from her shoulder a small screen which she handed to Rejoice. "A present for you."

"Oh, so Rationals do allow the giving of gifts."

"For truth. But do not think this lays an obligation on you. It contains math puzzles and games."

"How wonderful!" Rejoice pressed the screen against her heart. "Sister Guthry used to give me math puzzles. My father and I had so much fun working on them."

"Guthry is also a mathematician?"

Rejoice tried to keep the pain of a destroyed relationship out of her voice. "She's a meteorologist. We coordinate the weather forecasts. She lives in Promise because that's where her husband moved."

"Hmm," said Jax. "We have been informed that we are not wanted in Promise."

"Your information is correct. Don't look her up."

"Only where we are invited."

Not quite. Rejoice shifted her gaze away from Jax and into the brown and gray jungle. Then she pointed to the brown trunk of a camel knee tree. "Jax, there's something you should like. A camouflaged worm."

Jax turned and peered. "Where? I see nothing."

"Of course not. It's small and camouflaged. Right below the second knob." She pointed again. "None of these plants are poisonous, so you can get close enough for a good look."

Jax stepped through the knee-high clumps of lacegrass, stirring up the scent of ginger, and then bent to look closely at the trunk. "This brown and orange speckled worm? Looks like it swallowed a ball. Purpose for round—"

With astonishingly quick reflexes, Jax leaped back and threw up her hand to intercept a sudden stream from the worm.

"Oh!" Myra cried.

Jax leaped again and turned to show her dripping hand to Rejoice. "Acid? Poison?"

Laughter interfered with her words as Rejoice answered, "Just water. Plain, simple water. When Pastor Cruz showed me the worm, I was hit right in the eyes. I was sure I'd been blinded for life. When Brother Hancock showed Pastor the worm, he got squirted up his nose."

Jax stood rigid a moment before smiling. "An initiation?"

"I guess it is. We show the squirt worm to every newcomer."

Jax whirled and threw. Thock! A knife struck the camel knee tree under the second knob. A small shape fell from the trunk.

"Why did you do that?" Rejoice cried. "That worm is the least offensive creature on this island!"

Jax shrugged. "Not hurt. Only frightened it. Equivalency." She walked back to the tree and tugged out her knife.

"Careful," called Rejoice. "The sap is extremely irritating and sticky. You'll want to wear gloves while you wash off your knife with a solvent." Jax looked disgusted as she walked back holding the knife away from her body. The red sap smeared on it looked like blood and smelled like burnt hair.

Rejoice smoothed down her brown dress. "I'm visiting the Ti village today. Would either of you like to join me?"

Jax shook her head as Myra said, "I don't have any scuba gear."

"We have several outfits for guests. Do come, Jax. I would love to introduce you to everyone."

"I have a class to prepare for and a knife to clean. Myra, you go. Inform me what you learn." She walked around the statue.

With a puzzled look on her face, Myra watched Jax go, and tugged at a black strand of hair.

Rejoice leaned close to Myra and whispered, "I hope I didn't offend her."

Myra now tugged on a white strand. "Nothing for offense."

"Is she afraid to dive?"

"Jax is afraid of nothing. The reason why Henley likes her so much."

Myra stepped over the lacegrass to reach the road and walked toward the elevators that descended to the dock far below the cliff. She added wistfully, "Henley likes strong women."

"And mathematicians. So I heard." The elevator doors whooshed open and they stepped inside. "How can she throw a knife so precisely?"

Myra leaned against the transparent wall to watch their descent. "She practices an hour a day. I practice also, but an hour is too long. I cannot sustain my focus."

Where did they find so much time to waste each day? Right, they didn't have children. "May I ask why Jax wanted to talk only to me at first?"

"Henley wanted to meet with the more intelligent of your colony. Your father's test scores were far higher than any of the other emigrants."

"My father's scores? Scores of what? Where did you get them?"

Myra continued to watch the cliff-side slide by. A black bumblefly chased the elevator a few meters. "I don't know. I was only told they were high. When we found that his daughter ran the spaceport, he decided you would be the one most likely to be reasonable."

"When do we meet Henley Roberson?"

"I don't know. He does not care to be prominent."

Not like Elder Smith, then. Or maybe exactly like, pretending to be humble. "If that's so, how was he able to attract seven hundred people to follow him across the galaxy?"

"Many more than that wish to lead rational lives."

Why did they think they owned that word? "I should think so. Everybody I know wants to be rational."

Myra frowned.

Rejoice's stomach fall as the elevator stopped and the back door opened to the iodine tang of the sea.

A few minutes later, they were in the women's changing room. As Myra waited for the seal of her mask to mold itself around her face, Rejoice struggled into her tight suit. When she finally sealed the last seam, she sat on the bench exhausted.

Myra watched her with concern. "Are you ill?"

"I'm out of shape. Staying in bed for several months always does that to me."

"You are so often ill?"

"Only when I'm pregnant." With an effort, she stood. "Let's go. Meeting with the hexacrabs will be more interesting than listening to a litany of my woes." She adjusted the radio translators in their masks.

When they stepped outside, Sa-Issi and Sa-Isti were trundling toward the elevator doors with two rifles in their LV claspers.

Rejoice waved. "Sa-Issi! My eyes extend to see you!" The translator in her screen squeaked and grated.

Sa-Issi turned his LV about. His chitin covered legs controlled the steps of his LV while his tentacles pulled prostheses that governed the claspers and sensory data. His translator transmuted his melodic whistles and clicks into a monotone, "I perceive the one to whom I expose my soft parts. I cannot recognize the other air-ocean female."

Myra stepped forward and bowed. "Name, Myra Hower."

Without replying, Sa-Issi turned his LV with a nearly noiseless whirring of gears and walked down a ramp into the ocean. Sa-Isti continued toward the elevator.

Rejoice followed Sa-Issi into the sea. "Sa-Issi, I heard that the Sa ordered many rifles yesterday."

The LV submerged as Sa-Issi clicked, "Yes."

When the water closed over Rejoice's head, every muscle within her relaxed. She let her arms float while she watched the hexacrab maneuver his LV into its berth and connect it to a charger. As he flowed out of his vehicle, she asked, "Why? There aren't any pack bats or churtree at Sole."

Myra accidentally churned up some sediment as Sa-Issi disconnected his scooter from its charger. He snapped two tethers to the end of the scooter and placed the handles within easy reach of the humans. "The Sa and Ti have decided that all the water-ocean people shall learn to shoot."

"I understand that. I don't understand why."

The hexacrab did not reply. The wavering light glimmered on his blue, iridescent shell as he set his scooter at a gentle pace.

Rejoice enjoyed the effortless flow of warm water over her bare feet and arms. Hardheads ducked into the shadow of the dock as Sa-Issi towed the humans through an undulating forest of fishtail kelp. He steered between a silvered surface above and soft darkness below, through a hazy turquoise glinting with salmon fingerlings and diatom giants. Sa-Issi slowly arced toward the left.

"Excuse me, Sa-Issi, but I wanted to show Myra the Ti village."

Again, Sa-Issi did not reply.

Rejoice chose not to worry about it. Perhaps Sa-Issi did not feel he could expose his soft spots to the newcomers yet. A diaphanous sea veil bumped into her shoulder, slid down her back, and tumbled like a white leaf in her wake. Myra stared at everything with wide eyes. Save for the faint vibration of the scooter and the soothing sound of bubbling, a profound quiet enveloped Rejoice. She relaxed into the water stroking her skin.

When the tether line fell slack and a surge of pressure from Myra's fins washed over her legs, a school of glow bits surrounded them. Sa-Issi stretched out a tentacle and delicately plucked one green glowing bit from the school of drifters, and stretched back to present to the women the tiny, intricate glass box stuffed with emerald feelers raking the sea with an incessant rhythm. They bumped masks as they looked at it. Myra's grin reflected hers.

* * *

Back in the changing room, as they showered and dressed, Myra spoke with an animation Rejoice had not seen in her before. "Permission to bring the entire B Family someday?"

"I don't know why not, unless Jax has to throw a knife at everything she sees."

Myra laughed.

"If I start to violate your privacy, let me know, but who is in B Family? How does that work when none of you came with your parents?"

Myra tilted her head and studied Rejoice. "For truth do you hate sex?"

Rejoice choked. "Heavens, no. We just want it to stay in its proper place. Why do you ask?"

Myra fluttered her fingers toward Rejoice. "Why do you wear so many layers of clothing, pants and dress and everything?"

Rejoice in her turn had marveled at how Myra had slithered into her single piece of clothing and had wondered at how the girl could stand to walk around next to nude. "There's no point in enticing anyone but your husband. Don't the Rationals marry?"

Myra sat and tugged on her boots. "Marry is a bondage word. I am linked to Medesto, Wilson, Ernest, Carl, Jax, Lita, and Tammy. But if the rest don't ask Carl to leave soon, I'll go. Maybe I'll go back to the M Family. Carl is despicable. We are his eighth family. He should stay single like Zack."

To save her life, Rejoice could not think how to respond to that. She pulled on her shoes and sealed them. She picked up her computer and the screen Jax had given her. "So you move from family to family and, um..."

"Better to move than stay and quarrel."

Rejoice shook her head. "I would hate that. How do you cope with comparison and jealousy?"

"Only insecure people are jealous."

"Never knowing when you're going to be walked out on strikes me as a recipe for insecurity. And confusion. How do you coordinate—I'm sorry. I shouldn't violate your privacy like that." She transferred the screen to the other hand. Maybe linking did not mean some weird kind of multiple marriage the way she was hearing it, but she could not think of a discreet way to ask. In a group linking, how did you iron out the irritations that go with any relationship? Multiple interpretations meant multiple misunderstandings. And with no incentive to stay, there would be constant splits. "I like knowing that whatever problems we have, my husband will never leave me."

Myra's mouth twisted. "Like rats trapped in a cage. That's disgusting."

Rejoice sat back, appalled.

* * *

At supper, over a bowl of carrot soup, Noble announced, "Starting tomorrow, Young Man Ernest will be helping with the sports club. I like his enthusiasm. He listened respectfully to the prayers today and—"

"Resist didn't," Mark said.

"It's not polite to interrupt," Rejoice said. She took a slice of cheese bread and scraped off the black crust while she listened to Opportunity pace in her room with the baby. The closer he came to the door, the louder his insistent cries. She flinched. That screech was exactly the same pitch as baby Makepeace's cry.

She pushed the thought from her mind, took a bite of the bread, and grimaced. For the sake of their marriage, He Gives had better know how to cook. Opportunity must have dumped in the entire canister of baking soda into the bread mix. When she was growing up Mother had been busy nursing Father and watching Makepeace. Maybe no one ever took the time to show her how to cook.

Makepeace tilted his water glass and studied it.

"I think he'll be a real asset to the club." Noble said.

"He's strong," Mark said. "His muscles are almost as big as yours."

"He wants to learn all he can about us. And the kraken."

Mark kicked the leg of his chair. "Is it true that a kraken ate all the missing hexacrabs? Submit says so."

Noble reached for a sunflower seed muffin. "It may be. I don't know. I wonder how he can know."

"Submit's canary had babies. They look funny with no feathers on. One is purple, my favorite color. Can I have it for a pet?"

Rejoice thought of bird seeds and feathers all over her floor. "May you. No."

"His name is Peep."

Her computer beeped. "Cruz here."

"Status report."

"Oh, give me a moment." Mark looked sad-dog eyes at faher as she pulled herself up and trudged to the front door. Sometimes she hated gravity. Rejoice opened the door, stepped outside, and leaned against the curved white wall. The slanted sunlight gleamed on the yellow brick road. She twisted off a tomato from the vine over the doorway. A cloud of gnats whirled in an indecipherable dance about the perforated bole of a gray swiss tree across the road. "Go ahead."

"The shipments from Asteroid Ambling have been spotted. They're right on track and should splash down in three months. Crew reports all are well. Everything on the Starflower is in good repair."

"How could they repair the left anterior lock?"

"Excuse me. Except for that. And the bridge chairs etcetera. I meant that nothing new had broken."

Rejoice thumbed up the roster as she popped the tomato into her mouth. She read down the names. She should have gone to bed to do this. She swallowed and flipped the image on the screen back to the face of Brother Tse. "You need to recruit harder. I still don't have enough volunteers for the next mission. It's only a few months before the Starflower returns."

"Nine months is more than a few."

"Couldn't you tell the young men and ladies in Promise that they won't get any more plows and threshers if they don't do their share of volunteering?"

"I don't think so. We have enough iron stockpiled to last for years."

Rejoice's knees shook with fatigue. Why hadn't she brought a chair? A black manypede crawled over her shoe. She sighed, "We still need other metals."

"Your sister hasn't gone on a mission yet."

Rejoice rubbed the bridge of her nose. She could see Opportunity carelessly forgetting to close an airlock. "Sorry. We need her to watch Makepeace." Hmm. After Harmony died and Opportunity married He Gives, could she persuade He Gives to go up one more time? With Oppie of course. That would fill two slots.

"Everybody is needed somewhere."

Maybe Rejoice would volunteer again. Getting away from gravity and the baby sounded good to her. "All right. Are planet-bound flights going well?"

"No maintenance problems. Sister Strength is pregnant now, so we'll be shorthanded in the mechanic department in a few months."

"I thought you said nine months wasn't a few."

Brother Tse smiled.

"Thanks for the good report. Carry on."

She returned to the supper and slumped in her chair as Noble said, "Brother Zystra says the Orange Scar are extremely agitated. The chief's sons are theatrically threatening each other two or three times a day. The quartets are running riot in the woods, stabbing every bush they meet. They must be anxious about all the building going on this side of the ridge. Brother Zystra hasn't been able to leave his post for more than a week."

Rejoice suppressed a groan. She had forgotten that next week Noble started his month-long turn at the observation post. She badly needed to think about something else. "Back to Ernest. After what you said," She glanced at Mark. She shouldn't frighten him about things no eight-year-old can control. "I mean, I'm surprised that you would allow Ernest to attend sports club. He can't be a good influence."

"Influence can work both ways. I'll try him out for this week and then I'll be gone for the month with the churtree. I'll pray about it while I'm there. Look, it would have been best if they had never come, but they came. We have to deal with that reality and not waste time on wishful thinking."

"Ho, ho. Let me tell you about some wishful thinking. I took Myra diving and she tried to persuade me that these 'families' of eight or more people who randomly, uh," she glanced at Mark, "get together dwell in serene unity with no bickering, jealousy, or hurt feelings. I don't know how stupid she thinks I am. But unless they found a way to delete sin from the human genome, that's just not possible."

Noble laid aside his spoon and drew his brows together. "Did you fight with her?"

"Of course not. We had an intense disagreement."

Noble spread his hand across his face. Then he interlocked his fingers, laid his hands on the table, and said carefully, "You're correct. However, these people are so defensive that arguing with them will only cause trouble we don't need."

"Why is it that the only way to maintain peace is for them to say whatever they think and for us not to say what we think?"

"Let me finish. We need to model truth and love before them. As they see that, they will be drawn to God."

"I don't think they care about truth the way we do."

"Deep down, they do. Ernest does."

Rejoice chanced a spoonful of soup. Cold. She didn't feel like eating anymore anyway. "If you don't mind, I'd like to go to bed."

The main screen beeped. Noble walked over and opened the screen to the grief-stricken face of Elder Chin. His wet eyes gleamed. "Another kraken visited the sea mine. Ti-Taksi was too far from the shelter. Don't tell the others yet, as Sa-Itsa will tell the story as soon as he has composed it."

Mark squeaked, "A kraken ate Ti-Taksi?"

"I'm afraid so," Elder Chin said.

Rejoice rushed around the table, sat, and pulled Mark onto her lap as his face crumpled. He and the hexacrab were the same age. That they were twins was a standing joke.

"Why did God even make kraken?" he cried.

Noble laid his hand on Mark's head.

Rejoice rubbed his back. "I don't know, my sweet one, I don't know." She didn't know why God made churtrees or Rationals either. "I'm so glad He made you."

Mark's and the baby's cries melded into one futile protest against the universe.

PACIFISTS' WAR CHAPTER SEVEN

"Rejoice, you're not being reasonable." Noble set the box of food on the table and sat down to look into Rejoice's eyes. "This isn't like you."

"How is it unreasonable to ask you to stay and help when I still feel so weak and ill?"

"I'm paying half my salary to Opportunity so that she can take care of you and Jubilee. You need to let her do it. I've already missed two turns at the Observation Post. Brother Zystra can't cover for me anymore. His wife is due next week. If I can't start doing my share of the work, then I ought to go back to the Mainland."

"Maybe we should."

Noble studied her face as he took her hands and stroked them with his thumbs. "I don't plan to move back every time we have a baby. You can do your work anywhere on the planet. To do what I'm called to do, I need to be here."

Rejoice shifted her eyes away from the pressure of his intense gaze. "You didn't mind the last furlough we took. I think it's time for another one."

"Yes, I did mind. I was miserable the entire four years we wasted in First City."

"You never told me that."

"It wasn't relevant. I had to keep you and Mark safe. Now we have the motion sensors and cameras on every trail. And the churtree have learned to avoid confrontations with us. The pack bat attacks are far fewer now."

"So all those good times we had, you were faking it."

"No. No. I don't assume that because you love astronomy, you can't love Mark and me. You've always been the joy of my life. And being a father to such wonderful sons like Mark and Jubilee is supremely satisfying. However, just as you had to study astronomy or die, so I must evangelize the churtree and hexacrabs."

He was trying to drink the ocean. She studied his strong hands engulfing hers. "I feel so sick."

"I'm not surprised. You won't stay in bed the way you are supposed to and you won't let Opportunity do the work until you recover. You're up even now. I want you to go to bed and stay there until I get back."

Rejoice said nothing. She listened to the wails of the baby behind the closed doors and the faucet dripping water, *plink*, in the sink. Her heartbeat pulsed along weary bones.

"I wish you would try to love the churtrees."

"I do try," she breathed. "I don't succeed." His hands were so warm, hers so cold. "I can't make myself love the people I know are going to kill you."

"Is that a word from the Lord?"

"No. Or . . . I don't think so. It's what I feel."

Pause. "It's what you feel." He waited.

Rejoice also waited. That was irrational. She would not try to justify it.

"I can think of worse ways to die. You do know that even if I knew the date and place, if it was doing the work that God has called me to, I still would go."

She nodded briefly. She knew. The yeasty smell of bread dough rising in the bowl on the stove failed to comfort her as it usually did.

"Please stop trying to persuade me to abandon my calling."

"I'm not. I'm just asking for more help."

"You have lots of help." He stroked her hands. "As long as I am complaining at you, let me add one last thing. Please remember to control yourself when you talk to the newcomers."

"Excuse me. I'm only talking to them the way they talk to us."

"My point exactly." His grip tightened. "What do you remember of Old Earth?"

She looked into his dark brown eyes. "The moon's reflection on a lake. A bonfire. A beach and seagulls. Two pennies under a short table. They tasted funny. That's about it."

"Happier memories than mine. What I remember mostly is being pounded on by the neighborhood kids because my parents were different."

"You never told me that. Did you fight back?"

"Only once. I learned fighting doesn't make any difference when it's ten to one."

"And the point is?"

"The point is that I determined that I would never be like those boys, no matter what they did. The determination still holds. No matter what these newcomers do, they will not provoke me into violence with words or deeds."

"I see." She lowered her gaze again.

He leaned forward to kiss her on the forehead. "I will call you at least twice a day." He stood and picked up the box. "Who knows, maybe this is the week we'll have a breakthrough with the churtree."

Did he mean when they broke through the perimeter and slaughtered them all? "God be with you."

"And with you. Go to bed." The door closed behind him. Rejoice watched him through the window as he finished packing the runabout with replacement cameras and food, and drove off toward the pass.

She did not want to go back to bed and listen to the baby scream at her, but neither could she think of something else to do. Lassitude kept her in her seat for long minutes before she rose to collect a bowl of cherry tomatoes from the vine over her door. She set the tomatoes beside the keyboard and sat in front of the screen. Time to check the asteroids. She twisted the little green cap off a warm tomato, popped it into her mouth, and savored the acidic flavor. The baby still screamed behind the door. She needed to check the weather patterns too and see if Hurricane Malice had reached the Broken Lands yet.

Instead, she tapped in the code for Mother. A few seconds later Mother combed her curly, gray-streaked, brown hair on the screen. "Good evening," Rejoice said.

"Good morning," replied Mother. "Or is it? You don't look well."

"I'm just tired."

"I imagine so. How is sweet little Jubilee?"

"Loud as ever. How is Harmony?"

Mother set down the comb. "Sick as ever, I'm sorry to say. I don't suppose the Hancocks and Doctor Carlson have come any closer to discovering a cure for lung rot?"

"You'd be the first to hear."

Mother nodded grimly, then forced a smile. "He Gives has finally finished his vineyard. Next week, Harmony and I will go to the house raising."

"Good. I think I'll send Opportunity and Makepeace home next week."

"Do you think that's wise?" Mother looked at the bottom of the screen. "May I call you back later? Elder Smith is calling me."

"Okay." She closed the connection and the screen blanked. Why would that old bigot be calling Mother? Rejoice didn't hate him; she just didn't like him. Maybe he was calling for medical advice. But Promise had its own nurse. On the other leg, Brother Petronni, the nurse of Promise hadn't spent every day at the Smith house as Mother had when Sister Smith lay dying of multiple strokes.

Her fingertips skittered on the keys. She didn't feel like calling Sister Guthry at Promise for the weather coordination they did every thirteen hours. It hurt too much to engage in the short business chats that were all Brother Guthry allowed his wife to have with Rejoice since the Hollys and Cruzes had chosen to ally themselves with the pagan hexacrabs. Father dead and Sister Guthry muzzled, there was no one to discuss math or astrophysics with.

Just outside the window, a chicken scratched under the closest apple tree. Maybe . . . maybe what? Her mind felt as blank as the screen.

The chicken flicked up its head and squawked away. Jax jogged into view in a cherry red sweat suit. She headed straight for Rejoice's door and banged on it. Behind her came Opportunity dragging Makepeace with a half-filled basket of apples.

Rejoice opened the door to Jax panting, drops of sweat darkening her bristled hair. "Do the hexacrabs listen to you?" Jax gasped.

"Of course. No, wait. Do you mean do the hexacrabs hear me and obey?"

Jax nodded as she gulped in air.

"No. They tend to do whatever they feel like. But come in and sit down and tell me about it."

Jax brushed past Rejoice and dropped onto a chair.

"Hexacrabs are crawling everywhere in our dojo and asking, asking questions. They are carrying rifles and poking into everything."

Dojo? "Would you like some tea?"

Jax shook her head vigorously. "Please make them leave."

Rejoice sat across the table from Jax as Opportunity and Makepeace came in to stare. "Are they hurting anything?"

"I don't know."

"Why do you hate the hexacrabs?"

Jax glared at her. "Why do you hate the churtree?"

Rejoice almost laughed. Got her there. How could Jax tell? "When you viewed the vids last week, did my husband show you what happens when Orange Scar and Yellow Scar churtree meet?"

"No. Only weapon making, canoe carving, dancing."

Opportunity gave glasses of ice water to the two women.

Jax guzzled hers as Rejoice said, "I'm sorry about the heat. It takes several months to acclimatize." After a sip of her water, she moved to the screen. "Let's see." She tapped keys as she said, "How do you like their double vocal cords?"

"Like constant cat fights."

"Their screeching gives me a headache, but Elder Chin discovered their speech is sophisticated, multi-tonal, and complex, in that it's highly metaphorical and dense in, oh, here we go. This took place eight years ago near the bladder tree grove." Rejoice moved aside so Jax could have a clear view. She watched Jax's face. Rejoice had seen the vid many times and didn't want to risk triggering a flashback in front of Jax. So she only glanced at the screen occasionally to remember the sequence.

Opportunity pulled Makepeace into her bedroom. They had never let him see this. Then she hurried back.

A churtree, which still looked to Rejoice like a black weasel with a giraffe neck and hydra-like head with four arms, pattered up a trail on its stubby legs. Its four eyes between the four long arms atop the neck scanned the jungle with jerky movements. The arms radiated about a red circular maw lined with hundreds of teeth, and the two upper arms held spears. Bands of gold glinted on some of the arms and fingers. In the patches where the black fur had been shaved off, bright yellow scars in the patterns of spirals, dots, and starbursts marked the black skin.

The creature stopped, twitched its eyes, and turned. Four churtrees with orange markings leaped out of the bush. Their black arms flailed as they parried spears. Screeching rent the air. First one foot, and then the others of the Yellow Scar churtree were pierced and pinned to the ground. In the frenzy, the Yellow Scar churtree pulled one spear out of a foot, lunged at the Orange Scar in front of it, and gashed its neck.

Orange blood splattered over the trail. Orange Scars seized the arms of the Yellow Scar and pulled in opposite directions until the Yellow Scar was splayed out and unable to move. Then, in unison, they began eating up its arms. When they reached the neck, they each plucked out an eye and dropped the bloody prize into the maw of the warrior on their right. They hacked the body into bits and devoured it with much yowling. From time to time, one would cough up a gold band and toss it into a net bag. When the Yellow Scar had been reduced to blood splatters on the dirt trail and black hair tufts caught on the bushes, the Orange Scars gathered up the spears. One took the net bag of jewelry and flung it down the trail toward where the Yellow Scar had come from.

Rejoice closed the vid at this point. "That's why I don't like the churtrees. Now, why don't you like the hexacrabs who are nothing like this?"

Jax fingered her lip. "What is the purpose of torture?"

"No purpose other than they always try to eat things that are still alive. Except for fish, they eat dead things only if they're starving."

Jax leaned forward frowning. "With a height of a meter and a half, they have a low center of gravity. Four hands for holding weapons. Formidable in battle. Interesting problem, for truth." She scratched the bristles over her ear. "Is there a purpose for throwing away the gold armbands?"

Jax slowing her speech and including articles reassured Rejoice. Perhaps she was trying to get along. "The purpose stumped us for years. What we finally figured out is this. Every churtree wears distinctive jewelry based on rank and experience and, ah, taste. When the net of jewelry is discovered by the tribe, the message received is this: We have eaten you know who, and when we catch you, we'll eat you, too. And that fate is what every churtree spends most of its life desperately trying to avoid. If one thinks it is outnumbered and about to suffer that fate, it will kill itself first if it can."

Opportunity added, "And that's how Sister Hancock killed an entire village of Red Scar churtree."

Jax glanced from sister to sister. "What?"

"Long story," Rejoice said. "Now, why do you fear the hexacrabs who are nothing like that?"

"No fear. I don't like them."

"Why?"

"Why should I like them?"

"Because they're wonderful. They're incredibly intelligent and beautiful."

"Beautiful!" spat Jax. "They look like spiders."

"I don't think so. Not with those tentacles." Rejoice leaned back in her chair and idly ran a palm along the edge of the dusty keyboard. "It's funny how two people can view the same thing so differently. I thought the hexacrabs were beautiful from the first moment I saw one." She laughed. "Even though Ur-Veena at that moment was trying to kill me."

Jax still frowned. "Ur-Veena the one I viewed shooting pack bats?"

"That's the one. But we've been good friends now for almost two decades." Rejoice smiled. "He is a most remarkable person." She sighed.

Jax made a face and ruffled her eyebrows.

"What?" Rejoice asked.

"For truth, it is incomprehensible to me that anyone would call an alien crab a person and a friend. You said it tried to kill you."

"Oh, yes, but only because he thought I was a churtree threatening the nursery. I'd better show you their life cycle so you'll know what to avoid." She tapped the keys and the screen showed an underwater scene of seaweed and armor-plated, three-eyed fish. "You see these, ah, blue sea anemones with a little star atop a stalk and bulbous below. Those are the babies in the nursery. If you ever run into these while diving or boating, say goodbye as fast as you can. You touch their babies and even if you're good friends, they'll go berserk. They don't care if they die protecting their babies."

Jax nodded.

"When the babies mature, the bases split open and these little triangles swim out and head for the deep water. That's Child Departure Season. Something happens to them in the deep sea, we don't know what and we don't know how long. We think that it's highly variable. There are abandoned clusters that children are still returning to hundreds of years later. We're thinking that the minimum is three to five years. That's because talking females started returning at about that time after the hexacrabs discovered a talking female."

"Clarify, please. Talking females?"

"Oh, I'm sorry. The first hexacrabs that we discovered were all males. After they learned to trust us, they showed us their corral of mute females."

"Only male hexacrabs talk?"

"Back then, yes. Before Dark Death, all the females talked. But some mutation or something happened after it and all the females became unintelligent and mute. It was a great tragedy and sorrow for them."

"But their females now talk?"

"Yes, some of the young females do. The older mute ones, they still take care of. But they no longer mate with them. Ur-Veena and Sa-Issi traveled with us on the *Magellan* fifteen years ago in search of talking females. We found one surviving in the waters off this Archipelago, Ti-Ista. She was the mother of all talking female hexacrabs for about ten years."

"Genetic Diversity requirements?"

"Well, that's kind of a mysterious puzzle. We've never been able to figure out any lineage of any sort. It's probably because of all the life stages that I was talking about. Where was I? Oh yes, I hadn't gotten to that part yet. As I was saying the triangular children swim off into the deep and somehow three of the triangles fuse together. Then they return as a group in Child Come or Child Return Season.

"This is Ur-Siti catching one of the returning children. Here he puts it into a niche and covers the opening with rocks. A few weeks later, when the metamorphosis is complete, he opens the niche, and there's the sweet baby. This was a male so he ties him to his shell. That one grew up to become Sa-Tisi. The females are now usually tied to talking females' shells until they show that they won't talk.

"Starting twelve years ago, Ur-Veena and Ti-Ista netted talking females, but they don't become sexually mature for ten years. So it's only in the last couple years that more talking females have been laying eggs. Anyway, the babies stay tied to the shells of the adults learning speech and manners and whatnot, until they're strong enough to break the ropes."

"You have not shown the mating habits. How are these babies made?"

"We don't know, and we don't ask. The hexacrabs are a very, how to say it, reciprocal people. If we asked permission to record their mating, they would allow it only if they could join us in our bedrooms. And that we would not allow."

Jax snickered. "What harm in showing them a vid of—"

"No," Rejoice said as heat flared on her cheeks. "They can't see or can't interpret flat images. And we don't have those kinds of videos."

"Hmm," Jax said, tapping the table. "Not me, but if price is right, perhaps some of us could demonstrate the process for these friends of yours."

"I don't think so," Rejoice said, the heat spreading to her neck.

Jax clapped her hands once. "So how can they see to shoot pack bats?"

"I should have our brother explain it to you since he invented the LV."

"Makepeace?" Jax said, astonished.

"My brother Stronghold back on the mainland. Anyway, the hexacrabs sense on more levels than we do. They sense electricity, pressure, magnetism, taste, and smell a thousand times more acutely than we do. Their range of hearing is much wider than ours. We can't translate most of their vocabulary that involves those senses. They, on the other hand, have much lower color sensitivity and can't interpret flat images.

"Brother Holly studded the frame of the LV with revised sonar chips which feed into a grid of thousands of tiny rods that shift up and down to provide a 3-D image inside the LV. The hexacrabs have to correlate the visual image of what they see outside their tank with the 3-D grid inside. It takes a couple of months for them to get the hang of it, but catch on they do. You should see them at the shooting range practicing for hours at a time."

Jax looked again at the image of the blue hexacrab with a tiny hexacrab tied to its shell. "So many stages."

"That's how Brother Hancock had his arm paralyzed," Opportunity said. "He killed a baby hexacrab that he thought was a sea anemone and Ur-Nissi stabbed him."

"Bloodthirsty for pacifists, these Hancocks."

"Not at all," Rejoice said. "They're the gentlest people on this entire planet." She wiped the dust on her hand onto her brown dress. "New Earth taught us that you have to have more than good intentions. You need knowledge. That gaining of knowledge has cost us, the hexacrabs, and the churtree. That's why we hope you consult with us before you start any projects." Rejoice stopped.

Dimly she could still hear the baby's wails and she could see the women in front of her, but everything seemed momentarily obscured by a sudden insight. "Oh—I just realized why Brother Hancock never got a prosthesis. It's a reminder, like stones of remembrance. It reminds the hexacrabs of his offer to submit to their justice and of the time he went out to shell his soft parts with courage. And it reminds us to assume nothing."

Jax shook her head. "The words were English, but I don't understand."

"I guess you wouldn't. I'm sorry. You need to read our history."

"We are here for the breaking of history. And our computers are not compatible."

"We have some extra computers at the store."

"I have nothing to buy them with. Your people will not want my lessons in martial arts or anthropology."

The gymnasium was for martial arts? Martial arts! Dojo; a school for martial arts training? The Rationals had told the colonists they were building a school. Rejoice fumbled over her words. "We have a printer on the mainland. Since Sister Constancy needs to add another few chapters to the history anyway, I'll see if she can give you the galleys of the new edition. That would be free." Rejoice took a deep breath. "You and the hexacrabs are much alike. They would never dream of asking for something for nothing. That's why they're so eager to work in the fish hatcheries, kelp farms, mining, and shipping."

Jax grunted and stood up. "Why so eager to invade my compound?"

"Curiosity. They love learning. For the past three years they've been studying Old Earth history the way a child eats candy. Hmm. Both the air-ocean and the water-ocean people want to hear what's happened in the time since we left Old Earth. We could trade histories. Would that be acceptable?"

"Let them be curious elsewhere."

What would it take to make Jax answer a direct question? "But why?"

Jax glared again. "Why do you stay here when you hate the churtree?" Rejoice ran a thumb down her jaw line and answered slowly, "I'm here because my husband is here. I lost my heart to the hexacrabs when I saw

Ur-Veena; Pastor Cruz lost his to the churtree when he saw the Red Scar village cut into the cliff at Half Moon Bay. But you appear to love neither."

"Correct. What must I do to keep the hexacrabs out of my compound?"

"Let me talk to them. I can't promise any particular result, but I'll ask them to leave. Was Ur-Veena among them?"

"Five legs, white blotches on tentacles?"

"The blotches are scars from sun burns."

"For truth?"

Rejoice cleared the screen to call Ur-Veena. He whistled and clicked in reply, and a few seconds later the translation followed. Rejoice spoke in English so Jax could understand. "Ur-Veena, this is Rejoice. My gills huff to see you, but you do not come. Is it to breathe air for you to creep over and feel my little one?"

"I had heard that you were weak and must rest in your niche."

"I am swimming. Please come and bring everyone. I must eat maggots to tell you that these new air ocean-people have a trail long used that only invited peoples may crawl into their cluster."

"They swim in a new ocean."

"Yes, but they still need time to taste the currents. Delicate babies need siphoning."

"We will come."

Rejoice closed the connection and looked at Jax. "They're leaving your compound and coming here. Opportunity, how much salmon do we have in the freezer?"

"Enough to clog gills."

"Good. Could you—" Rejoice saw movement out of the corner of her eye and she turned to the window. Makepeace hummed by in the runabout in the direction that led to the airstrip and cliffs, steep cliffs with sharp rocks below. "Stop!" She hurtled out the door without pausing to put on shoes and raced after the runabout. "Makepeace, stop! Stop!"

The runabout swerved erratically on the lane. Rejoice gained on it and snatched at the door handle. Out of breath, she caught it and snapped open the door. Makepeace still drove forward, his hands clenching the wheel. Rejoice grabbed the door frame and pulled herself in. She fell on Makepeace's arms. Something in her abdomen ripped. Fire ripped up her stomach.

She stabbed the ignition button, and screamed as she fell out of the runabout and rolled alongside. She and the machine stopped at the same time. When she curled up reflexively, her knees hit the wire mesh wheels.

Awareness became a confusion of voices and crying and being lifted and carried and tasting blood and agony that didn't stop until cold metal at her neck hissed as Doctor Carlson held her chin and everything faded.

PACIFISTS' WAR CHAPTER EIGHT

Rejoice grabbed the computer with both hands and pulled it close. Jax scooted her chair over so she could see.

Rejoice's heart beat and breath whistled past dry lips and a wooden tongue. Sensation expanded to an itch on her nose; a soft, indistinguishable murmur of someone's voice; the pressure of a pillow on the back of her head. Then swooping down came the pain, burning in the abdomen, sharp stabs on the toes, prickling on the elbows, a headache dancing on the temples and between the eyes. So, looking at a computer with Jax had been a dream.

She opened her eyes. Above her arched the shadowed, curved white ceiling of her bedroom. Her hands lay like lead weights on her chest. She gazed at the ceiling a long time. Should she move? If so, what should she move?

She experimented, and one hand fell to her side. A buzzer sounded, and a few moments later, the door opened into a white rectangle outlining the dark shape of Noble. Rejoice squinted against the light he turned on.

"Do you need anything?" He sounded aggravated.

Rejoice's eyes adjusted. He looked aggravated, too. "Water?" she whispered.

He left and came back with a glass of water. Kneeling beside her, he gently lifted her head so she could sip from a straw. After a few swallows, she could speak. "What's wrong?"

Noble set the glass on the end table. "I hope you're happy. You've managed to pull me away from the churtree once again."

Astonishment was swallowed up by rage. She tried to keep her voice level. "Excuse me, but I was trying to save Makepeace's life."

"That was Opportunity's job. Why won't you let her do it?"

"If she had been doing her job, he wouldn't have taken off in the runabout!"

"You know how difficult it is to keep a constant eye on Makepeace. You should stop being so hard on your sister. She feels terrible about it."

Rejoice swallowed. "I didn't even think about her. All I could see was Makepeace driving right over the cliff and smashing on the talus."

"Why? We have a fence where the road runs along the cliff."

"As if we didn't design the runabouts to climb over everything!"

Noble looked at her with his mouth set in a line.

Rejoice breathed out. She needed to calm down or this headache would kick her head apart. "So, how is Makepeace?"

"He's fine."

"How am I?"

He took her hand and patted it. "You tore some muscles, ripped off some toenails, and cracked your elbow. Why did you refuse to realize that you were in no shape to go chasing after runabouts?"

"I'm sorry I didn't do a cost-benefit analysis before trying to save Makepeace. I didn't think; I reacted. When you were lying on the deck trying to hold in your guts after you threw yourself in front of a churtree to save me, maybe I should have kicked you for being so stupid."

Noble stood. "I'll be in the living room working. If you need anything, wave in front of the motion sensor."

What right did he have to be so angry? Were only males allowed to be heroes? "Oh." She sucked in breath. "I delayed the day that we can make love again, didn't I?"

The line that was Nobles mouth turned up on one side.

Bingo. Poor man, it had been months. No wonder he was so edgy.

Silence caught her attention. "Where's the baby?"

"Jubilee is being wet-nursed by Sister Carver. You'll have to start nursing again or you'll dry up."

Right. That also meant she should not take any more medications, or at least nothing that could affect the baby. This was going to hurt. "Could I have some tomatoes?"

Noble left and returned with a bowl of cherry tomatoes he set beside the hand that wasn't in a sling. Then he raised her up with some pillows behind her back and placed the screen on her lap. "In case you want to work." The door closed behind him.

After staring at the door a long time, Rejoice ate the tomatoes one by one and concentrated on their flavor and aroma. The occasional tear brimmed over her lids and ran down her cheek. Why was it so hard to think? Perhaps it was the residue of medication she had already had, in which case she did not trust herself to work with weather statistics anyway. A quick check on asteroids showed nothing dangerous had been sighted for a week.

She should call Sister Carver and see how the baby was doing. On the other hand, if he was doing poorly, what could she do about it? Impulsively, she tapped in the code for Harmony.

The computer's little screen showed Harmony sitting in a wheelchair with an oxygen tube snaking into one nostril. Her third daughter, Peace That Passes Understanding, the only one with red hair like Harmony's, hung on her arm and showed her a quilt block that the little girl had sewn crookedly.

"Later," whispered Harmony. Little Peace stomped off. Behind them, Mother, formed a cat's cradle for Reconciliation, Reason Together, and One Faith. She handed over the string to One and walked to the screen.

"Where are you?" whispered Harmony. "I can't see you on the screen."

Rejoice was glad Harmony couldn't see the sudden grief on her face. Theoretically, Harmony was supposed to live another four years, but already she was turning sallow. She was as thin as Father when he died. Her beautiful golden-red hair had been cut short to make it easy to manage. "I'm in bed. Noble is using the big screen."

"How are you?" Harmony coughed feebly and Mother rubbed her shoulder. Harmony typed in the rest of the question. [U frightened us badly. Opportunity cried like U had died.]

Rejoice shook her head. She could bet Opportunity cried. Now she'd be stuck on the island with Rejoice for another month or two.

[Are U in a lot of pain?] Harmony typed.

"Some. I guess I'll live." *Good grief. Did I need to say that to someone who won't?*

Mother spoke. "Dear love, please take care of yourself."

"I'll try. Harmony, how is your new memorization project going?"

She typed, [Slow. I'm working on the book of Job. I'm learning some things that are hard to put in words. But Noble is so patient with me and Stronghold is always encouraging me. I still type out the Gospel of Luke by memory once a month.]

"How are you coping with the new people?" asked Mother.

"I don't know. Half the time I can't figure out what they're saying. When I do understand, I'm appalled."

All the little girls screamed, "Daddy! Daddy!" and like chickens chasing after a thrown cherry they scurried off screen. A minute later, Stronghold waded on screen, dragging two giggling girls on each leg. He bent forward to kiss Harmony, then turned to face the screen. "Hi, Sis. Looks pretty dark where you're calling from. What's floating in your life?"

Rejoice smiled with relief. Perhaps he had forgiven her for being the one person the Rational People wanted to talk to. It had taken him a year to get over her assuming the management of the Space Agency, even though the assignment had been at Father's request. "Apparently, for a while, nothing. I'm stuck in bed again. How are things flowing in First City with your cluster of newcomers?"

Stronghold held up his hands. "We never see them. They stay on their side of the river except when they come over to load up on food, and then they look ashamed."

"I suppose we should be grateful they don't want to be guck suckers."

Stronghold moved behind Harmony and placed his hands on her shoulders. "Have they told you anything about their lab?"

"What lab would that be?"

"Surely they brought a medical lab. They had nineteen more years of medical research on Old Earth than we did. And if they didn't have to leave before they got all their equipment like we had to, they might have the machines that could find a cure for lung rot." Harmony reached up to weave her fingers among his.

A hope tinged with bitterness rose up within Rejoice. She picked up the glass to wet her lips and took several deep breaths before she could answer. "The next time we meet, I'll bring it up."

Mother spoke, "Dear love, I hate to cut you off, but Stronghold had to work late, and I need to feed these starving people. I'd like to say I'll call you later, but I remember what happened that last time I said that."

Rejoice started to laugh, but sudden pain choked it to a gasp. "I'm not going anywhere for a while. Goodnight." She tapped the edge of her computer. *Oh God, let there be a cure.* She had given up hope. Fifteen years the colony had spent looking. Hot tears scalded her cheeks. She needed to get out of this mood. Maybe it was time to call Constancy and start up another chess game.

Rejoice checked the time. No, Constancy would have just started her shift. Mark wouldn't be home for another hour. Poor little guy. She hadn't seen him at all yesterday. She tuned her computer to his and saw he was working on elementary algebra. That made her smile.

Then she tried to tune to the main screen, but couldn't, because the transmission was scrambled for privacy in case the colonists' strong mores about privacy weren't strong enough. She flipped the view and watched Noble, his dark eyes thoughtful as he listened through earphones to his parishioner. Every few seconds he glanced up to the corner of the screen.

When he closed his eyes to pray with whoever it was, she switched to the churtree channel he had placed in the corner of the screen and split into four views that changed every ten seconds. Oops, there was a blank corner. Camera 37 was out, so were cameras 42 and 43. Noble would have replaced them last night if he had not been called back. The fifty-two camera sequence began again. Camera 2 in the main hall of the Cliffside dwelling was half-obscured by a crud wasp nest. Tricky thing to go into the village grounds at night and extend one of Stronghold's spider bots to clear the mess away and get the bot back before the churtrees discovered the small machine and smashed it to bits. Cameras 5 through 12 showed the churtrees doing their usual canoe carving, weapon sharpening, child beating, and grooming.

Rejoice checked the time again. Noble used exactly twenty-five minutes for each session of Scripture memorization and counseling, and then five minutes for private prayer and preparation for the next session. She didn't want to interrupt him until that five minutes came up.

Noble opened the door and then shut it as he came in.

She startled and instantly regretted the movement.

He strode to the bed and knelt at eye level. "Are you up for a visit from Jax?"

Rejoice considered. Yes, she wanted to talk about their lab. "Sure."

Noble reached forward and buttoned a gap in her brown pajamas. His hands suddenly trembled. She reached up with her free hand and grabbed one of his. "I'm sorry."

A number of expressions flicked across his face before sadness stayed. "Well, life isn't always a bowl of cherry tomatoes." Then he smiled weakly and glanced at Rejoice's empty bowl. "You derive a lot of pleasure from them."

She squeezed his hand. "When life denies you great pleasures, take delight in the little ones." A quote from Elder Chin.

They both sighed. He reached over and wiped her tear with his thumb. "Are you sure that you're up for her?"

"Well, as aggravating as Jax is, I think that visiting with her beats boredom."

"Use wisdom and discretion, joy of my life."

She nodded.

He left and Jax entered.

She wore red today, red with black piping, red lips with a black outline, red nails with a black diagonal line slashed across each one, and red hair.

How much time did she waste each morning painting herself? "Good morning."

"For me," Jax said. "Not so good for you I think." She moved to the crib and ran her hands along the headboard and the star mobile. "I didn't know you were so sick during the initial talks."

"It wasn't relevant to the discussions."

"Maybe truth. But I'm sorry I pushed you to exhaustion." She moved to the foot of Rejoice's bed and rubbed the plastic post as she said carefully. "I have been thinking about our supper conversation. How old were you when you realized the electromagnetic mass driver would push away the oncoming asteroid?"

"Twelve."

"I apologize for speaking without thought. There is much I don't understand." She fingered the triangular painting of the photovoltaic-sailed ship *Magellan*, dove white against a gray-green sea and blue sky, with two tiny figures leaning on a railing. "Why did the adults not think of it first?"

Rejoice was beginning to feel as nervous as Jax looked. "Because Sister Guthry, the meteorologist, was the only Old Earth-trained scientist among us."

Jax rubbed the edges of the painting of the Potatoes, the three moons of New Earth as seen through the branches of an apple tree. "Stupid not to send scientists to a new planet."

"We had seven years on the way over to study and did, and still do. My father became a geologist. He had always wanted to be one, but graduate schools didn't accept Christians like us."

Jax shrugged. "If irrational in one area, perhaps irrational in science also."

Rejoice's fingers twitched. Jax was the kind of person who had strangled Father's dreams on Old Earth. She breathed deeply before saying, "We did the best we could with what we had."

Jax walked over to stand by Rejoice. "We've decided. To pay for food we will share our satellite information with you."

"If that will make you happy, that's fine by me." More than fine. Now Rejoice wouldn't be required to stand before the Senate and explain why satellites were more important than roads or warehouses or refineries or or or. "You do realize that it is to your advantage as well as ours to seek ways to keep this planet from being shattered to bits?"

"For truth. But for now, knowledge is all we have to sell. So we sell. But we don't know the language to format the information."

"My brother will be happy to help you."

"Brother who?"

"Ah, right. My biological brother, Stronghold Holly. He's the computer and robotics man of the colony."

"Our main computer is at Freedom."

"And Stronghold lives in First City. No problem."

Jax nodded distantly as she peered out the window and traced the frame with her fingertips. "I see Makepeace and Opportunity picking apples."

"We jimmied the genes so the trees would bear all year and have no chilling requirements. That means we have to pick a little bit every day. What we don't eat goes to the store. The Hancocks grow herbs, and the Carvers grow cucumbers. We all grow something as a spiritual discipline and as a way to cut costs and have fresh food."

Jax continued to stare out the window. "So much I don't understand. Yet I'm afraid to ask and offend."

She was joking, right? "So are we. Go ahead."

Jax pulled up the light plastic chair and sat with her hands between her knees. "You hurt yourself badly yesterday. Are runabouts so valuable?"

Rejoice stared. Were these people even human? If they weren't human, what were they? Her mouth hung open and she forced herself to close it. Last time she'd tell Jax to go ahead. No: wrong response. How were they ever to understand one another if Rejoice turned her eyes at every revelation? "No. Makepeace is. I was worried about my brother hurting himself."

Jax shook her head, stood and moved to the window again. "I try not to judge, for you are to live as you choose. It is hard to face another's immorality and not flinch." She seemed to be searching for another topic in the window frame. "May I tell you that you are not treating Opportunity as you should?"

Rejoice laid her head back on the pillow and listened to the rustle of bedclothes. She must need this lecture or she wouldn't be getting it twice in one hour. "How so?"

"Your co-wife possesses great talent, but you don't allow her time to paint and you don't encourage her."

Rejoice rubbed her forehead as the headache renewed its tap-dance between her eyes. "Is co-wife a word for sister?"

"Term of status, yes."

"No. Opportunity is my sister, my biological sister. She doesn't paint here because all her supplies are back in First City."

"It can be even harder to be co-wife to a sibling. You should treat her more gently."

Rejoice understood in a rush, and she exploded. "You think Noble is married to my sister?"

"We are not offended. Here we are free from Old Earth false moralities."

"We're not free from biblical morality. One man, one wife, for life."

A look of disgust crossed Jax's face. "Jacob married two sisters."

"And nothing good came of it."

Jax shrugged. "The twelve tribes of Israel."

"God could have made all the tribes He wanted another way. Since you know the Old Testament story, you know it's about reaping what you sow. Jacob sowed deception and he reaped plenty of it in return." The headache throbbed. Why was she arguing instead of engaging in peaceful discussion? "Excuse me. Opportunity is not my co-wife. She's here to help me and the baby."

"So she is free?"

"No, we pay her."

Jax smiled and then covered her mouth with her hand. Her gaze fell on the computer screen with the shifting images of jungle and churtree life. "Oh. Real time?"

"Yes. This week is Pastor Cruz's turn to monitor the churtrees."

The woman's eyes glowed with a glee that Rejoice could not understand. "So it is permissible to spy on sentient peoples."

Rejoice adjusted her sling. Did Jax think she had caught them at an amusing hypocrisy? "We do it only because it's the only way we can learn about them. They don't talk to us and won't tolerate us near them. The hexacrabs, on the other leg, were overjoyed to have language and culture lessons with us. We ask permission before we record anything the hexacrabs do."

Something besides the headache nagged at Rejoice's mind. "Ah, about that sequence I showed you yesterday."

"About the Orange Scar eating the Yellow Scar churtree?"

"The one. Could you not talk about it with the people on the mainland? All of us at the Mission have seen it, but we haven't released it to the general public."

"Your purpose?"

"Well, when we first recorded it, we didn't think the 'Come Ye Outers' needed any more ammunition."

"Come Ye Outers?"

Shut up, Rejoice! Shut up! "Ah, colonists who think we shouldn't have anything to do with the churtrees." *And the hexacrabs. And you as soon as they find out you think it's okay to have two wives.*

"Like you?"

"No, not like me." She didn't hate the churtrees for the same reasons Elder Smith and the people of Promise did. *Please, God, don't tell me I'm just as bigoted as they are. God, have mercy.*

Jax waited.

"Why do you hate the hexacrabs?" Rejoice could change the subject as fast as Jax could.

Jax sat again and watched Rejoice. "Are you capable of keeping a secret?'

"I'm a pastor's wife."

"Meaning?"

"Meaning I get to practice confidentiality a lot. I don't think Pastor Cruz tells me even one percent of what goes on in his counseling sessions, but what he does tell me, I keep secret."

"I am wondering. What does a pastor do all day?"

Rejoice smiled. She might as well try questioning barnacles. "I don't know what the others do. I can only tell you what my husband does. He wakes at five and exercises for half an hour, showers, and eats bread and fruit for breakfast. At six he goes out to pick apples and pray for an hour. At seven he reads Scripture to Lad Mark and me while we eat breakfast. Lad Mark goes to morning school and I do my work while Pastor Cruz works on his sermon for Lord's Day. From eight to twelve, he puts on the earphones and counsels with eight people on a weekly basis. He talks to thirty-two people a month this way. After a year he switches to a new group of thirty-two."

"So many people are troubled?"

"No, not troubled. He works with them on projects like memorization or overcoming bad habits or growing good habits. They discuss life and theology. At noon, Lad Mark comes home and we eat lunch. I teach Lad Mark in the afternoon while Pastor Cruz spends one hour being pastored by Elder Chin and talking about the churtrees. From one to three, he calls on people who aren't on his morning schedule. That's another twenty people or more per month. From three to four he gathers all the lads and young men for training in exercise and obstacle courses. From four to five, he prays and works on the sermon again and deals with hexacrab issues. From five to six, he and Lad Mark do what Lad Mark wants to do, except when it's time to take out the Deng boys for male bonding sorts of stuff. At six, we have supper and house maintenance. From seven to eight, we go for a walk if the pack bats aren't out. From eight on it varies with meetings with the deacon board or the hexacrabs or holiday and wedding planning or whatnot. From ten to eleven he does language study: Churt or Hebrew or Hex or Sign."

"Not much time for fun."

"That is fun for him."

"And for you?"

Rejoice shifted in the bed. Now she could identify the pain in her toes. Maybe she should get some medication after all and wait on nursing the baby. "Are you asking what I do for fun?"

Jax looked at the ceiling a moment before answering, "Yes."

"I like my paying jobs of asteroid searching, weather reporting, and running the space missions. I like my nonpaying jobs of teaching Lad Mark and cooking."

"You never rest?"

"We're commanded to," Rejoice said. "Because our duties are many on the Lord's Day, our family takes sixday as our day of rest. Pastor Cruz stays in bed until ten o'clock or so."

"With you, I hope."

Rejoice rubbed the bridge of her nose. Noble had told her not to antagonize these people, but for pity's sake. "Jax, excuse me, but I can't imagine how you could think that's any of your business."

"For us it does not offend to express concern for one another."

"We would prefer you not to express concern over sexual matters. On the eve before our weddings, our parents give us The Talk, and we're given the code to the manual of sexual techniques. If there's any difficulty thereafter, it is discussed privately with an elder, pastor, or doctor."

"All that repression must be painful."

"Were you still interested in what I do for fun that isn't private?"

Jax snickered and sat back. Her red chain earrings swung. "Yes."

"On Sixday, if we have a churtree all clear, we sometimes hike to the library and picnic."

Jax leaned forward. "What is this library?"

"Oh. We made three of them when we saw we weren't getting any germanium or gallium soon, and we might lose the entire computer system as it aged. One is here, high on an extinct volcano; one is at First City; and one is in the central plateau of Sole, about a thousand kilometers due west of your settlement. We downloaded every single file on the Starflower and printed them. We wrapped each book in nitrogen gas and an impermeable membrane so oxygen and insects wouldn't ruin them. Then we put them in a windowless building with double stainless steel walls a meter thick with an air-gel sandwich, like our panels for the Meetingplace."

"Including the sex manual?"

"Including that."

Jax nodded. "Intelligent."

"I'm glad we did something right." Rejoice rubbed the smooth rim of the empty bowl. "Ah, what else? Sometimes we go boating in the bay. Sometimes we go see what the Hancocks are doing in their lab. We visit with our friends. I read poetry and novels and continue studying astrophysics and the like."

"Before you left, had the subwavicles stranger, gorgeous, and most charming been discovered?"

Rejoice's breath caught. "No! Tell me about them. When, who, and what are their characteristics?"

Jax laughed. "And what will you pay me?"

"Pay you?"

"For now, information is all we have for sale."

Rejoice studied Jax. She was joking, right? Maybe not. "Wait. You might have something we want badly."

Jax arched her eyebrows.

"Did you bring an extensive medical lab?"

"For truth. But it is too late to grow new nerves for your deaf person or repair your brain-damaged brother."

"We need to find a cure for a fungal disease we call lung rot. It has already killed forty-one people. Last week there were a hundred and twenty-seven people in one stage or another of the disease."

Jax jumped up so fast, her chair tipped over. "Why not tell us sooner?"

"There's so much to tell. One hardly knows where to begin."

Jax stood with clenched fists. "Symptoms, length of illness, death rate, cause: tell me all."

"What will you pay me?"

Jax whitened as she spread her feet out and narrowed her eyes.

"I'm sorry," Rejoice said. "I was joking, and lung rot is nothing to joke about. Please relax. Even if you caught it today, you would have ten years to find a cure."

Jax still frowned, but her shoulders lowered and she brought her feet closer together.

"We can't tell who's going to get it. The spore is omnipresent and its source is still undetermined. So we've all been exposed. Even after HLA typing and tons of medical tests the medical people know—and I don't—we have no good predictors of susceptibility. Nobody in the Mission has it, and no one who has handled the food given to your people has it. It's something all of us test for every six months. My father was the first person to contract the disease. We thought it came from a cave my father was exploring when his filter mask broke, but when we went back to the cave, we couldn't culture any fungus from it."

"His filter mask broke?"

"Well, I guess that's something we never told you about either. For our first six years on this planet, all of us wore filter masks at all times while outside."

"Why?"

"There were high concentrations of toxic gasses. That's why we worked so hard at re-seeding the oceans and the land. The sooner we restored the plant life, the sooner we could do without those horrible masks. Our family burned ours in a bonfire when the elders finally voted to discontinue their use. Makepeace was the only one who missed them. He kept wearing his for another year. Mother finally started cutting pieces off it, a little at a time. Sometimes he'll still put on the left-over strap from the mask as a head band."

Jax shook her head. "But after you discovered the fungus, you discontinued the filter masks?"

"Oh, yes. We found that the filter masks made no difference with the spores. We now think the fungus spores float in the air, like they do in the hundreds per cubic centimeter in Old Earth air. As I said, we still haven't discovered the fungus source."

Jax set the chair in place and sat on it. "We may be infected already, and you couldn't think to tell us this?"

"I'm sorry. We were working so hard to keep you from killing yourself from the immediate dangers on this planet that we forgot to mention the less-immediate risks. The people you really should talk to here are Doctor Carlson and the Hancocks. They're focusing on a lot of the basic research and searching for the source. Doctor Cruz's lab in First City is focusing on the treatments. We'll tell our labs to give you everything we have on the fungus."

"Ten years."

"More or less. My father took ten years. Some take shorter. Brother Merganzer offered himself as a control and took no medication to see how long it takes to die without the medications we do take. He died in six years. My sister-in-law, Harmony, may not last more than six years, even with all the medication we can stuff down her."

Jax studied her knuckles. "World-crusher asteroids, killer fungus, hexacrabs, churtree, naspy, blight, poisonous plants, no germanium. What else?"

"I don't know at the moment. I told you we were stuck on this planet. We were just grateful that our amino acids were compatible with the New Earth proteins. When you're stuck with no alternatives, you become committed to solutions. We assume the same is true for you.

The computer on Rejoice's lap beeped. "Joy of my life, look at the churtree channel!"

They looked at a back view of four Yellow Scar churtree as they pattered up a trail that led from their village to the Orange Scar churtrees. They carried two spears apiece; and net bags hung about their necks held sharpened stones.

Rejoice turned the screen so Jax could see without craning her neck. "The churtrees always go out either as single hunters, or in groups of multiples of four. The Yellow Scar churtrees almost never forage in the jungle between their village and that of the Orange Scar. You saw why yesterday."

The view switched to another trail with four Orange Scars trotting along.

"Oh, no." Rejoice laid the computer down and squeezed her eyes shut. God, she did not need to see this. She should have stayed unconscious a few more hours.

Jax lifted the screen and stared avidly at the images. She glanced up. "Will we see another fight, but one more balanced?"

She hated these churtrees. Anybody who lived that stupid deserved to die that stupid. Why did they need to watch and care? She licked dry lips with a dry tongue. "Probably. They're headed straight for each other. On the other leg, churtrees seldom continue in straight lines for very long." Jax shifted the computer so both could see the split screen of Yellow and Orange moving toward each other. As the camera viewpoint switched, the Yellow side went gray.

"That camera's out, too."

"Cause of camera failure?"

"Oh, just about anything. Sometimes howler bags eat them. Beetle monkeys like to pry them off the trees and smash them. Twenty kinds of insects build nests on them."

The Yellow Scar churtrees came within range of another camera.

"If they meet, will they take turns?"

"No. It's a free for all. You would think they would try to find a way to not fight. Both tribes are dwindling; the Red Scar churtree are gone. Why can't they see that this warfare is useless?"

"Perhaps instinct for war is stronger than intelligence."

"Could be. Yet we know the Orange Scars can learn. When they hear our runabouts coming they decide that something off the trail is more interesting and they leave before there is a confrontation. They don't attack our ships that are delivering schools of salmon to their bays anymore. Instead, they go spelunking after pack bats."

"You said they always try to kill you."

"They still do if we get within thirty meters of them. That's why we made sure the runabouts were noisy. When the churtrees hear them, they move themselves out of the automatic attack range."

"Thirty meters. Hmm," Jax held her chin.

"The range is a meter for members of the tribe who aren't hunting bonded or immediate family."

Jax snickered. "One man, one wife, for life?"

"Hardly. There is no romantic love among the churtree. The females mate with the strongest whenever they can sneak away from whoever is providing their food. Since the males go out to sea to fish about half the time, the females have a lot of time to play the harlot. If whoever she is living with at the time she gives birth can tell the quadruplets aren't his, he chops up the babies and throws them in the bay."

"How can he tell?"

"I don't know. They all look the same to me."

"The mother allows this?"

"No. But the male usually wins the fight. After all, he hasn't just given birth. Sometimes, after all is said and done, they stay together and produce a litter that is his. Sometimes they separate. Oh."

The churtrees in each view stopped. They screeched in unison.

Rejoice tensed. Jax held her breath as her eyes widened.

The churtree abruptly stopped screeching and stood like statues in the brown and gray jungle.

Her heartbeat measured time.

The Yellow Scar churtree in front of his line threw down one of his spears and charged toward the distant Orange Scar churtree. The Orange Scars did not move.

"What?" asked Rejoice.

The Yellow Scar skidded to a stop about twenty meters from the Orange Scar troop, and with a howl it slammed its remaining spear into the ground. The Yellow Scar pivoted and raced back to its group, which then squatted on the trail.

The lead Orange Scar now threw down one of his spears and galloped to the spear in the trail. When he reached it, he too howled and plunged his remaining spear into the soil. When he rejoined his troop, they squatted and screamed, each dual vocal cord at two tones. The two bands alternated screaming at each other. Then slowly and deliberately, the two bands turned and walked away from each other.

Noble whooped in the next room. Rejoice used her hand to push her chin up until her teeth clicked.

"This is not usual?" Jax asked.

PACIFISTS' WAR CHAPTER NINE

A drop of water hung from every apple leaf tip, shining like crystal in the sunlight. Rejoice unrolled a bamboo mat onto the wet clover. Steelware clinked against a jar of soapy water as Opportunity set a basket on the mat.

Ignoring the shiny spoons, Makepeace plucked a rosy apple, shaking a shower upon himself. He lowered to the mat to study the apple's contours as he rotated it between his fingertips.

Rejoice grabbed a branch to steady herself as dizziness swirled her vision for a few seconds. Water spots darkened her brown sleeves. She twisted off a purple apple.

"Oh-oh," called Opportunity beside the yellow New Edo apple tree. "There's a stinger nest being built here."

Rejoice watched for stingers. "Let Noble get that." Beyond her sister, on the yellow brick road, Jax walked toward them, wearing her black oriental jacket, black lipstick, and red eye shadow. She rubbed her wrist against her neck, a motion that nagged Rejoice until she remembered where she had seen it before: on an Old Earth vid where the leading character had put on perfume. But when Jax came closer, Rejoice could not smell any special scent. Perhaps the Rational was just fidgeting again.

Jax stepped into the cool, wet shade . "Up already? I brought you something to occupy yourself while in bed."

Makepeace peeked at Jax over the curve of apple. "The shadows creep along the wall."

Jax turned her back to him as she handed Rejoice another small screen.

"Problems in topology."

"I don't know," Rejoice said. "I think you have to be a little crazy to truly understand and like topology. I prefer a firmer math."

Opportunity rolled her eyes and quoted Rejoice, "With crystalline structure and beautiful order, God's language of creation."

Rejoice wondered why when her sister said it, it sounded silly. Was that what she sounded like to Opportunity?

Jax reached up and tore off an apple and the fruiting spur it was attached to as well. "Quantum fifth level diffusion is ordered?"

"Once you accept the discontinuity between macro and micro and learn its logic, it is. Hmm, not logic, language."

Jax's fingers tightened around the apple as she stretched, catlike, with every muscle of her body. The black sleeves slid down her arms. Dappled sun and shade showed the tiny hairs on newly-tanned skin and shifted across the fine network of fold lines on the fabric. Abruptly her hands dropped to her sides. "I like the elasticity of topology."

Rejoice laughed. The smells of apple, moist soil, how the shadows moved over the curves of Jax's ear and dangling red earrings delighted her beyond words. "I guess I should be willing to learn the logic of topology." She slipped the screen into her pocket. "As soon as I catch up on air and space-port businesses, I'll get started on it."

"Start a heart," crooned Makepeace. "Stop a heart. Step into my parlor said the spider to the fly."

Opportunity jerked an apple off a tree. "Oh, hush. You've never even seen a fly."

"On vids he has," Rejoice said as Makepeace said, "A hundred ways to see and flee."

Jax bit into her apple. "For truth, a basket of these for my students would be a good exchange."

Rejoice pulled the screen back out of her pocket. "I'll return it as soon as I'm done with the program."

"For rent. Twenty apples then."

Rejoice shook her head. The colonists never haggled. Why did Jax en-

Joy it so?

"Fifteen then, and a half liter of tomatoes."

"Take whatever you want." Anything to stop the process.

Gracefully, Jax swiveled and leaped to snatch two apples higher in the canopy. Rejoice marveled at how fast Jax could dart from tree to tree. In two minutes she had her apples in a black drawstring bag pulled from a sleeve and then slung over her shoulder. With one foot before the other, she bowed toward the sisters. "I'll come back for the tomatoes later."

They watched as Jax pirouetted and headed back to the dojo. "My," said Rejoice, "the next time she does that, I want to record it."

"I wish you looked at me with such awe," Noble said behind them.

Rejoice jumped. "Oh, Noble, I do sometimes, but it's hard to maintain a steady state of ecstasy. Eventually you run out of endorphins."

He picked up a basket and moved to the tree with candy-green apples. "You sound like my mother." Jubilee slept peacefully in his backpack.

Rejoice picked up a few purple apples. "Not to be rude, but why are you out here?"

"Sister Cytowitz is on a private retreat. I have a few minutes."

A disgusting jelly rested on an apple. Rejoice shook it off to let it splat on the clover. "A private retreat. That sounds heavenly. I wish I could do that."

"You could retreat to your bed." After a moment, he added, "Sister Zystra just delivered a baby boy."

Rejoice smiled. "Any problems?"

"Nope. Mommy, Daddy, and little Overcomer are all doing well."

Rejoice sighed and tried to suppress her automatic envy of women who carried and delivered healthy babies with such ease.

Noble apparently noticed her reaction. He placed his arm around her shoulder and kissed the top of her head. "The churtree peace still holds."

She looked up at him. "Remind me again who took Brother Zystra's place with the churtree."

Noble watched the sky. "Brother Carver switched months with me. So I'm scheduled to go out in seven weeks, remember?"

"Oh, yes." She repressed another sigh.

Rejoice watched Opportunity picking apples and tossing them into her basket, bruising them so that Rejoice would need to turn them into applesauce. Everything her sister did to help ended up creating more work for Rejoice. That she liked a clean and well-ordered house led to disliking what Opportunity did to her home. Rejoice had said it before and she knew what Noble would say, and what was the point of repetition?

Rejoice lowered her arms gone leaden from exhaustion. "It's a mystery to me why I like Jax so much when she's for everything I'm against, and against everything I'm for." Hmm. Was there some way to extend the same grace to Opportunity?

Opportunity moved to the Blue Paradise apple tree. "There's no mystery to it at all. We're both lonely. You're the only physicist in the colony. I'm the only artist. You finally found somebody you can talk to without their eyes glazing over."

Rejoice leaned against a tree to keep her knees from buckling. "Why do you say you're the only artist when ninety percent of us embroider or stencil or sew?"

Opportunity threw down her basket and the apples bounced and rolled through the clover like so many yertles. "I'm talking about art! Art that says something! What does quilting say? What does stenciling wheat heads around a doorway say? I'm not talking about Mother embroidering holly leaves everywhere like a dog marking its territory!"

Hearing Mother denigrated broke Rejoice's patience. "Opportunity, I absolutely do not see any difference between what you do and what the rest of us do. You just—"

Opportunity flung her hands into the air. "That's exactly my point! I'm lonely!" Her glossy black hair swung and rippled as she turned and ran to the house.

"Clashing, crashing," Makepeace said.

A bubble drifted in front of Rejoice's face and popped. Her brother was blowing bubbles. His apple bobbed in the jar of soapy water.

Noble said. "Rejoice, I want you to go to bed and stay there until you recover. Look how your hands are shaking."

Rejoice shoved her hands into her pockets. "Now you sound like my mother." On her way to the house, she stepped on a forgotten, rotten apple.

* * *

A month later, Rejoice squinted against the sunlight sparkling on the swells of Ti Bay. The edges of the blue canopy on the barge rippled gently in the breeze. The moist air smelled of seaweed rotting on the shore and fish scales smeared on the deck. Sitting in a barge on Ti Bay felt like slipping on comfortable slippers after a day of wearing shoes that pinched.

Beside her, Opportunity helped Mark adjust his scuba straps. His wetsuit bagged about his knees. Rejoice's suit strained around her middle, reminding her she still had weight to lose.

"Bye, Mother!" Mark flipped backwards over the railing of the barge. Water splattered on the baby's face. His little fists jerked as he gasped.

"Oh, oh, oh, what a surprise for Jubilee," Noble sang as he jiggled the baby on his lap.

The baby screamed as Rejoice adjusted the hard casing on her remodeled flipper that was supposed to protect her toes during her dive to the Ti cluster to visit the babies newly out of their niches.

Noble leaned over the railing and dipped the baby's feet in the warm water. "Look how well Jubilee can hold his head up."

Opportunity helped Ernest with his apparatus. Then she slipped on her mask, and together they splashed into the bay. Bubbles roiled the water. Noble swung the baby so his feet plowed the sea. The baby hiccupped and watched the glinting light. Suddenly a blue tentacle wrapped around his tiny foot and then dropped back into the water.

"Whoa-ho!" Noble pulled his son back over the railing. "Who was that?"

Rejoice swiveled on the orange cushion and tapped on the screen connected to the underwater cameras of the barge. A hexacrab on a scooter darted after Opportunity and Ernest. "A youngster. Yes. Ha! It's Ur-Chantot. He's six now, isn't he?"

Opportunity snatched at the scooter and a slow motion wrestling match ensued.

Noble laughed and lifted the baby to his shoulder to pat him. "Every day Ur-Chantot looks more and more like Ur-Nissi."

Rejoice studied the screen. "You're right. Their mottling is identical. I hadn't noticed that before. Now, there's an irony considering what Ur-Nissi thinks of Brother Hancock. Do you suppose we'll ever see Ur-Nissi again or even find out what happened to him?"

Noble sat down and continued to pat his son. The baby's cheeks jiggled with every pat. "Not until they feel like telling us. Hexacrabs keep secrets better than anybody I know."

"Sometimes I'm tempted to listen in on the hexacrab channels to see if I can catch them talking to the missing hexacrabs."

"Ah, ah, ah. We gave our word, and I intend to keep it."

"So noble."

Noble wrinkled his nose momentarily before nibbling on his baby's ears and nuzzling his downy cheeks. The baby's face lit up with a slobbery, toothless grin. Noble glanced at the screen. Opportunity and Ernest swam shoulder to shoulder. His face fell. "I think I made a huge mistake when I asked Opportunity to stay longer."

Rejoice cleaned under her fingernails with her thumbnail. The extended stay was her fault.

Noble continued, "I'm going to talk to her tonight about being un-equally yoked and then hand her the tickets home. Do you mind?"

"I already asked her to leave next Oneday."

"And what did she say?"

Rejoice swallowed. "That she wants to stay longer and continue to practice being responsible. That she thinks I still need help. That the accident proves she isn't mature enough to marry yet. And she wants to stay under your pastoring to help her mature."

Noble shook his head. "How much of that was sincere?"

None of it. "I don't know." Same parents, such different lives. Rejoice held memories of a strong father, and a cute little brother. Opportunity had always had a sick father and an older brother with many difficulties. Rejoice could not understand how Opportunity thought.

Noble and Rejoice gazed at each other sadly as the baby fidgeted and burped loudly.

"You haven't eaten in the last two days," Rejoice said. "How long is this fast going to be?"

Noble sighed before he kissed the soft spot on his son's head. "Pastor Wiseman says the young men of his congregation are enthralled by the Robersonians, excuse me, the rationals. Those people sauntering through town with their knives and guns and glitter."

"I should think the problem would be the half-naked women."

"That too. My counseling sessions with the men have taken a radical change in the last month. I've quoted Job more in the last month than in the last decade."

"Job?"

"I have made a covenant with my eyes. Why should I look upon a young woman?"

"Good verse."

"Pastor Wiseman was telling me about all the counseling that he used to have to do on Old Earth with men with wandering eyes, addicted to pornography, living double lives of adultery in the dark of night. He was hoping that he wouldn't have to go back to those bad old days."

"You've counseled men with wandering eyes before."

"Of course. Men are sexually stimulated by their eyes and their imaginations. But our church community is small. And accountability is tight. Our founders chose our dress style accounting for those weaknesses of men. Loose-fitting brown dresses and pants are the least stimulating styles to a man's eye."

Rejoice laughed. "The elders might have made us all wear chadors like some Muslims."

Noble shook his head and smiled. "Now that's something Deaconess Redhorse would never have agreed to. She still carps about the dress code every five or so years. And she always loses the vote. The men here dress modestly and plainly also."

"Uh-huh. You kept taking off your shirt on the *Magellan* to incite lust in me."

"That's not why—" Noble cleared his throat. "Did it work?"

Rejoice smirked. "My mother's grandfather was in the army before he became a pacifist. He told her the only good part of being in the army was that you never had to decide what to put on in the morning. You only had to have a clean uniform. I must take after him. Even if it were allowed, I don't believe that I'd ever wear anything but a sister's brown dress."

Noble smiled. "And you look beautiful in it."

Rejoice snorted. "Well, I'm glad you think so."

"It's not as if the Robersonian women were flirting or attempting to attract our men. In fact, they walk and talk like men. But some men will become dissatisfied with their wives."

Rejoice took a sharp breath. "What about your eyes? Are you being tempted by all these tight, skimpy outfits?" She thought of her slumping midriff and Jax's sleek, toned form.

Noble paused. "Not really. I naturally look people in the eyes. So that helps. Many shy men's eyes naturally look elsewhere. It only took me a couple of times of walking behind these women to learn to look at the back of their heads."

He paused again. "There's only one body that I've ever loved or will love." He sighed deeper. "I hope you get well soon."

"You don't need to sound so desperate."

"I'm not desperate, but I'm getting there. Don't you miss it at all?"

"I'm so exhausted, the only thing I miss is sleep."

Noble smiled and squeezed her shoulder. "Are you sure, then, that you should be diving?"

Despite the oppressive air, Rejoice repressed the urge to sigh because he might misinterpret it. "I've never missed a Hatching Day yet."

Noble stuck his finger in the baby's mouth and rubbed the gums so vigorously, they squeaked. The baby smiled around the finger. "What did Jax say when you told her to make sure her compound was tied down?"

"She told me not to worry. They don't need to huddle in the Meeting-place because all their buildings are hurricane proof."

"You did tell them the winds could gust up to two hundred kilometers per hour?"

"I gave them all the stats on Hurricane Pernicious. They didn't even blink."

"Proud people." Noble shifted and his flipper squeaked on the deck with a noise much like the one he was making in the baby's mouth. "Jax enjoys visiting you."

Rejoice leaned back and listened to the deceptive, gentle sea. Jax didn't visit her any more than Ernest visited Noble. Ernest reminded Rejoice of a puppy as he followed Noble and helped him with the exercise training. She wiped a trickle of sweat from her temple. "I have to admit I enjoy her visits. In some ways, Opportunity was right. After Father died and Sister Guthry moved to Promise, there's been no one to talk to about physics and math. I have to keep telling myself that even if we had stayed on Old Earth, I still would not have been allowed to work in research."

"Research is what this Mission is about."

"Well, yes. But I prefer clean gamma rays to squishy guts or death rituals. Anyway, I enjoy her visits. We play logic games and talk about physics. You can't imagine what Old Earth discovered at the Moon Collider."

"You're right. I can't."

Rejoice smiled and looked out on the smooth sea with its quicksilver colors of green and gray and blue and pale gold. "So, can you tell me how things are going at work? Yesterday, after one session, you ran to the sink and splashed your head with cold water. What was that all about?"

"I was trying to wake up. I don't know what I'm going to do with Sister Peace With God Sharmat."

Rejoice fanned her face as she tried to remember. Yes, three years younger than she, a pale woman who never said anything, never did anything Rejoice could remember except for sitting in the back row in morning school. She grew up and married that loudmouth Walk In The Ways Of God, and they both worked in the textile mill. "What's the nature of the problem?"

"I was the one who called Sister Sharmat to initiate a project because she posed a challenge to me."

"What do you mean?"

"I've known her for years, and not once had I heard her say anything but one syllable replies to direct questions. It doesn't usually take me long to figure out people's motivations and likes and dislikes. But I couldn't figure out anything about her. She's a mystery. What does she think? What does she feel?"

"And?"

"I still don't know. She might like cake decorating." The baby spit up on Noble's hand and Rejoice laughed.

He fished a towel from the bag next to him and wiped the baby's front. "She memorized scripture slowly, because I told her to, but her heart wasn't in it. I came up with a dozen projects. She did them all without enthusiasm. Then she told me Brother Sharmat had complained that she was boring. I didn't think it would be helpful if I agreed with him.

"So I tried to tell her that most men are simple minded. If she made sure to feed him lots of protein calories, not gripe at him, and use some of the more exotic techniques in the Sex Manual, he would likely be happy. I thought she would get embarrassed, or indignant, or something that would give me clue as to what was going on inside. But she simply nodded and said she did that. So I gave her a list of twenty-five hobbies and told her she had to start one or else."

Rejoice laughed again. "Or else what?"

"I don't know, and she didn't ask. She never does. Yesterday, I asked her what she had chosen. She spent twenty minutes telling me how she made a frosting rose in that dull drone of hers. It was obvious she was telling me this just to get me off her back. I think I snored twice, but she never noticed. I need to hand her off to somebody else for counseling. But I can't think of anybody I don't want to stay on good terms with."

Rejoice pressed on her side where the muscles ached from her laughter. "As bad as that?"

"If she could be bottled, she would make a perfect sedative. I feel wicked even thinking that."

"Oh, dear." She wiped her eyes. "Do you suppose your mother would be willing to take her on?"

Noble spread his fingers across his broad chest. "My mother? She's as good at counseling as you are. No. I don't sic my mother on anybody except as a last resort."

The baby fussed and Noble rubbed the toothless gums again.

Rejoice watched the shifting colors of the sea. The cliffs surrounding the bay glared in the harsh sunlight. She wiped away another trickle of sweat and listened to the soft sea gurgle under the barge.

"What about your work?" asked Noble.

She blew out through pursed lips. "Let's see. Things continue as before on the Starflower and the Asteroid Ambling Mine. I don't have enough volunteers for the next mission yet. You already know the Robersonians added five satellites to ours and that doubled our asteroid surveillance rate."

"Uh-huh. You could finish in a decade, right?"

"The basic charts, yes. But we'll always need to keep a lookout for the odd asteroid with a five hundred or five-thousand-year orbit."

Nobles' dark eyes narrowed as he looked at the sea. "It was better in some ways before the Robersonians deployed their satellites."

"They were a lot humbler when they were receiving charity from us, weren't they?"

"I think it's incredible that we've managed to survive on this difficult world for nineteen years, and when these people show up, they instantly know we've done it all wrong. I think I know how the Native Americans felt when the European settlers showed up."

"Hmm. Will our fate be the same?"

Noble shrugged and shifted the baby to the other knee. "Elder Chin thinks so. I can't tell. I'm not responsible for the future. I'm only responsible for my ethical behavior today." His lips brushed the top of the baby's head. "However, the prudent man looks ahead. I have not been prudent about your sister."

"There are more Robersonians in First City than there are here."

"Salient point. But He Gives is there to hopefully keep her focused." He sighed. "So many of us had no choices before, and now we have several. Are we strong enough to make the right ones?"

Rejoice looked at the screen view of water and kelp. "I wish they would hurry up. Oh, speaking of choices, almost every time Jax visits, she urges me to leave you and join her 'family'."

Noble's feet thumped on the deck and the baby jumped. "What? I've been extending hospitality to someone who is trying to make you leave me?"

"She's just teasing, the way she does to see how far she can push us."

"And what do you answer her?"

"I tell her it wouldn't do any good. I'd still be on the same island as the churtrees."

Noble's face darkened as he scowled at Rejoice. "That's your answer?"

"Why answer nonsense with reason? I don't argue with her because you told me to get along with her."

His face darkened further. "Getting along should not require capitulation."

"What are you so angry about? I haven't surrendered anything except the right to rebuke her because you told me not to. You do remember telling me not to antagonize her, don't you?"

The muscles in his jaw shifted. The baby wailed as Noble said flatly, "What I feel about Sister Sharmat is what you feel about me."

Rejoice gasped. She looked about wildly.

Noble startled. "What? Do you hear a pack bat?"

"No. I'm looking for where that thought came from. It certainly didn't come from me."

"This isn't funny, Rejoice."

Mark whooshed out of the sea and grabbed the ladder. He pulled off his mask to shout, "They got more babies than ever! Wait 'til you see them! Ur-Siti even gots two tied on his shell. And they're both girls!"

Noble thrust the baby at Rejoice and then reached down to help pull Mark up the ladder. "Come on up, hardhead. My turn." No sooner did Mark stand dripping on the deck than Noble splashed under the surface of the sea.

The baby wailed and squirmed as Rejoice clutched him close.

"Mother! Look!" Mark thrust a pink shell under Rejoice's nose, and she leaned back to admire it. "Mother, can I watch the hexacrabs sink the barge this afternoon?"

Rejoice calculated. To keep the vessels safe the hexacrabs would sink all the vessels an hour or two before the strong winds began. "You'll have to ask your father. We still have some trees to tie down before the hurricane hits."

"Can I stay up and watch it? We won't have school tomorrow."

It was hard to hear her older son over the cries of the baby. "We'll see. Would you please open the locker? Father forgot to take the baby presents."

Mark skipped to the locker and pulled out the bag of shiny bobbers on short cords with catches on the end. "Can I have one for me? Since I can't have a dog for a pet, can I have a crab? Would a crab play with a bobber?"

"Crabs don't play."

"Can I have a yertle for a pet?"

Opportunity and Ernest surfaced and splashed up the ladder.

Ernest took off his mask and brushed his blonde hair out of his eyes. "Incredible! Hexacrabs are fundabulous. Can I buy one of those spears with teeth in them?"

Opportunity laughed heartily as she took the baby. "Silly, you have to dance with death to earn one of those."

Rejoice kissed Mark as she took the bag of bobbers from him. "Let's make sure all the babies get one before we talk about how many you get."

The warm waters closed over her head, and she relaxed in its embrace. A cloud of hexacrabs on scooters engulfed her, and together they drifted to the oozy bay floor. Tentacles wrapped and unwrapped about her knees and wrists as dozens of hexacrabs jostled around Noble and her. All the older hexacrabs carried smaller, uncoordinated versions of themselves tied to their shells. Rejoice clipped a bobber on the ropes tying down each tiny hexacrab. The youngster hexacrabs clambered over the older to fondle the bobbers with delight as the babies squeaked and the older ones clicked and whistled greetings to the humans.

Ur-Veena crept calmly through the surging mass of hexacrabs and scooters to position himself before Noble. One of his vision eyes stayed trained on the little one on his back and the other two fixed on Noble. "You have said that most of the Crusaders were not Christians."

Rejoice bit her lip to keep from laughing. Never one for small talk, the hexacrabs always picked up the discussion where they had left off, even if a year intervened.

Noble wrapped his fingers around two of Ur-Veena's tentacles. "Only God can truly judge. They were responding to the atrocities of the Muslims and the call for help from the Byzantines. But their response did not advance the Kingdom of God."

Rejoice paused in her dispersal of bobbers to watch. She loved hearing the actual hexacrab words and how their idioms were translated into English by Elder Chin's program.

"You say that St. Francis of Assisi was a true Christian."

"We think so. He walked unarmed into a Muslim camp to talk to their leader about Christ."

"I name this little one Ti-Assisi."

Rejoice released a bobber, and it shot up. A youngster joyfully whizzed after it on his scooter.

"Shall Ti-Assisi be the first hexacrab to live in peace with the churtrees?" asked Noble.

Ur-Veena rippled a tentacle until the tips snapped out straight, a gesture of dismissal. "There will be no peace until all the churtrees are dead."

Amen. Rejoice looked away. *I'm sorry, Noble.* She needed to try harder. Yet if she hadn't learned to love the churtrees in fifteen years, how would she ever?

"Our listening to your histories tells us that you think most of the Puritans were true Christians."

"Yes. We take many lessons from them. And the Quakers, Mennonites, and Amish."

"However the Puritans also carried many weapons."

"We don't agree with everything—"

"Gotta check my air," choked Rejoice, and flippered quickly to the surface. She tore her mask off when she reached the ladder and clung to the rungs as she gasped and laughed.

Opportunity leaned over the railing. "Are you all right?"

It took several tries before Rejoice could finish the sentence, "Were you following the conversation?"

"No. Do you want me to turn it on?"

Rejoice nodded. "I don't know if the hexacrabs or Elder Chin did it, but their translation for Puritans means one who wishes to taste currents no one has excreted in."

As Rejoice struggled to regain a normal breathing pattern so she could re-descend, Opportunity turned on the screen and listened. After a minute, Opportunity shut it off and leaned over the railing. "It's the same old argument. If we admit that some of the people who killed other people were Christians, then why don't we let the hexacrabs walk into the churtree villages and slaughter everybody?"

Ernest leaned over the railing. "How can you stop them?"

Rejoice lowered herself one rung so she could float on her back while talking. "We told them that if we ever caught them killing a churtree when they had a way to avoid it, they would never receive another bullet or charge from us. They're smart enough to realize that guns without bullets are pretty useless."

Mark joined in. "Did you pass out all the bobbers?"

"Oh, Rejoice," Opportunity said, "Ernest wants to know when we're going to try to make peace with the churtrees by doing the 'impaling the earth that births us to fight' ritual."

Rejoice grabbed a rung and pulled herself upright. A muscle in her abdomen twinged. "Not soon. Elder Chin has translated only the bottom harmonic of the first sentence. First he has to translate the entire transaction between Yellow and Orange Scar. Then we have to answer hundreds of questions like: Must this precise speech be used in the peace treaty? What are the necessary preconditions? What breaks the treaty? Can treaties be formed between different species? It goes on and on. We're moving slowly because we don't want to precipitate another mass suicide."

Ernest leaned over the edge. "You're always careful and holding yourselves back. Why bother? Why not let the two species fight it out?"

"Excuse me. We'll talk later," Rejoice fitted on her mask. Why bother to be polite to such rude people? Indeed, why were they bothering to tell the Good News to hexacrabs, churtrees, and Robersonians? No one in any of the three ever changed. She dismissed her brooding to give herself to the delight of water pressure, the flow of sea between her fingers, and the sight of mottled blue, indigo, and pearl hexacrabs, the embraces of strong tentacles, the swirl of festivity for the new children and friendship between the air and water-ocean peoples.

PACIFISTS' WAR CHAPTER TEN

That night, as Rejoice wearily scraped rice from the bottom of her bowl, she studied Makepeace sitting across the dining table from Mark. How could she cut his hair differently? Her heart had skipped a beat when she had gone to the Hancock's to pick up Makepeace and saw Brother Hancock and her brother walking in the garden. Makepeace had looked exactly like Father. Perhaps if she cut his hair much, much shorter, she wouldn't have so many of these heart-stopping episodes.

Noble stacked the bowls and Mark collected the steelware. While Opportunity rinsed, father and son disappeared down the hallway for a few minutes. When they returned, Mark took his uncle's hand and led him to his room to play pickup sticks.

Noble set three cups of apple-mint tea on the table. "Opportunity, please sit with us. We need to talk."

Opportunity carefully dried each finger with the dish towel. "I was expecting this. You need to preach at the wayward daughter."

Rejoice wrapped her hands around the warm, fragrant cup, but her arms were too tired to bring it to her lips. The baby fussed in his crib, and outside, the wind rushed over the bubble house and its sealed windows and doors. If only she weren't the adult that must do the confronting and comforting. How much better to be the child that is tucked in. Noble considered his words. Opportunity examined a thread in the towel.

Noble said slowly, "I would rather not preach until I'm in the pulpit tomorrow morning. Why don't we just talk tonight? I want to know what you're thinking. Do you think you're wayward?"

"I don't know." She picked at a thread. "I've been doing a lot of thinking about the things we do in the colony, and suddenly a lot of things don't make sense."

Noble murmured, "Such as?"

"Such as . . ." Opportunity paced back and forth behind the table and twisted the towel. "You want me to go home and marry He Gives Eternal Life, don't you?"

"It would be disastrous for both of you to do that if you're not sure you want to."

"I'm not sure. I'm not sure of anything. The rationals don't believe in God and they have a lot more fun than we do. They don't have 'don't do this' and 'don't do that' dogging their every step."

The walls of the house shivered under a gust.

"Which don'ts are bothering you?"

"All of them."

Noble raised his eyebrows in mock surprise. "You mean, don't jump off a cliff and don't stick your head in a combine?"

"Don't make fun of me. I'm not a child."

Rejoice turned her head so Opportunity wouldn't see her roll her eyes. The pungent smell of the green berry tomato vines tacked to the interior walls filled the room. Jugs of water, in case the desalinization plant fell, and emergency batteries filled the space under the computer counter. Maybe now, when there was no way to escape each other, was not a good time to have this discussion. Something thumped outside.

"You do understand my point. The rules that God gives us may frustrate us for a time. But in His love He gives them to us for our protection and eventual joy and fulfillment. Are we talking about sexual don'ts?"

"I guess so." Opportunity's face flamed. She glared at Rejoice. "I haven't done anything. The people at the dojo can't decide if that's pathetic or hilarious. I can't decide either."

Rejoice glared back, but kept silent. Let Noble handle it.

Noble rubbed his upper lip. "I'm worried about you. I could not stand to see you thrown out as pearls before swine and trampled into mire." "I can't believe you said that. Ernest helps you every day in your exercise class, and you just called him a pig."

"I don't know if he is or not. You, I do know. When you give your heart away, you're going to give it all. The Robersonians don't give their hearts to anybody. I don't want to see you hurt."

"You're wrong. They love as much as we do. They love more than we do and they aren't judgmental."

"It's wise to judge between mushrooms and toadstools when you're cooking dinner."

Opportunity frowned and sat down. "And what do you do when you find out you've been lied to about which is which?"

Rejoice squeezed her cup. Fear caught at her breath. What wreckage would they find when this storm had blasted through?

Noble sat silent, his brows drawn together, his breathing growing slower and deliberate.

Yes, she should be calming down, too. *God of peace, God of light—*

Makepeace tiptoed into the dining room. "The sea rages and pounds the crags with thousands of hooves," he quoted.

"This is a bad storm, but we'll stay safe in our home," Rejoice said.

"Mother? Mother?"

"Mother is safe in First City."

Opportunity watched him with narrowed eyes as he ambled about the room, touching every place a reflection gleamed with his forefinger. Mark came out and tugged him back into his room.

Opportunity said distantly, "The people at the dojo don't understand why we work so hard to keep someone so brain-damaged alive."

"So what are you suggesting we should do?" Rejoice said. "Should we shoot our brother?"

Opportunity shifted in her seat. "I don't want to shoot Makepeace."

Her voice rose. "What then? Should we leave him outside so the hurricane can blow him away and do our dirty work for us?"

"No. I'm not saying that."

Rejoice stood, knocking over her tea, and shouted, "What *are* you saying?"

"I'm not, well, if, if he had died as a baby, our lives would have been a whole lot easier."

"Murdering Father when he first got sick would have made life easier too! And maybe Stronghold should smother Harmony some—"

"Rejoice!" Noble commanded.

She stood panting and staring at her sister. The spilled tea spread across the table and dripped off the edge.

"Joy of my life," Noble said softly, "Jubilee needs to eat. Why don't you take care of him?"

Outside, a roar preceded a blast of wind that made the walls quiver.

Rejoice walked stiffly toward the bedroom door as she breathed through clenched teeth. *God of peace, God of light.* Once inside the bedroom door, she leaned against the printed slab and trembled.

The baby screamed. Reluctantly she moved toward him and clutched the sides of the crib. Would all the children she had miscarried have been as awful as this one? If he had died as a baby, would she miss him? *God, why does this baby hate me?* The baby's wail reached the pitch that bored a hole in her brain. Her heart still pounded from her anger at Opportunity.

A sudden weakness in her arms almost made her drop the baby as she shuffled with him toward the bed. Outside the door, the gentle voice of Noble continued, low and slow; and Opportunity's staccato voice rose higher. She blinked out tears as she tried to nurse her struggling baby.

Much later, when the wind outside was screaming and the wall of the house vibrated and the door frames creaked with tension, Noble entered the bedroom.

As Rejoice absentmindedly patted her fitfully-sleeping baby's back, she watched her husband undress in the low light. Strong arms, strong legs, the beginning of a gut he did not have when they first married, scars on his chest and abdomen from his encounters with kraken and churtrees. He pulled on pajama bottoms and slid gently into bed so as not to waken his little son lying between him and Rejoice. He picked up his computer and called up a lesson in Hebrew.

"Well?" Rejoice whispered.

He kept his eyes fastened to the screen. "I don't know." After a pause, he added. "You need to be careful about what you say to your sister, or you will drive her right into the arms of the Robersonians."

"She wants to kill our brother."

"She does not. She's feeling overwhelmed. What she needs right now is the blessing of our love and our prayers. I told her she could stay a few more months until she sorts out her feelings." He flipped the screen to another section.

The screaming wind became a chorus.

Rejoice watched the handsome profile of his face. He always looked intently at her when he talked to her. Why was he looking away now? "I want to talk about this morning."

"I've thought about it. There's no utility in discussing it. I'm sorry I said it. The case is closed." He highlighted a word in the passage on his screen.

"May I make one statement?"

"I've never been able to prevent you from doing as you please."

He made her move to Largest Archipelago. She took a deep breath. "You lied about me thinking you're dull, and I don't like that."

After a few moments, he said. "Objection heard." He scrolled down the screen to another passage.

So. She lay back on the pillow and stared at the ceiling. Overwhelmed. All of them. She thought of Makepeace and his sweet almond eyes, like Father's eyes and now Jubilee's eyes. She thought of how Makepeace had cracked rocks on Ocean Shore Boulder, the flashes of wit that shone through a fractured understanding. What kind of genius would he have been if he had not been conceived and born during warp?

She turned her head to watch Noble type. Case closed. He thought she was hopeless. Rejoice slid out of bed. "I'm getting a drink of water. Can I get you something?"

He glanced at her, and then scowled. "Why can't you keep yourself buttoned up properly? Your brother might be out there."

Rejoice looked down at the gap. "I guess the baby stretched the buttonhole. I'll sew it up tomorrow." She fumbled with the button. What did she need to do to get him out of this funk he was in? She faced him and began unbuttoning.

Noble looked up. "What are you doing?"

"I think the proper thing would be to unbutton all of them. What do you think?"

"I think you ought not tease me. I don't need that right now."

"I'm not teasing." She sat on the edge of the bed. Oops. She'd need to move the baby, and that would wake him up.

"I don't want to hurt you. I'm not touching you until Doctor Carlson gives his okay."

"I feel fine," Rejoice lied.

His computer beeped. He sighed before he opened the connection.

Pastor Wiseman looked distraught on the screen. "I'm sorry to bother you like this," he glanced at his watch, "this late at night for you." His image wavered. "You need to go over to the Green's and talk to Sister Redhorse right away."

"Not possible," Noble said. As if to punctuate his words, a thump shuddered the walls. "I don't know if you heard that, but I think we just lost one of our apple trees."

"That's right. You're in the midst of a hurricane." Pastor Wiseman rubbed his face. "Call her and talk to her. Today, her brother, God Is Our Provider Redhorse abandoned his wife and children and ran off to the Robersonians. Deaconess Redhorse is calling her daughter now because she wants to let her know before the rest of the colony hears what her brother did. You know how Sister Redhorse tends to carry on."

Noble rubbed his forehead. He knew. She had lost her voice for a week when she scolded the dojo students for an hour after she caught them trying to break into the library to use it as a base in their war games. She had followed them scolding all the way to the dojo and did not stop until Jax promised to set up surrounding warders twenty meters away from the library to mark it off-limits to the students. Then Sister Redhorse had complained another hour at Noble. "I'll call her right now." He cut the connection. "And so it begins," he murmured, and waited one breath. He flung aside the quilt, threw on his black shirt, and walked out to the main screen.

Rejoice slowly buttoned up her pajamas again as the baby woke and soiled his diaper. Slowly she changed him and laid him screaming in his crib. She lay staring at the ceiling, listening to the storm raging outside and the baby crying inside, until a nightmare-filled sleep claimed her.

* * *

Rejoice started awake, her mouth dry and her heart racing. She blinked her eyes and patted the bed beside her. Noble was gone. The baby was missing, too, and clear sunlight streamed through the unsealed window.

What a nightmare. Noble had pushed her off a cliff. Or had she tossed the baby over the cliff and fallen after it? The images faded, but the sense of dread remained.

She rolled out of bed and dressed. In the empty kitchen, a plate of toast and a bowl of sugared tomatoes and cream awaited her. She ate in front of the screen as she checked monitors to all the mission's systems. Water, electricity, warehouses, they all looked functional. Half the churtree cameras had disappeared. Noble's announcement that the Lord's Day service had been delayed three hours blinked in one corner. No families reported emergencies, and all families were still on-line. Good and good. Each season found them better able to cope with the hurricanes that scoured the islands of New Earth.

A quick weather analysis: no ships in the hurricane's present course. Nothing new with the Starflower. Several dozen new asteroids, none of them in New Earth grazing orbits, none of them big enough to matter if they were. Good, and good again.

Outside, Rejoice tiptoed over the litter of burst bladders from the bladder trees, shredded leaves and branches, blistering jellies, and thorny vines. Most of their apple trees still stood, though denuded. The outer skin of their home bore a few more dents, but no cracks.

Opportunity and Makepeace raked the debris from the roadway.

Noble, wearing overalls, no shirt, and the baby on his back, held together a broken limb and wrapped tape around it. At his feet lay the pruned branches too shredded for repair.

Rejoice kissed him on his bare shoulder, the one with the circular, jagged scar. "You didn't get much sleep last night."

He wiped his forehead with his forearm. Dark circles showed under his eyes. "How would you know, sleepy lady?"

"Every time I woke up to nurse or to keep from crashing on the rocks, you were awake."

"Crashing?"

"Nightmares."

"But not the churtrees?"

"Not this time."

"Yes, a lot to think about. Could you sit beside me during the service and poke me if I fall asleep during meditation?"

"Why don't you let me take the baby and you take a nap before the service?"

"The cells in the bark might die. I need to fix the trees while they're fixable. I'll take a nap after service though. If you'll let me."

"Why wouldn't I let you?"

"You usually want me to do something with Jubilee."

Rejoice blinked. Why he would say that? She had assumed he had wanted to spend his Lord's Days with his sons. "Have you eaten?"

"No."

"Don't you think you should?"

"No."

"Since Opportunity is staying," she said, "and the baby has such a hard time nursing, I think it's time to invest in some synthesized milk and bottle-feed him. Then Opportunity could feed him at night and we could get the rest we need."

"And then you could have even less to do with Jubilee."

She opened her mouth to protest, and then forced it shut. He was exhausted and incapable of thinking straight. She could argue with him later when he was rested. She moved to the road to watch her sister gingerly scrape some jelly from her rake.

Mark danced up and hugged Rejoice. "We're going to have a bonfire and roast apples and popcorn over the fire. Right after service. My job is to find good sticks."

Rejoice stroked his hair. "Look before you touch. There're a lot of jellies here."

The squashing sound of wheels running over wet leaves and jellies interrupted them. Jax drove an unshielded jeeper toward them. She wore something black and baggy, and her pale face seemed curiously bland without her usual paint.

Jax pulled up even with Rejoice. She mumbled toward her hands on the steering wheel, "May we borrow some water from you?"

"All you want," said Rejoice. "Our pipes and plant held up. Can we help you any other way?"

"No."

Rejoice and Jax piled the water cartons from under the counter into the back of the jeeper without another word exchanged between them.

They had nearly filled the jeeper when Rejoice's computer beeped. She sat thankfully on the jeeper's front seat. "Cruz here."

The voice was Brother Petrovich's, the man in charge of the water plant. "Sister Cruz, can you reach the people at the dojo? We've got a body in the bay. It looks like one of theirs."

PACIFISTS' WAR CHAPTER ELEVEN

Rejoice turned to Jax.

The woman put in the last canister and said wearily, "You want me to confirm?"

"I think it would be a good idea. Yes."

Jax moved to the driver's seat and started the jeeper. Rejoice grabbed binoculars from the house. As they drove toward the bay cliff, Rejoice beeped each house to ask for men who had nothing urgent to attend to. As they neared the cliff, Rejoice looked up from her computer screen and paused. "I don't see the roof of your gymnasium."

"Good eyes." Jax stopped the jeeper.

They walked to the railing and Rejoice handed the binoculars to Jax. The woman studied the body broken on the talus for a few seconds. "For truth, it's Carl. I thought he was hiding to avoid the work of cleanup."

"I'm sorry. We'll help you retrieve the body."

"Why bother? He was not wanted by any of the families. Instead of changing his behavior, he chose to kill himself. As you would say, let the dead bury the dead."

Rejoice froze, her mind rejecting what she had just heard. "Were there other people killed?"

"No, no. All showed for breakfast, even Carl."

"So he—" Rejoice looked unwillingly over the railing again. "How horrible."

"Not so. Suicide is a fundamental human right." As Rejoice gaped, Jax added, "However, his right cannot incur an obligation for me. I have other work."

Rejoice walked slowly to the jeeper and sank onto the front seat. Jax slid behind the driving wheel and handed the binoculars to Rejoice. "Necessity to drive you back?"

"No," Rejoice said faintly. "I'll wait here for the others." The binoculars pressed against her lap. "If you need to, you can still set up temporarily in the Meetingplace. This island is too dangerous to go without a strong shelter."

"We have shelter," Jax snapped.

Rejoice started to slide off the seat, but stopped. "Is this fundamental human right why you came with fewer people than your warp-ship could hold?"

Jax scowled. "You are too clever. For truth, two, and one was executed."

"Executed? For what?"

Jax's eyes smoldered. "Sabotage." She set the jeeper in motion as Rejoice pushed herself off the seat.

No sooner had the jeeper disappeared around the curve than the Hancocks in a runabout pulled up behind Rejoice. Behind them came Brother Popowich and Deacon Carden.

"What do we have here?" Brother Hancock said when he came up to the railing.

Rejoice clutched the binoculars and stuttered, "His name is Carl. He jumped, I guess. I forgot to ask for his last name. Jax doesn't want the body." *Stop babbling.* She inhaled. "I guess we'll need to bury him ourselves."

Brother Popowich ran thick fingers through his curly, russet hair. "We'll need to have the hexacrabs raise a boat for us. If we approach from the bay, we'll have fewer boulders to climb over."

Deacon Carden laid slim, sienna-colored fingers on Brother Popowich's shoulder and pointed. "If I recall correctly, there are sinkholes there, and barnacles the size of your fist. If we stay close to the cliff until we're opposite the body—"

Brother Popowich interrupted, "I thought the hexacrabs kept the bay clear."

"The barnacles are in their test plots," Brother Hancock said. "They saw the three-meter squares the Greens set up in the jungle for monitoring natural ecological changes, and they decided to set up some of their own. When they grasped the concept of the scientific method, they were excited for weeks."

Brother Popowich paled. "Naspy there, too?"

"I haven't seen any yet." Brother Hancock's faded blue eyes sobered as he looked over the railing.

Sister Hancock slipped an arm around Rejoice. "You look rattled. I wish your husband had come instead."

"Jax doesn't trust him. She's convinced all pastors are con artists."

"Do you know what a con artist is?"

"I do since Jax explained it to me."

Deacon Carden patted his fist into his palm. "Okay, I'll get a stretcher from the clinic and two more men. It'll take at least four of us."

"And I'll brew tea," Brother Hancock groused.

Deacon Carden slapped him on the shoulder that still had an arm attached to it. "Before we're through, we'll all wish we had as many arms and legs as the churtree."

Rejoice and Sister Hancock heard the high-pitched cry at the same time. "Not now!" Rejoice wailed.

The men looked at the women.

Sister Hancock said, "Pack bats," as she entered into the computer the code that set the pack bat alarms shrieking.

The men dashed into their runabouts.

Sister Hancock steered Rejoice into the seat behind the driver's seat, then closed and locked the doors. Gravel pinged against the railing and the monstrous statue as the vehicle accelerated. As they drove toward the mission compound, Sister Hancock said, "There's one silver lining in this dark cloud, I suppose. The pack bats should take care of our problem with the body."

"That's gruesome," Rejoice cried.

"I'm sorry," Sister Hancock said, "Were you fond of Carl?"

"I only saw him once, and he was unconscious at the time." She laid her head on the back of the seat. Clouds floated over the clear ceiling. "But I felt sorry for him. Ernest and Myra said that he didn't fit in and wasn't welcome in any of their 'families.'"

Sister Hancock slowed the runabout's pace and tugged her long braid of red hair turning gray out of the collar of her blue Lord's Day dress. "Rejoice, are you aware that your mother is worried about you?"

"She hasn't told me."

"She wishes you would call her more often."

"Every time I do, I'm interrupted by a call from Elder Smith."

The Hancocks looked at each other with lifted eyebrows. Sister Hancock said, "How hard it is when I am dying to know what is absolutely none of my business."

Brother Hancock said dryly, "Bethany, my dear, it ill becomes you to go fishing."

Sister Hancock said, grinning, "I'm sure it does." After a pause, she added, "I've been uncomely for a long time." They both laughed.

If only the ride could take much longer as Rejoice relaxed in the Hancock's infectious cheer. They entered the road running along the apple orchard.

"Why don't you let us take you to our house and have Resolved brew you a cup of his famous chocolate mint tea while I comb your hair?"

Rejoice touched her matted hair. She had forgotten again. Why hadn't Noble mentioned it? Maybe she should cut her hair as short as Jax's. "Sure. No. The baby is due for a feeding."

"After service, your sweet sister is coming over for a late lunch. Why don't you come too?"

"Maybe I could. But the baby squalls so."

Sister Hancock winked a sea green eye. "We'll wear ear plugs and sign to each other. Here you go, Sweetheart." The runabout halted in front of the door to Rejoice's bubble.

They scanned the sky for a long time. "There they go." Brother

Hancock pointed toward the horizon. "Sure enough, they're heading for the bay."

"I think I will come this afternoon. That will let Pastor Cruz catch up on his sleep."

"And let me obey your mother's command that I keep my eye on you."

After one more glance at the sky, Rejoice scurried out of the runabout and into her home.

The stifling air reeked of tomato leaves. Makepeace paced the central room, from the stove to touch a gleaming spot on a dial, to the table to study a pattern he had made with spoons, to the computer wall to examine the green cherry tomatoes drooping from wilted vines. Opportunity sat at the table clasping and unclasping her hands next to gloomy Mark. The boy tore a thin strip of bark from a long stick.

Noble sat before the screen and raised a hand to stay Rejoice when she tried to sidle past him to get to the baby crying in the bedroom. "Jubilee can wait. We're talking to Harmony."

Rejoice looked at the screen. She tried to keep her face neutral at the sight of her sister-in-law, ashen-faced and disheveled, sitting in a wheelchair with an oxygen tube in her nose, but the muscles of her face contracted in worry to mirror the worry Harmony radiated. Rejoice carefully sat. "Where is Stronghold?"

Opportunity gasped. "Taking the girls for a night walk to look at the stars."

Noble said, "I'm afraid I don't understand what you think is the problem."

Harmony spoke so quietly, Rejoice had to strain to hear. "Whenever we see one of the Robersonians saunter by, Stronghold stops and watches, and he gets this look on his face that frightens me."

"What kind of a look?"

"I don't know. Like he's thinking hard, maybe."

"Why not ask him what he is thinking about?"

"I'm afraid to."

"Hmm. Does Stronghold ever talk about the Robersonians or his work with their computer systems?"

"Once, he said they had beautiful labs, but he only got a glimpse. They won't let him into any of them. They bring out their computers for him to work on."

"Anything else?"

"He said they're disgusting. They grow pigs and live like pigs."

"Hmm. So, when Stronghold sees these disgusting people, he stops and stares. And this worries you."

Harmony bent her head and whispered, "Yes. He looks . . . so strange."

"But you refuse to ask him what he's thinking."

"I'm afraid to."

"Do you want me to ask him what he is thinking?"

"I don't—" She moved her trembling hand on the armrest. "I don't want him to know I was talking about him behind his back."

Noble put his hands together and supported his chin. "Can you see how this puts me in a bind? You won't ask, and I must not ask, but until we know, you're going to worry."

Harmony nodded miserably.

"I'll talk to him," Rejoice said.

Harmony's eyes widened as her forehead wrinkled into a mask of fright. Noble placed his palm on his mouth and wiped down quickly, a gesture that would be unnoticed by all but Rejoice. Years before, they had designated that gesture as a signal that Rejoice had just said something she ought not to have said, and needed to drop the subject.

Rejoice frowned and settled back in her chair. Noble's patience and ability to wait for weeks while his people took forever to puzzle out obvious solutions drove her to distraction.

"What does Pastor Wiseman say?"

"He doesn't know about my worry." She glanced toward the door. "Maybe you should know. Stronghold hasn't talked to Pastor Wiseman in six years."

"Why?"

"I don't know. He doesn't make it obvious, but whenever Pastor Wiseman gets near, he needs to change somebody's diaper. Or he sees someone on the other side of the room he needs to talk to."

"Is he leaving the faith?"

"No, no. He reads the Bible to the girls and helps them memorize. He prays. He attends services. He's very kind and gentle to me. As I type out Luke from memory, he watches and helps." She paused to breathe. "When he's in service, he looks, um, angry perhaps. Like he wishes he was somewhere else."

"Stronghold has always felt confined by the colony."

"I know."

"Have you talked to him about it?"

"I'm afraid to."

Noble leaned forward and said gently, "What are you afraid that you will hear?"

Harmony caught her lips with her teeth and traced the keys. "I—I don't know."

"You're living your life dominated by fear. You're letting fear master you."

She looked up at the screen. "Excuse me, but you're wrong, you know."

"I wouldn't be surprised. What am I wrong about?"

"I'm not always afraid. I'm not afraid to die. I just don't want to leave my little girls." Harmony cried breathlessly.

Rejoice's throat hurt as she watched Harmony struggle to breathe. She clenched her fists helplessly. If only she could turn up the oxygen or could at least hug her. How do you comfort someone on the other side of an ocean?

Finally, Harmony gained enough control to wipe her face, and she typed a sentence that scrolled under her image. [But I know God loves my girls and holds them as securely as He does me.]

"Amen," murmured Noble.

[I remember talking with Sister Deng before I got sick and her husband was killed. She thought that maybe after we had accomplished all God had sent us to this planet to do, all the human people would die of disease.]

Noble sat back. "That's a grim theory. Perhaps I should talk to her about that."

[Sister Deng might not feel]

A door opened, and then Stronghold came on screen with a sleeping girl lying on one shoulder. At the same time a light flashed in one corner to show someone else was trying to place a call.

"Hi, Sis and Other Sis, Pastor. I see you managed to hang on through one more storm. Say, shouldn't you be in service now?"

"Delayed," Noble said, "for emergency clean-up. But the pack bats came. We would have been better off sitting in service."

One Faith whimpered. Stronghold transferred his daughter to the other shoulder. "Sorry to be rude, but I have to put these cranky people to bed."

"Not yet, Daddy," wailed a chorus.

Harmony typed, [Tomorrow, I will recite the book of Ephesians for U.]

"That would be wonderful. God be with you." Noble broke the connection and looked at the number flashing in the corner. "Ready for a call from your mother?"

"Sure," Rejoice said.

But the face that appeared on the screen was not Mother's.

He Gives, with a furrowed brow above an arched nose, said, "What's happened to you? Oppie won't answer her—Opportunity! I see you!"

Opportunity shrank in on herself.

"Excuse me." Noble rose from his chair. Mark scurried down the hall.

"Oppie, why won't you answer my calls? I'm about to go out of my mind worrying about you."

"I—um," Opportunity's face flushed.

"I sent you pictures of the house. Isn't it what you wanted?"

"Well, I . . ."

"Well, what? Even your mother doesn't know when you're coming home. I don't mean to complain, but it's hard to make plans. I bought tickets for you to come home with, but I don't know what date to put on them. You won't answer my calls."

Noble tugged on Rejoice's arm.

Opportunity cried, "I don't know when."

"But—" His hazel eyes widened. "Oh, no. Don't tell me. God has called you to be a missionary to the churtrees."

"No, not that."

Confusion crossed his face. "Then what?"

She stuttered, "I've been thinking."

"About what? All I can think about is how much I love you and how much I miss you."

Noble jerked Rejoice, and she fell into the bedroom. The door clicked shut as he whispered in her ear, "Why are you watching what is none of our business?"

Red-faced, Rejoice picked up the bawling baby and sat to nurse him. "I can't believe she hasn't called him. That's cruel."

"She's embarrassed."

"She should be." It was impossible to talk over the baby's screaming and impossible to sign while nursing him. He sucked angrily, protesting every half minute or so, until he spit up. She changed him and rolled him onto her knees, where she patted him as he kicked feebly.

Noble sat on the bed, staring, perhaps at the picture of the *Magellan* in front of him. When the screaming had turned to grumbling, he switched his gaze to Rejoice. "You should be embarrassed about listening in."

Rejoice swallowed. She had known there would be days like this when she married him. He had infinite patience and could take forever to get to the point, but once he got to the point, he expected his flock to listen. "I accept your rebuke."

He nodded and looked at his screen.

Rejoice sighed. "Do we have time before the service to discuss one point brought up yesterday?"

"Not that."

"No, not that. Another point. You think Jax is really visiting me so that she can persuade me to run away with her. I don't think so."

Noble stood, stripped off his overalls, and watched Rejoice as he dressed in black.

"I think she visits for better salads." She paused, but he didn't laugh as she had hoped he would. She plunged ahead. "Jax is so persnickety about getting paid for every little thing. Every time she told me about another discovery in physics, I had to give her another half-liter of tomatoes. I got so sick of the constant barter, barter, barter, that I bought a new computer and gave it to her."

Noble stopped buttoning his shirt. "You what?"

"So she downloaded all the Independence files on physics and I've been as happy as a maggot in kelp. I'm getting all the math I need now."

Noble frowned as he sat and used his screen to pull up their financial records. "All our money is gone."

"I haven't touched our retirement."

He breathed out with a whoosh. "We can't afford your sister." He finished buttoning his shirt. "I wish you had considered consulting me before you made such a large purchase."

"A computer isn't such a large purchase."

"It was large enough to deplete us."

"At the time I bought it, I thought Opportunity was leaving soon, and I thought I couldn't stand it if I didn't hear about all the new physics."

Noble stood and looked out the window. "And how will that benefit the rest of us?"

"I wouldn't know. How did my study of astronomy benefit the colony?"

He rubbed his face. "So what do I tell your sister?"

"I don't know. How about, 'We can't afford you, and since your fiancée already bought the tickets for you, why don't you go home?' And after she leaves, then you could take some vacation time to help me."

"Vacation time? I used it up nursing you through the pregnancy."

"Then take some future time."

"In a month, it'll be my turn to watch the churtree."

Rejoice clenched her teeth. "Can't you switch with someone else again?"

"No. Not indefinitely." He turned from the w indow to face her. "I don't understand this. Is it because I'm stupid? You spend our last credit so we can't pay Opportunity. Then you ask me to spend time I don't have to help you. Why? You said you were fine last night. Why don't you take care of your boys and the household then? Why do you keep asking me to drop everything and take care of you? I have never known you to be selfish before. Why now?"

Rejoice's cheeks heated. The baby wailed. "I apologize." Please let her be loud enough to be heard by Noble, but not loud enough to be heard by anyone else in the house. "I should have talked to you about the computer. Maybe we should ask the government to pay for it because it allows direct communication between Jax and me. And maybe I should draw ambassador's pay since dealing with Jax takes so much time."

Noble looked exasperated. "With Elder Sims and Brother Jefferson in the Senate, you can ask, but you won't get. That's not the point anyway. The computer is a symptom of a deeper rot."

She squeezed her eyes shut and clenched her teeth against the explosion building within. "Is it such a crime to ask you to pastor your own family?"

The blood rushing in her ears almost covered the sound of his footsteps and the door opening and closing. She moved the screaming baby to her shoulder and rocked as she patted him. *God of peace, God of light,* she prayed with each bounce off the back of the chair. The baby never stopped crying and she never got past the beginning of the prayer.

PACIFISTS' WAR CHAPTER TWELVE

Twenty minutes after the two-hour service during which Noble said nothing but "Let us pray," twice, and Rejoice paced the nursery holding a whimpering baby, she sat at the cluttered table of the Hancocks. The soothing aroma of chocolate mint mingled with the sharp odor of specimens the Hancocks had dissected the day before and the dusty smells of drying herbs, pegged thickly on the ceiling. Over the door hung one of the hexacrab stone blades with triangular torpal teeth glued in a groove to form the cutting edges.

"Ernest wants one of those," Opportunity said.

"Let him dance his own torpal to death," Brother Hancock set down a tray of seaweed crackers. "Did you tell him he might not like the price?" He gestured toward where his other arm had been.

Makepeace sniffed a cracker before he licked it.

Sister Hancock set down a platter of cheeses ornamented with sprigs of sage and rosemary, and placed a jar of honey in front of Rejoice. Rejoice finished her sesame breadstick dipped in mayonnaise, and spooned honey into her tea.

"Good service today," Brother Hancock picked up a limp carrot stick.

Rejoice lifted her eyebrows. "Do you mean to say that the less the pastor says, the better?"

"Sometimes that's true."

Rejoice sipped her tea. Sweet enough. "When are you furloughing back to the mainland?"

"Never," Sister Hancock said. "The grandchildren can visit us here.

Every time I go back, I get elected to the Senate."

"Oh. That's why I was hoping you would go back. You have a special gift of making Elder Sims reasonable."

Sister Hancock smiled and shook her head. "Sister Cruz, Elder Sims is imminently reasonable. It's merely that his reasons are not your reasons. What is it you want from the Senate now?"

"Jax won't sell us any of their spacesuits, and all of ours are at least twenty-six years old. They need to be replaced. So do the shuttles. So does the Starflower if truth be told."

"Aye-aye-aye. It took Old Earth with all its resources and billions of people and industries to build the Starflower. I don't think we'll have the resources to build a spaceship for another five generations. But if you permit, I'll call Elder Sims and talk to him about the shuttles."

"And the spacesuits."

"Eh, economics, the dismal science," Brother Hancock said. "Wouldn't you rather talk about the chordate we discovered off Craggy Island? It everts its stomach over its prey, the glop-mounds, and—"

"No," Rejoice said.

"Opportunity," Sister Hancock handed her a bowl of molasses cookies. "You seem subdued today. Were you a friend of Carl's?"

"Not really. I saw him twice. Sometimes, Ernest or Zack would mock him for being clumsy. Not to his face. Well, Zack would, I think, but mostly behind his back."

"Pray excuse me. I didn't mean to pry. I thought you might want to talk about your feelings."

Opportunity rolled a radish with her fingertip. "I keep slipping up. I have to act one way and gossip to get along when I visit the dojo, and another way here at the mission. We have so many strictures about gossip that we can't say anything about each other."

"Last month's sermon about gossip was good," Brother Hancock said. "It keeps us out of 'he said that she said that I said' conversations. When you think about the damage that gossip did to Old Earth religious colonies, you can see why we don't allow it."

"I know. Colonists talk about the weather and crops and Scripture and what they think God is doing with them and hexacrab culture and books and quilts and music. But we never get to talk about what we're really dying to know. The Robersonians talk about each other and sex. Oh, and strategy, fighting techniques. When I'm not there, I suppose they talk about us."

"We talk about them from time to time," Sister Hancock said, "as we are today, so I suppose it's natural. And I imagine their talk isn't very flattering, since we hold inimical worldviews."

"We talk carefully. We're always afraid to offend. They're not. They're free to say what they think."

"The chickens always think freedom looks more attractive than their coops. They don't understand about pack bats." Sister Hancock said.

Opportunity frowned and continued to roll the radish. "They're super-intelligent. Most of them were genetically altered to form more glial cells in their brains than, well, us."

The adults stopped, then took deep breaths. Sister Hancock said in a voice that quivered slightly, "So they think to conquer nature, to overstep the boundaries that God hedged about us."

"I guess they do."

They sipped their tea in silence. Makepeace crunched his crackers.

A beep from her computer made Rejoice jump and the baby howl. "Cruz here." Opportunity snatched the baby and hurried him into the lab.

"Jax here. Can I pick you up in a few minutes? Necessity to talk to you."

"Is there a problem?"

"No."

Rejoice looked at Sister Hancock.

"You go right ahead, dear. I'll take care of your boys."

"Pick me up at the Hancocks. Inner ring, number 8." She sipped her tea. What now? How many years had this day lasted already? A memory showed up. "Did Jax ever contact you about your research into lungrot?"

"Doctor Carlson said that he was asked about it and gave them all of our data. But they haven't asked any questions or talked to us about it."

Fifteen minutes later, Rejoice and Jax sat in a covered rover parked at the place where the road overlooked the bay.

Rejoice looked about. "Did you want me to call the men and try to retrieve the body again?"

"No. I wanted to speak with you privately."

Rejoice had watched Jax's face during the short ride. Jax had seemed nervous? Preoccupied? What? Noble could have read the expression, but she could not. "Well, go ahead." Oops. She had forgotten what Jax might say when given permission.

Jax fingered her bare earlobe. "Tomorrow, is that a good time for landing our jets?"

"I think so. Churtrees usually stay holed up for three or four days after a hurricane."

"Tomorrow, Henley Roberson is coming to oversee the repairing of the dojo."

"So, he's finally coming down from the Independence."

"He's been down for weeks."

"Really? We hadn't seen him, so we assumed, ah, we shouldn't have assumed. We don't know what he looks like."

"He prefers anonymity. However, he plans to visit you. He likes mathematicians."

"Is there to be a negotiation?"

"No. Visit only." Jax looked at her with pale eyes filled with a message Rejoice couldn't fathom.

"Well, let's see. From ten to eleven forenoon, my duties are their lightest."

"Today is Sunday. Necessity for a day at the dojo. So ten in the morning on Tuesday?"

"Twoday it is"

Jax gripped the steering wheel. "Why do you bury yourself?"

"Pardon me?"

"Why do you bury yourself with people who are dumber than dirt? You are far above these people."

Rejoice pressed her hands between her knees. "Jax, we don't judge people by their number of glial cells; we judge by character. God loves us equally."

"Always we, we, we. When do you say I?"

"I identify with the goals of my colony."

"You weren't old enough to choose the flight to this world. What would you have chosen?"

Rejoice looked away from Jax's angry face. Could she have her heart's desire, she would have been working at either the observatory on Pluto or the collider on the moon. But heart's desire collided with physical reality. There was no going back to Old Earth.

"It doesn't matter. If I had been born a fourteenth century peasant, I wouldn't be working on Pluto either. All of us live bounded by physical reality and social circumstances."

"You could escape those boundaries."

"Are you offering to take me back to Old Earth?"

Jax slowed her staccato speech to say earnestly, "I'm offering you a chance to live with like minds, a chance to learn and research without needing to justify yourself. My family or Henley's family or no family. We would welcome such as you."

"Sure, you'd welcome me and the baby."

"Not the baby."

Rejoice shook her head. The heat and the smell of hot plastic in the vehicle stifled. She rolled down the window. "How do you hope to continue your families, if you hate babies?"

"We love babies. But it's cruel to continue the life of your defective."

"What?"

"No normal child cries so much."

Did Jax think she didn't know that? Rejoice viewed the far horizon where sky and sea smudged into each other. "You ask me to live with a people of like mind. My life is built around people of like heart. A wise man once told me when I was very young that we all have a choice. Separation from God is always an option. But not for me. Not today. Not ever. So stop it. Don't ever ask me to leave my people again."

Jax sighed and tapped the steering wheel. After a moment, she said, "Is your husband the same as No Confidence In The Flesh Cruz?"

Rejoice brushed back sweat-dampened hair. "I told him I wouldn't marry him unless he changed his name. I was tired of telling him no, when I meant yes. He picked a name he thought his mother could remember, but she still calls him 'No No Noble.'" Rejoice smiled, but Jax didn't.

"I've been reading the colony history. Impressing me most is your ingenuity. Impressing Ernest is your husband's courage."

Impressing Rejoice were their appalling morals. She wiped her hands on her blue dress. "If you've brought up all you're going to bring up—"

"Many things impress us about your colony. The dispersal of the colony into three different ecosystems, so if disaster befalls one group, the others may continue."

Rejoice smiled grimly behind her hand. Jax would be less impressed with the reasons for the dispersal.

"And despite the contamination of your genetic pool, you have strengthened it by good racial mixing."

"Whoa," Rejoice said. "Do you think we have the racial variety in our colony because we picked people on the basis of race?"

"Why else?"

"On Old Earth, seventy fellowships drew lots to see who in their congregations would go."

Jax frowned. "Lots?"

"Lots. Now I admit, to enter the trial, you had to meet basic criteria. The pastor had to agree the family was godly. Both husband and wife had to want to go. The family had to be free of any chronic disease that wasn't easily treated. Let's see. And unless you were Elder Smith or Elder Chin, you couldn't be over forty."

"Stupid!" Jax said. "The cause of so many old too soon and so much imbecility. You should have considered genetic contribution potential and intelligence."

"As you did?"

"Yes."

"Hmm. Do you think only Caucasians are intelligent? That's all you brought."

"Absolute negativity. We brought many sperm and egg samples of many races. We tried to recruit the most intelligent of all races, but requirements for our society were too stringent for most applicants."

"A perfect mind in a perfect body."

"For truth, that, and social requirements for rational living."

"Like our requirement to be godly."

"Nothing so foolish. Every male had to agree to not be jealous, to father only one child per woman, and to help raise all children alike. Every woman had to agree to carry one child by Henley Roberson."

Rejoice choked. "What kind of monstrous ego—"

"Roberson is a genius past measurement. His genes are a gift to any child."

The blood rushed in Rejoice's ears.

"I began my required pregnancy the day I landed here."

Rejoice fumbled with the door handle and exited the rover. She took three steps. Uh-oh. She was too tired to walk back.

Somehow, Jax stood beside her. "I am explaining this to you so we can be friends."

"Friends?"

"For truth. Friendship requires understanding."

"It requires more than that. There needs to be some commonality. You hate what I love and love what I hate."

Jax sighed again. "You have been much damaged by your upbringing."

"Please take me home."

Jax returned to the driver's seat and laid her arms and chin on the steering wheel. Rejoice tottered into her seat.

"You took no pleasure from my visits?"

Rejoice had never heard wistfulness from Jax before. Where was Noble when she needed him? What was she supposed to do now? "Much pleasure, believe me. It's so much fun to have somebody to talk to about math and physics. I wish—I might as well tell you. I wish I didn't have to bargain for every morsel of information from you."

Jax sat up. "The purpose of that is to keep the friendship clean. No hidden expectations to cause disappointment. You should understand. You have chosen capitalism."

"Oh!" Rejoice sat and thought intently. New pathways branched in a hitherto blank landscape. "We use capitalism for our money system, not our relationships. I see friendship as a relationship when I give what I think is good for the other person and never count it, while the friend does the same for me. And we share secrets. And we share something we like; in our case, physics. I'm feeling my way here about things I've never defined before."

Jax studied her, then smiled. "May I tell you the cause of my hatred for hexacrabs?"

"Only if you want to."

"For private consumption only, you understand?"

"Go, um, ahead."

"What do you know about Texas?"

"A state in the old United States. I read about it."

"I lived there with trillions of horrible insects. Poisonous scorpions, poisonous ants, poisonous spiders. At age ten, my best friend, Carmine, became angry. Some disappointment in me, an expectation that I should applaud her every idea, perhaps. We quarreled; I slapped her. She asked her brother's gang for revenge. Next day they caught me, tore off my shirt, held me down, and emptied a jar of black widow spiders on me. The spiders crawled on me until each one was slowly crushed by a stick. Some bit me. Carmine and boys laughed. When I came back from the hospital, I stabbed Carmine and she stopped laughing. Then I ran away."

Rejoice shuddered. "How ghastly. I'm so sorry."

"Don't be. It made me strong. I found a martial arts academy that let me train in exchange for daily mopping. Never again would I be helpless. Never."

"But your parents. What did they do?"

Jax shook her head. "Of no concern. I'm telling you what no one else has heard so you can understand why I hate spiders and spider-likes."

Rejoice lay back on the seat and swallowed. She shouldn't have eaten quite so much for lunch. Poor Jax. What story explained why she couldn't trust pastors? Did Rejoice really want to know? She squeezed her hands together. Take the story of Jax and multiply it by four or five or six billion and hear the misery of Old Earth.

"You look ill."

"I am ill." She opened the car door again and walked to the railing. Oh, what Jax had been forced to live through. "Let me catch my breath." She gripped the hot railing. The jungle behind, stripped to sticks and shredded foliage, offered little shade. She sucked in the sea air and looked down the cliff. "Jax, did your people decide to retrieve the body after all?"

In a moment, Jax stood beside her with binoculars, staring at the man below them. She grimaced. "Zack! He keeps forgetting who's the teacher and who's the student. No matter what I say, he challenges it. Twice I petitioned to have him sent back to his father, but even Henle y can't tolerate him. Please, what habitable island can I send him to?"

"What will you pay me for a habitable island survey?"

Jax smiled. "If it results in his departure, as much as you ask. Perhaps some embryos of animals you don't yet have?"

"We don't want pigs."

Jax still smiled as she leaned against the railing. "Moas?"

"Hmm. We already have ostriches. Are moa eggs good?" Rejoice's peripheral vision caught something. She gasped, snatched the binoculars from Jax, and leaned over the railing to examine the sea.

Jax looked toward a splotch of white on the blue sea.

Rejoice pulled out her computer and frantically punched in numbers. "Ur-Veena! There's a kraken in the bay!"

PACIFIST'S WAR CHAPTER THIRTEEN

Rejoice shouted, "Ur-Veena! The kraken alarms must have been destroyed in the storm. You've got to get the children to safety! Ur-Veena!" Her knuckles turned white as she gripped her screen. Nothing. She groaned, "Oh, no. They must have stopped breathing already."

She grabbed Jax's hand. "We've got to get down there. Put them in the filtered shelters. We—" She broke off and punched in a general alarm and broadcast. "Brother Hancock, there's a kraken in the bay. The hexacrabs need help!" A surge of adrenaline gave her the strength to pull Jax toward the elevator doors leading to the dock in the bay. A whistle from her computer stopped her in mid-stride.

"We are confused by your words. We breathe."

Rejoice slumped against the door. "My gills flutter to hear your voice. I ask you to carry your children to safety."

"Perhaps your eyes see what is not there. We taste nothing new."

Rejoice gritted her teeth and seized the binoculars again. While she studied the distant spot, the whirring of wheels filled the road behind her and runabouts slewed into spaces by the railing.

Brother Hancock reached her first. "May I see?"

"It's not moving." Rejoice handed him the binoculars. "Do you suppose it's dead?"

Elder Chin shuffled up behind Noble, who still had red marks on his face from sleep, and Brothers Madison, Popowich, Nguyen, and Green, and Deacons Carden and Volkonsky. With shining eyes Young Man

Grass Under Sky pressed against Brother Hancock. Several Sisters and Deaconesses joined the swelling group. Sister Hancock drove up with a camera on her shoulder.

Brother Hancock handed the binoculars to his apprentice, and tapped Ur-Veena's code into his screen. "Ur-Veena, we ask your people what we should do. We see a kraken floating on the sea, but it does not move. We think it is dead. May we examine it? What do you want us to do if it is dead?"

The connection clicked shut.

Brother Hancock gripped the hot railing and stared at the white spot. The crowd parted for Elder Chin who shuffled up to him and clasped his shoulder. "You taste the desire to dissect that kraken."

Brother Hancock sighed. "You said it. I missed my chance fifteen years ago when the dead kraken drifted away from the ship, just because we got busy patching up our future pastor and reviving the hexacrabs. I had to settle for only a few tips of tentacles to analyze."

Jax's gaze flicked from person to person as she watched the people who watched the sea. She exclaimed, "The Human-Hexacrab Treaty of Contact Year Five!"

"That's right." Rejoice resumed leaning on the door. Noble pushed through to her and placed his arm around her.

"What is purpose of withdrawing from kraken and ceasing all deep sea dredging?" Jax asked.

Rejoice rubbed her face. "Okay. The hexacrabs are afraid that we might inadvertently kill some of their children during deep sea dredging or sampling. The hexacrabs don't remember their deep sea stage of life. So they don't know which creature to protect. The compulsion to protect babies is so strong that it overrides every other consideration."

"How can they tell whose child is whose? Smell?"

"No, actually they can't tell and don't care. A child is a child. Even before Dark Death, the rare times one cluster would war on another, the children were never harmed."

"Cause of rare war?"

"Usually, when a cluster reaches a certain size, the cluster splits and half crawls off to start a new cluster elsewhere. So there weren't many resource quarrels. But a cluster surrounded by other clusters sometimes had difficulty finding a place to send its excess people." Rejoice leaned onto Noble. Her hands trembled. The strong odor of fermenting foliage oppressed her.

Jax tilted her head. "Purpose of leaving kraken alone?"

Rejoice sucked in the humid air. Half the people were watching her and Jax now. Some looked with distressed faces over the railing at Zack on the talus with the skeleton of Carl. She tried to push herself up straighter. "We don't understand what the hexacrabs feel about the Ancient Ones, as they call them. They won't tell us. It was after we—after I—killed a kraken, that the hexacrabs broke with us. And it wasn't until we made the treaty that our relationship was restored."

"And you haven't encountered a kraken since?"

"Oh, yes. They arise from the deep frequently. We've arranged alarms for us and the hexacrabs. We get out of the way and they crawl to safety. But sometimes a few hexacrabs will be too far away from the alarms and will be taken by a kraken. We believe that the one we encountered on the maiden voyage of the *Magellan* ascended from the deep because it sensed the hexacrabs. Since then the hexacrabs sail around the deep as much as possible."

Brother Hancock's computer whistled. "We allow you to look at the kraken. If The Spear lives, you must leave. If The Spear has died, we ask you to pull her to deeper sea and release her. Most of us go to the shelters. Some will raise boats for you. What do you need?"

Brother Hancock studied the crowd with narrowed eyes. "The barge and two gigs."

"We hear you." The connection clicked shut again.

Brother Hancock grinned. "All right. Let's see. Doctor Carlson, you've got your kit, good. Make sure you have your stuff for punctured lungs in case it decides to hug any of us. You, Young Man," he poked Grass Under Sky in the chest, "where's my sampling kit? You've got five minutes to get it here or watch from the dock in disgrace." He turned again as the Young Man raced toward a runabout. "Elder, will you accompany us?"

"My pleasure." Elder Chin shifted his hands on his cane.

Brother Hancock headed for the doors and wrapped his arm around Noble's neck. "What are you waiting for? Push the button and let's go. I want to see if you got any smarter when you got older."

Noble grinned back. "If I hadn't poked it, you would have been its lunch. You should be showing me what gratitude looks like."

"I will show you. This time Young Man Grass gets to poke it. You get to sit in the barge with your lovely wife and watch from afar."

Noble's smile stiffened. "That's it?"

"That's it. You're a father now. Let the young men idiots, a redundant phrase if ever there was, let them break their bones and learn to be smart like you and me."

The elevator door opened, and the first ten people filed in. On the dock, in the changing halls, Jax stripped next to Rejoice. She felt like a bowl of risen bread dough next to Jax's muscular, lean body.

"You're coming, too?"

"Why not? If it is such a rare event to view a kraken, then I should take advantage of the opportunity." Jax held her black clothes and pulled open a locker door.

"I'm sorry, but guests use the lockers on the other side, over there. The middle lockers might have suits your size." Rejoice pulled on her diving suit and pondered how to answer while surrounded by women and yet not betray Jax's secret. "I thought you might not like, ah, sea things."

"I will cope."

The other women, as they dressed in diving suits and checked their buckles and shrugged into life vests, watched Jax from the corner of their eyes. Their conversations were muted, truncated.

Rejoice's hands still trembled and her legs felt heavy, the aftermath of her fright, she assumed. "Sister Deng, when we get back could you give me a thorough physical?"

Sister Deng flicked her straight black hair over her shoulders and finished buckling her vest. "But it's the Lord's Day."

"Right." Would Rejoice be able to push herself up from the bench? "It doesn't feel like the Lord's Day with everything so disordered. I'm sorry. I feel so tired."

"Staying in bed for six months will do that to a person. Any fever?"

"I don't think so."

"You look flushed. It might qualify as an emergency. I'll see what I can do." She picked up her medical kit and left. All the women but Jax followed.

"Aren't you coming?" Jax pulled on a zipper.

"The spirit is willing, but the flesh is weak."

Jax smiled. "Bear one another's burdens." She took Rejoice's hand and pulled her up.

Rejoice's heart warmed toward Jax. God had blessed her with beautiful parents and the love of hundreds of people besides. Jax had been given what? Parents of no concern, parents that allowed their daughter to be so traumatized that she grew phobias anyone could understand. "Jax, do you mind if I ask how you know so much Scripture?"

Her face lost the smile. "You're asking. Maybe someday I will say." She turned away and marched out the door.

Rejoice tottered after her and caught the doorway for support. Noble waited for her and she signaled to him. When he got close, she let go of the doorway and grabbed him. "Could you help me to the barge? I don't think I can walk that far."

One side of his mouth lifted. "If you can't walk, how do you hope to rescue me if need be?"

"I don't hope to." Creases formed between his brows. "Wait, that didn't come out the way I meant it."

"Hup!" He swung her into his arms and carried her down the dock to where water sluiced out of dozens of holes in the barge's hull and Brother Hancock passed out electric prods to six of the men, two for each boat. The *chug chug chug* of air compression filling the hulls vibrated the dock.

Jax examined a prod. "I thought you agreed to not kill kraken."

"This shouldn't," Brother Hancock said. "We hope these will discourage it from attacking us, and not just rile up the monster." His voice rose suddenly, "Young Man, what use are you going to be to me if you stick that thing in your eye?"

Red faced, Young Man Grass Under Sky lowered his prod.

Jax covered a guffaw. "You people need training in the use of dangerous weapons."

"We all train on rifles. But we haven't used prods in fifteen years," Brother Hancock said. "I hope you don't point rifles in your face like that," he yelled to Young Man Grass, who shook his head and reddened more.

Brother Hancock grinned. "Brother Popowich, rope and tackle? Good. Deacon Carden, pole hooks? Good. Brother Madison, you have those holes plugged yet? Good. Doctor Carlson and Sister Deng, the med kits? Good. Pastor, you have Sister Rejoice. Good. Let's go!"

The human people filed into the boats and squelched down on wet benches. Rejoice flicked some seaweed over the side as Noble and some others pulled on the tarp canopy. Her eyes released their tension as she relaxed in its shade. Sister Deng passed out the orange floater cushions which everyone snapped into place. Four men each in the smaller craft sped toward the kraken. The barge followed slowly. Foul smelling mud puddled around their feet.

Jax settled next to Rejoice. "Please tell me about the kraken. In exchange, I will download the last world almanac."

Rejoice doubted the almanac would carry any information about the fellowships they had left behind. Still, news was news, and she saw no reason to hide information about the kraken that the Robersonians ought to know. "In nineteen years of contact with the hexacrabs, we have only seven recorded sentences about the kraken. Once it was called the Sword of the Creator. We think it used to be customary for the hexacrabs to end all their major planning discussions with, 'May the kraken let us live.' In times past, when the kraken ascended from the deep ocean, the hexacrabs stood still and let the kraken eat whoever it would. We couldn't understand that, because the hexacrabs are fierce warriors. They lose body parts to the torpal and churtree, and they keep on fighting to protect their children. They don't stop until they're dead."

Jax nodded. "You understand it now?"

"Yes," Noble interrupted as he sat down on the other side of Rejoice. "The kraken exude a neurotoxin that paralyzes the hexacrabs. The neurotoxin has a lesser effect upon hardheads, and torpals. I think the hexacrabs are embarrassed that we showed them the kraken was a false god."

"But they still revere it," Rejoice said, "hence, the treaty. Brother Hancock and the engineers designed alarms that can recognize minute traces of the neurotoxin. When the alarms sound, the hexacrabs crawl into their filtered shelters, and we withdraw. That's one reason why the mining at the undersea smokers on the other side of the island is going so slowly. There's a continental shelf not far from there, and at least once a week, a kraken comes up to investigate. If the hexacrab doesn't make it to the shelter in time, we're not supposed to intervene. That's how we lost Sa-Criti and Ti-Taksi."

"The hexacrabs make you dance a pretty dance," Jax said.

"I'm sorry. I don't know what you mean," Rejoice answered.

"They say go, you go, stop, you stop."

"That's the treaty we made. We like to keep our word."

"It's bad enough that you let an old book tell you how to live. Why let talking crabs tell you how to live?"

"Because they're our friends. Don't you ever do anything inconvenient for a friend?"

"When I want." Jax shaded her eyes and looked out at the body of the kraken.

Rejoice fingered her flippers. Should she put them on? She examined her toes and the toenails slowly growing over them. Another month and she might have something to clip.

Noble radiated disapproval. Before, he had wanted her to get along; now he wanted her to not capitulate. She took a deep breath. "Love and want aren't always connected. I don't want to wake up at thirteen o'clock, or two, or four; but I do it anyway because I love my baby and he needs to eat." *I hope I love him.* Noble squeezed her a little closer. "So it is with the hexacrabs. We want the mining to go faster so that if there's any germanium in the planet's crust, we can find it. We want to investigate the deep sea. We want to dissect the kraken. But because we value the hexacrabs much more than those things, we don't."

"What value have hexacrabs?"

"What value does any soul have? God loves us all."

"I value productivity. Why waste life on wasted lives?"

Rejoice bit her bottom lip. A number of people on the barge prayed. She turned to Noble. This was his province.

Before Noble could answer, Sister Hancock turned on the screen and continued to record the two boats in front of her. The view on the screen showed the view of the camera in Brother Hancock's boat. The kraken swelled larger and larger as the boat neared the monster. It still did not move.

Brother Hancock gave them a running commentary. "We're coming up on it. What I can see of the body appears to be three meters in diameter, smaller than the first one humans ever saw. It's still not moving. The tentacles . . . No, it's not going to move. It's dead. Look, no, point the camera here." A swooping view settled on the image of a tentacle being gently lifted from the water by a pole hook. "The little beaks have been nibbling on this. See the pockmarks here and here?"

The monster wouldn't attack them. Good, and yet neither would they have a chance to learn more about them.

"I see no signs of decay, so the death must have been recent. Deacon, do you think the easiest way to tow this would be to put some hooks through the arms close to the body?"

A muffled consent could be heard, and then an unintelligible question. "I think they would forgive us. We wouldn't be dissecting it, just setting in the hooks firmly. It's so big it should take all three boats to tow it."

The bulk of the white body filled the screen. One of the glazed yellow eyes replaced the main body.

"That makes me shudder," Sister Popowich said. "That eye is as big as the palm of my hand."

The gig sailed in a tight circle around the kraken, and the people in the barge watched the rotating image. Sister Hancock set down her camera. "No dramatic sea battles to capture, for which I'm thankful."

Jax sat back. "Are we expected to adhere to this treaty?"

"You are human, aren't you?" Rejoice asked.

"We were not present during negotiations. By what means are they enforcing the treaty?"

Noble's lips tightened. "We gave our word. They gave theirs. We don't need noncompliance-penalty clauses."

"The hexacrabs don't lie," added Rejoice. "They don't always tell you everything, but what they say they will do, they do. They can't even imagine breaking a treaty. Wait, I bet they can now that they've studied Old Earth history. But they have no cultural precedent for lying, bluffing, or even kidding."

Sister Hancock laughed. "They studied human humor for three years before they gave it up as too alien and worthless to even try to understand."

Jax avoided the eyes of the passengers.

"Time to earn your keep," came the voice of Brother Hancock. "Over you go." The screen showed a froth of silver bubbles, and then the underside of the kraken and the frightening half-meter-long beak.

"Hold it!" Brother Hancock shouted. "Zoom in on that. Yes, that."

The camera zoomed in on a protuberance behind one of the tentacles.

"Brother Fox, do me the favor of cutting that out along with ten centimeters of skin all around and a couple of centimeters deep into the flesh. Yeah, then we'll insert a hook in there. Handle it gently. It could be a poisonous parasite. Young Man, after Brother Fox gets that, you check every square centimeter to see if there are any more."

The people watched the operation while Rejoice fought down nausea. The Hancocks had a positive preoccupation with parasites and could calmly eat lunch while playing with the most disgusting specimens. She looked back to the cliffs. The tiny figure of Zack clambered over the rocks. Maybe he had a streak of decency in him if he wanted to bury what was left of Carl.

Exclamations caused Rejoice to look at the screen again.

Brother Hancock held the blue protuberance on his lap reverently as he gently sliced the skin around where the thing adhered. "Yes. You can see here where the mouth parts have grown into the blood vessels." He gently rotated the dead creature, stopped, and rotated it again. With a changed voice, he said, "One, two suture lines where the triangles have fused incompletely. The deep sea stage of the hexacrab is a parasite of the kraken."

* * *

Two hours later, as they approached the dock, Noble nudged Rejoice who was sleeping on his chest. She yawned and sat up straight. The sounds of conversation in the barge and the slapping of waves and the sound of the engine blurred together in a monotonous, soothing tone. Noble said, "Nature keeps sneaking up behind us and shouting, 'Surprise!'"

"That it does." She twisted. Elder Chin sat with both hands and his chin on his walking stick. "When do we tell the hexacrabs?" The other people stopped talking and faced him.

He blinked for a minute as his wrinkled jowls quivered. "I see at least three possibilities. The hexacrabs don't know, and don't want to know. The hexacrabs don't know, and their lively curiosity impels them to know. The hexacrabs have always known, and they are determined that we should not."

Rejoice rubbed an eye. "I don't think that third possibility is true. The hexacrab don't always tell us all the truth, but they don't lie. They told us that they don't remember what happens to them in the deep. We don't remember our time in the womb. Besides, if they knew, I can't understand why Ur-Veena would have let us near the dead kraken the first time."

"Perhaps he didn't expect us to examine it so closely. But you're probably correct. I would like the time to have some discrete discussions with our molluscan brothers before we broadcast this discovery. None of us wish to precipitate another crisis."

Certainly Rejoice didn't. She glanced at Noble. Would they ever have a spare moment to talk to each other in private?

The barge bumped gently into the side of the dock and several men jumped out to secure it. Noble carried Rejoice onto the dock and toward the changing hall.

"I can walk now. I just needed to rest. Thank you." He set her down. A few steps proved she had been mistaken, but he had gone ahead, leaving her with Jax. Zack strolled toward them grinning, his hands behind his back.

He halted in front of them and then flourished the discolored skull of Carl. "An interesting incense burner."

Rejoice gasped. Jax glanced at her, then whirled and kicked in a movement so fast that Rejoice could not follow it. *Thwack!* The skull arced and splashed into the bay. It sank, releasing bubbles, the white turning to a wavering green, then fading from view. The colonists who had seen stood motionless.

Jax thrust her face a few centimeters from Zack's. "Not in my dojo!" She stalked toward the changing hall.

PACIFISTS' WARCHAPTER FOURTEEN

The next afternoon when Rejoice reached the second ring road, she stopped and shifted her bag of cheese, flour, oranges and lettuce to the other hand and listened to sharp clicks. The sound reminded her of the percussion sticks used during the singing for the Lord's Day, but it came irregularly and was suddenly joined by a boy's howl.

She dropped the bag and darted to her right. When she rounded the curve, Resist held his hand and cried on the road in front of the Madison's bubble house. "You weren't supposed to hit my fingers!" A stick lay at his feet.

Mark saw her and threw his stick onto the road. Submit and Charitable turned and ran toward the playing field.

Rejoice caught her breath while she examined Resist's hand. The skin had abraded off four knuckles, and flecks of blood oozed in the scrapes. "What were you doing and why weren't you doing it on the playing field? Where's your adult supervision? Hold it right there, Mark. You aren't going anywhere because I'm talking to you next."

Resist howled loader, and between his sobs and denials and broken sentences, she pieced together that it was all Mark's fault and he was only hitting Mark's stick and Mark had hit him and now it was bleeding and he needed meshflesh, lots of meshflesh. She turned her glare to Mark who didn't mean to do it but Resist had moved wrong and he didn't hit him that hard anyway and both of them thought of it.

Rejoice took a deep breath, pointed, and watched Resist run to the field. Not sure that she would be able to get up after she got down, she lowered herself to eye level with Mark. "So what is it, exactly, you were doing?"

Mark looked everywhere but at her eyes. "We were practicing sword fighting. Like Ernest."

With an effort, she pitched her voice lower and said calmly, "Did you forget we're a people of peace? We are not churtrees. We don't fight each other with swords, so you don't need to practice."

He twisted his hands as he scuffed the road. Tears made tiny blotches in the road dust. He quavered, "Would you let the churtrees eat me?"

"Oh, honey, no!" She hugged his stiff body. "We have the watch posts and cameras now." She stroked his hair, hot from the sun. "We have the shelters every half kilometer along our paths, and the shatterproof runabouts."

He sniffed and leaned into her. "The hexacrabs have shelters."

Rejoice inhaled the smell of dust and burnt rosemary as she traced the connections Mark was making. "You still miss Ti-Taksi, don't you?"

His forehead rubbed against her shoulder as he nodded. His shudders revealed how hard he was working to not cry.

She sat on the road and attempted to pull him onto her lap, but he pushed away from her. She said, "Ti-Taksi had to think his death was worthwhile. As Christians, we have the hope of being with God after we die." She pulled a handkerchief from her pocket and dabbed his face. "I wish I could put the confidence I feel about your safety into you. We won't let the churtrees hurt you."

He howled, "You let them eat Resist's father!"

"We have more safeguards now. But let me tell you, Resist's father went to face God with clean hands that never shed blood."

His lips wobbled before he cried, "But why can't we fight to protect us?"

She looked into his eyes, so intense like Noble's, and grasped his thin shoulders. "You know what? I had this same conversation with my father when I was sixteen. And nothing he said satisfied me then. Now I understand that he was right. But I don't think I can tell you anything that will satisfy you either. I think you should talk this over with Father."

Mark scraped the road with his shoes. "He doesn't talk to us anymore."

"What do you mean?"

"He's always talking to Ernest. We don't play games anymore. Father just makes us run laps while he talks to Ernest."

"If you're running laps, it's because it's good for your body. Now go back and do what you're supposed to do." She tried to kiss him, but he ducked away and raced to the field.

Watching him go, Rejoice swallowed tears. She prayed that God's peace would fill her son's heart, would fill her. She rose, dusted off, and returned to her bag. There she was reminded why they couldn't grow oranges on the island. Yertles wrestled within the bag and yertles outside the bag strewed orange pulp across the yellow bricks.

* * *

At supper that night, as soon as grace was said and before Rejoice could tell Noble about Mark's fears, Noble stood. "Good news! I'll be starting a Bible study with Ernest and five of his friends next week."

Her glass of raspberry tea clicked softly as she carefully set it on the table and glanced at her son and sister. All but Makepeace were looking at Noble. "So what were you planning to cancel so you can fit this in?"

He too glanced at the other people at the table before saying, "Excuse me, but I do believe that I can handle my own scheduling."

"I'm just curious to know how you plan to slow the rotation of Shatterworld so you can have more time per day."

His mouth twitched before he answered. "Since our family walks are truncated by your inability to walk farther than a quarter kilometer, I decided that skipping it twice a week would do no one harm and could do great good." He walked toward the computer.

"You're not going to eat with us?"

He stopped. "I will fast for a season. There are hearts that God wants to touch and I want my heart prepared to touch them."

For once, Rejoice was relieved to hear the baby scream. Wordlessly, she rose and retreated to her bedroom.

That night Rejoice rubbed her eyes that couldn't see the text anymore. Was Noble ever coming to bed? The baby thrashed on the blanket next to her and protested fiercely; about what Rejoice still had no idea. Earplugs. What could she use for earplugs? Noble had a hole in one of his socks. Maybe she could cut that up and stuff the fabric in her ears. She looked at her screen. Where was he? She had good news for him if he would show up.

She pulled back the quilt and padded to the door. If he was still speaking with Elder Chin about ways to approach the hexacrabs about the discovery with the kraken, she had no wish to interrupt him, so she pulled the door open a crack, and peeked.

Noble paced before the blank screen with his head bowed and his lips moving silently. After several turns, he opened the front door and stepped out.

Rejoice opened her mouth and raised her hand to call out that he had forgotten his rifle, but she stopped and lowered her hand. Pack bats seldom hunted at night. What had so upset him that he had not eaten supper and now could not go to bed? He passed by the window with his head still bowed.

She dimmed the light and shuffled back to bed. *I'm sorry, Noble.* She couldn't wait up for him. Those last two days of clean-up had exhausted her. Oh, badness, she had forgotten to get the scissors for the sock.

Her screen beeped. Who would be calling so late?

Mother looked through her screen with a face furrowed by worry. "Rejoice, how do you feel?"

"Mother, I—Just a minute. I can't hear you." She picked up the squalling baby, dumped him in the crib, and shoved the crib into the living room. Even that small exertion left her panting. She collapsed onto the bed, blinked at her screen numerals until they came into focus.

"Mother, shouldn't you be at choir practice?"

"I left early. I had to call you. You don't sound well."

"It's late and I'm tired."

"Has Doctor Carlson seen you lately?"

"Today, as a matter of fact. He says I'm fine and he can't see any reason for the fact that I want to go to bed for a week. I think that if I had no responsibilities for just one week, I would recover and be okay."

Mother nodded gravely. "I was afraid of this, sweet-love. You're depressed."

"Mother. I'm tired."

"And depressed. Let me check." Her fingers moved on the keyboard. "Your pharmacy doesn't carry the right medication. I'll make sure some gets to you on the next flight."

"Mother!"

"And that week's rest, I'll see you get that too. If there's room on the next flight, I'll be bringing the medication. You hold on until I get there, honey-love."

"You're chasing a hardhead with a cannon. How can you up and leave Harmony?"

Mother's entire face squeezed in agony. With an effort, she smoothed it and said haltingly, "I'm bringing Harmony. Please add another module, make it two, to your bubble. I'll pay you back once my apartment is sold."

Random syllables formed and died before Rejoice could utter them. Finally, "I don't understand. There's no work for Stronghold on this island."

Mother's face contorted. Her shoulders shook and tears splashed on her keyboard.

Rejoice watched, immobile. Mother never cried deeply. Tears, yes, but not this shaking. She had not cried when Rejoice had miscarried her babies. She had not cried when Father died nor when she sang at his funeral. The only other time Rejoice had seen Mother, who was always cheerful and always singing, cry like this was when Stronghold had denounced Father and stormed out of their home. "Stronghold. What's he done this time?"

Mother drew in shuddering breaths and stammered. "The First City Fellowship agreed to shun Stronghold and Brother Redhorse. This morning, while we were still asleep, Stronghold ran off to join the Robersonians."

"No," Rejoice said, "No. No. No. He can't."

Mother typed, [can't talk about it now will call u later.] With a shaking hand she cut the connection and the screen went black.

"No," Rejoice whispered. "He can't." How could Stronghold be such a maggot? How could he? She shivered internally. What had the Robersonians offered him? Had they persuaded him that he shouldn't bury himself with people dumber than dirt? During their three years on the Starflower Stronghold had been so in love that he sometimes forgot to finish sentences and sometimes stabbed his cheek with a fork when he forgot he was eating. There had been a time when every sentence began with "Harmony. . ." and every time he called Rejoice to tell her that he had become the father of another little girl, tears of joy had run down his face. How could he throw that away?

The screen fell flat on her lap as she lay back and cried unrestrained. Long minutes later, she dragged herself to a sit, wiped her face, turned the pillow over so the wet spot faced the bed, and turned on her screen. She looked at it a long time until she remembered why she had turned it on. Two modules. No. Three. Two bedrooms and a bath. With all those girls, Mark and Noble would never get in the bathroom if they didn't add another one. Opportunity and the four girls in one bedroom, Mother and Harmony in the other. Likely, Opportunity would welcome moving out of Mark and Makepeace's bedroom.

Rejoice wiped her face again and sighed deeply. Check the Archipelago warehouse inventory. Three bedroom modules and two baths. And no more to be made for another year. Enough. Price? Oops. No money left, and the pay they received on a daily basis wouldn't cover the cost for months, even if they consumed nothing during those months. The chance of Mother paying it off soon was remote. Every credit beyond her grocery bill already went straight to the work of the mission. And who would buy her apartment? Everyone was building homes with separate bedrooms. Rejoice needed to talk to Noble.

She pressed his number. His computer beeped in the living room. He had left without his computer as well as his rifle. "Where are you when I need you?" she snarled. "All right, I'll buy them, and you can veto it tomorrow if you dare." She unlocked their retirement savings and transferred the money to the warehouse and the factory that had made the modules. What was left would pay for a comfortable retirement of one month.

She shut off her computer again and let her fingertips drift over the screen. *God, why would Stronghold do this*? He had always been arrogant, quick to anger, and oblivious at times to other people's feelings. But never had he been deliberately cruel. And he loved his girls. How do you dump your family?

The bedroom door banged open and angry Noble strode in with the baby crying on his shoulder. "How could you let Jubilee lie out there, shivering and wet?"

Rejoice's hands flew to her mouth. "I forgot the baby!"

"I can't believe you, sitting in here reading physics while your little boy is crying his heart out!"

Rejoice's cheeks burned as she watched Noble lay the wailing baby on the changing platform and strip off his urine-soaked clothes. She shouted to be heard, "I was not. I'll have you know I was spending the last of our savings."

He turned, keeping one hand on the baby. "What did you buy this time? You already purchased all their physics. What else could you buy?" He turned back and pulled off the sodden diaper.

Guilt piled onto her anger. When had she last changed the baby? "I bought—" Her throat closed.

He wrapped the baby in a towel, hoisted his son to his shoulder, and turned to face Rejoice again. "What made you think you should spend our savings on your own pleasures all the while Jubilee is suffering?"

"Stop." She closed her eyes. "Stop. Stop! STOP! STOPSTOPSTOP!" As she sat panting, it trickled into her consciousness that she had screamed. And the door was open. And everyone in the house had heard them. She opened her eyes. Noble had backed against the wall with the brown towel bunched in his fists. She took a deep breath and said in a quavering voice, "Could we start over again? I can't figure out how to say what I need to say."

The anger in his face was replaced by something Rejoice had not seen in Noble for years. It took a moment to interpret his expression: fear.

What was he afraid of? "Please, give me the baby so I can feed him and let's try this conversation over again."

Noble handed over the baby without a word and left the bedroom, closing the door behind him.

The poor baby; he was cold. She unbuttoned so she could lay his bare skin against hers and warm up. For once, he latched on quickly to nurse and didn't let go. She wrapped her arms and the towel around him and looked into his almond eyes. He watched her intently until his eyelids drooped shut. Rejoice felt an inner knot uncoil at this moment of peace; the first she had had this day. When she gently stroked his head, she saw the time on her screen. Thirteen fifty-seven! Twoday had already started. Where had Noble gone?

Minutes later, he opened the door slowly and forced a smile. Drops of water from a hasty shower dangled on the ends of his dark hair. "My own Madonna and child. I like to see that."

"I like to see you, too. I was beginning to wonder if I ever would."

"What time—oh." He edged toward the bed and took off his bath robe. He said hesitantly, "Were you with Jax when you sighted the kraken?"

Rejoice found it hard to think that far back. Her fingertips traced the tiny whorls of the baby's ear. "Yes, I was."

"I thought you were having lunch with the Hancocks."

What did that have to do with anything? "I did. Jax called while I was there. I saw no purpose in waking you to tell you we were going to talk for a few minutes."

Noble released a peg on the wall and hung his robe on it. "I see."

Ah, perhaps he was trying to pick a neutral topic so they wouldn't argue again. He slid under the quilt.

He pressed against her, pulled her hand away from the baby's wispy black hair, and kissed each finger. Then his knuckles softly followed the contours of her jaw and shoulder. His sun-darkened fingers tangled in her sun-bleached hair. He said with longing that could be felt. "You are so beautiful."

Rejoice smiled sadly as she watched him study the top on his son's head. Or perhaps he was studying elsewhere. She could translate that even easier than hex.

His gaze and his hand lifted to her cheek and stopped. "You were crying."

"I know." She placed her free hand on top of his.

"Why?"

Despair rose up and strangled her anew. She could not say it yet. "You first."

"Pardon me?"

"First you tell me what you're so upset about that you've stopped eating."

"Part if it is a feeling. I dislike that; I choose to live my life according to facts, not feelings. But I have this feeling. Elder Chin does too. I feel like an enormous, heavy, black cloud is lowering over us. And any minute now it's going to break into a downpour." He pulled her to him even tighter. "And when it does, we're all going to drown."

"Oh, Noble!" Rejoice cried. "That cloud just broke!"

PACIFISTS' WAR CHAPTER FIFTEEN

The next morning, Rejoice blearily washed off the table. Her chest felt heavy and her mental processes felt mired. Behind her, Noble murmured into his throat mike and listened through headphones to Brother Koch. He had refused to cancel the sessions, saying, "If I beg off once because I'm tired, they'll feel free to break off their appointments whenever they're tired. I want to avoid that kind of dynamic because we've committed to each other." The man was going to "dynamic" himself right into the ground.

She sank into a chair and stared out the window. She could not see Opportunity and Makepeace cleaning up the orchard. The baby howled in the bedroom. The wretched morning looked as if it would drag into a wretched afternoon. Opportunity and Mark had tiptoed around Rejoice and Noble until they heard about Stronghold. Then Mark's eyes had grown wide and frightened and stayed that way even after Noble had promised that he would never leave Mark. Opportunity grew silent and brooding. Makepeace had shouted and smashed plates and glasses on the table. Even after Noble had made him sweep up the shards, Makepeace still quivered with distress and chewed his thumb bloody.

Rejoice rubbed her face. Laundry. Yes, she should do laundry. How lucky the hexacrabs were to not need laundry or linen. The baby went through his clothing and sheets at a prodigious rate. No, she should do her work first; see where Hurricane Pernicious was now, check on the asteroids, monitor the Starflower. Had she done that yesterday? She ran her fingers through her hair. She had forgotten to comb it again.

A stranger walked past the window, a man with light skin, reddish-blond hair that was curled and cowlicked, and dressed in a yukata of blue and gold, patterned with relativistic equations. He knocked on the door. It took her slowed reflexes several seconds to respond. When she opened the door, she was startled by his intense green eyes flecked with blue and brown in a rugged face. He had the same ability Noble did to pierce through a person with his gaze. He smiled and bowed deeply. She bobbed her head back as she tried to think who he could be.

In a deep voice with a pleasant rumble, he said, "Here I am for my appointed ten o'clock visit. I'm pleased to meet you, Sister Cruz. Jax thinks highly of you."

Rejoice tried to keep from gaping like a goldfish. *Henley Roberson! Oh my goodness!* She was losing her memory. "Come in, please. I'm sorry. In all the excitement, I quite forgot." She backed up and bumped into the table. "You may hang your rifle there above the door. We have an eight-year-old, so we try to keep the guns up high. If you'll give me but a moment, I'll have some tea for you. Would ginger tea be all right?"

"Certainly." Though of average height and weight, he seemed to fill the room as he entered.

As Rejoice stumbled through the tea preparation, Noble blanked the screen and ripped off his headgear. After typing and sending a brief message, he stood and advanced toward Mr. Roberson. After a moment's thought, Noble extended his hand, but Mr. Roberson ignored it and bowed instead. Noble slowly bowed back. The two men studied each other until Rejoice set the tea on the table. "Please, sit. Please excuse me for being unprepared, but Jax neglected to tell me the purpose of your visit. She may have been distracted by the kraken in the bay. I know I was."

"Why don't you sit and relax?" He had a voice one could listen to for hours. "I have no agenda. I simply wanted to meet the most famous person on the planet."

"I don't know who's most famous. We all know each other."

"Excuse me," Noble said, "but who are you?"

The man smiled, revealing even, white teeth. "Henley Roberson. I brought in some more supplies for the dojo and wanted to visit with you for a short while."

When he reached for the tea, his hand brushed Rejoice's, and she felt a surge of desire that startled her with its intensity. She forced herself to breathe normally as she poured honey into her cup and stirred. *Whoa.* Was that charisma, magnetism, what? She avoided Henley's eyes as she handed a cup of tea to Noble. Did he affect all women this way? What was he? She swallowed some tea and scalded her tongue. Ow! Good, a different physical sensation to concentrate on. She scraped the scalded part against her teeth to increase the pain before she said, "I'm surprised to see a Rational above thirty years old."

Henley chuckled. "I'm fifteen years older than the next oldest in the group."

Late forties, then. A decade younger than Elder Smith when he arrived.

"It's been fun to watch, really. I had an entire shipload of raging hormones all the way over." He took a long draught of tea. "However, we need to deal with an issue I hadn't planned to deal with when I was preparing to come."

The door opened and Opportunity pulled in Makepeace. "Hello. May I join you?"

Rejoice waved toward a chair.

Henley stood and bowed. "Ah, the lovely Opportunity. I had the joy of seeing some of your paintings at our clinic."

Opportunity blushed as she moved to the cupboard.

She had sold some of her paintings to the Robersonians? What had they given her in exchange?

"The issue?" Noble said, still seated and not once moving his gaze from Henley's face.

"Ah, yes, the issue." Henley sat. "Do you believe in religious freedom?"

"Yes." Noble did not elaborate.

"I'm glad of that. It seems that a fuss, an unhappiness, exists in First City because two men have fled to our little settlement for asylum. It seems they no longer wish to live under the strict laws of your colony."

Rejoice blinked tears and her stomach tensed with nausea.

"This presents us with a dilemma. We, too, believe in religious freedom and we would be happy to welcome these men into our families. But we find ourselves wondering if the unhappiness of First City will have repercussions on our food supply."

Rejoice tasted bitterness. "We promised a six-month supply of food. We keep our promises." Stronghold hadn't. The Robersonians could keep the maggot who would vow to love, honor, and cherish and then turn back when life got hard.

"For that I am grateful. Again, I do not wish to annoy you who are gracious hosts, but I do need a point clarified. If one of these men had to, say, run an errand into town, would he be stoned?"

Noble grimaced. "We don't stone, hang, or burn those who fall away from the faith. We will shun them, so it will do no good for you to send them into town for errands."

"What is the nature of this shunning?"

"We will neither buy nor sell nor speak to them until such time as they repent."

"I see. It's not good, but it could have been worse."

Noble's gaze never wavered. "Are you thinking of the historical examples of the Puritans in the New England colonies?"

"As a matter of fact, yes."

"Then consider this: the Puritans immigrated to America for the express purpose of setting up a society that would reflect their doctrines. Then Pilgrims who had other goals moved in with them. These other people had an entire continent to choose town sites from, but they chose to move in with people they disagreed with and then quarreled with them."

"I see the point you're driving at. If we hadn't been starving, we would have settled on the other side of Sole. We want to be good neighbors and we want to live in peace."

"Do you? Then you will move your houses to the other side of your fields and your people will stop roaming our streets armed for war and half nude. We can help you move if you need."

Henley regarded Noble. "I can talk to the people of Freedom about it. Since I'm not a dictator, I can't guarantee the reaction."

Noble continued as though Henley had said nothing. "The second thing you can do to be a good neighbor is to tell Jax to stop bothering Rejoice. If your people have a request of my people, then you need to go straight to our secular authority: the Senate."

Alarm coursed through Rejoice. What was Noble doing? And why? Did he think she was incompetent and needed him to speak for her?

"The third thing you can do is start work on a cure for lung rot."

"Who says we're not?"

"Our lab people have tried to talk to your lab people for a month. We're getting no cooperation."

"Ah." Henley slouched back in his chair. "We figure we have at least a decade before we need an answer. Of course, in universe there are no guarantees except death and gravity. We may not find a cure. I think we will, but we will find it only by using the correct method. Premature excitement over false cures is not conducive to peace. Not until we've tested and double tested all possibilities will we be making any announcements."

"We have dozens of people who cannot wait a decade."

"I'm truly sorry, but you're angry at the wrong person. It's your God who isn't healing these people."

Noble stopped long enough for one deep breath. "Why do your lab people refuse to talk to our lab people?"

Henley half smiled. "When information is all you have to sell, you tend to guard it closely. When we have a product to sell, believe me, we will put it on the market."

"If we had a cure, we would not hide it from you."

"Nor will we hide it from you. When we have one. Until then, offers and counter-offers are premature. May I?" He reached for the teapot to refill his cup. The strong odors of wilted tomato leaves mingled with that of the ginger. "Is there anything else you want me to do to be a good neighbor?"

"One more thing for now. Whatever you have for a government structure needs to meet with our Senate so we can map out a set of common laws for both of us to live by."

Henley rubbed his brow. "The best government is no government. We won't bow to your infantile god. And we won't live by the laws with which you shackle yourselves."

"If you insist on being lawless, we shall forbid you from our cities."

"Oh come now. Hysteria is unwarranted. We are not lawless. We simply don't need laws."

"Would you be opposed to a law that said, 'Do not steal'?"

Henley rubbed his chin. "Not at all. I'll even concede your point. We might have some laws in common. We who came in the Independence hate theft of every kind." He grinned and leaned forward. "And how about a law that says, 'He who does not work, does not eat?'"

Noble's frown deepened. After a moment's pause, he said, "Yes. That Scripture is a fine basis for a law, but we need exemptions for the infirm and infants."

"Yes, we too exempt the infants who will someday grow up to be productive."

"You don't exempt the infants who won't."

Henley sat back again. "You won't catch me apologizing for living a rational and moral life. It is immoral to foist a miserable existence on any human."

The baby's cries pierced Rejoice's brain. He was certainly foisting a miserable existence on her. She inhaled the ginger and tried to force her thoughts away from the evil tracks they were following.

Opportunity watched Mr. Roberson with shining eyes that never left his face. Rejoice's foot nudged Opportunity's, but her sister didn't even blink.

Makepeace chewed his thumb and moaned, "Alas for Babylon."

Rejoice looked over at him. What was Little Brother thinking?

Henley sipped his tea and watched them with eyes that seemed to miss nothing. He set down his cup with a click. "I thank you for your hospitality. We continue to be grateful for the food, for the water, for the information about this world we are now sharing. I'll talk to the people in the dojo and in Freedom, and we'll see what we can do to ease tensions. As soon as we have gained some self-sufficiency, I'll see if we can't move a good distance from First City."

He stood. "All of us have much work to do. I hope that I can invite you over for a longer visit next time. Until then, good day." He bowed slightly to Rejoice and Opportunity. He walked out the door before Noble had risen from his chair.

With a grim look, Noble watched him walk past the window before he muttered, "It is precisely that kind of monster that makes me doubt the wisdom of pacifism."

"Monster?" Opportunity cried. "He was polite and reasonable. You were tearing at him like a torpal."

Makepeace groaned again, "Alas! Alas!"

Rejoice spread out her hands and said deliberately, "Let's stay calm for the sake of our brother. Noble, I too was surprised at the amount of hostility you showed Mr. Roberson. I have never seen you this hostile before." Her jaws hurt from the effort to speak quietly and slowly.

"What hostility?" Noble said. "These are a people who push until something stops them. All I did was set the boundaries."

Rejoice slowly folded her arms. "I thought you were looking forward to evangelizing these people. You just chased them away."

"I'm still looking forward to it. But these people hold us in utter contempt. As long as they hold us in contempt, they will not listen to us about God or anything else." His jaw worked as he stuck his hands in his blue overall pockets. "You're forgetting that I'm more than a missionary to the hexacrabs, churtrees, and Robersonians. I'm also a pastor. The spiritual welfare of this mission and the people I pastor in First City are my responsibility."

Rejoice shook her head. "Each person makes her own decision."

He hissed through his teeth. "Yes. To state the case more precisely,

I am responsible to help guide people as they make those decisions. The influence of these "Rational" people is not good."

This slow motion arguing wearied Rejoice. "What kind of faith is it that swims away through the first hole in the net?"

Opportunity stood. "And what kind of faith is it that tells me I'm supposed to shun my own brother? How can you say that all of us will shun him? The mission hasn't even voted on it."

"We will vote soon."

"I'll vote against it."

Noble sighed. "You do that."

Opportunity grabbed Makepeace's hand. "Come on. Let's finish the orchard." She glared at Noble all the way out.

At the moment Noble looked at his screen, Rejoice said, "I don't know why you presumed to speak for me when you said that Jax was to stop bothering me. When I feel bothered, I tell her to stop."

"I don't have time for this," Noble said. "The next session is in four minutes."

"Cancel it. We need to talk."

"We talked most of the night. We can talk at lunchtime. You should take care of Jubilee. He sounds hungry to me."

"Why did you tell him that Jax was to stop bothering me? I know I'm not called to be an evangelist, like you. But all Christians are called to share their faith. She's listening to me."

Noble watched her with his mouth set in a line. Finally; "Are you sharing your faith with her or is she sharing her faith with you? As a husband and pastor, I have the duty to intervene when I see you getting worse after every contact with Jax."

"Worse at what?"

"Every time you meet with her, you get moodier and more dissatisfied. Your care for the baby is more erratic."

"Noble, I'm depressed."

"We're all depressed. These people are disrupting our lives. You know, I'm glad Elder Chin and I decided to let the hexacrabs study our history. We wanted them to be prepared in case our grandchildren became untrustworthy. Now it looks as if it's going to happen sooner than that. I almost hope Sister Deng is right, and lung rot claims all the humans before they can harm the hexacrabs."

"No, I'm—" She stopped. The only person he had ever pastored who had been clinically depressed had killed herself even after he spent two hours a day for months helping with her babies. If he took her seriously, it would be one more fish in the net already frayed and ready to burst. Already he was showing a side she had never seen and did not like.

"You are what? You have thirty seconds."

"I'm thinking. Why do you think the Robersonians are going to hurt the hexacrabs?"

"A feeling. Just a gut feeling."

"Well, you were right last night, I mean, this morning. The cloud is breaking and we are drowning." He looked so weary. Why wouldn't he rest? When would she get rest? "I'll go feed the baby."

He nodded brusquely and seated himself before the screen.

Dismissed and chastised, she walked into her bedroom echoing with the cries of the baby. *No normal child cries so much.* Mr. Roberson considered it a moral duty to kill such children. What kind of future did this baby have? Would he ever be a pleasure? She gripped the side of the crib. She hated him. She didn't want to, but she hated him with all her heart. She had gone through so much to have him, and he wasn't worth it.

She whispered to the screaming child, "I think I envy Jax. She could take your pillow and smother you and then sleep at night with a clean conscience. Life is so much simpler for them. It's not fair that we who love God should have to swim against the strong current. I'm so tired."

She stopped and stared at the pillow in her hands just over the baby's face, the one that had been propping the baby on his side. What was she planning to do? She turned and threw it against a wall. The apple branch painting clattered on the floor beside the pillow. She strode to the window and clutched the sash and looked at the naked branches of the apple orchard. "God, why don't you supernaturally give me some love for this child? I could take anything if I loved him just the tiniest bit." Her fingertips hurt where they pressed into the hard plastic. "God, I need to hear from You before I lose my mind."

The door opened behind her, and Noble shouted above the baby's cries, "I thought you were going to feed Jubilee."

Rejoice laid her head against the glass. "I thought you were doing a session."

"One of her children playing tag knocked over a beehive. She's tending the casualties."

She listened to his footsteps, the creak of the changing platform, and the soft sound of snaps. A sudden stench filled the room.

"His bottom is all blisters. He needs to be changed more often."

"Yes." She turned to watch him wash the flailing boy. "I'm sorry. Let me finish the job."

"What were you doing?"

"Thinking. Praying. What you were doing last night on your walk?" She slipped a new diaper on the baby, and he promptly wet in it. After replacing it, she looked up to Noble watching her with an expression she could not fathom. Was it regret? She sat on the bed to begin another chaotic nursing. "What are you thinking now?"

"You don't want to know." He left.

* * *

Three days later, Noble, Rejoice, Mark, Opportunity, and Makepeace stood on the end of the dock in a drizzly rain watching the first barge filled with passengers from the sea jet being ferried in by hexacrabs.

Beside them stood Ur-Veena in his LV that glistened with raindrops. Little Ti-Assisi tied to Ur-Veena's shell played with his bobber and squeaked. Ur-Veena's gills flared when the barge slid next to the dock with the barest kiss.

After the ramp unfurled itself and became rigid, Harmony was the first to roll onto the dock in her chair. Noble bent to kiss her on the cheek. Her tremulous smile dissolved as she signed, {Your life have women many. Hope you don't mind.}

Noble dropped to one knee and swept the four still girls into a group hug. "I always wanted a little girl. I can't tell you how happy having four will make me." Then he stood and embraced Mother who looked as though she hadn't slept since the day Stronghold had run away. "Mother Holly! It's always good to see you."

Mother turned to embrace Rejoice, who relaxed and laid her head on Mother's shoulder as they swayed back and forth.

She whispered in Rejoice's ear, "I'm here now, sweet-love. We'll have you feeling better very soon."

Rejoice stepped back and looked into Mother's eyes. "I missed you so much."

"I missed you too, love." Then she said in a louder voice, "Where's my newest grandbaby?"

Noble answered, "With Sister Hancock until we get you moved in and you've rested a bit."

Mother looked down at Mark behind Noble's leg. She released Rejoice and swept him up under his arms and twirled in a circle.

She set him down and held him by the shoulders. "My, haven't you grown big. What are your father and mother feeding you?"

Mark grinned. "Good food! I'll show you the door at our house where Father measures how much bigger I get every month."

Mother loosed Mark and walked over to Opportunity and embraced her. She whispered in her ear, "Thank you for your sacrifices. Thank you for taking care of my son and my daughter. You are a good and faithful servant. Your father would be very proud."

Opportunity stepped back and looked in Mother's eyes and bit her lower lip. Then she looked down and turned away.

Mother watched her for a moment and then scanned the dock. "And where is my well-beloved son, in whom I am well-pleased?"

Makepeace ambled up mechanically, with his eyes on the ground, grinning.

Mother engulfed him in a hug and whispered in his ear, "I missed you so much! I love you so much!"

Makepeace kept his arms at his side. Then bounced on his toes and Mother bounced with him. He sang, "I got the joy, joy, joy, joy down in my heart."

Mother lit up. She grabbed his hand and that of One Faith and hopped in a circle with him. The other girls and then Rejoice and then Noble and Mark joined in the hop-dance circle, singing and grinning to the end of the song. Opportunity looked embarrassed as other passengers squeezed around them and smiled at the sight.

Rejoice panted. She was so out of shape. They had needed Mother there. If only Rejoice had inherited her happy gene so that her default position was joy.

Mother stopped and put her hands on her knees and puffed, "Okay, that's all the joy this old lady can handle at present."

She looked up with tears in her eyes. "I wish your father could be here too. He would be so intrigued by what you've done here."

Ur-Veena trundled up and the girls smiled as they jostled in close to see the baby hexacrab on his back. Mother pressed her palm and cheek against the glass side of the LV, and Ur-Veena pressed a tentacle on the other side. He whistled, "I am told that air-ocean people need to rest after a journey."

Mother fanned herself. "Well, I certainly need to rest now." The lines of exhaustion resettled on her face.

Ur-Veena's silver blue eyes swiveled as he tracked the 3-D board in front of him, the baby on his back, and the humans surrounding his LV. "When you have rested, I will sing you a new song."

"Thank you," Mother said. "My gills huff at the thought."

They moved toward the cliffside elevator, when Makepeace grabbed Mother's arm. "Stronghold?"

Mother stroked him gently on his cheek. "You look so much like your father." She looked down and coughed, and then gazed at him again. "And Makepeace, you pray like your father too. Pray for your big brother, with whom I am not well pleased."

Makepeace moaned, "Alas, Babylon!" He turned away and chewed on his knuckle.

Rejoice's chest hurt.

As the elevator doors closed behind them, Rejoice thought she glimpsed He Gives leaping from the second barge onto the dock. No, if he had come, Mother would have said something. "Mother, how was your trip?"

"I don't know. I wasn't paying any attention. Harmony had some problems."

"They put us in a special section and put a curtain around us," Reconciliation, the oldest girl, said. Her black hair looped out of its tattered braids.

"That was so we wouldn't stare at people," One Faith, the youngest, said. "I slept for twenty hours."

"You did not," Peace said. She lisped through the gap left by her lost incisors. The mist beaded into spangles on her red hair. "The curtains were so people wouldn't stare at us."

Opportunity fidgeted in the corner of the elevator. "Mother, did you bring my art supplies?"

"No, sweet-love." She ran a hand over her gray-streaked curly hair. "We only had room for our clothes and medical supplies. The rest is coming by hexabarge."

"But that could take months!" Opportunity cried. "You never know how long they'll dilly-dally doing whatever it is they do."

"I almost hope they do. I asked and they still have the agreement that if they take longer than two months, the shipping is free. That would help our financial situation."

"I've already waited so long!"

The doors opened at the top of the cliff.

Mother stiffened at the sight of Ernest leaning on his rifle, wearing a red shirt that seemed more cut-out than fabric, his blond curls dripping. Mother's gaze darted to Opportunity before she closed her eyes and took three deep breaths. Her mouth twitched as she left the elevator. "Young

Man, I am Sister Holly, the mother of Sister Opportunity."

He smiled as he extended his hand. "Much pleasure."

She gently grasped his hand and said faintly, "Please forgive me. I'm very tired."

He backed away. "For truth." He and Opportunity walked side by side behind the others as they walked down the road toward Rejoice's expanded home.

When Rejoice turned to ask if Opportunity had put the apple juice in the refrigerator to chill, He Gives came out of the elevator. He saw Opportunity and Ernest together and stood as though stunned for a moment. Then he darted back into the elevator. She opened her mouth and tripped over a yertle dashing across the road.

The girls squealed. Mark pounced on the creature. Noble and Mother were helping Rejoice up almost before she knew she had fallen. The girls clustered around their mother and kept on squealing as Mark flipped the yertle over to show its many legs beating in a frenzy. He kept his hands well away from where the stinger probed at one end.

Noble squeezed Rejoice's shoulders.

"How badly are you hurt?" Mother asked.

Rejoice couldn't answer, for the wind had been knocked out of her.

"Eew, what is it?" Reason said. She twisted her auburn hair around her forefinger.

Noble laughed. "We call them possums on the half shell. Everybody runs over one eventually."

"Well, that's an Old Earth reference that will fly over the heads of the younger ones." Mother laughed as she examined Mark's prize.

Rejoice sucked in a painful breath.

Mother said, "Can those hurt Jubilee?"

"Oppie," gasped Rejoice, but no one heard her over the clamor of the girls. She tried again. "Opportunity!"

"What do you want?"

Rejoice sucked in more breath. Would she need to shout to be heard for the rest of her life? "Oppie, I just saw He Gives."

Opportunity frowned. "He called again?"

"No. I saw him by the elevators."

"Here?" Opportunity's voice rose to a squeal. "On this island?"

As Rejoice nodded, Ernest said, "Identity of He Gives?"

Opportunity's mouth opened and her eyes grew wide as she turned to face the way they had come and then back to Rejoice. "When?"

"Just now. He ran back into the elevator."

"Mother! Why didn't you tell me he was coming?"

"I didn't know, sweet-love. I was busy with Harmony."

"Oh! Oh! Oh!" Her black hair streamed behind her as she ran back to the elevators.

Noble grabbed Ernest's arm before the young man could follow her. "Please excuse us, Ernest. Could you visit us tomorrow after we have taken care of family business?"

Ernest watched Opportunity running until she reached the elevators. She pounded on the doors until they opened. He shrugged, adjusted the rifle on his back, and sauntered away.

The girls huddled around their mother and looked frightened again.

"Come, little ducklings," Mother said, patting them on their heads. "Let's go see your new bedroom."

PACIFISTS' WAR CHAPTER SIXTEEN

As they entered the house, Peace pinched her nose. "It stinks in here!"

Harmony slapped the side of one flat hand into the palm of the other. {Stop.}

"You'll get used to it," Mother said distantly. "It's the honest smell of tomato vines that had to be brought in or blown away in a hurricane. See, there's one turning ripe. We'll eat it when it is ready."

Peace jiggled. "I don't like tomatoes."

"You'll eat what is set before you. Rejoice, will you lead me to the bathroom?"

When Rejoice did, her mother pulled her into the cubicle and handed her a small container. "One every morning, and one every night. I'm going to watch you swallow one now."

Rejoice opened the container filled with tiny white pills. Mother was a nurse, not a psychiatrist. What did she know about depression? "Excuse me; I think you may be overreacting."

"This is your mother speaking. If I have to hold you down to make you take it I will. I've had a lot of experience with Makepeace."

Rejoice took a pill, put it in her mouth, and swallowed. "Happy now?"

"Getting there. Next I want to talk to Noble about a treatment plan."

"No. Don't tell him."

"He has the most right to know. I imagine he's already figured it out."

"He hasn't. Right now he's carrying the world on his shoulders. If you tell him I'm depressed, he'll be afraid I'll do what Sister Olson did. He doesn't need that."

Lines that Rejoice had never noticed before deepened on Mother's face as she thought. "You're ashamed and want to keep this secret."

"No, I think you're wrong and I'm just tired."

Mother rubbed her eyes. "All right, on one condition. I will watch you take each and every pill."

"Oh, Mother!"

"We didn't do that for Sister Olson, and too late we found out she wasn't taking her medication."

Rejoice blinked. "I never knew that."

"Doctor-patient confidentiality. Afterwards, Doctor Cruz decided to expand the nurses' education. We hadn't expected mental illness because all of us were stable people before we boarded the Starflower."

"So what happened to me?"

"Honey-sweet, I'm sure this is a one-time thing. You had a difficult pregnancy and now you have a child with colic which I never heard of anybody enjoying. On top of that, those awful—" She stopped and forced in several breaths. "What does Opportunity see in that young man?"

"I don't know. I honestly don't know." Unless it was that Ernest was handsome and He Gives looked like a mud pie next to him.

Mother twisted her fingers together. "I thought I had taught all of you to love God and His law." She pulled a handkerchief out and dabbed her eyes. "There I go again. Why don't you give me a few minutes to collect myself?"

Who was depressed here? Rejoice retreated to the cacophony of shrieking girls chasing each other around their rented cots. Appalled Harmony pleaded silently at them to stop. Even Mark had forgotten his inside manners. Finally, Noble came into the bedroom, gathered the children, and herded them outside to run and shout while he scanned the skies for pack bats. The ensuing silence weighed more than the noise had.

Rejoice was shoving a box of clothing under a counter when Harmony plucked at her sleeve. She sat back on her heels. "Yes?"

Harmony whispered slowly, "He left me this note," and extended a folded sheet of paper.

Rejoice took it with some wonder. She hadn't touched writing paper for at least twelve years, not since she had helped place paper books on the shelves in the library. Where had the paper come from? A shock halted her momentarily as she unfolded the frontispiece of a Bible. She read the hand-printed block letters with growing disbelief: Remember Devotion.

She scrutinized gaunt Harmony wiping her nose and struggling for breath. Behind Harmony, Mother entered the room and her face darkened. "Why are you showing her that note from the pit of hell? You should burn it."

Rejoice shivered. She had never seen Mother with that type of anger.

Harmony reached toward Rejoice and pleaded with her eyes.

Rejoice gave the paper back and stood. "Mother, your room is through here. I'm sorry we had to make the girl's room your hallway, but it was the only way we could connect the modules and keep the bathrooms from being the hallways." As Mother walked into her bedroom, Harmony tucked away the note.

The room seemed to swirl. What possessed Stronghold?

The front door opened. Rejoice entered the living room, where Opportunity slumped into a chair.

Opportunity rubbed her forehead. "He's already gone. He was halfway to the jet before I got to the dock. I tried to call him a hundred times and he's not answering my calls. Do you think he saw Ernest?"

"I know he did."

Opportunity covered her face with her hands. "Oh, what am I going to do?"

There was a knock on the door and the sound of a baby screaming on the other side. "I believe that you'll be heating some water for tea and setting out some places for our guests, while I attempt to feed Cranky Pants," Rejoice said.

Opportunity shambled to the stove, while Rejoice went to the door. Elder Chin tapped the street with his cane, his granddaughter Heart's

Desire stood at his elbow, and Doctor Carlson behind him held the writhing baby.

Why Elder Chin? "Come in," Rejoice said. "Where are the Hancocks?"

"They spied Pastor Cruz with their great-nieces and went to greet them." Elder Chin shuffled in.

Doctor Carlson followed behind him and handed Jubilee off to Rejoice. "This little guy misses his mommy a lot."

She hadn't missed him. He squirmed in her arms. But if she didn't nurse him pretty quick, she would burst.

Mother ran out of the bedroom. "I hear my new grandbaby." She plucked the baby out of Rejoice's arms. "Let me hold him for just a minute before you feed him."

Mother held the baby up and snorgled him up and down. He stopped yelling. "My, aren't you a handsome young man?" His eyes focused on hers and he made half a gummy smile. Then his eyes clouded and his happy face was transformed into his gargoyle face in half a second.

It hadn't taken long for him to assume his default position.

He took a long, deep breath and Mother said with a laugh, "He's winding up for the pitch."

Jubilee's screams echoed down through the room and Rejoice's head.

"My, but you've got healthy lungs," Mother said. "Well, I can't meet your urgent needs, but I know who can." She handed him to Rejoice.

Rejoice took the screaming baby into her darkened bedroom and sat on the bed to nurse him. She left the door open so she could see the table and listen to the conversation. She was grateful when the baby actually calmed down and earnestly sucked.

Mother walked over to Doctor Carlson and took both his hands. "It's good to see you, Brother Established. How is your research coming?"

"That's one of the reasons that I came," he said. "If you're not too tired, I wanted to tell you about an interesting development."

"I'll hold up for a few more minutes before I collapse." She laughed. "Elder Chin. You look tired. Have a seat."

"I confess, Sister Holly, this old man is beginning to feel the weight of the times." He groaned as he lowered himself into a chair.

"As we all are." Mother turned and grasped a chair.

Doctor Carlson touched her shoulder. "Carol, I don't understand what is going on in Stronghold's mind at present. But for three years on the Starflower he opened his heart to me. I watched him grow from a boy to a man. I cannot believe that the kind of passionate love that he has for Harmony can be so easily quenched."

Mother's face crumpled and she spun away from him. "I can't speak of it now," she croaked and walked over to the cupboards. "Opportunity, please set the cups on the table and I'll get the tea tins out. And set the screen on captioning for Heart's Desire. Where are the Hancocks?"

"I see them walking up now." Opportunity glanced toward the window and set down the pottery cups she had formed back on Sole.

Mother set the table with the tea tins and spoons as Opportunity carried over the hot water.

"Established, Dr. Cruz sends her regards to her favorite student." Mother said.

"I thought you were the teacher's pet." He laughed. "Didn't you get your daughter to marry her son just to curry her favor?"

Mother laughed. It was her musical laugh that Rejoice had grown up loving.

Dr. Carlson said, "Sister Deng is diligent in her studies. She'll complete her P.A. in a few months and says that she wants to keep studying, become a doctor, and help find that cure."

"Well, God bless her." Mother said.

For the first time, Rejoice thought of Dr. Carlson and Mother as a potential couple. They were both lonely. Sister Carlson had died only two years after Father. Her heart lurched at the double grief.

The Hancocks burst through the door. Sister Hancock cried out to Mother, "Don't get up." She ran over Mother's chair, crouched behind her, and threw her arms around her neck. "I'm sooooo glad you're here!" she cried. "Where's my beautiful niece, Harmony?"

Mother kissed her cheek. "She's exhausted. I tucked her in just before you got here. Her eyes closed and she was asleep before I put her respirator on. Let her sleep for an hour or two."

Brother Hancock sidled up behind them and threw his arm around both ladies. "Eh, it's just like old times on the *Magellan*." He winked at Elder Chin. Then he looked over to the sink. "Of course, that Young Lady Opportunity was just a rugrat then."

Rejoice grinned even though she didn't know what a rugrat was. She enjoyed listening to the banter of those who had been adults when they came to New Earth even with the odd phrases they tossed about. The love and joy in her crowded living room warmed her heart.

* * *

That night, after an evening of putting girls into bed who kept popping out because they needed water or they needed to potty or they were afraid of the dark or they weren't sleepy or they thought they heard something, Rejoice and Noble crawled into bed and leaned on each other. The baby grumbled on Rejoice's lap, but he wasn't screaming, so they could talk.

Rejoice rubbed her cheek against his shoulder. "Are you tired?"

"I am so tired," he croaked, "my blood cells are napping in the capillaries."

At that moment, Noble's computer beeped. Jubilee screamed.

"I can't believe you didn't pull it off-line," Rejoice moaned.

Noble shouted over the baby's cries. "I did. It's been overridden!" He slapped open the connection as he snatched it from the bedside shelf. "What?"

Pastor Wiseman looked sad. "Once again, I apologize for calling so late for you."

Noble scowled and pointed toward the door. Rejoice hastily wrapped the baby in a blanket and went out to lay him under the main screen where he wouldn't be stepped on by somebody stumbling about in the dark. When she crept in the bedroom, Pastor Wiseman said, "Is Young Lady Holly still living with you?"

"So far as I know. She was here an hour ago."

And what a sad lot they looked at supper. After the adrenaline of the reunions wore off, the exhaustion and despair returned with a vengeance. All four women were on the verge of tears and all four girls so sad and scared they kept wetting their pants. Surely Mark would never want to get married.

"Then I'll leave it up to you to give her the news as you see fit."

"No," Rejoice said.

Noble sagged onto the bed and Rejoice sat beside him.

"An hour ago, Brother He Gives Eternal Life was walking through the terminal when he saw three Robersonians. Witnesses attest that he attacked them unprovoked. One of them got a broken nose. Several of our people got hurt pulling the Robersonians off He Gives."

"No," Rejoice said.

"He Gives is in the clinic now having emergency surgery to remove the spleen the Robersonians kicked to bits. He almost bled to death. They also dislocated both his shoulders and broke both arms. He's going to live, but he's badly hurt."

Rejoice pulled up her knees and squeezed herself into a tight ball. Jax must have taught them how to do that.

Noble rubbed his face. "Thank you. Keep me . . . keep me posted."

He broke the connection and carefully laid the screen back on the shelf. "Tomorrow, I must rise and have an appropriate response to every situation. But I . . . don't . . . know . . . what . . ." He slid off the bed, lay face down on the floor, stretched out his arms, and prayed aloud in Hebrew, his language of privacy.

Rejoice retrieved the baby and laid him on the bed. She carefully positioned herself around him. Father God, what would they do next?

* * *

Rejoice sat on the half-way stone and panted. Would she never get back in shape? The blue sky shone through the gray lace of shroud tree fronds.

A howler bag gulped and swooped away. Her rifle chafed one shoulder.

Mark whacked the gravel on the trail with a stick. "I don't know why I can't have a yertle because Reason got stung. I told her where to pick it up, and she said I wasn't her authority."

Noble pulled at the straps of the baby backpack. Tiny snores issued from the bundle on his back. "She paid for her thoughtlessness. However, it won't be long before Jubilee starts getting into things. I won't allow anything in the house that could harm Jubilee."

Mark stopped pounding the gravel. "Does that mean we can't have candles for Birth of Christ Day?"

Rejoice laughed. "We can have candles if you keep them away from the baby." She inhaled the warm pepper scent of the brown and gray jungle. A wind whisper and the tiny clicks of semi-beetles formed a background of quiet.

If only she could bottle this peace and bring it back home. Six adults and six children filled the house more thoroughly than volume would indicate. The girls would not understand that they could not go outside without an armed adult with them. "They are sure good forgetters," Mark had said.

One terrible day when they had refused to come in despite calls and searches, Rejoice had sat them down to watch a vid of pack bats in action. After that, it was two weeks before they would go outside without being carried. Eight years of dealing with a single child who had always listened to explanations had not prepared Rejoice for the bubbling silliness of four nieces whose minds must have left with Stronghold.

Most suppers were chaos. Most nights were punctuated with nightmares. For some reason, Rejoice's churtree nightmares returned and she would wake up in a panic. Noble would need to hold her tightly for five or ten minutes before the trembling would stop. It was odd because the churtree peace still held and she hadn't been thinking about them in particular. Brother Popowich had even agreed to switch months at the churtree observation post with Noble until the family situation was straightened out.

Mother's nightmares of those left behind on Old Earth also returned, but now she had no husband to comfort her.

Harmony, a pallid ghost with anguished eyes, rolled aimlessly from the bedroom to the living room and back again. Noble was discouraged because he couldn't help her focus on her memorized scripture. Her sleep was also interrupted by nightmares that she refused to describe.

Worst of all, Mother had stopped singing. She refused to start a choir at the mission, though everyone petitioned her to do so. She did not sing while cooking or cleaning. Nor did she chant lessons for the girls as she had before. Even the baby got no lullabies from her.

Once, Rejoice had seen her staring out the window with a blank gaze, and had asked her what she was thinking.

"Stronghold wanted to stay behind on Old Earth. He wanted to be adopted by the Apgils and stay with his friend Ricky. Perhaps I should have let him go."

"Oh, Mother, he was frightened. Ricky had told him he would die in outer space. He was just a little boy."

"And what is he now? Does a man abandon his own children? His own wife?"

Rejoice had tried to hug her, but she stood rigid and unrelenting. Until that moment, Rejoice had not known Mother was capable of bitterness.

Stronghold should see what he had done. Her palms pressed against the rough rock. Rejoice inhaled deeper. *God of peace, God of light.*

Almost a month of crying and confusion. Makepeace now required daily medication or else he tantrumed when tension tightened the air. Opportunity hardly spoke at all and never smiled. She went through the motions of doing her duties. Half-hearted and half-done. It would have been nice if she could have at least played with the children a little instead of just chaperoning them.

Ernest never came around. Noble had told him that he could continue to help with the sports classes, only if he stayed away from Opportunity. He grudgingly agreed. And Jax had stopped calling. Jax, she did miss. Rejoice tipped her head back and studied the clouds floating slowly by.

Listen to her whine. The brothers and sisters were helping. Every other

Worship Day the Hancocks would take care of Harmony and entertain her daughters. On the other Worship Day, Sister Redhorse was trying to take care of Makepeace the way her mother had.

Unfortunately, the attempted respite was having limited success. Makepeace would only stay for an hour or two with Sister Redhorse before making it obvious that he wanted to go home despite the chaos. They needed to pay her back for those broken dishes. Rejoice sighed.

"If I can't have a yertle and I can't have a fuzzy snake, can I at least have a chicken for a pet?"

Rejoice chuckled. Mark looked so serious. "We can't afford to get a hen her very own coop, but if you take a chicken from the flock to play with, and then put it right back, I suppose you could. If you promise to not bring it into the house."

"I want the black one. I'll call it Shiny because its feathers shine in the sunlight."

"Good name. Now I have an idea. Why don't we picnic here instead of at the library?"

Noble pulled her up. "Because you need the walk." His computer beeped. He smiled apologetically at Rejoice before turning on the screen. "Pastor here."

The dark, broad features of Brother Lerner, the man in charge of the deep sea mine, filled the screen. "Sorry to bother you, Pastor, on your day of rest, but I wanted to run this by you before it goes to the Senate."

"What is it?"

"Well, it's good news and bad news. Which do you want first?"

Mark squeezed in between his parents, and Noble lowered the screen so his son could also see. "It's been a long time since I've heard good news. Start with that."

"We found germanium."

"That's wonderful!" Rejoice exclaimed. "Now we can rebuild computers with some capacity to them!"

Noble glanced from Rejoice to the screen. "You don't look as excited as my wife does. Is that because of the bad news?"

"You got it. Not ten minutes after the last test drill, the hexacrabs shut the whole thing down and declared the smoker a forbidden-to-air-ocean-people zone. They say there are too many kraken there, and they don't want them disturbed anymore."

Rejoice groped for some hope. "If we found germanium in one place, surely we can find it someplace else as well."

The prominent furrows on Brother Lerner's face deepened. "And maybe they'll shut down that one too. The Treaty says they can close off up to five percent of the ocean. They aren't close to that limit yet."

Noble scratched his cheek. "The investors aren't going to be happy."

"I'm not," Brother Lerner said heavily. "My wife told me not to invest my entire retirement in the mine, but I was convinced that good things would come of it. Now I have to go home and tell her we're wiped out financially. I think I liked it better when we were communists."

Rejoice sighed. "Maybe we should cut off their access to some of the air-ocean and see how they like it."

"I suppose we could," Noble said. "But to what end? Besides, they don't need our land."

Brother Lerner ran a blunt fingernail along the crease between his nose and eyebrows. "You sure about that? There must be some reason why they placed an order for three hundred LVs."

Noble glanced at Rejoice before looking back at Brother Lerner. "When was this?"

"Yesterday. Drained every credit they have."

"Did they say what for?"

"Not a click. Oh, they ordered two rifles for each one, too. The firing range should grow to be a busy place. Maybe I should get out of the mining business and open another rifle range instead."

Noble said, "I think I'll talk to Ur-Veena about the moral obligation to pay you some compensation for taking your mine."

"I would appreciate it, though how they'll pay me when all their credits are tied up in LVs and rifles, I don't know. I'll talk to you again on Oneday. God be with you."

Noble frowned as he placed the computer back in its case. "What do you suppose is going on?" His eyes widened as he grabbed the computer again and tapped a code. "Elder Chin. Have you informed the hexacrabs that their larval stage is a parasite of the kraken?"

Elder Chin's sagging face turned toward the screen. His lips moved in and out for a few seconds. Behind him, Young Lady Heart's Desire approached with a cup of tea. She knelt and waited as he said, "No. I'm not sure that it's our place to be the current on which such a revelation should flow into their culture."

"Did you know the hexacrabs have ordered three hundred land vehicles?"

"I believe I did hear about that a few hours ago, but I was then deep in thought about the churtree peace. One of the spears is tilting. When it falls, will the peace end?"

He reached for the tea, and his granddaughter placed it in his hand. "The urgency in your voice tells me that I should have paid more attention."

"I was trying to think why the hexacrabs would require so many LVs. They purchased two rifles for every LV and emptied their accounts doing it. Perhaps they intend to raid the churtree villages."

Rejoice held her breath. She wanted to think that would be a terrible thing, but she could not. Like a sore that would never go away was the memory of seeing stacks of hexacrab shells in the Red Scar village, Noble bleeding on the deck of the *Magellan*, the bloody footprints leading from Father's room. She had often hoped a plague would wipe out both the churtrees and the need to love a people she could not.

Elder Chin touched his wrinkled lips to the tea and blinked, "They may."

"I'm going to call Brother Hancock. Will you stay on to advise me?"

Elder Chin nodded slightly and his jowls quivered. Noble split the view and Elder Chin's face shrank as bald Brother Hancock's face filled the other half of the screen.

"Eh, I'm glad you called. I just now discovered a new alga that's motile.

Want to see it?"

"What does motile mean?" Mark asked.

Noble placed a fingertip on Mark's lips. "Not now. I wanted to know if you knew why the hexacrabs bought three hundred armed LVs."

"Did they now?" He frowned as he rubbed his bulbous nose. "That's a puzzler. Hmm. They are keen on exploring. They loved hearing about the earth *Magellan* and Cook expeditions. Maybe they're mounting an expedition to the North Pole."

"Maybe they're planning a war."

Brother Hancock's blue eyes widened. He shouted. "Bethany, come here!"

Noble tapped in the code for Ur-Veena. Minutes passed as they waited for Ur-Veena to answer. Sister Hancock sat next to Brother Hancock. Elder Chin sipped his tea. Rejoice sat on the rock again and Mark resumed whacking the gravel.

Ur-Veena whistled and grated, "I wait to hear."

"Like a pebble between joint and shell is a question on which I meditate," whistled Noble.

"Bend toward me."

"Why have the water-ocean people traded for three hundred air shells?"

Water swished past the microphone. "We are growing in population. Our future requires air shells."

"Will there swim into your future the killing of the Orange or Yellow Scar churtrees?"

More water swished. "We will death dance only the churtrees who desire."

Noble looked relieved, but still puzzled. "Have the water-ocean people discovered other churtrees?"

"We do not search for churtrees. Urgent motions compel my vision, therefore I cease speaking with you." The connection clicked shut.

Elder Chin smiled. "Therefore we gain another mystery to keep us up late at night."

Bother Hancock grinned. "No mystery about what keeps the Pastor up. Where's your little noisemaker?"

"Asleep on my back. God be with you." He slid the computer into its case again. "Why am I not satisfied?"

When they returned from the picnic, the girls were dancing in the shady orchard circle while Opportunity played the flute. Well, that was an improvement. Maybe Opportunity was feeling a little better too.

Harmony sat in her wheelchair with them. God of Peace, grant her peace. Her sister-in-law's hands were shaking. God grant she wasn't coming down with some illness in addition to the lung rot. Makepeace also sat nearby, rocking as he studied the shiny parabolic surface of a flashlight. Mark ran to the girls.

Inside the house, Mother snapped off the screen when they entered and rushed up to take the baby. Her lips brushed Rejoice's cheek. "You lie down and rest, honey-love, and I'll give Jubilee his work-out. Come here, precious boy."

Rejoice shrugged off the rifle and dropped it in its rest. "Who were you talking to, Mother?"

"A friend. Hibiscus tea is on the stove. Jax called and said she wants to talk to you."

Rejoice and Noble looked at each other. "What do you think? May I call her?"

Noble placed a hand on his chest. "You're asking me?"

"You're the reason I haven't called her in a month. Tell you what. You stay with me when I call and when Jax says something untoward, you can tell her to stop."

Noble shifted his feet. "Have you been wanting to call her?"

"Yes. I can't solve a puzzle she gave me."

"Oh." He watched Mother take the baby into the back bedroom. "I was hoping to take a shower and join you for a nap."

Rejoice smiled. Eventually, they'd nap. "I promise to make it a short call if you promise to take a short shower."

He smiled back. "That's a current I'd like to swim."

A few minutes later, Rejoice lay on the bed, calling Jax.

Jax answered, out of breath, as though she had run to the computer. The screen stayed black. "Rejoice?"

"You called for me? I hope it isn't about government matters." Rejoice heard her gasp a greater volume of air.

"May I visit you tomorrow?"

Rejoice was surprised at how very much she did want to see Jax again. "Will you visit me in my home and allow my husband to listen in?"

A long silence made Rejoice check to make sure they were still connected. "For truth."

"And when you come, bring the solution to the puzzle, will you? I'm stuck on level 99."

Suddenly the image of Jax flared on the screen. She had moved into view of the camera in her office. Black and white zebra markings on her face reflected on a silver tunic. "Level 99. How long?"

"For two months."

"But I gave it to you two months ago."

"Well, actually, it was a week and two months. It took me a week to get to 99, and I haven't budged since. I can't understand the question."

Jax looked sick? Awestruck? It was hard to tell with the stripes obscuring her face. "Mr. Roberson himself devised that test."

"Test? I thought it was a game."

"There is no answer for 99. But it is easy to find an incorrect answer."

"And you let me waste two months trying to make sense out of a senseless problem?"

"Most never reach even problem fifty, not with months of effort. Necessity for you to consider future generations. A child of you and Mr. Roberson would be a prodigious genius, a child of much power."

"Did you say what I thought you said?"

"You should ask him for a chance to strengthen your genetic posterity. He likes to be asked."

"I'm sure he does. Forget it, Jax." Maybe Noble was right. "I don't like it when you urge me to commit adultery."

"Adultery is a no-sense word."

"Noble and I don't agree. Don't visit us if that's all you can talk about."

Panic flashed across Jax's face before being replaced by anger. "It's evil, especially for you, to be owned as a slave by your husband as though you possess no mind or rights. He tells you who to talk to, what to believe, what to do."

"We both have a higher Master that we're responsible to obey. Better enslaved by Him and our laws than enslaved by passions."

Jax forced a laugh. "Passions make life enjoyable. No better master." "I know you don't believe that. No matter what you feel like doing, you exercise every day. You work hard even if you want to laze about."

Jax tapped her lip. Rejoice's eyebrows lifted. Jax had colored her teeth black and silver. "Speaking of working hard, your brother labors eighteen hours a day."

Good thing Jax could not see her face. "I hope he's happy," she muttered. Oops. She had said that aloud.

"He seems to be, though he is disappointing many women. Nothing they do can pull him out of the lab."

"I don't—the lab? A computer lab?"

"Medical. He says he does not want to die a miserable death like your father did."

"But he doesn't know any medicine."

"He's a fast learner. I was rechecking the files of your family—"

"Those are private."

"—and your father was a remarkable man. I can't understand why you let him die."

Rejoice's throat hurt. How could Jax sting her with so many emotions in so short a time? "It wasn't a matter of letting him. There was nothing we could do about it."

"You don't possess the ability to transplant? Doesn't Makepeace possess two healthy lungs?"

"Makepeace happens to be using them. Father would never have allowed such an operation."

"Both could have lived on one lung each."

"Until the fungus invaded the new lung. Even if that weren't so, Father would never have made Makepeace go through an ordeal he would never understand. We don't transplant nonrenewable parts from people who are alive without their consent."

"You rely on God."

Rejoice stopped. Was she being led into a verbal trap? "Yes, and what medical skills and equipment we do have. We believe that God can guide the doctor. Look, I don't want to argue about that. I don't want to hear about my sinful brother. And I don't want to hear about improving the genetic pool by polluting the moral pool."

"So you want to be as deaf as Heart's Desire. Ultimately, only that which encourages life is moral."

Noble came in and elaborately locked the door.

"Um, Jax, I have to take care of something. Oh, and you still owe me an almanac for the information about the kraken."

"I'm sorry, but Henley vetoed that bargain. We'll renegotiate."

"Why don't you call me tomorrow, and we can argue some more. God be with you." She turned off the reception.

When Noble kissed her on the neck, she laughed.

"Does that tickle?"

"No. I'm thinking about Jax and how outrageous she is. The thing is, she doesn't even know she's outrageous."

His words were muffled as he kissed her shoulder. "I don't know a soul who doesn't think he's right and everyone who disagrees is wrong."

"Why does she keep trying to make me see things the way she does?"

Noble propped himself up on one elbow. "Because the urge to convert is not confined to Christians. Could we talk about this later?"

"Later you'll be asleep."

"I hope so."

Rejoice laughed again. "I remember a wise pastor once saying that men are simple-minded. Let's amend that to single-minded."

Someone knocked at the door, and Mother's muted voice floated in.

"I'm sorry. I'm out of diapers, and Jubilee needs a new one. It can't wait."

Noble growled and pulled up the quilt.

Rejoice hurriedly re-buttoned her dress. "There's a button missing. You must have pulled it off."

"Not me. Must have been Jubilee."

"Uh-huh. Now roll over and pretend you're sleeping."

As soon as the door opened, Mother bustled in with the baby and a putrid smell. Rejoice pulled down the changing platform and squirted cleanser onto a washrag.

"What's this?" said Mother, unpeeling the diaper. "How did he get a tomato in his diaper?"

"Oh, Mark was trying to feed him our salad. I'll have to tell him to be more careful."

"You'll have to tell him more than that. Look at the rash where it pressed against his skin. That explains the rash around his mouth, too." Mother gently cleaned the baby. "Sweetheart, you eat tomatoes every day. What if Jubilee is allergic to them?"

"I don't know."

"I'm sure that's why he has such horrendous colic. You are not to eat tomatoes for a week, and we'll see if that doesn't improve things."

"Mother. Raw tomato juice is acidic and I'm sure that's what irritated his skin."

"No tomatoes for a week. Come here, little grandson. Let's go for a walk," she bustled out and the door clicked behind her.

Rejoice folded her arms. Had Mother been this bossy before and had she simply never noticed it? Or was Mother clinging to simple solutions in a complicated time? Or were they all reaching the breaking point with each other? A noise brought her out of her reverie.

Noble had just flipped his computer onto their mood music and turned up the volume. He tossed her computer into the crib and shoved both the computer and crib outside the door. Again he locked it elaborately and turned to face Rejoice. He walked over, swept her up into his arms, and looked her straight in the eyes. "Now then, joy of my life."

Rejoice laid her head on his shoulder and whispered in his ear, "Yes. Let's have some joy."

PACIFISTS' WAR CHAPTER SEVENTEEN

Late the next morning, a little before service was to end, Rejoice let herself in the house and settled with a groan in a chair. The crying of the Green and Zystra babies had driven her out of the nursery. Still, she had gotten a half hour of peace before fussbudget decided he had had enough service. She reached for a tomato, but stopped with a hiss. No tomatoes for a week, and if that solved his colic, none for a year and a half.

As the baby nursed, beads of sweat formed on his brow. Rejoice's stomach contracted with hunger, but only the tomatoes were within reach. She sighed again before saying gently, "You are such a pain."

The computer beeped and Rejoice jumped, making the baby let go and wail. She wavered in indecision before rushing him to his crib and shutting the door. Every Lord's Day, they kept the computer off-line, so an override meant disaster somewhere. Rearranging her dress, she sat before the screen and took one deep breath before pressing acceptance.

Sister Mfume looked at her from the bridge of the Starflower. She wore a spacesuit minus the helmet and gloves. Some tufts of matted hair had pulled out into odd angles when she removed the helmet. She blinked as she choked through sobs, "We just lost Brother I Know."

"What do you mean lost?" Rejoice's skin swarmed with cold spiders as she waited the several second delay before the response came.

"His suit blew. I got there in twenty seconds, but he was already dead!

I tried—Oh God!"

Seven seconds was all it takes in vacuum. "Is everyone in the ship?"

A dreadful time passed before Sister Mfume nodded. "We brought his body in. What do you want us to do?"

"Have you called Pastor Wiseman?"

She shook her head. "We called you first. What should we do?" She wiped her face with shaking hands.

"Come home. Now. Don't over-accelerate, but instruct the Starflower to come home in the most efficient route."

Sister Mfume wrung her hands that had paled some in a year of spaceship living, but were still the color of apple seeds. "Should we retrieve—"

"No!"

"—the mass accelerator?"

"No, no, no! All your suits are old. I'll call Pastor Wiseman. You concentrate on getting home. Do you understand?"

The seconds felt like days. Sister Mfume nodded.

Rejoice cut the connection. Call Pastor Wiseman. He would call the family. Did I Know have any family at the mission? No, nor potential in-laws. With a calmness that surprised her, she tapped in the code for the pastor of First City.

A blank screen hid his appearance, but she could hear the grogginess in his voice. "What—Oh, Sister Cruz. What's the difficulty?"

At that moment she broke. She cried until she got up and drank a glass of water. When she returned to the screen, she squeaked, "You need to notify the Toshiba family that Brother I Know Whom I Have Believed Toshiba died from suit failure while carrying out his duties at the mine on Asteroid Ambling. The Space Mine has halted all operations and will not restart until such time as the Space Agency has new space suits, new shuttles, and the Starflower is completely inspected and refurbished. Brother Toshiba's body shall be returned to New Earth in approximately," she checked the Starflower computations, slow, slow, "four months. I'll have a firmer date tomorrow."

She closed her eyes while she took three more deep breaths. "I accept full responsibility for allowing the miners to work with unsafe equipment, and therefore resign my post as head of the Space Agency. Please extend my sincere regrets and apologies to the Toshiba family."

"Sister Cruz, this hurts all of us. You must not blame your—"

Rejoice cut the connection and paced for several minutes. That poor family. Death in a vacuum was so quick that it had to be nearly painless, but what of the pain of those left behind? His family had nurtured him into an intelligent, courteous, and considerate man. Engaged to, yes, to Sister As The Deer Sidwell. Rejoice should have halted the space mining sooner. She should have known that spacesuits couldn't last so long. She should have told the Senate that there would be no more metal for tractors until the space program had new equipment.

Her fingers automatically tapped in the code for messages to the Senate. When a polite recording asked for her message, she said, "This is Sister Cruz with two items. One: there has been an accident at the mine on Asteroid Ambling. Brother I Know Whom I Have Believed Toshiba is dead. I received word of this a few minutes ago. At the time of notification, I closed the mine and ordered all the survivors to come home. I shall have a full report within twenty-four hours."

Her throat closed and she choked down some more water. "Two: effective immediately is my resignation as the head of the Space Agency." Her hands tightened around the glass. "My recommendation is that I not be replaced until such time as the colony decides to treat the Space Agency with the respect, equipment, and funds that it needs. If new spacesuits had been built when I asked for them ten years ago, and eight, and six, and four, or even two years ago, this would not have happened. I will not risk any more lives in the search for needed resources if you can't figure out that spaceships and shuttles need as much maintenance as barns and power plants. I hope you're happy, Elder Smith. You saved money for your breakaway city, and because of that, Brother Toshiba died. I hope you can sleep at night knowing that your credit pinching and lack of vision caused the death of a fine young man who gave his life so you could have metal for your hoes! Tonight a family weeps because you—"

The front door banged open, and Noble stood by her, holding her shoulders before she realized that she had screamed the last several words. He scrutinized the screen, and before Rejoice could stop him, his hand darted to the keyboard and deleted her entire message. The children, wide-eyed, filed in and watched Rejoice.

She sagged, and groped though a haze of tears to a chair. She still held the glass. Indeed, she could not let it go.

Noble bent to whisper in her ear, "You will control yourself. You're frightening the children and your brother." The chair scraped across the floor when he sat beside her and said in a louder but gentle voice. "What are you upset about?"

"A few minutes ago, Brother Toshiba died when his spacesuit fell apart."

Mother gasped. "Oh, oh, no."

Noble pressed his fist against his mouth. "He was on one of my exercise teams when we lived on the mainland. He was a good person."

Opportunity sat and laid her face on her arms. "He was He Gives' best friend."

"Right. He was," Noble said. He reached over to take Rejoice's hand, but she could not pry it loose from the glass.

Mother briskly walked to the refrigerator and pulled out the box of sandwiches she had made the day before. "Come on, children and Makepeace. Let's go to the dock and look for hardheads." She shooed them out before her.

She called back over her shoulder as she closed the door, "Opportunity, would you please see to Harmony's needs?" Harmony had taken a bad turn during the service and Mother had returned her to her bed. Mother had set her silent wrist alarm for Harmony to push if there was a problem. It would also vibrate if any of the monitors' markers decreased to dangerous levels.

Silence filled the house. Rejoice studied the empty glass and the refracted light about its smooth rim. She had cut her income by one- third with this resignation when they had six extra people to care for. But what else was honorable? She had allowed the conditions that killed I Know. Oh, God, why hadn't she done something sooner?

Noble turned from Rejoice and gently rubbed Opportunity's shoulder. "Do you want me to try to call He Gives again?"

Opportunity refused to raise her head. "What's the use? It's been a month and he still won't accept calls from me or Mother. He hates me."

"I don't think so. He's not talking to anybody, not even to Pastor Wiseman when he visits. I think he's ashamed of his actions."

Rejoice watched him with slit eyes. Why was Noble trying to comfort her? Why didn't he tell her the clinic had put a suicide watch on him? And now this death would really help him out. Why couldn't the colony have given her the suits when she asked for them?

Opportunity sobbed, "I never meant to hurt him like that."

Rejoice snapped, "In what way did you mean to hurt him?"

Noble scowled. Opportunity jumped up and ran wailing from the room. One door, and then another slammed. Stereo wails from behind closed doors permeated the living room.

"Rejoice! You are spinning out of control. What is wrong with you?"

"What's wrong with me? What is wrong with this colony that Elder Smith and Elder Sims can dictate the Space Agency into obsolescence and death? Do they think that by closing their eyes, they can keep the asteroids away?"

Noble stood and held out his hands. "All right. Be angry at Colony politics and grieve for I Know. But why be cruel to your sister?"

"She didn't mean to hurt him? What did she expect? She kept him dangling on a line. Did she think the hook wouldn't rip his lip? She thinks she can do anything because she's an artist. She's above mundane chores like dusting and cooking. We're all supposed to gather around her paintings in adoration and comment on how artistically she makes us bleed."

"Is that why you knocked Opportunity's painting off the wall a month ago?"

"No. I was throwing the pillow away before I could use it to smother the baby."

"What?" he shouted.

She closed her eyes against the shock and anger on his face. She took a deep breath. "I'm depressed. I've been on medication ever since Mother moved in. I should have told you sooner, but I didn't think you needed any more grief."

"Did you think I wasn't man enough to handle it?"

She opened her eyes. He leaned on the table with his knuckles pressed against the dark plastic surface. "I wasn't sure that Mother was right."

"I don't think much of using medication to solve life's problems, especially when you're nursing. What is the stuff doing to Jubilee?"

"Nothing, according to Mother."

"In how much danger is my son from you?"

"None. None whatsoever. I concluded that Mother was right. The medication is helping. Wanting to do something doesn't mean I will do it."

Noble straightened as he studied her face. "You've become a stranger. Please see to Harmony." Abruptly, he stepped into their bedroom and emerged a few seconds later with the baby strapped to his back.

As he reached for the rifle over the doorway, Rejoice said, "Where are you going? I haven't finished feeding him." She stood and followed him. "You haven't had lunch either." The front door shut in her face.

She hit the door and the forgotten glass in her hand shattered. The bright bits of glass cascaded around her head. She stood in shock as the shards scattered on the floor. How did she do that? She turned her palm toward herself. Blood ran down her hand from a gash in her index finger.

Screaming and breaking didn't honor I Know. She had broken peace with Opportunity. She had destroyed the trust of her husband. She had frightened Mark. Lord God, things had been getting better. How had she destroyed so much in so short a time?

Because she was barefooted, she tiptoed to the sink, washed her, hands, and bandaged the gash. Slowly, slowly, she swept up the pieces of glass. *God of peace, God of light.* She felt no peace nor light as the glass rattled into the trash. She stood with both hands and her chin atop the broom.

The main screen beeped. *Please, God, not more bad news.* She moved to it reluctantly and pressed accept. The bearded face of Brother Popowich filled the screen. "Good afternoon, Sister Cruz. Is Pastor Cruz available?"

"He, he went for a walk."

"When he gets back, would you please tell him to call me as soon as possible? There's a big ceremony going on at the Orange Scar Village."

"Certainly." The screen blanked. How were they supposed to evangelize the churtrees and hexacrabs when their own lives were so muddy?

She listened, but could not hear Opportunity. Maybe she should start by apologizing to her sister. Even if she had been right, and she had been, she hadn't needed to be right at that moment.

She examined the red stain spreading thread by thread on the meshflesh wrapped about her finger. The broom clattered on the floor.

She walked slowly to the children's room and knocked. No answer. She quietly opened the door and found it empty. Opportunity must have gone out the back door. She trudged through the room, quietly opened the door to Mother's room, and peeked in. Harmony slept peacefully, as the respirator slowly rose and fell. She could wait for Mother to get back to wake and feed her.

Rejoice returned to the kitchen and wilted into a chair. "Father God, give me the right words and the right attitude." Her face grew hotter. She needed words of peace, not words of grief and anguish and anger. She needed, she needed, she needed. "Father God, hear my baby cry to you." *I need.* Turning her hands palm up on the table, she breathed slowly, in an effort to calm herself so she could think clearly. She couldn't be His light when she was this angry. Even the breathing was too hard to accomplish.

Someone knocked on the front door. Rejoice squeezed her eyelids together. *Go away.* The knock came again. She slapped the table as she rose.

Jax stood in the doorway, dressed in baggy black clothes and with a black scarf wrapped around her head and another around her neck. Black gloves and knee-high black boots completed the outfit. "Am I sufficiently unnude?"

Rejoice gaped, and then laughter bubbled up until she snorted. Suddenly, she felt very glad to see Jax. She gasped, "Would you like some tea?"

"For truth."

Still laughing, she sorted through her bins until she found her mint and cinnamon blend.

"We should require you to meet our dress code for your visits."

Rejoice thought of the naked people in the gym. "You could, but guess who wouldn't ever visit you again." She set down the cups, spoons, and honey. A giddy gladness at anything cheerful suffused her.

Jax smiled, and Rejoice was relieved that her teeth were white again. "I missed you."

"Me too." She sat across from Jax. She couldn't talk to her about I Know. She couldn't stand to think about it for one more second. "Do you have any more puzzles, ones with answers?" Answers, yes. That was why she liked math. Those problems had answers. Would that the problems of life did.

Jax blew on the tea cup cradled in her hands. No nail polish either. "I was hoping to ask you about pregnancy. Is it normal to be so tired?"

"Everybody I know found it exhausting at times."

"Henley says that with good physical training and proper attitude, there is no fatigue and pain."

"I'm glad he knows so much about it. I daresay he's carried lots of babies."

Jax chuckled. "Perhaps he's not infallible."

"Isn't that blasphemy on your part?"

"We don't worship him."

"No? He's got some kind of hold on you. How else could he get your parents to agree to send all of you away on a ship with a ratio of two women for every man and with your ridiculous requirements?" She inhaled the scent of cinnamon mingled with mint. The tea seemed a great deal more calming than all the breathing exercises she had tried. She inhaled again and felt another surge of goodwill toward Jax.

"We were the hope for a better future on another planet. For me, there were no parents. Not until Henley found me in the dojo."

"Did he rescue everybody? Everybody is following him out of gratitude?"

"He's a great man."

The cup radiated warmth into Rejoice's fingers. "So, it's good to follow a great man and not so good to follow the Bible, or perhaps I should say a pastor and his exegesis."

"The first is telling the truth."

"And the second isn't. What is your problem with pastors?"

Jax set the cup down and looked out the window. "Once, as a teen-ager, I was fostered by a pastor and wife."

After a few seconds, Rejoice said, "A number of our colonists did that before leaving Old Earth."

Jax's eyes lost focus. "All day the wife was praying and sermonizing. At night, the pastor was having other uses for me."

The tea slopped over Rejoice's fingers. "Oh, my." Her throat hurt. Oh, if there were some way she could gather up Jax and rock her. "I'm so sorry. I wish I could undo that. Oh, Jax." Hesitantly, she reached across the table. Jax did not protest when she squeezed her hand. "But I don't understand. How is that any different from what Henley does?"

Jax whipped her hand away. "All the difference. No hypocrisy. Henley waits to be asked. When you want to leave, you can leave. No slavery."

Rejoice rubbed the creases forming on her forehead. "And no security either."

"Security, slavery, same thing. All people grow tired of each other. It is better to part than to fight."

Some people just grow tired. Rejoice retrieved a towel and wiped up the drops of tea on the table. What made her so happy when she saw Jax? Rejoice had wanted to lie on the floor and die before Jax came in.

"Think of the misery between your sister and foolish He Gives. Why did he think he owned her?"

"They were engaged."

"Engaged, married, adultery—all no sense. No necessity for self-imposing of hardships." Jax blew on her tea. "But I'm arguing with you again, and I didn't wish to."

"I suppose it's pointless. If you don't accept the existence of God, why would you accept His rules?"

"For truth. In you is capacity for rational thought."

"Well, thanks." Rejoice added more tea to her cup, and then to Jax's.

"Your people are hard bargainers," Jax said. "Our three young men are learning far more about production of raisins than they ever wanted to."

Jax sounded as though she admired the bargain, though how the mediation between the colonists and the Robersonians about the injuries of He Gives could be construed as bargaining, Rejoice didn't know. "Do you think it's unfair to require them to work in He Gives' vineyard until he recovers from his injuries?"

Jax flipped her hand. "Hard work is good for them."

"Did you think requiring them to pay for the spleen operation and broken arms was excessive?"

"No. The price was worth the lesson."

"You mean the lesson that once they had disabled their attacker, they had no right to continue beating on him?"

"No. The lesson to the colonists that they cannot think to hurt us without retribution."

Some of her joy at seeing Jax evaporated as old grief hammered in her heart. "He Gives wasn't thinking. He was feeling."

"Wrong thinking, wrong feeling."

The hot cinnamon warmed Rejoice's throat. She studied the mud-colored tea. In an hour she needed to call the Starflower again, confirm they were coming, order an inspection and documentation of every suit, prepare a report for the Agency files and Brother I Know's family, and for the Senate. And then she should call He Gives. She should be relieved he would refuse the call.

"Rejoice?"

Oh, and she still needed to apologize to Oppie, and she needed to talk to Noble. Why had she told him about the depression and the pillow? She had known he didn't need to hear it.

"Rejoice?"

"Hmm? Oh, yes. What?"

"For truth your people discovered germanium and now the mine is being closed?"

"Looks like it. It's going to take the hexacrabs a long time to pay back Brother Lerner. They're out of credit."

"In such a manner, you allow the hexacrabs to cheat you?"

"It's in the treaty. Your people have reason to be glad we keep our word."

Jax tapped the table with her sharpened fingernails. "You are satisfied with lowered technology. Not us."

"The world is a big place. If we found germanium once, we'll find it again."

"How long did it take to find the first time?"

"Fifteen years."

"I don't want to wait fifteen years."

"I don't want to either, but I'm not breaking faith with the hexacrabs."

"Your faith is asking too much of you."

"As least it's not asking me to be a part of a harem."

"You are not all the bride of Christ?"

Rejoice choked on her tea. After coughing, she grabbed the towel to wipe up the table and the front of her dress. "I don't know whether to be mad at you for misusing Scripture or to laugh because you're so witty."

Her computer beeped. Now what? "Cruz here."

"I'm sorry, sweet-love, but Makepeace is tantruming. Could you and Noble come to the dock and help get him home?"

"I'll be right there." She turned off the computer as she moved toward the door. "I'm sorry, Jax; you'll have to visit another time." She pulled on her shoes and shouldered her rifle. On her way out, Jax smiled as though pleased.

PACIFISTS' WAR CHAPTER EIGHTEEN

ark and the girls were waiting by the elevator doors at the dock. Mother danced out of the reach of the fishing rod Makepeace smashed on a pylon. "Where is Noble?" said Mother in a quiet tone that belied her eyes.

"On a prayer walk. I'll handle it. It's my fault." She ducked as a shard of rod flew toward her, then walked up to Makepeace and hugged him loosely. She crooned, "I'm sorry, Makepeace, that I was so angry when you came home. I'm not angry now, so you can calm down."

"Where is the lost sheep?"

"I don't know." She reached up to place her hands on his cheeks and gazed into his lovely eyes. "Can we go home and this time I'll be quiet? We'll look at kaleidoscopes on the computer. Come on."

He tilted his head and studied her face. "Breaking. All is breaking."

"Not everything. Come on."

He dropped the rod and, with a puzzled look on his face, grasped Rejoice's hand and followed her to the elevators. The girls watched him solemnly as they rode up the elevator. When Rejoice put him in the runabout and offered the girls a ride, they shook their heads from side to side like pendulums.

"How is Harmony?" Mother asked.

"She was still sleeping the last I looked."

Mother fretted. "I'll need to wake and feed her when we get back."

Rejoice struggled to look cheerful and calm during the drive back. Would there never be an end to crises? Makepeace needed a calm atmosphere. He didn't need an older sister screaming about the Senate and a younger sister pouting about her missing paints. He didn't need a sister-in-law weeping constantly as she clutched a scrap of paper or the constant bickering of girls with more time on their hands than sense. He didn't need it. She didn't need it. Nobody needed it. No wonder Noble was taking increasingly longer prayer walks.

In the house, she gave one of the leftover bobbers to Makepeace and set his screen on neon stars kaleidoscope. She sat to drink her now tepid tea. Odd how the good feelings she had felt when first drinking the tea had so thoroughly dissipated. Would doubling her medication make her not care that Brother I Know was dead and that she lived in a house of chaos?

Noble entered with the baby screaming on his back. Rejoice pushed him into the bedroom with the hope of not disturbing her brother. Noble propped the rifle on the wall and slid the baby pack from his shoulders. "Jubilee's hungry."

"I'm sure he is." She peeled the pack from him and sat on the bed to nurse.

Noble leaned against the door and watched for a minute. "You won't have to bother with that much longer. I ordered a huge batch of synthetic milk and it should be here by Sixday."

"Oh, honey. That wasn't necessary. Mother and I are trying an experiment that might end the colic."

He did not reply as he continued to watch her with a sad face.

Rejoice dropped her gaze and concentrated on the little boy sucking her breast. While she was finger rolling some of his sweat-soaked hair into curls, he abruptly fell asleep. His little head lolled back and milk dribbled out of his mouth. His lips pursed over toothless gums as he feebly dream-sucked air.

While Rejoice was still watching the baby's face, Noble moved in and extracted him from her arms. Then he settled on the other side of the bed with the baby sleeping on his chest. Gently stroking the infant's back, he kept his gaze on the far wall.

Rejoice buttoned up and tried to lean against Noble, but his hard flesh would not yield to her at all. She drew back and said in a controlled voice, "Please stop treating me like a monster."

He stared at the wall for several seconds before turning his face to look at her. "I don't like talking to a chemical. I don't understand. What kind of mother wants to harm her own child?"

Rejoice traced the outline of a button with her fingertips. How do you unsay words that should never have been said? "I don't know. I've tried so hard to like him, and I can't manage it. Something's broken, and I don't know how to fix it."

He clenched his hands a few times. "The woman I married cared about people and would never think to harm anybody. She was unacquainted with selfishness."

"I thought you married me."

"You were tough. I knew that when I took off my headset at the end of the day, I could relax because you wouldn't be clinging to me for help. You could run a marathon in one day, take a nap, and run again the next day."

"Nobody can run a marathon with a broken leg."

Noble placed his hand on the baby's head and sat up. "I can't take this kind of emotional blackmail. Unless I do what, you're going to stay broken? Both Opportunity and your mother are here to help you, but you still keep after me to reduce my work hours. How much help do you need? Now I'm afraid to do my turns at the churtree observation post. What will you do to Jubilee while I'm gone?"

"Nothing."

"I don't get it. What is so depressing about living with me?"

Rejoice's head snapped up. "Oh, Noble, no. The depression has nothing to do with you. Its hormones or something like that."

"When you're looking for an excuse, anything will do."

Rejoice bit her lips against the rising wrath that struggled with pity for Noble thinking her problems were his fault and with a sense of profound failure. No prayer, no breathing, no counseling would patch this hurt that hung like a haze between them. Did Father and Mother ever hurt like this? They loved each other. How could they hurt each other like this? Makepeace was right. All was breaking.

Noble leaned back against the headboard and directed his gaze to the ceiling. "How do I face the people on the Lord's Day to proclaim the Word of God when my own family is out of control?"

A frenzied knocking rattled the door as Mother cried, "I'm sorry, but Noble, you must see this."

In two strides he was out the door, still holding the baby and with Rejoice hard on his heels. She bumped into him when he stopped suddenly to study the main screen filled with the images of Orange Scar churtrees. Had the Orange Scars started killing the Yellow Scars again?

The old chief of the Orange Scar churtree, named Big Killer by the colonists, hobbled in a circle between his two sons, Pride and Prejudice. His two daughters, from the same quartet as the sons, finished clamping the last of the gold rings that ran down the upper spines of the sons. With his four-fingered hands, the chief ripped the rings from his own spine. Dark orange blood dripped down his black fur and spattered on the sand. Two spear lengths away, the rest of the tribe howled with dual voices, a cacophony of ripping metal and screaming cats.

Rejoice covered her ears. The girls covered their eyes. She wanted to move them, but she herself could not turn her back to the screen. The leaning spear on the trail had fallen several weeks before but the peace between the Yellow and Orange Scars had remained intact. Was this a ceremony that would renew the conflict?

Big Killer picked up four spears, one in each hand, and staggered to the center of the ring. His eyes rotated between his arms, and then withdrew into little knobs of wrinkled flesh. The screaming stopped. Rejoice held her breath as the chief swung the spears toward one son and then the other. Then, he stood and barked once.

Instantly the sons descended on him, grabbed two spears apiece and skewered their father through the throat. The churtrees wailed like sirens and Harmony's girls screamed. Prejudice and Pride drew the bloody spears from the still vibrating body of their father and circled each other warily, jabbing and pulling back from each other. The watching churtreess flailed their arms.

They weren't aiming for each other's bodies, but for each other's feet. Rejoice flinched as the jabbing escalated and the spears clashed.

A sudden flurry and Prejudice had impaled Pride's foot. With tremendous shrieks, the entire village descended on him, stretched out his long arms and stubby legs as far as they would go, and pounded stakes through each hand and foot.

The girls' screams mingled with the churtrees'. Puddles appeared under two of the girls.

"Death and destruction!" Makepeace shouted.

Rejoice should be comforting her brother or nieces, but she couldn't move.

The shrieking churtrees swept the victorious son over the beach and into a canoe. They pushed the canoe into the waters of the bay. Prejudice grabbed the pointed paddles, swept them in great arcs in four directions, and then paddled the canoe toward the mouth of the bay.

"I recognized a word," Noble said over the howls of the baby. "Testing, like what they do to a newly carved spear. This is what the testing of the chief means. We just saw the churtree version of the king is dead, long live the king. That explains the crucified Red Scar we saw in the first village we came to."

Rejoice laid a shaking hand on the back of a chair. She had spent the last fifteen years trying to forget the image of insects crawling over the emaciated churtree. That nightmare was sure to come back tonight. But would Noble be willing to hold her until she recovered?

The flanks of the staked churtree heaved as the other churtrees lifted the body of the old chief and carried it to the caves carved in the cliff. The internal cameras showed the churtrees dumping the body of Big Killer into a sinkhole.

When the view returned to the beach, Noble counted the canoes. "Only the new chief has gone to sea. Remember when the Red Scar would not use their canoes to reach our ship? My guess is there is a taboo against using canoes until the chief returns. Since seventy percent of their diet is seafood, they should become extremely hungry. Then if they eat when the new chief returns, they would participate in a symbolic meal that demonstrates all is well in the world and that a strong chief insures food for the tribe. This'll be interesting to watch to see if this follows that scenario."

Opportunity swallowed hard. "So what happens to the churtree pinned to the ground?"

"He dies," Rejoice said. "They let him starve to death. It's just what I saw fifteen years ago at the Red Scar village. The churtree that Ur-Veena killed just off the boat was the new victorious chief. The starved, staked churtree that Elder Chin and I found was the brother that lost."

Distress wrinkled Opportunity's face. She tugged on her long, thin fingers. "Shouldn't we do something?"

"Like what?" Rejoice snapped. "If you tried to feed him, he would eat your arm."

"Come on, little honey muffins," Mother broke in. "The show's over. Let's clean you up."

Mark giggled nervously as Makepeace moved closer to the screen, chewing on his thumb.

Noble glared at Rejoice. "For you, the only good churtree is a dead churtree."

Her voice rose. "You knew how I felt about them when you courted me. Now's a little late to fault me for it."

"The Lord of the flies," moaned Makepeace.

Rejoice retreated to the bedroom. Would she ever want to leave?

* * *

The next morning, Rejoice yawned as she looked through the satellite weather photographs. Hurricane Riot was dying on the southern coast of Sole. Lots of rain for First City and a fair amount for Promise, but moderate winds. She fought to keep her eyes open as she flipped to another part of the world.

What a terrible night. They had both lain in bed, but she doubted either of them had slept. Every time she dozed the churtree nightmare rolled in her head. She forced her eyes open and tried to not cry. She took deep breaths to calm herself, but pushed away thoughts about Noble or God's great hand engulfing hers. The visualizations she used to utilize didn't calm her. They only made her angrier.

Whenever she nursed the baby, Noble snatched him away as soon as he was done, changed him, and bedded him in the crib. "Don't do that," she said each time, but wordlessly he ignored her. If the baby was crying any less, she couldn't tell.

She received three calls that night: first from the Senate accepting her resignation and neutrally reworded report without comment, second from the crew of the Starflower petitioning that she not resign, and third, the worst, from the Toshiba family saying that they did not blame her but rested in the sovereign will of God.

Through all those calls, Noble talked with Elder Chin and replayed the churtree ceremony dozens of times. Not once did he touch Rejoice.

Now he knelt in the living room praying for church members as the baby cried in Mother's room. Makepeace paced around the table, muttering from time to time, "Hungry," as he had all during breakfast despite all the pancakes Mother placed in front of him. The morning felt quiet after Mother and Opportunity had carried the girls to morning school. They hadn't gotten much sleep either, what with wet beds and nightmares punctuating the night.

Harmony was rallying and seemed to be feeling better that morning. She signed to Rejoice asking why the girls had such a hard night. When Rejoice told her about the churtree ritual she whispered that she was glad she missed it. Then she asked why they had let the girls watch it? Rejoice apologized and confessed that they had been in too much shock to think about the girls.

Rejoice tapped on her screen. Why were the churtrees so fascinating? What made that level of evil so compelling that they couldn't turn away from it? Oh, what was this? A flattish spot on the sea, a place where the wave structure changed, occupied a rough circle, perhaps a kilometer in diameter. A coral atoll in the making? Since the colonists had restored the ozone in the upper atmosphere a hundred thousand atolls had begun to grow in the last decade. Why had she stopped to look at this one?

She flipped to view Hurricane Tyranny near the Southern Dipper Islands. Wait, that flattish circle was in deep water. There couldn't be an atoll there.

She flipped back to the section and ran a week's worth of satellite photos of the area. The spot was moving slowly eastward. A clump of floating seaweed perhaps? If it floated near Largest Archipelago, she would tell Brother Hancock so he could sample it.

Back to the hurricane. No ships in its path.

Her computer beeped, and she replaced the view of swirling clouds with the bearded face of Deacon Rabbinowich. "Cruz here."

"Yes, Sister. The hexacrab barge arrived with your family's belongings. They deleted all charges because they were late."

"Oh, good. We'll pick up everything tonight, if that's all right with you."

"Of course. God be with you." The clouds returned to the screen.

Too bad her work was more interruptible than Noble's. She tapped in another code. "Opportunity?"

Opportunity looked around the door. "Yes?"

Rejoice startled. "Sorry. I wouldn't have beeped you if I'd known you were so close. Your belongings just arrived."

Opportunity squealed with delight. "I'm going down right away to get my paints."

"Okay," said Rejoice at the same time the door clicked shut. "Wish she'd do the dishes that fast." Rejoice checked the clouds over the Broken Lands.

An hour later, Mother brought in the crying baby. "Do you mind, dearest-love, if Harmony and I go to lunch with Sister Hancock? She missed her visit yesterday and wants to visit her auntie. I have lentil rice soup on the stove."

"No. Go ahead."

Rejoice fell asleep while nursing the baby, and did not wake until she heard the girls playing tag in the living room. Groggily, she rose and straightened her brown dress. Lunch, yes, she needed to feed everyone. She blinked, trying to clear her vision, as she shuffled into the living room. One Faith ran into her. "Tag is played outside." Why couldn't they remember that? "Set the table."

The children complied and Rejoice filled bowls with savory soup. She frowned in concentration as she put the bowls on the table and shoved aside Makepeace's computer. Mother was at the Hancocks. Where was everyone else?

"I don't like onions," Peace said.

"Shh," Rejoice said as she tapped in Noble's code on her computer. "Noble, I'm serving lunch."

He sounded out of breath, as though he were exercising hard. "I'm on a prayer walk and skipping lunch today."

"You didn't eat breakfast either."

"I can fast if I choose to."

Rejoice flushed at having the children hear him speak so sharply to her. "Excuse me for annoying you." She shut the connection and called Opportunity. "It's time for lunch."

"I'm giving Ernest a painting lesson right now. Unless you need me, I'll come later."

Ernest? She hadn't seen or heard from Ernest since He Gives left the island. Noble had let him back in to help with the children's sport's class hoping to evangelize him, but had told him not to call Opportunity. She must have called him.

"Well, do bring in Makepeace. He was talking about being hungry all morning."

There was silence for several seconds. "I left him with you."

Something in Rejoice's abdomen squeezed. "Excuse me, but I don't remember you telling me that."

The girls stopped giggling.

"I told you I was getting my paints. Surely you didn't think I was going to take him with me?"

Rejoice cut the connection without replying. Why not? He could have helped her carry something.

She called the Hancocks. "Mother? Is Makepeace with you?"

"No, dear. I believe he's with Opportunity."

"Thank you." Rejoice laid the screen on the table. A sick feeling within her spread. "Mark, you and the girls search the house while I look in the orchard."

Outside, she scanned the sky for pack bats, and then jogged around her bubble house. Not there. Back inside, Mark said, "He's not here. But somebody left the freezer open."

She sent an urgent to all the houses except the Hancocks' and asked who had seen Makepeace lately. Most replied within a few minutes that no one in their house had. She sent an urgent to the stores, warehouses, and plants. The swift replies were all negative. She bit her lower lip and called the dojo. No.

Her fingers stumbled over the keys as she called Opportunity again. "Start looking for Makepeace. He's missing."

"But—what a bother he is. Of course I'm not allowed to paint. He—" Rejoice cut it off. She struggled to take deep breaths, but her lungs would not expand.

She called Noble. "I'm sorry to interrupt you again, but you've got to help search for Makepeace. He's missing."

"Did you look outside?"

"Of course I have! He's not here!"

"Calm down. I'll look for him on the way home." The screen clicked.

Yes. Calm down. Somebody would find him in a few minutes. She should not frighten the children with this panic that was pushing her heart into double-time. Her fingers twisted about each other. Why this dread? Someone would find him in a minute. Calm down. "Children, you go ahead and eat."

"We should pray first." Mark said.

"Yes. Pray and eat while I go outside to look some more."

A few minutes later she stood outside the Madison's chicken yard. Not in the inner ring. Not in the Meetingplace. *God, please protect my little brother.* She scanned the skies again. Where was he?

She met Noble going into the house.

He stopped in the act of shrugging off his rifle. "I thought you had taken the runabout. Where is it?"

Her gaze darted to the place they parked it. "I didn't notice it was gone. Makepeace must have driven off in it."

They entered the house and Noble entered a general alarm on the screen.

Rejoice deleted it. "I don't want to worry Mother until we need to." She entered an urgent for people to drive out and look for him. *God, keep him away from the cliffs, please.*

Noble had gathered the children into a circle to pray when Opportunity walked in laughing and holding hands with Ernest. "Sister Rutherford nearly ran me down on the road. Is there a race going on?"

Rejoice tried to count slowly. "Everyone is looking for Makepeace."

Opportunity flipped her black hair over her shoulder. "He'll show up. He always does."

"We think he took the runabout."

"He did that once at home. He drove a tractor down Main Street and almost hit a truck full of chickens."

"It's not funny. He could get hurt."

Opportunity sighed and laid her paint box on the counter. "Ernest, will you go with me to the dock to look for him?"

Before Ernest could reply, an emergency override flashed Brother Popowich's round face on the main screen. "Are you aware that Makepeace is driving straight to the churtree village?"

"Oh, no!" Rejoice cried.

"Is anybody following him?"

"We just started our search here," Rejoice wailed.

Brother Popowich's eyes widened, "I'll try to catch him." He dashed out of the observation post without cutting the connection.

Noble stepped up to Opportunity and whispered, "Please take the children to Mother Holly's room. We don't need a repeat of last night."

He then whispered into Ernest's ear, "Please return to the dojo. Now." Then he sat in front of the screen. His fingers flew over the keys as he activated the various churtree cameras until he had a view of the runabout winding down the steep and narrow path to the Orange Scar village.

Opportunity grabbed Ernest's hand, pulled him with her, and herded the somber children through the bedroom door.

Rejoice held the back of Noble's chair. "Please, God, please. Noble, Brother Popowich won't reach him in time, will he?"

"Depends. Makepeace is going slow, but he's pretty close to the village. But then, so is Brother Popowich."

"As the bat flies. Brother Popowich has to go around the ravine."

"Rejoice, what do you want me to do? I can't fly either."

She checked the schedules. No jets for the dojo or mission due today. No shuttles, no ships. All the mining equipment was still far out to sea. No mechanism for her to arrange for Makepeace to slide into the ravine.

He wasn't answering the com-unit in the vehicle. No way to stop him.

And every single churtree save the one at sea were milling around the village. She pressed her screen against her forehead. *Think, Sister, think.*

Nobel switched views. "They hear him coming. This is bad. They're all getting spears."

Rejoice clasped her hands. "Makepeace, keep your door closed!"

Behind her the bedroom door quietly opened and closed. Opportunity stole up beside them. "What are you watching? Oh, no."

The vehicle stopped at the edge of the village, and Makepeace emerged from the vehicle with a large pink block in his hands.

"The salmon from the freezer," Rejoice said.

Opportunity reached for Ernest's hand.

Makepeace headed straight for the churtree staked to the ground.

Rejoice cried, "Hungry! He wasn't hungry. He was worried about Pride being hungry!"

The churtree in the village raced, screeching, toward him. He stepped carefully over one of the black arms of the staked churtree and broke off a piece of salmon. He knelt to drop the piece into the maw of the shuddering churtree.

The howling mob engulfed him. He jumped up and then fell backward. Multitudes of black arms rose and fell.

Rejoice screamed "No!" She turned so she would not see him being slaughtered, and saw Opportunity back away. "Why didn't you watch him?"

Opportunity flared. "Why didn't you? Why didn't he use common sense? Why were we spending our lives trying to keep him alive?"

Rejoice slapped her across the face. Noble grabbed Rejoice's arms from behind.

Opportunity staggered against Ernest. Her hand flew to her cheek. Tears spurted from her eyes. She turned, ran for the door, and jerked it open.

Mother stood there, reaching for the handle.

"Oh-h-h!" Opportunity cried. She bolted past Mother. Ernest followed.

Noble pulled Rejoice after him as he lunged for the keyboard to shut off the view of the bloody, screaming churtree dancing on the body of Makepeace.

Mother stepped into the house. "What's going on?"

PACIFISTS' WAR CHAPTER NINETEEN

Rejoice laced her fingers together as she looked at the image of Jax on the screen. "I called to ask you to please give a message to my sister."

Jax looked at her with eyes surrounded by glitter. "No guarantee she'll listen."

"I'm not asking you to guarantee anything. I just want you to tell her, to tell her . . ." She bowed and pressed her forehead against her hands for a few seconds. A deep breath and she raised her head. "Tell her the funeral is tomorrow. At noon. Tell her I regret the violence I committed yesterday. I don't know an adequate way to apologize for what I did to her. Please. We want her to come. Both of us said and did what was not right. I don't think she meant what she said."

Jax watched her without expression. "Anything else?"

"I'm sorry. Mother desperately wants to see her. We, I—I don't know how many ways to say I'm sorry."

"Message understood. Necessity to return to students."

"Yes, yes, of course." Rejoice was talking to a blank screen. Unable to think of a reason to move, she sat for a long time. Somewhere, Noble walked with the baby. Sister Hancock was caring for the children by showing them her tanks of naspies, hardheads and slinkies. The deacons were all taking a day off from normal duties to arrange the funeral, and the deaconesses had already come and gone, having cleaned the entire house, done the laundry, and left two weeks of meals in the freezer.

A call surprised her, though she had received dozens that morning already, and it took a moment to press accept. He Gives' arched nose loomed even bigger in a face grown haggard. "Sister Cruz? I listened to your message yesterday. I appreciate the call." He looked down. "I wish it had been me instead of I Know."

"You took your turn. It could just as easily have been you."

He sighed. "Then I heard about your brother. I called to tell you I'm sorry."

Rejoice tried to smile, but those muscles weren't working. "Thank you."

They sat in silence for several moments. "Is Opportunity there?"

Rejoice shook her head.

"She's not answering my calls again. I don't blame her. My records show she tried to call me eighty times. Could you ask her to call me one more time? I promise I'll answer."

Rejoice licked dry lips. "She's not answering my calls either. We had a fight yesterday."

"But I need to talk to her. I finally figured out what the problem was. I was taking her for granted. I want to ask for permission to court her again."

Rejoice looked into his hazel eyes and hated what she was about to say. "She moved to the dojo. Her friends came to get her belongings this morning."

His lips moved several times before he burst out, "Then it's hopeless? Is she going to be shunned? But I finally realized that I'll never love anybody but Opportunity. I tried to hate her, but I couldn't do it. She owns me."

"Listen. Listen. I know I'm not a counselor and I don't know how to say things without making everything worse, but listen to me. I speak from experience. You can learn to love someone else when the first one you love turns you down."

He shook his head. "No. I'll wait. If it takes sixty years for her to repent, I'll wait sixty years." He raised arms grown thin from disuse. "I'll fly out and go to the dojo. I've got to tell her how much I love her."

"You signed an agreement that you wouldn't go near a Rational for five years."

"What can they do but kill me? Without Opportunity, I'm already dead."

"If you don't keep your word, who will trust you with a marriage promise?"

He shrank into himself and sat in mute misery.

"Do this: make a message, squirt it to me, and I'll send it to the dojo. Maybe she'll come to her senses."

He nodded and whispered. "God be with you," before he blanked the screen.

Rejoice shuddered. She bowed her head, exhausted. Her old nightmare had taken a new shape last night. The spears rose and fell as the churtrees clustered around her brother. Noble would run up to stop them. Then the spears were rising and falling on him. Then she ran up to stop them. Then she was looking up as the spears were descending on her. She woke repeatedly, screaming. But Noble kept his back to her.

She forced herself to rise and heat bean soup for lunch and take it into Mother and Harmony's bedroom.

Harmony listlessly embroidered a kitchen towel with a fishtail seaweed motif.

Mother lay on her cot reading the Bible. She looked up at Rejoice's approach and blanked the screen. "Thank you, sweet love. I should have been out there helping you."

"The deaconesses made this."

Harmony rolled her chair over to sit beside Mother and whispered, "Thank you."

Rejoice didn't want to watch Harmony's slow eating with breathing rests between each bite. Soon her sister-in-law would require intravenous feeding. She watched Mother instead. "Where were you reading?

"In Psalms. They remind me how God notices what happens to us. And they remind me how poetic Makepeace was."

"He wrote poems?"

"No, dearest. He saw things with a poet's eye. If you listened to him and watched him, you could learn to see the light and all its manifestations."

This was beyond Rejoice's comprehension, but she had learned a long time ago that explanations never helped. She merely nodded.

Mother crumbled her cornbread into a thick bean soup. "Did you reach Opportunity?"

"Not yet."

Mother poked at the soup with her spoon. "I think. I think I need to face squarely the fact that I have only one child left. I try to think how I failed in the raising of my children."

"No, Mother."

"I dedicated each of you to God, and each one of you seemed so precious and different. Stronghold, strong-willed. I thought that when he finally comprehended what God had called him for, he would be a mighty man for God.

"You, you took after your father and can understand how God structured the universe. You both have that rare gift of intuitively seeing and comprehending the most complex mathematical problems. Your Father called it the language with which God spoke forth all creation.

"Makepeace was my poet and sweetheart. His brain was fractured, but his heart was whole. And Opportunity, my last baby, who took after me with her love of music and beauty. Makepeace died a martyr, and I can comprehend that. I can. But the other two . . ." Her voice trailed off.

She studied the spoon as if it were a puzzle. "If I didn't have all these granddaughters depending on me, I would just as soon join Theophilus." Rejoice's throat hurt, and she could not swallow. She had not known that grief came in so many forms; a terror, a crushing weight, a gray blanket, a helpless waiting for a new dread, a blindness and deafness to previous pleasures, and now this clawed hand strangling her.

Mother's computer beeped. "Holly here." She sighed.

"Sister, is this a good time to talk?" came the strong voice of Elder Smith.

"Excuse me a moment." Mother pressed mute. "Do you girls mind if I ask for some privacy?"

Rejoice couldn't eat anyway. She rose and kissed Mother on the forehead before leaving with Harmony. When they reached the living room, Harmony wheeled around to look out the window at drizzle, and Rejoice brewed some chamomile tea. "It's been calls all morning. I've heard from people I haven't talked to in years. Even some in Promise." It had been bittersweet to hear Sister Guthry's voice again.

"My mother called," said Harmony in a thin, wavering voice. "She wants me to move in with her. She thinks it's too dangerous here."

Rejoice set the tea on the little wheelchair table and dropped a straw and two molasses cubes into it. "Maybe she's right. Will you go back?"

"I'll think about it. I don't know, Rejoice." Her breath failed her and she typed. [Sometimes I think if I went back and saw Stronghold one more time, maybe he would change his mind. I want to ask him what his letter means.]

"What kind of an answer could he give that would make you happy?"

Harmony tapped the edge of the keyboard as she sucked in breath. [Do U want me to go?]

"No. Please, do whatever you need to do. I've never been in your situation and I don't know what you should do."

[I don't want to see the house that Stronghold and I shared for fifteen years. I don't want to see everyone at First City looking at me with pity.]

Another guilt. "I look at you with pity."

Harmony tried to speak again. "I know. But I can still annoy you enough to make you forget."

Rejoice hugged her. When she straightened up, she turned to the window and bit on her thumbnail. Then she remembered Makepeace chewing on his thumb. *Father God, would it have been so hard to watch over that little sparrow and make the runabout break down or run out of charge?* "My father has no patience with children. My girls so miss their father. Nobel is so good and patient with them."

But not with Rejoice. She stood and gazed out the window at the gray forest and the gray rain. Her hand pulled the rifle from its rest before she realized she was leaving. "I'm—" What was she doing? "I'm going for a walk."

The drizzle darkened her brown dress as she walked out of the mission compound. A yertle bleeped as it scurried from under her feet. The forest shifted and drops of water splattered Rejoice as an erratic wind fussed over the island. Her eyes seeped. Her heavy breasts leaked. She should be home nursing the baby, but Noble had taken him only God knew where, and only God knew where she was going. Instead of entering the elevator to the dock, her feet stayed on the road. To the dojo then. She wiped rain from her eyes. Yes, she was going to see Opportunity, beg forgiveness, and talk to outrageous Jax who always managed to make Rejoice feel better despite her outrageousness.

Her teeth chattered by the time she stood dripping before the open gymnasium door. Within, rows of dojo students sat in lotus positions, silent as the colonists during prayer. The rifle pressed against her back and the wet dress clung to her skin as she shifted from foot to foot, trying to figure out how to interrupt and ask for Jax. The woman burst out of her office, rubbing her wrists together.

"Class is over. Join me." She backed into her office.

Rejoice stood rooted for a moment before following. The right side of Jax's face glowed red and her right eye had swollen shut. When she had closed the door behind her, Rejoice exclaimed, "What happened to your eye?"

Jax dropped into the chair behind her desk and pointed to the chair opposite her with one hand. The other hand rubbed her wrist against her neck. "Zack was over-exuberant in his match."

"Over-exuberant? He beat you! And you're pregnant."

"No cause for glory for him."

"And everyone stood by and let him do it?"

Jax settled in her chair.

Rejoice reached out to hug her, but stopped when she thought of her wet dress.

Jax popped open a locker and tossed Rejoice two towels and a white canvas robe. "Put on something dry."

Rejoice shivered as she stripped off her clothes, wrapped a towel around her head, and pulled on the robe. Jax hung the dress on the locker door. A tiny oven beside her desk produced two white cups without handles filled with a green tea.

Rejoice wrinkled her nose after tasting it. "It's so bitter. What is this?"

"Green tea."

"I see it's green and I know its tea, but what is it made from?"

"The unfermented leaves of the tea plant, the green bushes inside the dojo compound."

Rejoice chanced one more sip before setting it aside. Nasty stuff, yet already she could feel some muscles loosen. "Our men would never think to kick or hit a woman. They're taught to cherish women."

"The way you cherished Opportunity?"

Rejoice bowed her head and slid her cold hands into the sleeves of the canvas robe and sat without moving.

After a minute, Jax spoke with deliberation, "I am sorry. You do not need confrontation at this time."

Not this time. Not any time. And yet so needed. "If you know of another way to repent, I'll do that too."

"Crawling on your knees?"

Rejoice slid off the chair and onto her knees.

"No, no!" Jax hurried around the desk. She grabbed Rejoice's hand and pulled her up. "Don't do that. Necessity for you, for your sister, is freedom."

"What did Opportunity say when you gave her my message?"

Jax retreated to her desk, sat, and picked up her tea with great care. "She does not wish to speak with you or your mother."

Rejoice sat. The muffled thumping of her heart filled her ears. Why did her heart keep on beating? "You must be pleased to have another Holly join you."

"Your sorrow does not please us. But, yes, we are always glad to have another extraordinary person join our families. There's still room for you."

"Jax, why? You think we're genetically contaminated, yet you're always trying to convert us."

"Not truth. Only intelligent ones."

"Why any of us?"

"Why should you die with the rest?"

Rejoice's heart stammered and dread raced along her capillaries. "A massacre? Your people are planning to massacre mine?"

"No, no, no." Jax fingered her lower lip. "The lung rot."

"We breathe the same air. Why should we die of it and not you?"

"No. You're misunderstanding me. I phrased it badly."

Rejoice tried to read Jax's face, but the hugely swollen eye made it impossible.

"Your life is being wasted. Your people are dying in slavery." Jax shook her head, and then winced. "For truth. Why should you die before you have tasted freedom?"

Rejoice rubbed her forearms covered with minute bumps. Stronghold's freedom was devastating quite a few lives.

With pauses to think, Jax said, "You're being treated as a child. You're not even allowed caffeine."

"What is caffeine?"

"A natural drug in coffee and tea for alertness. A simple thing like that you can't have. You're not allowed alcohol, or the fun of sex with each other, or freedom in clothes or thought."

Rejoice wished she could tend to Jax's eye. She wished she could throttle Opportunity; no, beg her face to face to come back. If only she could go to bed and never wake up. So many wishes and none to come true.

What had Jax said? After a moment's thought, Rejoice said, "You do physical disciplines; and we do spiritual disciplines." She fixed on a dent on the edge of Jax's desk.

Jax inhaled. "I am sorry about the death of your brother."

"You are not. You wanted him dead."

"I'll say it again. I am sorry for your grief."

"So am I."

Jax sat back and watched her. "Why do you people fear death so much?"

"We do? What do you mean?"

"Whatever lives, you prolong into misery. Where is the mercy in forcing old, feeble people into continuing debility and pain? Where is the mercy in forcing handicapped children into never-ending agony? Where is the mercy for the able who must spend their lives watching the agony? For an intolerable life, you demand continuance. Is death so terrible?"

The bitterness of the tea still clung to Rejoice's tongue. God, this was frightening. Jax was beginning to make a perverse sense. "My question is: why do you love death so much? It seems like your only answer. Here's a deaf child. Don't learn to sign. Kill the child. Don't care for the old, feeble person. Kill him. Don't persevere through difficulty. Kill—"

Rejoice pressed the heels of her hands against her forehead for a moment. "I think I see. We don't fear death. But neither do we like it. We grieve for our losses. Yes. And you, on the other leg, fear life. You're afraid that life might give you something you can't handle."

"For truth. Universe doesn't care. Physical events happen. As Henley says, never enter a room with only one exit."

"And death is your exit."

"It's one exit. Another question. Why aren't you punishing the churtrees for eating your brother? Now they will think that humans are an easy target. More danger for us all."

Rejoice quoted Scripture, "Vengeance is Mine. I will repay, says the Lord of Hosts."

"He's slow."

Rejoice rubbed her face. She knew. Oh God, she needed an exit now.

Jax set down the cup and pushed it aside. "This is hard for you and creating a difficulty for me. What should I tell Ernest? Can Noble still welcome him for sports training?"

"I can't speak for Pastor Cruz. Ernest will have to ask him directly." Silence filled the room which smelled of bitter tea, salve, and damp. What was she doing there? Why did she like Jax so much when she was everything Rejoice opposed? Rejoice forced herself to stand. "I came here to talk to Opportunity. Since I can't, I may as well go home and be useless there." She slid her arm out of one sleeve.

"Wear it home. It's yours."

Rejoice held the robe. "I've never worn anything but the brown or blue dresses, or brown pajamas. I'd feel strange walking around outside in this."

"Perhaps it's time to expand your choices."

Rejoice looked at Jax's lopsided face, "Not today," and laid the robe across the back of the chair. The cold, wet dress resisted being pulled on. The cold pants made her legs ache. The fabric clung to her chilled skin and interfered with walking. As she was reaching for her rifle, she glanced back at Jax. The fury in the woman's distorted face halted her hand.

Jax leaned back in her chair and folded her arms. "I will not ask again. If you choose foolishness, then live with it."

Rejoice backed away from the angry eyes.

The dreary trudge through the drooping, gray and brown jungle and erratic rain seemed endless. Dreary thoughts coursed the same paths endlessly in her brain. If Jax had an abnormal child, she wouldn't need to endure its crying. She could snap its neck and be done with it. If Jax had a husband who didn't like her anymore, she could leave and find someone who did like her. If Jax were sick and tired of life, she could end it. She needn't walk forever like Rejoice, through a volcanic valley filled with the ash of sorrow. *God, I can't run this race anymore.* She would need to limp through the course He set before her. Wasn't it pitiful when the best thing one could look forward to was dying?

She pushed wet hair from her forehead. Yet what kind of freedom was the freedom to hurt people?

When she entered the house, Noble, screaming baby held over one shoulder, turned from the screen to face her. "Rejoice I was worried about you. Why were you gone when Jubilee needs to eat?"

Before she could answer, Mark rushed up to hug her. She dropped to her knees and pressed him against herself.

PACIFISTS' WAR CHAPTER TWENTY

Rejoice watched the hexacrabs in their LVs congregate in the open portion of the Meetingplace. The humans sat in pews facing the dais which held the coffin covered with roses, lavender, and rosemary. Though scarcely needed, the coffin stretched full length. The churtree cameras had recorded the monsters discarding the remains of Makepeace into their dump at the edge of the village. Brother Popowich and Brother Hancock had courageously recovered what they could of them that night.

The serene, cool sunlight, filtered through the white walls of the dome, evenly illuminated every petal, every face, every fold of skin upon her knuckles. Her fingers searched for something to do. Perhaps that was what rosaries were for. A random thought to match the hundreds that had scattered through her brain in no discernable order.

The faint squeaking and grinding of gears and treads brought her gaze back to the hexacrabs: sun-scarred Ur-Veena with Ti-Assisi still tied to the back of his shell, Sa-Issi, Sa-Pita, and Ti-Ista, the first talking female hexacrab the humans had ever seen. One had to listen hard to hear the humming of their water filters. The smell of iodine competed with the lavender.

Rejoice thought again of the customs left behind on Old Earth. The colonists had chosen to be a plain people, but the images that filled her mind were of priests swinging censers as they walked in rich robes, of women in shawls kneeling in unison and crossing themselves, of farmers shouting under great tents, a panoply of the hundred generations before

Rejoice who had worshiped the Son of God and who stood, like her, before the gate of death saying farewell to the ones they loved.

They had kept the custom of flowers. Why?

Mark looked so puzzled. She folded his small hand within hers. On the other side, One Faith kicked her legs in a steady rhythm. Then came Noble, Reconciliation, Mother, Reason Together, Peace, and Harmony in the aisle on the other side of the pew.

Rejoice jumped when the door opened. Only Brother Madison bringing in more roses. He dropped one pink blossom into each land vehicle, and the hexacrabs examined them with unblinking silver-blue eyes.

She turned her eyes back to the simple, plastic coffin and bit her lip until she noticed that it hurt. She had hoped it would be Opportunity coming in. How could Opportunity and Stronghold skip the funeral of their brother? She glanced at Mother who looked grimly ahead.

Brother Madison helped Elder Chin to the dais, and then stood behind and to the left of the elder to sign what he said. The translator wore service black, and his sepia-colored hands folded into a waiting mode in front of his chest. As apprentice linguist to Elder Chin, he knew Sign, English, Hex, Hebrew, Latin, Greek, Mandarin, Aramaic, Swahili, and as much as any human of Churt. How odd that a man with so little to say could have so many ways to say it.

Heart's Desire wriggled behind her to get a clear view.

Elder Chin wore black. His skin, the faded yellow of dead pea vines, sagged. His jowls quivered as he slowly recited the fifteenth chapter of the book of First Corinthians. He said, "O death, where is your sting?"

In my heart.

Elder Chin continued, "Brother Makepeace Holly was twenty-four years old when he died of compassion. In God's wisdom, He blessed us with this very special life of love. After his short pilgrimage with us, Makepeace is now united with his cohorts, resting in the Everlasting Arms of his Lord and Savior."

Rejoice bowed her head as her eyes filled with tears. But she was startled when she heard from the always silent congregation behind her a wave of murmured Amens.

Elder Chin fingered the pulpit while his lips sucked in and out. He studied the coffin. Heart's Desire signed {Makepeace} to him. He nodded before continuing. "God made His ways and thoughts understandable to us by sending His Son. He was the Word of God made flesh; the Light that lights everyone that comes into the world. We have all been blessed by having the privilege of knowing Brother Makepeace Holly. Our brother Makepeace saw more, heard more, and perceived more than appeared on the surface. He loved light. He was a natural theologian. He studied light: light reflected, light diffused, light refracted, light broken into the colors of the rainbow. The sign with which God made peace with men."

Oh Lord of Peace, fulfill my brother's name, prayed Rejoice. *Make peace in my heart and among Your people.*

"As his body was failing, Theophilus Holly, taught his son to play chess. He saw more in the mind of his son than others thought possible. Makepeace saw patterns others did not see. He saw behind strategies and changed situations. He now stands with his father, Theophilus, who truly was a lover of God. They stand as brothers before the One Father, whole in body, and whole in mind."

Mother sobbed. Noble reached over Reconciliation to place his hand on her shoulder. His eyes were red.

"Brother Makepeace's perceptions of this world were different; but not necessarily inferior. He understood much more than we knew. But he did not understand danger and malice. He did understand how we must respond to need. He loved those that hated him, as did our Savior."

Mark pulled his hand out of hers. She had been squeezing too tightly.

Sa-Issi jerked in agitation. The hexacrabs had already offered to help the mission by spearing all the Orange Scar. That the colonists would not avenge their own troubled the hexacrabs greatly. This was the fourth death, and still the colonists would not allow the hexacrabs to remove the danger. Might as well throw naspies into the nursery. "Perhaps," Ur-Tsetse had suggested, "breathing air damages even air-breathers."

On this, the Robersonians and hexacrabs agreed. How long before they joined forces and did what they wanted, no matter what the colonists said? Rejoice wasn't sure she would try to stop them.

Elder Chin stopped speaking and gazed at the people, water and air-ocean alike. When Brother Madison touched him gently on the shoulder, Elder Chin repeated his last sentence, stopped, and looked around in confusion again. Brother Madison signed, {Let us pray.} Heart's Desire rushed up to join him in helping the Elder navigate to a pew.

After ten minutes of silent meditation, the six deacons carried the coffin to a grave site dug where the apple grove met the jungle. As the coffin was lowered into the ground, the humans sang *Rock of Ages*, and the hexacrabs paced around them, watching.

Far down the road, a little group of Rationals watched them also. Rejoice tried not to stare. No, Opportunity was not among them. Myra, co-wife of B family, with her hair striped black and white, was, and she looked different. Oh, she didn't look pregnant anymore, which likely meant she wasn't. Rejoice averted her eyes. Not another sorrow.

She focused on the people taking turns throwing a shovelful of dirt on the coffin. The Holly girls clung to adults and jumped at every sound. Deacon Jordon set a simple, white stake at the head of the grave that had engraved on it the name of Makepeace Holly, the dates of birth and death in Old Earth and New Earth time, and the Scripture: Blessed are the peacemakers.

Sister Redhorse came up and engulfed Rejoice in an embrace. As she had once laughingly said, she was only half the woman her mother was, but she was still large. "My mother just called and told me to tell you that the Meetingplace in First City was full to overflowing. Many from Promise were there also watching the live relay of the service at one a.m.. Sister Guthry told my mother to tell you that we all mourn with you and that she loves you very much. Makepeace was like a son to my mother and a brother to me. He will be greatly missed."

Rejoice whispered in her ear, "Thank you." Like a trapped animal, she wanted to flee, but where could she go that pain would not follow? She pressed Mark against her hip and absentmindedly stroked his smooth, black hair. Death was a drumbeat, the theme of her recurring thoughts. The people in their blue dresses or gray suits, moved slowly back to the Meetingplace. Rejoice was required to eat and then thank everyone who embraced her and then take back the baby from Sister Carver. It all was more than she could do.

Ur-Veena left the colonists and directed his LV toward the Robersonians. With thoughts that moved as slow as maggots, Rejoice watched him go. The hexacrab would probably ask why they hadn't joined them. He had more questions than a room full of four-year-olds.

A far-off howler bag whooped, and the breeze bore the warm sage and clove scent of the jungle. Steam tendrils rose from the wet ground to meet the glare of the sun. Rejoice's eyes ached. She wiped them, sad she could not produce more tears.

Ur-Veena reached the Rationals. After some conversation, he backed up his LV and crashed straight through the jungle toward the dock elevators. After a few seconds, all the hexacrabs wheeled about and followed him. The Rationals watched the exodus.

Why had they done that? The hexacrabs had said they would join them for the mourning meal.

A few hours later, she found out. Noble woke her from a nightmare-filled nap by taking away the baby she had nursed to sleep and handing her the computer. She rubbed grainy eyes as she sat up and looked at the image of Jax dressed all in black, her right eye slightly less swollen.

"With what have you been poisoning attitudes of hexacrabs?"

"Excuse me?"

"Did you think we would stand by and allow this damage?"

"I'm sorry, but you haven't given me enough information to know what you're talking about."

Jax leaned on her desk with her palms flat on its shiny black surface. She glowered into the camera as she spoke each word distinctly, "The hexacrabs dumped our cargo in the middle of the ocean."

Rejoice frowned and blinked as she tried to clear her mind. "You mean a storm broke one of their cargo ships?"

"Are you listening? They purposely jettisoned our birthing center, tea fermenter, and barracks."

"I can't imagine why they would do that. Did they tell you why?"

"They said they will not deal with same-churtree. What does that mean?"

Alarm burned away the residual drowsiness. As she tapped in the codes for Elder Chin, Brother Hancock, and Noble, she said, "Uh-oh. What did you do to the hexacrabs?"

"Nothing."

"Excuse me, but your people did do something. We've been called same-churtree only twice. The first time was when Brother Hancock accidentally killed one of their children. He had to offer himself to their justice to avert war. The second time was after we had killed a kraken and then berated Ur-Veena for killing a churtree. To restore peace, we made the treaty. We've had fifteen years of peace since. What did your people do?"

"Nothing. We paid them the rates you established."

"It wouldn't be the money. Have your people been scuba diving, putting chemicals in the ocean, anything that could affect them?"

"No."

Rejoice's heart hammered in her chest. The funeral? No, they had gone to the funerals of the first three people killed by churtree. The flowers? They had examined flowers before. What was different? "I saw the hexacrabs talking to some of your people at the funeral. Were the hexacrabs angry then?"

"Wait. I will ask." Jax moved off-screen.

Noble's voice came over the link. "I'm calling Ur-Veena now."

A minute later, they heard the whistles and clicking of Ur-Veena. "I am called."

Noble said, "Ur-Veena, do we still expose our soft parts to each other?"

A simple click, "Yes."

"Who is same-churtree?" The baby howled. Mother carried away him away, and a door slammed.

"The new air-ocean people from the warp-ocean." His whistles stuttered with anger.

Jax appeared on the screen with Myra. "Ur-Veena asked Myra a question."

"Same-churtree!" grated Ur-Veena and cut the connection.

"What?"

Rejoice gripped her computer. "Hexacrabs consider the churtree the most despicable thing on this planet." So did she. "Same-churtree means to be just as despicable. What did you do?"

Myra waved limp hands. "I don't know what the problem is. The one with the baby on his shell asked me if I had miscarried like Sister Cruz often did. I told him I aborted the fetus because it was defective. Then I defined abortion because he didn't know that word. Then it called me same-churtree and left."

Rejoice fought to keep her revulsion from her voice. "That's it then. The churtrees sometimes chop up their babies and throw the pieces in the ocean. The hexacrabs can understand why the churtrees like to eat hexacrab eyeballs. They're enemies and both hate each other vehemently. What they can't understand is why the churtrees would kill their own children. The hexacrabs have such a strong protect-the-child instinct, that anything else without that instinct is considered, uh, same-churtree."

Jax placed her fists on the desk. "Hexacrabs cannot require us to bear defectives. What do they do with their defectives?"

Rejoice sat back and thought. "They don't seem to have many defective children that survive. At least that we know of. Entire generations of female hexacrabs returned mute and simple after Dark Death. The male hexacrabs continue to care for them even after the talking females returned."

"They will pay us for that cargo."

God of peace, God of light. "We'll talk to them. Do you understand that they are out of credits and even if they do agree to pay you, you come after repaying Brother Lerner?"

Jax turned her head and ground her teeth for several seconds before looking at the cameras again. "Why are you depending on these sea spiders for shipping and mining?"

Rejoice waited for Elder Chin or Noble to answer, but neither did. "We let them do ocean work because that lets them earn credit. They spend the credit on scooters and such, and that ensures that we keep communicating."

"They cannot do this to us. You communicate that to them." Her hand darted forward and the screen went blank.

Rejoice stared at the blank screen

Then came the tremulous voice of Elder Chin; "Let us pray."

* * *

In the dark living room shortly before dawn, Noble recited in a strong, clear voice, "In the beginning was the Word, and the Word was with God, and the Word was God. He was with God in the beginning. Through him all things were made; without him nothing was made that has been made. In him was life, and that life was the light of men. The light shines in the darkness, but the darkness has not understood it."

The faint hiss of the lighter sounded next to Rejoice, and the flame of a beeswax candle shone on the solemn face of Mark, who recited, "The people walking in darkness have seen a great light; on those living in the land of the shadow of death a light has dawned."

Rejoice swallowed hard as Mark turned and carefully lit the candle Reconciliation was holding. As Reconciliation recited her verse, Rejoice tried to concentrate on the flickering light instead of on the shadow of death. This had always been Makepeace's favorite ceremony. He would watch the flame until the soft candle had burnt down to his fingertips and the fragrant wax coated his hands.

Thin Harmony shook as she held her candle and whispered her part about the birth of Christ. Stronghold had gone to something worse than death. Rejoice doubted Harmony would see another Birth of Christ Day.

When Reason held aloft her candle and recited the verse about the angels, Rejoice had to work at moderating her breathing. This was where Opportunity usually played a carol on her flute.

Around the table, one by one, the candles were lit and the story of the birth of Christ recited. The baby stared at all the dancing lights as he drooled on Noble's knuckles. Mark had looked like that.

What kind of mother was she? The baby's crying had dropped to approximately four hours a day, but she still didn't like him. Noble seldom let her be alone with him. Why did the baby always cry when she held him? She didn't like him, and Noble didn't like her. Makepeace was dead. Her other brother was a traitor.

Mother leaned over and touched the tip of her candle to Rejoice's. Both candles flared together. Rejoice blinked as a spot of wax burnt her thumb. "I can't," she choked.

Noble slid his hand across her back. "You can. It doesn't matter what we feel. The truth is the truth, and we must proclaim it."

For truth. She sucked in as much air as her constricted lungs would let her. "Simeon took him in his arms and praised God, saying: Sovereign Lord, as you have promised, now dismiss your servant in peace. For my eyes have seen your salvation, which you have prepared in the sight of all people, a light for revelation to the Gentiles and for glory to your people Israel." She extended her candle toward Noble's.

As his candle caught the flame, the frankincense and myrrh imbedded in the wax filled the room with their heavy odors. One Faith sneezed. Noble recited the rest of the story of the birth of Christ. Then they placed the many candles into white ceramic holders. In the soft, warm light, Noble slid back the shutters and announced, "Rejoice, for the light has come." The rising sun shone over the tree tops and into the window.

Rejoice and Mother set out little bowls of honey, date, and almond candies that they served only at this time. The children dived on them. Mother set a vase of clove-scented, dark blue roses on the table, and then walked about, kissing each grandchild.

When she kissed the baby, he lunged and sucked on her chin. Laughing, she pulled him away from Noble, and handed him to yawning Rejoice.

Rejoice walked into her bedroom so she could lie down to nurse. She had half an hour yet before the Birth of Christ service.

As she knew he would, five minutes later, Noble came in with a tray of apple cinnamon buns. "You'll want some breakfast before the service."

She sat up. He would never lose those shadows under his eyes so long as he woke up for every feeding to watch Rejoice and kept the baby on his back wherever he went. The only times he let the child out of his sight were when he could hear him crying behind the door. As soon as the baby stopped crying, Noble would excuse himself from counseling and check on him. It seemed a petty victory that the baby had proved to be even more allergic to synthetic milk than he was to Rejoice's milk with or without the taint of tomatoes. Were it not that he needed to nurse, she might never be allowed to touch him.

She stroked his silky hair. Poor thing. How would she ever bond to him and stop hating him? It was his fault Noble didn't like her anymore. Yet, it wasn't as if the baby had intended for that to happen. She said to Noble, "Have you had breakfast yet?"

"Of course." Noble set the tray beside her.

There was no of course about it. He watched the baby, and she watched to make sure Noble ate. He skipped at least half his meals and had lost the tiny paunch he had started. Soon she would need to take in all his clothes. They were driving each other crazy. How had that happened? "Noble, it's been over two months now. Tell me what I need to do to prove that I'm not a monster."

"I never said that."

Rejoice sighed and picked up a bun to bite into the soothing, warm bread. She licked the sweet glaze from her fingers. "Okay, what proof do you need that I'm not a stranger?"

He grimaced. "We're going to service soon. We shouldn't upset each other. This should be a happy day for Mark. For all of us."

"I'll go to any counselor you name."

He studied his hands. "Elder Chin is suffering from little strokes.

Doctor Carlson does what he can for him. He's only seventy-five Old Earth years old, but a tendency to have strokes runs in his family. Pastor Wiseman is not very good at marriage counseling, I'm sad to say. He gives all his cases to me. I know what Pastor Stayer would say, and neither you nor I are ready to turn our backs on the natives of this planet and move to Promise."

"We could still talk to hexacrabs if we moved back to First City."

He stood as still as a rock. "It's hard enough knowing that I will spend my life studying churtrees, and it won't be until I'm an old man that I'll be able to walk up to them and say the equivalent of "Hello." We learn of them so slowly. It took fifteen years to learn how they make peace. And while I study, two more generations of churtrees will die without knowledge of Christ. It's hard enough to know that eighteen years of study and preaching have resulted in a zero response from the hexacrabs. It's hard enough to see that we aren't converting the Robersonians. They're converting us. Four more from First City last week. But when you add to all that a wife that won't support me or love the child that's an answer to prayer, then—"

Her computer beeped. She cut if off. "Then what?"

He removed the baby from her breast. "Go ahead and answer it."

"No," said Rejoice. "We need to—" The door closed behind him.

She turned on the screen as she straightened her dress. "Cruz here."

The face of Jax painted like a kabuki warrior mask appeared on the screen. "I grow impatient. When will the hexacrabs pay us for their damage?"

Rejoice pressed the screen against her forehead for a second. "Jax, this is the Birth of Christ Day. In a few minutes, we're going to service, and after that, the hexacrabs are coming for a feast. Please bother me another day."

Jax tapped her desk with her pointed fingernails painted black. "You're on their side. Perhaps it is hopeless to expect rational behavior from you."

Rejoice clamped her lips between her teeth. She should not provoke

Jax or any of the Robersonians. "Perhaps I am irrational. I won't deny that I love the hexacrabs very much. But I will also agree with you that they had no business dumping your stuff in the ocean. We're continuing to talk." For all the good that would do. The hexacrabs had paid off Brother Lerner, but they weren't about to pay off the same-churtrees. The Ur, Sa, and Ti wouldn't budge. The Senate wouldn't cover the costs because humans should not cover the wrongdoing of hexacrabs. She couldn't pay for it because they were barely scraping by. Noble wouldn't let her ask the rest of the missionaries to pay for it out of their retirements, and even if she could, that likely still wouldn't be enough. Why was she the only one who saw two ships on a collision course? She was screaming and everyone else was sunbathing on the decks.

Jax continued tapping the desk. The lines of makeup scowled ferociously. "Bureaucracy!" Jax snorted.

"I agree," Rejoice said.

Jax's smile distorted the kabuki lines. "Something we can agree on besides the infinitude of the square root of two."

Rejoice covered the microphone with her thumb so Jax wouldn't hear her sigh of relief.

Jax tilted her head. "Birth of Christ Day? Christmas?"

"For truth. We follow the Old Earth calendar for church events because the days and years on New Earth are longer than on Old Earth. So our church events happen earlier and earlier every year until this year we're celebrating two Birth of Christ Days in the second and thirteenth months. Then next year we're back to one. It's a way to keep ties with the Body back on Old Earth."

"The body? You're always denying the body."

Good. Back to banter instead of chilly silence. "I suppose so. I'm glad your eye has gone back to normal. You'll take better care of yourself as you get further along in your pregnancy, won't you?"

Jax drawled, "Yes. For caring, I thank you." She sat on the edge of her desk. "You are such a bizarre people."

Rejoice rolled her eyes. That from Jax, whose face was painted like a mask. But she replied with an even voice. "The probabilities of that being a true statement are high. St. Peter did call us a peculiar people."

"Why are you shunning Opportunity and not Ernest?"

"Because it's what St. Paul commands in the Bible. He says we can't disassociate from sinners or else we would have to leave the world altogether."

"Which you did."

Rejoice blinked. "We did, at that. Then he says we are to disassociate from those who called themselves Christians, but don't act like they are."

"I am wondering when the scars will fade."

Rejoice croaked, "I hit her that hard?"

Jax tapped her forehead. "Mental scars. She thinks she can own Ernest. She showers only when it is dark. She blushes often."

A blush heated her own cheeks. "Unless you want to tell me that they've repented, I don't want to hear about Opportunity or Stronghold."

"You don't want to hear about your own nephew?"

Rejoice pressed mute as she struggled with her breathing. This would kill Mother, yet, yet, yet, what was to be expected? The child was not the sin, however the child was conceived. She rubbed her forehead against the pain of thinking of any child growing up among the Robersonians. Wait. It had been only a little over two months. If Opportunity was pregnant, how could they know so quickly and know its sex? Right, they had better medical technology. Hold it, whose son? Opportunity's or Stronghold's? She did not want to ask. The silence stretched out.

Finally, Jax hopped off the desk and before she cut the connection, she said, "Merry Christmas, Rejoice."

CHAPTER TWENTY-ONE

Rejoice descended slowly to the bottom of Ti Bay, welcoming the warm water flowing past her relaxing muscles. Another month of chaos and stress and sadness with nothing much changing, but the growing feeling that the pressure would build until something exploded. Another month of an angry husband, a crying baby, a mourning mother, a declining sister-in-law, and multiple fragile nieces was taking its toll.

She had really needed to get out of that house. She closed her eyes and sank in silence. A house full of sad eyes and whining girls was the backdrop of a life centered on the screaming, demanding, insatiable baby boy.

Joyful baby hexacrabs waved bobbers at her. Why did she like baby hexacrabs so much better than her own? She greeted little Ti-Assisi who had broken his bonds the day before and could now join the cluster as an independent hexacrab. Ur-Veena watched as his little one clambered up Rejoice's legs. She grasped two of his tentacles and swung him through the warm water while he squeaked in delight. Maybe she liked them better because their babies sounded like dancing piccolos and her baby sounded like a blaring off-key clarinet.

The sediment swirled as Noble settled beside her and stroked the tentacles of the hexacrabs large and small surrounding him. Silver bubbles flattened in their race to the surface. Three little hexacrabs still remained tied to the shells of their guardians, and they strained mightily against their bonds, hoping to break them that day so they could join in the festivities.

Rejoice passed out bits of salmon to the little ones who had won their freedom.

Tiny Ti-Keeti piped from Ur-Teeki's back, "Me, too. I am hungry, too."

"No," clicked Ur-Teeki, and deliberately crawled away from the group. Ti-Keeti's legs drummed on the shell.

Rejoice hoped Ti-Keeti wouldn't burst his little hearts with all that jerking. Sa-Issi hummed by on a scooter, snared Ti-Assisi, and pulled him to a blurry distance. Eighteen years ago, Sa-Issi had been tied to Ur-Veena's back. Now he acted like the proud uncle of Ti-Assisi.

Ur-Veena grated, "The same-churtree have scanned our cluster."

Rejoice and Noble looked at each other. Bad news or non-news?

"Yesterday," added Ur-Veena. "They did not find the nursery. Tell them the next time they swim over us, their boats shall gain many holes."

Bad news. Rejoice shifted the hexacrab in her face to behind her back. "Like a torpal in a school of slowbobs, so the water-ocean people love to explore. The same-churtrees also love to explore."

Ur-Veena's breathing siphon rhythmically opened and closed. Rejoice had used a poor choice of metaphor. The two hundred seventy-year-old hexacrab slowly turned and crawled away.

Stubborn, stubborn, stubborn. She motioned to Noble, and together they finned slowly to the surface. After they had clambered onto the barge, Sister Deng, her two boys, and Mark plunged into the sea to visit the hexacrabs.

Noble grabbed a towel and blotted his face. "I guess we should call them right away."

Rejoice sat and listened to the distant crackle of gunfire at the firing range. As salt water puddled around her feet, another hexacrab in an LV lumbered toward the dock elevators. "I'm so worried about this, I can't think straight. The Hancocks said they were willing. Why don't we use their retirement to make a down payment for the dumped cargo?   That would give us a few more months of negotiation time."

"What negotiation? Neither side is backing down." He threw the towel onto the bench opposite him. "It's hard to understand those people. They owe us their lives."

"They think they paid that debt a long time ago. Or were you thinking of the hexacrabs? It's true for both."

Noble took off his fins, padded to the cooler, and returned with two bottles of lemonade. He handed one to Rejoice. "I'm trying not to be, but I'm still irritated that you asked that of the Hancocks."

The cold bottle grew instant drops of condensation. "It came up before I knew I was doing it."

He unzipped his suit to the waist and pulled off the sleeves. She studied the scars on his broad chest and sunken abdomen as he tilted back his head to drink. The reflected light from the sun vibrated on the tarp overhead and slid along the bottle. Rejoice floated on a surge of sorrow. Someday she would notice a reflection and not think of Makepeace, but she couldn't imagine when that day would be. "Do you think things will ever be right between us again?"

He abruptly lowered the bottle. "Between who?"

"You and me."

He gritted his teeth as he screwed the lid on the bottle. "You have an absolute gift for picking the wrong time to bring up things. Sister Deng and the boys will be back at any moment."

"You're right. I'm sorry, but I can't find the right time. Our talking time was consumed by the Robersonian Bible study and everything else. I miss you."

"I'm home all day."

"You're home working all day. You're exhausted. You've lost nearly fifteen kilos. I've taken in your pants twice. When you're not working you're praying. Most nights now, you fall asleep on the floor praying."

He shook his head and held up one hand with the fingers splayed and the other with his finger and thumb a centimeter apart. "There are five people that close to conversion. I expect Ernest to repent any second now.

My question is why aren't you praying with me? Don't you care about the souls of these air-ocean people God has placed in the midst of us?"

Shame heated her ears and neck. "You're right again. I'm selfish, and I am sorry." She pressed the cold bottle against her hot cheek. "Still, I wish I could stop missing how you couldn't keep your hands off me whenever the door was closed."

His gaze shifted to the cliffs of Ti Bay. "I know my duty," he said, "and I will perform it." He set the bottle on the bench. "I just figured out what the difference is between when I wear my headset and when I don't. When I'm wearing my headset, my work is appreciated."

Rejoice rolled the bottle between her hands. "Noble, I do appreciate your work. I only wish that you would do less of it for a while and rest."

"I don't find boredom restful. I don't understand why the solution to every problem is for me to stop being a pastor. You knew what I was when I married you. I intend to stay a pastor until the day I die."

Mark bobbed up next to the ladder. "Mother, guess what! Ti-Assisi wants to play hide-n-seek with me and Submit and Resist. Can we, I mean, may we?"

Rejoice bit back laughter. Didn't he know that Ti-Assisi could see their bubbles? "As long as you come up when your alarm goes off."

Mark plopped back under the water, and Rejoice turned to talk to Noble, but he was already at the far end of the barge doing back-strengthening exercises. She pressed the cold bottle against her eyes to forestall tears. Would he ever love her again?

Back at the house, Rejoice called Jax, but Zack answered. He looked beyond her, as though he was examining the kitchen behind her. She shrank the image on the big screen because he was standing too close to his camera, and his face hugely magnified intimidated her. He looked very like his father minus the kindness that Henley seemed to exude. "The hexacrabs of Ti Bay have asked us to tell you that they don't want you to boat over their cluster or nursery. My guess is that would include the solar cells as well."

"Do they think they own the ocean?"

"Yes, they do. We sail it or farm it by their permission."

Zack dropped his head and shook it. "If they want to give us a message, they can call us directly."

"Hexacrabs don't talk to same-churtree."

His head snapped up and he glared at Rejoice. "Contract-breakers have no cause for accusations. We go where we wish. Can they stop us?"

"Maybe. But why precipitate a fight?" A shout from off-screen startled Rejoice.

"Zack! Get out of my office!"

Zack quirked up one side of his mouth. "Her highness has spoken." He sauntered out of camera range.

A door slammed and Jax stepped into view. "Your purpose?"

Rejoice tried hard not to stare at Jax's rounding abdomen or think about how she got that way. "Well, your dojo students may have misunderstood where they could and could not go with your new boat. They went past the buoys yesterday and over the Ti Cluster. The hexacrabs are not happy about that."

Her black eyelids slid shut once. "I should care?"

"We did tell you that we would accept you getting a boat only if you avoided the areas marked off by the hexacrabs."

"Where is the payment for the destruction of our goods?"

So that's what they were doing. "We have lived with the hexacrabs for nineteen years now. One thing we learned is that you can't annoy the hexacrabs into doing what you want."

"And neither should they annoy us."

Movement caught Rejoice's eye, and she turned to watch two hexacrabs stilt past the window holding rifles to practice with on the firing range. Prickles raced along her neck. "I think we might be able to get a down payment to you next month. But if you provoke the hexacrabs, who knows what might happen? If we, their friends, sailed over their nursery, they would have a fit. You won't like what happens if you sail over it. Please, can you wait another month?"

Jax lowered herself into her chair and locked her fingers together atop her swollen abdomen. "I will wait one Old Earth month."

Rejoice stuttered, "I thank you for your patience." She was afraid to ask what Jax would do if the money were not forthcoming. After the call ended, she sat and chewed her lip while staring at her dark reflection on the main screen. Perhaps she should have argued for a New Earth month. She might need the extra four or five days. Noble would be furious, and so would the Hancocks' grandchildren, but the Hancocks had said they were willing. And she could pay them back as soon as Mother sold her apartment.

A new thought struck her. Elder Smith called Mother all the time. Maybe Mother could talk Elder Smith into making a donation to keep peace. All her life she had pictured Elders Smith and Sims as twin pillars of the irrational, uncompromising portion of their church. The force of their personalities maintained the original vision of the colony and opposed any flexibility in the face of the unexpected contingencies that New Earth forced upon them. They broke away and founded Promise to keep that original vision intact.

Rejoice had pictured Father and Elder Chin as the other two pillars of the church, the side that saw God's hand in those same unexpected contingencies and embraced them. Now one of those pillars was gone and the other was beginning to crumble. Both Elders Sims and Smith despised the hexacrabs, but Elder Smith might be willing to do Mother a favor.

Once Rejoice had asked Mother why Elder Smith called so constantly, and Mother had gotten misty-eyed. "Remember that I cared for Sister Smith during her last years after her stroke. There at the end, we became very close. Such a precious saint she was. Elder Smith likes to call and talk to me about Naomi. Then he listens while I reminisce about Theophilus. And now he listens while I talk about Makepeace." Mother had pulled on a loose thread in a kitchen towel. "We both know a lot about pain. You expect life to be hard, but you never expect it to be quite this hard. Losing half of yourself is more than you can imagine ahead of time. I'm so glad God holds us in the palm of His hand and remembers we are dust. Still,

I hope you never need to know such sorrow." She looked up suddenly. "I'm so sorry, Rejoice. You've lost the same number of children I have."

She threw her arms around Rejoice and squeezed. Rejoice hugged her back. She had regretted losing the babies that she had miscarried, but that grief was nothing like if she was to lose Mark. Theoretically she should feel the same, but she didn't. How wicked was she that she would gladly lose another? She dared not tell anyone these thoughts.

The baby's crying brought her back to the present. Before getting up to feed him, she tapped a memo to Mother's computer that they needed to talk. It would be perfect. Elder Smith had no children, and he surely had a lot of wealth. He fled a world wracked with war, and he surely would want to maintain peace on this world. Surely.

In the bedroom, the baby sat crying in his crib as though all the miseries of the world had come to claim him. His wispy hair reached his shoulders. His chubby fists beat helplessly on his knees.

"Come here, little boy," Rejoice cooed as she reached into the crib. Like someone had pushed his mute button, he stopped crying and pawed at the front of Rejoice's dress. Rejoice walked to the window. Noble stood talking with Ernest in the apple orchard. Where was Mark? Maybe he had gone with the girls for their turn at diving. If so, so much for family time together.

No, the girls were family, even if temporary. That brought up another sad line of thought as she unbuttoned and sat in the chair to nurse. Last week Noble had come in after settling the girls in bed and had lain back on his pillow with a wistful look.

"I'm going to miss those girls when they go to My Soul's. I wish Harmony had named us as guardians."

Rejoice had covered a yawn. "Deaconess Copulos would have contested. Too dangerous here. It's hard to believe Sister Hancock and Deaconess Copulos are sisters. Everything scares Deaconess Copulos and nothing scares Sister Hancock. Except Brother Hancock." She had shut off the image of the flattish part of the ocean coming closer to Largest Archipelago and slipped the computer into its case. "Hurricane Torrential should miss us by three hundred kilometers."

"That's good."

"For us. Not so good for the people at the Broken Lands refinery."

He had fiddled with his screen without looking at it. "Harmony doesn't look good. She's turning yellow."

"I know."

He had sighed and gazed at the closet door. "I wanted to have a little girl so badly."

"Me, too." Though living with this batch might have changed her mind. More thoughts that weren't fair. Those poor children had their father run out on them, their uncle murdered, and now were watching their mother die. It was a wonder that they were as good as they were. "Maybe the next one will be a girl."

Something had hardened in Noble's face, and without a word, he had stalked out of the bedroom and had not come back for several hours.

The baby grunted as he nursed, his eyes intent upon her face. She placed her forefinger into his palm and he gripped it. His tiny fingernails needed clipping. When the nursing, changing, burping, and clipping were done, she carried him to the window and looked out again. Noble still spoke to Ernest, his hands making large motions.

Noble was emaciated. His face had become all planes and lines. His overalls hung limply from his shoulders. Rejoice tried to think. Yes, he had eaten breakfast yesterday, but not lunch or supper, nor anything today.

She stuffed the baby into the now tight back pack and pulled it on. In the kitchen, she prepared a tray of poppy seed bread, pickled cucumbers and eggs, cheddar cheese, dried figs, and two glasses of chilled and sugared ginger tea. If she fed Ernest, maybe Noble would eat to keep him company. May God grant somebody converted before Noble starved to death.

Her shoulders hurt by the time she nudged open the door with her foot and walked out to the orchard carrying the heavy tray. When she rounded the bedroom bubble, she almost dropped the tray.

Noble and Ernest were hugging each other. Rejoice's heart stuttered.

Had Ernest become a Christian? Opportunity would have a fit. Or maybe she would return. Joy and doubt chased each other so quickly that Rejoice could not move.

Noble saw Rejoice and dismay crossed his face. He gently pushed Ernest's shoulders until the young man let go and backed up a step. Noble turned him so that he still could not see her. While sliding an arm around Ernest's shoulders, Noble flicked his fingers at Rejoice in dismissal. Slowly, the two men walked toward the road as Noble talked into Ernest's ear.

Rejoice stood perplexed. Noble's rifle still leaned against the trunk of an apple tree. She took a breath to call to him, but checked herself. He had made it plain that he didn't wish to be interrupted.

The baby grabbed a fistful of her hair and crammed it into his mouth. On the other side of the Inner Ring, a rooster crowed. A semi-beetle landed on the tray with a click. Rejoice blew it off, turned reluctantly, and walked back into the house.

Half an hour later, Mother, Harmony, and the children burst into the house with chattering and squealing enough to almost cover the sound of the baby crying. One Faith squealed when Harmony accidentally rolled over her foot. Peace sulked when Mother reminded her that she couldn't have cookies until she had eaten the rest of her lunch. Reconciliation and Reason got the giggles and could hardly eat at all. Mark made faces at his little brother who never stopped crying for a moment. Rejoice sat sipping chamomile tea and staring out the window.

"Where's my son-in-law?" Mother moved One Faith's glass of milk away from the edge of the table.

"He went for a walk." Rejoice swallowed the "with Ernest." The mention of Ernest always made Mother irritable for at least an hour.

"Children," Mother announced, "if you will take Jubilee to the back room and entertain him for half an hour, I will take you all to the store for a treat."

"Hooray!" they shouted.

"I want a peppermint," Peace said.

{Polite must you,} signed Harmony as the children moved noisily into the back room.

"What did you want to talk about?" said Mother.

Rejoice started. "Did I want to talk about something?"

"Somebody named Rejoice left a message to that effect on my computer."

Rejoice frowned and studied her cup of tea for inspiration. *Oh, right.* That had been only an hour ago. How could she have forgotten so quickly? "Yes. I wondered if you could talk to Elder Smith about something for me."

"Probably, dear heart. About what?"

Rejoice ran her fingertips around the rim of her cup. "The Robersonians are becoming more and more upset that the hexacrabs aren't paying them for the buildings they dumped in the ocean. I'm afraid they might harm the hexacrabs."

"Why would they do that? It's just stuff. It can be replaced eventually." She brushed back her hair that had seemed to have grayed considerably more since she had moved in with them.

"The Robersonians care more about stuff than you do, Mother. They also place a high premium on keeping contracted agreements. What I was thinking was that since Elder Smith fled Old Earth because of war, he would want to insure that war never broke out here. I was hoping he would donate some of the cost of the buildings to the Robersonians as a payment on behalf of the hexacrabs."

Mother peered at Rejoice. "Ah!" She reached for her cup of tea and swallowed some. "My dear love, I don't think that there would be any way he would do such a thing."

"Does he hate the hexacrabs so much?"

Mother sighed, pushed away her cup, and folded together her hands. "He does have an unfortunate dislike of the hexacrabs. I daresay we all have our quirks. I also don't think that's why he would turn down your request. I think he would say that he doesn't have a dog in that fight. The people in Promise won't have anything to do with either party. And I don't believe he would be willing to give one credit to those disgusting Robersonians."

Rejoice's swallow slid past a sharp place in her throat, and her vision blurred. "How am I going to keep the hexacrabs safe?"

Mother took her hand. "Oh, sweet love, why do you think it's your responsibility alone? Don't you think the hexacrabs should bear it?"

"They don't understand how bad it could be."

"After churtrees, Dark Death and studying Old Earth history for three years, I think they must have a pretty good idea of how rough life can be." She pulled a handkerchief from her pocket as her eyes unfocused. "And how sudden death can be." She stood. "Honey, you've got your hands full now. Don't take on more weight. Harmony, sweetest, will you go to the store with me and the children?"

Harmony looked at Rejoice as Mother gathered the dishes. She moved the oxygen tube that ran into her nose and typed. [Will U come too?]

"No," Rejoice said. "I think I don't pray enough. I think I'll rectify that this afternoon if you're willing to take the baby with you."

Mother paused in the wiping up of some spilled milk. "If he's eaten recently, I see no problem."

Rejoice saw nothing but problems. With a mind blanked by dread, she watched Mother wash the dishes and Harmony roll around the table picking up the milk and pickles to return them to the refrigerator. Her bubble house suddenly felt as fragile as a soap bubble. Any minute now, a booted soldier could step on it and crush all of them.

She visualized the hexacrabs in the bay and walking to and from the firing range, the students in the dojo wheeling and kicking and running through the forest with rifles and knives, the churtrees and their new chief plunging spears into the bushes as they searched the jungle for live meat. She tried to sense God's hands holding the planet and its peoples, but all she could see were the asteroids tumbling in space as they looped from the frigid outer regions to the orbits of the inner planets. Time and physics dictated when one would crack the shell of New Earth.

No, God had placed the asteroids where He wanted, and had used Dark

Death to clear a space for the humans. Too bad he had forgotten this corner, though. Why had He made her love the hexacrabs so much if she couldn't save them? Why hadn't He given her love for the bawling baby He gave her?

The six children like a riot of sixty passed by Rejoice and jostled out the door as Harmony led and Mother herded from behind.

God, forgive me for rebellion and grumbling. She rose and walked into the bedroom, resolved that she would seek the mind of God, and whatever He told her to do, she would do.

She laid a pillow on the floor to kneel on so that she wouldn't be distracted by pain in her knees. But whatever it was God had to say to her, she missed, because as soon as she had knelt and leaned over the bed, she fell asleep.

She woke up three hours later as Mother banged on the door and the baby cried. Her eyes focused on the quilt pattern. How had she ended up half on and half off the bed? She stumbled to the door to retrieve the baby and clambered back into bed to nurse him. She promptly fell asleep again for another three hours. When she woke up the second time, she stretched and thought that was the best night's sleep she had had in months. Oh! She had slept the day away.

She fed and cared for the baby. Where was Noble? His computer lay on his pillow, so she couldn't call him. And when she emerged, rumpled, from the bedroom, everyone but Noble sat at the table eating a supper of spaghetti with cheese and mushroom sauce.

Mother set down her garlic bread. "It's good to see you finally took your day of rest seriously. Give me little Jubilee fussums. I made him a rice pudding I hope will last him through the night."

Rejoice handed over the baby. "Have you seen Noble?"

"Not since this morning." Mother waggled a spoon in front of the baby's face. "Hey, big boy, today you learn about solid food." She whistled a hexacrab chant about the six kinds of seaweed that are good to eat. That was the first melody that she had heard from Mother since she arrived.

The corners of Rejoice's mouth turned down as she remembered that tune being whistled to baby Opportunity. And now Opportunity might be having a baby of her own. How could she tell Mother? Would Mother ever be able to whistle that tune to that grandson?

Rejoice put green beans and garlic bread on her plate, but hardly knew what to do with them. Where was Noble? She kept seeing Noble putting his arm around Ernest's shoulder, and Ernest leaning his head onto Noble's shoulder as they walked away. Why did that alarm her? Noble often hugged and patted the boys in his sports teams and Bible Study clubs. She thought about the rifle propped against the tree. That shouldn't be a problem. The last pack bat attack had been last week, and twenty hexacrabs from the rifle range had shot down half the pack within five minutes. The rest of the pack had fled and likely wouldn't return for weeks, maybe months.

"Excuse me," Rejoice said, and returned to her bedroom. Oh, of course. This complaint of the hexacrabs should lead to a discussion with Elder Chin about it. She tapped in Elder Chin's code and saw Heart's Desire on the screen. Since it was difficult to hold the screen and sign simultaneously, Rejoice typed in the inquiry. [Sister Cruz here. Have U seen Pastor Cruz today?]

Heart's Desire clapped her fingertips together. {No.}

Rejoice typed, [Sorry to bother U. God be with U.] and sat brooding a minute. Perhaps he had taken the Deng boys out again. Another inquiry showed he had not. Nor was he at the Hancock's or Madison's or Rabbinowich's.

Well, fretting wouldn't bring him home any faster. She almost called Constancy on the mainland for a chat to take her mind off Noble, but then remembered that Constancy had switched to a day shift. So she sorted through weather photos until she stopped seeing them. She set the computer down and then picked it up again. Who else could she call? No, he was likely on an extra-long prayer walk. She should relax.

She paced the bedroom floor. Might as well pace outside where she might run into Noble.

Mother fiddled with some of Harmony's equipment, and Mark played a game of chess with Reason, while Reconciliation jiggled the baby on her lap. Rejoice walked through the living room and slung on her rifle. "I'm going for a walk."

"That's nice, dearest." Mother checked another reading. "We have an hour yet before the Lord's Day begins."

The sun cast long shadows, and the golden light illuminated clouds of hovering insects and the papery flutter-hawks that ate them. Rejoice first did a circuit of the Inner and Outer Rings.

As she walked, she called Ur-Veena who also had not seen Noble since that morning and who wanted to know if the same-churtree had agreed to stay on their side of the boundaries.

"They have trouble seeing lines drawn on water. They had not smelled your anger and were surprised to hear of it. I will talk to them again tomorrow."

Ur-Veena whistled a dissatisfied dismissal.

She was dissatisfied too. Blessed are the peacemakers unless neither side wants peace. Makepeace and bloody spears. She walked faster.

When a yertle zipped out from under a sticky bush, she kicked it into a grove of bubble leaves. Perhaps he had gone to the library. It sat in a sheltered fold between two ridges and was a quiet place to pray and meditate. If you stood on the roof, you could look one way and see Ti Bay scalloped into the coastline, and the other way you could see far off the other side of Largest Archipelago and the ocean where the churtrees fished.

Sweat dripped from her face, her knees trembled, and the sun kissed the horizon when she pulled, panting, into the clearing in front of the library and then tottered to a stone bench and plopped onto it. The giant cube gleamed in the slanted light. Not here. Where was that man? She was used to him keeping confidence with half the colony. She never asked and he never said where he went on his prayer walks, but this was the longest she had ever been out of touch with him.

She contemplated the trail back down to the mission and how she would need to walk most of it in the dark. Stupid not to bring a flashlight.

A shadow moved in the jungle, and her hand tightened on the rifle. *Oh, God. Not a churtree, please. Let it be a leaf stripper.* She peered at the place. Yes, there.

A human dressed in brown and gray camouflage stepped into the path. Rejoice let out her breath with a whoosh, and then her heart froze again. Opportunity!

Rejoice stepped forward, and then stopped as Opportunity flipped up her goggles and scowled at Rejoice.

"Shouldn't you be running away since you all decided to shun me?"

Rejoice paused. Opportunity's stomach swelled under the camouflage. *My nephew. I'm sorry. I love you. Have you seen Noble? My brain has crashed and I don't know what to say.* She removed her hand from her rifle. God, what was she supposed to say?

Opportunity marched into Rejoice's face. "You tell Noble one thing for me. He can't have Ernest. Ernest is linked to me. You got that?"

Rejoice blinked. The words could not find traction in her brain.

Opportunity snapped her goggles back into place and darted into the jungle.

Rejoice stared after her until she couldn't see her anymore. What did that mean? Rejoice hadn't said a word. Why hadn't she apologized? Why hadn't she said something? Anything?

The gold light graded to gray. Twilight, and dark soon. Rejoice started down the trail, and then halted. Had Ernest converted? What would the Robersonians do if one of theirs converted? Perhaps Noble was searching for a safe place to hide Ernest.

She jogged down the trail. The Robersonians claimed to believe in freedom of religion, but they also had the temper of a torpal. What a stir this would make in service tomorrow. Would Mother, who could forgive churtrees, be able to forgive Ernest?

Rejoice's heart pounded in a fractured pattern. All those messages she had left at the dojo, and her sister still looked at her with hatred in her eyes. Ernest is linked to me.

Rejoice stumbled in the deepening dark as a different and terrible interpretation came to her. She saw again Noble sliding his hand along Ernest's shoulders and Ernest leaning his head against Noble. "No!" she wailed and fought the urge to vomit. No, it wasn't possible.

She ran with the rifle bouncing on her back. She ran with the air tearing out of her lungs and the warm smell of spice flowing past her and the blurred jungle looming over her. God, oh, God, when she reached home, let Noble be there fuming because she wasn't there feeding the baby. She tripped on an unseen stone and floundered back to equilibrium and a slower jog. Let Noble be on the floor praying his heart out.

A night screech flitted over the trail ahead of her, its gray wings seen only in their movement. Oh God, let him be anywhere doing anything but what she was thinking.

Her legs, her side, her chest, everything hurt, but still she careened through the dark. She was staggering by the time she reached the road and its low footlights. Noble's rifle still leaned against the apple tree, illuminated by the glow from their bedroom window.

She fell onto the side of the runabout and sucked in air. Her legs trembled so much, how would she make the last few meters to her front door?

Tiny moons sailed serenely across a black sky studded with stars. A sudden streak, fading from vision almost before it was registered, crossed the Hand constellation. Part of the Comet Ice Follies showers. The sweat dried on her face as she sought and found the gas giant Harfang near the Andromeda Galaxy. The Milky Way, with its myriads of stars and glowing gasses, banded the sky.

Oh, if only she could incorporate the beauty of physical matter and the passionless recurring patterns of numbers into herself; could focus on the DNA within her cells unzipping in a dance to allow messenger RNA to receive the coded instructions for the formation of enzymes; could lose herself in the contemplation of infinity; and never again need to cope with despair and its aftermath, depression.

Despair was not doing, and she needed to do! But what? She needed to feed the baby. She needed to mother Mark. She needed to do the duty God set before her.

She pushed herself off the runabout and stumbled to her front door.

Mother leaped up from the table where she had been rocking the baby. "Sweet love, what's wrong?" The baby squalled.

Rejoice gasped. "I can't find Noble."

Mother plopped the baby into his high chair and supported Rejoice to the bathroom. "Here's your medication. Let me see you take it. Good. While you're showering, I'll get your pajamas and towels."

After the shower, Mother escorted Rejoice to bed where she nursed the baby and listened to a lecture about not letting her worries nibble at her like little beaks and that Noble was an adult and surely knew his way home in the dark or otherwise.

Rejoice listened to it all and understood none of it as she played over and over in her mind Noble's dismissive flick with his fingers. The baby kept twisting away his face and spitting. The poor thing must not like the taste of fear. When he would suck no more, Mother took him away to spend the night with her. Rejoice sat in bed and looked at the painting of the *Magellan* with two tiny figures on the deck.

He had nearly died when he tried to protect her. She clenched her hands and willed away the image of Noble on the *Magellan*'s dining table as Mother reassembled him and blood, God, blood everywhere. She chose to remember the walks on the deck, kilometer after kilometer, round and round. Oh, precious Lord, once they had walked together. Today he walked away.

She pulled the Bible onto the screen, but she could not read the words. She pulled up satellite photos, but the clouds swirled in meaningless patterns. She called up asteroid surveillance data, and that too spiraled down into smashed fractal bits. She checked the time. Twenty-four p.m. Before, she would have said that only death would keep Noble from observing the Lord's Day.

Now she knew why Harmony had fled First City. Some things were too hard to bear.

Twenty-five o'clock. The baby cried and Mother moved in the kitchen preparing rice for him.

One o'clock. A sick certainty settled in her bones. She could call Jax to confirm it, but Rejoice's hands would not place the call.

PACIFISTS' WAR CHAPTER TWENTY-TWO

She must have fallen asleep after three a.m. when she had sent a message to Elder Chin that he needed to lead the service. The six o'clock beeping of her computer woke her up. She wiped eyes that refused to focus and fumbled across the quilt until she felt the computer.

Brother Zystra's plain, round face filled the screen. "Sister Cruz, I don't know what happened, but I found Pastor Cruz collapsed on the trail close to the Orange Scar Village."

"What? What?"

"He keeps saying he's okay, but he can't move so I don't think so. I don't think he's going to lead the service today either. I guess your runabout must have broken down somewhere on the road. Can you borrow a runabout and come get him, or do you want me to drive him in?"

"I'll be there." She threw off the quilt and pulled on her clothes and ran out the door. The runabout still stood in its place. She drove past the Outer Ring and on the road to the observation post before she thought of Mother. And she had left the front door open. As she jolted over the road, she keyed in a message for Mother and set it to beep. Rejoice couldn't talk to her. She didn't know what to say.

The hour-long drive to the post seemed to take three days. Once she ran over a yertle and twice she almost slid off the road while going too fast on the curves. What had happened to Noble? Where was Ernest? Collapsed.

And close to the Orange Scar. "I don't understand," she muttered like a chant. Her fear rose in sour waves from her body. Was it fear or hunger that made her hands tremble on the steering wheel?

Air puffed out and lurched into her lungs while she pounded on the door of the observation post. Brother Zystra opened the door and then jumped back. Rejoice ran to the cot where Noble lay and fell on her knees beside him.

Brother Zystra cleared his throat. "He looked dehydrated to me, so I've been trying to fill him with orange juice. Where did you find the runabout?"

Noble opened his eyes and gazed at nothing. "I'm fine. A little tired is all."

Rejoice held his thin hand in hers and frowned at him, but the presence of Brother Zystra held her tongue. She had never been able to read minds, but if it were possible, she felt deep shame emanating from her husband. "Could you help me get him into the runabout?

"Sure thing." Brother Zystra supported Noble on one side and half carried him to the passenger side of the runabout. He wrapped a blanket around Noble's legs and handed him a bulb of juice.

Through it all, Noble said nothing and would not look at either person.

Rejoice waited until they were out of sight from the post. "Well?"

He did not answer for he had fallen asleep. The bulb dripped on the blanket. She set the bulb in the tray and drove in silence all the way home.

Everyone had gone to service when they arrived at home. Good. One embarrassment deleted. Rejoice held Noble up as he shuffled into the bedroom and fell onto the bed. Then she took off his shoes and gasped. Broken and bleeding blisters covered his feet. The cleaning, salving, and bandaging of his feet took twenty minutes of glum silence.

"Excuse me a moment." She carried their computers out of the room. A few minutes with each one and several more with the main computer rendered them incapable of receiving any signals. Then she locked the front door, locked the bedroom door, and faced her husband. "Now, you will tell me what happened."

The man who always looked everyone straight in the eye studied the back of his hands and whispered, "I went for a walk."

"I want to know what happened before you went for that walk and decided to kill yourself."

He continued to look at his hands and whispered, "I did not decide to kill myself."

"Excuse me, but you did. Why else would you run unarmed into the Orange Scar Village?"

He sighed. "It was dark, and I became lost."

She moved closer. "What happened before that walk?"

He breathed and rubbed his fingers. A minute passed. "You will despise me."

Rejoice licked her lips as she studied his black hair, dark eyes, handsome nose, and turned down mouth. She waited for him to elaborate. He did not but continued to stare at his hands. Rejoice took a deep breath. "So, did you have sex with Ernest?"

Now he looked at her. "No. I have always been faithful to you."

Rejoice had braced herself to lift a heavy box and instead found it full of air. She smoothed her dress and backed up. "Then what did you do that could make you try to kill yourself?"

He spoke louder. "I wasn't trying to kill myself. I was thinking. I was walking and thinking and praying. I walked to the library and back maybe four or five times. I didn't notice I was at the pass until the sun set. The observation post was closer, and I thought I had a better chance of reaching that unharmed than home. I ended up on the wrong road by mistake."

"Don't lie to me. I'm your wife. You couldn't have taken that hairpin turn by mistake. What in the Name of God did you do?"

He closed his eyes. "Ernest propositioned me. I told him all the reasons that it could never be. He left. Believe me, Rejoice, I did not—" He swallowed. "But I wanted to." He rubbed his face with skeletal hands. "I want to vomit when I think about it, but God help me, I still want to."

Rejoice stood still.

Noble's chest heaved. She sat on the bed and embraced him as deep sobs wracked his withered frame.

When the sobbing finally slowed, He whispered hoarsely, "Rejoice, I never anticipated this. Women, of course, yes. But I've always been so careful. I made sure you were in the background or potentially in the background when I counseled women. It's why I do most of my counseling by screen. I'm never alone with any woman except you. I didn't coach girls' teams because every thirteen-year-old in the colony seems to spend at least six months infatuated with me. I needed to make sure no touch of mine ever kept a girl in that stage. But I've never had any thought of temptation toward men. I never, never expected an onslaught from that direction."

Rejoice wove her fingers together behind her back. Her poor, tortured husband. No wonder he wasn't eating. She prayed, *God, if you never answer another prayer of mine, I don't care, but this time, this once, let me say the right thing.*

His voice broke. "Who is ever going to trust me with their sons again?"

"I will." Rejoice lay on the bed beside Noble and turned his face toward her. "I never should have made you change your name."

Until that moment, Rejoice had not known that someone could look frightened and puzzled at the same time. "I don't . . ."

"No Confidence In The Flesh. When did you decide to neglect that truth? You got that upset because you were tempted? Then it's the death penalty for me because of what I'm tempted to do to the baby. Maybe instead of beating ourselves up because we're tempted, we should be thanking God that He gave us the strength to do what we should have done instead of what we wanted."

He laid his head on her chest and his arm around her. There they lay for a long time.

* * *

Rejoice hefted an orange at the store. Too light. She wanted oranges heavy with juice.

Sister Rutherford, prim and thin in brown, came around from the only other aisle and stopped beside Rejoice. "I do hope Pastor Cruz will be feeling better soon."

"I'm sure he will. He's been swimming across the current, and some time in the cove should refresh him."

"Do tell him that we're all praying for him."

"I will." Sister Rutherford moved away. Rejoice checked the limes. The grapes looked good. Rejoice picked up a cluster and then quickly set it down again. They likely came from He Give's vineyard. The poor man. She thought of Opportunity and the rage that had filled her eyes the night before last. She looked at her hand. If only she had cut it off before she ever hit her sister.

A gentle touch on her elbow startled her. She turned. Great-bearded Deacon Rabbinowich turned his broad brimmed hat in his hands. "Might I have a word with you in private?"

"Sure." Puzzled, she followed him out of the tiny store and into the alley between the building and the elementary school.

Deacon Rabbinowich scanned the area before bending down. "We need to speak to your husband. All your computers are so far off-line they can't be overridden."

"That's correct. Pastor Cruz is exhausted. I intend to see to it that he gets the rest he needs."

"The deacon board has an urgent issue to discuss with him."

"It'll have to wait a week."

"It cannot wait."

"What is so important that Pastor can't rest for one pitiful week?"

The portions of his cheeks above the gray beard darkened. "I must speak directly to Pastor right away."

Rejoice shifted her canvas shopping bag to the other arm. "You can't. You tell me what the issue is, and I'll decide whether or not Pastor should be bothered." *Sister, that was rude.* But what could she do?

He twisted his hat and darkened some more. "The deacon board wishes

Pastor to resign until we have investigated the charge of . . . of sexual misconduct on his part."

Rejoice's fingernails dug into her palms. "Who brought these charges?"

Deacon Rabbinowich looked around again as though searching for escape. A hexacrab stepped by the mouth of the alley and waited with the stillness only wild creatures can achieve. The deacon cleared his throat. "Ernest Roberson claims Pastor used him sexually on Sixday, and then threatened to harm him if he ever told anyone."

"And you believed that liar? No, I won't tell Pastor that you've lost your senses. I will tell him that the board decided to give him a two-week paid vacation in gratitude for all the work and prayer he has invested in all your lives. I don't want to talk to you again until you begin the conversation by saying that you repent of your baseless suspicions."

She charged out of the alley and nearly collided with another hexacrab. The hot sun burned her back as she strode toward home, and anger burned her face. Brother Higashi swallowed his greeting as she stormed past him. Seconds after banging through the front door, she stood under a cold shower. She could imagine the water flashing to steam as it hit her skin. She stayed in the shower until she shivered, her scalp ached from contraction, and her fingertips had shriveled and paled. Then she slowly dried and dressed and prepared a lunch for Noble.

Rejoice took the tray into the bedroom. She said with a smooth face, "The deacons order you to take a two-week vacation." Then she fed him by hand.

* * *

Noble hobbled toward the table and seated himself before a bowl of applesauce. Mother and Harmony had taken the children to service. Rejoice set the tableware gently on the table. The silence felt so precious, she was reluctant to mar it with even the innocent clinking of table setting. She placed a plate of Noble's favorite cinnamon peanut buns beside him.

"Are you sure the deacons said I wasn't even to attend service? Why did they tell you instead of me?"

"I suppose they feel guilty about letting you overwork yourself." Rejoice sipped lemon balm tea and tried not to think of the pitying glances she received from the deacons' wives whenever she stepped outside. So much for confidentiality from the deacon board. Most everyone else seemed only worried and supportive. Maybe the accusation hadn't gotten beyond the board and their wives. Certainly Mother and Harmony didn't know.

Noble tapped his spoon against the rim of the bowl. "I'm about to die of boredom. I can't call even Elder Chin. One week should be enough."

"I already cancelled your sessions." *Lord, please call the board to its senses.*

Noble spooned up the applesauce, but looked as though he took no pleasure from it. "I feel like a prisoner."

"Spending time with your wife and children is a prison?"

"No, no. I didn't mean it that way." He reached for a bun. "I like being with you. But you have your work and the children have school and then home studies. I can do only so much reading and sleeping."

"I'll talk to the board."

"That's funny. That's how you say you'll talk to the hexacrabs and the Senate and the Robersonians. I want you to fix the computer and I'll talk to them myself. Or maybe I'll go for a walk."

"Your feet!"

"They're almost healed. I'll get out of shape if I stay in bed much longer."

The bubble always bursts eventually. "One more day, okay?" Rejoice watched him. What would happen when this bubble burst?

When the sun set, Noble and Rejoice sat up in bed with their door open to the living room. He worked on the grammar of a sentence in Hebrews. She sewed on popped-off buttons. The girls liked to grab each other's dresses and jerk while playing tag. In the living room Mother and Harmony helped the children with their memory verses and the baby in his high chair gnawed on a rice cake.

Mother's computer beeped and she quietly rose and moved into her bedroom to answer it. The baby pounded his rice cake into bits and cried. Reconciliation handed him another rice cake, but he cried louder. Rejoice pricked herself with the needle and sucked on her finger.

Mother came through the open door. "Excuse me. Deacon Rabbinowich wishes to speak to Rejoice."

"I'll take it first," Noble said. "I want to tell him to please cancel the rest of the vacation." He leaned forward to take the screen from Mother's hands. Mother gave it over, stepped back, and closed the door.

Noble kept his thumb on mute. "Rejoice, what's wrong?"

"Answer the call," she said faintly. *God, I lied when I said I didn't care if you never answered another prayer of mine.*

He smiled at the face of Deacon Rabbinowich even though the other man couldn't see him. "It's good to see you. I'm rested now and ready for work."

The man rubbed fingertips across his lips. His gray eyes shifted his gaze from spot to spot. "Ah. Is, ah, Sister Cruz there?"

"She is. But as I'm rested, I think you can speak to me."

He looked off-screen for a fraction of a second. "Ah, yes, we were going to ask her if it is all right for you to join us at a board meeting at my house."

"I don't know why you need to bother her with church details. When is the meeting?"

"Now."

"I'll be there as soon as possible." He shut the computer, rose, and grabbed his black shirt from its peg. "Hmm. The next scheduled board meeting is a week and a half from now. I wonder why they're having a special meeting?" He buttoned the shirt.

"Noble?"

He paused at the middle button. "Yes?"

"I lied to you."

He blinked a few times. "About what?"

"About." She took a deep breath. "About the vacation. What the board really wanted you to do was to resign until they investigated Ernest's charge that you had sex with him."

His arms fell to his sides. "Why would Ernest do that? I told him we couldn't because it's forbidden and because it would ruin my ministry. He knows my ministry is my life. Why would he destroy me like that? I thought he loved me."

Rejoice froze. *Noble thought Ernest loved him? My God, he isn't over it yet!* "Noble, it's obvious. Hell has no fury like a woman scorned. I suppose it works that way for young men, too. Remember Potiphar's wife. If you're ostracized by the colony, he may think you have no place to go but to his arms."

Anger kindled in Noble's eyes. "Why didn't you tell me?"

"I was trying to protect you. I thought that with time they would reconsider."

Noble pressed his fists against his forehead and shouted, "I'm not your little boy! Who do you think you are to lie to me and tell me how to eat and how much work I should do? You have a little boy! Maybe if you took care of him, he wouldn't cry so much and you'd be too busy to interfere with my life!" The door slammed behind him and a second later the front door slammed. The baby howled and One Faith wailed with him.

Rejoice laid aside the dresses and buttons. Of course he was angry. She had trespassed onto his territory. He understood people and she understood quantum mechanics. Her skin heated down to her toes. Everyone had to have heard every word he shouted. He had never shouted at her before. Even when she had shouted at him, he had never shouted back. But what could she have done?

Suddenly, she knew. She could have let the Deacon board do its work and vindicate Noble. Again. She had done it again. How did she unsay words she should never have said? When would she gain foresight instead of hindsight? *God, help me think before I speak.*

One Faith had stopped crying, but the baby still wailed. She should go out and take care of him. But she felt too humiliated to go and face Harmony and Mother yet.

Why couldn't Noble have told Ernest no because he loved her, and not because it would ruin him? She picked up a small dress. She didn't notice until she had finished the row that she had sewn on the wrong size buttons.

Two hours later, she woke up when someone stroked her face. Noble whispered in her ear, "See if you can disentangle yourself from Jubilee without waking him up. We need to talk."

Gently, she rolled the baby onto his back, and, wonder of wonders, he did not wake. She rose, straightened her pajamas, and let Noble take her hand and draw her through the living room and into the soft night. Her sandals made soft flipping sounds on the paved road, and a hush followed the silent path of the three moonlets overhead. They walked until they reached the cliff overlooking Ti Bay. Under the star-sprinkled black, the boats and dock glowed ghostly white in the dim moonlight. The scents of mace and salt enveloped them.

Noble held her hand and watched the ocean for several minutes before he said, "That was the most unusual board meeting I've ever attended. When I left to go to the meeting, I felt more violent than I have ever in my life. I must have looked crazy to you."

Rejoice bit her lip and tried to read his face, but all she could see were shadows. A yertle snuffled by.

"When I walked in, they were all in a circle on their knees praying. I joined them on the floor and tried to calm down. After a long time, Deacon Rabbinowich said that after talking to you, the board had done some deep soul searching. Then he asked me to forgive him for his lack of concern about our financial hardships during the past several months. He said he would pay for our grocery bills next month. And would I please let him take two of my clients to counsel? Deacon Jordan asked me to forgive him for hating the Robersonians and questioning my work with them. He would pay our power bill next month and could he take two of my people to counsel? Deacon Volkansky asked me to forgive him for a judgmental attitude and said he would pay our water bill. He wanted two of my clients also."

Rejoice calculated in her head. That would take them out of all but the house addition debt by the end of the month.

"Deacon Carden asked me to forgive him for being so self-absorbed that he paid no attention to the difficulties of our family. He said would pay for Harmony's medication. He wanted two clients and specifically asked for Sister Sharmat. Deacon Kim asked forgiveness for not showing the gratitude I deserved and said he would pay for all the shoes and clothes we will need this year. He wanted three clients."

Noble's grip on her hand tightened. "Then Deacon Rabbinowich asked me if I had any sins I wanted to confess to the board. I told him I did."

Rejoice jerked her hand away and backed up. He had lied to her! She bumped into the railing and grabbed it. He had *lied* to her!

"And then I confessed my sin of neglecting you."

PACIFISTS' WAR CHAPTER TWENTY-THREE

Noble let the baby grip his two forefingers and helped him walk between his legs. Rejoice set the weather photos on slow flick and took the time to smile at Noble as the two inched across the living room floor. The baby stared with perpetual astonishment at everything, as though he had not seen it all every day of his life. Rejoice hoped the baby would think the smile included him. Why did he still look ugly to her when the images of beautiful baby Mark exactly matched the images of this child?

"You seem pensive this morning. What are you thinking about?"

"Ah." She was never going to discuss that again. "Seeing Myra pregnant again. I have such a hard time having babies, and she could just abort one in cold blood. That must have been a shock to Mr. Roberson to have one of his babies turn out defective."

Noble winced before he bowed deeper to kiss the top of his son's head. "It wasn't one of his, but rather a donor baby. A lot of people on Old Earth paid a lot of money for the outfitting of the Independence in exchange for the promise that one of their children would be born on a new world."

"My word."

"Charley told me they think a saboteur damaged some of the donor embryos and the food synthesizers. Something about that doesn't sound right to me."

"Nothing they do sounds right to me."

"I meant logically. That was one busy saboteur. And since she was executed, we aren't able to hear her side of the story."

"The saboteur was a woman?"

"That's the impression that I got from Ernest. I keep thinking that a state of crisis is an effective vehicle for promoting societal cohesion."

"You think Mr. Roberson did it?"

"I don't know. But Elder Chin assumes so."

Rejoice didn't know either, but rather than argue over how unlikely that seemed, she returned to the screen. She squirted a message to Brother Hancock that the flat spot on the ocean had drifted close enough for a day trip to sample. Then she pulled up the previous day's surveillance of asteroids.

"Guess what I saw on the dock this morning," Noble said.

"A horde of invading naspy."

"Nasty guess," Noble said. "I saw Ti-Assisi learning how to drive his own land vehicle."

"That's foolish. Ti-Assisi is far and away too young. What is Ur-Veena thinking of?"

"I suppose he's thinking it's not foolish or he wouldn't have been standing there watching. Ti-Assisi did drive off the dock, though. Brother Petrovich laughed so hard, he fell in, too."

Rejoice chuckled. "Too bad you didn't get a recording of it."

It was so good just to be enjoying relaxing banter with Noble again. Most of the funk he was in broke during their time together on the short visit back to First City when Starflower finally returned I Know's body. They had attended his second memorial service and dedication of the school's laboratory in his name.

With just them and the baby, they had time to talk with each other face to face. At first Noble hadn't wanted to accept the gift of the air fare from the crew of Starflower and several past crew members. But all of them had wanted Rejoice and Noble there, so they pooled their money to fly them in for two days. Rejoice had been shocked by seeing Elder Smith brooding in the corner by himself after the service. She still couldn't believe that he had the audacity to have come to the funeral. He was the one most responsible for the accident.

She checked a few more photos. "Two hurricanes birthing. Where am I in the alphabet? I name them Hurricanes Vain-glory and Vanity. And rain here tonight."

Mother came in from the bedroom humming and paused at the front door. "Sister Hancock, Ur-Pita, and I are going for an organism count at the tide-pool today. Harmony isn't feeling up to going out, so she'll be watching RealTime Research if you want to join her. I won't be back in time for lunch, so don't wait for me, dearies. God be with you."

When the door closed, Rejoice said, "She seems cheerful this morning. It's good to hear her make music again."

"Truly," Noble bent over the baby. "I hope she asks me to do the ceremony."

Rejoice mistyped and had to delete. "What ceremony?"

Noble looked up, grinning. "She hasn't announced it yet, but I'm expecting it any day now."

Rejoice swiveled in her chair. "Announce what?"

"Goodness, Rejoice, but you are oblivious. Your mother's in love."

Rejoice grabbed the sides of her chair. "With who?"

Noble laughed and swung the baby up to his shoulders. "Elder Smith, of course."

"No!" Rejoice covered her mouth. All those calls. "Oh, please, no." It should have been Doctor Carlson.

Noble pulled up a chair to sit in front of Rejoice. "Why not? Why is it impossible for you to be happy that these two wonderful people are finding happiness in each other?"

"I." He was responsible for the death of Brother I Know. "I." He had opposed Father at every turn. "I." And he didn't think much of her either. "But that means Mother would move to Promise and I'd never get to talk to her again."

"That's a ridiculous statement."

"But she needs to care for Harmony."

"She knows that better than you do. I believe she won't marry until after Harmony dies. Either that, or she'll take Harmony with her."

"But, but . . . don't tell me my worst nightmare is about to come true."

"After what we have been through this year, if *that's* your worst nightmare, then you're one blessed woman. When will you learn you can disagree with someone without hating him?"

The day he apologized for all his wrong decisions. She stammered, "I don't know. I repent of my lack of charity. Ah, could you give me some time to get used to the idea?"

He looked at his screen. "Oops. You have it. It is almost time for my next session. Excuse me while I boot you off the main screen." He handed the baby to Rejoice.

She walked into the bedroom with the baby stretching his arms toward Noble and then crying when she shut the door. *God of peace.* She had already lost her father and brothers and sister. Must she lose her mother, too?

"Da da da da da," the baby wailed.

"Dada's working, so you must not bother him. I'm working, but me you can bother. The statistics don't have to hear me." She handed him a purple and white striped rattle which he tossed away. She could see it now: the first wedding feast in their history where the groom and stepdaughter broke peace by strangling each other.

She sat on the bed, and as she flipped open her computer, it beeped. The sight of Jax in something shimmery purple surprised her. She had not talked to her for nearly three weeks. Come to think of it, she hadn't seen Ernest either. Noble had assigned the Bible Study to Deacon Jordan, but when only two of the Robersonians showed up and found Noble wasn't there, they left and never came back. So what could Jax want now? "What can I do for you?

Jax's mouth slowly spread into a smile, but her eyes did not join in, "I am calling to remind you about next week."

Rejoice watched her son crawl over to the crib and pull himself to a wobbly stand. Next week? After next week came Resurrection Day, but that couldn't be what she was calling about. And her baby couldn't be due yet. "I'm glad you called to remind me, because I don't remember what you're talking about."

"The first payment for our goods."

She dropped the computer. *Oh, no.* She'd forgotten. Where was she going to get the money? "Just a minute," she stammered, and pressed mute. Roaring filled her ears. Her breath accelerated.

She couldn't get the money. The Rationals and hexacrabs were going to fight and the hexacrabs would die. She picked up her computer and set it down again. Sister! Panic wouldn't let her hear God's peace. She couldn't lie and put it off again. She gazed at the little cloth stars of the mobile above the crib drifting in small circles. You break God's command and everything goes wrong. She had never lied before the Robersonians came. It was time to do things God's way and let Him handle the consequences. Rejoice prayed, *God, with Your help, I will never lie again.*

She picked up the computer. "I'm sorry. The hexacrabs don't seem to understand how serious this is."

Jax looked straight at the camera. "We will not allow this."

"Look," Rejoice said as the baby flopped to the floor on his padded bottom. "If a hurricane had destroyed the ship and all its goods, you would have accepted the loss and gone on. Why don't you view the hexacrabs as a natural force you'll stay away from, and go on?"

Jax shook her head, and the sparkling streamers radiating from her ears whipped back and forth. She pulled out a knife, flipped and caught it one-handed. "That is accepting oppression."

"No. It's reality. Reality has to be accepted."

Jax smiled again. A red lipstick smear shone on her canine tooth. "No. This reality will change. We will fight this to the last drop of blood." The screen turned black.

Rejoice frowned at the blank screen. What was Jax planning to do the hexacrabs? How could Rejoice stop her? *God, whatever it takes to save the hexacrabs, do. Whatever knowledge I need, give it to me.*

She hugged the computer to her chest and shivered. Wait, wait.

How did she know Jax was going to slaughter them? Maybe she would only destroy some of their property. Why was she always panicking? The baby cruised along her footboard. She must need a counselor. She couldn't think straight anymore. The baby gnawed on the corner of the footboard. Rejoice needed to calm down and be, ha ha, rational.

Her computer beeped again and she flipped it open. A plaintext message crawled on the bottom of the screen. [Please leave your house and go somewhere secluded at least twenty meters away. Tell no one. Your house is full of ears and eyes. Repeat, tell no one.] The message scrolled off the screen and left it blank.

Rejoice started. What? Did this have anything to do with Jax? An electrical sensation pricked along her skin and a sudden sweat trickled down her sides. She rolled off the bed. "Noble!" Her computer beeped again. Another plaintext message. [Please, I need U. Sis ter. Now.]

She narrowed her eyes as the message scrolled off. Sis ter, a typo, or her brother who always called her Sis?

Noble came in with his headgear slung around his neck. "What?"

Rejoice jumped, snapped shut the computer, and stammered, "Oh, I'm sorry. I forgot to check the time. I wanted to take a short walk. Real short. Maybe you could watch the baby for a minute."

"You're white. What's wrong?"

"I'll, ah, tell you when I get back. At lunch time. Okay? Then I won't interfere with your clients."

He stooped to pick up his joyous son. "Can't you wait fifteen minutes?"

"No. I'm sorry. I'll be back soon." She brushed past him, snatched her rifle, and exited before he could say anything more. In the center of the orchard, she stopped and flipped open the computer again. An apple blossom detached and settled on the screen. An orchard mason bee crawled onto the tip of a leaf and launched itself. Hot sunlight glared on the curve of a pink and white streaked apple and glowed green through the leaves. She waited.

Plaintext crawled on the screen again. [Alone and away from house yet?]

[Yes] she typed.

There appeared on the screen the face of her brother much altered. Unkempt long hair hung to his shoulders, and his dark eyes appeared sunken above a long beard. "Sis, where's Harmony?"

"Did you call to repent?"

He scowled. "When I've done something to repent of, I'll repent. Now, where is Harmony? The house is locked up with a For Sale sign on the door. Nobody here will talk to me."

"Why should you care? Did the orgies grow tedious?"

"Sis! I don't have time for this. Where's my wife?"

"Where are you? Where have you been for the past six months? Don't you care how much you've hurt everybody? I'm not talking to you until you sit down with Pastor Wiseman and straighten out your life. Over."

"Wait! Stop! Don't cut out. I need, please, only one piece of information. Where is Harmony?"

"Are you going to talk to Pastor Wiseman?"

He scowled again. "I haven't talked to that windbag since he asked Father what sins he wanted to confess before he died."

"Father wasn't offended."

"I was. Now, are you going to tell me where Harmony is, or do I need to swim over there and strangle it out of you?"

She examined his angry face and tried to ignore her competing emotions. "Did you know Makepeace was killed?"

Was that moisture in his eyes? "The maggots didn't tell me until two weeks after the funeral. I couldn't do anything about it." He looked offscreen as he waited for Rejoice to reply. When she did not, he paled. "My God, don't tell me Harmony died!"

"No. Not yet."

"Then in the Name of God and all that's holy, tell me where she is!"

Rejoice looked up at the mosaic of green leaves and blue sky, and then down to the screen. In the Name of God and all that's holy? "She's here. With me."

"What? With the churtrees? Where are my girls?"

"Here."

"My God, my God, my God. What do I— Rejoice, I've got to get there. I can't even buy a ticket. How will I—You've got to buy a ticket for me! Now! On the soonest flight out. Sis, tell me you're doing it right now."

She split screen and pulled up the flight schedule. As her fingers danced over the keys, she said, "What do I tell Harmony? What do I tell Mother?" "Nothing! Tell Harmony nothing! There are eyes and ears all over your house. Keep this a secret from everybody!"

Rejoice paused when she saw the ticket price. How could she pay for it? Right, the bank still held one month's retirement She sighed, unlocked the money, and sent it to the airline. "Secret? You know I hate secrets."

"Believe me. I know. But you must keep this secret. Don't tell Noble. Don't tell anybody. Did you buy the ticket yet?"

"Yes. Can you make it to the airport in an hour? That's—"

The screen blanked.

Rejoice pinched the bridge of her nose and closed her eyes. What was her brother doing? She could well imagine why he wouldn't want the little ears and eyes of his girls learning about his coming if he wanted to slink in and, and what? Why was he coming if he didn't want Harmony to know? And how could he think he didn't need to repent for all the anguish he had splattered over everyone? How deceived was he? Wait, wait, wait. What if the ticket was not for him, but for someone else? Who? And why? No, that didn't make sense either.

"Excuse me, but Jubilee just chipped off the microphone from my headset."

Rejoice jumped and opened her eyes.

Noble stood holding the baby in front of her. "Do you mind telling me what that was all about?"

"I can't betray this confidence. I'm sorry."

"Oh. If you're through, would you please take Jubilee back? I have another ninety minutes of counseling to do this morning."

She took the baby who instantly twisted to hold his arms out toward his father. "Aren't you even a little bit curious?"

"I'm a lot curious, but if it were my business, you'd be telling me about it. Bye-bye, Jubilee." He turned and strode through the dappled shade toward the house.

The baby strained toward him and wailed. Rejoice stood, wishing she had the discipline of Noble, wishing she could make peace between the Robersonians and hexacrabs, wishing she knew what Stronghold was up to, wishing she could like this baby even a little bit. "But wishing isn't doing," she murmured into the baby's ear. "Let's, oh, let's go visit the chickens." Then she needed to figure how to get over to Ti Bay in about six hours to meet that jet without lying and while keeping the secret. "I hate secrets," she muttered as she carried the baby to the coop.

PACIFISTS' WAR CHAPTER TWENTY-FOUR

The cliffs of Ti Bay looked cool in the late afternoon shade. Rejoice leaned over the railing and watched the silver flash of the sea jet land past the floating solar cells. Tiny, rectangular barges moved toward the jet. In the north, blue sky joined blue sea on a faded horizon line. In the south, black clouds massed with sudden, inaudible flashes of heat lightening in their crowns. A low-pressure front pulled the clouds toward Largest Archipelago.

She gazed down at the water ruffling around the boulders. On the dock ramp, an LV broke the surface of the sea and walked, dripping, onto the dock. She watched until the first barge neared the dock, and then walked to the elevator doors.

When the doors slid open, someone behind her shouted, "Halt!" Six Robersonians in camouflage and with rifles in their hands jostled past her into the elevator and turned to grin at her. One was Zack with his chestnut hair pulled back into several braids. He patted his rifle. "You catch the next one." The doors slid shut.

Rejoice stood a moment before she gasped and pulled out her computer. With trembling hands she called Jax. "What are your students going to do to the hexacrabs?"

After a minute of silence, the screen blinked on. Jax sat herself on the edge of the desk and laced her fingers over one knee. "Nothing unless they are attacked by those contract breakers."

"And what would make the hexacrabs do that?"

Jax affected a yawn. "Don't waste my time. You think we we're stupid. You're wrong." She cut off the call.

Rejoice charged through the doorway when the elevator returned and agonized the entire way down. *Father God, stop them.* God must stop them. When the door opened, she burst out and nearly ran into a hexacrab holding two rifles and calmly waiting for its turn in the elevator.

Rejoice stepped aside. "Excuse me."

The Robersonian's boat floated empty and moored to the dock. What, then, were they up to? *Slow down, heart.*

Several of the passengers who had debarked stood with their heads facing the barge and watching the Robersonians leap onto it. The Robersonians ran from one end to the other and jumped back onto the dock. Then all but two clustered at the point where the second barge would come in. Two of them ran to their boat and gunned it toward the sea jet, roaring away with spray flying behind it.

Rejoice bit down on her knuckle as she tried to make sense of what she was seeing. The other colonists watched for a while also, then turned to walk to the elevators. The wide, gray-haired man in front of Rejoice turned, and she gasped again. Elder Smith!

He seemed startled to see her as well. He set down the folded cot and duffle bag he was carrying and extended his firm, broad hand. "Ah, Sister Cruz. I did not expect to meet with you quite so soon. Are you here to meet someone?"

Three of the Hancock's grandchildren loped by, caramel-colored with tightly-curled blond hair, shrieking and laughing about the one of them that had gotten seasick on the barge ride.

Smile. Shake hands. He might be her stepfather soon. Rejoice pulled her lips into a smile, placed her hand in his, and murmured, "I had heard that my brother might be on this flight." Oops. She wasn't supposed to tell anyone. Why had Stronghold thought she could keep a secret?

He let go her hand. "Not on this flight. Aren't you shunning him as the rest of the body is?"

Rejoice clasped her hands behind her back. "Well, yes. But . . ." She looked past him to the barge loaded with boxes touching the dock. The Robersonians jumped on it. "I want . . ." What did she want? A chance, any chance to bring her brother back. She looked into his accusing eyes. "Were you always a Christian?"

His gray eyebrows lifted and he straightened a bit. Behind him, the Robersonians helped unload the boxes, and then opened them and peered inside. "You're right. Only God knows when and how a man may change his mind. I've let my anger at your brother keep me from loving him as I ought."

He fingered his sparse beard and his gaze wandered to the vertical cliffs, the gray jungles, and the fast moving clouds. "I became biased when I saw him hurt your mother. With God's help, I intend to do all I can to keep her from being hurt again."

Oh, no, it's true. Smile, Sister. "Does Mother know you're coming? I can call."

"No, no. Don't do that. I'm coming as a bit of a surprise. I'll visit after I get set up at Elder Chin's."

"Elder Chin? But you haven't talked for, um."

"Years," he supplied. "Two surprises for the price of one. I've decided that I'm too close to eternity to allow disagreements to come between me and the people I love. I'll never understand how so many of us could lose our original vision of what we were to be. But I need to let it go." He looked up at the cliffs again.

His vision had nothing to do with what they had found on New Earth. But smile, Sister, he might be apologizing.

"You know, when I attended Brother Toshiba's memorial, I sat there and did a lot of thinking.

"Yes, I saw you there too. I'm sorry we didn't get over to you." *Oops, sorry God. I said I wouldn't lie again.*

"Yes, I'm sorry too. But at that time I came to the conclusion that you were right"

She was? "About what?"

"You were wise to close down the space program. It seemed like such an easy way to get metals. It took a death to show us that we should have spent our efforts looking for places on the planet's crust to mine."

That was the wrong conclusion!

"We should park every single one of our shuttles and forget about space for a while."

You fool! She should save them both time and strangle him now. "Excuse me, but that ignores the fact that we don't know where the next asteroid to hit this planet will come from." Her face hurt from smiling.

"We had a three-year lead the last time, and we weren't even looking. We can gear up again if need be."

Double fool! Who told him asteroids came with guarantees? "Excuse me again, but we cannot count on that."

He shook his head, then pulled out his computer. "Will you forgive an old man? I'm tired and I need you to show me how to get to Elder Chin's."

She took his computer, pulled up the mission map, and highlighted the bubble on the Inner ring that belonged to Elder Chin. "You can take my runabout at the top. It's the one with the baby blanket on the back seat."

"Thank you, Sister." He touched his forefinger to his lips. "Let this be a surprise."

Hadn't Mother told him she hated surprises? She nodded.

He picked up his things and trudged toward the elevator.

She should be helping him. Instead she looked at the indentations her nails had left in her palms. The gold light winked out as the sun fell below the ridge. The shadow of the island reached to the boat bouncing back from the jet. What kind of cargo were they in such a hurry to get?

She glanced toward the changing rooms. Maybe she should dive for an hour. If she went home now, Noble would want to know what was wrong, and she would start crying, and then he would be angry when he found out what she was crying about. Maybe he should be happy. She had just gained an incentive to make her stay on the island forever.

Scowling Robersonians surrounded her. Zack leaned into her face. "Where is that scum?"

She met his narrowed eyes. "Scum?"

"Stronghold!"

"I don't know."

"For truth, you were here waiting for him."

She squeaked, "I haven't seen him."

Abruptly they clattered away toward the elevators. One stayed by the doors as the others went up.

Rejoice stood in place. What had Stronghold done now to swim between a torpal and a naspy? Had he planned to run back to Harmony as the only person left on this planet who would welcome him? If so, where was he? And why had he called Rejoice instead of Harmony? And what had happened to the retirement money she'd just spent on his ticket?

Deacon Rabbinowich rumbled by with a load of boxes for the warehouse.

Yes. A dive. Warm water. Maybe some hexacrabs. A chance to drift in a gentle current. A chance to practice forgiving an old man. Yes, she would dive for an hour. Maybe two.

Ninety minutes later, she yawned as she pushed the button on the elevator. A Robersonian moved out of the shadows. "Why were you diving?" She had blond hair pulled back to a ponytail and brown blotches painted on her bread dough-colored face.

Rejoice didn't like that the woman carried her rifle in her hands instead of slung on her back. What if she tripped in the dark? "I wanted to float. It felt good."

"Why now?"

"It's always felt good. I got to play with some string-glows. Did you notice how shimmery the water is tonight? The string-glows are in a mating swarm."

The woman bared her teeth with a hiss and stalked away.

Rejoice watched her melt into the shadows. The Robersonians were so confusing. No one had ever questioned her about diving before. What peculiar people they were. And furious at Stronghold. Her stomach twisted and her heart raced again. Where could she find out what was going on?

She stepped out of the elevator at the top. Another Robersonian paced the edge of the lighted area around the doors and carried his rifle in his hands. Oh. What were they planning to do to her brother? The young man watched her as she walked up the road toward home.

Three-fourths of the way there, someone whispered, "Sis!" from the jungle. She whirled to face the sound, but saw nothing in the dark beyond the footlights. 'Shh," came the whisper. "Come in here."

She glanced both ways, saw no one on the road, and stepped into the darkness.

Suddenly strong arms were around her, almost crushing her. Stronghold whispered in her ear. "Sis, this is going to be hard, but you need to find an excuse to take Harmony into the orchard. Don't mention me. There are eyes and ears all over your house."

"You keep saying that. Do you mean the children? What did you do?"

"Shh. There are microphones and cameras, bugs, all over your house. The maggots have been spying on you from day one."

"What? Where?"

"Your bedroom mostly. The Noble and Rejoice show is quite a hit."

Rejoice could not breathe. The Robersonians had been watching them? Every argument? Every time they made love? Every time they dressed and scratched and sprawled? Everything? She shook. "Did you like it?"

"Shh. I want to kill them too, but I can't and remain true to who we are. If it's any comfort, the worm I left behind should have destroyed all those records. Now, please, get Harmony, but don't tell her. She can't hide anything and I've got to get to her before the maggots catch me."

"Where will you and she hide? How will you live?" She stopped and felt his wet shirt. "How did you get here?"

"I rode with the cargo so I wouldn't contaminate the passengers and bailed out as soon as the jet hit the water. I swam in and climbed the cliff. I expect to be caught at any moment. Get Harmony before I'm caught." He pushed her toward the road. "Take her someplace dark and I'll find you."

She forced herself not to look back and to walk toward her bugged house. Jax had said she wanted to be friends. The liar! Even if Stronghold did destroy the records in Freedom, what did that mean for the records at the dojo? What else had Stronghold done? Would they be hunting him like this just because of a worm? Well, that would depend on how destructive that worm was. And once they did catch him, what were they going to do to him? Fear and shame chased her down the road. How was she going to pretend that everything was normal?

Fortunately, she walked in at the moment that Mark swung One Faith around and cracked her head against the corner of the table. With all the screaming and crying and blood and Mother tending the cut and Noble lecturing his son, no one thought to ask Rejoice why her face was red. She picked up her baby and carried him into the bedroom.

Rejoice tried to keep her eyes focused on him and not searching the walls. Where were the cameras? Then the memory of the time that she had invited Jax into her bedroom struck her like a glass of cold water to the face. "Oh, Father God," she stuttered as she recalled Jax stretching weirdly and running her fingers along things. *I'm going to kill her.* What would Noble do when he found out?

A few minutes later, Noble came in and stretched out on the bed. "Whew. What an evening. What happened to our daily walk?"

"I'm sorry. I needed a break, and the dive felt good."

He moved closer. "I know what else would feel good."

"Ah, Noble, I was thinking as I was diving and walking home."

"Mmm?" He kissed her shoulder.

"I want to have a private talk with Harmony. Here. You take the baby." She bustled out before he could protest.

Every girl popped up in her bed as Rejoice walked past. Mother was beginning to undress Harmony when Rejoice walked in. "Harmony, the night is so pleasant I wanted to go for a walk with you."

Mother looked puzzled, and Harmony shook her head before whispering, "I'm too tired to go out."

"Just for a few minutes, please? I want some one-on-one time with you and it's going to rain hard in another hour or two and the moons are beautiful with haloes around them. Please?"

"Are you pregnant again?" asked Mother.

"No. I want a private walk is all."

"Sweet love, you have been acting strange all day. And you just had a huge time of privacy."

"And during it, I thought of something I want to say to Harmony. Privately."

"Well, then. Don't stay out too late." She straightened Harmony's brown blouse and skirt.

Rejoice smiled over gritted teeth. *Yes, Mother.*

As Harmony rolled out into the moist, warm dark of the evening, Rejoice asked, "Did you have some company while I was gone?"

"No," Harmony whispered. "Was someone supposed to come over?"

Reconciling with Elder Chin must have taken longer than Elder Smith thought it would. "I don't know. I met someone on the dock who said he might."

"Who?"

"Can you keep a secret?"

"No."

"Oh." Then Rejoice said a sharper, "Oh!" as the crackle of gunfire reverberated across the mission.

Harmony craned her neck and studied the empty road. "We should ask them not to practice at night."

Rejoice gripped the back of the wheelchair and swallowed. Yes, the sounds were coming from the firing range and not at the dojo.

Harmony worked on breathing as they stood in the dark. "What did you . . . want to say?"

"Let's go to the middle of the orchard first."

Harmony's chair bumped over the ground, and she whimpered with every breath by the time they reached the center. Rejoice took Harmony's hand and wrapped it around hers as she finger-spelled, {Wait}

They waited as the wind shuffled the dark leaves. One moon, and then another disappeared as black clouds overgrew them. The third moon skirted a scalloped edge. It grew too dark to see the white stake that marked the grave of Makepeace on the border of the orchard. Rejoice shivered.

She jumped and gasped at a tentative touch on her arm.

"What?" Harmony wheezed.

Something moved beside her and then hissed.

Harmony jerked and whimpered, "What did you do?"

Rejoice could barely hear the whisper, "My love, I gave you a shot that will kill the lung rot. Only God knows how much I've missed you."

Harmony choked.

Rejoice reached for Harmony and smashed her hand on Stronghold's shoulder.

"Take it easy, love. I don't know how much time I have with you."

Harmony's strangled cries slowly subsided. "How?"

"I had to pretend to join them to get into their lab." His hand found Rejoice's. "Sis, you're not going to like this. The antibiotic molecule requires germanium, just like the computers do."

The mine the hexacrabs closed. If they refused to reopen it, which group of humans would be the first to open it with violence? "Arsenic is close to it on the periodic table. Can't you substitute arsenic?"

"We tried. One of the folding angles is a few degrees off, enough that it won't bind to the lung rot cell wall."

Harmony pulled away his hand. "Why . . . hide?"

A harsh cry split the night. "I see you! Don't move! Over here!" Light from a flashlight struck Rejoice in the face. She turned from the glare. Stronghold knelt in front of Harmony with tears on his face and his hands cupping her face. He moved not a muscle.

He whispered, "Whatever happens, remember that I counted the cost and I was willing to pay it. I love you. Tell our daughters that I love them."

Two more lights shone on them and came closer. Rejoice could not see who held the lights, but she could clearly see the rifle barrels pointed at her. The lights stopped three meters away. "Stand slowly."

Stronghold rose as Harmony clutched at him. He carefully stretched out his hands and turned to face the lights.

"Where is it?"

His right hand slid into his pocket and withdrew an injector tube. He extended the small rod.

Someone in camouflage stepped forward and snatched the tube. He turned it over in his hands. "Discharged!"

"These women had nothing to do with it. They had no idea what I was doing. I turn myself over to you, but let these innocent women go."

"Move, thief!" A rifle tapped him on the chest, and, still holding his hands up, he stepped away from Harmony. She reached after him.

"Name?"

Rejoice squeaked, "Her name is How Good Harmony Is Holly."

A voice behind one light snickered, "The brain-dead Holly. You?"

"Rejoice In The Lord's Salvation Cruz."

A different voice groaned. "Jax told us to leave her alone."

The rifle tapped Stronghold on the shoulder. "Move."

"No," Harmony wheezed. Rejoice reached for her hand and watched with tear-blurred vision as Stronghold, in the center of the lights, walked out of the orchard and down the street toward the dojo. Harmony choked again. Rejoice fumbled in the dark for the switch on Harmony's power chair, steered it between the tree trunks, and hurried her into the house.

"Mother! Noble!" she called as she ran to the screen and activated a general alarm.

Mother burst through the door in her pajamas. The girls peered through the doorway. Noble came in wearing pajama bottoms. His gaze swiveled from Mother dealing with Harmony's choking to Rejoice typing furiously. Her words flashed in large letters. [I want every man to go to the dojo as a witness to what they do to Brother Stronghold Holly.]

"Stronghold is here?" asked Noble.

"The Robersonians just took him prisoner."

"Daddy!" screamed Reason.

"I don't understand. He went to live with them," Noble said.

"He went to find a cure for lung rot. The Robersonian s think he stole it."

Harmony's struggle to breathe rasped through the room.

Noble ran into the bedroom and came out a minute later dressed in black. He grabbed his rifle and ran out the door. Rejoice tried to put her arms around all four girls who kept crying, "Daddy! Daddy!"

* * *

An hour and a half later, Noble came into the lighted bedroom and slumped onto the chair. "Here's the agreement. The Rationals have promised to not hurt your brother. Yet. As soon as Henley Roberson arrives tomorrow, there will be a negotiation or a trial or something. We never did agree to a common justice system, so . . ." He stopped and looked at Rejoice running her fingers along the bottom of the footboard. Two rocks lay on the floor by her knees. "What are you doing?"

"I'm cleaning house. Would you help me tip the bed over?"

He blinked. After watching her a few seconds, he squatted by the side of the bed, placed his hands under it, and heaved. Then he grabbed it to keep it from rolling over and smashing the wall. "Do you think you could finish this tomorrow?" He scanned the room. "Where's Jubilee?"

Rejoice rubbed her hands over the bottom of the bed. "With Mother. Aha. This must be a crawler, for I'm certain Jax never touched there." She stooped to the rocks, placed a glittery white fleck on one, and with the other smashed the fleck to a glassy powder.

Now he noticed a small pile of powder beside the rocks. "What was that?"

Rejoice resumed rubbing the underside of the bed. "Are you calm?"

"Not anymore."

"Then wait a minute." She stroked every square centimeter of the surface. "Okay. Let it down."

He did so and continued to watch her with wariness wrinkling the skin around his eyes.

"Sit."

He sat in the chair.

"I have confirmed what Stronghold told me. Our entire house has been bugged by the Robersonians."

He gaped. "Even the bedroom?"

"Especially our bedroom. I've found ten so far. Most of them are white and attached to Opportunity's paintings."

"Since when?" His voice sounded hollow.

"According to Stronghold, from the moment they met us. But I remember now when Jax bugged our bedroom. It was the time that I allowed her in the bedroom to talk, just after my accident with Makepeace on the runabout. I remember that she was very nervous and was stretching like she was exercising and touching odd surfaces around the room with her fingertips. When we started talking about our cameras observing the churtree, her eyes lit up. She seemed relieved that we thought it ethical to study the churtree unawares."

The muscles of his jaw tightened. Through gritted teeth he muttered, "This is one of those times . . ." His fist squeezed rock-hard and white, his biceps swelled huge, the veins in his neck bulged and pulsed. "That I truly wish I was not a pacifist."

CHAPTER TWENTY-FIVE

The pain in Rejoice's hip woke her in the morning. She pushed herself up, brushed her hair away from her face, and contemplated what a miserable place a floor was for sleeping. She hurt all over.

Noble's folded blanket lay on the floor beside her. She scanned her bare, white chamber as she stretched. Noble had disassembled every bit of furniture and thrown the pieces outside in the hard rain. The paintings had almost joined them, but after mounting a tug of war for several minutes, Rejoice had persuaded Noble to leave the paintings in the main room. She stood and rubbed her hips.

Yawning, she stepped into the main room and looked out the window. Their belongings sprawled by the side of the road in multiple pieces and spattered with mud.

Mark crept in from the hallway. His tousled hair framed his wide eyes. "Is Father angry?"

"Oh, honey," she bent to hug him. "Not at you. The Robersonians put spying devices all over our house and furniture. And now we're looking for them."

"What's going to happen to Uncle Stronghold?"

"I don't know, sweetheart. But we should find out today. Oh, look at the time. You need to be going to school."

"I haven't had breakfast yet."

"You get dressed and I'll make toast and get the girls." The next twenty minutes were a flurry of dresses and shoes and combs and crumbs. Finally, Rejoice plodded through the rain with them whining behind. Rejoice did not envy Brother Wu's job of teaching that morning. Trudging back, she tried to remember what Noble had said before he left. He was taking the baby to the Carver's, right? And that was why she hadn't heard the baby that morning?

A roar shook her bones. The Robersonian's jet lowered to the runway. She hoped all the churtrees had stayed on their side of the ridge so they wouldn't panic and kill themselves. Rejoice stopped and marveled at herself for wishing anything good to the churtrees. At this moment, she preferred churtrees to human treachery.

"Ur-Veena is right," she muttered, "they are same-churtree. No, worse-churtree." The churtrees were stupid, blatant, and evil. The Rationals were smart, subtle, and evil. And you knew the churtrees would try to kill you. You didn't find out about the Robersonians until too late.

When she reached sight of her home, Sister Deng dashed into the house with several cases under her arms.

Rejoice followed her into the back bedroom where Harmony, limp and mottled, breathed irregularly on her bed. The sour smell of sickness gripped her throat. A band on Harmony's forehead flashed a temperature far too high. A screen beside her traced a faltering line connoting heart failure.

Doctor Carlson and Mother fitted together tubing and needles. White-faced, Mother snapped, "Stay out of our way. We need to oxygenate and dialyze her blood."

Doctor Carlson took the cases from Sister Deng, set them down, and then gave her a needle to insert into Harmony.

Rejoice backed out with her hands at her throat. That injection was supposed to cure her, but Harmony was dying. What had Stronghold done? She sat on one of the girl's cots and shuddered.

Her computer beeped. She couldn't hold it, so she tipped it out of its case and jabbed at it until she hit the receive button. Noble's voice said,

"Mr. Roberson is here, and we're assembling at the gymnasium. Please bring Harmony as soon as possible."

Rejoice tried to speak but couldn't. She typed [I caant]

"Rejoice? Hello?" A pause, and then, "Elder Smith?" The connection ended.

Rejoice stood and wobbled out the door.

When Rejoice reached the part of the road where it skirted the cliff, the rain had stopped. She leaned on the railing and watched the sky crowded with clouds. A tiny dot that had to be a puffin swooped between the lumpy sky and wrinkled sea. The breeze cooled Rejoice's neck as she thought about Harmony.

Except for three or four random images of Old Earth, Rejoice's memory went back to the seven-year voyage to New Earth. Every day Harmony had been there with flowing golden-red hair that Rejoice envied. Every day Harmony insisted on being Rejoice's friend and dreamed of being a mommy and got into trouble for talking out of turn. When she became a teenager, she used her friendship with Rejoice to stay close to Stronghold. She had planned to name her first girl after Rejoice, but Stronghold had intervened.

Rejoice's grip on the railing tightened. Harmony shouldn't be dying for another four years. Rejoice had held Father's hand a few minutes after he died and thought what an ugly enemy death was. Who should she be with? Harmony or Stronghold?

A hexacrab ascended the ramp. Another followed it. Stronghold had designed their LVs. She had never thought to ask the hexacrabs what they thought of Stronghold joining the same-churtrees. Except he hadn't. Or so he said now.

Rejoice took a deep breath and pushed away from the railing.

At the dojo entrance, she wavered a moment and leaned against the open gate. A sour-smelling Robersonian in rumpled camouflage and stubbled face, watched her with narrowed eyes. His fingers stroked the knife strapped to his thigh. The barrel of the black rifle behind his shoulder scraped the door jamb. She averted her gaze and thought. Maybe she would see Opportunity. If she did, she knew what she would say now: "Please forgive me. I love you." Did Stronghold know about Opportunity?

She stepped in and the first person she saw was Jax dressed in black turning away from Myra. Jax saw her and stopped.

Rejoice clutched her hands behind her back so she wouldn't do anything violent with them and walked up to Jax. "Why?"

Jax walked out of the auditorium and Rejoice followed. Jax shrugged. "You're studying the churtrees, and I'm studying your culture. Remember, I became an anthropologist on the journey over here."

"You could have interviewed me." *You maggot!* "We spy on the churtree because it's the only safe way we have to learn about them! Safe for them and us!"

Jax shrugged again. "Equivalency. You would not have told us all we learned."

Rejoice's fingers ached. "You had no right."

"I didn't hurt you."

What did she call hurt? The high-pitched cry of a pack bat pulled her gaze to the sky. She backed up and bumped into the compound wall. Jax, too, searched the sky. Then they both saw Zack leaning on the gymnasium buttress and laughing as he pocketed a whistle. "That's not something to cry wolf about!" Rejoice shouted. She glared at Jax who was scowling at Zack. "Why were you hiding a cure from us?"

Jax leaned forward. "Your brother lied." She spat on the ground. "We thought there was hope for the Hollies." She leaned closer. "He wanted to end the prolongation of her misery, a moral action, for truth. But why he chose his other actions, perhaps your god knows. I don't care why. I want justice."

Rejoice pressed her elbows against the wall as she fiercely held onto her hands. What did people like these know of justice? Jax's words penetrated her anger. What else had he done? Her knees weakened. Jax had said that he was deliberately trying to kill Harmony. That could not be, not the way he had looked at her last night. Not unless they had taught him to see such killing as a mercy. But then why would they be so angry at him?

Jax entering the gymnasium. With tentative steps Rejoice followed.

Forty-one colonists sat on the floor on one side and the fifty dojo students and staff sat on the other side. Everyone but Stronghold and Elder Chin wore a rifle on their back or a gun at their hip. In the center, against the back wall, Stronghold knelt with his hands behind his back and a Robersonian on each side with rifle drawn. He looked at the floor with no expression on his face.

Nowhere could she see Opportunity. Sister Hancock peered through her camera as she scanned both sides of the gymnasium and made an adjustment. Brother Hancock, his face wrinkled with concern, sat gazing at Stronghold with his lips moving silently in prayer. Most of the other colonists sat with bowed heads. Noble rushed up to Rejoice. "Where's Harmony?"

Rejoice hung onto him for support and laid her head on his chest.

Henley Roberson's pleasant, low rumbling voice rose above the multiplied discussions of the students, who instantly fell silent. "Since we are all here, I propose that we begin by deciding whose jurisdiction this man falls under."

Noble sat and Rejoice followed him. The hard floor pressed against her bones.

Henley stood in the center of the gymnasium wearing a dark gray suit with scarlet piping. Black straps visible only when he parted his suit jacket held a massive pistol under his left arm that must weigh as much as a rifle. His rugged face looked solemn. "Who is here to represent the colonists?"

Elder Chin rose and shuffled to the front. Tremors activated his head and hands. His jowls gently vibrated to an inner rhythm. "I shall make the attempt. The Senate is attending by screen."

"So. Is he yours or ours? If he is ours, then things are simple. We take him back to Freedom and execute him for his crimes. If he is yours, then—" He stopped at the outbursts from the colonists.

Rejoice pulled on Noble's shoulder to rise and shout, "Why? What has he done?"

Henley stood facing the colonists with one hand folded inside the other and he waited until they had stopped talking. "If he is yours, then we enter into a negotiation, for the city of Freedom has a great grievance that needs to be addressed, a claim against the colonists that have conspired against us."

Looking puzzled, Stronghold watched Henley.

"We suspect he is yours, else the distress call given out last night would not have called him Brother Holly. Else Sister Cruz, who supposedly was shunning her brother, would not have been waiting for him and aiding him in the evasion of justice. Else the mission would not have responded with dozens of men violating our boundaries and invading our privacy." *Privacy? What do you care about privacy?* Rejoice screamed in her mind.

"Else we would not be having this meeting today." He spread out his hands. "So. Do you accept responsibility for his actions or do you not?"

Rejoice shouted aloud, "Since when did 'stealing' the results of one's own labor become a crime worthy of death?"

The voices of other colonists erupted from behind her as Noble pulled her down and spoke in her ear. "Let the Elder do his job. All we'll accomplish by speaking out of turn is a riot."

The Robersonians sat in a stolid, silent mass, watching the colonists with eyes squeezed by anger.

Deaconess Rabbinowich reached forward and gently rubbed Rejoice's shoulder. The colonists quieted and looked at Elder Chin.

Elder Chin repositioned his hands on his cane. "You claim a grievance and a conspiracy. I must confess that I know nothing of either charge. We cannot accept corporate guilt for an individual's acts until we know what those acts were and how the corporate body impelled the individual to those acts."

"So. Do you deny sending "Brother" Holly to our city to sabotage our labs and computer systems?"

"I deny doing this, yes." He peered at Henley from under folds of skin. "Does the Senate have knowledge of anyone commissioning such a deed?" From the computer on his hip came two voices in swift answer, "No."

Henley folded his hands together. "If you will not accept responsibility, then we will consider his acts those of a lone madman and take him back home to be shot."

"I'll take responsibility," Rejoice said.

"Stop!" Noble clicked in hex.

"No, Sis," Stronghold said.

Henley stepped over to face Rejoice. "So. You are part of the conspiracy."

"I don't know what you're talking about. But whatever he did, I'll try to find a way to pay for it."

"As you did for our destroyed goods?" Henley sneered. "And do you deny telling the hexacrabs to destroy our goods because we violated your petty morals?"

Rejoice opened her mouth, but Noble squeezed her hand, and she shut it while glaring at Henley.

Elder Chin's voice quavered. "Excuse me, but we still do not know the exact nature of the charges."

Henley held up his fingers and ticked off the points. "One: he lied to us about his intentions in order to gain access to proprietary materials, specifically knowledge, one of the few things we have to trade with you. Two: he purposefully trashed our computer system. Three: he destroyed many of the lab samples we need for ongoing medical research and care. Four: he caused the death of a thousand human embryos."

Rejoice sat stunned. Behind her dozens of people sucked in breath. *Oh, no.* If the hexacrabs heard that Stronghold killed a thousand baby embryos, they would consider him same-churtree and worthy of death.

"That's not true," Stronghold said. "Nothing I did could have harmed the embryos."

"Oh, but they have received the ultimate harm. They are dead, and by your hand." Henley looked from Stronghold to the colonists. "There is no justice in a society that does not require the fulfillment of contracts. To use your terminology, we hold contracts to be sacred. We contracted to raise those embryos on whatever new world we landed on." Henley lowered his voice. "And this person murdered every one of them."

He didn't even mention the cure for lung rot. "But they were damaged and you were going to discard them anyway!" Rejoice shouted.

"Rejoice!" Noble said.

Henley smiled at Rejoice. "You are referring to a separate batch of embryos. We carried two thousand in total and kept them in two separate freezers so that if anything should happen to one batch, the second would be safe. Your brother's worm had the freezers thaw the embryos, and then freeze them again slowly so that ice crystals disrupted every cell."

Rejoice gagged.

"Not true," Stronghold said.

Several of the Robersonians hissed.

Elder Chin tapped his cane on the floor twice. "I would like to hear his side of the story."

Henley opened his hand toward Stronghold.

Stronghold started to rise, but his guards pressed down on his shoulders. "I did crash their system, but only long enough for the worms to do their work. I knew which freezer held the embryos, and my worms didn't touch it. They did delete files the maggots had no business having."

The Robersonians hissed again.

"I'm proud that I destroyed their stores of black fever, yellow fever, measles, and more. If the lung rot didn't kill us fast enough, they intended to loose those diseases on us."

"Liar!" several Robersonians shouted as the colonists exclaimed.

Stronghold shouted, "They were keeping the cure that I discovered secret so the colonists would die off and they could take over the planet with a superior race. But I wormed instructions for manufacturing the drug into our clinics and every computer that was connected yesterday. I made copies of the instructions and hid them in a dozen places. The secret can't be kept."

Rejoice held Noble's arm and squeezed. Henley stood silent with a small smile on his face. How could he stay so calm? She looked at Elder Chin, and saw that he, too, was calm. But then, he would have been expecting this kind of response. But why was Henley unconcerned that his plot had been uncovered?

Henley shook his head and broadened his smile. "I believe your Scripture says that a false witness lies. Perhaps he has come up with this story hoping that you will protect him. Where do I begin the refutation?"

"With the viruses," Elder Chin said.

"So. There is no need to put a sinister interpretation upon our possession of disease organisms. I am surprised that you don't have a store of them." He held up a finger. "Consider: two, three, eight generations from now and all our descendants have naïve immune systems that have never been challenged by an Old Earth disease. A ship from Old Earth comes, much as we did, and one of the passengers is an innocent carrier of a virus that spreads like wildfire through our population. We had those viruses so that we could make vaccines if need be. Our future generations may not thank this fellow. I would not be surprised if Stronghold became a curse word."

"The lung rot cure," Elder Chin said.

"There is no cure." Henley paced slowly as he looked each colonist in the eye. "Not yet. We are working diligently on it, as we promised. None of the drugs we have developed so far have passed even a third of the protocol. We have begun animal trials, and we may have something in a year, maybe two, maybe three. You cannot hurry this kind of research or raise false hopes."

"Then what did he inject into Sister Holly?" Rejoice said. Noble tapped her knee.

Henley pursed his lips a moment. "You'll have to ask him. But it's an odd cure, don't you think, that leaves his wife dying of liver, kidney, and heart failure even as we speak?"

The muscles in Stronghold's face sagged. Then he surged to his feet. He twisted away from the guards, revealing his hands tied behind his back.

The guards exchanged glances, then moved in unison to clip him behind his knees.

His knees cracked against the floor as he collapsed. He shouted, "You have no authority over me. I must see my wife!"

Several of the colonists jumped to their feet. An equal number of Robersonians rose and faced them.

Henley opened his hand toward Stronghold. "The issue of authority comes up again. Do you, as a corporate body, accept responsibility for his acts, or is he ours to deal with?"

A noise in the doorway caused all to turn. Ur-Veena entered the gymnasium in his gleaming LV. Behind him came another and another and another hexacrab, each holding two rifles in their claspers.

Half the Robersonians stood and pointed rifles at the hexacrabs. Henly held out a hand, palm down, and they lowered their rifles. A Robersonian ran to the door and squeezed his head between the door frame and an LV. When he pulled back, he announced, "At least thirty in the courtyard."

Jax looked sick as she studied the hexacrabs with eyes narrowed to slits. "Contract breakers!" some of the Robersonians shouted. One of the guards left Stronghold and sprinted to a back door. He looked outside, nodded to Henley and then slipped outside.

Never enter a room with only one exit.

Sister Hancock handed the camera to Brother Hancock and leaned over to whisper at Rejoice, "Is it true that Harmony is dying?"

Rejoice nodded. They must not have found all the bugs in the house. She swallowed.

Sister Hancock rushed to the door. A hexacrab moved aside, allowing the woman to exit.

If only Rejoice could wake up from this nightmare.

Henley stood before Ur-Veena. "Have you come to offer reparations?"

Ur-Veena whistled, "We come to speak."

Henley spread out his hands. "So speak."

"The air-ocean people who swam to us out of the warp-ocean protected us from the space-ocean asteroid. We do not understand why these air-ocean people will not protect themselves from the same-churtree. We do not see the heaven-ocean people that they say should protect them.

Therefore, we will protect them."

Jax jumped up and shouted, "If you spider slugs spill one drop of our blood, I promise that with your blood the seas will run red."

Henley motioned her down. "My dear, their blood is orange. There's no need for hysterics." He turned his back on the hexacrab. "Have we decided whether or not this fellow is same-churtree or is one of yours?"

"They're not responsible," Stronghold said. "None of them knew what I was doing. If they had, they would have tried to stop me."

"Then why do they call you Brother?" Henley's gaze flicked to the colonists and to the hexacrabs with calculating caution, and then back to Stronghold with contempt.

"Old habits are hard to break. Please, let me see my wife and children one last time before I go back with you."

Elder Chin tapped the floor again. "Brother Holly is one of ours, mistaken perhaps, but one of ours."

Stronghold twisted around. "Elder, no. He's trying to trick you. He'll use this to harm the colony."

Henley crossed his arms. "Brother Holly, you lied to both us and your people when you said that you repudiated them. You learned about our computer system and labs so that you could destroy them. We welcomed you with open arms, but you refused to share your marvelous genetic heritage with us and claimed that you had been injured."

Rejoice laid her head on Noble's shoulder as relief that her brother had been faithful to Harmony washed over her. She looked at Jax and her rounded belly. The Robersonians thought the colonists were neurotic because they cared so much about faithfulness.

"You lied when you said you were bringing home a cure. You, Brother Holly, are in no position to accuse me of trickery."

At the back of the gym, Elder Smith rose. "Excuse me, Elder Chin, but you cannot make a unilateral decision of this magnitude. The body voted to shun him. We need to have the body vote again."

Rejoice clenched her hands. "Do you *want* him to be shot?" Noble's hand over her mouth shut off the rest. She slapped his hand away and glared at him.

"Thank you, Elder Smith. You are correct. We have a quorum here of the mission. I imagine there is a quorum in both First City and Promise listening. Is Brother Madison here? If you would be so kind as to tally the vote." Elder Chin's head bobbed as he repositioned his hands on the cane. "I move that Brother Holly be readmitted into the body on a provisional basis for a week. No, make that until such time as this matter here has been thoroughly investigated, after which another vote shall be taken."

"I second the motion," Brother Hancock said.

"Let us pray," Elder Chin said.

The colonists sat with bowed heads. Noble watched Rejoice until she sat on her hands and lowered her head as well. The jointed feet of an LV touched her knee. The Robersonians wanted to kill Stronghold, and everybody was acting like they were discussing what shape to make the Meetingplace windows.

Henley paced slowly between Ur-Veena and Stronghold. His fingers rhythmically tapped on the holster strapped to the left side of his chest. The people on the other side of the hexacrabs joked and snickered.

A shiver crawled up Rejoice's spine. He still smiled. *Sister, you need to calm yourself and think*! This was bigger than Stronghold. They intended for all of them to die. What was Mr. Roberson's gambit? He seemed willing to let natural causes destroy them. Wait, wait, wait. Did this make sense? Bullets were simpler and faster. Maybe he wanted something from them first. What?

Elder Chin tapped the floor. "Let us vote."

The hexacrabs rotated their silver blue eyes as their siphons opened and closed. The humming of their circulation pumps was obscured by the sound of computers being slid from their cases and flipped open.

A minute later, Brother Madison announced, "We have a quorum with six hundred twenty-seven for and forty against."

Rejoice shook with hatred that forty people had decided that they would rather see her brother executed. Had Elder Smith voted no?

"So," Henley rumbled. "What will the colony pay for all the

damage done to us?"

"The colony is innocent," Stronghold said. "Don't punish them for what I did on my own. If you want servitude, I'll give you servitude. I'll work for you for free for the rest of my life."

Henley glanced briefly at the ceiling. "If you think that we will ever let you near one of our computers or labs, then you are less intelligent than you think we are. No, Mr. Holly. You are banned from our towns and our property. If you ever trespass, we will shoot you on sight."

Rejoice tried to rise, but Noble wrapped his arms around her.

"Please excuse me," Elder Chin said. "You are asking the colony to pay for what one of its members has done. On what basis is the corporate body responsible?"

Henley clasped his hands behind his back and paced with deliberation. "I see. You claim him so we cannot obtain justice. Then you say you are not responsible and we can eat our losses. Can you see the error in this equation? I grow weary of you colonists. You have judged us by your petty standards since the day we arrived. We have paid for everything you have sold us, paid without quarreling over the price. We have undertaken the research you have asked us to do. We have respected your ridiculous laws and mores every time we stepped foot on your land.

"So how have you rewarded our good neighbor policies? You assault us without provocation and then fine us when we defend ourselves. You stand by when our property is destroyed. You send in someone to spy on us and destroy our industry. Now, you tell us to turn the other cheek so you may hit us again.

"Let me review our losses. The system crash cost at least a day's productivity for most of us and several months for some of us. Our lost viruses are irreplaceable. We still have some others on the ship, Ebola, Red Death, Simian X, and such like, but now we need to go through the hazard and expense of reproducing and splitting the samples before bringing them down. The erased files were all backed up in a separate memory on our ship, so the cost there is the time of downloading the copies."

Rejoice put an arm around Noble. *God, no.* They had a back-up of their bedroom conversations! She buried her head in Noble's shoulder and gritted her teeth. She couldn't stand these threats. *God, Elder Chin was right. Why do You permit such an evil man to exist?*

"Now we come to the thousand embryos. They were our insurance of genetic diversity. They were our contract with the people of Earth. They were our children. How can you replace one thousand lives?"

Stronghold said, "I am not the one that killed them."

Henley glanced at the guard who then placed his foot between Stronghold's shoulder blades and shoved. Stronghold fell forward. Since his hands were tied behind his back, his face smacked onto the floor.

Several of the colonists shouted, "Stop that!" as Rejoice and Noble rushed forward to pick up Stronghold. Blood leaked from his nose. Some of the Robersonians jeered. The guards backed away and held their rifles pointed at the ceiling. Rejoice pressed her handkerchief against Stronghold's nose as she frowned at Henley. His eyes caught hers. He tipped his head to one side, smiled broadly, and winked. Her blood froze. She clenched her teeth so she would say nothing. Noble struggled with the knots in the rope binding Stronghold's hands.

Henley watched them until everyone had stopped shouting. "With the loss of these precious lives, we shall need to utilize another method to ensure genetic diversity." He smiled briefly at Ur-Veena. "Therefore, this is the demand we make of you colonists. Twenty of your most intelligent women shall bear my children."

Rejoice dropped the handkerchief. A quarter second for everyone to take a breath, and then Rejoice and every colonist shouted, "No!"

In the midst of shouts, "That's outrageous!" and "No!" Henley turned to face Ur-Veena. "Do you have a problem with my requiring twenty colonists to bear my young?"

Ur-Veena whistled, "It is good to bear children."

"That's all I'm asking for," Henley said. "We won't hurt your pet colonists."

The Robersonians hooted, banged the butts of their rifles, and slapped the floor in applause.

"That is our demand," Henley said. "You have one day to present to me your plan to comply."

Elder Chin leaned heavily on his cane, motionless.

PACIFISTS' WARCHAPTER TWENTY-SIX

Rejoice stared at Henley as Noble pushed her and her brother toward the door. Every colonist stood and filed after them. The hexacrabs turned their LVs as the Robersonians continued their thunderous pounding. Rejoice's last glimpse of Henley was of him standing, rocking gently on his feet, and grinning.

Rejoice wanted to run, but they were surrounded by LVs. Noble and she worked their way through the crowd jostling in the courtyard and jamming the gates. The smells of spice and sea and churned dirt and tea surrounded them. Silver-blue eyes studied them from all sides. Rejoice tried to stay calm as they pushed past the hexacrabs. Henley's monstrous demand would mean nothing to the hexacrabs. They mated during mating season and no other time. The entire cluster cared for the nursery. When the anonymous children swam back, whoever caught them raised them, each child raised by a single parent.

They could not understand marriage and families that humans grouped into. They tried to understand, for they were fascinated by the concept of growing one child at a time within oneself, but fidelity and rape were concepts they had given up asking explanations for. Tentacles pressed against the glass sides in greeting, but Rejoice ignored them as she pushed through the gate.

Her panting obscured the patter of water dripping from the shroud-like foliage onto the runabouts parked on the side of the road.

Noble jerked to a stop. "How did our runabout get here?"

"Elder Smith must have dropped it off. You drive and I'll try to finish untying Stronghold."

They threw themselves into the runabout, and with mud splattering behind, Noble accelerated down the road. In the back seat, Stronghold leaned over Rejoice's lap so that she could reach the knots.

"I'm sorry, Stronghold. Your wrists are bleeding. I don't think I can undo this until I get the scissors at home."

The jungle blurred past as he levered himself upright. "That's okay, Sis. Noble, can you drive any faster?"

"Oh, oh, oh!" Rejoice said. "I think I know what his game is. He's trying to provoke us into violence so they can slaughter us with clean consciences."

"He's succeeding," Noble said. "I am extremely provoked."

"Not one of them has a conscience," Stronghold said.

The runabout slid to a stop on the gravel by the front door. Stronghold was out and in the living room saying, "Where is she?" before Rejoice could get out of the runabout. She followed him into the back bedroom. Mother, Doctor Carlson, Sister Deng, and Sister Hancock looked up at Stronghold from where they sat around the pale, limp form of Harmony.

Machinery piled on Mother's bed hummed and tubes filled with blood ran from Harmony to the machines and back again.

Tears and sweat and blood dripped from Stronghold's face. He collapsed onto his knees.

Rejoice ran to get her scissors, and when she came out of her bedroom Mother was by the front door pulling her rifle from its hold. Lines etched Mother's face. "Mother! Where are you going?"

"I did not raise my son to be a liar. I will not share a roof with him." The front door slammed behind her.

Rejoice jumped when Sister Hancock touched her on the arm. "I'll go with her. Harmony has stabilized, for now at least. Doctor Carlson and Sister Deng will stay with her." She pulled out a handkerchief and wiped her eyes. "I'll call the deaconesses to make sure the children are fed and cared for until it's time for them to come."

"Thank you," Noble said as he held her shoulder. When she had gone, he ran his fingers through his black hair. "Ah, you go and cut him loose. I guess I'll keep looking for bugs. I wish we could move her to someplace private. I need to talk to Stronghold and I don't want to be overheard."

Rejoice wet a towel and went into the back bedroom. Sister Deng stood by Harmony, while Doctor Carlson took a scalpel and cut Stronghold's ropes. Then he knelt and put his arm around Stronghold's heaving shoulders. Doctor Carlson looked up at Rejoice. "I heard you talking about the bugs and I think that Brother Hancock has a piece of equipment that should be able to detect any broadcast frequency."

He stood up and touched Rejoice's shoulder. "Harmony's stable." He turned to his nurse. "Sister Deng why don't you take a break, while I run over and talk with Brother Hancock? Let's give the family a little privacy." Rejoice nodded. He whispered, "Call me if anything changes and I'll be here in two minutes." He walked over to Stronghold and squeezed his shoulders before he left.

Stronghold paid no attention to Rejoice wiping his face. Slowly his sobbing subsided and he crawled on his knees to the head of the bed and laid his hand on Harmony's cropped hair. His thumb stroked her forehead.

Rejoice stood, holding the scissors that she had never used and severed bits of rope that she had picked up off the floor. What could she say that would comfort? "Didn't you expect this to happen?"

"No." He swallowed. His gaze never wavered from Harmony's face. "A fever, yes, as the fungus died and released toxins. It worked perfectly in the animal trials." He swallowed again. "All she ever wanted out of life was a chance to finish raising her children. I wanted to give her that chance."

The chemical smells seared Rejoice's nose. She blinked rapidly. A bit of rope dropped to the floor and she picked it up. She backed away from the monitors with their horrible numbers, away from the humming machinery and the acrid smell of sickness, away from the sight of her brother gazing with despair at his wife.

In the kitchen, Sister Deng sipped a cup of hot lemon balm tea. Her fingers trembled as she looked at nothing through the steam curling up from the cup. "Your husband left for a conference with Elder Chin," She blew on the pale green tea.

Rejoice threw the rope into the trash and poured a cup of the lemon balm tea. They had to stand, for all the furniture still lay in pieces outside. She had never seen Sister Deng when she was not calm. "How long do you think she has?"

"Harmony?" Her thin, finely wrought eyebrows pushed toward each other for a moment. "I don't know. I don't know how long any of us have. Those viruses they brought . . . Simian X . . ." Her voice trailed away.

"You were listening to the meeting?"

She nodded.

"Is Simian X bad?"

"Many months ago, Elder Chin exhorted me to be brave. He was sure that some of us, maybe all of us would die within a year or two." She blew on the tea again. "It's difficult to be brave about Simian X." She shook her head and stroked her smooth, black hair tied back into a glossy bun. "The dialysis seems to be helping Harmony."

The hot teacup made Rejoice's hands slippery with sweat. She sipped and burnt her tongue. Ur-Veena walked by the window several times. Guard duty?

About a half hour later, Rejoice was wiping the pieces of a chair to be reassembled, when Doctor Carlson returned with Young Man Grass Under Sky right behind him, carrying a piece of equipment over his shoulder and a wand of some sort. The doctor said, "I'm here to relieve Sister Deng and bring you a little good news."

Rejoice leaned on the back of the chair and smiled, "Any little bit will help."

"You tell her," Doctor Carlson said to Young Man Grass as he walked to the back bedroom.

The young man looked embarrassed.

"Well?" Rejoice was irritated that she needed to prompt him.

"Well, Doctor Carlson told me about the bugs and Brother Hancock was busy, so I figured out a way to detect even the smallest transmitter. We'll need to turn off all of the computers while I do it."

Rejoice threw her arms around the young man and hugged him. "You have no idea how much better you just made me feel."

Young Man Grass turned red. He and Rejoice turned off all of the computers and he swept the wand over every surface of the house. It took a small knife to scrape out a few of the creeper bugs that had wedged themselves into the cracks between the wall and ceiling. Then he sucked them up with a little vacuum.

After half an hour, he proclaimed the house bug-free. Rejoice tried to hug him again, but he backed up too quickly. As he left, he told Rejoice that he would go over all the furniture outside and make sure they were clear. Then he'd go get some help to reassemble all the furniture and move it back in place.

As the young man was leaving, Sister Carver walked up with a crying baby. "I'm afraid that I ran out of milk for two hungry babies," she said.

Rejoice took Jubilee. "Well, I'll gladly take him, because I'm leaking all over." Rejoice sat on one of the reassembled, cleared chairs to nurse him.

"I'll be back when Jubilee is done nursing and take him again so you can get your house back together." Sister Carver left.

Thank You, God, for Sister Carver. Thank You, God, for Sister Deng. Thank You, God, for Sister Hancock.

As she was nursing, Stronghold stumbled into the kitchen. "Is there anything to eat or drink with caffeine in it?" He wiped his face. "I lived on coffee in Freedom. Withdrawal is giving me a headache." Rejoice shook her head. He slumped into a chair. "Where do you keep your towels?

Rejoice looked up from Jubilee. "Have you met my son?" She unhooked him and rearranged her dress.

Stronghold's eyes focused on her and he shook his head. "Sis, not now. My head is going to explode."

He stared blankly for a few moments before he rose and stared blankly some more. "Right. New nephew." He walked over and gently laid his hand on the baby's soft head, engulfing it. His muscles relaxed a little. "So this is Jubilee. You get the boys and I get the girls. He's beautiful, Sis."

Stronghold's swollen, red eyes filled with tears. "I remember how beautiful Harmony was whenever she nursed our girls." He turned away quickly and dropped back down into the chair. "Where do you keep your towels? I want to wash Harmony."

Rejoice started and the baby stirred, but didn't cry. "Is she . . ."

"No. She's still stable. But you know how fastidious she is. Before she got too sick, she showered twice a day. I think she'd feel better if I cleaned her up." He pulled his shirt away from his chest. "I know she'd want me to clean up."

"Is she awake?"

"No." He blinked slowly.

"You shower, and I'll get you some of Noble's clothes. When was the last time you ate?"

"Yesterday, I think. No, day before. I was busy."

"Do the Robersonians really have Simian X virus on their ship?"

"Not if I was successful. And I believe all those back-up files on the ship are destroyed. He was blowing hot air. He does that a lot, even more than Pastor Wisemen."

Oh, thank God. "Is there any way to tell the files were destroyed?"

"Not from here."

"Why did you do it?"

He looked up at her. "Do what?"

"Leave your wife and children. Break Mother's heart. Lie to the Robersonians. Think that God would bless a lie."

Stronghold looked at her with fierce eyes. "You really want to know?" He rubbed his hands over his face, composed himself and looked straight in her eyes. "I did it right after I talked with Sister Joy and Crown."

"Harmony's cousin? The Hancocks youngest daughter? She told you to do it?"

"No. But she gave me the idea. Their youngest daughter died of leukemia."

Rejoice remembered now. Brother Hancock had told her that their youngest daughter, Devotion, had died on Old Earth.

"She was visiting and we were talking about Harmony and feeling hopeless. Then she told me that she remembered her sister dying when she was a little girl and how the Hancock's tried everything possible to find a cure for her. They spent all their savings, traveled around the world, even tried some illegal treatments. None of it worked and she died. But Joy and Crown said she grew up to understand just how much her parents loved her by remembering all that they did for Devotion."

He rose unsteadily and slouched toward the bathroom. "I looked over at my girls and the decision was made." His voice was cut off by the door.

Rejoice resumed nursing. The baby fell asleep and she laid him on the blanket in the bedroom. "So, that's what his note meant," she whispered. "That's why he capitalized the word Devotion."

An hour later, Sister Carver returned and took the sleeping baby. The men outside reassembled all the furniture and Rejoice directed them where to place each piece. It felt surreal to be moving furniture while Harmony was dying.

The men left. Rejoice sat and laid her head on the table. Someone knocked on the door.

"Now what?" Rejoice rose and opened the door.

Elder Smith held a box.

"I'm sorry, but Mother isn't here at the moment."

"I know exactly where she is. May I come in?"

She backed up and let him in. "Could I make you some peppermint tea?" *Smile, Sister.*

"Don't bother yourself," he said stiffly. "I am bringing you some sandwiches for your family and the ones helping Harmony. I will pick up your mother's things and get out of your way."

Rejoice took the box and glanced at her screen. Fourteen o'clock already? She hadn't eaten yet. "Um, her things?"

"Her clothing. Her bed. She's moving in with the Hancocks for a while."

"That's one crowded house with the grandchildren there. Let me see. Her cot is holding the medical equipment now and giving Doctor Carlson a place to sit."

He seemed unable to know where to look. "I'll give her my cot then, and I will sleep on Elder Chin's floor. A few nights won't kill me."

"May I ask you a question? Why did you want my brother to be executed?"

He shook his gray head. "I'm guilty of much, but not that. I didn't bring all of you a thousand light years from home so that one of you could be executed by these, these, wicked people."

Rejoice dropped the box on the table. "Then why did you call a vote on what should be obvious?"

He tugged at a strand in his beard. "To forestall a revolt on the part of Promise. They also needed a say, something they haven't had for years. I knew that if I slowed things down and the people of Promise had a chance to pray, most of them would remember that God loves the unlovely. I was gratified that only forty voted no."

Only forty! Rejoice gripped the edges of the box.

"You have no idea how angry your brother made a lot of people. Myself, I still can't believe what a bonehead stunt he pulled, and him so smart, too. He thought lying would show him the way of God. He could have spent these last precious months with the woman he pledged his life to, but he wasted them and dirtied the name of Christ. If I had my way, he'd be dropped on a rock in the middle of Widest Ocean with a ten year supply of food so he could take the time he needs to meditate on his folly." He sighed and pressed his blunt fingertips on the surface of the table. "On the other hand, I don't know how you can punish a man more than with the sorrow he's walking through right now." His voice lowered. "How is she?"

Rejoice held the box and breathed deeply. Perhaps he wasn't such an ogre. "Stable, last I heard. It's hard for me to go in there. She looks ghastly."

"That's only the body."

How much longer would any of them have bodies? "Elder Smith, what do you think will happen? What are we going to do about Mr. Roberson's demand?"

"Don't fret about it. He was biting our tails to see which way we would swim. Tomorrow, he will ask for a sum at least twice reasonable in the hopes we'll be so grateful for his backing off the first demand that we'll cave. It was a nasty negotiating tactic from a nasty man. I convinced Elder Chin and the Senate that the rest of the negotiations should not be public."

Elder Smith had run multiple corporations on Old Earth. "Maybe you're right." But her stomach still hurt. And he wasn't one of the twenty intelligent women he intended to breed like sows.

Elder Smith cleared his throat. "It looks like you'll get your way and the colony will pay for the dumped buildings. I'd take it out of your brother's hide if I could, but his lifetime earnings won't pay for the damage he has done." He thumped the table. "However I feel about it, the milk is spilled. Let's not cry over it."

Laden with towels and soap, freshly shaved, his wet hair tied back, and wearing Noble's overalls with the pants legs rolled up, Stronghold stepped into the living room and halted. "Elder Smith! Why are you here? Did you decide to vacation among the infidels?"

The old man looked at Rejoice before slowly forming the words, "Brother Holly, I am sorry about this time of sickness."

"But not sorry enough to understand why I did what I did to keep my wife from dying."

"You cannot achieve God's purpose outside of God's law."

"I should have achieved God's purpose by staying home and watching my wife wither away like you did?"

Rejoice reached for her brother. "Stronghold!"

Elder Smith swelled, but his words were mild. "Perhaps I should come back at a later time."

"If the Senate or the church wants to shun me or condemn me, I want to know now. What did you come here for?"

"To retrieve your mother's belongings. She's moving in with the Hancocks so that you can move in here."

Stronghold looked from Elder Smith to Rejoice and back again as a puzzled look rearranged his scowl. "When did you become my mother's errand boy?"

Elder Smith clasped his hands behind his back. Was he trying to keep from punching Stronghold in the face? He took a deep breath before answering. "Since I asked her to marry me and she answered yes."

Stronghold's face darkened. Abruptly, he turned and strode into the bedroom, slamming the door behind him.

Rejoice bit her lip and studied the table. She should apologize for Stronghold. She should congratulate Elder Smith. She should think peaceful thoughts. She should, she should make lunch for everybody. No, that's why there were sandwiches there. She should—

The soft click of the front door closing interrupted her thoughts. Rejoice sat. She should get the children. No, Sister Hancock said that she would take care of them and she needed to give Stronghold time to recover.

Sister Deng looked in from the bedroom. "Would you mind monitoring while I check on my boys?" Rejoice startled. She hadn't noticed when Doctor Carlson had left and Sister Deng had returned.

"No. Go ahead." Wait, why couldn't Stronghold monitor? Maybe she meant he was the one she was supposed to be monitoring. Rejoice shuffled into the bedroom.

Stronghold rubbed a raspberry-scented soap along Harmony's neck with a soft touch. That gentle odor collided with that of sickness and of the ion generator that precipitated floating bacteria out of the air. The sharp smell of antibiotic foam that covered all of the needles and tube entry points brought tears to Rejoice's eyes. "Can I help you?"

"Sure. I need a basin or something to wash her hair."

Rejoice fought revulsion in silence as she helped Stronghold with the chamomile shampoo. Harmony's eyes were bruised and sunken. When that was done, Stronghold filed her fingernails. As he concentrated on a thumbnail, he said in a low voice, "Will I be allowed to see my daughters?"

Rejoice paused in her gathering of comb and towels. "Of course. Whenever you're ready. I'm sorry you thought we were keeping them away from you."

"I don't know what to think. Do they hate me?"

"They love you passionately."

"I'm relieved somebody does." He moved to the other hand and stroked her knuckles.

"Do you know anything about Oppie?"

He looked up for a moment. "I know that she left you to join the maggots. They told me that right away. I know that He Gives lost his mind and nearly lost his life. They were laughing about that for weeks. I talked with her the first time she called, for a minute. I had a hard time controlling myself and told her that I was busy and would get back to her. I never did. She left messages for me a few times, but I never bothered to return her calls and she gave up."

"Did you know that she was pregnant?"

He closed his eyes and dropped Harmony's hand. "Oh, my God, she mated with a maggot." He stood up and walked to the wall and leaned against it with both arms extended, lowered his head, and moaned. After about a minute he muttered, "I'll never see her again or her maggot offspring." Then he straightened, returned to his chair, picked up his wife's hand, and filed again.

Rejoice sat stunned for another minute. "Will you go to the wedding?"

He grimaced. "Huh. You mean Mother and Elder Smith?" He shook his head. "Mother wanted to show me she was angry, and I guess she did."

Rejoice frowned. "What?"

He grimaced again. "Tell you what, Sis. Give me a half hour of peace, and then I want to see my daughters."

"Do you think she's marrying Elder Smith to spite you?"

"Why else would she marry that egomaniac?"

Rejoice counted to ten. Why had Harmony married him? "Compare him to Mr. Roberson."

"I do." Stronghold dipped into a jar of lotion and rubbed Harmony's hands. "Harmony hates fighting. Must we fight here?"

Rejoice retreated. Grief and exhaustion were scrambling his brains. Worry was scrambling hers. *God of peace, grant us Your light, and soon.*

In the living room, Noble stood eating a sandwich. The baby snored on his back. "There you are. We need to pick apples."

"Now?"

"They'll spoil if they're left any longer."

Crazy day, crazy people, crazy requests. She threw the towels in the washing machine and followed her husband to the far corner of the apple orchard. There she spread out a blanket on the damp ground for the baby, while Noble fetched the wagon and baskets. Overhead, the sun shone through clear patches of thin clouds oozing west.

Noble tied the baby's leash to the trunk of an apple tree. "We need to talk and I don't want to be overheard."

Finally, something she could smile about. She told him about Young Man Grass Under Sky and their bug-free house.

"Well, that's a relief," Noble said. "Now that the meeting is over, I'm sure Brother Hancock has him busy de-bugging the Meetingplace and their homes."

"Yes. What have you and Elder Chin been doing the past several hours?"

"I can't tell you yet. For all I know, there could be listening devices out here too. Our discussion was done by signing in Greek to each other."

The baby began that high-pitched wail that always made Rejoice grit her teeth. She carved him a slice of apple, which he took with both hands and gnawed on with fierce determination. She took a basket to the tree nearest the road. "So what can we talk about?"

"I have several problems I need to solve simultaneously. I keep praying, but as yet I don't see a solution for any of them."

The round fruit felt good in her hands. Warmed and aromatic, they should have delighted the eye and nose. Problems? Calculating velocity and force of impact is a problem. What they had there were horrendous situations. "There may not be a happy solution," she said. "Oh, did you want me to sympathize or did you want me to give you advice?"

He reached high into the canopy and pulled on a purple apple. "My foremost problem is keeping you safe from that monster."

Rejoice rubbed a pink and white streaked apple against her cheek. "Elder Smith thinks Mr. Roberson is trying to shock us into paying him off."

He rubbed the purple apple on his shirt and took a bite out of it. "Elder Smith is a smart negotiator. I'd be willing to put him across the table from any businessman. But Mr. Roberson is not a businessman. He's the leader of a cult."

"They think we're a cult."

"We have an outside standard, the word of God, to live by. Elder Smith cannot violate that standard and expect more than a handful to follow him."

"Promise is more than a handful. And forty of them voted to let the rationals murder Stronghold."

"Elder Chin and I both agreed that vote was exactly the right thing to do."

Rejoice frowned.

"Elder Smith understood that too. We need to come together in our one Lord and our one faith. Otherwise we will not stand against this onslaught."

"But they . . ."

"I'm not going to argue with you about Promise. They believe that washing clothes and milking cows by hand is a more fulfilling way to live. That's not a heresy. They're not claiming that the way to salvation is through mucking out stalls. They only claim that their lives are more meaningful than ours. Let them say it. They're still trying to live by the same outside standard we are. We agree that the Bible is our standard. The Covenant of our Colony is our promise to each other.

"Roberson, on the other hand, is free to make it up as he goes along. What happens to cult heads is that they get caught in positive feedback. They wind tighter and tighter in a delusional self-referential loop until something blows. The question is: how do I keep you from getting caught in the explosion?"

Rejoice set the apples in her basket gently so they would not bruise. "Hide?"

Noble moved to the tree with oval, red apples. "It may come to that. It may." He wiped his forehead with the sleeve of his blue work shirt. "The next question is: how do I comfort my congregation, reduce the shock, and provide for my family?"

"I thought the deacons settled that. Hmm. If Stronghold gets his old job back and they move out, our costs will drop dramatically." Assuming a plague hadn't wiped them out. Of course, that reduced costs, too.

"I've been thinking that perhaps my parents would loan us the money to set up a farm on the outskirts of First City."

Rejoice tripped over her basket. "What? A farm? You don't have to take me back to First City. I want to stay here now. And I have enough to do with a baby and my jobs and these apples. I don't want to milk cows, too."

"Ow!" Noble flung something brown to the ground and stepped on it. "Father Time beetle."

Rejoice shuddered. She hated the hairy creatures with scythe sharp mandibles. "It can't be mating season already. Should I take in the baby?" "The season won't be for another month. My fault for not first shaking the tree." He examined the cut on his index finger. "I know you're not fond of livestock. Since there's a predicted shortage of blue cotton, I was thinking that maybe we could farm a few hectares south of First City. When the bolls open, the fields of blue are beautiful."

The baby wailed, but Rejoice ignored him to study Noble. The pattern of leaf shade and light mottled the planes of his face. "Noble, what are you talking about? What does farming cotton have to do with your mission work and your pastoring?"

Noble reached up with both hands to grasp a branch. He smiled crookedly. "What am I going to do with you? You're so sweet that you can't imagine the routine evil that other people do."

Jubilee hiccupped and his wailing rose to screaming.

"I wish that were true. I wouldn't be growing such an ulcer." She glanced at the crying baby. He didn't look hurt, just angry, so she returned her gaze to Noble.

He shook his head. "I didn't realize you wouldn't think out the implications of that farcical trial." He looked past her and his expression turned grim. "Go into the house and seal the door."

Rejoice turned. Henley Roberson ambled along the street, whistling a tune she did not recognize. He stopped and smiled at them. "Exactly the people I wish to speak to."

CHAPTER TWENTY-SEVEN

Noble's back blocked her view of Henley. "Elder Chin wishes to renew the negotiations tomorrow."

Henley moved closer. His smile never faltered. "We finished the negotiations this morning. There is nothing left to discuss except the timing of the payment."

"We have told you, as clearly as we know how, that we do not agree."

Rejoice peered around Noble. Henley shook his head as if rueful, then moving so quickly his hands blurred, his rifle pointed directly at Noble's chest. "We will not be cheated by you people again."

Rejoice's knees weakened. She reached up to clutch Noble's shoulders. The baby screamed.

"Go!" Noble whispered hoarsely.

"I can't." Her legs could not move. She looked around his back again. "Really now," Henley said. "You are making a fuss about something not worth fussing about. The price I ask is minuscule compared to what I should be asking. We intend only to make sure that you never defraud us again."

Rejoice could not take her gaze from the rifle. The black bore seemed to swell and envelop her in darkness. Noble moved to shield her again.

"You are making mistakes on several levels. For one thing, my wife should not have any more babies. Physically, she cannot cope. The next child could kill her."

"Bearing your screaming defectives might be a problem. No one has ever had a problem with my children."

"No. Even by your standards, it is immoral to rape."

His shoulders twitched. "What is immoral is allowing defectives like that to live. Can't you shut it up?"

"His name is Jubilee, not defective. Go away."

Henley's smile broadened into a grin. "You really are a fool." He stepped closer. "Let's not make this any messier than it has to be. Step aside."

"No."

The gun blast sent Noble staggering against Rejoice. She tried to hold him up, but he fell through her hands. Her ears rang from the report. She gaped and could not breathe as she stared at her husband lying on the leaves. His hands went to his chest as he looked at her. Then his eyes closed and he slumped.

Rejoice stood with her hands out that had failed to hold him. She could hear shrill screaming: the baby, not her. She had yet to take a breath. Could he be gone so fast? A haze, like cotton batting, clogged her ears, filled her mouth, clouded her eyes. Could he be gone so fast?

The muscles of her neck moved and she looked up. The rifle pointed at her.

From a far distance he spoke. "I trust there will be no more nonsense from you?"

Her gaze slid along the sunlit cylinder to the hands to the man's face. He still smiled.

"No need to look so stricken. Whatever your husband said, I don't intend to rape you. I want to do a simple blood test to see where in the cycle you are. You can opt for artificial insemination."

He still smiled. Why didn't God smite him with His fist? Air soughed through her lips. "No."

He angled away his gun and reached out his hand with a small, glittery device in it. "Come now. It won't hurt a bit."

The muscles in her neck flexed and tightened as she shook her head.

"No."

He shook his head in turn and laughed. "What will it take, girl? Do I need to put you over my knee and spank you?"

Her heart beat in staccato time. Insane. He was insane. *Noble! God! Take anybody— take me—but don't take Noble!* Her first breath was a moan.

His face turned grim. "Do you need more persuasion that paying up is in your own best interest?" He glanced toward the baby. "Who can think with that infernal screaming? Shut up, defective." He shouldered the rifle and swung it toward the baby.

"Not Jubilee!" Rejoice screamed. She threw herself toward the howling baby.

Another blast. She thudded to the ground. The baby stopped howling a moment, and then shrieked. She curled around him and panted. Had she been shot? Had Jubilee? He seemed all mouth and quivering throat, but she saw no blood. Holding him, she rolled to look. Where was Mr. Roberson?

She pushed herself up, and her breath caught. Henley Roberson sprawled on the clover next to the road, his head a ruin of blood and bone and brains.

She bit on her fist. How? A movement caught her eye. Ur-Veena stood on the road with his rifle pointed at the body.

Scarcely aware of her movements, she laid down the screaming Jubilee and rose to her feet. She tottered to the road and stared at the bodies of Noble and Henley.

Ur-Veena whistled, "The same-churtree planned to hurt the child."

Her thoughts staggered in slow motion. *Yes, he planned to hurt the little one tied to my shell. But first he shot my heart.* Like a rusted gear, she turned to face the hexacrab in his LV. Like another blast, she remembered what Jax had said that morning, an eternity ago, when Rejoice lived in a universe that made sense. "If you spider slugs spill one drop of our blood, I promise that with your blood the seas will be running red." *God, no. Not the slaughter of the hexacrabs.* They would fight, oh, yes, they would fight, but in the end they would lose.

She thought of little Ti-Assisi curling his tentacles around a silver bobber. She looked into Ur-Veena's three silver-blue eyes.

She pulled her rifle from her shoulder. "Ur-Veena, we need to trade guns. Here."

He clicked. "Why?"

"If the same-churtree find out you killed Mr. Roberson, they'll kill every one of you, every child, every egg. Do you hear me? They have poisons you don't understand. They will kill your babies!"

"To thrust the knife is not to pierce."

Rejoice wrenched Ur-Veena's rifle from the claspers of the LV and jammed her rifle in its place. "Remember human history—the terrible weapons we have made. Trust me! Go quickly. Tell nobody what happened. Let this be a human matter. Please, hear me. Tell nobody!"

The LV backed up.

"Tell nobody! Promise me!"

Ur-Veena turned the LV and walked back the way he had come. Rejoice focused on the rifle in her hand. Could she persuade the Robersonians that he had accidentally shot himself in the head? No, their rifles and ammunition were different. Could she hide the rifle? Where?

They would still want to know where the bullet came from. And they would wonder why she didn't have her rifle. Should she put it in Noble's hands? No, no, no. She couldn't let the people think their beloved pastor had died while committing violence. That left her. But she had vowed to never lie again.

The rifle vibrated in her shaking hands. She dropped it and held her head. She saw with febrile clarity the overturned basket and apples rolled out. One bore the curved gash left by a Father Time beetle. Jubilee shrieked again and again.

A shout brought up her head. Robersonians. Jax, Zack, Myra, Modesto, and Wilson ran toward her. She stood, numb and detached, watching as it were a vid of them stopping when they saw the body.

Myra's screams joined Jubilee's. Shouting words that Rejoice vaguely recognized as evil words for women, Zack flipped his rifle to his shoulder and aimed at Rejoice. As he squeezed the trigger, Jax whirled and kicked the gun. The bullet whined past her ear.

He aimed again. Jax grabbed the barrel and shouted. "Don't you hear the hexacrabs right behind us? They'll shoot us if they see you shoot the murderer! We'll make them pay, but not now! Look!"

He turned. Eighteen hexacrabs marched in formation, holding rifles before and behind themselves. Zack snarled and lowered the rifle.

Myra kept on screaming.

Then Jax's face, mottled with rage, filled her vision. "Why?"

Rejoice backed a step. Myra fell to her knees beside Henley. Rejoice choked on her words. "He killed Noble."

Jax screamed, "He will recover in fifteen minutes! Thus for Henley?" Rejoice gasped. The anesthetic bullets! That was why Henley could smile after shooting down her husband. Noble wasn't dead! She turned, and in the act of turning, collapsed.

Zack and Modesto grabbed her arms and hauled her up to face Jax.

"Justice to you!" Jax spat.

Rejoice gasped again when Zack wrenched her arm and pushed her along the road. "We can't leave Noble and Jubilee! What if the pack bats come?"

Zack wrenched her arm again.

Four hexacrabs in LVs lumbered past them.

She looked back toward the orchard. Tears obscured the sight of Modesto and Wilson picking up the body of Henley Roberson. Myra still screamed. Her black and white hair fell across her face and Roberson's chest.

"Ow! Let me call someone to watch over Noble and the baby!"

Zack tore the computer from her side, lifted it high, and smashed it on the road.

"Jax! We can't leave them out! Jax!"

Zack twisted her arm until she stood on tiptoe and panted with pain.

Jax ran black-nailed hands over her red, bristled scalp. "Who has anesthetic bullets?"

"Me," Zack said.

"From you silence! No shooting unless I say so. Modesto, you?"

Modesto looked sick. "For truth."

Zack pulled a whistle from his pocket with his free hand blew on it.

'You idiot!" Jax snapped. "You shouldn't call the bats until we reach the dojo!"

"No!" Rejoice sobbed. She tried to twist away.

Jax pointed at Modesto. "Shoot her."

Modesto laid down Henley's legs and braced his rifle against his shoulder. His multiple braids bent over the barrel.

"We can't leave him here!" Rejoice screamed. "I'll go with you after he recovers. I'll—"

A heavy fist slammed into her ribs. "Don't leave—" Her mouth quit working. Her knees buckled, and as she fell, she lost consciousness.

* * *

When Rejoice awoke, she lay in impenetrable darkness on a hard floor. With consciousness came an awareness that the back of her head, her shoulder blades, her hips, everyplace that touched the hard floor, hurt. A fetid, sweet film coated her tongue. When she tried to move, the pain in her right arm streaked colors across her vision and swamped over all the other pains. When she could breathe evenly again, she inhaled the smell of dust, fabric worn too many times, bitter dried plants, and fear in her sweat-soaked dress. A closet then. Was this where they had kept Stronghold? She listened, but all she heard was her breathing and the internal whine of tinnitus.

She counted to three, held her breath, and forced herself to stand. Rejoice stood with gritted teeth until the streaking colors and pain subsided. They had said he would recover in fifteen minutes. The odds of pack bats showing up in any particular fifteen-minute stretch of time were low. With all the screaming and shooting, somebody was bound to investigate, find Noble, and drag him to safety.

Groping in the darkness, her left hand found a ledge, a shelf with folded canvas on it. She laid her hand on the edge of the shelf and tried to push away the image of black bats tearing at Jubilee's eyes. *I believe they are safe.* She must believe or go mad, and she would not give these wicked people that kind of satisfaction.

She extended her hands up and down. A series of metal shelves. Sliding her hand along a shelf, she came to a corner, shelves with boxes, another corner, more shelves with boxes, some hard items wrapped in cloth, a wall, doorframe and door with a lever handle. Locked. No second exit? Probably a trap door in the floor or ceiling. No light switch.

Something clicked against her foot. Gritting her teeth again so she wouldn't groan, she stooped to pick up the metallic object, aha, a knife.

Why would they leave a knife with her? Did they think she would use it to attack when they opened the door and then they could shoot her in self-defense? Or did they think she would consider everything hopeless and kill herself? She cautiously tested the edge. Dull. She would mangle herself long before she died with this knife. Such convoluted people. She laid the useless weapon on a shelf. Whatever their currents, she wasn't swimming along with them.

She pulled the canvas that felt like robes onto the floor. If her arm didn't hurt so much, she could have climbed the shelves and tried to escape through the ventilation shaft, if they had one. She restrained herself from laughter. And then what? She couldn't live on roots and berries in this jungle. The botanists had found one edible leaf and one edible tuber in the thousands of plants they had cataloged, and both tasted nasty and lacked some of the essential amino acids. Even if she could live in the jungle, she wouldn't. What was the point of living merely to continue pumping blood?

Opening the boxes, she groped inside them for candles or flashlights. He Gives had punched one of the Rationals in the nose and had gotten his spleen and arms broken. For messing up their computers, they wanted to kill Stronghold. What would they want to do to her?

She held onto a shelf for support. *God, I won't do well if they torture me. Oh God, help me.* She thrust her hand into the next box of dried leaves. Jax wasn't the kind to torture, maybe. Zack was. *Justice to me. Oh, God, make me brave.*

A box of mugs. Good. Little chamber pots which she needed badly. Her mouth felt dry and hunger made her knees tremble. She would die of hunger before she told them what she needed. She hoped.

Rejoice came to hard objects wrapped in cloth. Knives and swords. These were sharp.

Start with the premise that she was dead. She would not give them an excuse to slaughter the hexacrabs. She also would not lie. But if she kept silent, they would assume that she had killed Henley.

Rejoice kicked the canvas robes into a long pile. Ur-Veena might tell them. Why he thought the Robersonians couldn't slaughter his people she couldn't imagine. If he did confess, at least her hands would be free of their blood. *Oh, no, what am I thinking? God, keep them safe.*

She lowered herself to the canvas pile. The Robersonians might kill them anyway to gain access to the germanium mine. Well, not if the cure wasn't a cure. *God, my God, has Harmony died yet?* What could Rejoice do before she died? She could pray. She lay back on the canvas. *God, have mercy on little Mark. Comfort him as he loses his mother. Be with Jubilee and heal his colic. Provide for him somebody who will love him the way he needs.*

She prayed for each member of her family and for each person in the mission and for all the Ti, Sa, and Ur she could remember. As she prayed, a thought came to her that glowed like a candle. She did love Jubilee after all. She had been confusing emotion with love. She might never like him, but she loved him enough to have laid down her life for him. That's what kind of mother she was.

Oh, Father God, how sad to lose him when she had finally discovered that she did love him.

She was praying for the colonists in First City when she fell asleep.

* * *

Rejoice blinked at the dark figure outlined in the bright doorway.

"Get up."

She croaked through cracked lips. "God be with you this morning, Wilson."

Wilson backed up. His gaze darted everywhere but to Rejoice's face. "You have a visitor in Jax's office."

Rejoice flung aside the robes and ignored her aches as she barged through the door. "Is Noble all right? How is Jubilee?"

Wilson said nothing as he led her down the hall, across the deserted compound, and into the gymnasium. Clouds half-covered the sky. The walls shook with the roar of a jet taking off.

Rejoice crowded past the guard in her hurry to enter the office and then slowed at the sight of Brother Hancock sitting at Jax's desk, looking miserable.

"Thank God," he said as he rose and put his arm around Rejoice.

"Where's Noble? Where's Jubilee?" The panic she had suppressed in the dark seeped into her voice.

"Here, sit." He pulled his chair close to hers. "You haven't seen Noble yet?"

"No. What time is it?"

"Fourteen o'clock. I've been waiting for two hours to see you. I thought maybe he was with you."

"So where is he?"

"I don't know. He tried to see you last night, and I believe he ripped one door off its hinges before they subdued him and dropped him off at your home. Did you hear it?"

"No. I'm being kept literally in the dark."

Brother Hancock picked up a ball from Jax's desk and squeezed it. "You look pale. Are they treating you well?"

She nodded briefly.

"Is there anything you want me to get you?"

Out of here. Her husband. "I could use some water."

Brother Hancock's knuckles around the ball whitened. "They haven't given you anything to drink since yesterday? Nor anything to eat, I suppose."

"It doesn't matter." She was dead anyway. What did it matter if she got a little hungry first?

He rose and strode to Wilson. "This is outrageous. You will give Sister Cruz food and drink."

"Henley Roberson is not eating and drinking."

Brother Hancock brushed past him.

"Halt or I'll shoot."

"Shoot then. I'm getting her some water."

Wilson shrugged.

Brother Hancock returned with a mug. Rejoice drank the water with a greediness that embarrassed her. He felt about in his pocket, then handed her three hard candies.

Wilson left the doorway and stood over Brother Hancock. "Better give her the news. In five minutes you leave."

Brother Hancock's lips twitched. "So we still haven't found all your bugs in our Meetingplace? No, I'll come back after Sister Cruz has eaten."

"Then I will tell her."

"No." Brother Hancock rubbed his eyes.

The only time Rejoice had seen him look so miserable was at Father's funeral. Her throat hurt. "Did Harmony die?"

Brother Hancock smiled a wobbly smile. "No. Good news there. She recovered."

"You mean she's healed?"

"Well, we don't know that yet. She still needs oxygen, but she is off most of the machines now. My niece is tougher than anyone thought."

Rejoice rubbed away tears. So they did have a cure. How wonderful. Oh, but now there would be a desperate demand for germanium. And the underwater mine the hexacrabs controlled. "I think you came to bring me bad news."

Brother Hancock surveyed his fingers and tapped the desk. "I'm required to ask you some questions. We didn't know for sure you were here until four hours ago when the Robersonians announced that you were indeed here and that you had killed Mr. Roberson. Did you know he was dead?" His sea-blue eyes looked into hers.

She nodded.

"And did you, indeed, kill him?"

She looked down at her hands.

He waited for about a minute and then said, "I see." He shifted in his chair. "Will you tell me whether you shot him out of self-defense or by accident?"

She shook her head.

"The mission church met and voted. I volunteered to break the news to the daughter of my best friend."

She studied the faint blue pattern of veins on the back of her hand. How she wished she could tell him, the best friend of Father. He had always been good to her.

"Until you repent of the killing of Mr. Roberson, whether it was murder, man-slaughter, or self-defense, the church will shun you."

How did you repent of what you haven't done? The pain in her throat sharpened. "Was Noble there?"

"No. And we did not send for him. We would never ask a man to vote on shunning his wife."

She must not ask. She had no business knowing. "How did the vote go?"

"Rejoice," he whispered. "The vote was unanimous."

She couldn't breathe. She had thought how the Robersonians would react. She had not considered the feelings of the colonists. This would destroy Mother. "Does Mother know?"

He took so long to answer that she looked up at him. "Your mother made the motion."

Rejoice laid her head on the desk. Not only was she dead, the boys would grow up thinking their mother was a killer. She must tell him, but if she did, the hexacrabs would die. *Oh, God, will Noble shun me too?*

"Time to leave," barked Wilson.

"Excuse me, but Sister Cruz needs time. I want to be with her until she comes to a decision."

"You promised to abide by our rules." Wilson pressed the muzzle against Hancock's temple.

His chair scraped across the floor and his hand rested lightly on the back of her head. "Farewell." Footsteps, and then the closing of the door.

He had said 'farewell', not 'God be with you'. She was cut off. Father God, must she destroy her family to save the hexacrabs? Tears spilled over her eyelids.

* * *

As she sat in the dark, sucking on the last candy as slowly as she could, Rejoice ran through the equations, each time coming to a dreadful answer.

If she admitted that Ur-Veena had shot Henley, either the Robersonians believed her or they did not. If they did, the slaughter of the contract-breaking spider slugs began. If they did not, Rejoice ended up dead not only as a murderer but also a liar.

In this coming war, what would happen in the hexacrabs ran short of ammunition? Would their war instincts kick in? Would the hexacrabs perhaps even kill colonists to force them to supply ammunition?

If she could somehow get a message to her family—But if she signed, there were cameras everywhere. Infra-red ones for the dark. If she did find a computer, any message she sent would be tapped.

Sudden light flooded the closet. She glanced up. An oversize ventilation grate covered much of the ceiling. Ho, she could escape; if she was agile, had she a place to hide, and did she not suppose the Robersonians would do something like execute ten colonists a day until she returned.

Wilson entered with a tray of some noodle and meat sauce mess and a glass of water. Without looking at her, he placed it on the floor and left. The water and noodles were covered with a layer of dirt. Rejoice tried to keep her face still for the cameras. They could say they offered her food. Tomorrow, she might eat it gratefully. Then again tomorrow she would probably be dead.

She leaned back against a shelf. Actually, the Robersonians were showing remarkable restraint. Why weren't the colonists' towns ablaze and the colonists' bodies being bulldozed into heaps? Rejoice had not been raped or tortured yet. Why not? Did the Robersonians have some decency in them after all?

Of course, they had been threatened by the hexacrabs, but why would that bother them? All it would take to nullify that threat would be some poison thrown into the right spots in the ocean. Ah, but the Robersonians probably wouldn't know what would poison the hexacrabs. She could bet they were researching the question. But again, they wouldn't know where all the clusters were, and they knew the hexacrabs would fire back.

Perhaps they felt they couldn't afford to lose any more people without problems of inbreeding. If they were afraid of the hexacrabs, then why should she sacrifice her family to protect the hexacrabs for what, a week, a month, a year until the Robersonians felt they were ready to take them on?

The door opened and Jax came in, dressed in black with a red ribbon tied around her scalp. One hand held a knife shaped like a serrated claw. She looked pregnant enough to burst but moved with an agility and menace that made Rejoice's mouth go dry. She stood tossing the knife and catching it for a minute while watching Rejoice with hatred in her eyes. "I tried to save you."

Rejoice licked her lips with a dry tongue. *I don't have the courage for this.* She opened her mouth and closed it again. If you spider slugs spill one drop of blood— "I could save us both time and start screaming now."

Jax slid the knife into a sheath strapped to her leg. "You will have a trial."

Rejoice willed herself to stop shaking. "Why haven't you executed all of us for this crime?"

"Diversity requirements. In a generation, your sick religion will die in the light of our rational living. Your children will join us."

"What if a hexacrab—" *Shut up, Sister!* "opposes you?"

"Let them try. Churtree like the eyes of hexacrabs as a delicacy. I am looking for delicacies to trade with churtree." Jax touched her chin with a blackened and sharpened fingernail. "For truth, they will protest the trial. Good excuse may be coming."

Surprise poked through the terror. "Why would you want to trade with the churtree?"

"They know where gold is."

One part of Rejoice's mind tried to make sense of the reply and could not. Gold was useful in a number of industries, but there were many common metals that could replace gold and do nearly as efficient a job. The other part of her gibbered with relief—a trial. Perhaps they would only shoot her instead of skinning her first. She shook and tears squirted out her eyes. *Stop it, you coward!*

Jax's look of hatred altered into contempt. She picked up the tray. "Why did I ever love you?"

Another surprise. Rejoice pulled out her handkerchief and wiped her eyes. "Like Ernest loved Pastor Cruz?"

"For truth. I cannot explain Ernest or you for staying with a hypocrite."

"Not Noble. He let himself be shot."

Jax threw the tray onto the floor and the red sauce splattered. "He said he loved you even when he wouldn't touch you."

"That wasn't hypocrisy. That was obedience. Love is what you do, not what you feel. He was keeping his contract with me and with God."

Jax drew out the knife again. "Three hours until trial and execution, murderer." As she departed she shut the door behind her with a thud, and the light flicked off.

PACIFISTS' WAR CHAPTER TWENTY-EIGHT

Hours later, when the light came on, Rejoice pulled herself to her feet. *Please, please, let it be Noble.* But, no. Elder Chin, dressed in Lord's Day black, shuffled in, leaned on his bamboo cane, and blinked at Rejoice.

Rejoice held onto a shelf for support and attempted to keep the disappointment out of her voice. "Since I am being shunned, I suppose you have come to ask me to repent."

His head bobbed as he thought. "Repentance is always good, my dear daughter. If you wish to repent, I will listen. However, that's not why I came. I have come to be your lawyer."

"But you're a linguist."

"I had some lawyer friends and sat in on a case or two on Old Earth." He smiled and smelled of mint. "It is a bit far to send for someone better."

"Where is Noble?"

"Taking care of business. Now, my business requires that I ask you what happened."

Rejoice pressed her lips together and held them together with her teeth. Jax was looking for an excuse to feed hexacrab eyes to churtree.

"Your husband told me that he saw Mr. Roberson enter the orchard to talk about impregnating you. Noble told you to leave, but you clung to him from behind. After Mr. Roberson shot him, he remembers nothing."

Rejoice looked at her hands.

"If Noble had shot the man, I think he would have confessed it. Please look at me, my favorite daughter."

Rejoice glanced into his shadowed eyes and then looked down at her hands again and dropped some tears on them.

"I knew death was coming, but I never thought it would come through you. I feel as though water has turned dry." Chin moved closer.

What do I do, God? What do I do?

Soft fingers caressed her jawline. "I am thinking that more happened there than we are considering." He sat back and rubbed the knob of the cane. He said thoughtfully, "Rejoice in the Lord's Salvation."

Her voice cracked, "Yes?"

"I am not calling you. I am giving you a command. Rejoice! We shall see salvation."

If only salvation did not involve so much blood.

After several minutes of silence passed, Elder Chin sighed. "Would you be so kind as to take my arm and help me to the runabout?"

Rejoice reached for him. *I hope I can do this.* They might both end on the floor. With one hand on his cane and one on Rejoice's shoulder, Elder Chin creaked forward.

The sunlight outside made her squint as they shuffled toward the gate. A silent crowd of Robersonians in black and with drawn rifles escorted them. "Where are we going?"

"To the clearing in front of the elevators." Elder Chin wobbled a bit. "Both your brother and husband will be shot if they step foot on Roberson property. We, in turn, are shunning these Rational People except for what must be done at the trial. They, in turn, have broken every window on Main Street in First City. At this moment they are moving the contents of all our warehouses into Freedom. Brothers Song and Eagle Flight offered to help them and are now in the hospital."

Rejoice gulped. She could not go on with this farce. She couldn't let her people be hurt like this.

"It's just stuff, dearie," jeered the male Robersonian escorting them. "It can be replaced."

They passed through the gate. Brother Madison helped Elder Chin into the runabout. Myra, with smoldering eyes, clicked a band around Rejoice's ankle. "Transponder and microphone. We won't lose you," she said in clipped words.

A need for privacy as strong as the hunger cramping her stomach chewed on her mind. She had seen the dojo students wearing these bands in the jungle and had assumed they were decoration. She couldn't whisper the truth to her people, or the Robersonians would hear. If she spoke in Hex, they would be able to translate.

No, why was she thinking of a secret message? She needed to tell the truth to everybody. But if she did—*God, You've got to tell me what to do. I don't know what to do.*

"Move." A rifle prodded her in the back.

The hot ginger and mace odors of the jungle on either side and the smell of fear rising from her wrinkled dress threatened to choke her. The close circle of dojo students harried her down the road. She was concentrating so hard on not falling that she stumbled into the student in front of her when he halted at the edge of the clearing. Past the elevators, Stronghold sat alone on the railing, staring out to sea.

She rushed past the dojo students to reach him. "Stronghold, where are my children?"

He disentangled himself from the fence. "How would I know? Noble whisked them off to somewhere. He doesn't talk to me. Nobody talks to me except Harmony. I bring home a cure and instead of being welcomed as a hero, everybody treats me like a pig with leprosy."

Didn't he care that she was about to be executed? "Maybe that was part of the cost you didn't count."

Stronghold slammed his fist into his palm. "Sis, sometimes you are the most irritating person on the face of this planet. No matter what I do, you find a way to top me. You can't stand for me to be in the limelight." Rejoice gaped. How could anybody so egocentric keep from imploding? She sucked in a deep breath. If he was not aware or did not care that she was about to die, she was and did. She did not want to leave a legacy of bitter words. She sucked in breath again. "I'm glad that Harmony is getting well." Breath. "I am grateful that no one else has to die like Father did."

He braced himself against the top railing. "It won't do any good if we are all killed because of what you did."

Enough. She would tell what happened. Mr. Roberson threatened Jubilee and hexacrab instinct kicked in.

She turned away from Stronghold. Elder Chin stood in the center of the clearing with Jax, who stood with her back to him, sucking on a black bulb. Beyond them, the elevator doors opened. Ur-Veena, in an LV and with Ti-Assisi clinging to his shell, stepped out. He carried guns in his front claspers, and spears in his back ones.

The Robersonians in front knelt and the ones in back stood and braced, and all pointed their rifles at him. Ur-Veena ignored them.

Jax tucked the bulb into her pocket, and scowled, "Spider slug! Your purpose?"

Ur-Veena whistled and grated. "I come to taste the currents."

Could Ur-Veena read the loathing on Jax's face? If looks were lasers, her stare would have melted through the glass and vaporized the water breather. "Stand in my way once and you are dead." Her fingers traced the outline of the bulb in her pocket.

Elder Chin tapped his cane on the gravel. "If I represent Sister Cruz, and you represent the prosecution, who is to be the impartial judge? Shall we defer to Ur-Veena, the leader of his species?"

"Never!" Jax said. She looked around the circle of humans. Most were dojo students. Zack and Ernest stood side by side, Zack with fury animating his face and Ernest with red eyes. Beside them stood three more young men with identically shaped eyes and noses. Behind them stood fifty or sixty students. They all looked as though they wanted to push her over the cliff now.

Rejoice searched the faces. No Oppie. Her last memory of her sister's face would be one of sheer loathing. The last time she had seen Mother's face, she was full of anger at Stronghold. And Stronghold's face was full of disgust. *Lord, at least give me the strength to make You smile.*

By the doors stood the Hancocks looking morose and holding cameras. Next to them stood Brother Madison and Elder Smith.

Noble, why have you abandoned me? Elder Smith could come, but not my mother?

She looked to the hexacrabs and watched Ti-Assisi fondle a small stele, a stone sliver with spines glued on in specific number, arrangement, and angles. Ti-Assisi scraped his beak across the top of the stele.

Dear God, the colonists were the ones committed to His peace. They were the ones who were supposed to place their bodies between harm and the ones He commanded them to love. Mother and Noble would die before allowing harm to the hexacrabs. They would agree with her if they knew what she was doing. But how could she make that decision for Mark and Jubilee?

"Let Elder Smith judge," Jax announced.

Elder Smith looked horrified. He held out his hands, palms forward. "I can't be the judge of my step-daughter."

What? Had they married while she was imprisoned in the closet?

Jax chuckled. "You hate the mission. You hate us. Are you not a fair man?" She waved unsteadily at the circle of people. "You requested a trial. If no judge, then no trial, and we impose the justice."

Elder Smith moved into the circle. He intertwined his fingers. "Will you accept my verdict?"

Jax grinned.

What was wrong with Jax? Had everyone on the island gone insane?

"For truth, if you give us justice."

Nausea joined hunger and pain. Jax was looking for a reason to start a war. She didn't care who with.

Noble shouldered his way into the circle. She ran and hurled herself upon him, pressed her face against his chest, and listened to the beauty of his heartbeat.

Jax pulled them apart. "Stay away from the prisoner." Rejoice stepped away, afraid of what Jax might do with her knife. Jax smelled strange, like disinfectant.

"We are one," Noble said. "What she did, I did. Whatever you do to her, do to me."

Jax nodded. Her eyes glittered. "If you want it so. Most gladly, Pastor."

One of the students slipped a band from his ankle, ran over, and snapped it around Noble's. "Your funeral," he said.

Rejoice clung to Noble again. Jax didn't care because this was all a show. They had already decided what they would do to them.

Elder Smith pulled at a strand in his beard. "Our tradition does not call for anyone to be punished except the person who committed the crime."

"Your Christ was doing what then?"

Ur-Veena stepped forward. "Do the same-churtrees think defending a child is a crime?" he whistled.

No, Ur-Veena, say no more.

Jax marched to Ur-Veena's LV and peered into the glass case. "From you, silence. This is a human matter. If you intrude again, I will fillet you for sushi." She pressed the tip of her knife against the glass.

Rejoice hastened to place her hand against the glass. "Ur-Veena, please, don't—" Don't what? If she said "Don't tell," everyone would want to know what he shouldn't tell. "Don't crawl into this quarrel between the air-ocean people. Retreat to your niche and keep your children safe."

Ur-Veena did not reply, but with a whirring of gears he did back up his LV two steps.

That left Jax and Rejoice facing each other. Jax fingered the handle of her knife, then strode back to face Elder Chin and Elder Smith. "We believe in punishment in proportion. Like what your Bible says about eye for eye, tooth for tooth, life for life. We demand death for the murder of humanity's best hope."

Rejoice put her arm around Noble's waist and leaned her head on his shoulder. Noble, her love, she was so glad he was there, but, oh, how she wished he weren't. *Please, God, let them be satisfied with my death.*

Elder Chin scanned the circle of people. "I defend Sister Cruz with three arguments. One. Without witnesses, we do not know who shot Mr.

Roberson."

The Robersonians roared with indignation. The few that had not yet pulled out their rifles or guns did so now. Zack stepped out of the circle and shouted, "She was standing next to his body with her rifle with one shot missing at her feet. Who else?"

"Order, please," said Elder Smith. "Sister Cruz, do you have a statement to make about the shooting death of Mr. Roberson?"

"No, Elder," breathed Rejoice as she looked at the gravel.

"Two, Rational law allows for killing in self-defense."

"Against a blood test?" Jax sneered.

What could be seen of his eyes glinted as Elder Chin said, "Sister Cruz may have thought that she had just seen her husband killed. She may have had reason to think that Mr. Roberson intended to kill her and her son as well."

"Dead women don't bear children." Jax brushed the long end of the red ribbon that hung near her ear over her shoulder. "Anesthetic bullets are harmless. Henley Roberson never hurt anyone. Never. Not ever."

"Excuse me," Elder Smith said. "Sister Cruz, do you have a statement to make about that?"

"No, Elder." Noble's arm around her tightened. She breathed shallower, but did not tell him how that hurt her wrenched arm.

"Three. Even if Sister Cruz did shoot Mr. Roberson, and even if she was not justified by fearing a threat to her life, all she did was hasten Mr. Roberson's demise. With the Rational propensity for executing defectives, Mr. Roberson's date of execution was not far off."

The Robersonians hissed and shouted. Jax thrust her face within a few centimeters of Elder Chin's. "You are senile."

"That is possible. Nonetheless, Mr. Roberson, if not insane, was definitely irrational. What sort of man tries to achieve genetic diversity by attempting to have all the children be his?"

Silence, and then shouting. Myra stood with her hand over her mouth, her eyes growing wider and wider.

Jax held out her hand palm down.

The Robersonian quieted, but they continued to point their rifles at Elder Chin.

Jax rubbed the knife handle with her thumb. "His genetic code was perfect; all disease traits were deleted. He was the most intelligent person on Earth."

"So he claimed. It may even have been true. But I find it interesting that he was the first one to discover the deaths of the embryos in both cases. With his vast intelligence, he could easily have destroyed the embryos and the evidence of who did it."

The hissing and shouting swelled. Jax and Elder Chin stood with their gazes locked onto each other. Rejoice watched them with panic clutching her throat.

Elder Smith spoke something that only Jax could hear. In response, she held up her hand and the Robersonians fell silent. Then he said, "The third point is irrelevant. Mr. Roberson is not the one on trial."

"Now sentence," said Jax. "Death."

Elder Chin tapped the gravel with his cane. "Even if Sister Cruz were guilty of killing a hundred of us, we would not accept a death penalty."

"For truth?" said Jax. "Again you will deny us justice?"

"Death of a killer does not restore the lives taken. The most we would accept is a life sentence of exile. But considering the extenuating circumstances and lack of direct witnesses—"

"For us the least acceptable sentence is death."

God, stop it, please, stop it! I can't see a solution that will keep them from slaughtering us. "I accept death," she squeaked.

Noble lifted his voice. "Exile us to live among the churtrees."

Everyone stared at Noble. The Robersonians lowered their rifles from their shoulders and their mouths gaped.

A bubble of silence surrounded them. Not the churtrees! Rejoice placed her hand on his chest, but he did not look at her. He watched Jax. *God, that isn't the right solution. Why did he say that?*

Jax grinned. "Without weapons."

Elder Smith cleared his throat. "Do you accept such a sentence? To live without weapons among the churtrees?"

Rejoice tried to swallow and couldn't. "Yes." *NO! Somebody say no and put a stop to this! Why would Noble do this to me?*

Elder Smith stood with his palms together and the fingers pressed against his nose.

Elder Chin lifted one hand from his cane and stood, shaking. He turned a bit and looked at the circle of people.

Oh, no. He looked confused. What was God doing?

Brother Madison stepped up to Elder Chin and whispered to him. Elder Chin's head bobbed as he leaned on Brother Madison. Brother Hancock dropped his camera and rushed over to hold Elder Chin's other arm. Elder Smith did not move as the two men led Elder Chin to his runabout. Rejoice watched them go the same way a yertle watches the approaching runabout.

The dojo students cheered.

When the ring of people closed behind them, Jax still grinned. "We would accept this compromise."

Elder Smith sighed and lowered his hands. "You have thrown your lot in with those cursed creatures. To the churtrees you shall go."

But they would eat her! They would eat Noble! She would rather jump off the cliff and feed the pack bats. Rejoice eyed the fence. There were too many people between her and it.

The Robersonians laughed and cheered except for Myra, who stood with wide eyes, and Ernest, who wiped his eyes. Brother Hancock entered the circle, laid his hand on Elder Smith's shoulder, and spoke urgently into his ear. Elder Smith nodded and motioned to Noble, Rejoice, and Jax.

Rejoice could not move. Noble carried her closer to Elder Smith. Her feet dragged on the gravel.

Elder Smith watched as Brother Hancock said to Jax, "Give them a night's rest before the drive to the Orange Scar Village."

"Rest, fine; drive, no. All their property is forfeited to us. House, runabout, all. Let them walk. For them no computers, no weapons." She slowly slid her knife under Brother Hancock's chin and let the point barely rest on his throat.

He swallowed. His voice rose in pitch. "They need guns for the pack bats."

"No. She is not trustworthy with weapons."

"It doesn't matter," Noble said. "The pack bats shouldn't be back for weeks."

Brother Hancock backed a step and shook his head. "When he said they would live with the churtrees, you understood that did not mean within their tunnels, right? The tunnel roofs are too low. They can build a house on the beach, right? Behind the cliffs?"

Jax laughed. "As long as they don't walk more than one kilometer from center of village, I don't care. We will monitor. Exile means no contact, for truth?"

Moisture filmed Brother Hancock's eyes. His voice hitched. "You must allow food deliveries."

Jax shrugged.

Noble stroked Rejoice's hair and gazed with unfocused eyes.

Jax laughed again. "No human contact. They can speak with the spider slugs and churtrees. I don't care."

"Pastor Cruz," Brother Hancock said. His face twisted. "Is this what you meant when you asked for exile among the churtrees?"

Noble continued to look over everyone's head. "Fine."

Brother Hancock turned to Jax. "Ms. Lindsey, will this satisfy your people? Or do your people intend to begin shooting us after they have finished looting our things?"

Rejoice clutched Noble's arm even tighter. What would the Robersonians do with a warehouse of filter masks from when the atmosphere could not be breathed long term? God, what had she done to her people?

Jax tapped her fingertips together. "You can bring your children and mothers out of hiding. Justice brings satisfaction."

"Okay." Brother Hancock looked at Rejoice and Noble. His eyes searched their faces as though trying to memorize their features. "God be with you," he said huskily and then turned away. Sister Hancock stumbled toward him with her handkerchief over her eyes. He guided her feet onto the road and Elder Smith joined them in walking away.

Rejoice searched, but could not see Stronghold. Ur-Veena looked at her with eyes that could not blink. *Be worth it, Ur-Veena, be worth it.* Did He understand that she had just sacrificed the colony for him?

The barrel of a rifle pressed her cheek. "Move."

Rejoice held her breath so she would not give way to hysterical laughter. They couldn't threaten her. Shooting her would be far kinder than sending her to the churtrees. She took one step and collapsed.

Several of the Robersonians clapped and laughed as Noble bent to scoop her up and carry her toward the dojo.

* * *

In the dark closet, Rejoice listened to the steady heartbeat and inhaled the male scent of her husband. Her mind skittered, as it had for the past many hours, around the vision of the churtrees stabbing Makepeace and of his blood flowing over the sand and mud. This precious flesh, this precious heart; could God truly allow that to enter the red maws of the churtrees? History gave her no comfort. Nor did Scripture. *Precious in the sight of the Lord is the death of his saints.*

His hand stroked her hair and shoulders.

All they had been doing was picking apples.

"Noble," she whispered, hating that every word was taken up by the receivers on their ankles. Would Jax play their conversation for laughs at parties? "I never got to say 'God be with you' to my sons."

He stroked the side of her face. "I did it for both of us. I took Mark out for a few hours and whittled a heart for him and one for him to give to Jubilee when he is older. I told him it represented our love for him." He took a long breath. "After I married your mother and Elder Smith, I gave them guardianship of the boys. They will be good parents. In Promise, Mark will have a horse and as many dogs as he wants."

Another regret. Would it have hurt so much to let Mark have a pet?

The Robersonians should have shot her then and there. "Mother didn't come to the trial."

"She's tough, like you. She will recover. She married a good man, and that will help."

Rejoice swallowed hard. "How is Jubilee? Did he get sun-burnt sitting out there all by himself in the sun?"

He shifted on the canvas robes. "This is the first time I've heard you call Jubilee by name."

"I love Jubilee. I do, you know. I threw myself on Jubilee to keep Mr. Roberson from shooting him as he threatened."

"Shh, Love, it's all right." He stroked her hair again. "You cannot imagine how I felt when I woke up and saw your smashed computer and blood all over the road. I thought it was your blood. After I made sure Jubilee was safe, I went looking for you."

"I can too imagine it. It's how I felt when I saw you shot. I thought that he had murdered you. And he kept on smiling. I forgot about their anesthetic bullets."

"You also forgot we were people of peace. When the Robersonians announced that you had killed Mr. Roberson, I nearly went out of my mind. On one level, I can understand. On another level I don't understand at all. Is life so sweet that you're willing to purchase it at the expense of another person's life? Do you distrust our Lord and Savior so much?"

If only he knew. Her body could not manufacture any more tears. She rubbed her cheek against his chest. "Why, then, did you come back for me?" she whispered.

"Because I love you more than life." He continued to stroke her hair in the dark.

PACIFISTS' WARCHAPTER
TWENTY-NINE

The morning sun shone with a watery brilliance that offended Rejoice. Father God, why weren't the heavens weeping with the tears she couldn't shed? Breakfast lay heavy in her stomach. The back pack filled with water bottles and fruit pulled on her shoulders.

Jax had said they needed enough strength to reach their destination. Then she had winced, placed her hand on her forehead, and stumbled from the room. Perhaps her pregnancy was as hard for her as it had been for Rejoice. Do good to those that hate you. Pray for them that spitefully use you. Rejoice prayed for Jax with mechanical words. *It's not the dying,* she thought, she hoped, *it's dying like that.*

Her fingers interlaced with Noble's, she walked toward the gate through a double line of dojo students and staff, all still dressed in black, all with hate-filled eyes, all with drawn rifles. Rejoice felt acutely the lack of a rifle on her back. Noble walked as though he noticed nothing. When they passed through the gate, the Robersonians marched behind them. The wind blew in from the sea and shushed through the gaunt, gray trees. A gray bark hugger chirped at them to warn them away from its hoard of galls.

Noble said, "Joy of my life, please, repent before we reach the mission."

Rejoice watched their feet, stepping every step closer to the churtree. She repented heartily, but she still couldn't say the words that would destroy the hexacrabs. *Father God, why isn't there another way?*

She tightened her grip on his hand.

When they reached the elevator clearing, the doors opened and two hexacrabs stepped out, Ur-Sinni and Sa-Kisi, each bearing two rifles.

Jax yelled at them, "We are not harming your pets."

The students separated and formed a semi-circle around hexacrabs and aimed their rifles.

Sa-Kisi said, "We do not come to harm you."

Jax motioned and the students reassembled themselves into a marching formation.

The hexacrabs stood and watched the humans march by. When the line had passed, they quietly turned their LVs and followed after.

Jax kept glancing back at them with narrowed eyes. "Call off your dogs," she ordered Rejoice.

Father God, don't let the hexacrabs do anything stupid. "I'm sorry, but hexacrabs do what they decide to do." She stammered, "Likely they are headed for the practice range."

Jax slapped her thigh and stepped away from Rejoice.

They passed Rejoice's house. The door hung open. Piled on the ground lay Rejoice's clothes and sewing projects. The painting of them on the *Magellan* lay dented, scratched, and splattered with dirt. The smashed purple and white rattle protruded from the mud. Her boys. God be with her sons. Rejoice averted her eyes. An LV gleamed ten meters within the jungle.

They came to the Meetingplace plaza. Every adult except Rejoice's family and the Hancocks stood in a line watching them. Most of the women and some of the men had tears running down their faces. Rejoice's eyes welled with tears. She had thought that she had run out. She sighed, as she wiped them away. Noble ignored everyone. A chorus of "God be with you, Pastor," rippled along their path across the plaza. Though many tearful gazes turned her way, no one said anything to Rejoice.

She watched the bricks they walked over. All she needed to do was say, "I'm sorry I shot Mr. Roberson," and she would get to say "God be with you," to the people she loved. Or she could tell the truth and not go to the churtrees. She could tell the truth and see her sons again. She could tell the truth and restore at least one child to Mother. Rejoice clenched her teeth.

Halfway across the plaza, Noble halted and Rejoice looked up.

Ur-Veena and a long line of hexacrabs entered the plaza from behind the Meetingplace. From behind each house and building ringing the plaza stepped hexes of hexacrabs in wedge formations.

The double line of students reshaped into an oval of students standing back to back. Their eyes and rifles darted back and forth as they tracked the hexacrabs pouring into the plaza.

Jax whirled and suddenly her knife glinted at Rejoice's throat. The other hand held Rejoice's hair. "Ambush?" she hissed at Noble.

Noble's head swung from side to side as he took in the growing number of hexacrabs. "I have no idea what they are doing. Ur-Veena! Where are you swimming?"

Rejoice could think of nothing but the knife at her throat until she saw the occupant of the LV closest to her. "Look! There's Ur-Nissi!"

The older colonists called out, "There's Ur-Visi." "There's Ur-Sitvi." "There's Ur-Savi."

Rejoice's eyes widened further when she saw the hexacrab next to Ur-Nissi. She was speckled with brown! Suddenly the pattern of the pieces clicked together: the missing rods, the lost scooters, the purchase of three hundred LVs. "The missing hexacrabs! They built a floating city and I've been watching it come for the past three months without knowing what I was seeing. They found another cluster."

Ur-Veena whistled and clicked, "The same-churtree do not need to skitter at shadows. We will not shoot them unless they harm our air-ocean friends."

Jax withdrew the knife and muttered to herself, "We're badly outnumbered."

At least one hundred fifty hexacrabs thronged the plaza. All held at least two rifles.

Ur-Veena clicked, "The Ur, Sa, Ti, and Chuu will protect our friends from the filth-eating churtree."

"No," Noble said.

"No!" Zack screamed. "For the murder of my father I want justice!"

"Wait," Jax said, looking from side to side and licking her lips.

One of the students cursed, then shouted, "Message from Freedom. Two hundred, maybe more hexacrabs are patrolling the road between Freedom and First City. They are halting the confiscation."

"Shooting?" Jax called.

The student spoke urgently into his wrist-com, then listened a second. "No. The hexacrabs there say they are waiting for us to sting first in deference to friends."

"If you want war, I'll give you war," Zack said. He raised his rifle.

"Not now!" Jax commanded.

Zack fired.

A glass cracked and the hexacrab inside jerked. Orange blood swirled as the Sa slid a patch from under the controls.

Jax flung her knife. Zack dropped his rifle, clawed at the knife protruding from his throat, and collapsed. Water and blood sprayed onto the bricks from different directions.

The hexacrab inside the LV slapped the patch against the hole and stopped the water from pouring out. Orange continued threading the water, but his claspers brought up both rifles and aimed them at the students. They aimed back.

Jax shouted as she ran between Zack and the shot hexacrab and threw wide her arms, "We're not shooting! We're not shooting!"

Sister Deng pushed through the LVs and raced to Zack. "I need help," she called.

Young Man Grass Under Sky joined her and together they knelt in the blood.

Zack's legs thrashed against the bricks.

"We're not shooting!" Jax shouted again. She shoved down the barrel of the rifle held closest to her. The student stepped back but kept her rifle down.

Sister Deng pressed against the artery as Zack gurgled. Young Man Grass held down his flailing limbs. Doctor Carlson came in from the back and took Zack's hand to feel his pulse. The students stared at the hexacrab rifles pointed at them. Several of the colonists dropped to the ground and prayed aloud for peace. A minute passed. Sister Higashi ran to the three with a medical case in her hands.

Doctor Carlson said, "I have no pulse and I believe the trachea and artery are severed." Sister Deng drew back bloodied hands. The spurts of blood had turned into a trickle. Doctor Carlson examined the neck. "We won't be able to establish blood flow to the brain in time. He's dead."

Young Man Grass looked up. "You murdered one of your own people."

"It was not murder. It was execution for treason."

The students huddled together, looking from Jax to the hexacrabs to Zack.

Jax faced Rejoice and Noble with her hands held out to her sides showing she held no weapons. She screamed, "Go to the churtrees now! If you think you can circumvent justice this way, you're wrong!" She stepped closer. "If you refuse to die, I'll make sure all of these people die. Move!"

Noble grabbed Rejoice and pushed her across the plaza. People and glass tanks parted before them. Her ragged breath and the click of LV feet against the bricks were all she could hear.

As they climbed the first hill that led to the pass, Rejoice looked back. The colonists scattered to their bubble homes and the Robersonians jogged back to the dojo. LVs swarmed over the plaza like semi-beetles on a fallen apple. Behind them, a pack of hexacrabs mounted the road.

"Come on, Rejoice. We need to reach the Orange Scars before the hexacrabs do."

"So we can be safely slaughtered before the hexacrabs arrive?"

He winced and hunched his shoulders. "The churtrees might not kill us. Even if they do, think about it, Rejoice. Even if they do, our deaths would help show them that they don't need to be terrified of us. We won't seek revenge. Instead, we come to them open-handed, again. That should make them think."

"Of how to get more tasty treats. Why are you doing this?"

His tread lengthened and Rejoice trotted to keep up. "Please, you don't have to do this," she said. "Our boys need one of us. The church needs you. There may be horrible suffering ahead. I can do this alone." *Oh God, I can't.* "Please go back. Be a daddy. Be a pastor. Don't make me watch you die again."

He focused on the ground as he paced ahead. He said so softly that Rejoice could barely hear, "I can't be a pastor anymore."

"What? Slow down. Why? Because your wife is shunned?"

He did not slow his pace. "Maybe that, too. No. Because once the Robersonians show everyone my confession to you about Ernest, no one will accept me as pastor anymore."

Rejoice gulped in air and sweat trickled down her face and sides. He had said he intended to be a pastor until the day he died. So he had decided to die the day he couldn't be a pastor. "There isn't a man in the colony who hasn't struggled with lust in his heart."

"Not that kind."

Rejoice stumbled and stopped. She called after Noble. "You might be surprised. The Hancocks and Elder Chin would understand. So would my mother." Maybe. "And your parents." He turned and walked back to her. "So would Stronghold and—"

"Stronghold would be the first to pick up a stone. Haven't you noticed how judgmental he is?"

Her hair hung like tangled strings before her face. She pulled it back with trembling hands. There must be a way to keep him from committing suicide like this. "I notice mostly how judgmental I am."

A sad smile lifted the corners of his mouth. "I love you so much. One reason is that you always acknowledge the truth. I guess that's why I don't understand why you won't confess and repent of the murder of Mr. Roberson. You've always been the quickest to speak in the colony. Why do you say nothing about this? We may not have much time left."

Rejoice looked down the road. Trees hid the hexacrabs from view and she could not tell how far away they were. "There aren't any churtree monitoring cameras here, are there?"

"Not for another two kilometers."

Rejoice looked at the band on her ankle.

Noble sighed, "Joy of my life, by now they know more about us than we do."

{Here is my confession} she signed. {Roberson I kil l him not} an R tapped on the head and then the sign combination boy child for son.

Noble grabbed her shoulders. "Who?" he mouthed.

Rejoice tapped the five sign on her leg. {Ur-Veena. Baby he protect.}

He held her for several seconds without blinking. Then he spun away and strode several meters up the road where he shouted in Hebrew at the sky.

Rejoice had forgotten the little Hebrew she learned in high school, and she hoped the Robersonians did not have a translation program that covered that language. She watched him shout for a minute, and then another fear jabbed her heart. Maybe he would think that what she had done was evil. Her silence certainly brought evil to hundreds and hundreds of innocent people.

Maybe her inaction had been evil. Maybe she had helped destroy the colonists to stave off the Robersonian-hexacrab conflict for only one day. What had she done? She covered her face with her hands. What had she done?

And then Noble's arms wrapped around her squeezing tighter and tighter. Her ribs bowed under the pressure and her arm was an agony. She could not breathe.

"I love you so much," he murmured over and over as they swayed back and forth.

He released her and she staggered. He caught her. "I was thinking. On the way to the Orange Scars I can rip off a branch somewhere and try to make it look like a spear. When we reach the village, I will stab the ground and—ah. I wish we had access to the recording of the peace treaty between the Orange and Yellow Scars. Maybe if we screech together, the churtrees will figure out we are trying to talk to them about peace."

Rejoice blinked away the spots dancing before her eyes. "Screaming. Yes. I'm sure I will scream."

A noise made them turn their heads. Less than five meters away Ur-Veena stood watching them. Two hexes, a dozen hexacrabs filled the road with sun glare flashing from their LVs and their rifles.

Noble placed his palm on the glass of Ur-Veena's case. When Ur-Veena pressed a tentacle on the other side, Noble said, "Ur-Veena, you must go back. You agreed years ago that your people would leave the churtrees alone."

"Will you crawl to the churtrees?"

"We must. That was the agreement that brought peace."

"We will crawl with you."

"Ur-Veena, we love your people. Retreat to your niche and protect your children."

The hexacrabs marched past Noble and Rejoice. Noble jogged to the front and stopped. They swerved around him. He walked beside Ur-Veena and pleaded with him for an hour to turn back. The hexacrabs said nothing as they continued their steady progress toward the Orange Scar village.

Finally, Noble grabbed Rejoice's hand and pulled her to the front of the troop. As they trudged up the long slope to the pass, Noble said hoarsely, "Leadership: find which way the crowd is going and get in front."

Rejoice thought her heart would burst with love as she studied his sweat-streaked face. She handed him a water bottle, and as he marched and drank, she said, "The last thing I want to do at this point is anger you, but there are two questions I want to ask you."

He poured some water into the palm of his hand and splashed it on his face. He handed back the bottle. "What do you want to know?"

"Why did you volunteer for exile to the churtrees?"

He wiped his face. "Before and during that mock trial, I was pounding on the doors of heaven, screaming for God to show me how to rescue you, how to keep our people safe, how to cushion my congregation against the shock of discovering my illicit desires, how to do His will." He took several deep breaths. "And then suddenly I saw a way through the impasse, a way to stay with you, a way to continue at least part of my work. I don't know how much time we have before the Robersonians kill the last of the churtrees and hexacrabs. We must get the gospel to them before they enter eternity."

He glanced over his shoulder. "I didn't guess the hexacrabs would do this. Now we're really swimming between a torpal and a naspy. If we don't go to the Orange Scars, the Robersonians will kill all of us colonists. If we do go and the churtrees do what churtrees do, the hexacrabs will slaughter them. What should we do?"

"Rest," Rejoice said. She spotted at a small sandy space between the trees lining their path and turned into it. The hexacrabs behind her swerved into the jungle. She slid off her back pack and sat on it.

Noble joined her. The hexacrabs formed a circle around them facing out. "What was your second question?"

"How do you manage to love the churtrees? I need to know how to do that real soon."

Noble pulled a water bottle from his pack and poured some of the water over his head. Then he took a long drink. When he capped the bottle, he said, "If I don't love the churtrees, who will?"

"Oh!" She leaned against him. "I think I just discovered why you fell in love with me."

His hands brought her face up and his lips pressed against hers.

Ur-Veena whistled, and the hexacrabs radiated away from the humans into the jungle, perhaps to keep their LVs shaded, perhaps to give the humans privacy. It had taken them years to learn that humans craved privacy, especially when they started taking each other's clothes off, but they had never learned why.

PACIFISTS' WAR CHAPTER THIRTY

About three hours later, at the hairpin turn on the other side of the pass, Rejoice stopped to examine some snapped branches and trampled vegetation. "Something big came through here last night."

Noble shrugged and kept on walking as he broke twigs off the branch he had torn from a shroud tree to form his ersatz spear. Then he pulled Rejoice's elbow and whispered, "If we pushed together, I think we could knock over one of those LVs."

Rejoice felt short of breath. Twenty minutes or less and they would be there. In the village. With monsters she had nightmares about for fifteen years. She kept seeing Makepeace trying to feed the salmon to the staked churtree. She saw him fall under the spears. "That leaves eleven to follow us."

"I can count," he snapped.

"I'm sorry." Rejoice reached out and snagged a handful of gray anise tree leaves and sniffed. *Thank you, God, for this wonderful smell. Thank you for beautiful sunlight and all things beautiful. Thank you that I got to know love before I die. Show these fearful churtrees Your love.* Was it God's grace or numbness that kept her feet on the shady road to Half-Moon Bay and the Orange Scar village? Her ears buzzed. *Thank you, God, for your son Jesus and for salvation. Keep my sons safe in Promise.*

Noble clasped her hand, hefted his stick, and took a deep breath. "I hurt a churtree once, and I vowed I would never do so again."

"You weren't the one that killed him. You've done nothing to be ashamed of."

"I was afraid he would kill you and baby Opportunity. My reflexes took over. I'm afraid that might happen again. And that fear pales beside that of knowing what these hexacrabs are going to do. We are paddling toward a waterfall. God help us all."

"Amen."

Noble squeezed her hand. "In heaven, we will look back on this and laugh."

Okay. Her mouth felt so dry she would have reached for her last water bottle, but the coordination to accomplish that escaped her. Her feet moved of their own volition.

"To die safe in the hands of God is a great blessing."

Okay. She glanced up at him and tried not to see spears ripping through that handsome face, through those hands that brought her such ecstasy.

They passed the empty hidden observation post and rounded the last curve before the descent to the Orange Scar village. They stopped and gazed out over the clear, turquoise waters of Half-Moon Bay. They looked down the steep path into the narrow crescent valley with its small creek flowing down the center. The towering cliff rose on its other side pockmarked with the tunnels of the churtrees.

Rejoice shuddered at the memory of the Red Scar corpses and the empty hexacrab shells that had filled that same village fifteen years ago.

Noble pulled her close and embraced her. They hugged each other for a time she could not count and was not long enough. They released each other to start the final leg of their final walk together.

Then they both halted. Two LVs following them cracked into each other.

Rejoice found her voice first. "Who brought a house here?"

A white bubble house sat where the beach edged into the forest about fifty meters from where the small creek flowed from the trees. The churtrees moved on the beach on the other side of the creek as though the house was not there.

Surprise fixed their feet on the road. Behind them came the multiple clicks of safety catches being released. Noble spun and pounded on Ur-

Veena's case with his fist. "No! You must not hurt the churtrees."

"It is our gift," Ur-Veena grated.

"I think they saw us," Rejoice said. *Make me brave.*

Faint yowling and screeching were carried to them on a salt breeze. The churtrees scurried in all directions.

Let her die praising His Name. She reached for Noble's hand. "Either we go down or they come up. Why don't we see how that house got put down there?"

The road ended and the trail began. Transporter treads had churned mud and vegetation into a stinking mess.

Rejoice stopped praying. "I don't understand. Why didn't the churtrees kill themselves when they saw the transporter coming and they couldn't stop it?"

"Maybe they are finally got used to us."

Maybe they would find a bunch of human bones in nets around the cab of a transporter. Dear God. The buzzing in her ears grew.

They reached a new clearing made by a transporter turning and mashing the vegetation as it backed and deposited the house.

Beyond the clearing, the mud and sand beach began, stretching to the stream and the bay. On the right of the house rose the sheer walls of stone with its clinging jungle. On the beach massed dozens of churtrees yowling. They splashed through the stream screaming and jerking their spears. Then they stopped, just on the other side, and did not come into the clearing.

"Look at that." Noble pointed.

Between the clearing and the beach, about twenty meters from the stream, two spears stuck up from the ground. One was churtree, made of fire-hardened wood and sharpened bone. The other was of stone with torpal teeth glued into grooves on the sides.

Rejoice's hands dropped to her sides. "That's Brother Hancock's spear."

"Brother Hancock has more courage in his little finger than the rest of us do in our entire bodies. This is incredible! We've broken through!

Peace with the churtrees! Thank you, Lord, for what You have done!"

Rejoice swayed. Relief and adrenaline made her heart skip. Then Ur-Veena lumbered past them and Rejoice stood frozen before screaming. "No! Stop!"

Noble threw himself upon one of the claspers and rifles. Ur-Veena dropped that rifle, pinned Noble against his case, and continued toward the spears in the ground. The churtrees screeched and waved their spears.

Noble kicked at the LV legs. "Remember your promise!"

Rejoice ran and pushed the side of the LV.

The LV wobbled but Ur-Veena continued until he reached the spears. He raised the rifle.

"No!" Rejoice screamed and pounded on the glass.

Ur-Veena plunged the rifle into the ground, barrel first next to the two spears. He released it and backed away. Five steps away, he dropped Noble who rolled and sat up facing the churtrees.

Together, they watched the churtrees flail their thin, black arms. Then Pride, the new chief, ran forward with one spear and planted it beside the rifle. The humans, hexacrabs, and churtrees watched each other.

The hexacrabs backed away some more. The churtrees turned with deliberation, and then ran screaming toward their tunnels.

The hexacrabs turned their LVs. "We will return," Ur-Veena said. They walked back up the trail.

Rejoice dropped by Noble on the churned ground. She embraced him with trembling arms. "I wet my pants."

Noble grabbed her. He began to laugh, or perhaps it was crying, who could say? Rejoice joined him in the hysterics. They laughed or cried for a long time.

Finally, when they could draw deep, shuddering breaths and wipe their faces, Rejoice said, "Well, that was anticlimactic."

"Thank God, thank God, thank God." Noble slowly stood and reached down for Rejoice.

"I am thanking God." She took his hand.

"Rejoice in the Lord's Salvation!" he exalted as he lifted her up under her arms and spun her around three times.

He set her down and embraced her tightly again.

Would her ribs survive this day? "I hope there's water in that house." He took her hand and pointed to the house. "Should be. I see they arranged the solar cells to catch rain and dew and divert it into a cistern."

"Look!" she said. "There's a tomato plant by the door."

They walked toward the door. He took a noisy breath. "Baths for us. And then we're going to bed for a week."

"I thought you needed rest."

Noble stopped and leered, "Woman, you are insatiable."

"You haven't proved that yet." She took his hand and led him into their new home.

PACIFISTS' WAR CHAPTER
THIRTY-ONE

"He is risen!" Rejoice said when the first morning light entered their bedroom window.

"He is risen indeed!" Noble replied. He lay in bed, studying at the ceiling.

Rejoice caressed his shoulder. "You don't feel like getting up and celebrating Resurrection Day, do you?"

Noble pushed himself up on one elbow. "It doesn't matter how I feel. The truth is Christ is risen from the dead. A sermon, then, after breakfast, on being surprised at the tomb." He rolled out of bed and began his hundred pushups.

Rejoice pulled on her dress and padded into the kitchen. She usually made waffles on Resurrection Day morning. She checked the ingredients: flour, yes, powdered eggs, yes, butter, running low. Perhaps when they were re-supplied, someone would think to throw in an extra dress and pajamas for her. She looked out the window.

Crooked Arm beat on Helpless until Helpless scooped up some sand and stuffed it down Crooked Arm's maw. He almost lost some fingers doing it, but while Crooked Arm spit, Helpless scurried away.

She felt sorry for Helpless. At the realization, she nearly dropped the bowl. Was it possible that she could feel compassion and not disgust for every churtree?

Rejoice sat and looked at the bundles of herbs hanging from the ceiling. She missed Mark and Jubilee, who would be lighting purple Resurrection Day candles on this day. Well, Mark would be lighting them. Jubilee would be staring at the candlelight and sucking his little fist. She missed the Hancocks who gave them their house, and Elder Chin and Sister Deng and everybody. She ached to talk to Mother even if only once more.

As she peered out the window again, her fingers typed out her thoughts on a non-existent keyboard. She missed her work, the weather, the asteroids, the space agency. The chore of washing their single set of clothes once a day consumed little time. Cooking and sweeping took a little more time. Pollinizing the tomato flowers took a minute a day. They had lived here less than two weeks, and already she feared that she would die of boredom. Not much appreciation for the miracle that she still lived. *I'm sorry, God.* Maybe she should exercise as much as Noble did.

"Any unusual behavior?" Noble said as he stepped into the kitchen.

On her part, perhaps. But her new feeling of pity for a churtree still felt too fragile to discuss. "No. The Moab quartet aren't back yet from fishing."

Noble began his leg stretches.

Rejoice stirred the batter. This had to be far worse for Noble than it was for her. She had always wanted time alone to think. He had spent his days immersed in people. Now he spent his days in prayer, in exploring precisely how close he could get to the churtrees before one of them hissed and raised a spear, and in preaching to the unseen Robersonians on other side of his transmitter band. "If they are going to be listening in, then I want them to hear something," he had said. He looked as twitchy as Rejoice felt.

He stopped on his sixty-fifth curl-up. "Joy of my life, is something wrong?"

Rejoice tried to smile. "Isn't it amazing how quickly we take the miraculous for granted and in return for God's provision, start whining and crying?"

He held his shins and panted. "Yes. Within days of the miraculous crossing of the Red Sea, the children of Israel were whining for meat and drink and longing for slavery. If I had known how things would turn out, I would have arranged to take our sons into exile with us."

"It's like an itch you can't scratch. How are they? Where are they? What's happening to the mission?"

"I hope somebody thinks to send a recording of us here to our mothers." Rejoice stirred some cinnamon and cardamom into the batter. Not all the recordings. *Please.* "I keep expecting to see Jax coming down the hill to enforce the justice that the churtree did not. I hope the reason she hasn't is not because she is too busy fighting the hexacrabs. Not knowing what is going on is going to drive me crazy."

"I'd like to know why she can kill a Roberson and get away with it."

"Maybe nobody liked him. Or maybe she's in exile or executed. If she hadn't stopped Zack, all of them, the dojo students I mean, would be dead today." So would they and a lot of colonists. Her gaze traveled involuntarily to the rifle propped up against the door frame that Ur-Veena had dropped and said nothing about when he left. They never mentioned it nor a great many things because of their monitoring bands.

They did discuss elementary theology using memorized verses from the Bible. Her fingers twitched again. No Bible, no reading, no chats with friends, nothing that required a computer. Maybe it was time to experiment and find out what leaves could be turned into paper and what she could use to make ink and ink pens.

A thought made her stop stirring. "I would guess the churtrees can see flat images. Without a computer to analyze their tones, we won't understand a thing they say, but what if we taught them a sort of written language?"

Noble lifted rocks he kept by the window as weights. "Draw a simple icthose to represent a fish. We would need to use huge letters since I still can't get closer than thirty meters. Oof. They don't want us to swim in their bay, so it will be difficult to catch fish. I like that idea. It may take a while to work out the logistics."

The rocks thudded to the floor. "Something's happening."

Mothers whipped their children toward the caves and the males picked up spears. Pack bats?

Noble opened the front door and Rejoice joined him to listen for the high-pitched cries that Noble's ears would miss. What she heard were female human cries and runabout wheels scraping over gravel from the hill trail that led to the road above and behind the cliffs.

Then Opportunity burst into the clearing and raced toward them. She wore camouflage stretched over a round belly and carried a basket.

Noble darted out of the door and shouted. "I'll watch the churtrees—you get her!"

The churtrees bunched behind the spears and rifle in the ground. Thirty meters from them, Noble skidded to a stop and held wide his arms. Rejoice ran to meet her sister.

Opportunity fell panting into Rejoice's arms. "They're chasing me." Her long black hair lay in streaks across her face and open mouth. Rejoice supported her, and together they stumbled across the clearing and into the house.

"Who's chasing you?"

"I don't know," she wheezed, "but they nearly caught my runabout until they slid off the road a while back. They were driving crazy."

Rejoice grabbed a chair and thrust it toward Opportunity.

She put the basket on the floor, dropped into the chair, and pushed the hair away from her face. "I came to join you in exile."

"What happened?" Rejoice said as Opportunity sobbed and tried to catch her breath. Rejoice stepped to the sink to get her a glass of water.

Then the door crashed open. Stronghold stood in the doorway. He grabbed the doorframe with one hand and with the other clutched his shirt over his heart.

Noble pushed past Stronghold standing in the doorway and took the other chair to sit next to Opportunity and took one of her hands in his. "We want to help you."

"Thank God." Stronghold gasped. "Other Sis, I thought you were going to kill yourself." He staggered over to Opportunity, pulled her up, and embraced her. "When I saw you tearing through the mission, you had death on your face."

"What happened?" Noble and Rejoice cried together.

"They're leaving," Opportunity sobbed.

Stronghold continued to hold her and pat her on the back.

Rejoice wet a cloth and wiped her sister's face.

Stronghold said, "Their jet is coming and going constantly from the dojo. It sounds like they're packing it up and moving to Freedom."

"No." Opportunity sniffed and wiped her eyes. "I don't know where to start. Everything is chaos. Brother Redhorse was killed when he tried to keep the Rationals from shooting the hexacrabs. In Freedom, three women and one man killed themselves after the funeral. Henley's I mean. One man shot and killed two of the men in his family. His wives executed him for murder." She blotted her eyes again. "Ur-Tasiti and five Rationals were killed when the J Family tried to run the hexacrab blockade."

Opportunity stopped and caught her breath. They watched her. "Then Myra stole Henley's private computer and hacked past his security codes. She found his secret recorded diary. He said why he had destroyed all the embryos. 'Quality trumps diversity', he said. Many defective incestuous imbeciles might have to be destroyed, but the geniuses produced would save the universe."

"God save us," Noble said.

"What do those rationalists think now?" asked Rejoice.

"I don't know. A bunch committed suicide. Most of Henley's children hate Jax. She was supposed to take over if anything happened to Henley. And, and—" Her face crumpled.

Rejoice got her a dry cloth. "I love you. Please forgive me."

Opportunity blew her nose. "I missed all of you so much. You'll never know. When Jax told me you were calling to tell me not to bother coming to the funeral and you were shunning me, I nearly died."

"What? I crawled on my knees before Jax asking for a chance to tell you I was sorry. We didn't vote to shun you until after you didn't come to the funeral. All of us left messages begging you to come back."

Opportunity pressed her fist against her mouth. "I hate them. I hate them all. They talk and talk and talk about love, but they love you only as long as you're beautiful or useful or intelligent. The minute you lose any of those, you're supposed to kill yourself so you won't be a bother."

The band on Rejoice's ankle weighed heavier and heavier. "You do know that we're being monitored? If you thought you could hide here, they already know where you are."

She nodded. "I was told to come here. And now that I'm here, I want to stay."

"Who told you to come here?"

"Jax. They're leaving. Almost all of them. All of Henley's children except Ernest are moving to the Crater Lakes region in northern Sole. About a hundred of them. I mean the children and their families. And—" She stopped and wiped her eyes.

"So Jax and Ernest are moving to Freedom?"

"No. They're leaving the planet!"

Rejoice stopped breathing a moment. "Jax and her people are willing to live another seven years on their ship and return to Old Earth sixty years after they left? They have enough fuel for that?"

"They're going to another planet a hundred seventy-light-years away."

Rejoice wanted to scream. "They have the star map the government wouldn't let us have. That's only two and a half years on ship." Never enter a room with only one exit. "But most of the women are pregnant. They saw what Warp conception and development did to Makepeace."

"Oh, they found out about that within a few months after their original launch," said Stronghold. "As soon as their monitors showed all their babies to be defective they aborted them. Then they made sure none were conceived for the rest of their trip here."

Opportunity picked up another cloth. "They're all having abortions again. They wanted me to have one, too, but I couldn't do it. I couldn't kill this child." She wiped her eyes which refilled instantly. "Ernest thanked me for wanting to keep his son. But he still decided to leave me! And I thought he loved me! How could I have been so foolish?"

Holding her even tighter, Stronghold said, "You were seduced, Other Sis. Most of them wear engineered pheromones."

"What are pheromones?" Rejoice said.

"They're biological chemicals you can't smell, but when you sniff them, you have a sexual response. It makes you fall in love and you don't even know why. I'm glad I found their computer file about it before their women started trying to seduce me. If you're aware of what's going on and focus, you can fight it off."

A chill settled in her stomach as Rejoice said slowly, "Could a woman wear pheromones?" Sometimes Jax rubbed her wrist on her neck like putting on perfume as she walked up to her.

"Anybody can. A rock wearing pheromones would be interesting."

Noble stood rigid. "Do pheromones affect men as well?"

"The right ones do."

"God have mercy on me," Noble said. "Is everything they do a lie? Everything?" He raised his fists. "He was using me! I thought he meant it when he said he loved me!" He looked over and saw them all staring at him.

"Excuse me," Noble said, "I'm going out to break something." He stalked out the door.

Breaking something sounded like a good idea to Rejoice. "Those . . . those frauds!"

Stronghold and Opportunity switched their gaze to her.

"Those con men! Those wimps! They think they're so big and tough because they swagger around with knives in their boots. But as soon as things get tough, they leave. When living with somebody gets hard, they walk away."

She sat and pulled her ankle up toward her mouth. "Are you listening, Jax? I hope you are, because I'm telling you that you're a coward. You can't even earn love legitimately. You have no idea what love and courage are. Your people are pathetic." She let go her foot and panted.

"Sis, you're shouting."

"When life gets unpleasant, they kill themselves."

"Sis."

"When they get outnumbered they run!"

"Calm down, Rejoice."

"Yes, Stronghold. Why don't you tell me to calm down?"

Wide eyed, Opportunity backed into the table. Stronghold studied the floor for a moment and cleared his throat. "Can I explain about the trial?"

"I doubt it. But you're welcome to try."

Stronghold shifted his feet. "I was angry. I thought that all I had done was for nothing because Harmony would be killed, I would be killed, all of us would be killed because of what you'd done. I was so angry I couldn't see straight. But I couldn't stand what they were going to do to you either, so I left. When I reached your house I could hear Mother screaming and sobbing several houses over. I nearly ran back to shoot as many of the maggots as I could. But then I thought of Harmony. So I didn't. Rejoice, I'm sorry. I was a maggot. I don't know what to say."

"Say what happened to my sons. How is Mark? How is Jubilee?"

"They're back in Promise now. The jet made a special trip to evacuate some of us. Harmony wasn't well enough to travel yet, so I sent the girls with Mother and Elder Smith to live with Harmony's mother until we can get back to First City. In the meantime, we're living at Doctor Carlson's house."

"You haven't answered my question. How is Mark?"

"Harmony says that Mark looks sad and Jubilee cries most of the time. Mother and Elder Smith won't talk to me, so I get everything second-hand." He sighed. "I feel sorry for your boys. Their plight starts with my running off to the Rational lab. Mother and Elder Smith are going to swim up a waterfall to make sure those boys don't turn out the way we three did: a liar, a fool, and a killer. The only innocent one is dead."

Rejoice signed furiously, {Roberson I kill him not} Then she pointed to the band on her foot and then to her ear.

Stronghold glanced out the doorway. A steady thunking came from the jungle. He mouthed, "Noble did?"

She tapped the five hand on her leg. {Ur-Veena} She tapped the five hand on her chin, {Mother secret please tell her}

He looked away and seemed to be counting.

Rejoice pulled his computer from his pocket. Then she typed: [Roberson was going to shoot Jubilee to stop him from screaming. I jumped in front of him to take the bullet. I forgot they used anesthetic bullets. Ur-Veena saw what Roberson was doing and his instinct to protect the young kicked in.]

Stronghold's eyes bulged. [That dose of anesthetic would have killed Jubilee,] he typed.

Rejoice bit her lip to keep from screaming. {Roberson he knew?} she signed with the toss over the shoulder to indicate past tense.

{Yes} he signed back.

Rejoice shredded the towel she was holding.

When she had calmed, she said aloud, "Please find someone to negotiate with the Robersonians about sending Mark and Jubilee to us. And paper. And a change of clothes for us."

Anger made his signs choppy. {Robersonians leave. You leave permit. Stay why?}

{Ship warp it need at least three months for start. Emotions fade must. Wait must}

He looked away as his jaws clenched.

Rejoice spoke aloud, "Opportunity, if Jax sent you to us, do you think she would mind if our sons were sent to us?"

"I don't know. Everything is in an uproar. Myra left too. This morning she told me that she wants to become a nun."

"A nun?" Stronghold and Rejoice repeated in unison. Rejoice continued. "Does she know our tradition doesn't have nuns and convents?"

"I told her, and she said she would start one. She said if she can't have a marriage like you and Noble have, then she doesn't want to see another man as long as she lives."

Rejoice sat on the edge of the table. "She saw us at our worst, and that's what she wants?"

Opportunity wiped her eyes.

"I don't understand that. And I don't understand why Jax didn't come and kill us after the churtrees didn't."

"She's been busy dodging assassination and I don't know what else. This morning after Myra had her abortion and I refused mine, Myra told me that the love that you and Noble have for each other is the most beautiful thing that she can imagine. Then Jax screamed at her that she didn't love her anymore and she couldn't come with them. Myra yelled back at her that she was going to Elder Chin so he could teach her what love really was."

Tears rolled out of Opportunity's eyes again. "I threw it away. I could have had a pure courtship and then given myself to He Gives on our wedding night. I could have had everybody so happy for me. And every baby we had thereafter would have been a cause to celebrate. Now all I will ever bear is shame. Let me stay with you, Rejoice."

Opportunity had no idea how soon she would be dying to get out of there. Rejoice opened her mouth, and then paused, uncertain what to say.

Stronghold enveloped Opportunity again. "No, Other Sis. You won't bury yourself here. What you will do is ask for a special service. When we meet, you will repent publicly and be voted in as a member again."

Opportunity pressed her face against his shoulder. "How do I face everybody?"

"I'll go with you and repent first. There's always something to repent of. Ah, pride, yes. That's a good one." He looked at Rejoice and his eyes filled with tears. "And arrogance and cowardice and despair and selfishness and thoughtlessness and hatred and lying. Other Sis, by the time I'm finished, the congregation will be relieved that your confession's so short." He swallowed. "Then you'll marry He Gives and have as happy a life as one can have on this side of death."

Opportunity wailed, "He must hate me! Who could blame him?" "Then why did he call me two days ago, begging to know if you were safe in the turmoil? Why did he tell me to tell you he loves you and always will? Why did he tell me he doesn't care what you've done? He wants you back."

"Oh, no!" she sobbed. "He deserves better!"

"He doesn't want better," Rejoice said. "He wants you." Her face flooded with heat. That had not come out right. "He called me before all this started to say the same thing."

"Does he know I'm pregnant?"

Stronghold stepped back and held Opportunity's shoulders looking in her eyes. "I told him," he said and paused. "He gulped. Looked down for all of ten seconds and asked if it was a girl or a boy. I told him that I didn't know. He said that he wanted lots of kids, sons and daughters, and now he'd get one a lot quicker than nine months after the wedding."

Opportunity wailed again and buried her head into Stronghold's shoulder.

"Then he messaged me ten minutes later," Stronghold said softly in her ear, "and said that the name would be Accepted In The Beloved Schmidt if she was a girl and Well Pleasing Son Schmidt if he was a boy."

When she finally stopped sobbing, Opportunity stepped back and smiled weakly through her tears. "Well Pleasing Son it is."

Noble came in panting, with streams of sweat dripping from his face, and holding a many-splintered stick. He threw it into a corner of the kitchen and dropped himself into a chair. "Okay." He gulped. "I don't know how much trouble we'll gain by your coming here, Stronghold." He panted some more. "But I'm glad you came. How are our sons doing? How is Mother Holly, uh, Smith now?" Rejoice handed him the wet cloth and he wiped his face. "Tell me before these Rationalists come to drag you away."

A tiny cry from the basket pulled all their gazes toward it.

"Your paints just cried," Rejoice said.

Opportunity's crying turned into part laughter. "This isn't paint." She picked up the basket and set it on the table. "It's Jax's farewell present to you."

Rejoice lifted the lid and stood there, unable to believe what she saw.

Inside the padded basket and wrapped in a black blanket, a tiny, wizened, red-faced baby with a red ribbon tied around its bald head scrunched its eyes and opened its toothless mouth to wail feebly.

Did she dare touch anything so frail? "It's so tiny. Whose?"

"It's Jax's. A girl. Premature instead of aborted. She weighs almost two kilograms."

Noble scooped her out of the basket and laid her against his sweat soaked shirt. His face shone. "I name her Rescue The Perishing."

Rejoice stroked the baby's soft skull with two fingers.

"Jax said you had better take good care of her. If they don't like the next planet, they're coming back," Opportunity said.

Rejoice calculated. "That could be as soon as thirteen years."

"Speaking of coming back," Stronghold said, "you have other company coming. We passed a line of fifty hexacrabs on this side of the pass."

Noble looked up from the baby. "I am not at all sure how the churtrees would handle that. When should they get here?"

"I think we have at least an hour."

Rejoice threw her arms around her brother and sister, so happy to have them back, so grieved that her sacrifice had put off the fighting between hexacrab and Robersonians by only a few days. She hadn't known what to do, and so of course she had done the wrong thing. Mentally she groped for what to say, what to do. "Breakfast. How would you like some breakfast?"

In the flurry of domestic activity, her brain stopped whirling and rested on the joy they shared and the marvelous new baby with her tiny fingers and tiny toes and tiny nose. They laughed at the syrup dripping off Stronghold's chin. They laughed at Opportunity's big burp. They laughed because the sun was shining. They laughed because they were laughing.

Rejoice finally got over her fit of giggles and rubbed her sore side. Outside, the churtrees bunched around the weapons on the ground. "I think we should walk you back to your runabouts and wait there for the hexacrabs."

A meter past where the trail met the road, a white stick pounded into the ground marked one kilometer from the center of the churtree village. They stood near it, reluctant to part. When Rejoice hugged Stronghold, he whispered, "As soon as Harmony has regenerated enough lung cells, we'll go to Promise and talk to Mother."

"Is she getting better that fast? Won't she need more medicine? How will we make any with the mine closed down?"

Stronghold laughed and held her tighter. "You won't believe this, Rejoice. The hexacrabs have agreed to let us reopen the mine."

"If you're lying to me."

"It's true, Sis. When Brother Hancock told them why we needed that mine, they agreed. All we have to do is erect some fences around the mine."

Opportunity gave them a box of baby supplies that Jax had sent with the baby.

More hugging, more tears, and finally Stronghold and Opportunity drove the runabouts away. Rejoice gazed at the empty road, torn between joy that the mineral had been found and anger that it had not been discovered in time for Father. So many emotions in one short morning exhausted her. Noble rubbed his face over the tiny girl in his hands.

A few minutes later, Ur-Veena walked into view. Rejoice took the baby and nested Rescue into the hollow of her throat. Surprised by how good and satisfying that felt, she stroked Rescue's downy, soft back. So soft, and Jax so hard. She gave this gift to her. Did that mean Jax still loved her, or did she think looking into Henley's eyes every day would push her into a guilty suicide? Would Rejoice ever understand why?

The hexacrabs gathered around them, trampling the brown bushes and scraping against the gray trees. With one hand holding the baby against her neck, and the other touching LV after LV, Rejoice moved among the hexacrabs. Such beautiful eyes, beautiful mother of pearl blue shells, beautiful markings on their crustacean legs, and beautiful, expressive tentacles.

Rejoice whispered, "Little Girl, from Jax and Henley you got your genes; from Noble and me and hundreds of hexacrabs, you will get love." Noble grinned as he slapped one tank after another.

After all the greetings, Ur-Veena positioned himself before Noble and whistled, "You have a new little one tied to your shell."

"Yes," Rejoice said. "She belonged to Jax and Henley, but she floated into our net."

"You have learned from us to net the young that are not your own and care for them."

Rejoice and Noble glanced at each other. Was it worthwhile to refute that?

"Yes," Noble said. "Thank you for your lesson."

"We too have learned from you. Now we understand the current of the innocent taking the punishment for the guilty."

Rejoice's hand stroking the baby stopped. She looked at Noble. What was this?

Noble glanced down at his ankle. "The same-churtrees can hear everything that is said."

"Then let them hear that the Ur, Sa, En, Ti, and Chuu choose to become Christians that carry weapons to protect."

Noble and Rejoice stilled.

"We ask you to be our pastor and explain why the heaven-ocean God was so angry at us that He threw the asteroid Dark Death at us."

Rejoice moved close to Noble. He put his arm around her.

"We ask you to explain the kraken, naspy, and torpal."

Noble stuttered, "We can explore these questions together. I don't know if I have answers for everything, but I can talk about them with you. Could we start with what your people have said about God in times past? You never would tell us before."

"We have come to ask of you."

When Rejoice could breathe again, she said, "I think your first sermon should be on the book of Job. Or maybe you should do a catechism of some sort. Oh my goodness, where will we begin?"

"This is Resurrection Day and my first sermon as pastor to the hex-acrabs will be of God's great love in giving his Son, of His Son's great love shown by His great suffering, and of the hope that comes from an empty tomb."

"But first, I have another question," clicked Ur-Veena. The hexacrab that Rejoice had never seen hesitate, now hesitated. "How will you baptize us?"

Rejoice and Noble peered into Ur-Veena's water tank for a moment, then laughed so hard that they had to sit on the trail. The hexacrabs, who had never understood human humor and had decided that they never would, waited patiently for them to finish.

EPILOGUE

Rejoice sat on the wide porch bouncing baby Dana Zystra on her knee. The glorious shade that restricted their crops to mushrooms made it easy to watch Noble and Mark swinging in a hammock studying Hebrew together. Noble looked up at the baby's laugh and smiled at Rejoice.

Three more houses surrounded their house on the edge of Half Moon Bay. Up on the cliff, Myra's cell overlooked the bay and Mission Point Two. She prayed the Hours and followed the church calendar by herself and wore only black and white. How she could do this day after day and then year after year without dying of boredom baffled Rejoice, but that was her business. The woman helped with everyone's mushroom gardens, and once a week lowered a rope ladder and climbed down with a bushel of mushrooms from her own garden to send to the mission. She took care of the Cruz's three children while Rejoice and Noble hiked and talked.

The missionaries had built a bridge over the churtree trail so that both could access the shoreline without colliding into one another. Then the churtrees built a ropeway over the bridge. The children loved to watch the churtrees swing through the trees. Humans and churtrees still stayed a careful distance from each other.

Dana squirmed around to look at her house. A few dead leaves fluttered down onto the roof and slid down to the duff at the base of the house. The Zystras had gone into town to pick up supplies. So Rejoice played with the baby while watching Jubilee and Rescue throw a ball back and forth. The embroidered red and blue flowers on Rescue's dress made it easier to see her in the brown and gray jungle.

Rejoice stood and hugged Dana to herself. She hummed *Rock of Ages* and paced the length of the porch. Pipsqueak frolicked around her feet in an apparent attempt to get squished. Bitty shifted her belly swollen with puppies into the corner of the porch. The hairless kilogram- sized dogs amused Rejoice. The amount of engineering that had gone into the making of Mark's dogs had to have made Elder Smith choke. Theoretically, it was an investment that Mother Carol had made on his behalf. But while she spent his money on their development, she retained the patent. Once Rescue and Jubilee got their dogs, any profit made from the sale of the highly-desired puppies would go straight into the mission; as had thirty percent of Elder Smith's vast holdings.

Rejoice had not seen it, but she had heard several versions. Elder Smith had howled right there in the bank, "Carol! You married me for my money! How could you do this to me?

Mother had kissed him gently as he stood there red-faced and vibrating. "I love you so much, my dearest. You know I don't give a fling about money except for what it can do. Why wouldn't you want to contribute to the best missionary in the whole world?"

"But, but, thirty percent?" His voice had cracked on the cent.

"They need support while they teach the hexacrabs and work on the churtree."

He had swallowed several times, breathed deeply several more times, and then quietly asked Mother where she wanted to go for lunch. He was a man who was used to having a wife tell him to do the right thing. He never mentioned the Great Gift again.

But when Mother gave ten percent to the space program, he locked the account and gave her a weekly allowance which she usually gave away within the hour. He seemed content and relaxed every place he went, and Mother seemed to live in bliss.

The conversion of the hexacrabs had removed the largest complaint between First City and Promise. And some in Promise, who found farming a lot harder than they had dreamed, moved back to First City.

When some of the newlyweds in First City realized that they would be allowed to use a good bit of technology after all, if they kept quiet about it, moved to Promise.

And some of the colonists formed a third city named Grace. That city required fewer spiritual disciplines and allowed a great deal more color in their clothing. Opportunity's art store there might make a profit any year now.

Most of the Robersonians left behind, about two hundred, moved to the other side of Sole. Some few stayed in Liberty and never set foot on the original colonists' land again.

Rejoice sighed happily. Peace was good. Then she shouted, "Jubilee, Rescue, you're too close to the border! Move away!"

The border represented by sticks staggering in a rough line was respected, but it was easy for children to be distracted. They knew what could happen if they strayed over the line. The children had watched what happened to some of their chickens who had less concrete ideas of boundaries. Jubilee and Rescue moved a few more steps away from the border.

One Of Four stood watching them. Rejoice hoped the young churtree wasn't salivating. It moved a step closer and rolled its eyes in the direction of the dogs.

"In, Pipsqueak! In, Bitty!" Pipsqueak bounded into the house, and Bitty trudged.

One Of Four sat. Its eyes followed the arc of the ball the children were tossing back and forth.

What, oh what, did they understand? For a year the missionaries had tried Rejoice's idea to communicate with picture boards and word boards. The churtree had studiously ignored them. Then Brother Madison had pointed out that a more natural way to communicate would be by sign. Rejoice had asked, "How would they read the Bible if all they know is sign?"

"Why don't we communicate first, and then teach them how to read?" Brother Madison had answered.

Four years of miming and signing had gotten the missionaries a little more attention, but the same response. It felt odd to be watched by so many eyes that seemed to hold no comprehension. Sometimes a little churtree would make a sign to a sibling, but the signs were not used with meaning.

Rejoice moved to the rocker. Tomorrow, the Cruzes were heading to the hexacrab dock for their weekly service and teaching. Now there was a responsive people. Just thinking about the hexacrabs made her happy. She sang a hexacrab lullaby Mother had translated from Hexacrab into Human English. Dana gurgled.

Jubilee dropped the ball again. As could be expected for any child born to Rejoice, five-year-old Jubilee was a little clumsy. As could be expected for any child born to Jax, Rescue had astonishing reflexes. And as can be expected for any child born anywhere, Rescue liked to rub it in that she was superior in ball throwing and catching. As soon as she caught Jubilee's wild throw, she shot it back like a rocket. The ball bounced off Jubilee's head and soared over the crooked line of sticks.

"Don't move!" Rejoice shouted and startled the Zystra's baby. She threw out her hand as though she could hold back her son with it.

Jubilee stood still and looked sadly at the ball.

"Rescue, stay where you are!"

Rescue crossed her arms and jutted out her chin.

Noble glanced at Rejoice, and then returned to the vocabulary test with Mark.

She propped Baby Dana on her hip, walked to her younger children, and rubbed Jubilee's hair. "I'm sorry. We'll get you another ball."

"It's not my fault," Rescue said.

"I don't remember saying it was."

"It wasn't *my* fault. She threw too hard," Jubilee said.

One Of Four crept to the ball and picked it up. He held it close to one of his upper eyes and rotated it. He tasted it with one of his feet. Then he popped it into his maw. He choked and coughed it out. The ball, with its outer skin slightly shredded, rolled a short distance.

One Of Four's mother and three siblings slouched over to see what it was doing. One Of Four snatched the ball and held it in all four hands so the siblings wouldn't be able to touch it.

Rejoice snickered. "Let's back up before somebody over there gets scared. Then I want you to watch and then tell me if selfishness brings happiness."

Jubilee suddenly remembered that Rescue had hurt his head, so Rejoice kissed the bruise and told Rescue that she needed to throw balls underhand to her brother so that he could have time to see the ball.

Rejoice didn't need to look to know what all the hissing, squalling, and screeching on the other side of the sticks was all about. After she made her children hug and shake hands, they returned their attention to the churtrees.

One Of Four sat hunched on the sand, bleeding a little, still holding the ball. The three siblings play fought with sticks on a boulder several leaps away. The mother churtree, Twitchy, hovered nearby, glancing from humans to her children and back with the nervous twitching that earned her the name.

"Maybe we should go into the house for a minute."

Jubilee signed, {Ball give me.}

One Of Four focused all four eyes on Jubilee. One arm jerked and the ball flew over the sticks and thumped Jubilee's chest.

The world stopped spinning for a moment. Every churtree within sight froze. Rejoice stopped breathing. Don't, don't, don't, what?

The missionaries had been so careful to give the churtree nothing that might cause them to kill themselves. They had been so careful to introduce no more than one new person per week to this outpost and one new visible activity per two weeks. It had been a year before Rejoice let the children out of the house for more than five minutes at a time. They had been so very careful for five years, and now this child churtree had literally thrown the ball into the missionaries' court.

Jubilee grinned, completely forgetting to keep his teeth covered, and he threw the ball back.

One Of Four easily plucked the ball out of the air and tossed it to Jubilee.

Rejoice glanced at the frozen mother and saw her staring back. Rejoice lowered her gaze lest the mother churtree think she was challenging her.

One Of Four signed, {Fish give me}

Jubilee placed the ball between his knees to hold it and signed, {Ball Ball give me}

One Of Four signed with his upper arms, {Ball give me} and blared, a noise the colonists thought meant laughter.

Jubilee threw the ball.

Noble glanced up at the silence and followed the gaze of Rejoice just in time to see Jubilee throw the ball and the churtree catch it. Then he fell out of the hammock and Mark landed on top of him. Pipsqueak ran out to be part of the excitement and leaped on Mark and Noble as they scrambled all over each other to stand up.

Twitchy shrieked.

Noble froze in place so that he would not frighten her further.

One Of Four blared again. It threw the ball to Rescue.

The ball bounced off her shoulder. She picked it up and looked at Rejoice.

"Go ahead," Rejoice breathed. "Slow and easy, not like a weapon."

Rescue threw the ball slow and easy to the churtree.

Many churtrees ran up, stopping ten meters away to stare at the humans and churtrees no more than three meters apart. One Of Four would sign wrongly, and then would repeat the humans' corrections with much blaring. The ball soared back and forth.

The siblings came closer to the line. Two Of Four signed, {Ball give me}

Jubilee threw the ball to it.

Two Of Four grabbed the ball and ran, screaming, with it. One Of Four screeched and chased after it. Twitchy snatched her other children and dragged them away.

"But I was playing good," Jubilee said.

Rejoice arms ached from Baby Dana's weight. She gathered in her children and slowly walked them into the house. "Jubilee, you were playing very good."

Noble and Mark followed them in. Noble latched the door and made sure all the windows were closed and covered. Rejoice laid Dana on the floor between the wall and the sofa, a safe place from children's feet. She lined up the three children on the sofa. Safe. Everybody was safe.

And then, then Noble and Rejoice clutched each other. When they broke apart, both of their faces were streaked with tears.

Rejoice motioned, and the three children joined them in a circle. Holding hands, they danced around and around. Rejoice made up a song. "Jubilee threw the ball at churtree, at churtree, at churtree. Jubilee threw the ball at churtree and the walls came tumbling down." The children sang the words enthusiastically. The dogs bounced around their feet.

When they stopped and leaned on their knees for breath, Noble puffed, "A little child shall lead them."

Rejoice laughed. Jubilee had been named rightly after all. Praise God!

Author's Note

I hope you enjoyed this book. You are welcome to join me at www.leliaroseforeman.blogspot.com and tell me what you think. There you will find questions for discussion and a free story.

If you are interested in helping people who have been devastated by violence, there are a number of organizations that help the survivors of the genocide in Rwanda and civil war in Burundi.

One of those organizations is Samaritan's Purse

http://www.samaritanspurse.org/

I have seen some of their work and love these people.

Another organization is Come And See Africa www.comeand-seeafrica.org/

If you like stories about real missionaries, you might be interested in Forgive Like a Rwandan: A Memoir of Love, Loss, and Letting Go by Chris Alan Foreman.

About the Author

Lelia Rose Foreman

When she was in the fifth grade and working her way through the Long row of Reader's Digest Condensed Books on her mother's shelf, she ran across *A Fall of Moondust* by Arthur C. Clarke. It was though a fuse had been lit and fireworks went off. Next she read every speculative fiction book in her small town library. (There were a lot fewer then.) In high school she discovered J. R. R. Tolkien and fell in love with fantasy as well. As for horror, she's still working on appreciating the genre.

She obtained a B.S. in Medical Technology, raised and released five children, all of whom survived, and followed her husband in the U.S.A.F to bases in Japan, Texas, and Alaska. She is the author of *A Shattered World* and a number of short stories in anthologies.

Publisher Information

Glad to support the

original work of Lelia Rose Foreman

and other great Christian authors:

http://bearpublications.com/